# LEGACY

# LEGACY

An Event Group Thriller

DAVID L. GOLEMON

THOMAS DUNNE BOOKS

ST. MARTIN'S PRESS ◆ NEW YORK

This is a work of fiction. All of the characters, organizations, and events portrayed in this novel are either products of the author's imagination or are used fictitiously.

THOMAS DUNNE BOOKS.
An imprint of St. Martin's Press.

LEGACY. Copyright © 2011 by David L. Golemon. All rights reserved. Printed in the United States of America. For information, address St. Martin's Press, 175 Fifth Avenue, New York, N.Y. 10010.

www.thomasdunnebooks.com
www.stmartins.com

Library of Congress Cataloging-in-Publication Data

Golemon, David Lynn.
  Legacy : an Event Group thriller / David Golemon.—1st ed.
      p.   cm.
  ISBN 978-0-312-58079-7 (alk. paper)
  1. Event Group (Imaginary organization)—Fiction.   2. Moon—Exploration—
Fiction.   3. Human beings—Origin—Fiction.   4. Outer space—Exploration—
Fiction.   5. Quests (Expeditions)—Fiction.   I. Title.
  PS3607.O4555L43 2011
  813'.6—dc22

                                                                2011011260

10   9   8   7   6   5   4   3   2

This novel is dedicated to the men and women who have given their lives in the American Space Program

*Theodore Freeman Elliot See Charles Bassett*—training accident
*Virgil Grissom, Edward White, and Roger Chaffee*—Apollo I
*Clifton Williams*—training accident
*Michael J. Adams*—X-15 accident
*Robert H. Lawrence, Jr*—test accident
*Francis "Dick" Scobee, Michael J. Smith, Ronald McNair, Gregory Jarvis, Judith Resnik, Ellison Onizuka, and Christa McAuliffe*—STS-51-L
Space Shuttle Challenger
*M. L. "Sonny" Carter*—accidental death
*Rich D. Husband, William C. McCool, David M. Brown, Kalpana Chawla, Michael P. Anderson, Laurel Clark, and Ilan Ramon*—STS-107
Space Shuttle Columbia

And also to the astronauts and cosmonauts the world over who have given their lives for the chance to make us a far greater species than we are—we will always need heroes!

And finally—
To a brilliant British author and one of the more intelligent writers of any genre—James P. Hogan personified science fiction and gave it a human face. And he was right; we have a chance to inherit the stars.
Let's not blow it.

# Acknowledgments

*Legacy* has been my most challenging novel to date, simply because it involves something close to the heart of this author—the space program.

As there are close to twelve hundred men and women who offered their expertise on the future of space travel, I found it impossible to single them out one at a time without my editor and publisher complaining about the length of the book; that is how many pages I would have to add just to thank everyone who assisted me in the technical details of this novel. Suffice it to say I would have been lost without the valuable input of some of the most amazing people at NASA, DARPA, and the defense department.

There is one thing I want to add on a more personal basis—we have to continue our endeavors in the arena of space—without that challenge we will wither and die as a people. We are explorers, so let's get back to exploring—it's what we do best above all else.

DLG

# PROLOGUE
## TO GAZE INTO THE FACE OF GOD

The old shack stood in stark contrast to the gleaming new structure that towered over it. The larger structure, a two-story house, had been built at great expense following the gold strike in the Superstition Mountains two years earlier. It had been occupied for exactly seventy-two hours before the old man and his houseguest decided it just wasn't their style to live in such opulence. Much to the consternation of the military police and the security team that patrolled the property at the base of the mountains, Gus Tilly had moved back into his original shack along with the small being who had become his closest friend. The one-room shack had been repaired and a few creature comforts, such as new lamps and two new beds, had been added, but other than that the walls still leaked cold air in the winter.

Gus Tilly's net worth was something in the neighborhood of $160 million according to close government sources, but he still worked by himself at the Lost Dutchman Mine with occasional help from his houseguest and the young man who lived in Chato's Crawl. The boy in town was named Billy Dawes and he could only assist Gus on the weekends and holidays now because of his college schedule—a schedule that was paid for by the proceeds from the mine.

The Lost Dutchman, discovered by accident in 2006 during the incident in the desert, had been bestowed on Gus by the U.S. government after his assistance in that event had been deemed invaluable, but that wasn't the reason for the massive military presence that guarded not only the mine but the shack and the empty house as well. The real value of the property was the creature that Gus watched over. Tilly had sat with his friend for hours at a time during the ten thousand hours of debriefing by other friends based many hundreds of miles away in the desert sands beneath Nellis Air Force Base, Nevada. Four years' worth of valuable intelligence, covering a period that had begun in the time of Harry Truman and ended in a battle that had claimed hundreds of lives in 2006.

The existence of this small being was known only to a few people. He was referred to by the code name he had been given as part of the highly classified Operation Case Blue. Mahjtic, or Matchstick as he was nicknamed by Gus, was the most valuable and precious being the world had ever known. Only the president of the United States, the chairman of the Joint Chiefs of Staff, and an organization known as Department 5656 knew of his existence—an existence that provided the intelligence that would assist in safeguarding the world from a threat that had been coming for many generations, beginning one stormy night in 1947 in a small town in New Mexico named Roswell.

Gus Tilly rolled over on his oversized bed as he heard the whimpering sound coming from the child's bed to his left. He raised his head and looked down at the small creature lying restlessly beneath the thick covers. Mahjtic kicked at the blanket that had been draped over him, his movements violent at first, then gradually slowing. The Mickey Mouse night-light that Mahjtic loved glowed softly in the wall socket only a foot away from the small bed. The old man watched as Mahjtic's large green head and small hands and feet became still, but in the dim light he could see that his large slanted eyes were working beneath the almond-shaped lids—the small being was dreaming, an extremely rare occurrence that only happened when Mahjtic became aware of the enemy known as the Grays.

Gus was just about to lie back down when Mahjtic sat bolt upright in the bed and began screaming, kicking the covers free of his small body. He pushed himself into a sitting position and stared wide-eyed at the far wall of the shack. Gus's heart raced as he saw the terror that filled those large, obsidian eyes. He jumped when the front door opened and two men came into the one-room house with nine-millimeter automatics drawn. They looked around and saw that all was still except for the otherworldly screeching of the small being they were there to protect. They looked about as if they had no idea what to do. The first plainclothes soldier reached for the light switch.

"No!" Gus hissed. "No lights. He's dreaming. He's still asleep." The old man tossed his own covers away and eased out of his much larger bed. The two security men watched as Gus lowered his eighty-four-year-old frame next to the small bed and took the creature's hand. They all noticed that the cowboy-and-Indian pajamas that Matchstick wore were soaked through with the tiny being's perspiration. "Hey, old boy, wake up," Gus said as he gently patted Mahjtic's small, long-fingered hand. "You're having a doozy of a nightmare."

Matchstick was shaking and his eyes were still focused on the far wall, or on something far beyond it that the men couldn't see. Outside the shack's thin walls the winter wind blew cold against the aged wood and made a moaning sound that didn't add any comfort to the strange situation.

"Hey, big fella, now you come on and wake up. You're scarin' old Gus."

Mahjtic blinked and then screamed once more. It was a piercing sound and something that Gus hadn't heard since 2006. Mahjtic was terrified.

"Oh, shit," the tallest of the security men said. "Should I get a call into Director Compton?" he asked Gus.

Gus ignored the question, instead placing an age-spotted hand against the soft green skin of the alien's cheek. "Come on, old boy. Come back to Gus, I ain't goin' to let nothing get ya."

Finally Mahjtic blinked. A large tear rolled from his right eye and soaked quickly into the yellow pajama top. He blinked again and then his eyes opened wide and settled on Gus's craggy face.

"There ya go, son. Gus is here."

The eyes of the small creature drooped as they took in his friend's features. He placed its hand over the old man's.

"They come, Gus."

The old man's heart froze in his chest. He knew exactly who "they" were. He closed his eyes and nodded his head. "I thought it had something to do with those bastards."

"The Moon."

Gus opened his eyes and saw that Matchstick was again staring off into space. "What's that?"

"The Moon."

Gus turned toward the man who had spoken earlier. "Get on the radio and get Director Compton out here. Tell him to hurry."

The two men quickly left the shack and disappeared into one of the six trailers that circled the two houses.

"Now, tell me what's so important about the Moon, and then we'll talk about those other fellas that are coming."

Mahjtic moved his eyes and looked at Gus once more. The shaking had stopped and in the dim glow of the Mickey Mouse night-light Gus could see Mahjtic trying to focus.

"The Moon, Gus. The Moon—"

## 700 MILLION YEARS AGO

The war had lasted exactly three years, two months, and twenty-one days and had ended civilization as they knew it. Never again would the voices of children at play be heard, or those of men and women expressing thoughts or feelings of love.

Now the last desperate hope of their species had dwindled to a small outpost on a moon orbiting a hostile world—a blue, volcanic planet with a shifting crust and so harsh an environment that even their enemies wouldn't want it for millions of years. The moon orbiting this explosive and angry world had once had a larger twin, and that had been where the last hope of the people had been found. Their salvation had been an ore of amazing quality and properties. It had been mined, smelted, and turned into the magical energy needed to fight the invader. This great moon, where the powerful ore had been found, was now gone. Its sudden, system-wrenching death had taken with it the hope of an entire civilization, causing a home world of red sands, green oceans, and emerald skies to be voluntarily reduced by its own people to a dead and drifting planet with all traces of life erased from its face forever, and the survivors had found that there is no honor in death—just death.

The destruction of the large moon Ophillias had been intentional. The ignition of its mineral mines did just what the planners of the final solution had intended. The enemy fleet and their devilish mechanized invasion troops were blotted out in a nanosecond of stunning violence. Only things didn't go as planned; they seldom do in wartime. Instead of the eruption taking out only the mineral mines and the enemy saucers in orbit around the moon and their home world, the moon had been shattered. First the mineral deposits ignited. Then the core of the moon, rich with energy, had exploded, slamming the nearby home world and this, the lone surviving moon. First one world and then its larger twin were hit so hard with debris from the exploding Ophillias that their orbits had been ripped apart, while the home world was sanitized of all life and pushed deeper into space. Entire cities, oceans, and continents were wrenched into the vacuum. The other blue and still burning world with its small moon, Phobos, was nearly thrown into the sun. It was now the third planet in orbit around the large star.

The large man thanked the heavens above him that this desolate and barren rock was only a brief stop before the planned jump to the giant blue and green colored world 240,000 miles away. The new orbit taken by that world and its moon was still unstable, but the survivors of their race had little choice in the matter. They were going to call it home, volcanic environment or not.

The helmeted man, standing on the edge of an enormous crater, stared upward into the face of what would be their new home. The days it had taken for the surviving warships to follow this rock and the giant volcanic world below to their new orbit had been harrowing, but the new orbits had finally stabilized just as their scientists had said they would.

In a billion years, the great world below could possibly have become a twin to their home planet. He could see its single great supercontinent, partly hidden beneath billowing white clouds. The man could even make out its hundred thousand volcanoes spewing fire, gas, and steam. This world was a familiar giant that once was so close to their home world that they could see its oceans moving at night through telescopes. Now it was the only planet within ten light-years that had breathable air. The scientists at the base were saying that the great landmass was still in motion, destabilized by the sudden push toward the sun provided by the explosion of Ophillias.

The man looked away and down, kicking at the dust that covered the old moon as its new parent watched over it. He knelt and retrieved a piece of rock that didn't belong on this moon's surface. As he examined it, he knew it was the one element that had been their deliverance in defeating the invaders—Trillinium, an amazing ore that when laced with oxygen and water produced vast amounts of pure, clean energy. That energy had allowed them to create new light weapons that had proved invaluable in the fight with the saucer people and in the end it had become the instrument that destroyed both the defender and the conqueror. He rolled the stone over and looked at it. Then he took a deep breath, though it sounded hollow and empty in his helmet.

He knew this moon would be inundated with massive amounts of ore from the Ophillias explosion, as would their new home on the hostile planet below. Perhaps on their new world they could recover some of the magical ore and put it back to work producing energy.

The man let the small rock slip from his fingers and fall into the lunar dust. He wasn't used to regrets, but he had come to learn that even a man like himself, someone who always looked forward in life, could not ignore the fact that they had destroyed their own civilization. *Oh yes*, he thought, *he was capable of regret.*

The three remaining battleships of the home fleet were in orbit around the moon. He could see them high above as they made their hourly circuit across the inky, star-filled sky. They were only small specks of light, but he knew them for what they were, the last haven of a self-vanquished people whose home world was now void of air and sea, a rotating ball of red dirt orbiting the same star as the hostile planet he now looked upon. Sister worlds, one smaller than the other, ripped apart like conjoined twins, killing them both. He kicked at the chunk of Trillinium, sending the rock out into a low trajectory. He watched as it sailed through the airless environment and landed a hundred yards away.

He shook his head and looked at the readout on his sleeve. The needle indicated he was starting to run into his oxygen reserve. He glanced up one last time at their future home and knew this would be a good place to salvage what remained of their civilization. *Hell*, he thought, *it's the only place.*

As he started down the steep slope feeling the pain of guilt once more as he had on other days since that horrible moment when his own red planet had come to an end, the man slid to a stop and reached over to his left shoulder. He pulled the small flag from his suit, not caring that he risked damaging the vital material that protected him from the harsh environment. He looked at the small flag and its four circles representing the great society of twin planets and their two moons. He smiled without humor and allowed the stiff material that made up the flag to fall through his gloved fingers to the gray dust at his boots.

He shook his head inside his helmet as he continued to make his way down the crater's side.

"Gideon, are you receiving?"

As he reached the bottom outer wall of the crater he pushed the transmit button on his wrist. He started whistling and spitting, blowing air through his pursed lips. "I—unable—radio—static—"

"Knock it off, Gideon, I know you're hearing and transmitting just fine. The computer says you're low on oxygen, so you'd better get back. Things here are starting to get weird."

Major Gideon smiled at hearing the sweet and calm voice of the youngest member of their lunar team. Lydia was cute and sassy, but had a no-nonsense streak that was suffocating to men like himself. But she had the cutest pointed ears of any woman he could remember.

"Yes, mother, I am very capable of reading an oxygen gauge."

"Hmm, you could've fooled me. It seems I have to remind you on a daily basis. Dr. Joshua says you could hurt yourself if you get low on $O_2$ every time you go out on your little strolls."

"I get the drift, Doc," he said as he heard Lydia talking with someone on her end. Apparently she had inadvertently left her transmit key on.

"Major, I have a request from Professor Remiss to observe the eastern quadrant as *Guidon*, *Vortex*, and *Ranger* pass overhead. He wants you to measure their orbits with your laser range finder. Ours is malfunctioning at the moment along with everything else. Radar and sonar echoing is down also. Can you manage that while in transit back to base?"

Gideon heard the request and froze. He frantically looked at the timepiece on the lower portion of his left wrist and then back at the western sky. It was barren, devoid of anything but the immense star field.

"Damn!" he said, as he bounded forward using the elongated hops he had come to be very efficient at. He saw the deep crater that housed the base a quarter mile away and knew it would take him forever to get there. He should have recognized what was happening when he had seen the ships only moments before, but he was daydreaming about the planet below and hadn't made the connection, a sign that he was starting to lose his edge since the war with the barbarian species had ended.

"Lydia, get an emergency call out to the battleships. They have company coming their way from their stern."

"What are you talking about?" Lydia asked, confused, possibly thinking Gideon was joking because they all knew the enemy and their fleet of saucers had been incinerated along with Ophillias and their home.

He continued his loping strides, the lighter gravity of the lunar world making him fast and light. "Damn it, Lydia, I just saw three ships pass overhead not five minutes ago. They couldn't have been ours. Our three aren't due for another ten minutes. I'm betting it's three enemy saucers!"

"Oh, God—"

"Hit the emergency klaxon, get a call to *Ranger*, and then get the scientists and other personnel into the deep bunkers!"

There was panicked chatter on the radio, but Gideon ignored it as he fought his way toward the white shimmering base hidden in the crater ahead. He feverishly hoped that Lydia could get the men and women of the lunar science teams into the four-mile-long bunkers beneath the complex where the bulk of their technology and food was secured.

As he leaped from spot to spot he kept glancing spaceward, hoping to find their three warships still safe in their orbits. *How could three enemy saucers have escaped the destruction of their home world?* he thought as he tried in vain to lengthen his strides. They had thought the entire enemy force and their orbiting fleet of saucers had been incinerated by the suicidal act of destroying Ophillias, but now he knew that assumption had been wrong.

He had to stop. He went to his knees because he was finding it hard to breathe. He looked around as the moon became a wavy and jumbled relief of gray and white. The mountains in the distance shimmered and turned to haze. His head was hurting and he was now struggling for air. Gideon had the presence of mind to look at the $O_2$ gauge. The illuminated numbers and their backup needles jumped in his vision, so he brought them closer to his faceplate. He saw immediately that he had gone past redline on his reserve and knew he would never make it to the base. Loud and jumbled chatter pierced his ears as he slowly slid over onto his side. He should have known how much faster he would use up his oxygen by running. He tried to stand but only managed to roll onto his back, his survival pack digging into the soft soil. He felt himself let go mentally. He closed his eyes and waited for the end.

"Fool," he said with the last breath he could muster.

"Fool!"

He heard the echo and was confused. He smiled as his self-deprecating curse came through the speakers in the side of his helmet.

"I told you, but no—you have to take chances!"

As his eyes started dimming around the edges, he felt himself rolled onto his side and then jerked into a sitting position. He heard a slight hissing that hadn't been there a moment before. Cool air rushed into his helmet. He came around as the headache and agony in his extremities started gnawing around the edges of his brain, and then directly behind his eyes, fingers, arms, and legs.

"Maybe you'll listen to me from now on you idiot!" the voice said as he was shaken roughly.

His eyes opened and he saw the helmeted person kneeling at his side. He swallowed, trying in vain to get rid of the cottony taste in his mouth as he stared at his reflection in the gold-colored visor. He saw a small, gloved hand reach out and lift the outer glass of the helmet. Then he found himself staring into the soft features of Lydia. She wasn't smiling as she raised one of the empty tanks she had pulled from his backpack, then brought her arm back and launched it away into the light gravity.

"Next time I'll just leave you out here, Major."

"Okay, okay," he said and then remembered what was going on. Before he could ask about the status of the situation he looked up and saw three bright dots taking form just over the eastern horizon at about a hundred miles in altitude. He struggled to stand.

"Take it easy. Do you want to pass out? I can't carry you all—"

"Look—our ships," Gideon said. He pointed skyward and at the same time lowered a middle visor in his helmet that magnified the image of the three ships far above them.

Lydia turned in her overlarge suit and saw the bright specks of *Vortex*, *Guidon*, and the much larger *Ranger* as they hurtled on.

"Damn, they're still running in formation. Didn't the base contact them?" He turned an accusing eye on the young scientist.

"Everything is down, radar, sonar, communications, everything. I told you things were getting weird!"

"I should have known," Gideon said. "They're not down, they're being jammed, and I should have realized that." His eyes never left the three ships flying in a wedge formation toward the base. Their altitude wasn't even staggered. They were still about a hundred miles high and sailing wing abreast, the two smaller pocket battleships slightly behind their flagship, *Ranger*.

"Maybe—"

That was as far as she got as Gideon grabbed her and pushed her to the lunar dust. As he did so, the pocket battleship on the left side of the formation erupted silently into flame and floating debris. The eeriness of the enemy strike was so sudden and quiet it was surreal. Gideon saw another salvo strike what remained of the smaller pocket battleship *Vortex*, and her sizzling hulk vanished in a white hot explosion that sent chunks of lightweight metal flying in a torrent of faster-than-sound missiles of aluminum and plastic. The debris struck the lunar surface far below, sending up enormous geysers of dust and rock. The two remaining battleships were caught unawares and reacted far too slowly after taking hits from the explosion. *Ranger* started her turn, her bow thrusters firing at full throttle as she started to slow, and then *Guidon* did the same a moment later. Both were attempting to turn and face the sudden and unseen threat. The major shook his head, knowing they would be too late.

"They'll never make it," Gideon said softly. He lifted Lydia to her feet and pushed her toward the complex of huts hidden behind the wall of the crater.

The three enemy ships that Gideon had seen before reappeared. Without viewing them up close he knew the silverish saucers would be old and scarred from many engagements on and around Ophillias and their home world. He watched as their exotic weapons opened fire. The first six shots were evenly dispersed among *Guidon* and *Ranger* as they turned their bows around to bring their main batteries to bear. The large turrets swiveled to line up on the three enemy saucers.

Gideon watched in horror and then flinched as the first laser beams struck the larger of the two ships. Pieces of the ship's pressure hull and of the main deck composed of spiderweb girders exploded outward. Noiseless and horribly bright, *Ranger* returned fire with her twenty-inch twin forward cannon, quickly followed by a salvo from their number-two forward mount. A bright flash of greenish light exited the crystal-tipped barrels, followed by an expanding gas slug of nitrogen that was used for cooling the large bore and diamond tip at the end of the great cannon. The nitrogen froze immediately as it exited the barrels, creating a blanket of fog that from a distance resembled smoke. The twin laser shots from each mount were infused with particles made up of two thousand ball bearing–sized steel balls that passed through a hole in the crystal refractor. This volley was soon joined by twin shots of infused light from the smaller fourteen-inch cannon of *Guidon*. Major Gideon saw the first enemy saucer vanish in a gut-wrenching, metal-shredding wreck as the laser slugs punched large holes in it. The three-hundred-foot-diameter saucer started to lose its orbit, sliding toward the lunar surface in a silent death plunge.

The second saucer in the enemy line broke from the remaining twin formation. It made a run directly at the lunar surface and the small base inside the crater. The major heard the chatter and screaming on the radio. Whatever jamming had been placed on lunar-space communication was now inactive as the captain of *Ranger* was heard asking the condition of his sister ship *Guidon*. Gideon, still holding Lydia's hand, stopped and looked up as the battle raged directly over their heads. In the distance, maybe fifty miles away, they saw the silent impact of the first enemy saucer as it slammed into the lunar surface and blew to pieces. The eerily quiet death in the moon's vacuum belied the shaking violence of the impact.

Above, the enemy saucer that had broken away started firing toward the lunar surface. He could see the green-tinted intermittent lasers as they struck the outer walls of the crater.

Bright flashes overhead announced that *Ranger* had fired again. Finally, the heavily damaged *Guidon* answered the bell and also fired, producing the eye-fooling slowness of the faster-than-light weapons. It was still amazing to behold as the laser blasts streaked toward their target. The lone enemy saucer in a high orbit tried to maneuver out of the way of the particle weapons fired at it, but it was too late. The four rounds struck the top of the saucer's pressure hull in an enormous shower of flame and sparks fueled by oxygen released from the ship. Gideon and Lydia watched as the giant saucer broke into two distinct pieces and started an out-of-control fall toward the moon's surface.

As *Guidon* and *Ranger* started ejecting thousands of gallons of water that transformed into ice crystals in an effort to cloud and diffuse any return fire, they began turning toward the remaining saucer.

For the first time the major let out a yell of triumph. They just might fend off this last, desperate attack. But his joy was short-lived as two things happened simultaneously. First, five distinct lines of green laser fire struck the base camp inside the crater. All Gideon could see were chunks of moon rock and white pieces of composite material from the enclosures—and then, to his horror, un-space-suited bodies sailing into the black night. The crater looked like a volcano spewing forth not red-hot magma like the planet below but man-made structures and men themselves as the lasers struck their oxygen and weapons storage areas. The second thing that happened was that the saucer now cascading in pieces to the moon below had fired all of her advanced lasers in the last second before her own death. As Gideon and Lydia dodged debris from the base camp, *Guidon* exploded above them. The death of their battleship was so sudden and so complete they didn't realize at first what had happened.

The remaining enemy vessel was placing laser shot after laser shot into the base camp from a half kilometer up, where the saucer had slowed almost to a hover to maintain altitude long enough to destroy the last remaining enemy colony.

The major glanced skyward at the spot where *Guidon* had vanished. He could see no debris remaining larger than a city block. But he did see the burning and smoldering *Ranger* as it majestically righted herself after receiving the near-death blows from *Guidon*'s destruction. The reinforced armor of the smaller ship had peppered her hull with millions of particles as it exploded. The molten debris had set *Ranger*'s two forward turrets afire before exploding outward and sending the crews of the four massive guns spinning into the cold death of space. Gideon gripped Lydia's hand with first shock and then pride as *Ranger* fired her main engines and started her turn for the enemy saucer far below.

"She has no forward armament!" Lydia cried out.

Gideon looked at *Ranger* as she sped toward the enemy warship. The entire superstructure forward of her bridge was glowing red-hot from the dual assault of enemy fire and the brunt of *Guidon*'s final death rattle.

"What is she doing?" Lydia asked.

"The only thing she can do. She's going to ram the bastards."

"He thinks the base is still intact. Can we call her off?"

"She's doomed anyway. She's hurt too badly," Gideon said as he watched the terrible race far above him. Suicidal ventures were quickly becoming the norm of his civilization.

Lydia reached for the radio transmit button on her wrist and started calling frantically. The enemy saucer, apparently seeing the threat coming its way, had started to rise back into a higher orbit, blasting at the heavily damaged *Ranger* with her now retargeted lasers. Gideon looked down at the diminutive blonde, who had started crying as she failed to raise *Ranger*. The major reached out and pulled Lydia's arm down. She struggled and fought with him, finally collapsing against his chest, shaking, giving in to the hopelessness of the situation. Gideon's eyes went from the charging *Ranger* to the big blue planet below them. He shook his head and held Lydia closer just as *Ranger* slammed itself bow-on into the enemy saucer. The resulting explosion from the fuel and munitions of both vessels sent out debris in a deadly arc that smashed into the lunar surface, causing ten thousand small eruptions in the siltlike dust of the dead moon.

The final battle for his home world ended silently, with less than ten minutes from beginning to end. Over six thousand men and women had vanished in a final insanity-driven burst of mayhem.

Gideon let his knees fold. Both he and Lydia fell to the dusty surface and then they sat that way, holding each other for long minutes.

It was twenty minutes after the explosions subsided that Lydia stopped crying, and with effort raised her head. She saw the blue planet, which was just starting to set. Half the world was covered in fine white clouds and the other half lay in darkness. She turned away after a moment and clung to the major even tighter than before.

"What were they calling the planet?" she asked. "I mean, were they still going to use the same name as the one we were brought up with and learned in school?"

"As far as I know it was still the same," Gideon answered. He looked at the blue planet, setting for the lunar day. He suddenly stood and pulled Lydia to her feet.

"Come on, we have a lot of work ahead of us! Those downed saucers might have those mechanical sons of bitches on them. Soon they'll activate—and they don't negotiate."

Lydia didn't question the large man as he pulled her along toward the crumbling crater where the science facility once sat. She did turn and watch the last of the blue planet sink away to nothing.

"We need to name our new home something, maybe the essence of what it really is," Lydia said in her quiet and disillusioned state.

"We have to get there first, and then you can name it any damn thing you want."

It was almost two full months after the last surviving members of the human race left for the new world below that the war pods embedded in the destroyed superstructures of the downed enemy saucers activated. They came alive only because their programmed brains hadn't sensed any movement from the saucers that had crashed on the lunar surface. Designed as storm troopers for a race of cowardly yet advanced aggressors, the pods started dropping free of their modules into the lunar dust.

Only seventeen of the mechanical soldiers had survived the destruction of the saucers and their masters. Twelve of the ten-foot-diameter pods shot free of the mangled remains of the saucers and went to their programmed destination—the planet below. Their sensors immediately picked up advanced electrical sources that the primitive world should not have on its surface. They locked on to the signals and shot into space with fiery engine bursts, their destination Earth. The mechanical killers' programmed orders from their masters were to eliminate the last vestiges of mankind.

The last five pods rolled out of the wreckage in ball form. Three started roving the lunar surface searching for the enemy they had been programmed to kill, while the other two rolled toward the last place their telemetry had told them humans had been—the crater. Each of the five pods, after not discovering their enemy, settled into the lunar dust, their mechanical bodies curled into fetal positions inside their shells. Their duty would be to wait, no matter how long, for man to return to the surface of the lunar world.

BERLIN, GERMANY
JANUARY 1, 1945

The minister of armaments for the Third Reich stood silently in front of the most powerful man in Nazi Germany other than the Führer himself. The smallish, sheepish little man sat behind his desk with not so much as a single oiled hair out of place, and a uniform that had been recently cleaned and pressed. Even while his world was falling apart and burning around him, the small rat managed to maintain an air of superiority. The man behind the desk studied the last page in the brown folder that had been delivered to him only moments before. The reich minister for armament production, Albert Speer, stood waiting for a reaction by the former chicken farmer who was now serving as the head of the most powerful entity outside of the German army, the SS.

Heinrich Himmler adjusted his glasses as he read. When he was done he made a show of placing the paper perfectly in line with the previous pages of the report and then slowly closed the folder. He tapped the thick binder with a single finger as though he were coming to some monumental conclusion derived from careful thought. However much Himmler tried to disguise his demeanor, Speer knew the calculating little bastard did nothing, not even speak, without thoroughly thinking it through beforehand. The demonstration he was putting on, in the reich minister's view, had become tiresome.

"I must say that I do not appreciate being hijacked on the way to the Reich Chancellery."

Himmler smiled and looked toward Speer with a fatherly look. "Such a word—hijacked? I merely asked my men to inquire if you would join me before filing your report on Columbus prior to your presentation to the Führer, just so we could chat awhile. And since so much of the operational success of this project has come from this office, I felt a briefing by you, to me, was not out of the question."

Speer looked around the spartan office of this prolific mass murderer. He removed his brown saucer cap and placed it under his left arm, all the while feeling uncomfortable in the cold space of his surroundings. His discomfort was also due to his closeness to the chicken farmer—a nickname for Himmler that had caught on among the intellectuals of Hitler's inner circle, a group that Speer knew was ever dwindling.

"I have ordered the excavation stopped, and for the site to be destroyed immediately, the remains of the artifacts buried," Speer said, as defiantly and calmly as he could. He watched the practiced reaction of Himmler as the impish little man looked at him with a trace of a smile. "At least until we can negotiate our finds with the Allies. After all, I would rather think the Führer would prefer not to have the artifacts fall into the hands of the Bolsheviks, wouldn't you?"

"So I have read in your report, Herr Reich Minister," Himmler said, ignoring his statement about the Red Army. "I wonder if such an action is warranted at this time."

Speer noticed the comment wasn't phrased in the form of a question.

"The discovery of the bodies and of the technology came at too late a date. The properties of the ancient weaponry have yet to be unlocked, and coupled with the fact that we were unable to ascertain the age of the bodies I felt it necessary to destroy the site and bury all until we can turn the information we have over to the Americans or the British."

"I believe that to be a hasty conclusion to the excavation. After all, it has shown very much promise, yes?"

"If we are not careful the Russians will discover what we have failed to properly evaluate, and if that happens the West will be in serious trouble." Speer saw the twitching of Himmler's left eye under his wire-rimmed glasses but continued saying his piece. "We have no choice in the matter. In case you are one of the ones holding on to your glorious dreams of a Thousand Year Reich, Herr Himmler, I hate to be the bearer of bad news—the war is lost. It was lost the moment our beloved Führer declared war on Russia while still entangled with the Allies. The problem, as you know, was exacerbated when the United States came to the aid of the Allied cause. I have buried the mine because the technology and the truth of the world's past will not save our country now."

"A history lesson?" asked Himmler. "Political ideologies and our current military situation are not subjects I need to be briefed on, Herr Minister."

"Still, it seems a point worth reminding you of."

Himmler smiled, trying to bring Speer back into his rightful demeanor of fear and subservience, if only because he needed the reich minister now more than ever. Himmler knew if it hadn't been for this brilliant architect, Operation Columbus would never have been launched. A partnership had been formed in the early days before the war with the Allies between Speer and himself when the discovery in Ecuador had been made. It was the brilliance of this man that kept Operation Columbus viable right under the Allied noses. Himmler grudgingly respected the man, but like most intellectuals, Speer was weak when the hard truths had to be faced.

"Let's not quibble. I believe you need to be brought up to date on a few developments that have cropped up here at home since your clandestine trip to South America." Himmler folded his hands in front of him, trying to speak as clearly as he could. "The Führer has decided to personally conduct the operations concerning the defense of Germany from that monstrosity you designed and built for him below the Reich Chancellery."

Speer was taken back but tried not to show it. He closed his eyes momentarily and wished he had been sitting, as that would have made hiding his surprise much easier.

"He is going into the bunker?" was all he could say.

"Yes. It seems the Russian army will not allow us to conduct business aboveground these days. Very inconsiderate of them, wouldn't you say, my dear Albert?"

"Your point, please."

"My point is that we should not be so hasty in destroying the one element of our research that could be very beneficial to certain members of the Führer's inner circle. Columbus would be something that either the Americans, British, or in the most dire of circumstance, the Bolsheviks, would trade our lives for, wouldn't you agree?"

"That could be a possibility. However I see very many problems."

"Really? I see no such obstacles to our dealing away the one thing that will change all of history as we know it—possibly even the future."

"One such problem is that during my recent evaluation in South America, I barely escaped with my life. The man that you said should not be a concern to me almost caught me and my men on the beach in Argentina. He was informed of my being in country by that Harvard boy you said wasn't a threat to our operations in Ecuador. Thus far, Herr Himmler, you have been wrong on every count. And also may I remind you that the country of Ecuador is not one of Germany's allies. They are fully in the hands of the Americans, and the country is tightly controlled by this American colonel, this Lee—a man chosen personally by William Donovan of the OSS to head operations there."

"This Colonel Lee will cease to be a problem *before* we bring out the artifacts. His man in Ecuador, this Hamilton chap—well, we are arranging for that young man to cease being an annoyance. I suspect neither Colonel Lee nor this Hamilton fellow will interfere in the removal of Columbus." Himmler opened the folder and looked at the last page of Speer's report. "And I have ordered the last cave formation to be excavated."

"Why not trade Columbus for our purposes with the artifacts in place?

Why take a chance on allowing this very formidable man in South America to have even the slightest chance of discovering just what it is we have? I also believe opening the final cave formation to be a mistake. It will take too much time, and that is a commodity we have very little of."

"Because if we offer the trade before Columbus is on German soil, the Americans will just take it and then hang us all anyway. This way they have to strike a deal. And the last cave may hold the secret to this trove of technology, wouldn't you think? Now, perhaps you will step back from the project and let my capable offices handle the final phases."

Speer placed his cap back onto his black hair and stared at Himmler. The reich minister for armaments saw the small man's smile twitch once more as he calmly placed the carefully prepared report on Operation Columbus into the wastebasket.

"As I said, you will reap the benefits, as will I, after we trade our fantastic finds for our lives. When the time is right, perhaps when the inevitable becomes a reality, and after the American agent Lee and his apprentice are eliminated, our plans to bring both the technology and other artifacts out of Ecuador will be achieved. The delay will also offer the time we need to break into this last chamber inside the dig." Himmler looked up in a dismissive way as he slowly and deliberately reached for another report. Then he extended his right hand into the air with his palm facing out. "Heil Hitler! And please, Albert, give the Führer my regards, and tell him that I have been delayed by Party business. Frankly, that bunker smells rather bad to me."


RÍO LUJÁN, ARGENTINA
APRIL 30, 1945


The large man was stationed at the mouth of the Luján River just to the north of Buenos Aires. The night was warm and the sea calm as he watched the small breakers. Earlier he had seen not one, but two British destroyers as they passed on their run up the coast. His bosses in Washington had figured out the schedule for the patrols and discovered that the British pattern never varied. Unfortunately, the German navy had also figured out the same pattern and was using it to their advantage. They could have warned the British about the flaw in their patrol patterns, but the Americans liked being able to figure out when the U-boats would attempt dropping off a landing party just off the mouth of the Luján. The large man had already captured several couriers attempting to make it ashore with messages vital to the German war effort. On this night, and thanks to one of his most trusted informants in Buenos Aires, he would catch another.

The American adjusted his binoculars and scanned the area in front of him. As he turned left he frowned and cursed under his breath. The conning tower of a U-boat was just disappearing into the sea. He had missed the blackened silhouette in the distance, and since the boat was submerging it meant that its human cargo had already been delivered.

"Damn it!" the man said as he swung the binoculars to his right, watching for any telltale sign of the boat's cargo. There was nothing. He replaced the field glasses in their case and then reached into his leather jacket and brought out his Colt .45 automatic. He chambered a round as quietly as he could. Reaching behind himself he removed the safety on another Colt in his waistband, and then, as was his habit, he finally adjusted the dirty brown fedora on his head. After looking around with caution he started walking along the tree line that fronted the river and the sea beyond.

The OSS had had numerous successes gathering the information they needed on what the German high command and its inner circle planned on scurrying out of Germany after they surrendered. The plans included escape to Argentina, Venezuela, and Brazil. The large American figured this courier was delivering the same cargo as the last three: new identity papers forged through the offices of the SS and Gestapo. If not that, then it was probably the hard currency of the Allies, so the escaping war criminals could live the life of luxury and power they had grown accustomed to since 1933. He suspected the latter, thanks again to his female informant, who had overheard the plans from one of the SS operatives in the city.

The American stood six foot four inches and had the brown-colored skin of a man who had served long days in the extreme Southern Hemisphere. Since he had been transferred out of Germany two years before, he had successfully conducted operations for the OSS—the Office of Strategic Services—in six different countries with the assistance of his staff of ten men.

The large man suddenly stopped and knelt low to the sandy ground. The natural cover was something he wasn't comfortable with as he watched the barren area to his front. His backup had not arrived as scheduled and that made him apprehensive.

He heard a noise behind him as a small bush hit the trunk of a tree. There was no wind to make it do so. He immediately turned and pointed both Colt .45s at the dark silhouette in front of him.

"Don't shoot me, Garrison," said the female voice from the darkness.

"Damn it, Isabel! What are you doing? Get the hell out of here!" Lee hissed.

The woman he had known for two years, Isabel Perione, the very best OSS informant they had in the region, came forward cautiously. To Colonel Garrison Lee, she looked out of place in pants and shirt. Her usual attire was evening wear smuggled out of Paris by the OSS and used as payment to the Argentine spy.

"I am sorry, Garrison. I had to come. Two of your men were taken right from the Club Dubois in the city."

"What do you mean by taken?" Lee asked as he watched Isabel's eyes in the soft moonlight.

"All I know is that your men were removed from the club and taken away. I know they were supposed to meet you here."

"Haney and Rafferty are too damn good to get snatched from a public place," Lee said. His eyes never left the woman, nor did the guns he held waver.

"Nonetheless, Colonel, your men will not be here for you."

Lee was about to respond when he heard voices. He realized whoever they were, they were speaking a heavily accented form of the castellano Spanish of the Argentine region.

He risked moving two small branches of the bush they were hidden behind, using the barrel of one of his Colts, all the while keeping the other automatic pointed in the general direction of his informant. He knew beyond a doubt that the best thing to do would be to back away right then, call the operation a bust, and return to Buenos Aires to learn about the situation from his only two-man team in the region. However, he needed to see who he was dealing with.

Lee counted six men. They were only ten yards away. Four of them were Argentines; the other two men were dressed in dark clothing and woolen hats, the sort used by men just coming in from the sea. The smaller of the two was holding a satchel and the taller, a very lethal-looking submachine gun. Automatic weapons weren't the norm for anyone sneaking into Argentina. Lee looked at his .45 and shook his head, then half turned toward Isabel.

"We have to let this one go, doll face. I'd say the better part of valor tonight is—"

He heard the click of a hammer being drawn back and felt a gun being placed to his head.

"I would hate to put a bullet hole into what I know is your favorite hat, Mr. Lee. So if you would, please release the hammers of both of your Colts as gently as possible. I am not the only one with a weapon on you."

"I must say," Lee said, as he did what was ordered, "you were good, Isabel." He finally turned and saw the Argentine woman with the pretty face and perfect body holding the gun, now pointed at his nose. The more menacing view came from another man he hadn't counted in the small circle of men to his front. He was also carrying a submachine gun. Garrison added his and Isabel's number value to the equation—nine altogether. "Have you been accepting dresses from another man?" Lee asked as he slowly stood to his full height.

The woman smiled, showing her perfect white teeth as she backed away from the most dangerous man she had ever known.

"Yes, many dresses, and a small monetary amount to tide me over after the war."

The man with the submachine gun gestured for Lee to raise his hands.

The American did as he was told, feeling sick at being caught so easily. As he stood, the .45s were taken from him by Isabel, who watched for any sudden movement. The man with the heavy artillery called out in horrible Spanish and the six men stopped and turned as he was pushed out of the small grove of trees with his hands in the air.

"We have caught the Oso of an American who has been preying on your agents," Isabel said from behind him. He had to smile when he heard the nickname the Argentines had bestowed on him—Oso, Bear. He figured that compared to the short sons of bitches around him, he was a bear-sized American. Well, there was one German that was as big as he was, the one next to the small man with the satchel.

The Satchel Kraut, as Lee now thought of him, approached and looked him over. He turned to his colleague and muttered in German, "The OSS is getting more brazen every day. And attempting to take us right from the beach? Such treatment by a colleague." He laughed.

"Kill him and be done with it. We have to be in Quito for the second part of the operation in two days time. We have no time for this."

Their final destination: Quito, the capital of Ecuador.

The smaller German turned to face the American and tilted his head. His glasses and black leather jacket shone in the moonlight. He smiled as he removed the wool hat.

"Before you are disposed of, may I say that you have quite an admirer in Herr Himmler, Colonel Lee?"

The American reached up and tilted back his brown fedora, making the other six men, along with Isabel, flinch. The smaller Argentines brought up their only weapons—four large machetes. All of their uneasiness at his supposed killing prowess brought a smile to the American's lips.

"Anyway, I wanted to inform you of that fact, Mr. Garrison Lee," the small German said with a grin. "Before you are shot."

"That's Colonel Lee to you, Fritz."

"You fools, stop your playing. This man is a killer," Isabel said. "I know. I've watched him do it."

The American's smile was infuriating to the large German who stood behind the man he was there to protect, the smaller Kraut with the satchel. "According to our reports in Berlin, you were quite a thorn in our operations here in South America, Colonel Lee. It will be a feather in our caps, so to speak, to have been the ones to eliminate such a man who has caused our organization such hardship."

"Organization? You're being far too kind to yourselves. You must mean the SS, or what we in the states call Murder Incorporated."

"Witty, Colonel Lee—I hope that wit will be available to you in the moment of your death," the small man said. He turned away and whispered something to the larger German and then turned to face the woman. "As for you my dear, we are not in the habit of rewarding spies who assist in the killing of our agents."

The large SS man finally smiled. He brought up his submachine gun and shot three rounds into Isabel's head and chest. She fell backward and Lee caught her before she hit the ground. As he did so, his plan was formed.

Without a second's hesitation, Lee spun Isabel's lifeless body and tossed her into the third German. He dove for the sandy ground, grabbing for the small .32 caliber pistol that Isabel had dropped at the moment of her death. He shot before striking the ground, hitting the German in the chest. He twisted to his backside and fired another shot, hitting the nearest of the Argentine guides, dropping him and the machete he was holding.

The small German grabbed two of the Argentine guides by the arms and started running. The larger man knew his orders, but they were shouted out anyway as the man with the satchel made his way through the beach scrub.

"Kill him!"

Lee rolled as the submachine gun opened up. One bullet struck his calf as his own bullets hit another of the Argentine men. Lee grabbed the man's body and used it as a shield, bullets stitching the dead man's back. Lee was momentarily stunned when the corpse reared its head as one of the heavy caliber rounds struck its face. The head hit Lee's nose painfully, bringing a flood of tears across his vision. He fired blindly with the dead man still against his chest. One of the small bullets hit the last Argentine in the right eye, flinging him backward. Lee rolled again, knowing the last man standing, the German with the machine gun, was aiming right at him. Just as he expected several bullets to slam into him, he heard the loud click. The SS man's weapon had jammed on him. Lee suddenly found the strength to stand. Then he realized that somewhere along the roller-coaster ride of his derring-do he had lost the small .32. He looked at the German, who was trying desperately to clear his machine gun.

"Jamming right when you don't need it to is a common failure of that particular weapon type, isn't it, Fritzy?" Lee swiped at his eyes and then charged the large man just as he tossed his weapon away, grinning as he too leaned forward and charged Lee.

The two large men collided like charging locomotives. Lee lost his fedora from the impact. The German was powerful, but he was like most SS officers, unused to tangling with someone who fights back, giving Lee the advantage. Several blows to the German's back and ribs brought on a fit of coughing. Then Lee brought his hand up into the blond man's face and pushed up on his nose, crushing it into his brow. With the German grunting in pain, Lee took the man to the ground and then just as quickly brought up his right hand with the fingers extended outward. With every ounce of strength he had remaining he brought the fingers down and into the German's Adam's apple, sending his fingertips into the hardened cartilage of his throat. The pressure Lee brought to bear didn't stop until his hand had sunk to the SS officer's spine.

Garrison Lee, a former lawyer, and then one-term U.S. senator from Maine, rolled free of the dying man and lay beside him. His hand moved in the sand and he soon found one of his Colt .45s lying next to Isabel's body. Then he saw his hat and forced a smile, a tired expression that didn't come naturally at that moment. He slammed the hat onto his head and then cocked the weapon and waited, seeing nothing more threatening at the moment than the moonlit trees around him. He lay still as he tried to get his breathing under control.

He slowly reached out with his free hand and touched the wound on his leg. He knew the bullet had gone all the way through his calf just to the left of the tibia and assessed that the blood flow was of an acceptable level. He raised himself into a sitting position and was in the process of trying to undo his belt buckle for use as a tourniquet when he heard movement to his front. The man he had hit in the face with the .32 wasn't as dead as Lee had thought. The man was up and charging.

"This isn't my night," Lee said as he brought the .45 up and aimed as quickly as his adrenaline-drained body would allow. He aimed with his left hand and fired the first of three rounds into the man's face, chest, and abdomen. Still the Argentine came on.

Lee tried to roll to his left as he once more fired the Colt, but he wasn't fast enough as the machete arced toward his exposed face. At the last second he turned his head as far to the left as he could, letting the man's body fall upon him. The dying man's momentum brought the large machete down on the right side of his face. The steel blade sank to the cheekbone and sliced cleanly through his right eye, brow, and then his scalp, knocking the fedora from his head. The pain hit immediately as he fired two more rounds into the man out of pure anger and fright.

Lee rolled the Argentine off his body and then turned over on his back. With the smoking Colt still in his hand he reached up and covered his face. He felt the blood flowing freely through his fingers and knew he had lost his right eye. He screamed out more in rage than pain. He was angry because he had been caught off guard and then wounded so badly he would more than likely bleed to death before his men found him.

Garrison Lee struggled to shut out the pain. He tried his best to focus on the moon above him. It flashed in and out of focus as he closed his left eye and placed pressure on his right. He tried to keep the eye open but soon allowed the blood loss to take its revenge on his stupidity. His last action for the night was to reach out and take hold of his battered fedora, his large hand crushing it to his body. He had allowed the German courier to escape with another communiqué to Ecuador. As Lee slowly lost consciousness, he kept his hand over his face and cursed out loud about the large slice the man had put through his hat.

As he finally passed out, Garrison Lee had no way of knowing that Operation Columbus was about to receive its final orders.

## QUITO, ECUADOR,
## 37 HOURS LATER

Benjamin Hamilton watched the train station from a small café down the block. He alternated between watching the station and looking at the eleven snowcapped volcanoes that surrounded the capital city. He wished he were skiing instead of doing the most boring job of his life. He had made choices, and this was the inglorious end of the most important choice of his life. He'd had a chance at being a Regular Army officer after his graduation from Harvard Law School, but he had opted for the OSS, the United States intelligence service, and working for one of its more persuasive minions, Colonel Garrison Lee. Now he found himself far from the exciting life he had been promised, since Lee had sent him to the slowest, albeit most beautiful, region in South America. He had hoped for duty alongside the legend, Lee himself, in the south, but instead found himself watching for the occasional Nazi who just happened to wander into his operational zone.

As his green eyes went back to the train depot, he thought about the message he had received from the main OSS operative in Brazil, relaying the news about Lee being missing and suggesting he be on the lookout for a Nazi named Heinz Goetz, an SS general they suspected of being in this hemisphere. Goetz was possibly coming to take something out of Ecuador. Hamilton examined the only picture Washington could forward of Goetz and saw that the small SS man had cruel eyes. He figured that, between the cruel eyes and his small stature, Goetz should be easy to spot if his destination was, indeed, Quito. There was no information or even an educated guess about what this Goetz might be removing from Ecuador, just that it might be more than one item.

Ben placed the photo back into the inside pocket of his jacket and then zipped the coat up to his throat against the chill of the day. As he watched the train that had just pulled in, he raised the cup of rich coffee and drank.

As he sat there waiting, Ben thought about the only thing that had occupied his mind for the past three years—his new wife, Alice. He had only been with Alice for three days after their wedding before he was shipped out for training at Quantico, Virginia, and then to Fort Knox, Kentucky. He missed his eighteen-year-old bride more than anything in his own young life, and couldn't wait for the damned war to be over so he could get back to her. No matter what Garrison Lee said or how much he begged, the OSS was not the life for him, not if it meant being away from Alice.

His thoughts were interrupted by two large trucks speeding down the street. He half turned and watched as they pulled up to the loading platform at the station. He looked around, trying not to move his head, as though the trucks were of no interest to him. He saw three large Western-looking men start shouting orders in broken English to fifteen Ecuadorian workers as they piled out of the back of the first vehicle. They all ran for the covered bed of the second and started unloading crate after crate. Ben turned to his left and whistled. A man who was sitting at a shoeshine stand lowered his newspaper with the banner headline, *HITLER DEAD!* The medium-sized man saw Ben nod his head toward the trucks.

The man stood, tossing the boy shining his shoes a quarter, a real prize for the kid or for almost anyone else in the country. He stepped down and then gestured to his right. Three men joined him. They walked to a car parked along the street and opened the trunk. As Hamilton watched, he unzipped his coat and made sure the Colt .45 he had was there along with his spare clips of ammunition. He zipped the jacket back up as the four men removed two Thompson submachine guns and two large shotguns. They double-checked their loads and then the lead man walked casually over to the train station. Hamilton stood and tossed a dollar on the table, then slowly made his way out of the café, electing to go around the far side of the small station and its loading platform.

"One more mission, Alice, then your husband is coming home," he said to himself with a smile as he dodged the few cars along the main thoroughfare of Quito.

The four men approached the truck that was being loaded. Two men split off and checked the back of the first truck. Four wooden crates had already been placed on the platform. The first two approached a large blond man who was laughing with another European-looking man as they leaned against the back of the truck being unloaded. The third was in the back supervising the work.

The sound of a shotgun being charged with a lethal round brought all the activity around the trucks to a halt.

"Gentlemen, we are the United States Federal Bureau of Investigation. We need to see a bill of lading before you transport these items out of Quito."

The two men at the back of the truck straightened and the third poked his head out of the back and smiled.

"The FBI, in Ecuador?" the large man asked, hopping expertly down from the bed of the truck. The speaker's words were in very passable English.

"We're here at the invitation of the local government and the people of Ecuador, sir. Now, the bill of lading, please."

The third man kept smiling as he took in the guns and the other two men who came up from the first truck on either side. The Ecuadorian laborers stepped back as the confrontation ensued. The blond started removing a thick pair of gloves.

"Would you mind if I saw some identification, gentlemen?" The man's smile broadened as he shot a quick glance at the train station.

The lead agent slowly lowered his shotgun and reached into his leather field jacket. He brought out a green ID card with "FBI" written in bold, golden letters.

"Looks real enough," the man said, leaning closer to the ID card, "Agent Ferguson."

Two of the agents suddenly turned as the doors to the station house opened and a small man with a long black leather coat emerged. He carried a satchel and his glasses reflected the light of the afternoon sun.

"Is there a problem, gentlemen?"

As Ben rounded the far side of the platform, he saw the small man who stood on it looking down at the scene below. Hamilton fumbled for his .45 and at the same time he brought out the picture the OSS in Brazil had forwarded to him a day earlier. Ben smiled as he recognized General Heinz Goetz. The SS officer was even shorter than his description.

"No problems here, Mac, as long as you have the proper paperwork for these crates," the lead agent said, placing his ID back into his jacket. "Why, you boys didn't even have these things weighed in. I believe the Ecuadorian government requires the weigh-in of all freight."

"I have a bill of lading and weight certificate right here, gentlemen." Goetz half turned his head and nodded toward the interior of the station. Then he opened his satchel.

Ben saw movement and froze. Then he jumped forward toward the first truck.

"No!" he shouted loudly.

Just as Ben made his appearance, Goetz removed a Walther pistol and fired point-blank at the lead agent, then before the rest of the FBI team reacted Goetz slammed his body down onto the wooden platform just as the large glass windows behind him shattered as machine gun bullets started raking the three remaining agents and several laborers at the back of the truck.

As Ben ran around the blind side of the second truck, one of the agents was thrown backward into him. Ben saw that he was still alive and started pulling him back as bullets started to find their way back to his vulnerable position. Hamilton aimed as best he could with the wounded agent in his arms and then fired, but the agent's weight pulled his aim off considerably. Not that it would have mattered. As he stumbled backward he saw ten men emerge from the station house and all of them had machine guns. They were raking not only the agents, but the Ecuadorian workers who were trying to flee in a panic.

Ben lost his footing and went down, pinned beneath the agent's weight. Still, he was able to raise the .45 in his right hand and start firing low to the ground. He managed to hit the feet and ankles of the two men at the back of the truck. As they hit the gravel-covered ground, the OSS man placed two rounds each into their heads and then he ejected the spent clip and inserted another. Hamilton then started pulling the wounded agent along as best he could as he heard men taking position around the first truck. He knew they would soon be surrounded.

"Don't kill the American. We need him."

Ben Hamilton heard Goetz shout at the remaining man who had accompanied the trucks. Ben shrugged the agent, who was now dead, off him and stood.
He retraced his steps and then took quick aim at Goetz, who was standing on
the platform looking as if he were Julius Caesar. Hamilton placed pressure
on the trigger and that was when he was brutally pulled backward, hard enough
that the .45 flew from his hand. He lost his balance and fell, a strong arm pulling at him, his coat collar used like a suitcase handle to drag him through the
gravel. Ben tried to warn whoever was pulling him that there was a man taking
aim at them, and just as they reached the corner of the platform, the man pulling him to safety emptied a Colt .45 into the assassin. Finally, as they rounded
the wooden platform, Ben was pulled to his feet.

"What were you going to do after you shot Goetz?" a strong voice asked as
he was pushed toward the open door of an idling car. "Take the honorable way
out and blow your head off?"

Ben was pushed through the open door as the man hurried around to the
driver's side of the idling car and smashed the accelerator down. The car sped
away.

"I thought I taught you better than that. You live to fight another day,
dumbass!"

As Ben tried to get his breathing under control, the rear window exploded
inward and the driver swerved as he twisted the wheel hard to the right. Hamilton risked a look up at his rescuer. All he could see was a large bandage. Blood
was seeping through as Colonel Garrison Lee turned toward him and angrily
looked him over.

"Are you hit?" he asked. He then turned the wheel in the opposite direction
and slammed on the brakes, throwing Ben up against the dashboard. "Are you
hit, Hamilton?" Lee asked again, looking through the rear window frame.

"They said you were missing," Ben stammered, checking for any leaks he
may have sprung.

"Not missing—just beat half to death and cut up some. Now, are you hurt?"

"I don't seem—"

"Good, we'll talk later about how there seemed to be just about an entire
SS regiment in your country of responsibility and you not knowing about it,"
Lee said. He removed the empty clip and inserted another into the handle of
his .45. He tossed Hamilton another ammunition clip. Then, as Ben watched,
Lee laid his head against the steering wheel. He took some deep breaths. Blood
had started a pretty good flow through the thick gauze across the right side of
his face.

"Are you all right, Colonel?"

Lee laughed with his forehead still on the steering wheel.

"Do I look all right, Hamilton? I mean, I thought you were a Harvard grad."

"What happened back there?" Ben asked, nervously looking through the
windowless panel in the back.

"I don't know, Hamilton," Lee said, straightening as he heard the train pulling out of the station. "Do you have any idea what in the hell was so important to Goetz that he risked being shot or captured thousands of miles away from home?"

"Well, sir, there's the crates—"

Lee looked over and finally a smile broke out across his shattered face.

"Really, Hamilton. You think so?"

Ben caught on quickly that the colonel was making light of his obvious observation and he felt embarrassed having made it. Lee, with blood starting to course down his right jawline, put the car in gear and sped off in the direction of the eastbound train. Hamilton saw how gingerly the colonel was working the brake and the gas pedals, then he saw why. There was another bloodstain on his right pant leg at the calf. So the report was true. The colonel had indeed been ambushed and almost butchered in Argentina. How he could be doing what he was doing was far beyond what Ben could imagine.

"Look, we have one chance at this. You have to get on that train and stop it. The only thing I would be good for is throwing the car in front of it," he hissed. He turned onto the narrow gauge tracks and started riding the rail, with two wheels on and two off. The ride was bumpy and with each jolt Hamilton could see Lee grimace. "What has your training taught you?"

Ben charged a round into the .45 and then thought about what he had to do. "Can you run the front bumper of this thing right into the ass end of the train?" he asked as he rolled down the right-side window.

"That's my intention, Hamilton, and you can't jump onto that damn thing sitting in here."

Ben tucked the Colt into his waistband and then took off his thick jacket. As the car rumbled down the tracks its wheels were catching the ties, sending shockwaves through the suspension of the battered Ford. Hamilton slid easily if bumpily out of the window. He used his hands and feet and started to kick and pull.

"Hamilton? What in the hell are you doing?" Lee called out, trying to focus on ten things at once.

Ben glanced back inside as the car jumped once, then twice, almost throwing him from the Ford. He finally braced himself. "I'm getting ready to jump onto the train."

"Damn it," Lee said, shaking his head. Then he took the wheel with his left hand and with his right brought his own automatic up and fired three times into the windshield on the right side. Then he started punching the glass with the barrel of the gun until the glass was gone. "That may be a little easier, don't you think?"

Hamilton slid back into the car and then, feeling like a scolded school kid, pulled himself onto the hood. Ben immediately saw that this wasn't going to be like the serials at the movies. With the car being jolted first left and then right, and also up and down, he was finding it hard to stay in one place on the hood.

"Look out!" Lee shouted.

Ben turned and saw a man step out onto the back platform of the train to light a cigarette. It was one of the men who had opened up on them from inside the train station. His eyes widened as the match he was using blew out. He had started to reach for a sidearm when Ben, his reactions this time far faster, aimed his Colt and fired four rounds. The first three hit nothing but air as the car was jolted from side to side. The fourth caught the German in the center of his chest. Lee watched as the man's weapon fell. Then, in slow motion, he leaned over the small railing and plummeted from the train. Ben was almost thrown from the hood when the car ran over the man's body.

Lee gunned the engine. As steam started spewing forth from under the hood, partially blinding Hamilton, the Ford's front bumper slammed into the train. Ben was thrown forward, losing his grip on the single windshield wiper. He started sliding down, unable to grab on to anything because of his gun hand.

Garrison Lee saw what was about to happen. He slowed the car until there was twenty feet of distance and then accelerated once more with the engine screaming in protest.

"Get to your knees and get ready," Lee shouted. "Hold on to nothing."

"What! Are you nuts?" Hamilton pushed the Colt back into his pants, then stooped and faced forward, following his orders no matter how crazy they sounded.

The last ten feet between car and speeding train was covered in less than ten seconds. The front bumper slammed into the train once more. The impact was so hard that without a handhold Ben was shot forward like a catapult. His eyes widened as he passed through the steam of the overheating engine and then the railing was right there. He grabbed at it as Lee backed the car away. With his heart racing faster than the car's engine, Ben hung on to the thin railing as his feet bounced from railroad tie to railroad tie. Finally, he started to pull himself up as Lee's car bounced once, twice, and then hopped the tracks to the right side of the caboose. Ben started climbing up the railing to the platform. As he slid to the floor he tried to catch his breath. Looking around, he wondered how he was going to get inside with at least ten armed men waiting for him. Then he saw the answer.

Garrison Lee was using the last of the car's momentum to catch up with the passenger cars. As he looked to his left with his good eye, he saw the shocked face of the small SS general, Goetz, widen in astonishment. Lee grimaced, raising his .45 and shooting into the windows of the Pullman. Glass was flying as at least three of the wildly placed bullets hit their targets. The unsuspecting Germans never saw it coming. Lee didn't know if he had hit Goetz, but suspected he hadn't.

Ben knew when to act. He took a deep breath and then stood. His legs were no longer shaking and his heartbeat, while still fast, had calmed enough that he could put his makeshift plan into motion.

Hamilton turned the knob and stepped inside the caboose. He saw a shocked conductor and caboose man as they cowered in a corner. Ben placed a finger to his lips and then ran forward. He went through the next door and onto the open platform between the two cars. He once more took a deep breath and then stepped through the adjoining door. He saw men starting to pick themselves up from the center aisle, and at least two more firing their submachine guns from an open window. Ben opened fire, taking out the most obvious threats first—the men at the windows. Then he fired twice more at two men who were attempting to stand. Then, as he saw Goetz start to run down the aisle, Ben aimed. Click. His Colt was empty. He looked around. He noticed a wounded German prone in the aisle and Hamilton saw what he was reaching for. He kicked out viciously with his right boot, catching the man in the chin and sending him to the Thousand Year Reich. He reached down and recovered the machine gun. Without hesitating, he jumped over the dead and dying guards and ran after General Goetz.

Outside, Lee knew he had to get on that train. The car was as near to death as he himself had been four days earlier. He saw a break between cars coming up and slammed the steering wheel to the left. The Ford once more hit the berm on the tracks and jumped three feet. Instead of sliding back down, the small car hugged the side of the speeding train. Lee reached out and took hold of the railing that protected passengers going from one car to the next. The Ford suddenly jerked right and he lost his hold. Cursing, he tried again, once more slamming the slowing car into the side of the train. The engineer in front started blowing his whistle and the train sped up. Lee was fast losing his window of opportunity to get on the train and help young Hamilton.

"Damn it," he yelled, ripping the soaked bandage from the right side of his face. He reached out again through the window, this time holding the steering wheel steady with his wounded leg. He took a firm hold of the railing and pulled. As he did so his right leg straightened and the wheel began to spin crazily. Lee was pulled out of the window and left dangling by one hand as the speeding Ford turned sharply to the right and then simply rolled over, crashing into the tree line that ran beside the feeder road. The OSS colonel found himself in the same situation his onetime student Hamilton had been in a moment earlier as he dangled from the train. His right leg was screaming in agony and he knew his strength could not hold out much longer. He felt his fingers starting to lose their hold on the rail. He closed his eyes and felt the blood from the damaged stitches on the right side of his face begin to flow in earnest. He cursed himself for his lack of strength. Now he would fall and be crushed underneath the train's wheels. It wasn't dying that bothered him. It was letting young Hamilton down. He silently wished him luck as his fingers slid from the railing.

Just as he felt his hand let go, his fall was stopped. He was still dangling as he looked up and saw why. Hamilton had come from the car and reached out and grabbed Lee's hand at the last second. Lee saw him struggling with his weight and against the forces of the speeding train. Still Hamilton pulled. Finally Lee was able to grab the railing with his right hand. Then, before he knew it, he was pulled aboard. Both men collapsed and sat breathing hard. Hamilton swallowed and then looked over at Lee, who was sitting with his chin on his chest. Ben saw the horrible wound on the right side of the colonel's face. He grimaced and then stood with the help of the machine gun.

"If you'll excuse me, Colonel, I believe General Goetz went thataway."

Lee reached out and tried to grab Hamilton's pant leg but missed. He fell to his knees.

"Damn," he said, reaching into his waistband and pulling out the Colt. As he tried to sit up, he found he had to use the railing again since he had no strength left.

Ben cautiously opened the door on the next car. Looking back at Lee momentarily he saw the big man trying to sit up. He knew from looking at Lee's condition that he would have to take Goetz alone. He opened the door. He saw the crates that had been loaded and then he saw Goetz ducking behind the largest of them.

Hamilton closed the door and went to one knee. He watched, waiting for Goetz to show the top of his head. Ben had been first in his class in target shooting and hoped his skill hadn't diminished in the years he had been inactive here in Ecuador. As he waited, Goetz remained hidden.

"Mr. Hamilton, I believe?" Goetz called out.

He listened, but didn't say anything in return. Ben saw an opening and duck-walked to a crate that was against the far wall of the freight car. He took up a position behind it.

"Mr. Hamilton, my name is Goetz. I am aware of your record, my boy. I am also aware of the qualifications of the man that trained you. And I also know that Colonel Lee is still alive. Imagine my consternation seeing him driving a car at fifty miles an hour and shooting at me."

"I imagine you almost shit your pants. I mean, I would if I knew Lee was coming for me." Ben used the loudness of his voice to edge closer. He sped across to the next closest crate and hunkered down.

"Ben . . . may I call you Ben?" Goetz raised his head for a split second and then quickly ducked back and in that split second Hamilton saw that the right lens was cracked on Goetz's wire-framed glasses. One advantage of this was that the German would have a hard time seeing. Lee had taught him to quickly count down the advantages and disadvantages of any situation he found himself in.

"Sure, why not be on a first-name basis with the man who's going to kill you?" Hamilton said, looking away from Goetz so as not to give him his exact location.

"Those are hasty words, Ben, especially for what I have to offer the United States government."

Hamilton resisted the urge to speak again. This time he rose up as high as he dared and peeked over the large crate. He brought up the machine gun and waited for Goetz to show himself one last time.

"It's a miracle, Ben. In these crates I have a miracle. Your government would be happy to have what I possess, young man."

Hamilton knew Goetz wasn't going to risk another peek above his own crate. The young agent knew he would have to flush the general out. He aimed at a tight spot where he guessed Goetz would appear.

"What one man possesses one minute, another possesses the next," he said. "Whatever is here, General, we'll soon know all about it."

"That is true. But what comes with the crates, Ben, is five years of research by the best German minds. It will save you years upon years of study to come half as close as we in understanding what it is we truly have—as I said, a miracle."

"All right," he said as he aimed still tighter on the area he thought the voice was coming from. "I'll bite. What have you got, and why in hell should we care about it?"

"Because every human being on this planet wants to know, needs to know . . . and I dare say, would kill to know. Just a minute's truce, Ben, that's all I ask. Then I'll throw my hands in the air and I'll become your prisoner."

Hamilton thought a moment. The man was small and overweight and this was probably the only time he had ever fired his weapon against a real man and not at some helpless woman or child.

"Here is my only weapon," Goetz said and then slid out onto the wooden floor a small caliber pistol. "There, Ben, I'm unarmed. Now I will stand and I will show you a sight you will tell your grandchildren about."

Ben watched as Goetz stood up. He had his hands raised. His left was empty and in the right he carried the large satchel. Hamilton stood but kept the submachine gun pointed at Goetz.

"The satchel, drop it," Ben said as calmly as he could.

Goetz slowly lowered the leather case to the top of the crate he had been using for cover. He then raised the now empty hand over his head. "Perhaps you will be so kind as to lower that weapon, my young friend?"

"I feel better with it pointed right between your eyes, Herr General." Ben stepped out from his cover.

"Since the Führer has left the war effort, I think it a good time to surrender," Goetz said as he stepped further into the center of the car and slowly started to lower his hands. The car swayed as it went around a bend, throwing Ben's weight to his left. Goetz noticed that no matter how jumbled the ride, the submachine gun never left its mark.

"I'm sorry, General, but my company doesn't take prisoners. We keep score in other ways."

Goetz saw Hamilton in a light that made him feel very uncomfortable. "Young man, your organization and mine can do business in this matter. I am willing to offer these artifacts," he said with a gesture, which elicited a menacing forward thrust of the weapon in Ben's hands, making Goetz flinch. "As well," he added, "as the expertise behind their discovery and examination. To help you in your decision, I will say that over two hundred German soldiers were killed very recently by machines—machines designed to fight as men. Mechanicians designed millions of years before man walked our planet. Perhaps I may show you?"

"No, General, you may not. You and your kind may find sympathetic ears in my government, you may even find those that will turn a blind eye to what you and other murderers have done in Europe, but I'm not one of those people. I intend to kill you, and the only deal I'll make with you is if you want it easy or hard. I prefer hard, maybe both of your kneecaps first. What do you say?"

"You're insane, young man; you are throwing away knowledge that will astound your superiors!" Goetz said, his eyes never wavering from the machine gun.

Ben gestured for Goetz to move away from the large crate where he had placed the satchel. His eyes were drawn to the strange symbol marking the sides and top of all of the crates in the compartment. Four circles, each smaller than the one before it, each partially eclipsing the one behind it.

As the general moved to his right, Hamilton felt movement behind him. At that exact moment one of the guards sprang up from behind a row of crates Ben had not been paying attention to. The man must have been there the entire time. Ben turned and fired. The machine gun spewed forth bullets in an arc that caught the man across his chest. Too late, Hamilton saw Goetz rush forward, producing a long and lethal knife as he did. Before Ben could bring the machine gun to bear, Goetz brought the knife up and into the young agent's stomach, slicing deep into his abdomen. Several more shots sprang from the weapon Ben was holding but all they did was slam into the largest of the crates.

"You see, we are pretty good at conducting business also, my young friend." Goetz withdrew the knife and rammed it into Hamilton a second time. Ben felt his body go numb and he let his weapon fall from his hands. He thought he could smell the German's hair oil and the powder he used against being chafed by the South American wind. As he slid down Goetz's small frame, he tried desperately to stay on his feet. He reached out and grabbed for the top of a large crate on top of another the same size. Ben's mind started swirling, even the sound of the train seemed distant, but he could swear the crate he snatched at looked like a coffin. He finally held on hard enough that he thought he had arrested his fall when Goetz pulled the long knife free of his insides. As he continued to fall, he pulled the crate free and Hamilton fell along with it to the train's shaking floor. The crate broke open and its contents fell over Ben. It and he rolled and then all was still.

As Ben was starting to lose consciousness, he smelled dust, old mildew, and dirt. As he tried to focus he could see rocks and black shoes. The shoes moved as the sound of large caliber rounds filtered through Hamilton's dying breaths.

The shoes Ben was looking at started dancing and then they magically flew away. As he closed his eyes against the flying dirt, Ben thought he heard cursing. As he opened his eyes again and tried to sit up, he came face-to-face with a grinning skull. Ben blinked and tried to clear his eyes. When he opened them the skull remained. It was encased in something round—a helmet, he thought. Yes, a helmet. The view was confusing because everything—the skull, the helmet, even bits and pieces of clothing—looked to be made of stone. He was questioning what he was seeing when his body was pulled up. He blinked again and then he saw Garrison Lee was looking at him. His wounds had opened up and he was bleeding heavily.

"We better get you to a doc," Ben said, so low that Lee had to get close to his mouth to hear the words.

"I'm fine, Hamilton," Lee said as he shook his head.

"I guess I could have done better," Ben whispered.

"No, you did fine. You remembered your training. You helped capture the man who will probably have his way in the end as far as my life is concerned." As he said this last, he felt the river of blood pouring out of the open wound on his face. "I'm proud of you, boy."

Ben tried to shake his head but found he couldn't. He tasted the blood in his mouth and then tried to focus on the colonel.

"I think I bit my tongue," he said, the words trailing off to nothing, and the light in his eyes dimmed.

Garrison Lee looked at the young face of Ben Hamilton for the longest time. He brushed a strand of dark hair from his face and then after a few minutes lay him gently next to the strange body and even stranger-looking rocks that the Germans had unearthed. As he did he heard General Goetz moan and cough. Lee, without even looking at the injured German, raised the .45 automatic and emptied his remaining rounds into him. He then turned and slowly collapsed from his own wounds. His body slowly fell and landed next to Ben, and also next to the most important archaeological find in the history of the world. Lee saw they all had the same symbol stenciled onto them—the four circles in a straight line. As the blood flowed freely from Lee's fully opened wounds, his good eye fell on the symbols stenciled on the crates. He tried to focus, but the blood loss finally took him down into the black abyss of unconsciousness.

In the far corner a corporal, a clerk attached to the SS division in Ecuador, stood and with a frightened expression made his way out of the car. Joss Zinsser, who was no more than a boy, moved away, one of the last witnesses to what had been uncovered in Ecuador.

As the last visages of the real world twirled and spun, Garrison Lee wondered about the fate he had chosen for himself.

Operation Columbus had been momentarily halted on train tracks outside Quito, but would not remain there for long. Soon a secret that belonged to the entire world would be reburied behind steel and concrete.

## WALTER REED GENERAL HOSPITAL, JULY 4, 1945

The woman sat in the same chair in the same spot in the room that she had been in for the past three months. She sometimes read books, and at other times just watched the slow rise and fall of the patient's chest as he breathed steadily. He was no longer being fed oxygen underneath the small plastic tent. His wounds were healing and his color was improving. She watched patiently as Garrison Lee slowly recovered from the massive loss of blood he incurred while on duty in South America. The woman had waited day in and day out.

The young woman had dark brown hair that was usually tucked up under a large hat. For the first two months she wore one of many black dresses as she sat and waited, never standing and checking on Lee with a physical touch, but always watching. Gone now were the black mourning dresses and in their place were nice, clean, sensible skirts.

As she sat she heard firecrackers somewhere off in the distance. It was the Fourth of July and she was marking her sixtieth day at Walter Reed. As she looked down at her small and elegant hands, she heard something over the pop of firecrackers. She looked up and saw that Colonel Lee was moving under the blanket. His head turned first to the left and then slowly to the right. She saw the large bandage covering the entire right side of his face and the forehead area. The blood had stopped seeping through as soon as the doctors got the infection under control last month. The bandages were now clean and dry. His one good eye blinked in her direction. She could see that he was having a hard time focusing after so long a sleep. She stood and walked slowly to the bed, placing a hand on Garrison's cheek. She smiled.

Lee, as he finally focused on the young woman standing next to him, thought that the smile he received was a sad one. He tried to remember where he knew this beautiful face from. He had met this young girl before. He swallowed and tried to speak. The woman reached over and brought a large glass of water, using a straw to guide it into his mouth. Garrison took two long sips and then lay his head back. Once again the woman touched his cheek.

"You rest now. You've been hurt for a very long time."

As his eyes fluttered shut, he tried to see the woman clearly. Her face was partly hidden in shadow because of the big-brimmed hat she wore. He gave up and let sleep take him once more.


Garrison Lee sat up when the nurse brought in his breakfast. He examined her face closely. It had been two days since he had awakened for good and ever since then he found himself looking at each female face as they came in to feed him, take blood, or just check his wounds. The woman this morning was not the same one he had awakened to three days ago.

A knock sounded at the door and the girl stepped back. She smiled and then nodded that whoever it was should come in.

Lee, with a half spoon's worth of oatmeal in his mouth, saw a heavyset man walk into the room and remove his hat. He knew the man well.

"Well, it's about time you woke up." The big man stood over Lee as if examining him. "And, you don't look as bad as everyone made out. I've gotten worse wounds while getting a haircut and a shave."

Lee placed the spoon on the tray and looked the man over.

"Then you damn well ought to get another barber." He looked at the large man with his one good eye. "How are you, Bill?" Lee asked, his voice still raspy.

"Tolerable, Lee, tolerable. Everyone thinks we can relax now that the war in Europe is over, but to hell with that, I say. We've still got one hell of a problem in the Pacific." He leaned over after nudging the young nurse out of the way. "And to be frank with you, my boy, the Reds are starting to rear their ugly heads in Berlin, not to mention a dozen other places."

Lee closed his eyes. "Well, they can't say you didn't warn them about that one, sir."

"Damn right I did, Lee." William "Wild Bill" Donovan, the head of the Office of Strategic Services, shooed the young hospital nurse away and then sat on the edge of the bed. "Well, until you get out of here you can keep this in your pocket, my boy. Too bad you can't show it to anyone or wear it on some fancy uniform."

Lee was handed a small case. He clicked it open with one large hand while his eye studied Donovan. Finally he looked at what was inside the case. A set of silver stars gleamed under the harsh fluorescent lighting. He snapped the case closed as though he had discovered something distasteful.

"Congratulations, General," Donovan said as he stood.

Lee set the new rank on the table with his oatmeal and then pushed the table out of the way.

"Yeah, I thought you would be all enthusiastic and giddy as a schoolgirl over the promotion."

"Promoted for getting my agents shot all to hell? Getting a kid knifed in the belly? Yeah, I'm giddy as hell over that."

"Felt you let them down, huh?"

"Something like that."

"Well, for your information, our young Mr. Hamilton stopped one murderous bastard in that Nazi general." Donovan leaned over and looked Lee in his one good eye. "And you better damn well give that kid the respect he deserves for doing his job."

Donovan turned and started for the door.

"I'm afraid I fell asleep before the end of the book. What in the hell was in those crates?" Lee asked as he reached for the box containing his new general's stars.

Donovan turned and all humor and anger was absent from his face.

"By the time those Hoover boys got their tails back up, the crates were gone. We assume the German agents did what General Goetz couldn't. They probably made their way back to Germany somehow." Donovan looked down at his feet. "Anyway, we'll talk later. Right now there's someone who's been waiting to see you." He turned away as he buttoned his suit jacket and placed his hat on his head. "And try to use some of that etiquette you used to have when you were a senator. She's a classy young woman."

"Bill?"

"Yeah," Donovan said as he turned back to face Lee. He flinched as he was almost hit by the small jeweler's box Lee had thrown at him. He fumbled it and then caught it.

"Shove that star up your ass."

Donovan at first smiled, and then he laughed out loud.

"That would hurt, General Lee." Donovan turned and left as his laugh echoed back into the room. "By the way, I have another job planned for you, or rather the president has."

As Garrison turned away, not dwelling on what Donovan or the president was cooking up, he heard the footfalls of high heels on the floor. When he looked up he saw a woman in a large hat standing at the doorway. She hesitated only a moment and then stepped into the room, closing the door behind her. She stood planted just inside the doorway. The hat hid her face and the small veil attached to it made her look mysterious, but Lee knew who she was. She was the same woman he had awakened to three days before.

"I understand you've been a constant companion of mine these last couple of months," Lee said.

The woman pushed the veil up over her hat and centered her attention on the man in the bed for a few moments before approaching him.

"I just wanted to see if you're as big a son of a bitch as Ben said you were."

Garrison Lee looked for the longest time at the young, beautiful woman before him. Then he swallowed as the memory of their first meeting came into his mind. He had come to her parents' farm a million years before wanting to talk with her young husband about patriotism and how he could best to serve his country. His remaining eye could not hold her image any longer and he looked down.

"Mrs. Hamilton," was all he said.

She slowly sat on the edge of the bed where a moment before the man who was soon to be known as the father of the CIA, Wild Bill Donovan, had been. She removed a large hatpin and then her hat. Her hair was done up in a bun and her face was clean of makeup save for lipstick. Her face needed none as far as Lee was concerned.

"Tell me about Ben." She saw the uncomfortable look cross Lee's face. "Not about how he died, about how he lived. You knew him far better than I, you see."

Lee looked up and took the woman in.

"He lived, Mrs. Hamilton. In the short time he had, that boy lived."

The widow of Benjamin Hamilton looked down and saw Garrison Lee clearly for the first time. She knew him to be someone who cared about his people, but also a man who hid that attribute well. She felt she knew him immediately and far better than anyone else ever would. It was that single eye and its penetrating glow. She never shied away from it and would listen to him speak for hours.

"General, I think you can call me Alice."

PART ONE

# THE KILLING
# OF INNOCENCE

# 1

Alice Hamilton watched Garrison Lee sleep. She leaned closer when he mumbled, trying to catch the words he was struggling to say. She couldn't catch the soft words but she could tell he was distressed. He had been having nightmares of late and they were the first she had ever been aware of in their sixty-eight years together. Lately it seemed Garrison Lee, former senator from Maine, an OSS general during the war, and now the retired head of the most secret organization in the United States government—Department 5656, also known to a few as the Event Group—was having trouble with his conscience, rare for a man who never allowed anyone near his deepest thoughts. For sixty-eight years Alice had guessed at them, and on a few occasions had been right about his true feelings, but now she didn't know what was going on inside Lee's failing body and mind. The only thing Alice Hamilton ever really knew for sure was that Garrison Lee loved her, and she him.

She took Lee's hand and squeezed it gently when he turned his head first left and then right. He mumbled something again and then fell silent. Alice allowed the tears to flow for the briefest of moments before swiping them away.

"Jump, Ben, jump!" Lee shouted as he tossed his head to the right.

Alice froze at the moment her long dead husband's name was mentioned. It was a subject Lee and she had discussed on only one occasion and that was in the months after World War II had ended. It had never come up again and Alice never once asked him to repeat the story of how her husband had died.

"Oh, no, no, no—you bastard—you bastard!"

Lee sat up so fast that Alice had to lean back to keep from being knocked silly by the man's still large frame. He sat up and his left eye opened and he had a look of murder on his face. The ugly scar ran under the eye patch covering his right eye and ran pink into the gray hairline. Gone were the dashing good looks of the Hollywood leading man that was once General Garrison Lee. Now all that remained was a dying man with a guilt-ridden memory and a woman who had fallen in love with him in only a few short years after the war.

"Garrison, wake up," she said as she tried to gently push him back onto the bed.

Finally Lee took two large breaths and looked over at Alice, allowing his one eye to adjust to the faint light filtering into the bedroom. He blinked and then finally realized where he was. He slowly lay back, but not before taking Alice's hand in his own.

"Dreaming," he said as his eye closed.

"Yes, I know," Alice said, leaning over and kissing his brow.

"It's hell dying, old woman. All the ghosts start to pop open the tailgate to the welcome wagon." He opened his eye and looked at Alice. He tried to smile and for the first time in her life she saw that Lee had a tear in his good eye that he didn't try to swipe away.

"I tried to bring him home alive. I—"

"Stop, don't even think about it. Ben will be there waiting for you. After all that we've been through and learned at the Group, you have to believe he's there. Hell, he may even have a choice word or two for you about stealing his wife," Alice said, smiling.

Lee returned the smile. "The only reason I regret going is that I have to leave you." Lee half turned and lifted his free hand. He held her face. "You saved me. Every day you were in my life, you saved me from being that bleak man you met all those years ago."

"You're not gone yet and I'm still here, old man. You get some more rest." She let his hand go and reached for several large files that were spread across his blanket. "And no more reading material for you," she said, stacking the red-bordered files and then standing, but not before she leaned over and kissed the 103-year-old-man deeply. "If you get your rest, I'll give these back to you."

"You're such a bully," he said as his eye closed.

"Yeah, and you know where I got that training." She turned for the doorway and then stopped and looked back him. "Jack called and asked if he and Sarah could stop by later tonight, I told them yes."

"Always good to see Jack and his girl," Lee said, without opening his good eye.

Alice watched as the senator went to sleep, then she turned and went through the door, leaving it cracked open by a foot as she expected his sleeping mind to bounce back on him again.

Senator Garrison Lee was near death, and there wasn't anything Alice could do but watch him die.

## SHACKLETON CRATER,
## LUNAR SURFACE

For the first time since *Apollo 17* the United States had returned to the surface of the Moon. Peregrine, the code name for the package of four robotic lunar rovers, *George*, *John*, *Paul*, and *Ringo*, named for their resemblance to a large-tracked beetle, had landed safely with its air-cushioned (balloon) landing system that would eventually be used for all future lunar and Mars missions. The four rovers had deployed without incident. Their mission—find proof that the Moon had deposits of water embedded in its dead and lifeless soil and rock, possibly enough water to make the Moon a desirable launching platform for all future space travel.

Since the presidential order of 2010 to curtail NASA's intention of a manned return to the lunar surface in the next decade, it was decided to combine the exploration budgets of Jet Propulsion Laboratory and NASA to explore the possibilities of hidden water deposits on the Moon, left there by countless encounters with the frozen speeders of space, the comets, thus justifying a return to a place America knew well.

As the first landing spot chosen for the Peregrine program, Shackleton Crater was above all else a safe spot for the experimental rovers. Unlike the remote and preprogrammed rovers sent to Mars, *John*, *Paul*, *George*, and *Ringo* would actually be tasked to do heavy-duty work in drilling remotely from the safe plains surrounding Shackleton and operated by mission specialists from their distant confines in Pasadena and Houston. This program was a far cry from taking soil samples on Mars. Shackleton Crater was safe, soft, and conducive to success the first time out. And success was what the space program needed. Water equaled a cheaper way to get to Mars in 2025, the projected date of the first American attempt at gaining the high ground of the red planet.

Mission parameters called for the four rovers to explore the dips and valleys of the outer crater, never venturing down its steeply sloped sides and to its deep floor. They would measure and test for any moisture content in the soil surrounding the large rock formations. This fact was a running joke for the mission planners, as they knew they would find no water at Shackleton. That would be for a later mission at the southern pole when they had conquered the problems of deep-soil drilling.

As *George*, *Paul*, and *John* ran freely around the brim of the giant crater, *Ringo* was taking snapshots of the sky above Shackleton for GPS purposes. The programming for this had been completed at the University of Colorado in Boulder, and designed specifically for *Ringo* to skirt the outer rim and map the sky. The simple instructions for *Ringo* were to guarantee that the other three rovers stayed on mission, testing their sampling and drilling packages for telemetry relay back to Pasadena and Houston. The problem developed when a small glitch in the rover's programming had gone undetected by a sixth year grad student in Colorado. *Ringo*'s design for traversing the lunar surface outside the brim of Shackleton was flawed and was off by a mere three feet. As the other three rovers were performing their remote-controlled tasks flawlessly, *Ringo* was off on its own and running dangerously close to the giant crater's precipitous edge. As eyes 244,000 miles away watched the colorless broadcast coming from the small rover's stationary camera atop its four-foot-wide boxed frame, the roving beetle started to slide off the powdered edge of Shackleton.

## JET PROPULSION LABORATORY, PASADENA, CALIFORNIA

At 9:10 in the morning California time, the press room was full of reporters, not because of the excitement of America's robotic return to the Moon, but simply because it was a very slow news day. As everyone watched the rovers on four different high-definition monitors arrayed around the large press room, they saw one view go askew. The press on hand had no idea that *Ringo* was in the midst of what Pasadena called "a hissy fit." Inside the mission control room, a hundred men and women who had worked on the Peregrine mission for the past ten years watched as a problem they didn't need with the press on hand started happening right before their eyes.

"Ooh, we have *Ringo* going off mission here," said one of the men watching the telemetry board in front of him instead of the video being broadcast. "Jesus, according to my telemetry he's . . . oh, there he goes."

Stan Nathan, the director of the mission, switched his view to that being broadcast by *George*, the closest beetle to *Ringo*. As he watched, he saw the 450-pound rover slowly start sliding off the edge of the crater.

"Becky, stop that damn thing," Nathan said, trying to be as calm as he could. "If it gets down inside of there, we'll never be able to get its telemetry. Those crater walls will stop any signal from getting to it. Hurry up, because Houston's going to start screaming in just about one minute."

Dr. Becky Gilickson, remote operator and programming technician in charge of *Ringo*, turned to her six-person team and frowned. There was nothing she could do. She tried sending out a command to reverse its track and override its program, but with the one-and-a-half-minute delay in communication, all she could do was watch as *Ringo* started a head-first run down the steep incline inside Shackleton Crater. Instead of typing in the remote command, she turned toward Nathan, who was standing in the middle of the darkened room.

"Flight, our command just hit *Ringo*, but it's too late, he's starting to slide. We recommend we run with it. If he tries to reverse track now at that speed he may roll over."

Nathan hurriedly turned to the live shot of *Ringo* as it traversed the slope of the crater. For the moment it was running straight; its large six-limbed arms with the tri-rubber tracks seemed to be handling the rough terrain with ease.

"I concur. Let him go. I want a command sent now that once it hits the bottom of the crater I want it to turn—"

"Stan, Hugh Evans is on the line from Houston," his assistant said as he looked up from the large phone console.

"Put him on speaker."

"Stan, Hugh here," said the senior flight director calling from his personal console at the Johnson Space Center. "Look, this could be very embarrassing. Let *Ringo* run and do not, I repeat, do not order it out of the crater. It'll be down there, so let the press know that we decided to explore the base of Shackleton. Tell them it was my decision to send *Ringo* off mission, clear?"

Nathan was relieved that the flight director for the Peregrine mission had taken control. With the press watching this, it was a potential public relations disaster in the making. If they couldn't control their robots, how the hell could they keep men alive out there?

"Clear. *Ringo*'s running free. It looks like he's going to make the half mile journey pretty quickly."

"Okay, get your press people out there and explain that we intentionally sent *Ringo* off on its own to explore the inside of the crater, nothing more. That ought to keep the dogs away until we can figure out how to recover the rover."

The phone line went dead as Nathan turned his attention back to *George*'s video. The descending rover just went past its line of sight as it slipped and slid down the steep slope.

"Switch main viewer to *Ringo* so we can see what it sees." Nathan turned to his left at the last telemetry station in the long row. "REMCOM, start getting a communications relay established between *George*, *John*, and *Paul*. We have to align them so we can continue to receive telemetry from the little guy once it hits bottom, because it'll never be able to broadcast out of the damn hole."

The remote control communications station began sending out signals interrupting the programming of the three remaining rovers. The scientists would introduce a "burp" in their existing program and send another order to span that gap. They would arrange the rovers around the edge of the crater to receive the telemetry signals from *Ringo* and then relay that signal to earth. It had never been done before, but that was the business they were in.

"Estimate thirty-five feet, plus or minus a foot, until *Ringo* hits bottom," Communications called out. "Signal strength on telemetry is weak. Okay, signal lost at 0922 local time."

"Come on people. Let's get the rest of the Beatles in on this," Nathan called out as he closed his eyes, hoping that *Ringo* didn't go belly-up in the last thirty feet of its unscheduled walkabout.

"We have a patch through from *Paul*," Communications said. "Okay, we now have video from *Ringo* . . . it stopped. It looks like—"

"The damn thing's sideways—it's hung up on something," Nathan said angrily. He was trying his best not to take it out on his people.

On the monitor, the video streaming from *Ringo* showed the side of the crater. As they relayed a signal down into Shackleton from *Paul*, they ordered the camera to rotate 60 degrees. They wanted to see what they were hung up on before trying to extricate *Ringo* from its current 10 degree tilt position.

"Okay, at least we know it's on the bottom and in one piece," Nathan said as he stepped toward the large monitor, watching the area around the rover as it panned its view to accommodate its orders from Earth. "Goddamn big crater," he mumbled as he looked at the darker than normal picture surrounding *Ringo*. "We must be in the lee of the crater's northern wall."

As the camera completed its 180-degree sweep, it stopped. Its lens was automatically trying to focus on something that would be oriented to its left side. It was obviously the obstacle that had arrested *Ringo*'s run down the slope.

"Okay, there it is," Nathan said, as he tried to get a clear picture. "Is that all we have on focus?" he asked.

"Without the external lighting, that's it," REMCOM said as he turned in his seat and looked at the flight director.

"Well, the batteries be damned," he said, looking at the remote communications specialist. "We have to get *Ringo* into the sunlight anyway to charge the damn thing. Turn on external lighting and see what we're snagged on," Nathan said in frustration, because he knew battery life was *real* life when you're on the Moon.

"Relaying the order," REMCOM called out.

As they waited for the delay in communications, Nathan sat on the edge of one of the consoles and rubbed his face. He hoped this would be the only glitch of the mission, but he knew when you were dealing with robots and remote technology, anything could go wrong, so he figured this whole endeavor could take years off his life.

As everyone in mission control in both Pasadena and Houston watched, and with the press yawning, displaying their boredom in both press rooms, *Ringo* turned on the powerful floodlights rigged to the top of its camera tower. The lens refocused and the picture suddenly turned to red and blue.

"Color? What in the hell is color doing on the Moon?" one of the technicians said as she stood up to get a better view.

Of all the photos from the Apollo program and countless views from the Moon, with the exception of anything man-made or views of the Earth, there was never anything of color to be broadcast from the lunar surface, just the white, grays, and blacks of its geology. But here was *Ringo*, the little remote designed for the search and testing of water deposits, sending out a full color image of something that had reached out and grabbed it on its way into the crater.

"Pull the view back by a foot," Nathan ordered, as a sliver of recognition came into his mind. He stared intently at the color image

As the view pulled away from the object holding *Ringo* in place, more detail started to emerge. The colors were from what looked like some kind of material, possibly nylon in nature.

"Pan to the right," Nathan ordered.

After a minute the camera view turned away from the colorful material, eventually settling on something white. Then it focused its high definition camera onto something jagged and dark.

"Damn it, what the hell is that?" Nathan asked, his heart beating faster. "Pan back another foot."

A minute later the picture adjusted. That was when the first reaction was heard. Someone dropped a coffee cup and it shattered the stillness of the control room. The view on the screen was shocking to say the least. The jagged darkness the camera had picked up was the shattered remains of a sun visor attached to a white helmet, and the colorful material-looking pattern was an environmental suit, not unlike those every man and woman in the room had seen at one time or another in old footage of the Apollo program.

"Jesus Christ," Nathan said as he felt his heart start to race.

As the camera focused on the white helmet with the shattered face shield, the bone-white structure of a grinning skull came into view, the eyeless sockets staring at the camera as the bright floodlights cast eerie shadows on the skeletal remains.

Suddenly the speakerphone came to life, making most in the control center jump.

"Pasadena, this is Houston, do you realize that whatever this is, it's being shown to the press, cut the feed to your press center, now!"

"You got it, Hugh," Nathan said as he started shouting out orders.

In the press room a floor down in the JPL building, the members of the media stood dumbfounded as they watched the remote video of the skeleton, buried up to its waist in the lunar dust of Shackleton Crater. The image went from living color to a slow fade to black.


EVENT GROUP COMPLEX,
NELLIS AIR FORCE BASE, NEVADA

Dr. Niles Compton stood only five foot eight inches, but every man and woman in the massive hallway of the underground complex watching him cut the ribbon for the new vault section on Level 75 saw him as a much larger man. His reputation as the no-nonsense leader of the department was legendary. With his thick glasses pushed onto his forehead and his white sleeves rolled to the elbow, Niles looked the part of a harried and very tired accountant. As his predecessor, Senator Garrison Lee, once told him, when in this position of responsibility the director of the Event Group needed to relax and smell the roses; otherwise, what was the point in holding and storing the most prized antiquities in the history of the world and the knowledge that went with them. So today Niles took time out from his normal duties overseeing the blackest department in the federal government to be present at a ceremony to open a new set of storage vaults, and the excavation that housed them almost two miles beneath the sands of Nellis Air Force Base, just outside Las Vegas, Nevada.

He smiled for the first time that morning as his deputy director, Virginia Pollock, handed him an ordinary pair of office scissors. He looked past the tall head of the Nuclear Sciences Division and at the other sixteen department heads and tried desperately to smile. Then he nodded toward the men and women from the Army Corps of Engineers attached to Department 5656. He quickly reached out and cut the yellow ribbon that had been strung across the security arch leading to the new but empty vaults beyond.

"Now, let's get busy and fill some of these up before certain people in the federal government catch on to us and fire everyone."

The men and women of the Event Group laughed as Niles handed the pair of scissors back to Virginia. Then he turned abruptly to a thin man with a pair of horn-rimmed glasses similar to his own. He had the same harried look as Niles, but his smile was genuine while the director's was not. Pete Golding was the head of the Computer Sciences Division of the Group and held the same position Compton himself had many years before.

"What did Europa say about the images?" he asked Pete quietly, while taking him by the arm and walking him away from the milling men and women.

"We dissected that image from here to St. Petersburg, and all Europa had to say was the environmental suit was not of any known design. Not ours, the Russians, nor the People's Republic."

"You mean we have a Cray computer system worth two and half billion dollars and all it can do is agree with what we already know?"

Pete looked hurt and taken aback. He knew it wasn't just the images sent from Shackleton Crater that stunned and shocked everyone at the Group; it was the condition of Senator Garrison Lee that was weighing heavily on the director's mind. Pete took a deep breath and looked down at the man that he admired above all others.

"Niles, Europa only has an image from NASA to analyze. We need more data; she's not a miracle worker." Pete wanted to add *at least not all of the time*, because in his eyes and everyone else's, Europa was indeed just that: a miracle worker.

Niles pulled his glasses down from his forehead and before he put them on, he half smiled at Pete without really looking at him. "I know, Pete." He finally placed his glasses back on and nodded for Virginia to join them. As she walked up, the three moved off toward the elevators.

"Virginia, get our ex-NASA people assembled and give them to Pete, they're pretty much spread out among all the departments, so you'll have to dig them up. I want to know if someone has been hiding something they shouldn't have, or if we have a moon that was far more crowded back in the day than we realized."

"Has the president asked us to check into this?" Pete asked.

Virginia nodded and smiled, anticipating the answer that Niles was about to offer. The air-cushioned, glass-enclosed elevator arrived and they stepped inside.

"No, but he will soon enough, that is if I know him like I believe I do." Niles thought for a moment and then turned to look at Golding. "Pete, I hate to ask this but—"

"You want Europa to break into NASA's and JPL's secure computer systems," Pete said, anticipating the order from Niles as Virginia had a moment before.

"Yes. I don't know why NASA went dark on us and the rest of the world, but it bothers me that this may be kept secret. And in case my old friend the president wants to keep this thing close to the vest, I want to be prepared when it blows up in his face. And it will. He never was any good at keeping things under wraps. Besides, lately he has far too much on his mind, things you and I would never be able to fathom." Niles looked up at the two closest and brightest friends he had. "This is big, I feel it."

As the elevator traveled at over a hundred miles an hour up to the office level of the complex, the sexy Marilyn Monroe–style voice of Europa came over the small computer terminal beside the twin doors. "Director Compton, you have a communication request from Range Rider."

Range Rider was the day's code name for the most powerful man in the world, the president of the United States.

"Speak of the devil," Niles said as he punched a small LED screen on the panel. "Europa, I'll take it in my office."

"Yes, Director Compton."

As the elevator hissed to a stop a mile and a half higher than they had been a few moments before, Niles stepped off on Level 7 and looked back.

"Best guesses on what's happening on the Moon in an hour. Virginia, give Security a heads-up. We may have to cancel Colonel Collins's plans for dinner at the senator's house."

As Niles walked to his office doors and opened them, his eyes flashed to the ten-foot portrait of Abraham Lincoln, a thing that usually gave him a chuckle over what old Abe had accidentally started with the Event Group those many years ago. Today, however, with the thing on the Moon and the condition of his mentor, Garrison Lee, he just wished Lincoln was in charge of Department 5656 instead of him.

Niles walked to his overly large desk and tossed a pile of papers to his left. Then he hit a button. A small screen embedded in the back center of his desk rose from the polished wood. As he stood with his fists planted on the desk, his eyes looked into the lens on top of the monitor. The screen flashed blue, and then the seal of the president flashed on. Soon after, the man himself came into view.

"Niles," the president said.

"Mr. President." Compton greeted his old college roommate, who was the polar opposite of him in the area of politics.

"All right, I can see you're in a mood, but for the record, the vice president acted without my express authorization this afternoon."

"It's nice that you have such a handle on what your people are doing. I mean, with people running around with their fingers hovering over red buttons and all."

"All right, knock it off, smartass. I've changed the damn blackout orders. We fully intend on sharing information with the concerned parties of the world, and that does mean the general populace, at least for the immediate future. Now a warning, baldy. This new order could change at any moment if something else is found up there more mysterious than our thin friend in the red and blue space suit. To tell you the truth, and with all joking aside, this little discovery is a little unnerving, considering our recent past with visitors from out there."

Niles didn't say anything. He just watched his old friend.

"Okay, listen, you warned me about people keeping secrets back when I first took office. Do you guys out there have anything on someone reaching the Moon before or after us?"

"Well, I know that under Senator Lee this department was represented well on almost every Moon landing from *Apollo 11* to *17*. We had complete and trustworthy information on the Russian program, and we know they were nowhere near the surface of the Moon with a manned mission before or since."

"What do you mean your department was represented well on the Apollo missions?"

Niles had to smile for the briefest of moments. "Old Buzz Aldrin was Garrison Lee's man, as were many others, on those rickety spacecraft and in Houston."

"Goddamn old spook, was there anything he wasn't privy to?"

"Evidently there was, because we're in the dark on this one. If he knew something about what was found on the Moon, he would have told us."

"Do you think you can dig something up? I don't want to step on toes in a program I just cut to the bone. I'm not that popular at the moment in Houston and Pasadena, and God forbid my car breaks down in South Florida."

"Look, if this blows up, people will speculate that we were onto something up there, and your cover story about water surveys will be out the damn window."

"I know, but what can we do. Find out what you can—that's why those robots are there."

Niles relaxed and nodded his head. "We'll try and get something. I have Pete extending Europa's mission statement once again and we'll have—" Compton stopped when he saw the president hold up his hand.

"I don't want to know, Niles. Golding and his damn partner in crime are

not what a man in my position should know about. It makes me an accessory."
The president paused. "By the way, how is Lee doing?"

Niles looked at this friend, then said, "He's dying."

## FAITH MINISTRIES, INC., LOS ANGELES, CALIFORNIA

Rev. Samuel K. Rawlins had pitched his tent in what was known to a few of his closest followers as hostile territory. For the largest, most famous, and most profitable televangelist in the world to live in the very heart of the evil he preached against to over 600 million viewers worldwide every Sunday, Wednesday, and Saturday was an insane move. Nobody joked about this around the Reverend. Los Angeles was changing and Rawlins knew where the money was and forever would be.

Named one of the four wealthiest men in the world, Rawlins reserved one side of himself for the millions upon millions of his followers, and another for business associates. It was said that once you did business with Samuel Kenton Rawlins, you would rather sign a contract with Satan himself.

Today he wasn't at one of the four television studios he owned; he was at home in the palatial estate on Mulholland Drive that he had torn down a total of sixteen mansions to build. Most said he liked slumming it because he could have built his private home over any scenic beach in California, instead of the dry hills overlooking the city. But those that knew him best thought he just liked looking out over Los Angeles and marveling, just as Alexander the Great once had: "Is this all there is?"

The large and ornate study overlooked two of the four swimming pools on the estate. As Rawlins, all six foot eight inches of him, sat at his desk he watched the security guards standing at their posts. His dark eyes moved with every step of one of the uniformed guards and didn't stop looking even when the man became motionless to gaze out onto the hillside above the thirty-three-bedroom mansion. He finally looked away and went back to his sermon for the following Sunday morning at his Church of the True Faith in Long Beach. The three-block-long glass and steel tower would house 27,000 worshippers and another one billion would hear his words worldwide.

He was concentrating heavily, allowing his silver hair to fall across his tanned and unlined forehead. He had four assistants in his outer office who were prepared to offer their services, but the Reverend Rawlins liked to pen his own work in his own hand. The assistants would have plenty of time to copy and distribute the sermon to any one of the six publishing houses he owned from California to New York. The Reverend would also sell the handwritten sermons at auction at the end of the year. Everything was money to Rawlins—to a point.

Today's sermon was a special one that would air live that night on the evils of reach—the reach of mankind into God's house, the universe. How mankind would now face the long overdue wrath of God. The image of the skeletal remains found on the Moon played like a stuck recording in his mind's eye as he wrote furiously on his notepad. The contempt America was showing during the hard times this nation and the entire world were now facing was unforgivable. Now they were tempting God's anger by sending out mechanicians to the otherworldly bodies when so much more was needed at home. This foolishness must end and the Reverend had the power to do just that.

A knock sounded at his oak door. He continued to write, finally using his right hand to swipe at the silver hair that ranged across his tanned and unlined forehead.

"Yes," he said, still bent over his work.

The door opened and his first assistant, a striking woman, stuck her blond head inside. She watched the Reverend, marveling at the man's concentration. He finally looked up at her and gave her a smile. He could see her face flush and her knees slightly bend. He knew the effect he had on women, not only here but in the outside world, and he used that influence and sexual intensity to his great advantage.

"Susan, what a pleasant distraction," he said, finally laying his pencil to the side of his sermon. No one but he knew that her distraction was anything but pleasant. Beneath the blue eyes he thought about how pleasurable it would be to walk over to the doorway and slam the woman's head between the door and the oak jamb.

"Sir, you have a call from Vice President Darby. He's on line two."

"How are you today, Susan?" he asked, placing his large hands behind his head and leaning back in his thronelike chair, seemingly unconcerned about getting a call from the vice president of the United States. His smile remained as she returned an even wider, girlish grin. She looked him over. His light blue shirt contrasted with his dark tan and set his pale blue eyes off like a light on a darkened night.

"I . . . I am just fine today, Reverend. Just fine."

"And I must say you look just fine." Rawlins stared at her, his eyes moving down her red dress to her chest and then back to her green eyes. "Ah, but business calls." He had one last look and smile at his assistant and then he picked up the gold-plated phone. He punched in the correct number, maybe a little too hard in his anger at being interrupted.

"Harry, how are things this morning?"

"The president overruled my press blackout."

"Ah, I told you it wouldn't be as easy as you thought, didn't I, Mr. Vice President?"

"Yes, Reverend, you did. But bragging about your insight will not stop the public from gaining knowledge about Operation Columbus."

Rawlins sat straight up in the high-backed chair. He closed his eyes as he tried to compose himself. Then he opened them as the momentary tempest quickly and expertly subsided.

"Please don't use that name on the phone, even if we have a secure line. I've told you about that numerous times."

"I . . . I . . . am, uh, I apologize, Reverend. I am just frustrated. We have not only this headache, but the ongoing nausea inflicted by this Case Blue that's just a wisp of a rumor."

"I understand, Harry; you're in a very stressful business. Politics is something I wouldn't want to be in. We know this Case Blue is being handled by a department not in the norm of day-to-day business, but let's not get ahead of ourselves. What is the NASA and JPL plan of action?"

"For right now they are officially off mission. They are reprogramming the remote rovers: one more will join the first inside of the crater and the other two will be used as communications relays."

"Well, I must conclude that this little find *has* to be related to Columbus. I've never been a big believer in coincidence. The president knew there was something there and he hid it well by cutting NASA's budget, sneaky bastard." His anger was elevated once more, but Rawlins forced his rage back beneath the surface of his speaking voice. "I was hoping we had seen the end of it. I want to thank you for the instantaneous way you informed my office on this disturbing find on the Moon. Of course you will be rewarded in a suitable way, maybe far more than a monetary offering after the next four years is up."

"I just wish the president would have kept his head in the sand and allowed me to do what he assigned me to do. I can still control things to a point."

"My only question is, what about the press?"

"That's the worst of it. The president is going public with everything they find up there. It's like he was waiting for a big discovery to justify a major boost in the space budget. I'll admit he was good, but how did he know there was something in that crater?"

"The press is the problem right now; we'll get into how he knew what was up there later." Rawlins thought a moment, swiveling his chair to see his daughter through the twenty-by-thirty-foot plate glass window. The eighteen-year-old saw him and waved. He smiled and waved back with a glimmering smile on his lips. "I wish we could make the president disappear."

"Even though this line is secure, I didn't hear you say that," the vice president said hurriedly.

"Yes you did. I'll say it again in far more profound and legalese wording: the man is a pain in the ass and needs to go away. Another four years of his leadership is not part of the Lord's plan."

"We've known each other since seminary school, Sam. You know I love my country and my God, so you must understand me when I say those loves are in that exact order."

"And you must understand me, Mr. Vice President; we've managed to bury

Operation Columbus for seventy years. I will not allow the public to start needless speculation about its origins. I will not allow that. *I will not!*"

"Give me time. I can convince the president this is not in the best interests
of the nation. Hell, there may be national security issues to deal with. Give me
the time I need to discover what and who's running this Case Blue operation."

"Time is a commodity we don't have." Rawlins stood and watched his
daughter lay out her towel by the pool, and then his eyes went to the security
man who was watching her do it. He frowned and turned back to his desk without sitting. "I want that find on the Moon hushed up. Ever since I let you in on
the Columbus find in Ecuador, when we were in school, and—you're right—
since I was a seminary student and you were stealing books to sell back to the
school bookstore, we made a deal that the world will never be tempted by the
devil and the knowledge that Columbus would bring to humankind." Rawlins
furrowed his brow as he watched the security guard and the absolute shameless
way he ogled his beautiful daughter. He closed his eyes to shut out the sight.
"Now, I need you to start thinking ahead. The news about this find is already
all over the world. What if this nation, or any other power in the world, decides
to get to the Moon and they uncover the equivalent of Columbus? What are
you prepared to do?"

"Are you asking what if the United States tried to send a manned mission to
the Moon? Or someone else?"

"Of course that's what I mean, you moron. I will not allow that to happen. I
would spend fifty billion dollars to see that any attempt would be stopped. Now
tell me, are we capable of getting back to the Moon on short notice? Is anyone
in the world capable?"

"No, of course not. NASA hadn't planned a return for at least fifteen more
years. And other nations—well, it would be impossible."

"I hate that devilish word, impossible. That's why I'm in a position of power,
my friend, because I didn't listen to people who said that the things I wanted
to achieve were impossible. Nothing is impossible. So—" His eyes sprang open
and he glared out the window at the security guard, who didn't seem to care
who was watching him stare at his younger daughter. "What are you prepared
to do if the impossible happens?"

"I . . . I . . . don't know."

"You disappoint me, Harry. Maybe you shouldn't be in line for the job I
thought you were ready for."

The Reverend hung up. He had wanted to throw it through the window, but
caught himself before he allowed his explosive temper to fully vent. He slowly
and deliberately walked over to the large plate glass window and tapped lightly
on the thick pane, trying not to attract the attention of his lounging daughter.
The security guard, a large man himself, turned with his thumbs pressed into
his gun belt. Rawlins smiled and waved at the blond-haired guard. With his

smile still in place he gestured with his right hand for the guard to join him at the ornate French doors. The guard's face flushed, and then he pointed at his own chest and mouthed the word *me?*

Rawlins nodded his head enthusiastically. The big man in the blue security uniform walked away and disappeared around the corner. Samuel Rawlins walked back to his desk and pulled open the top drawer, retrieving a small item, then turned and opened the outside doors to his study. The security guard was standing there. His arms were at his side and he looked as if he were at attention.

"Yes, sir?" he said, looking from the smiling, silver-haired Rawlins to his right, and then left, suddenly wishing he wasn't the only guard on duty on the west side of the estate.

"How are you today—" Rawlins asked, as he bent at the waist to get a better look at the man's name tag—"Officer Wright?"

"Uh, just fine, sir, how are—"

"I saw you looking at my daughter a moment ago."

"Uh, yes sir, she is very—"

Rawlins's large hands shot through the air so fast that the guard never knew what was happening. One minute he was standing there facing the Reverend and the next minute his neck was being twisted brutally to the left. Before he even realized his words had been cut off, he heard his own neck snap in two. Rawlins grimaced and let the large man slide through his hands to collapse onto the concrete walkway.

"You were about to give an answer that would have gotten you in trouble, young man." Rawlins stepped out onto the walkway and looked around. Then he removed the object he had retrieved from his desk. It was a small digital camera. He adjusted the automatic focus, zooming into the shocked and now strangled security guard. He snapped a picture and then looked down at one of the hundred security men he had on staff. "Your services will no longer be needed at my home."

Rawlins turned and stepped inside the French doors and closed them behind him. His anger was totally vented and the relief he felt was just this side of ecstasy. He turned the small digital camera over and looked at the picture he had just taken on the small LED screen. He smiled and half nodded his head. "Not bad."

He picked up the phone as he placed the camera on the desktop. He punched in a number and waited.

"Security. Anderson speaking," the voice said as Rawlins picked up the camera once more and studied the picture.

"Ah, Mr. Anderson, one of your men seems to have had an accident right outside my study on the west side of the house. I think you better call for an ambulance—very quietly of course, I think he tripped and fell. Very good, no, please don't disturb me. I have quite a bit of work to catch up on."

Rawlins set the phone down and smiled at the small picture of the dead security guard. He finally opened the drawer and shut off the camera as he placed it inside. As he did he saw the small framed photograph he had placed inside a few months earlier, meaning to get the frame changed. He had forgotten about it. He picked it up once more as he had a million times in his life and looked at himself forty-five years earlier. He was standing next to his father in the black-and-white photo. He himself was as unsmiling as the man standing next to him. The dark-haired man wore the uniform of an Army lieutenant colonel. The uniform was spit-polished and fit as snugly as a tailor could make it. They stood in front of an old castlelike structure that looked as if it had seen better days.

"Nineteen sixty-five," he mumbled.

As he lay the picture back inside the drawer, he knew the old castlelike building was no castle at all. Nowhere close, in fact. It was a stone monstrosity made to keep men imprisoned and his father had been the gatekeeper of that fairy-tale place—the man with the key in a rotating nation-by-nation watchman's role.

He closed the drawer, shutting out the stern image of his father. Yes, his own flesh and blood had been the gatekeeper back in 1965, and that was how the events of today were related to Reverend Rawlins.

The keys of the gatekeeper opened and closed the dungeonlike cells of Germany's Spandau Prison.


## LAS VEGAS, NEVADA

Jack Collins and Sarah McIntire stood on the large front porch of one of the more modest houses high in the hills just off Flamingo Boulevard in Las Vegas. Collins was a former black operations guru and a man with countless incursions behind enemy lines, and that was why Sarah McIntire could not figure out exactly why Jack was nervous about seeing his old boss, Senator Garrison Lee. Jack knew he was never one for watching people he loved and admired slip away. Sarah, her stature exactly one foot four inches shorter than the colonel's, placed her hand through Jack's arm as they waited for the door to be answered. They both wore civilian attire; the colonel in a button-down blue shirt and Sarah in a green skirt and white blouse. They both felt odd and out of place without the blue jumpsuit of the Event Group uniform, or at the very least their desert BDUs.

Jack and Sarah were both officially on detached service to Department 5656. Collins was head of the large security force at the complex that provided security for all archaeological digs and the safeguarding of its valuable finds and equally valuable complex, while Sarah, an Army lieutenant, was head geologist assigned to the Earth Sciences Department. It had been the senator who recruited them both and all three, along with Alice Hamilton, had grown close over the years. They were both worried as much about Alice as they were about the senator.

The left side of the double doors opened and Alice stood inside the threshold smiling. Sarah stepped in first and hugged the older woman while Jack looked around, uncomfortable at the very least. Finally, without a word spoken between Alice and Sarah, they parted and then Jack tried to smile as Alice hugged him. The embrace seemed to go on forever, and instead of making Collins feel uncomfortable, he relaxed. He patted her back and then stepped back and looked down at the smaller woman.

"How are *you* doing?" he asked.

"I'm tolerable, Jack, come on in out of the heat," she said, stepping to the side to allow them access to the large but modest house.

Jack had been here on several occasions for dinner, just to talk with Lee about everything under the sun. He and Niles Compton went out of their way to update the senator from time to time on the current status of things at the Event Group complex. The former senator and OSS general seemed to appreciate the visits far more than he let on to Alice.

"Sarah, why don't you help me in the kitchen and let Jack and that old grizzly catch up with one another?"

Sarah smiled and looked at Collins. Then she followed Alice down the long entranceway.

"Go ahead, Jack. He's awake and in pretty good spirits—this being one of his good days. Oh, by the way, he insisted I ask Niles over for lunch also. He said he had something to discuss with all of you."

Jack watched as Sarah and Alice disappeared, then he grimaced as he turned and walked down the long hallway of the one-story house. As he moved, Collins saw not one bit of memorabilia on the walls. There were no personal pictures, nor was there anything to indicate that the senator or Alice ever had a personal life, much less a life spent together. There were beautiful prints of desert sunsets on the walls, and that was when Jack realized it was like walking through one of those model homes that set fake fruit on the dining room table and dishes inside cabinets. As he approached the senator's bedroom he also thought the reason the house was like a model was because the senator and Alice would never consider this their home, not after spending almost every day since 1946 underground at the Event Group complex. *Yes*, he thought, the complex under the sands of Nellis was their home, not this pile of wood and stucco. He stopped at the senator's door, took a deep breath, and knocked.

"Well, don't leave me in suspense. Open the damn door," sounded the gruff command from inside.

Jack turned the knob and looked in, feeling as if he was a young boy and was intruding on his father. He saw the senator standing at the sliding glass window watching the desert behind the house. He finally turned and took in Collins, and then he smiled. Jack nodded silently back. In all of his visits he still wasn't used to seeing the large senator in a pair of pajamas and a robe.

"Don't laugh, Colonel. The Queen of Mean went and hid my clothes on me. She says I don't need the aggravation of dressing."

Jack walked into the room and held out his hand. He was taken aback by how weak the return handshake was. He remembered the first time he had been greeted by the senator four years before and the powerful grip of the ninety-something man. The difference was night and day. Collins released his hand and looked around the large bedroom quickly as if the senator might have read his mind. The only thing on display on the walls was a large shelf. Sitting upon it was what looked like a collection of hats, fedoras to be exact.

"Nice collection," Jack said in true admiration.

"Yeah, I used to look good in hats. Reminded me of Mike Hammer, you know—the impression of toughness. Anyway, glad to see you, my boy." Lee looked behind Jack. "Where's that little girl of yours?"

"You mean Lieutenant McIntire?"

"Cut the crap, Jack. You two never put anything by me, or Niles. By the way, is he here yet?"

"I don't know."

"Well, you're supposed to escort this walking corpse to lunch. My cane doesn't do me much good anymore."

Jack could see the dilated left eye and knew Lee was under the influence of a powerful medication. He wondered if he was up to leaving the room at all. Lee settled it quickly as he reached out and took Jack's arm at the shoulder and then he and Jack made for the door.

"How has . . . everything been?" Collins asked hesitantly.

"What, you mean dying? It's like finishing off a roller-coaster ride, Jack. Scary as hell, but when you get to the end, you want to do it all over again."

"You mean life?"

"Yes, my boy. Never grow old, Colonel, it—what do the kids say? Oh, yes, it sucks big-time."

"Yes," Collins said as they approached the dining room. "That's what they say, sir."

When they entered the large dining room, Jack saw Niles Compton standing there. He was actually dressed in something other than his usual white shirt and black tie. His button-down shirt was blue with white stripes and his slacks were gray. Jack thought to himself that he had never before seen Niles in a civilian outfit that didn't consist of the most mundane black and white clothing.

"Ah, Niles, now it seems all the people playing hooky today from work have finally arrived for this very late lunch."

Niles Compton nodded a greeting, looking just like Jack had on the front porch. He pulled the senator's chair out and smiled as best he could.

"Everyone, please do me a favor," Lee said as Sarah came in carrying a large bowl of salad. "Stop acting like this is the goddamn Last Supper. I have something to discuss with you and I don't need all of these cow-eyed looks. Frankly, it doesn't help my appetite."

"What's he bitching about now?" Alice asked, coming in behind Sarah with a platter of sandwiches.

"I think he's saying that he doesn't want any sympathy from the likes of us," Sarah said, walking up to Lee's chair and kissing him hard on the cheek.

"Well, if he gets any, it won't be from me," Alice said, and placed the platter in the center of the table. She took Lee's napkin and tucked it into his pajama top. He fidgeted like a petulant child and then scowled, sending his eye patch askew and his good eye ablaze.

"Would you sit down, woman, for crying out loud?"

Jack, Niles, and Sarah knew the act between Lee and Alice very well, and it never grew old. If Lee had to live without Alice he would be happy to be dying. It would be living without her in his life that would have been unbearable and anyone who saw them together knew that.

"Niles, thank you, my boy, for coming to see me on such short notice. I know you absolutely hate leaving the complex."

Compton was putting salad in a bowl. He looked as if he were about to say something but caught himself. "Oh, it's kind of slow at the moment," he offered instead.

"You always were a poor liar, my old friend."

Jack watched the exchange between the senator and Niles. He felt he was not privy to something. He accepted the salad from Niles but remained silent. When he passed it to Lee, he waved it on.

"That was quite an event that happened on the Moon this morning," Lee said as matter-of-factly as he could.

Niles looked at Jack and then back at the senator. He nodded his head. "The president just asked our group to see what they can find out from NASA."

"Kind of spooky," Sarah said, looking from Niles to Jack.

"Ah, that is the gist of the matter, isn't it?" Lee said and then coughed. That turned into another, and another. "Scary . . . stuff . . . to say the . . . least," he managed to say through his coughing.

Alice, her fork paused halfway to her mouth, watched Garrison for a moment, and then continued eating when he seemed to get the coughing under control.

"Anyway, do you have a thought on the subject of this fantastic discovery on the lunar surface?" He looked at Jack first.

"I would say that we weren't the first ones to the Moon, or if we were, someone was a damn close second. I can't say I admire whoever it was for leaving a man behind." He looked at Sarah and then Alice. "Or a woman," he added.

"My thoughts exactly," Niles said as he laid his fork down, knowing Lee was leading them to something, like a horse to water. He had been in too many conversations with the man and knew his traps well. He wiped his mouth with his napkin and waited.

Garrison took his own napkin out of his pajama top and then pulled a pen from his robe's front pocket. Alice watched as he did this, and then looked at the others around the table. She knew what Lee was doing and was watching the reaction of the others. Garrison took the pen and started making a design on the white napkin. When he was done he held it up and showed Jack, Sarah and Niles.

"For the benefit of those around this table, and with the deep knowledge of world history bestowed in the heads of same, can you tell me if you have ever seen this design before?"

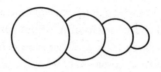

"I believe that particular design is linked to more than one culture," Niles said as he leaned back in his chair and examined the crude drawing Lee had scribbled on his napkin.

"I think one of the cultures was Mayan," Sarah said, her sandwich paused at her mouth.

"Yes, also the design has been found on cave walls and deserts from Mexico, the American Southwest, Peru, Ecuador, Uruguay, and as far south as Australia."

Jack looked over at Niles and then at Sarah. "Don't ask me, the only thing it reminds me of is the sign in front of Pocket's Billiard Parlor outside Fort Bragg."

Lee was silent for a moment and looked as if he were having a hard time catching a breath. His chin lowered to his chest and once more Alice watched him closely. Sarah looked at Alice and wondered how long she would let the senator fight through this visit. She lowered her eyes and then looked at Jack with worry on her face. Soon, Lee gathered himself and looked across the table at Alice.

"Maybe you better get ready with that needle you're so fond of wielding like Excalibur."

Alice excused herself and walked out of the dining room.

"Endless apologies. General Sherman was wrong. It's not war, but dying that's hell. Now, the symbol—of course you are all correct, except for Jack, who wasn't even close. And I know that pool parlor very well by the way." He looked at Collins and winked with his one eye. "All of these civilizations, or more ac-curately, the regions you spoke of, had depictions of this diagram in one form or another. All throughout history science said they were more than likely drawings of eclipses that these differing tribes of man witnessed at one time or another." Lee took a deep breath. "I also saw this exact symbol someplace where it had no right to be, at least as far as I was concerned."

Jack placed his napkin on his empty plate and watched the senator, who was growing visibly weaker.

"In 1945." His one eye good wandered over to Alice as she entered the living room with a small black bag. She did not look at the others as she pulled out a chair and sat next to the senator. "I saw this symbol on several crates we intercepted in Ecuador. They were in the hands of the Nazis and they were going to attempt to use their contents as a bargaining chip for leniency from the Allies after the war. They were excavated from a mining operation right under the noses of the Allies in Ecuador."

"What were the contents?" Niles asked, watching Alice fill a syringe with an amber liquid. As she did, Compton lowered his eyes when she pulled the senator's robe and pajama sleeve up, and then dabbed an alcohol swab on Lee's arm. Then she expertly jammed the needle home. They all watched as the old man's face cleared up. The pain eased almost instantly.

Alice sadly tossed the needle into the black bag and then stood, ignoring the senator's bravery. Lee watched Alice leave the room and then he became serious as he finally reached for a sandwich from the platter. "Everyone saw the extraordinary video from the Moon this morning," he said, taking a bite of the sandwich. He looked from one face to the other. Everyone nodded their head.

Alice returned and sat, replacing her napkin and stoically eating her salad.

"Now," said Lee, "you mentioned that the president has called his best friend for help." He looked at Niles, who in turn acted as though his friendship with the president was a bad thing. Lee nodded his head. "It's not a bad thing to be friends with the most powerful man in the world, Niles. I must say, I never achieved such lofty acquaintances in my tenure at the Event Group."

Everyone around the table knew that the senator was fudging on his own history, as every president since Harry Truman knew and respected Lee more than anyone in government service.

"Cruella, can you bring me the map please. It's on my desk."

Alice stood and made her way into the senator's study, again ignoring his jibe.

"She thinks I could have handled this on the phone. But what she doesn't realize is that I know this is my last, grand adventure, and I'm damn well going to see it through."

Jack, Sarah, and Niles all felt uncomfortable because they knew anything that Alice thought was bad for the senator, you could take as gospel. None of them looked at Alice when she returned with the map. Sarah finally smiled as Alice sat and lowered her head. Sarah placed her small hand over Alice's more elegant one and squeezed.

"Now," Lee said as he folded the map and pushed it toward Jack and Niles. "The Nazis dug up what was in the crates here." He tapped the map.

"Quito, Ecuador," Jack said aloud.

"Yes, there was an excavation just at the base of the Andes that the Germans carried out for years, at least since the spring of '38. We discovered, or I should say Cruella's late husband, Ben, discovered, the shipment and stopped it, for a while anyway. That mission cost that boy his life, or I should say my slow reactions did."

Alice looked up and gave Lee a dirty look.

"Slowed reactions because you were half dead at the time," she countered while holding Lee's singular gaze. "If you're going to tell it, tell it right, or what's the damn point?"

"I defer to one that's not tripping the light fantastic," Lee joked as he bowed his head in Alice's direction.

"As he said, he and Ben, my late husband, stopped the Nazis from removing the shipment from South America." Alice pushed her salad plate away. "The old man received his beauty mark there, and Ben lost his life. When the senator recovered enough to tell his story to his superiors, he was informed that the crates were gone, and no trace of them was ever found. It was as if Ben had died for nothing and Garrison was half butchered for the same result. Someone in either our government or the German high command had taken the crates from the train before an unconscious Garrison was found by members of the FBI."

"Do you know what was in the crates?" Sarah asked.

"Of course I do. As I said, each crate, about fifteen of them, were marked with that circular symbol, and during some unpleasantness at the time, one of the crates had broken open. Guess what was inside? None other than a skeletal corpse," Lee said, enjoying the moment as he watched his lunch guests closely, and then he finished when he saw that his statement had the right effect. "Inside were items coded by the Germans as Operation Columbus, and that quote came directly from a Nazi general named Goetz.

"Tell them, Garrison," Alice said, trying to hurry him on as she watched his good eye start to droop.

"As I said, inside the crate was a skeleton. The petrified remains I saw in 1945 wore the same kind of blue and red space suits as the one discovered on the surface of the Moon just this morning. And here's another tidbit: on the shoulder of this ancient bit of clothing worn by our visitor was that symbol right there," Lee said, tapping the drawing of the circles on the napkin.

The room was silent. Alice stood and walked over to Lee and stood behind him. She placed her hands on his shoulders and pressed.

The three guests sitting around the table were flabbergasted. Niles opened his mouth, wanting to ask something, but his voice failed him. It was left up to Jack to ask the obvious question.

"Columbus? Why that code name?"

Lee reached up and patted Alice's hand as she rubbed his shoulders. "I assume it's because the Germans believed, and I think rightly so, that the remains of the spaceman they found was a visitor, an explorer if you will, to this planet."

"How long ago?" Niles asked, finally finding his voice.

"I don't know," Lee said, lowering his head. "If only the OSS had had a chance to examine the crates more closely."

"And we don't know where the crates are now?" Sarah asked as she stood and started pacing.

"No. No trace of them has ever been found," Alice said with resignation. "The last known sighting was Ecuador. So, either Germany or Washington is where you should look." Alice removed her hands and then sat in the empty chair next to Lee's. "I think you need to start there."

"Start what?" Niles asked.

"Your investigation, of course. I assume it would be within the parameters of what the president has given you authorization to do," Lee said, smiling at Niles.

"Why not start at the excavation you spoke of?" Jack asked.

"Because it has been buried and the ground salted. The Ecuadorians allow no one near the site. I know. I was shot at years later trying to get in," Lee said.

"May I suggest, since we have a geologist on hand, that we use her to find out what she can about the excavation? And while Sarah is doing that, Niles and Jack can start the search for the crates. Because whatever is in those wooden boxes holds the answer to what they just found on the Moon."

As they watched Alice answer for a very tired-looking Lee, she stood and helped the senator to his feet. She placed her arm around him and started walking toward the hallway.

"That's enough for you for one day," she said. "Say good-bye and good night."

"Damn woman won't let me play no more."

"Get some rest," Niles said as Sarah walked over and kissed Lee on the cheek once more. Then she regretted the gesture; the senator had to bend low to accept it.

Jack turned toward Niles and shook his head. "I don't see the point of this. NASA will soon have the answers we need, and if the skeletons are indeed from one and the same civilization, why bother to find the crates? And we have to consider the big question here."

"What's that?" Sarah asked.

Jack stood and replaced his chair. Alice walked back into the room to show them out. Jack thought a moment and then came to the conclusion that Alice also needed to hear his question.

"Someone thought the find in 1945 was important enough to get rid of, and important enough not to announce. Now here we are trying to find out where those crates are. Whoever has them may want them protected at all cost, for reasons of their own."

Niles bit his lower lip and then his eyes settled on Jack.

"Good point."

# 2

Evans looked up from his clipboard to the monitor.

*Atlantis* was on its way.

Hugh Evans had worked his way up the chain of command from engineering to flight director. His normal duties called for his expertise on the space shuttle program, but eighteen months earlier he'd had a mild heart attack. Shuttle missions were well beyond his health situation at the moment, so when his superiors asked for a liaison and flight manager to work with JPL on the Peregrine mission, he jumped at the chance to get on the boards once again. He was working closely with Stan Nathan out at Jet Propulsion Lab, not interfering with his mission leadership but helping with some of the more NASA-based situations that sprang up. It had been his suggestion to Stan that morning to use *John*, *George*, and *Paul* as a linkup from *Ringo* and then up to REMCOM at JPL, completing the relay of the communications signal back to earth.

Mission control was running shorthanded. The Peregrine mission was squeezed in between STS 129, one of the last space shuttle missions to be launched before that particular program came to a close, and a Mars orbiter currently on course for the red planet.

Now, in the large monitor to the right-center of the main screen, Hugh Evans saw the shuttle *Atlantis* as it started making its journey from the barn to the launch pad. The large-tracked vehicle carrying the giant shuttle moved slowly and surely toward one of the final missions of the shuttle program. Hugh was looking at it longingly, as he knew he would never be a flight director again for one of the last few missions to the International Space Station.

Hugh turned his gaze back to the main screen in the center of mission control. He watched as *Ringo* started another grid pattern search of the center of Shackleton Crater. He glanced over at the large telemetry readout next to the image and saw that *Ringo* was beginning to show a power loss of over 65 percent.

He frowned.

If he had been in charge he would have cut the grid search down. He would have concentrated *Ringo* closer to the center of the crater for expediency. He had started to suggest just that four hours before, but he knew that Stan Nathan in Pasadena was having a far more harrowing day than he. So Evans had decided to keep quiet, even though as a second recommendation he would have used *Paul*, the second rover into the crater, as a search partner to *Ringo* instead of digging out the mysterious skeleton. After all, they knew what the damn thing was. So his priority would have been on finding other remains or something that could identify what it was they were dealing with.

Finally, Hugh switched his view from the interior of the crater to the rim, where *George* was watching with its long-range lens. He saw the zoomed image of *Paul* as it used its drill arm to scoop out deposits of lunar dust from around the left side of the half-buried skeleton. All of a sudden the robot stopped. He saw the image being streamed from *George* switch to the close-up view from *Paul*'s camera.

"What's that?" he asked aloud as several of the overnight telemetry technicians looked on just as confused.

On the large monitor was the left arm of the space suit. On it was a patch. It was not unlike the flag that United States astronauts wore on their left shoulder. This one, however, was a multicolored series of rings, eclipsed by each before it, the first being the only whole circle of the four.

"If that's a flag, it sure as hell rules out the remains being anyone from this side of the border," he said. He stood and tilted his head. There was something just underneath the shoulder blade of the now exposed left arm of the skeleton. He hit the small transmit button on his belt, and then adjusted the headset to his mouth.

"Stan, this is Houston, can you ask REMCOM to order *Paul* to zoom in on the object just beneath the arm. Yeah, do you see the black thing there? It's partly exposed."

As he waited for the time delay in communications, Hugh became a little anxious. Soon the image changed as the camera angle from *Paul* adjusted and focused on a long tubular object jutting from the dust. As it became clearer, Stan Nathan's voice came over the loud speaker.

"What in the hell is that?"

Stan walked a few steps down the steep steps leading to the control room floor and stopped. His mouth became a little drier. He knew exactly what the strange object was.

"Uh, Stan, we aren't going out live this time are we?" He looked around at the small staff of technicians inside his own facility as they in turn watched him.

"No, most of the press is dozing inside the press facility. Why, what is that thing?"

"The object at the very top of that tube is a sight, maybe a scope."

"I'm not following," Stan said from Pasadena.

"Sometimes having a history as an Air Force officer has its advantages," Hugh said, "because what we're looking at is a back sight and scope for a weapon."

"A what?"

"A gun, and look at the end of the tube. That isn't any sort of weapon currently available to any inventory in the world."

As they looked on, the camera view zoomed in at four times power. Everyone saw what Hugh was talking about. At the hollowed-out tip of the cylindrical object, just in front of what Evans had called the front sight, was a small crystal.

As everyone started absorbing the possibility of what they had found strapped to the back of the skeleton, loud warning alarms started sounding in Pasadena.

"What is it, Stan?" Evans asked. The screen on the main viewer changed to the outer rim of the crater. There, *George* had a shot that froze the hearts of everyone in both Pasadena and Houston. The rover *Ringo* had made its second major discovery of the day. At the far right center of Shackleton Crater was another red and blue space suit. As the camera adjusted its picture and zoomed in closer, the scene changed dramatically. As *Ringo* started backing away from the scene as it had been ordered to do, they saw the three skeletons that were ringed around the second space suit. They were more than three quarters buried in the lunar dust, and not one of them looked to be in environmental suits. They seemed to be partially dressed in burned and shredded lab coats of some kind.

"Jesus, what in the hell have we dug up here?" Stan Nathan asked from Pasadena.

"What we have here is a damn battlefield," Hugh answered.

"A what?"

The most experienced flight director in the United States stared at the most unsettling image he had ever seen from space.

Then he hit his transmit button.

"It's a killing field."


## EVENT GROUP COMPLEX, NELLIS AIR FORCE BASE, NEVADA

"What is the body count thus far?" Virginia Pollock asked from her seat next to Niles.

The entire divisionary infrastructure of the Event Group was seated around the large conference table next to Niles Compton's office on Level 7. They had been silent as Pete Golding played them the video of the last series of images he had just stolen with the use of the supercomputer Europa—or "hijacked" as he put it—on the large thirty-foot monitor on the wall.

Virginia Pollock had voiced what was on all their minds.

"Yes. The body count." Compton turned toward the lieutenant commander on detached service from the Navy. The Japanese American signals officer was tasked with infiltrating NASA and JPL communications. "Commander Yahamana, what have you found out?"

"In a secure message sent to the program's head, that being the vice president, we have learned they have uncovered parts of sixty-two bodies inside Shackleton Crater. Some were whole, some less intact. Most were without space suits. That is where we stand at the moment since JPL has ordered all four Beatles to stand down for solar recharge."

"I'll add this," Niles said. "There seem to be support structures from a destroyed composite environmental unit, or shelter. They don't know at the present time how many or how large these shelters were."

"I take it we are now leaning toward this site not being of Earth origin?" Colonel Jack Collins asked from his seat at the opposite end of the table.

Next to him Captain Carl Everett, the second man in charge of the Security Department, was at a loss for words, as were most in the room at hearing about what was happening on the Moon. He leaned over and whispered to Jack. "Okay, I spent the last eight hours off base—what in the hell did I miss?"

"Oh, you're going to love this one," Jack said. He turned his attention back to Niles.

"No," Compton answered with a slight shake of his head, "not unless someone made a leap in technology that would outpace the rest of the world by at least two to three hundred years."

"Have they uncovered any more weapons?" Charles Hindershot Ellenshaw III, the head of the Cryptozoology Department, asked from the center of the table.

"They think three," answered Yahamana. "One of them considerably larger than the weapon strapped to the back of the first skeleton."

"Do we have any idea the makeup of any of the weapons?" Virginia asked Niles.

"Jack, what does our resident military man have to say?"

"If I had to speculate, which is bad business in our world, I would say it was some sort of light weapon."

"Light? You mean in weight?" Ellenshaw asked.

"No, I mean it's a particle beam weapon. The crystal installed on the end of the first weapon is the tipoff here. Aberdeen Proving Grounds used a crystal that intensifies a particle or light beam upon discharge through the emitter."

Charlie Ellenshaw looked around the table and passed his hand over his head. "Okay, you lost me," he said, as a few chuckles and agreeing nods came from around the table.

"A ray gun, Charlie," Jack simplified.

"Oh."

"Which brings me to the next point," Compton said, standing and pacing in front of the large table. "How many nations have the capability to decode NASA and JPL transmissions?"

Jack turned to Yahamana and then to Captain Carl Everett. "These two would be far more capable at an educated guess than anyone else."

"Anyone with a ham radio could receive the data, but to decode?" Yahamana said, looking at Everett for his concurrence. "I would say maybe five or six nations can decode NASA's and Jet Propulsion Lab's communication codes."

"The imagery from the Moon would be far easier. It would be like piecing together a jigsaw puzzle," Everett said, still not understanding the full extent of what was happening on the Moon.

"What are you thinking, Niles?" Virginia asked, knowing her boss was ten steps ahead of everyone else in the room.

"What I'm thinking is, if nations, particularly the space-capable nations, find out we are digging up advanced weaponry on the Moon, how soon before they're crying bloody murder about us withholding valuable information from them? This could open up a can of worms we really don't need right now."

"What do you propose to do about it?" Virginia asked, seeing Niles's point.

"We have some work to do historically. And we have things we need to find out about what exactly happened up there on the Moon. I will have orders and instructions very soon for each department. Jack, you and Captain Everett may be able to get a jump on the rest of us and take a trip to Ecuador. Snoop around a little. Take whatever men, tools, identification you deem necessary and see if you can get a lead on Columbus."

Jack nodded his head as the meeting broke up. As he gathered his papers he looked at Carl, who was staring at him.

"We're chasing Columbus now? I think he's dead, at least that's what my fourth grade teacher informed me."

Jack smiled as he looked at Everett and then started picking up his notes and briefing materials.

"Far deader and for far longer than you may have been led to believe, Captain," he said.

This time the smile was missing when he looked back up at Everett.


Jack had made the arrangements for himself, Everett, Will Mendenhall, and Jason Ryan, to fly south to Ecuador. The two lieutenants, Ryan and Mendenhall, were thrilled to be getting out of the training schedule they had been facing with all of the new recruits in the Security Department. In their absence the training would be conducted by the Army and Marine noncoms under them. Ryan would be doing the piloting of the Air Force Learjet C-21A.

Collins stopped off on Level 7 to see if Director Compton had any last-minute orders before they lifted off from Nellis Air Force base a mile and half above the complex. Jack nodded at the assistants as he strolled through the outer office. From the way the three men and one woman were hunched over their computer terminals, it looked like Niles had them dealing with a heavier than normal workload. Jack knocked on the door, sparing the ten-foot-by-six-foot portrait of Abraham Lincoln a brief glance after being told to come in.

"Niles, we're getting ready to shove off," he said as he saw Compton switching his interest from a file in his hands to the large center screen monitor.

"Jack, good, you may want to see this before you go," Niles said, offering the colonel a seat in front of his desk. He handed Collins a copy of the report he was reading. "I had these typed up from memory and a brief conversation with the senator just an hour ago. Also, take along some of these photos of what was found in the debris of the crater. It looks like paperwork and pictures of star fields. They're made of the most unusual material; they look like paper, but seem to have a property like glass or dense plastic. I've passed them along to Virginia and Pete Golding to get their take on it. The public has no knowledge of these . . . at least for the moment."

Jack took the typed report and downloaded photos from Shackleton, glancing over them as they were printed out. The written report was basically everything they had covered at the late lunch meeting with Lee and Alice at their home. The photos sent by the probes from the Moon, however, were a different story. Some showed the Moon from different angles, some showed Earth in heavy cloud cover. One showed the star field deeper into the solar system. Some of them Jack didn't recognize. After he perused the report and the strange photos, he turned and watched the center screen. It was the grainy telemetry signal from Shackleton Crater. One of the rovers looked as if it had a small stone in its Canadian-built steel grips. It was rolling it over in its "fingers" as though examining it. Then Jack watched as the rover swung its arm around and deposited the stone in a pile that was at least two feet in height.

"With everything inside that crater, I would think JPL and NASA would be concentrating their efforts somewhere else instead of rock collecting."

"That's the thing I wanted you to see. Remember when the senator said that inside the crate that fell over there were skeletal remains and some strange-looking rocks?"

Jack looked at the report again. Then he found the spot where Niles's memory had recorded the senator's exact words. "I didn't until you just mentioned it." Collins looked at the video feed again. "Is this live?"

"Yes, they're running a special on CNN about the collections going on in the crater, that's why the picture is so grainy," Niles said. "It's streaming right to us before JPL's had a chance to clean it up. The point is, look at those rocks. I've seen Moon rocks before. Hell, I've probably held at least two hundred of them. They've always fascinated me." He stood and moved closer to the large screen. "I have to say this, and I think someone else also has noticed this at NASA and JPL. Those are not rocks indigenous to the lunar surface."

Jack stood. He tried to focus on the grainy picture. The rocks resembled lava. They looked porous. But he had seen Moon rocks that looked the same way.

"How can you be sure?" Collins asked.

"Look here," Niles said, pointing at the uppermost layers of rocks that the robot had piled in the center of the crater. "That silverish material looks like mercury, or possibly even lead. That's not a Moon rock."

"Maybe small asteroids or meteors then. That would go a long way to explaining the devastation inside the crater."

"I don't know, but point taken, Jack," Niles said, watching the robot pick up the rock it had just placed on the pile. "Maybe we'll find out something in a moment. It looks like they're going to try and get a spectrograph report."

## JET PROPULSION LABORATORY, PASADENA, CALIFORNIA

Stan Nathan had just agreed with Hugh Evans in Houston that they should run a spectrograph analysis on one of the stones. Stan was hesitant at first. Hugh had just sanctioned the use of a limited supply of bottled air and water to clean off the surface of the rock before running the analysis. The Beatles all had a very limited supply of air and water, and Stan hated the idea of expending the supply of *George* for the test. But as Hugh had pointed out, they had supplies from three other Beatles if they needed water or air.

"Okay, REMCOM, get the order out to *George* to start the centrifugal force rotation of its hands."

"Roger, Flight, commencing spin."

A full minute later they all watched as the two-handed *George* started to spin the rock in its three-fingered grip. They saw dust fly off the stone as the centrifugal force became too great for the small particulate matter to adhere to the porous surface. It spun for fifteen seconds and then came to a halt. By that time, the command to wash and blow off the small rock had been sent and received.

As the world watched live, a third arm located beside the small drilling derrick extended and came within two inches of the rock. The finger grips started spinning once more as a stream of heated water shot from a small nozzle embedded in the arm. The water struck the stone. Frozen particles of ice were thrown free as the centrifugal force forced them from the porous stone. A fourth arm extended. A burst of air hit the spinning stone. More particulate matter blasted away from the rock and then as quickly as it had started, the spinning and washing ceased.

"That went well," Stan said with relief as he reached over his console and patted one of the programmers on the back. "Pretty flawless, now we need to connect the spectrograph and see—"

"Flight, we have a glitch in the power readings for *George*. The stored battery charge has risen by thirteen percent."

"What?" Nathan moved rapidly to his console and looked at the telemetry streaming in from Shackleton.

"I'm also showing a rise from the stored battery power of *Ringo*, Flight."

"That's impossible. Where can they be picking up power? *Ringo*'s not even in sunlight."

"I don't know, Flight, but *George* is now back up to fifty-two percent power and rising."

As they watched, the grainy picture from Shackleton cleared and became crystalline in clarity.

"Flight, we have a one hundred percent surge in communications from *John* on the upper rim of the crater. Whatever is going on is affecting the remote from almost a half a mile up."

Stunned, Nathan looked at the programmers and technicians.

"Look!" someone said, louder than necessary.

On the main screen, the rock that was being held by *George* was glowing with a soft luminescence. The illumination was silverish in color and seemed to act as a halo around the stone.

"Pasadena, this is Houston," Hugh Evans called on the VOX system. "Stan, this reaction started happening when oxygen and water was added to that rock. For the time being have *George* drop the rock and get the hell away before we lose him."

"Right," Nathan answered as he nodded for REMCOM to pass along the order.

Technicians started to furiously type commands from their stations. They were ordering all three of the Beatles to get as far back from the stone as they could without climbing out of the crater. The rock on the screen was glowing brighter.

"Come on, come on!" Nathan said out loud.

"The batteries can't take this. The voltage regulators onboard are not shutting down the charge. We are at one hundred and twelve percent and rising on all three Beatles. John on the rim is at eighty-five percent recharge and rising."

Finally, on the television screens and in front of most of the world, *George* dropped the rock and immediately started backing away.

"Leave *John* in place on the rim, I want to get as many readings from the crater floor as we can," Nathan said. He wished the Beatles would move faster.

"We have no effect. Power readings are off the scale. We may have to—"

"Jesus, look at that!" another technician said. Nathan was glad that their reactions were kept in-house. CNN had left it up to JPL's science advisor for descriptions of what was happening. He wished he could hear how he would explain this.

The pile of strange rocks began to glow, apparently reacting to the air- and water-contaminated rock. They were much brighter than the first stone.

"That's it," the *George* remote leader called out. "We just lost *George*. Massive power surge and overload. He's dead."

On the main viewing screen the picture from a retreating *George* went to snow.

"That's it for *Ringo* and *Paul*!"

*Ringo* and *Paul* had maxed out at over 100 stored amps. Stan Nathan watched as his robots succumbed to the strange properties of the rock they had found inside of the crater.

"Jesus—"

That was as far as Nathan got in his exclamation over the event happening more than 244,000 miles away. The entire view screen, along with the picture coming from the rover *John* on the Shackleton Crater rim, turned to snow after a fantastic flash from the interior.

"What the hell just happened?" Nathan demanded. "Did we lose *John* to the same power surge?"

The room grew silent as the picture from *John* looked as though it wanted to come back on. Then it went white again.

"Pasadena, this is Houston," called the voice of Evans at the Johnson Space Center. "Pasadena, Houston!"

"Go ahead, Houston," Nathan finally answered.

"Goddamn it, get on the ball out there, Stan, we've just recorded a large detonation from the surface of the Moon. It was caught from orbit by *Peregrine 1*, over."

*Peregrine 1* was the mother vehicle orbiting the Moon as a relay platform for the Beatles. It had also been the vessel that brought the four lunar rovers to the launch point for their landing the day before.

"Say again, over," Nathan said, his mind racing as his eyes watched for the picture to return from *John*.

"*Peregrine 1* is reporting a large-scale detonation equal to two kilotons of TNT at 89.54 degrees, south latitude, and zero degrees, east longitude. That's inside Shackleton, over."

Before Nathan could answer, the picture from *John* flashed, and then flashed again, and then the picture cleared.

"We are receiving picture from *John*!" REMCOM called out.

"What in the hell is wrong with it?" Nathan finally found his voice at about the same time he regained control of his racing heart.

"He's been knocked on his side, Flight," the *John* remote team reported, as they started typing commands once again.

"Damn it! Give its camera arm a ninety degree turn. Now!" Nathan ordered.

A minute later the picture started to rotate. The view cleared and the camera pointed skyward with just the edge of the crater's rim in the picture. They all stood and stared, unable to believe what they were seeing.

"This can't be," Nathan said.

"Pasadena, Houston, we have a three-hundred-times-power picture coming in from *Peregrine 1*. It should be coming up on your screen, over."

"Roger, Houston," Nathan said, leaning heavily against his console.

The room was completely silent as the view changed from the bright, almost blinding, picture of *George* to that of *Peregrine* flying over 180 miles above the lunar surface.

"What the hell did we dig up?" Nathan asked, turning and sitting heavily on his chair as he realized that the Peregrine mission was now finished for all time.

On the screen, the mushroom cloud expanded into a silent and energy-filled cloud that rose from the lunar landscape, snaking into the airless void of space before dissipating sixty miles up.

# 3

## THE UNITED NATIONS,
## NEW YORK CITY

The emergency meeting of the Security Council unofficially started long before some of its members joined together inside their chamber.

The television cameras were shut down. The press was being kept in the dark by the Council membership. The arguments with the American ambassador had begun as soon he had stepped from his office thirty minutes before. The tirade had continued as he tried to make his way to the Security Council chambers. After finally reaching the Council doors, the American turned to one of his assistants and whispered something. At that moment, the ambassador from Great Britain slammed his palm on the podium. After receiving his instructions, the assistant turned and left the chamber.

"Gentlemen and ladies, we must conduct ourselves with a little more decorum," the British head of the chamber called out. "The gentleman from the United States has a statement he wishes to be read into the record."

Even more protests then erupted among the eight-member council.

"Tell me, sir, will the Russian Federation be able to question this so-called statement, or will this be a deniable dictate from the esteemed ambassador from the United States?"

"I'm sure he will try and answer any questions the Council has—"

"China echoes the request of the Russian Federation. We must be able to question this statement and have far more precise answers of what really happened on the Moon this morning. The introduction of nuclear material into outer space is unconscionable and will not be tolerated by the People's Republic."

The American ambassador sat stoically, waiting for the chamber to calm.

The two protesters to his statement did not go unnoticed by the career diplomat. Neither of them had used their interpreter to state their displeasure.

The French ambassador lowered his head in deference to the American on his left. He said, "France must concur with the sentiments of our esteemed colleagues, although we are willing to hear the United States reasoning, or explanation if you will, for this very disturbing development."

The small, bearded American diplomat had just been ambushed by the Frenchman. While guarding his closeness with the Americans on most items on the Security Council agenda, he was now stepping back and siding with China and Russia. He knew then that the French government was in the process of forming their own opinion. If Britain and Japan abandoned the United States, censure would be close behind.

"I have a brief note to read from the president of the United States. Although he is going to brief the country, and therefore the world, at six P.M. tonight, he wanted to send along a personal explanation to our friends around the world."

"Very well. Read your statement, Mr. Ambassador," the Englishman said as he gave the American the floor.

The ambassador didn't stand up. He simply opened the folder in front of him and started reading. He refused to use the dramatic move of looking tense. He was calm and cool, just as the president had instructed through his secretary of state.

"Gentlemen, as you already know, an incident occurred on the surface of the Moon at 1133 hours this morning, Washington time. It was witnessed by many of you live. It would seem that an unstable, but wholly natural element detonated on the lunar surface. As this incident was accidental in nature, but instigated by our robotic instruments, the United States must therefore assume responsibility for the event and will immediately start the investigation into what exactly happened. I must stress to the member nations that this was a natural element and not a device of American origin. We are fully compliant as per the United Nations treaty of 1966 forbidding the introduction of nuclear material into outer space."

The ambassador and every member of the Security Council knew this was a lie. The exploration spacecraft *Cassini* launched in 1997 had violated the treaty and almost ruined the reputation of the American space program. Its most staunch ally, Great Britain, dropped out of the project because of the nuclear reactor that would eventually be sent crashing through into Saturn's atmosphere. The American therefore wouldn't bring up the fact that the Chinese, Russians, and even the European Union had also violated the treaty.

"We again emphasize the fact that this detonation was accidental and was not caused by any material we introduced into the lunar environment."

The American closed the folder in front of him and waited for the tirade to start in earnest. He didn't have to wait long.

"I think an immediate vote to censure the United States is appropriate at this time," the French ambassador said, with a sober nod to his American counterpart. There was an instant smattering of yeses from around the large table.

"The Russian ambassador would like to read a statement," the distinguished British ambassador said, looking at his colleague from America with sad eyes.

The Russian stood and nodded to the Englishman, then faced the American ambassador directly.

"You take responsibility for the investigation upon the lunar surface, is this correct?" he asked.

"That was clear in the president's statement to this body, I believe."

"I see. And just how is the United States planning to conduct such an exhaustive endeavor, from the safety of this planet?"

"I have not been informed of the plan of action nor its timetable."

"Mr. Vilnikov, is this a statement or a cross-examination?" asked the chairman.

"I'll tell you how," the Russian said as he looked at the faces watching him. "You will simply guess as to the cause, or more to the point, you will lie to the people of the world. Therefore I will state that my government has every intention of conducting its own investigation, not from the safe confines of the Earth, but directly from the surface of the Moon!"

The Russian ambassador closed his briefcase. He turned and left the chamber with his assistants trailing behind.

As the American watched, the Chinese ambassador stood, nodded his head, and he also left. The meeting broke up with every U.N. protocol broken. The American ambassador sat and looked at the tabletop.

"What's happening?" one of his young assistants asked.

"I'll tell you," he said as he tapped his fingers on the folder that held the president's statement. "They're not doing this to investigate what happened on the Moon. They saw everything as clearly as we did. No, they're going because there is something up there that makes our nuclear technology as obsolete as a biplane. I figure they have two agendas, and I'm not even a scientist. One, they are going to retrieve the weaponry that was uncovered in that crater, if it's still there, and two, they want that material."

"But the images of the weapon were not broadcast to the public," his assistant said.

The ambassador shook his head, not even wanting to comment on how naive the young man was.

"Then what will we do?" the assistant asked, worry finally showing on his face.

"Nothing. We can't even begin to start planning a return trip. We stripped NASA's budget completely to the bone as far as the Moon is concerned."

"What does that mean for the country?"

The ambassador stood and placed the president's statement in his case and then turned and smiled sadly at his assistant.

"It means if everyone gets to that technology before we do and answers the questions concerning that mineral, the United States just may become a Third World nation."

## EVENT GROUP COMPLEX,
## NELLIS AIR FORCE BASE, NEVADA

Dr. Pete Golding watched the Astro-Sciences Division in frustration. They had invaded the Computer Center and were working frantically. Their assignment was to find out as much from the *Peregrine 1* mother craft, and from the last burst of data sent by *John*, as they could. The photos and strange paperwork absconded by Europa from NASA and JPL communications was spread out on the largest ten monitors at the Comp Center. The way Virginia Pollock and her hundred-person team were working the problem of finding out what they were dealing with on the Moon, Pete figured they would get nowhere quick.

Golding stood from his position in the observation seats arrayed in a semicircle high above the Computer Center floor. He was looking at the unusual language discovered on the plasticlike "paper" uncovered by the lunar rovers. He figured it would take Linguistics a full year even to figure out the alphabet of the alien tongue. The Chinese- and Cyrillic-looking characters had no rhyme or reason based on Pete's limited expertise. He wandered from screen to screen, his eyes fixed on what appeared to be a star field. Perhaps it was a photograph, though if it was he didn't immediately recognize the position of the stars. As his eyes roamed over the recovered material he saw another photograph taken from the Moon. He did see something familiar in this one. It was obviously Earth. He could see what looked like the west coast of North America, but that was as far as the recognition went. The rest of the globe was covered in clouds. Pete then looked more closely at the small un-detailed photo and corrected himself.

"Not regular clouds." he mumbled under his breath. "Looks like steam, smoke, maybe even ash." He stepped up to Virginia, who was busy arguing with a supervisor from Linguistics about the very problems Pete had thought about a moment before—the fact that they had little time to decipher the alien tongue.

Pete tapped Virginia on the shoulder and nodded his head toward an empty Europa terminal.

"Just take your linguistics team, Professor, and start trying to figure the common wordage of repeated phrases. You may have better luck in the short time we have," she ordered, watching Pete for a moment before joining him.

"What is it, Pete?" she asked finally, stepping up to the desk and terminal.

"This," he said, typing in a computer command. The small photo of Earth came up. It was only half a shot. He assumed the picture was taken during earthrise, when only half the globe is visible. "What do you make of these?" he said, pointing at the cloud cover.

"Clouds?" she asked, wondering if Pete was on the same level of observation as everyone else.

"I don't think so. There's no pattern to normal cloud cover. It looks like steam, smoke, maybe even ash. See the dark tinges embedded in the clouds and the way the center of some of them look deep and funnel-like?"

"Okay, I see it, but that could be moisture, maybe even a hurricane. Hell, Pete, it could be anything. Listen, we're worried about the Moon at the moment, not Earth," she said, her words trailing off as she leaned in closer to the flat screen monitor. She saw something she thought was familiar.

"I think it's volcanic activity on a massive scale," Pete said as he tapped the screen. "And look at this," he added, typing in another command for Europa to execute. The picture of the strange-looking star field came up and Pete leaned back in his chair. "Looks familiar, doesn't it?"

"I don't know. I'm not an astronomer," Virginia said, once more looking at Pete. She realized he was right about the strange cloud pattern depicted in the photo.

"Look," he said, pointing at a spot inside the same star field. "That's Venus."

"Okay, I'm not an astronomer, but I know enough to tell you you're mad. It's not in the right spot. I would say it's about, oh, maybe a hundred, maybe even two hundred thousand miles from where it should be."

"Nonetheless, it's Venus." Pete began to type and then thought better of it. He reached out and brought the terminal microphone closer to his mouth. "Europa, shut down all inquiries from other terminals and then act on the following requests only."

"Yes, Dr. Golding—overriding system for singular use."

As the sexy-voiced computer started shutting down all terminals across the board, they heard the complaints from everyone in the comp center as their stations shut down. With a withering look from Virginia, who still gave Pete Golding a lot of leeway when it came to playing hunches, the operators and her team quieted and watched Pete.

"Europa, clear and enhance photo 112. Can we get an estimation of moisture content in the cloud cover?"

"Attempting to analyze," Europa said, as the picture of an eclipsed Earth disappeared and then reappeared with grid marks and a multitude of overlaid colors. "In answer to your query, Dr. Golding, the moisture content of cloud cover cannot be analyzed with current data. However, Europa can correct a previous assumption of the objects tagged as clouds."

Pete smiled and then looked back at Virginia. "Go ahead, Europa."

"Objects viewed in photograph are of varying thickness. They are indicative of windblown contaminate, therefore they cannot be classified as cloud cover.

Europa will tag contaminate as volcanic activity from the Asian continent. The particulate is acting as though it is caught in the North American jet stream. The thickness of volcanic contaminate is sixty-seven miles. The Asian continent is estimated at eleven thousand, eight hundred miles distant as calculated from height of contaminate."

"That's impossible, Asia is not that far off the west coast of the United Sates," someone in the Comp Center said.

Pete smiled as his suspicions were confirmed. A few more of the technicians started making their way over to where Pete and Virginia stood. Seeing this, Pete switched all of Europa's calculations and depictions to the large thirty-five-foot screen at the center of the front wall.

"Europa, analyze the distance of object from present-day Earth coordinates depicted in the lower right hand corner of photo 171. I have designated object as Venus."

"Europa has confirmed the planet Venus as object depicted in data received."

Pete glanced back at Virginia and raised his brows. "It's not where, Virginia, but when."

Virginia Pollock was beginning to understand where Pete was going. She decided to join in on Pete's developing theory.

"Europa, overlay photo 171 with a recent star field photo of the current position of the planet Venus, and show the current position of stars in background, please."

As they watched, recent photos from Jet Propulsion Lab, the Hubble Telescope, and the Griffith Observatory in Los Angeles were placed side by side with the recovered Moon photograph, and then the four photos slowly blended into one. Venus was then clearly shown separated from its twin in the recovered photo.

"Estimate distance from the two planets depicted, please," Pete continued, as a shocked Virginia and her large staff watched in awe. Meanwhile the computer technicians under Pete's command looked at their boss with even more respect than they'd had just a moment before.

"One hundred fifty-six thousand thirty-two miles, plus or minus two hundred miles from current position of the planet Venus."

Pete stood and looked at the picture above them. "Estimate time of solar system expansion from current position of Venus subtracted from photo number 171."

"Photo marked as 171 was exposed approximately seven hundred million years prior to recent earth- and space-bound photography, plus or minus error factor of one million years."

The room was stunned. Pete was too shocked to gloat. He turned white and faced Virginia.

"Photo 171 taken of the Earth. The reason why the estimate of the Asian continent as being so far away from the North American west coast is because

Asia, at least in this photo taken from the Moon, was on the far side of the world at that time. The picture was taken—"

"Before the continents separated, and at a time when the world was inundated with volcanoes and explosive activity on its surface," Virginia finished for him.

Pete smiled, albeit uneasily, and then removed his horn-rimmed glasses. "Bingo."

## CHURCH OF THE TRUE FAITH, LONG BEACH, CALIFORNIA

The Reverend Samuel Rawlins knew when he had his congregation where he wanted them. The two-hour sermon had started out chastising America's foolish reach into space and continued with the accusation that the United States had introduced a weapon of mass destruction into God's universe. As his Hollywood-style speaking voice reached out to the thousands attending in Long Beach, it was also reaching record numbers in eighty-six other countries that had accepted the special programming after the day's events on the Moon.

"Were the mechanics and engineers of our wayward nation satisfied when we placed the footprint of mankind on one of the Lord's heavenly bodies five decades ago? No, we have to reach for unspoiled ground once more and taint it with the radiation of a blackened soul. I say we have sinned a great sin, and the nation, if not the world, will pay for this egregious affront to God almighty!"

The congregation stood and shouted their approval. "I say to everyone listening and watching around the world that this reach back into space cannot be tolerated. This so-called find on the Moon is nothing but a hoax perpetrated by the leaders of this morally bankrupt nation, and assisted by their so-called allies across the globe, a trick of humankind to once more gain access to the working-man's pocketbook—once again my brothers and my sisters, this trickery will not, cannot be tolerated, and I will fight this expansion into God's universe with every breath in my body, even unto my own death!"

At that point the three-hundred-member choir broke out in song and the gathered parishioners stood and started clapping and shouting out amens. The Reverend Samuel Rawlins stepped away from the magnificent golden pulpit and held his hands high in the air. Women seated closest to him came near to swooning, while the men looked up at the ten-foot-high stage that was filled with palm trees and flowers with nothing but reverence and admiration etched upon their tear-streaked faces. As the choir sang the Reverend gestured to one of his younger deacons to lead the congregation in final prayer. Then he waved as if he were Elvis leaving the stage and departed to the left.

There were three men waiting for him as he stripped off his white jacket, but he ignored them as he first went to his two daughters and hugged and kissed them. The older wrapped a towel around his neck and the younger gave him a tall glass of water. He smiled and then excused himself. First, wiping his brow, he went to a man in a dark business suit.

"Numbers?" he asked.

"Our own network is carrying a forty-eight percent share. We swept the major networks off the airwaves. And listen to this—we pulled fifties in most European countries."

"That's good, Elliott," Rawlins said after he drained the glass of water. "Give me real-time numbers, not percentages."

The president of Faith Networks Worldwide saw the intense blue eyes as they bore into him and he wanted to step away, but he smiled instead. "You were seen by no fewer than one billion people here and abroad."

Rawlins wiped his sweating face once more and then nodded. "Good. Now set up my special for Guiana. I have a sermon reserved just for our family down there. I want it to be beamed out to them no later than tomorrow evening. I've already recorded it."

"Yes, sir."

Rawlins turned to the two other men as he watched his daughters, who also loved the attention and the limelight, step out onto the stage. They started singing and clapping with his choir and deacons.

"Okay, what have you got?"

The two men were part of his security team and were ruthless. They collected intelligence on anything or anyone that could possibly hurt his ministry.

"We have a special telegram from the Vatican. It seems you've hit a nerve with the new pope. He demands that you use—his words here, sir—common sense, and he hopes for restraint on your part. It seems you are inflaming the populace of many nations."

"Is that right? Well, the pope and all of Catholicism haven't seen anything yet. What else?"

"The regional board of evangelistic ministries has echoed the complaints of the Vatican. The president of the United States has been mum so far on your attack on the space program and himself. We don't expect that to last after to-night."

"I tremble in my shoes," Rawlins said with a laugh, tossing the damp towel as he walked briskly toward his dressing room. "Keep up, gentlemen," he said, not bothering to look back over his shoulder as the two men turned and followed. "I am informed by a most reliable source that the European Space Agency, along with those godless Russians and Chinese, have contingency plans to reach the Moon." He stopped and looked intensely at the men. "Obviously they plan to attempt a recovery of both the human remains and the mineral samples. Of course, our contingency plans were predicated on something like this happening. Oh, maybe not such a worldwide attempt, but close. This cannot and will not happen, gentlemen."

"We are ready, sir," the largest of the two security men said, holding his own eyes steady on the Reverend.

"Now, the appropriate blame will be placed on nations and on organizations I have taken years to choose. The consequences of taking so many lives must not be traced back to me. We have spent more than two billion dollars over the years preparing our response and this is not the time to screw things up."

The medium-sized man, actually the security chief for Faith Ministries and a former Delta operative, finally cleared his throat. His goatee was closely trimmed and his hair was recently cut.

"You have hired the best men there are from all around the world. You have paid handsomely for the loyalty of all. We will not fail you or your church, Mr. Rawlins. We will kill all who try to blunt the word of God."

Rawlins finally smiled with true comradeship.

"God bless, Mr. Smith."

The man known to everyone who worked with him as Smith, nodded once and then turned away, his taller assistant following.

The Reverend Rawlins watched the two men leave as he slid down the knot in his tie. The smile was gone and he felt better for it. He looked up into the girder work of the giant cathedral.

"Yes, Mr. Smith, go about God's work. And, if need be, bring upon the heathen the Four Horsemen, for they shall deserve God's wrath."

## 300 MILES NORTH OF QUITO, ECUADOR

Will Mendenhall was up front in the cockpit of the Air Force Learjet taking his flying lesson from Jason Ryan while Jack and Carl studied the latest satellite images provided by the Event Group's own KH-11 satellite, code-named Boris and Natasha. The images were downloaded into a virtual reality map that showed real-time cloud cover and ocean tides. The in-motion virtual map showed and even measured the snowfall in the Andes. As Jack hit the zoom icon on the side of the plastic map, the image enlarged to the point where he and Carl could clearly see the indentation in the Earth made when the original German excavation was buried after the war.

"Let's see," Everett said, counting under his breath. "I count no fewer than four guard towers and three roving SUV patrols. And they claim it's all for public safety?"

"That's the claim. They say there are dangerous and eroding mine shafts and such. However, according to the senator, we know for a fact that the operation was an open pit mine, no shafts involved, at least none that can be found by hikers."

"Okay, do the Ecuadorians know what was taken out of the ground there?" Everett scanned the map for more detail.

"We have no idea. Even though relations are good, they're pretty hush-hush on what the site is hiding—or, what it hid at one time." Jack said, correcting himself.

"These SUVs, you notice something?" Everett asked, pointing to and tapping the three roving vehicles outside the thirty-foot chain link fence.

"Nonmilitary, black in color, and expensive," he said, adjusting the magnification on the virtual reality map. "Maybe a little bit beyond the resources of the Ecuadorian military."

"My thoughts exactly," Carl agreed.

"Colonel, we're starting our descent into Quito, so you and the captain better buckle up back there," Ryan said over the intercom.

Everett looked at his and then Jack's seat belts, which had never been undone from takeoff. "Nah, we won't tell him. He may think we don't trust his flying," he said with a crooked smile.

As Jack sat back in his seat and closed his eyes, his cell phone rang.

"Collins," he said.

"Colonel, Niles here. I have an update for you on several fronts. Number one, the rest of the civilized world has seemingly turned an ugly eye toward us. They are using the excuse that we introduced fissionable material onto the lunar surface."

"You're kidding. I suppose they didn't see the same footage we did on CNN?"

"Well, the president thinks it's just a red herring, several of the more capable countries seem to be hell-bent on investigating the event firsthand."

Jack sat up in his seat and then sat the cell phone down on the table between him and Everett. He hit speakerphone.

"Are they running a bluff? I mean, are they capable at this time of getting there?" Jack asked as he mouthed the word *Moon* to Carl.

"Well, the ESA claims they have not one, but two prototypes ready to go. I personally find that difficult to believe. They could never have hidden the budget from the European Union. But they did go on television just twenty minutes ago stating they were prepared to shuttle components into South America to start assembly of the two Ariane 7 vehicles."

"Damn, what does CIA have to say about the accuracy of this claim?"

"Jack, all of our intelligence services were caught flat-footed on this one, and I for one won't start pointing fingers; keeping tabs on the ESA hasn't been the highest priority. The same goes for China and Russia. CIA counts warheads and missiles, not lunar-capable systems. For all we know they could launch as soon as they get their systems online and their vehicles assembled."

"Is there anything we can do about it? I mean it's obvious to anyone who's been paying attention that there is a mineral up there that would be highly desirable. And the technology those remotes dug up, that's not a bad second prize either."

"The president wants me to get with DARPA and NASA to see if we have any alternatives," Niles said, speaking of the Defense Advanced Research Projects Agency. "I'm flying out in a few minutes to meet with the Defense Sciences Office in Arlington, and then I'm off to Houston."

"Do we have any capability at all to get back there since the budget cuts?"

"I doubt it, Jack. That's why you and Captain Everett had better come up with something. We need Operation Columbus and its artifacts found. One more thing, the excavation you're visiting is owned officially by Hans Dieter Brinkman, a German businessman who leases and sells land out of his Munich offices."

"What's the story on this guy?" Jack asked.

"Well, Europa ran a background check on him and it seems our Mr. Brinkman is the son of Field Marshal Karl Brinkman. We have learned that the field marshal was an engineer before and during the war. He died in 1963 in, of all places, Quito. Pete Golding dug deeper and found that our man was a mining engineer. His son took over the business end of things but has never once set foot in Ecuador. Europa, as is her style, surmises that Mr. Brinkman the younger is nothing more than a front for another owner that she can't find in the fine print of the property ownership papers. So, watch it, Jack. It could be anyone."

"Is that all?" Collins asked, shaking his head at Everett.

"There is one more little thing. Pete Golding analyzed the material sent from the Beatles and has come up with an approximate age for the lunar site and the remains found inside Shackleton."

"We're listening," Jack prompted.

"Right around seven hundred million years old," Niles finally said. "Give or take a month."

"A month, huh? Well, I can see you're beginning to develop that sense of humor, Mr. Director. We'll call when we have something."

"Okay, Jack. I'm meeting with the president and he tells me I'm going to be incommunicado for the next eight hours, so I guess something's pretty important. Anyway, good luck."


As Jack, Mendenhall, Everett, and Ryan waited for the only rental car available at the Mariscal Sucre International Airport, Quito's brand-new facility, they realized from the taxis and beat-up bus service that the airport had yet to see an influx of high-traffic rental car companies and high-end service industries. The services were somewhat lacking as the four men waited at the curb for their rental to be delivered. Ryan had gone to the only open rental counter inside the terminal and found sparkling new counters and floors, but only one company, Quito Express, was open for business. When Ryan returned he was unusually quiet as he waited beside Will Mendenhall.

"That was pretty quick," Will stated, peeling his Hawaiian-style print shirt from the small of his back. The heat wave that had struck the foot of the Andes had surprised them when they exited the executive jet.

"Uh, yeah," Ryan answered and then handed Will a brochure from Quito Express Car Rentals. The large picture on the front showed a shiny new Lexus SUV. The flyer folded out into three large panels of makes and models. "The choice was pretty simple." Ryan moved his feet uneasily as he looked at the colonel and captain out of the corner of his eye. They stood with their sunglasses on, stoically waiting for any sort of punch line Ryan might add to his statement. They didn't have to wait long.

Mendenhall was the only one to jump when a large bang sounded in the underground roadway that fronted the large and shining terminal. The backfire was soon followed by the squeal of an alternator belt as their rental pulled to the curb. Jack turned and looked at Ryan, who stood and stared straight ahead.

"I see your taste in cars is right in line with your taste in women, Mr. Ryan."

Everett just stood and looked from the 1986 Yugo to the brochure Will was comparing to the actual rental. The car was white and looked as if a giant tiger had raked large, sharp claws across its side and hood. The rental manager hopped out. With a gold tooth showing, he smiled and handed Jack the keys. Collins looked at the set of keys and saw the remote door lock. Out of curiosity he pushed a button on the key fob. Mendenhall jumped again as the horn blared and the emergency lights started blinking. Jack pushed it again and the horn stopped, the lights went dead, and they all heard the audible click as the doors locked. Jack lowered his head and handed the keys to Ryan.

"Hey, guys, this was the only thing they had," Ryan said, objecting to the looks he was getting from everyone as Mendenhall pushed the color brochure into his chest.

"Come on, Ryan," Everett said, opening the car door and holding the front seat forward for Jack. "Maybe we can find a used llama dealer on the way."

Ryan looked at Mendenhall, who was just shaking his head.

"Next time, you get the car."


An hour later, with Ryan driving and fighting the maladjusted wheel alignment along with the burning clutch, they reached the foot of the Andes. The paved roads that Ecuador boasted of in their vacation travel guide, which Will was trying to read in the passenger front seat, failed to mention that the roads had been repaved sometime in the early sixties, right around the time of the Cuban Missile Crisis. They hadn't seen repair since.

"Turn right on the next road you see, Lieutenant," Everett said, as he held the Global Positioning monitor. "Then another quick right and stop. That will put us at a safe distance from the first guard shack and place us behind the main road where the roving security patrols travel. We should be able to get a good bird's-eye view from there."

Ryan fought the steering as they approached the dirt road on the right side of the paved highway. With brakes squealing and the alternator belt in danger of piercing their eardrums, the Yugo made the turn.

"Jack, why don't we have a geologist with us? I mean even if we came across this mineral, we wouldn't know it from a granite countertop."

"I asked Niles if we could have one of Sarah's people, but he said they had all been assigned other duties."

Ryan made the other quick right ordered by Everett and for the first time they saw the high cyclone fence surrounding the excavation site. Ryan slammed on the brakes and then shut down the engine as fast as he could before the alternator belt told everyone from there to South Miami they were in the neighborhood. Ryan opened the car's door accompanied by loud cracks and squeaks and then stepped out to allow the colonel to squeeze out of the backseat. As Jack stretched his taxed legs, he saw the barbed wire that topped the high fence. Then he saw something coursing through the steel chain link.

"For a patch of dirt, someone sure doesn't want visitors, do they?" Mendenhall said. He removed his dark glasses and looked at the wire that led to conductors, then to the power pole nearby. He read the warning signs posted every forty feet along the electrified fence.

"Serious enough that someone's going to run up one hell of an electric bill," Ryan said, as he read the sign out loud. "Fifty thousand volts worth of persuasion."

Jack watched the interior of the old excavation and saw that the ground was bare. It was flat and with not one single bush, flower, or weed. He turned and reached into the car. He brought out a pair of binoculars and sighted the glasses on the silverish-looking Quonset huts that lined the sides of the fence. Then he turned and scanned two of the posted guards in their towers. They were carrying something else the satellite pictures hadn't shown them—AK-47 assault rifles.

"Jack, I'm not getting the best feeling here," Everett said, reaching behind him and making sure the nine-millimeter he carried in the waistband of his jeans was still in place.

"Definitely overkill for a large sandbox," Jack said as he watched two more guards exit the largest of the six Quonset huts. "I figure they have the facilities for over a hundred men. Complete with a self-contained mess hall, and God knows what else. Will, get the parabolic mike out and let's see if we can eavesdrop on one of these good ol' boys and see what nationality they are, because they sure as hell aren't Ecuadorian." Jack handed the glasses over to Everett.

As Carl zoomed in on the first set of guards he saw that one had blond hair and the other red. He turned the glass 100 degrees to the right and saw a second set of security men as they waved at the first and then said something he couldn't hear.

Mendenhall placed a set of headphones on his ears and pointed a short, very slim black microphone down into the compound. He adjusted the sensitivity when the words the guards were saying almost shattered his hearing. He then turned the set to external application and the words came out clear so the others could hear.

As they listened, they heard the first set discussing the horrid lunch they had just finished and that the second set of guards had that to look forward to.

"American," Jack said. "At least the one on the left, maybe from Georgia, I'm not sure."

"Yeah," said Everett, as he eyed the guards. "The blond-haired gentleman may be from the south too—south Berlin. What we have here, Colonel, is a multinational security concern, heavily armed and looking like they mean business. There is no way we get in there." Everett turned on Jack with a smile. "Unless you're feeling brazen today."

Jack took the glasses and scanned the interior again. "I am indeed feeling brazen, Mr. Everett," he said, and turned the glasses on the large main gate and the guard shack beside it. "Shall we pay them a visit?" He reached into the back of his shirt and pulled out his own nine-millimeter. He handed it to Ryan as he continued to look at the gate. Everett followed suit with his own weapon and Mendenhall accepted it, shaking his head.

"Why don't we give you a lift in something more comfortable than your rental car?"

Jack and Everett turned at the sound of the voice. A small man in tan work clothes and five others in immaculately pressed gray uniforms stood just on the other side of their Yugo. They had very lethal-looking AK-47s leveled at the four of them.

"Hi," Jack said.

"Hello," the small man said in German-accented English. "I predict you are going to tell me that you are four American tourists lost in the foothills of the Andes?" The small man gestured about the wilderness area and then came forward, as did his men.

"Boy, this guy's good," Everett said. "You get lost tourists all the time out here, then?"

The small man removed the set of headphones and parabolic microphone from Will's grip.

"Ah, but none so well equipped as you. Listening to the local wildlife as you try to find out where you made your wrong turn?"

"Silly hobby, I know," Jack said. "If you can just show us on our rent-a-car map here where we went wrong, we'll get out of your hair."

The man nodded at two of the guards and they stepped around the Yugo, deftly removing the four weapons that were being held by Ryan and Mendenhall.

"You know it is illegal in Ecuador to carry concealed weapons?"

"But they weren't concealed," Everett said. "Our two friends had them right out in the open." Everett's eyes moved from guard to guard. They didn't have much chance of escaping without being cut to pieces.

"You know, half of my men here at the Müeller and Santiago Mining Concern are American, but after all of the years I've spent with them, I have yet to understand American bravado when you're caught doing something you're not supposed to be doing. Is it to cover your fear or are you just that stupid in not knowing when you have been caught." The man shook his head. "I suppose it would be too much to ask if you have passports on your persons."

"Damn, I told you we forgot something," Everett said, looking at Jack.

The small man smiled and stepped as close to Everett and Collins as he could get. "To save us all a bit of time here, gentlemen, I will inform you that all private aircraft coming into Quito are thoroughly researched and checked out. It has been that way for over sixty-five years. You see, we like to know who's visiting our friends the Ecuadorians, and when an aircraft with registry numbers identifying it as part of the United States Air Force inventory lands in this country, we become concerned not only for our friends but for ourselves as well. Imagine our surprise when the occupants of that aircraft just happen to be found on our security cameras zigzagging their way onto our property."

"Well, we can always zigzag our asses right back out of here," Collins said smiling.

"That you can, but I think we should escort you to our facilities and have a small chat. That is, if you don't mind."

"Well, if it's all the same to you—" Jack started to say.

"Oh, but I insist. There's lunch in it for you. Today is Salisbury steak day."

"Then how can we say no?" Collins smiled at his three companions, then gestured toward the small man. "After you, Herr . . . ?"

The man's smile never wavered. "We'll save introductions for later. We have so much time to get acquainted."

"What about our car?" Ryan said as one of the larger guards took him by the arm.

The small man looked from Ryan to the Yugo, and then he broke out in laughter.

"Don't worry. I'll post a twenty-four-hour guard on your rental car. After all, its value is obvious."

"You'd better, pal," Ryan said, as he was shoved none too gently into the back of the car. "I signed for that piece of shit."


**From *CNN World News***

The reporter stood on the deck of the French aircraft carrier *Charles de Gaulle* (R91). The wind tore at his clothing and styled hair:

"*As the flagship of the French navy, the* Charles de Gaulle *is better protected than any other warship steaming from a European port. The great vessel has been moving at flank speed for the east coast of South America since the early hours yesterday.*" The camera pulled back to show six enormous tarp- and plastic-covered cylindrical objects. "Her task is to deliver the component parts for two Ariane 7 rockets and their corresponding top secret payloads. It has been speculated among the world's topmost intelligence agencies that an attempt is underway by not only the European Space Agency but also by the Russian Federal Space Agency and the China National Space Administration, or CNSA, to reach the surface of the Moon in a cooperative venture to find out the root cause for yesterday's high-yield explosion at Shackleton Crater. While the United States has fervently denied any wrongdoing, it has become apparent that they have not joined in this effort to reach the lunar surface, and many in the international community are asking, why? This is Frank Dance, reporting from the deck of the aircraft carrier Charles de Gaulle somewhere in the central Atlantic Ocean, for CNN."


## LOS ANGELES, CALIFORNIA

The Reverend Rawlins closed his eyes, but this time he couldn't contain the explosion that traveled from the pit of his stomach to his temples. He angrily threw the remote control for his television hard against the expensive high definition screen, cracking the plastic and sending shards of the remote control outward like shrapnel from a grenade. Rawlins stood and paced to the large window of his office in downtown Los Angeles. In the distance he could see the Hollywood Hills and the late afternoon sun playing off of the city's many billboards. He calmly ran a hand through his silverish hair and then took three deep breaths.

As Rawlins moved to his desk, he straightened his blue silk tie and made sure his white vest was pulled taut over his muscled abdomen. He hit the intercom on his switchboard.

"Tom, have you reached Mr. Smith?" he asked, in a far calmer voice than he felt he could muster at that moment.

"Yes, sir. He is on line one."

"Is the line secure?" he asked, looking down at his left hand and examining his manicured fingernails.

"Yes, Reverend. All lines were swept this morning and there were no compromises."

Without saying anything to his assistant, he reached over and hit the first flashing button on the console.

"May I assume you have seen the news reports coming out of Europe and Asia, Mr. Smith?"

"Yes, sir, I have. While the reports from Europe involving the ESA and the Russians are worrisome, they are not yet as worrisome as the developments in China."

"Meaning?"

"As I have explained to you many times, we can get to the European agencies and stop their launches. We cannot, however, do the same in China. We have no assets there, therefore we cannot stop them from attempting a Moon shot if they so desire."

"You told me, Mr. Smith, that you have the assets to stop them," Rawlins asked, feeling his temper start to get the best of him once again. "What happened to those?"

"And I do have solutions to these problems. But as I explained to you, the cost in human assets and monetary losses would be extraordinary if we have to strike at China."

"Cost is not my concern. I can outspend most nations. These blasphemers must not be allowed to bring back any evidence from the Moon. Am I making myself clear on this?"

His eyes flared, as though reflecting the fire of some burning bush.

## DARPA SCIENCE OFFICES, ARLINGTON, VIRGINIA

The director of the agency sat at his desk and read the letter Niles Compton had delivered to him. Next to Niles, Lieutenant Sarah McIntire and Deputy Director Virginia Pollock stood silently watching to see Jensen Appleby's expression when he saw the signature at the bottom of the White House stationery. They didn't have to wait long.

"Bullshit," he said, surprising Sarah and Virginia. Niles, however, seemed to take the anger and the rebuke of the president's letter in stride; he simply smiled. Sarah figured Niles had gone through this before. And ever since his seven-hour meeting with the president the previous night, he seemed extra tense, so the smile gave her some relief. "I don't know you. And your credentials, which you refuse to show me, would more than likely prove to be as false as this forged document." Appleby punched a button on his phone. "Get me a security team in here, ASAP."

Niles looked over at Virginia and Sarah and shook his head as he pulled out a cell phone and opened it. He hit only one button and then closed it just as the security team arrived. As the first man reached out to take Niles by the arm, Compton held his right index finger into the air, and then pointed at the phone on the desktop of Director Appleby—the phone buzzed.

Appleby hit the intercom to his outer office. "Yes," he said, while eyeing the small man in the black jacket and plain white shirt who wore his thick glasses down toward the end of his nose. Then his eyes turned to the two striking women next to him.

"Uh, sir, the White House switchboard is calling; the president has asked to speak with you."

Suddenly the blood drained from the man's face as he swallowed. He had just been cursing the president in the last few weeks for cutting his budget and that of NASA. He was wondering now if he had heard about his bashing and had sent these three here to collect his scalp. He slowly lifted the phone from the cradle.

"Appleby," he said meekly into the phone, as he held his left hand up to stay the security team from removing Niles, Sarah, and Virginia from his office. As the thin man with the lab coat listened to the president, he nodded and said, "Yes, sir." Appleby punched a button and laid the phone back in the cradle. Then he nodded for the security team to leave by moving his eyes toward the door. The speakerphone came to life.

"Mr. Compton, I owe you five dollars, you were right, he didn't believe the letter or the signature. I've got to stop betting with you. Mr. Appleby is now a believer and has recognized my voice, although he will undoubtedly run a trace program for further confirmation when no one is looking."

Niles took a step toward the desk. "Yes, sir, I'm sure he will," he said softly as he pushed his glasses back onto his nose and stepped back.

"Okay, Mr. Appleby. Dr. Compton and the two fine scientists in his company are there to evaluate any and all contingency plans DARPA may have on the boards for getting to the Moon in one hell of a hurry. If you remember the security briefing you attended at the Pentagon three years ago, you may recall the password Case Blue?"

Neither Sarah nor Virginia had thought that still more blood could drain from the scientist's face, but it did. Whatever that code name was it had scared the hell out of the director of the agency.

"Dr. Compton and his two assistants are to be given every consideration, and hold nothing back from them. If there is something on the boards, explain it to these three. I don't care if it's something your people have doodled out on the toilet wall, show it to them. At the moment, the general public and the world think that the United States is out of the investigation that is to take place on the Moon's surface; I want it to stay that way for the time being. Do you understand everything that I have said, Mr. Appleby?"

"Yes, sir, full cooperation. However, may I ask just who these people are, and just what are their qualifications to be in our facility?"

"Now you see, Director Appleby, that's a good, sound question, and in answer I'll say, no, you may not ask. Dr. Compton has been designated by me as a project director for findings on how we get to the Moon, and will lead any effort in this endeavor, if there is an effort. Now, is there anything more?"

"Sir, this Case Blue, is it really—"

"Have a good day, Mr. Director." The line went dead and Appleby slowly reached out and disconnected his end with the question officially unasked.

"He can be a bully; I actually think he enjoys it at times."

Virginia and Sarah looked at Niles and saw that it wasn't the president that had enjoyed being a bully, but Niles. They saw the quick little smirk that disappeared from his face before they could fully realize it had been there.

"Well, if the president says you're qualified to be here, then you must be up on your Astro-Sciences and Gaming."

"Yes, I believe between the three of us we won't make complete fools of ourselves with your staff," Niles said, nodding toward Sarah and Virginia.

As Appleby gathered his notepad, Sarah leaned in toward Niles.

"Director, if I may ask, what is Case Blue?"

"Lieutenant, as long as you live, don't you ever say those words aloud to anyone," Niles warned. "There are only a hundred men and women across the entire globe that know what that code name is for, so forget you ever heard it." Niles kept his eyes on Sarah until she felt intimidated enough that she just nodded her head.

Director Appleby walked to the door and held it open for his guests.

"Then I guess we'll start with any questions you may have about DARPA. I'll answer them the best I can on our way to Building 11 for a tour of our Industrial Necromancy Division."

"Excuse me?" Virginia said.

"It's a place where dreams come true, Ms. Pollock—heavy metal dreams."


As Niles, Virginia, and Sarah toured Building 11, they marveled at the mock-ups and engineering models they examined. There were seventeen different kinds of space vehicles that utilized everything from solid fuel to ion pulse generators for propulsion. There were over one hundred different companies currently bidding on the new Mars lander and environmental habitat and, best of all, there were full-scale mock-ups of the newest Ares I and Ares V rockets along with an Orion crew capsule from the Constellation program, which had just been canceled by the president. These were to have been used to return not only Americans, but also many other nations back to the Moon.

"Mr. Appleby, do we have anything that is real here, or are we becoming the world's best dreamers and toy makers?"

Niles cringed at the harsh way Virginia stated her question. As for himself, he would have tried to use a little more tact, but Virginia had her way and that's why she was with him.

"Ms. Pollock," Appleby said, rounding on her as men and women from DARPA's Industrial Necromancy Division stood and wondered what was happening. "I assure you these are not toys. With less than a full year's warning, we have companies out there ready to get started on these so-called dreams. In less than two or three years, with the right budget, we can have men back on the Moon not only for a few days but for longer, very much longer, durations."

"Mr. Appleby, you fail to understand, we may have to go back *now*," Niles said. "If we lag behind, the Russians or Chinese will get there first. Then they could have a substance that makes plutonium look like Silly Putty. May I also remind you that there has been a discovery of advanced weaponry found at that same location that we hope went up in the Shackleton explosion, but if it didn't it will set the United States back three hundred years or more in technology if somebody else gets to it first. You can see why the president is so concerned. He knows he may have made a foolish mistake by trying to be fiscally responsible in cutting your budget, but tell me who could have foreseen this happening? There are other areas of the military that the president has to concentrate on that have nothing to do with fighting our fellow man." Niles refused to look away after the harsh rebuke.

"That does not change the fact that we are nowhere near to getting there, even if . . ."

The three visitors watched Appleby's expression change as if a sudden gust of wind had blown away all previous thought.

"Mr. Appleby?" Niles asked.

"Follow me please," Appleby said as he spoke over his shoulder and raced down the main floor of Building 11. "As I said, we cannot get there with what we have on the design board. What we need is a proven and already built technology."

"And you have something like that?" Virginia asked, as she tried to keep up with Appleby.

"No, we do not," he said, opening the security door with his ID badge.

"Then—" Sarah started to ask.

"The very people who have been there before," the thin man said, as his guests filed out into the bright sunlight.

"Who?" Niles insisted.

"Why, NASA, of course!"


THE ANDES FOOTHILLS EAST OF QUITO, ECUADOR

Any hope of knowing exactly where they were had gone by the wayside as they were immediately hooded and moved into the back of a truck. Each of the Americans—Ryan, Mendenhall, Everett, and Collins—had a security man sitting next to him, preventing any conversation or touching, with the handcuffs making the ride that much more uncomfortable.

Jack was silent and had his eyes closed under the black hood. What he had hoped would happen was indeed happening. Given Niles's explanation of the short time frame they had to come up with something, what better way was there to get inside any heavily guarded facility than to be arrested and thrown in? It was a risk, and more than likely that risk had now tripled, but they had to play the hand they had been dealt. For the moment Jack was busy estimating speed and time as the truck made its way to wherever they were going. They had made three turns—the first left, the next two right—and they had stopped twice, so he took all that into account for his estimate. He knew all three of his men were doing the same calculations.

Every once in a while, Jack could hear the security men whispering to each other as they joked or spoke about one thing or another. The curious thing about their conversation was that they were speaking English in two distinct accents, one American and the other German. Finally, as Collins listened and calculated at the same time, the truck came to a sudden halt and the engine was shut off. Instead of being taken from the covered back of the truck, which was probably a Mercedes brand vehicle, they felt the bottom give way on their stomachs. Although the truck had ceased moving, it was now being lowered by elevator. The colonel figured any pretense about this being an Ecuadorian government-funded operation went right out the window.

After traveling downward quite a distance, all movement ceased. They heard the tailgate being lowered, and then they felt themselves eased onto a hard surface. Jack was the first to have his hood removed. He blinked in the bright fluorescent lighting. They were in a giant concrete tunnel of engineered beauty. It was rounded above the floor and traveled in a steady downhill slope, disappearing at least half a mile ahead of them. Jack remained silent as the others had their hoods taken off.

"Hey, I thought we were going to eat Salisbury steak," Ryan said, as a way of getting attention.

"Yeah, I'm hungry. What happened to lunch?" Mendenhall asked.

The distraction gave Everett the chance he needed. He slid in beside Collins.

"About three miles," he whispered.

"Yeah, three miles and some change, traveled in a roundabout way. We didn't go anywhere," Jack said, as he watched two menacing and very large guards staring down Will and Jason. "We zigzagged in a circle around the perimeter and then ended up right back at the main gate and then up a hill to the base of a mountain. They drove in here and then we took an elevator down to this marvelous place. I figure—"

"You, silence!" one of the guards said, approaching Jack and Carl.

"He was just explaining about how he just knew the Salisbury steak thing was too good to be true," Everett said, looking up at the guard. The man stood at least four inches taller than Everett himself, making him no less than six feet, eight inches. "But I don't want to get hit for it," he said, feigning fear at the man's intimidating size. The comment put a smile on Jack's lips as he lowered his head because he knew that the former SEAL could bust the man in two with his hands still tied behind his back.

"Is that what you came here for, Jack? Lunch?" a voice asked from behind them.

Collins turned and saw a small man signing something on a clipboard and then handing it back to one of the guards. The man with the mustache and well-trimmed beard and light blue suit looked familiar, though Collins couldn't place him at first. But when the newcomer smiled, recognition hit him like a brick to the stomach.

"Jim McCabe?" Jack asked as he tried to focus his eyes in the harsh lighting.

"Good to see you too, Jack," the man said as he approached.

"Has everyone you've ever known gone over to the dark side, Colonel?" Mendenhall asked, as he watched the smaller man join their group.

"Gentlemen," said Jack, "I'd like you to meet Lieutenant Colonel James Mc-Cabe, former United States Delta Force leader, supposedly killed in action 12 November 2004 in Iraq."

The man smiled again, this time even wider than before, and then turned as if he were showing off a new suit.

"Ah, the rumors of my demise were greatly exaggerated, old friend." Mc-Cabe approached the four men. "I am glad my little ruse to discharge myself from the employ of Uncle Sam was so successful, er—what is it now, Jack? Still Major?"

"Colonel," Collins said.

"I knew you would make it. Tell me, who in hell do you work for that would send you here, of all places? DOD?"

"You can ask," Jack said, "but you know me, Jim—hush-hush and full of mystery."

Again the smile and the shake of the head as McCabe turned his attention to Jack's three companions.

"I take it these three are as fully capable as yourself?"

"Nah, they just came along as valets."

"Now, let me guess," he said, turning back to face Everett, Mendenhall, and Ryan, "Jack and I used to play this game back at the Point, guessing the rank of military personnel in civilian clothing. They always look so out of place. Let's see . . ." He stepped up to Mendenhall. "A sergeant, maybe a master sergeant?"

"Off," Will said, although he knew the man to be right, up to a point. Will had only recently become an officer and a gentleman, a second lieutenant, and he had been promoted to that rank from master sergeant.

"Really? Well, we'll come back to you." McCabe then looked Ryan over and laughed out loud. "You're hanging out with Navy men, Jack. What the hell is the world coming to?"

"Hey!" Ryan said, taking a menacing step toward the man staring at him before the guards restrained him.

As McCabe turned toward Everett, his eyes narrowed to mere slits.

"Could I be looking at a Navy SEAL?" he asked Jack.

"Guys, don't let McCabe's mind-reading ability intimidate you. Ryan, you just look Navy, not hard to guess. Will, McCabe here is a puritanical bigot, who thinks black men are only capable of reaching noncom status. Mr. Everett, your SEAL tattoo is showing."

"Why, Jack, you *are* capable of giving away secrets," said McCabe.

"What now, Jim?" Collins asked.

"Oh, my employer will want to know what a multiservice group is doing on his property. And my name is now Smith, by the way."

"That's original," Jack said, eyeing the man in front of him.

"Jack, Jack, Jack! When will you get it through your head that the entire world is now a gray area? No white, no black, just gray. Gone are the bad guys and the good guys, and all that's left is men trying to survive in a world that only cares who is strongest or who is the wealthiest."

Collins tuned toward his three men.

"The former colonel's last psych evaluation said that he was off his rocker, maddened by an inability to control his temper."

"Just as I am having difficulty keeping that temper now, Colonel Collins. May I say, gentlemen—" He looked from Jack to the others. "—that you walked into the wrong fucking piece of property, and it will be my pleasure to bury you here."

Collins, Everett, Mendenhall, and Ryan watched the small man turn away and gesture for the guards to bring them along. They headed down the tunnel where the overhead lighting disappeared to nothing as it sank into the ground.

Leave it to Ryan to anger McCabe even more with his last question.

"So I guess lunch is out of the question?"

# 4

Jack, Carl, Will, and Ryan watched as the excavation dug back in the thirties and forties slid by the windows of their tram. There were three cars attached to the motorcar and they were riding in the middle six-wheeled conveyance. The road they traveled on was old but well maintained. The concrete poured all those years ago must have cost the German government a small fortune. As Collins tried to examine some of the deep depressions where men had once dug into the base of the mountain, he saw no evidence of anything that had been taken out years before.

Finally their journey came to an end. Although they had stopped in front of a large steel-reinforced gate, the paved road continued downward at a steep angle, indicating that there were further excavations beyond. The guards in the front and rear cars motioned for them to get out. McCabe was there and he was again writing on his clipboard. As the guards herded the four men toward a Quonset hut in front of the large gate, Jack saw several items that chilled his blood. Lined up neatly against the stone wall were approximately a hundred crates of varying sizes. On several of the smaller ones, stacked thirty feet high and sloppily covered in tarpaulins, the crate's markings had been exposed.

"Damn, Jack, do you see that?" Everett asked, just as he was pushed from behind.

Collins took one last quick look before he himself was jabbed in the back. *FIM-92* was stenciled on several of the exposed plastic cases. Jack immediately recognized what they were seeing. FIM-92 was a Stinger missile system, an infrared-homing surface-to-air missile developed in the United States and licensed by the Raytheon Corporation to be built by EADS, the European Aeronautic Defence and Space Company in Germany.

"Shit, there must be over eighty of those cases!" Carl said, as a door was opened and they were led into the hut.

James McCabe stepped in behind them and watched as Jack and the others were placed in seats. McCabe then gestured for the men and women who were sitting at several desks to leave. Once they were gone, McCabe sat on the edge of an empty desk and looked at the four men. He seemed confident, even though none of his captives was restrained. Jack supposed the eight large men in gray security uniforms holding AK-47s were a confidence builder for the former Delta officer.

"Okay, here we are. As you can tell, Jack, there's nothing much to see here but an old German mining company that was once a promising site for recovering uranium. The mining attempt failed, and the new owner is particularly worried about others digging around and finding something the old boys from the war didn't. A patriot, you might say, who doesn't want any undiscovered material falling into the wrong hands."

"I see, and that makes you a man who is concerned about the well-being of innocent people?" Jack asked, his brows raised.

"Ah," McCabe said, raising his hand and swiping it through the air, "You know me far better than that, Jack. It's the money, of course. I'm paid a lot by my employer to keep this place secure. It's not the rest of the world I care about—it's my world I'm concerned with, you should know that."

McCabe stood from the desk and walked up to Will Mendenhall and looked down at him.

"Now, I need to know who you work for." McCabe looked from Will to Ryan, and then down the line until his eyes rested on Jack. "Any volunteers?"

The room remained silent as McCabe glanced from face to face. He didn't seem disturbed that all four men kept their mouths shut.

"It's just a matter of curiosity. It makes no never mind to me. You came, you saw, and now you can report to—" He smiled. "—*whomever* it is you answer to that there is nothing in Quito that requires American involvement." He looked at his wristwatch. "Well, I have to be somewhere else in a few hours. I think it's time to feed you that lunch that my colleague promised you, and then you can get back to wherever you came from." He slapped Collins on the right knee. "Jack, it was good to see you, old friend. Take care of yourself."

They all watched as McCabe left the room. After he did, Jack and Carl exchanged a look and their unvoiced thought was that they would never see the light of the outside world again.

The security men gestured for the four to stand. The door was opened and they were escorted out into the massive cavelike gallery. Collins looked to the left at the large gate, and then to the right, where several workers were starting to load the crates and their contents onto the tram. The lead security guard pointed his AK-47 in the direction they had come from. Altogether there were just four of them and they had eight large men with guns. Jack was trying to think as fast as he could as they were led to a small excavated gallery that had been dug into the side of the large tunnel system. He remembered Sarah explaining to him that miners sometimes dug out side shafts for the discarding material that would save them loading it onto a conveyance to take topside. He knew this was where they would be shot and dumped. They were out of time.

"Colonel, I don't think this is the way to the kitchen," Ryan said from the front of the line as they were led into the darkened chute. "I hope you have a plan."

"Nothing comes to mind," Collins answered from the back. The security men were in two rows beside them, four on the left and four on the right.

"This job really sucks sometimes," Mendenhall said from behind Ryan.

"Shut up and move forward," the guard said. He turned around and faced Mendenhall. They could hear that he was one of the Americans in the security group.

As they moved further into the darkness, Jack could see that the excavation was getting smaller, and the walls rougher. He could also feel a much cooler draft on his face. Finally, they could see the end of the small shaft and the dropoff ahead. Jack kept his calm. He allowed his eyes to roam across the walls and the men that were watching them. He saw one advantage; most of the guards were aware of their surroundings and were uneasy in the semidarkness. Their eyes moved from place to place as they drew closer to the edge. Jack could smell water and hear the rush of a river somewhere far below. He closed his eyes as a plan formed. It was a long shot at the least and an expedient way to meet their death at the most.

The guards stopped and started pushing them toward the edge of a large rock outcropping—first Mendenhall, then Ryan, then Everett and Collins. They were being lined up.

"Gentlemen, it isn't much, but I suggest we keep walking forward," Jack said beneath his breath.

Before any of the eight guards could react, instead of stopping at the dark edge of the chasm before them all four men kept going and walked right off into the black void.

Falling side by side, Mendenhall cursed and Ryan prayed as the automatic weapons opened up above them. Tracers started filling the darkened shaft as they fell. One round hit Jack in the shoulder, barely grazing his shirt and taking an inch of skin with it into the blackness. Another three rounds struck the wall in front of them and ricocheted in all directions. It was like falling into an abyss with angry hornets buzzing around their heads. As they braced for a crushing impact, the four men were amazed as they kept falling, gaining speed as they fell feet-first into the great unknown death that awaited them.

Mendenhall was the first to strike the water, followed by Ryan. The latter had lost the battle with keeping his body straight and fell face-first into the rush of the river, the impact breaking his nose and shocking him into near unconsciousness. Everett managed to stay upright and hit the underground river with an impact that sent him straight to the river's bottom, where he jammed both knees on the coarse rock that made up the riverbed. Jack landed right beside him and veered off sharply after going under. The extreme angle allowed his feet to strike the left bank of the river. Collins thought he had broken his ankle as it came into contact with a large boulder, but he was aware enough to see red hot tracers stitch the water around him. He pushed with his legs and pulled with his arms, all the while assisted by the flow of the river. He finally managed to surface to the sound of rushing white water and the pings of bullets bouncing off rocks. In the darkness he bumped into someone who reached out and grabbed his right arm. Then he felt another man's hands and another's. Will and Jason were shaken as they coughed and spit out the freezing water.

"Damn," Everett shouted. "Are we all here?" The words were almost lost in the din.

There was no answer as they picked up speed and the current pulled them around a bend in the river. They struck a rock wall and then spun back into the center of the current. Then there was nothing, the sound disappearing as the walls and ceiling vanished above them. They were completely submerged.

Jack tried to hang on desperately to the man he was holding, but the twisting and rolling water separated them. He knew they had followed the river underground and figured that was it. He thought they could travel for at least three of four miles without the benefit of drawing air into their lungs. As he twirled underwater, he was sorry about leading his men into such a simple trap as the excavation, but knew his people well enough that they would rather die like this than be shot in the back and dumped into the blackness.

As the four men were battered by the twisting river, Jack was amazed to see the clean, cold water brighten. As he registered this in his oxygen-deprived brain, he was suddenly free of the river. He felt a free-falling sensation as he was ejected from the underground river and into thin air. The fall was from a height he would never have volunteered for. The waterfall noise covered the screams coming from all four of the men as they finally struck the white water below the falls. Jack struggled to the surface and realized then that through the entire length of his free fall he hadn't taken a breath. Finally reaching the surface of the roiling water, Jack took in the most wonderful breath of his entire life.

"Colonel, are you all right?"

As Jack gained his senses he felt hands lifting him up. When he looked to his right he saw it was Will Mendenhall who had taken his shoulder. In his other arm Will held Ryan by the back of his neck, keeping him afloat. There was a lot of blood clouding the water around Jason and that brought Collins back to complete consciousness as he reached out to see how badly hurt Ryan was.

"Mr. Everett?" Jack called out.

"Right here," came the answer. The Navy SEAL had taken both the fall and the water in stride, great swimmer that he was.

"Is Ryan all right?" Carl asked as he joined the three men holding each other up.

"He's breathing. I think his nose is broken." Will looked around to get his bearings.

At that moment they became aware of eyes upon them. Jack looked to his left and that was when he saw a man and two small boys. They were staring at the strange scene before them with fishing poles in their hands. Their eyes were wide and they didn't notice that the smallest child was getting a large strike on his pole.

Jack waved his hand at the three fishermen, and then out of the corner of his mouth said, "I think now may be a good time to get the hell out of here."

## FAITH MINISTRIES, INC., LOS ANGELES, CALIFORNIA

Rev. Samuel Rawlins paced the floor with the cordless phone held tightly in his hand. He was irritated at the two-second delay in the voice signal caused by the scrambled transmission. That was just another thing James McCabe, or Mr. Smith as he was called, had installed that had become an incredible waste of time.

"And what do your people say? Who is this man?" he asked the person at the other end of the line. He waited in frustration for the scrambled reply.

"We don't really know. We have a background check running right now and so far all we've come up with is that he was the highest-ranking student ever to come out of Harvard and MIT. After graduation in 1985, this Compton just fell off the map. That fact makes me suspect he's CIA."

"Mr. Vice President, you of all people should know that top MIT graduates do not go to work for low-paying intelligence agencies." Rawlins wondered why he dealt with men who had to have the smallest things explained to them. "Now, what did their visit consist of?"

The silence on the other end of the line was far longer than the scrambling could account for. Rawlins squeezed the handset even tighter.

"They were asking questions about how fast the United States could get to the Moon."

With the vice president's answer, the whiteness of Rawlins's hand on the phone increased and blood was forced out of it with the pressure he brought to bear.

"And?" he said, gritting his teeth.

"I don't know. All of this information was passed to me as the head of the space program, but I'm being kept at arm's length as far as the president is concerned. He's not taking me into his confidence."

"If that is the case, Harry, why the hell am I paying you so much money?"

"Look, this Compton can't get any information that won't eventually get back to me. Obviously the president has chosen this man to formulate a plan of some kind, possibly as a contingency only, so all we have to do is watch him."

"No, we can't take that chance. I want this man eliminated."

"What? He works directly for the president of the United States, Reverend. I think that would cause some very serious consequences."

Rawlins moved out from behind his desk and strode to a large couch fronted by an ornate coffee table. On the couch was a woman reading a magazine with her legs tucked underneath her. Rawlins placed his hands on her blond hair. The softness seemed to calm him considerably. He looked down at the family portrait sitting on the coffee table. It was a photo of Rawlins and his two daughters. The elder of which was sitting right in front of him.

"Use your imagination. If he is indeed on his way to Houston, as you say, any number of things can go wrong in flight. Am I correct?"

The young, beautiful woman on the couch, his daughter Laurel, lowered the *Esquire* and turned her head toward her father. She had a questioning look on her face. He smiled down at her.

"I wouldn't even know how to go about ordering something like that. I can't be caught committing what amounts to an assassination. That's tantamount to treason, no matter what you—"

"Do you really think I would put such an assignment into your lap, Harold? I'm not a fool. Just keep me informed about what this Niles Compton learns on his trip to NASA. That will give me time to make the arrangements. With luck, NASA and DARPA will tell him the same thing you've told me for years, that our space program is tits up in the water."

"Look, Reverend, we need to think this out. We need—"

Rawlins pushed the disconnect button on the phone and lowered it to his side. His hand continued toying with his daughter's blond hair until she finally became irritated enough to push him away.

"Are you going to keep me in the dark forever, Daddy?"

Rawlins looked down at his eldest daughter and smiled. "Just the usual incompetence with employees. You know the drill. They just can't see the things I do." Rawlins leaned over the back of the couch. "God's will can be an angry and ugly thing."

"I love your euphemisms for murder, Daddy, I always have."

"I will assume you mean that in the most respectful way, daughter." Rawlins straightened and walked back to his desk, tossing the phone into its cradle.

Laurel Rawlins stood and walked to her father's desk, perching on the edge. Her shapely right leg swung back and forth as she tilted her head low so that her father could see her eyes.

"I told you, you need more dependable people on your payroll. Now, give me your wish list and I'll get things done. I have the people, and I have the contacts. You said it yourself. Mr. McCabe will have his hands full in the coming days and weeks and can't be every place he needs to be. And we don't need the Mechanic getting himself killed before his usefulness is at an end, do we?"

Rawlins looked up at his older daughter. Her blue eyes were as blue as his own. Unlike his younger daughter, Laurel was all him. She was a woman who even as a child knew what made her world go around and that was the money her father could provide her. She had so much of it that her nighttime activities were a mere hobby to her. That fact alone should have concerned him, but he knew she had to have excitement in her life.

"I do things for the love of my God, daughter, but never for myself. Of course, the money is always nice, but it never seems to be enough."

"The money is good. And I have no doubt that you do what you do for the love of God," Laurel said, reaching out and touching his cheek. "And I do what I do for the love of you." She smiled broadly and batted her eyes. "And the money too, of course."

"I suspect that is not all you do it for. I believe I should be worried about your wicked ways, Laurel—for instance, your little affair with Mr. McCabe."

The young woman slid off the desk, hopping gently to the carpeted floor and straightening her skirt. "Believe me, Daddy, when I say that my relationship with our former Army friend had its little perks. I've met people who will be a benefit to us, even if our dear Mr. McCabe has to, well, even if he suddenly has to leave our employ."

"For now, I need him like no other. He devised a brilliant plan that will shift blame away from our actions to where it belongs. It's ingenious really. And he chose the perfect man in the Mechanic, a man who will set us on the road to everlasting glory."

Laurel raised her eyebrows, knowing that her father was as crazy as they come, but she still loved him in her own special way. She returned to his desk and became serious.

"Now, if I heard you right, you spoke of a Niles Compton?"

"Yes."

"And he'll be in Houston this afternoon?"

Rawlins saw the gleam in his daughter's eyes as she demurely took a notepad from his desk and wrote down the pertinent information.

"Yes, the Johnson Space Center."

"Now," she said, lowering the writing pad, "I take it you want him to cease his activities, whatever they are?"

Rawlins looked through the large window. His eyes fell on the smoggy afternoon outside his offices.

"Fine, if you want to know about the ugly side of God's work, I may have something even more thrilling for you when you finish with this. If what is happening is truly going to happen, we will not only be out many valuable patents on the technology in the mines, but the world could turn against the word of God for those damnable petrified bodies. The nonbelievers of the world are going to try to make my people, and others of our kind, turn from their faith. If it comes to that, we may have to commit ourselves to the salvation of our very souls, and that of the people who allow us into their homes three times a week."

"Sounds like we may be busy then," she said, moving her head to get her long blond hair behind her shoulders. She tore the page from the pad and tossed it onto the desk. "If you'll excuse me, I have a flight to catch."

"Not to ruin your good mood, my dear, but the Mechanic is coming in from Ecuador immediately and I will have him meet you in Houston. Use him. I do not want you directly involved if the Mechanic finds an opening against this Dr. Compton."

"Oh, I have many uses for our Arab friend. Using him to kill is just one of them," she said, shooting her father a demure look.

Rawlins watched his daughter leave the office. He knew Laurel was not a follower of his word, but there was a quid pro quo. She allowed him his own small peccadilloes as far as his religion went. As long as the money supply was up to a minimum level, Laurel was his forever. He smiled as he figured that it was probably time she earned her keep. He looked at his watch and frowned.

"All right, Mr. McCabe, where are you?"

## 30 MILES OUTSIDE QUITO, ECUADOR

Ryan had come around nicely. They made their way through the thick stand of trees as Jason asked Will Mendenhall one more time if his nose looked as bad as it felt. Collins raised his hand when he saw Everett suddenly stop and hold up five fingers, then clench his fist. He lowered his hand slowly with the palm facing down, telling through his fingers to stop, get down, and be quiet. Collins eased his way forward.

They had heard helicopters fly very low over the sparsely forested part of the foothills, and each time they had to scramble for cover, barely staying out of view of people who were obviously McCabe's men searching for them. For the most part they had been lucky. The bulk of the search was being conducted around the falls and the lake they had been near more than two hours before.

Everett turned around and knelt beside Jack. "Looks like a cop up ahead on that small road—looks local to me. He's parked next to a '66 Chevy Impala with a male driver and a woman passenger. Looks like they're changing a flat. The cop is just standing there, jawing."

"This may be our chance to bum a ride."

"That's what I was figuring," Everett confirmed, and looked back at the scene just below on the roadway.

Jack turned and held up a hand to Ryan and Mendenhall, indicating for them to stay put. As he watched, Will reached out and patted Ryan on the shoulder. He silently shook his head and made a face indicating that the nose looked real bad, causing the small Navy man extreme consternation.

"Okay, looks like we may be in business here, Jack. The cops are leaving."

"Okay, stay in the tree line. I'll see if we can get a ride."

"Well, they look to be pointed in the right direction," Carl said as he moved aside to let Jack by. "Watch your ass."

"Yeah, my judgment hasn't been real good today, so maybe you better watch it for me," Collins said, easing out of the trees.

"Hola," Jack called out. He raised his right hand and crossed the broken macadam of the old roadway.

The man was just lowering the large car from its jack. He paused and stood. He pulled the woman behind him as he looked at the bedraggled man crossing the road.

"Hola," the old man answered, as his eyes searched the area around Collins to see if he was alone.

"*Habla inglés?*" Collins asked, smiling the best nonthreatening smile he could muster.

"*Sí,*" the man said. "Little . . . bit," he said, holding up his index finger and thumb about an inch apart.

"Uh, I and some friends seem to be in a fix. Our car broke down a few miles back, and we need a ride into the next town."

The middle-aged man watched as Jack approached the car, hands held slightly out in front of him. He seemed to relax a bit as he stepped away from the car.

"You need assistance?" the man said, the words clearly understood by Jack.

"Yes," Collins said, looking around the car. All he could see was the woman standing behind the man, as though hiding.

"*Sí,* we will assist you," the man said. He pointed west. "Quito," he said, looking back at Collins.

"That's where we're headed."

"*Sí,* bring your friends," the man said.

Jack turned away and gestured toward the trees. Everett came first, followed by Will and then Ryan. As Jack watched them come down the small incline, he was shocked when he saw Everett dive into some bushes, quickly followed by Mendenhall and Ryan.

As he turned he saw that the small woman had stepped out from behind the older man. She held an ugly-looking UZI machine gun. Jack's eyes widened as she brought the weapon up and started shooting. The initial line of bullets stitched a path directly to Jack's front. He saw the gun move in slow motion. Without thinking, he jumped to the right and landed behind the car's rear bumper. He rolled until he was underneath the hot exhaust pipe. The heat was intense, but he kept rolling until he hit the right rear wheel, still partially suspended by the jack on the rear bumper. As he watched, the man went to one knee and the first thing Jack saw was the blue steel barrel of an automatic being angled toward him. Thinking fast, Jack spun on his back, causing broken pieces of blacktop to dig into his skin. The woman once again opened fire on Everett, Ryan, and Mendenhall across the road. Collins, mustering all the strength he had, kicked at the jack. It didn't take as much strength as he thought to make it break loose. The man had just spotted Collins and was about to open to fire when the car began to fall.

"Oh, shit," Collins said, flattening himself as low as he could manage. The large Chevy came down and the rear quarter panel caught his would-be killer in the side of the head, propelling the side of his face into the roadway. The weapon was knocked out of his hands just as the car's bottom hit Jack in the chest. The heavy-duty springs brought the car back up. Jack reached for the gun and fired into the woman's legs. Two bullets hit her in each thigh, dropping her to the ground. Jack saw her face twist in anger, shock, and pain. She desperately tried to bring the UZI around.

"Don't do it," Jack yelled, aiming at a spot between the woman's eyes.

Before she had a chance to fire her weapon, and before Collins managed to kill her, a large boot came down onto the side of the woman's face. Jack relaxed when he realized Everett had come up on her without her knowing it. He lowered his head and took a deep breath.

"You okay?" Carl asked as he knelt and looked at Jack's dirty face. "It's a damn good thing you don't have a beer gut, buddy. This car would have surely flattened it for you." Everett reached out a hand and pulled Jack out from under the car.

When Collins stood he saw that the woman was out cold not two feet from the man's body. Was the man her husband?

"Will, see what you can find in the car," Jack said, reaching down and retrieving the UZI. He tossed it to Carl. "Get her legs wrapped. You and Ryan can pull both of them into the trees. I suspect their friends will find them soon enough."

"Yes, sir," Mendenhall said, amazed at the close call the colonel had just had.

"May I suggest we take the car and get the hell back to the city?" Everett removed the ammunition clip from the UZI and checked its remaining rounds. He smiled as he slammed the clip back home. He went around to the driver's side, kicking the jack stand and crowbar out of the way as he did so.

"Let's go, gentlemen. I have a feeling our ex-Delta man may have more friends waiting for us."

Two hours later the old and battered Impala pulled into the main concourse area of the airport. Everett had taken all the back roads he could find into the outskirts of the city and the zigzag route had cost them time. The four men were sore and exhausted.

"Well, here we are," Everett said, slamming the car's gearshift into park. "Ryan, do you think you can fly with that swollen nose of yours?"

"Very funny. I want you guys to know that this thing hurts like hell—and the face Mendenhall makes every time he looks at me doesn't help."

Will turned away and opened the rear door without saying a word, but he was smiling where Ryan couldn't see him.

Jack stood and stretched as he tried to examine as much of his surroundings as he could.

"What do we do about the excavation, Colonel?" Will asked.

"There's nothing we can do about it at the moment. We don't have a clue how deep this thing goes. We may be dealing with the Ecuadorian government and their military." He turned and faced the others as he closed the car's door.

"What about the weapons inside?" Ryan asked. He gently touched his nose.

"They won't be there even if we do come back. We need to bring Niles up to date as fast as possible. This thing has to be figured out at management level."

As the men turned and headed for the private section of the new airport, James McCabe lowered the field glasses that he had been using to examine the parking structure across the way.

"We can shoot them before they board their aircraft," his assistant said.

McCabe raised the glasses once more and watched as Collins and his men moved into the terminal.

"Why in the world would I want to do that?" he asked, smiling. "When mistakes are made in field operations, you try not to compound them by making another equally disastrous move." He lowered the glasses and tossed them to the plainclothes security man. "You minimize the mistake by at least getting intelligence for the next round of battle. When they leave here, we'll know exactly where they will land."

"Yes, but instead of a tracking device, we should have planted a bomb onboard their aircraft," the large German said, turning to follow McCabe.

"That is why you are you and I am me. I need to know who Jack and his pals are working for, and I couldn't do that if he's dead, could I?"

McCabe opened the door of his limousine.

"I want those two fools who got shot up on the roadway eliminated for trying to kill them after they managed to escape. You should have passed on my orders far sooner than you did," McCabe said, looking closely at the large German before stepping into the limousine. "And that's exactly why I will kill you if my instructions are not followed to the smallest detail. You see, there must be discipline in the ranks or else there will be chaos. And then we could not do what we are paid to do." The small man climbed into the car and the German felt the heat of the man's glare.

"Now, I need to go to our private hangar. I feel like blowing something up."


## JOHNSON SPACE CENTER, HOUSTON, TEXAS

Director Appleby watched the face of Niles Compton. Although tired from his many flying hours in the past day, Compton seemed bright and eager. He was astonished to see what DARPA in its dark guise had to show him.

They stood in a small nondescript room and watched the large screen before them. Sarah, always one to show wonderment when faced with the unbelievable, walked to the screen and placed her hand on the image. She turned and looked at Appleby.

On the large monitor the director had instructed the NASA/DARPA computer system to bring up a split image of two different warehouses. One of the warehouses was active. Niles, Virginia, and Sarah saw men and women walking around in their white coveralls as they worked. In the foreground was the giant solid booster rocket that made up the heavy power stage.

"Mr. Compton, I give you the Ares I. The new platform is an in-line, two-stage rocket configuration. The vehicle's primary mission is carrying crews of four to six astronauts into Earth's orbit. However, Ares I may also use its twenty-five-ton payload capacity to deliver resources and supplies to the International Space Station or to park payloads in orbit for retrieval by other spacecraft bound for the Moon or other destinations. Normally this would have been in the *cut* portion of the president's budget restraint, but with the retirement of the space shuttle program nearing, the president pointed out a small loophole in the budget, some sort of secret black project that kept the Ares program operational."

"How many do we have?" Niles asked, looking at the giant booster and Ares's different stages as they lay prone in the massive complex housing the project. The director of DARPA saw that Compton had expertly sidestepped the issue of the president secretly saving the Ares system even though his budget cut had called for it. On the monitor everything gleamed in pure whiteness and the sight was so impressive that Niles had a hard time not looking at its beauty.

"One platform is available now, complete with the Orion crew capsule and the Altair lunar lander. All are highly advanced systems designed for Moon debarkation and extended habitation. The other Ares can be put together in a matter of a week and transported to either one of two launch facilities, complete with a three-quarters-finished lunar landing and transport system."

"We have two Ares and no other backup?" Niles turned and faced Appleby. "Those are all untried systems." Niles held up a hand when Appleby looked to protest. "That's not a rebuke, just an observation. What if the president gives a go to a Moon mission and the system fails?"

"That's exactly why I brought you here, Mr. Compton. I need to show you the only reliable backup we have."

Sarah stepped back from the large screen as Appleby punched some buttons on the computer keyboard. "My science offices axed this program many, many years ago, but NASA, in its nostalgia, hung on to it."

As they watched, the scene went from Ares to a view that was live but had none of the activity that the Ares I mission warehouse had. The giant hangar-like structure was dark and all they could see was four men standing near a giant object.

"This is a warehouse on seldom used grounds at the Cape—hidden away, if you will." Appleby looked at Sarah and Virginia. "That's Cape Canaveral."

As they tried to figure out what it was they were looking at, Appleby brought a phone to his ear.

"Okay, Dan, hit the lights and pull off the tarp. Let's show our guests what it is they're looking at."

Niles, Virginia, and Sarah watched as the bright lighting of the warehouse came up. The four men reached for the bottom of a giant red plastic tarp. They started pulling. Soon they were joined by several security men in white shirts in an effort to get the tarpaulin off without the massive hundred-yard material killing someone. As it finally gave, Niles recognized it immediately and fell in love all over again. He recognized the most amazing sight he had ever seen as a boy, an object that dwarfed the men who were uncovering it.

"I give you the Atlas V rocket, designed by Wernher von Braun, at one time the most powerful launch system in the world."

Niles examined the copper-colored features of the unpainted Atlas V. It was glorious in all its terrible beauty. The vehicle that had taken mankind to the Moon over four decades before was still a sight that sent chills down his spine.

"Are you telling me we have a complete system?"

Appleby smiled and stepped up to the screen. "We have this one and one other, but the second is hanging like an old out-of-date picture in the Smithsonian. NASA never had the willpower to dismantle this one. We have everything for the old girl. We have the Apollo capsule, which of course we couldn't use today for safety purposes, and we also have the lunar lander, or LEM, complete with upgrades for her systems on the design boards. But I'm afraid that would take too long to rebuild. We would probably have to go with a third Altair lander, if we can match the designs together."

"My God," Sarah and Virginia said simultaneously.

"This would be our backup for Ares, Dr. Compton." Appleby walked back to the control system and closed the image from Florida. "I guess you can tell the president that we weren't caught totally flat-footed on this one. All we need is a launch time frame and we can meet any challenge. Of course, we'll have to remove most if not all of the safety protocols."

Niles grabbed his coat and his briefcase. He turned to Virginia and Sarah as he neared the door. "Once aboard the plane, I need a direct line to the president." He held the door open for the two women and looked back at Appleby. "I hope you *can* meet any challenge, Mr. Appleby, because the Chinese have just informed the United Nations they plan to launch in three weeks. The ESA should follow shortly. But we will meet that challenge and beat them to the punch if at all humanly possible."

"So, what are you saying?"

"Begin preparations to get the two Ares systems up and get the Atlas ready to go. We'll need them in less than a month from today. That still puts us a week behind everyone else."

"That's crazy!"

"No, it's necessary, Mr. Appleby. If we like our way of life, we'd better beat those other powers to the Moon and bring back whatever is up there. Much more than falling behind is at stake here."

"Does the president know about this?" Appleby asked, as Niles turned and walked through the door.

"He soon will, Mr. Appleby. I suggest you get on the phone and start waking up about a million people, because we're going back to the Moon."

Appleby watched as the door closed. Then he turned and brought up the image of the warehouse at Cape Canaveral again. He watched as the men stood there, dwarfed by the powerful rocket, its five motors, and its engine bells. He shook his head.

"Impossible," he said. His eyes continued to dwell on the image of the old spacecraft, and then a smile slowly crept across his lips. With fist clenched, he hit the desk lightly. He didn't care if it was impossible. They were going back to the Moon and he would give it the best possibility of success. Finally he closed his eyes and shouted, "Yes!"

A front of rain clouds and wind had encircled the city of Houston. Niles, Sarah, and Virginia were forced to wait out the storm on the private tarmac at William P. Hobby Airport. As they waited they were informed by Pete Golding from the Event Group Complex in Nevada that Jack and his team were on their way home, and with that message the Department of State had received notification that an arrest warrant had been issued for Colonel Collins, Captain Everett, and Lieutenants Ryan and Mendenhall. The charge was two counts of murder and industrial espionage.

Niles sat in shock. Virginia and Sarah both exchanged incredulous looks, knowing that if Jack and the others had to kill, it was only as a last resort, and it would never be anyone who didn't intend them harm first.

"Who the hell did they supposedly kill?" Niles asked Pete. They were speaking over a secure video link between the private Learjet owned by the Event Group and Niles's office beneath the desert sands at Nellis AFB. Pete slowly removed his glasses and looked into the camera.

"Two Ecuadorian tourists, supposedly during a carjacking," Pete said, with a tinge of disgust at the accusation.

"But they are safely out of the country and in the air?" Niles asked.

"Yes, ETA Nellis in forty-five minutes," Pete said. He slid his glasses back on and continued with the report. "Also, the government of Ecuador has closed off the region that includes the old German excavation and has reinforced that closing with federal troops. That's something that particular government has never done before."

"Has Europa come up with anything about the true ownership of the excavation?"

"No, that information has been buried pretty deep, but we'll find them. We do have a lead on this Brinkman fellow in Berlin. It seems there is a connection between him and Operation Columbus, a pretty strong one."

"What's that?" Niles asked, always irritated at the way Pete had to have information dragged from him.

"It seems his father was a prisoner at Spandau Prison at the same time, for a few hours or so, as Albert Speer. Speer was Hitler's architect and one of the managers of Columbus. There's a smoking gun here."

"Tell Jack to contact me as soon as he settles in at the complex. We may need for him and the captain to take another trip."

"Germany?" Pete asked.

"It seems everything begins and ends right where it all started, and I'm afraid we need feet on the ground there to find out what everyone else knew that we didn't. Also, have Europa get into the Ice Blue computer system at CIA, the Pentagon, and the FBI. We need to pin down a connection between this Brinkman character and Columbus. Cross-reference all of the pertinent names Senator Lee mentioned. Get any information you receive into Jack's hands. I'll leave it up to him and his team to decide what to do with it."

Pete was writing furiously as he took down the instructions.

"Anything else?"

"Yes, it seems NASA and DARPA have been keeping secrets from the rest of the federal government—to our benefit it seems—but I need a complete workup of everything those two agencies have on inventory with the National Accounting Office. Also, get Europa into the House Ways and Means Committee and find out what secret funding NASA and DARPA have received over, say, the past thirty years. Anything that relates to a manned incursion into space. I don't want to have to pry information out of these people, especially about projects they want to keep hidden. We may need everything they have."

"Wow, is that all?" Pete finally looked up at the camera.

"No, get your coffee cups and lunch tray off of my desk," Niles said, disconnecting the view of a stunned Pete on his laptop.

Niles took his glasses off and rubbed his eyes. Then he looked at Sarah and Virginia.

"Okay, as for you two, you're dropping me off at Andrews Air Force Base. I have to pay the president a visit, and then you'll fly on to Nevada. Virginia, you take charge, assist Jack and determine if we need feet on the ground in Germany." He held up his hand to stop Virginia before she could say anything. "No, you are not to go on any field missions. Stay put at the complex." He put his glasses back on and looked at Sarah. "Lieutenant, I want you, Ryan, and Mendenhall to put together a team and start trying to figure out what this mineral is and how we can get a handle on controlling it just in case some other nation brings back a load of it. There has to be something in our own natural makeup that resembles it in some way. I suspect that earthbound samples of it exist. The Germans may have it lying around or maybe they've distributed it in some form."

"I don't think we—"

"Humor me, Sarah. Find anything, we'll need someone with an understanding of what we're dealing with where this mineral is concerned"—he leaned closer toward Sarah—"and to put it frankly, I want at least one of our people on any attempt to get a mission up there. Guess at what that mineral is and what it's made of. Your best guess will get you on one of those missions. I don't trust anyone I don't know to give me the straight dope on what it is we're dealing with. The president would feel better too. Virginia and I will explain further when the time comes."

Sarah leaned back in her seat, stunned as she'd never been stunned before at the suggestion that she could possibly be included on something like a Moon shot. Niles saw her dilemma and patted her on the knee.

"I suggest you don't mention what I just said to Jack."

"For *your* sake," Virginia said to Niles.

"Director Compton," said the voice of the Air Force pilot in the cockpit. "We've been cleared for runway three north. We'll be rolling in one minute."

Niles winked at the still shocked Sarah and then finally fastened his seat belt.

Laurel Rawlins watched the Learjet from the dry shelter of a private hangar three buildings down, where the small jet was spooling up her engines for taxiing onto the runway. She smiled as she turned to look at the man McCabe had recruited, someone from his antiterrorist days with the army. The bearded man watched Laurel closely. He never spoke much and when he did she could always hear the disdain he held for women of any religion or country. A man losing his faith was a nasty thing to watch.

"At what speed did you set the charge to go off?" she asked, watching the blue and white Learjet start moving.

She had nervously waited as the Mechanic—the name he was known by in every police agency in the world—placed a one-ounce charge of C-4 explosive near the aluminum rim of the nose wheel of the jet.

"The charge will detonate at one hundred knots, a split second before the jet reaches takeoff speed. That should be enough to send the plane off course and cause it to crash before liftoff. I have done this before. You may not wish to watch."

Laurel smiled and pulled her silk windbreaker closer around her upper body.

"Are you kidding? This is what I live for," she said. She was disgusted that the bearded Mechanic would even suggest such a weakness. She turned away and watched the Learjet taxi toward the runway. "You need to have faith in women, my friend. Your old ways of looking at things have never made you any true friends among your own kind. James and Daddy will be proud. They won't be using this Mr. Compton to coordinate anything having to do with the Moon. I'm afraid they'll have to get someone else."

She was so excited that she could barely keep her legs still.

As the Learjet taxied further into the misting gray fog of Hobby Airport, the cell phone inside Laurel's windbreaker rang. She shook her head, not wanting her glee at what was about to happen disturbed. Her blue eyes were glowing in anticipation. Her father's eyes had glowed that morning too, though what she was feeling was anticipatory wonder and excitement and what her father had been feeling was pure anger at not being able to control everything around him. Finally, she realized that the only people who had this particular cell phone number were her father and James McCabe, her Mr. Smith. She angrily tore into the coat pocket and ripped the phone free. She opened it hard enough that the Mechanic standing next to her heard the cover crack.

"What?" she hissed into the phone.

"Laurel, what are you doing?" a voice asked.

"I'm doing what you would do if you were here," she said into the phone. "And you know what, James? I'm a little busy at the moment."

"Listen, tell me what you've done, quickly." McCabe's voice was calm and precise.

"I'm helping you and Daddy, just like you taught me to do."

"Slow down and listen to me. If you are planning on hurting Compton and his team, you'll not be doing us any favors. Do you understand?"

"But—"

"Laurel, right now we have the advantage. We know about him, but he has no idea who we are. Stop whatever it is you are doing, right now."

McCabe's voice was so calm and measured that Laurel was taken off guard. She felt embarrassed and humiliated at having thought this was something that would have made her part-time lover and her father proud of her. She lowered the phone and looked at the Mechanic, who was still wiping his hands on the red rag and sneering at her.

"Disarm the charge," she said, not looking directly at the bearded man but at the distant jet as it rounded onto the runway. The man saw her face go slack, and the vitality she had displayed only seconds before had drained away. For the first time he saw through the young woman's expensive exterior and the ugliness that he saw was shocking. He nodded his head. Her eyes narrowed and she watched as the Event Group Learjet spooled up its engines to full takeoff power.

"You realize that the charge will be discovered when the mechanics check the aircraft?"

Laurel, instead of replying, just tossed the cell phone at the Mechanic, not caring if he caught it or not, and then she turned angrily away and stepped out into the misting air.

"Yes?" he said into the phone.

"Can you undo what you have arranged with that aircraft?" McCabe asked.

The Saudi-born Mechanic reached into his coveralls' front pocket and brought out a small transmitter. He hit the single red button on its face.

"It is done," he said into the phone.

"Now listen closely. You are never to engage in any wet work without my explicit confirmation of action. You are never to allow Laurel to . . . compromise herself again. She, like her father, needs to be protected. Do you understand?"

"Completely."

"Now, I assume you used a remote device on Compton's aircraft, yes?"

"This is correct," the Mechanic said. He watched Laurel as she stared after the streaking Learjet on the runway.

"Do you have the ability to track the device?"

"Up to three thousand miles. I am tied into the Faith—" The man stopped himself before saying the name of his employer. "I am patched through a reliable satellite service."

"Track-only for now. Gather your equipment and alert your ground personnel. We have duties in Russia and then down south in French Guiana."

The Mechanic closed the phone without saying anything. He watched as Laurel fixed on him with a look of hatred and failure.

"You will have to fly home commercially, madam," he said. "Or hire a plane. I have been ordered to another area of opportunity."

Laurel stood in the light rain and stared at the Mechanic. Her hair was drenched and her beautiful features were obscured by the stringy strands of hair.

"It must be hell for a man like you to lose your faith in yourself," she said. "So many of your brothers have been martyred and here you are, worse than your onetime enemies. Taking money from the people you once professed to despise, who you would have killed in a minute. You are worse than sad, and you hate me because I am a woman." She took a step toward the Mechanic. "Well, at least I have the courage of my convictions. You have nothing. I expect McCabe knew what he was doing when he hired you. You just may make that martyrdom yet, but don't expect your promised virgins in the afterlife. From what I understand they don't reward cowards."

The Mechanic watched her smile a lunatic's grin as she turned to leave. He knew that she was right about him. For a man once feared by the Zionists and the entire Western world, he was a skeleton of his former self. A man who thought his brothers in Afghanistan were weak and without conviction, enough so that they thought him unstable. He was banished from the movement forever and now he found himself in the employ of pigs, the very same people he had sworn to annihilate. Laurel Rawlins's words about achieving martyrdom echoed in his head and then just as quickly disappeared.

He turned away from the woman and watched the Learjet climb into the sky. Then he looked down at the remote device in his hand. He safed the system and placed it in his pocket to check the GPS later for the final destination of the aircraft. He smiled as he saw the landing gear retract on the expensive Learjet and pointed a finger at the plane. He made a motion as if he were pulling a trigger.

"Another time, my friend. Another time."

# 5

## BAIKONUR COSMODROME, SPACE LAUNCH FACILITY, KAZAKHSTAN

The jointly managed space facility run by the Russian Federal Space Agency and the Russian Space Forces was located 124 miles from the Aral Sea. Since the heyday of the Soviet space program, Baikonur Cosmodrome had seen occasional fits of activity, but since the Russian president openly declared that his countrymen would make an attempt at the investigation on the lunar surface, the facility had seen activity on a massive scale. Forty thousand workers had flooded into the old buildings in Kazakhstan, making the area near the sea once more a viable force in science and space exploration. A much needed transfusion of rubles and euros was flowing in.

As the world watched in wonder, the unveiling of Russia's top secret lunar program, Ice Palace, began to take shape, and it came far faster than any Western government could ever have imagined.

The giant first stage of a rocket known as the Angara A7, the most powerful launch system the world had ever seen, was being transported to the assembly building three miles from where the mission would be launched. The great system was strapped down and prone on the tractor system, looking like a scene from *Gulliver's Travels* as it crawled along at four miles per hour toward the waiting hands of its engineers. The seven RD-91 rocket motors were partially covered, but most of the bell funnel system was open for satellites the world over to see. Not since the massive engines of the Saturn V blasted America to the Moon had there been anything like the RD-91s.

The hydrogen-based rocket fuel was capable of creating almost double the thrust of anything Russian science had developed since the horrifying failures of its N series of rockets in the sixties and seventies. The new design was a source of pride for a Russian lunar program that was now twenty years ahead of schedule.

The man watched from two hundred yards away. His eyes studied the Russian air force security personnel who traveled beside the Angara A7 first stage. The security force was a hundred strong and each of the green-clad soldiers carried an automatic weapon. As the man watched, he could see massive gaps in the security line. The force of guards was just not enough to cover the giant launch platform as it moved out toward the assembly building on the huge caterpillar.

The man was dressed in an expensive Western suit. He pulled the equally expensive coat tightly around him as he turned to the shorter man at his side.

"Your martyrdom is assured. Your family will take with them through life the knowledge that your actions will benefit Allah and his glory. You are the man who will strike the first blow against the infidels and their mission to cast God into the shadows. Is your team prepared?"

The small man looked up at his benefactor. He knew the man as Azim Quaida, the former leader of the Islamic terrorist front Egyptian Islamic Jihad. In Western intelligence circles he was also known as the Mechanic.

"My men are ready. Allah be praised."

"You may proceed with your mission. The attempt to belittle God shall end in this godless country. *La illahah illalah*," he said with unbridled pride. There is no God but Allah.

The smaller man pulled his long coat around his thin frame. Tears streaked down his cheeks.

*"Allah Akbar,"* he said proudly.

The larger man placed his hand on his shoulder. "You will be in heaven this day, and you will proudly say you struck the first blow against the humiliation of Allah."

The smaller man turned away and gestured to the ten men who comprised his small unit. Several of them carried sound equipment and cameras. They would approach the slowly moving Angara A7, as many had in the past three hours, just a group of journalists using the new rights afforded to the Russian press.

They broke away into four different teams and separated into groups of two that would approach the crawler from both the near and far side. No chance would be taken that the experimental first stage could survive the attack. Two teams hurriedly crossed the massive fifteen-gauge tracks of the crawler and set themselves to filming on the far side. The other two knelt and started filming from the near side, taking care to zoom in on the proud Russian air force security element. The young men smiled, thinking that their pictures were being streamed live into the living rooms of friends, relatives, and lovers.

On the small knoll overlooking the scene, the Mechanic shook his head. He had once been as those below, but that was before the traitorous acts of men in a position of power, men who had sold out Jihad for safety in lands other than their own. Money was his driving force now. He felt a pang of guilt and shame at what he was doing to his loyal men. He turned away toward the small car that would carry him to the main gates of Baikonur. He knew the young men would carry out the task assigned to them. As he stepped into the backseat of the car he pulled out his cell phone and hit a speed-dial button.

"I suspect you are watching the glory of Russian science on your television?"

"I most assuredly am, as is the Reverend."

The Mechanic pulled up the sleeve of his coat and looked at his watch.

"Well, my friend, say good-bye to the tranquil, patriotic scene on your television."

McCabe didn't comment, he just hung up.

The Mechanic rolled down the window and, instead of disconnecting, pushed several buttons. The built-in scrambler started shuffling phone numbers to the forefront of its computerized memory—numbers that would lead Russian intelligence to a place that would surprise no one, the Islamic terrorist Jihad against the West. McCabe had provided the phone, but the Mechanic hesitated for a brief moment, wondering if he was doing the right thing. He shook his head at the way he doubted the plan. He looked at the cell phone and saw that the power was on and its signal intact. The authorities should have no trouble in recovering the small phone. The bearded man smiled and tossed the cell phone through the open window and then tapped the seat in front of him, just before the car sped away.

The first hint of trouble caught the young security force off guard. The group of newspeople on the far side of the crawler gently placed their equipment on the ground, smiling as they did so. The forty-five-man security unit was taken totally by surprise as the men rushed the crawler and its heavy cargo, the Angara A7 booster rocket.

A lieutenant colonel reacted first, bringing out his holstered handgun just before the younger air force personnel around him jumped into action. He fired six quick shots in succession as the first four-man team rushed the crawler. Two men fell and a third was hit in the right knee. The man staggered and went down, but not before he pulled the striker on the forty pounds of C-4 that had been meticulously strapped to his torso. The explosion rocked the security detail, sending most to the ground with bleeding eardrums. The large detonation on the far side alerted security. The Angara rocked on its railway car, straining the straps that held it in place. It quickly settled, but not before the second team had made shocking progress toward the railcar.

The last man threw himself underneath the car, but not before the security force fired thirty rounds into the bodies of his fellow team members. One of the men rolled over onto his back and screamed, "God is great!" He was struggling to pull the small wire that would send an electrical charge into his package of C-4. Just as he finally located the thin wooden handle attached to the silverish wire, the large steel wheels of the train car ran over both his legs. The young boy screamed and tried to pull himself from the path of the giant crawler, but only managed to tear his legs away from his body. He skewered onto the tracks just as the next set of wheels ran down the center of his head and torso. The C-4 remained undetonated.

The second and last team didn't seem as lucky at first. Security personnel downed all four of them almost as soon as they could aim their weapons. It looked as though the maddened attempt on the Angara A7 booster system had failed, but then the first of the wounded, the man closest to the crawler, looked to the sky and pulled the thin wire. The explosion rocked the ground and sent the railroad track twisting in all directions. The motion rocked the Angara A7. Its restraining straps broke free just as the fireball struck the polished white paint.

The security men, the gathered reporters, and the administrators of the Moon project were thrown back by the first attempt at stopping the lunar mission. However, more destruction was on its way. The second team, though down, detonated another eighty pounds of C-4 with their dying breaths, creating a blinding force of heated energy. This time the A7 booster didn't stand a chance. The force of the blast struck it just as it ripped free from its restraints. The impact tore the booster rocket from the car and pushed it onto the far-side security element. The aluminum and copper housing of the A7 rolled over, crushing a hundred men and women.

Finally the paint on the booster caught fire as the electrically powered crawler exploded in a burst of flame and sparks, blasting into a frightening future.

## EVENT GROUP COMPLEX, NELLIS AIR FORCE BASE, NEVADA.

Jack was fuming. Mendenhall, along with a bandaged Ryan and Carl, understood Jack's frustration when the Event Group ground crew discovered the small bomb that had been placed on the nose wheel of the Learjet twenty hours after it had landed. The device was sitting on Jack's desk and one member of the security team, Marine Corps Corporal Albert Espinoza, was in the process of dissecting its simple technology.

"Basically, Colonel, everything here could be bought at RadioShack or Walmart. We don't have anything that will lead us anywhere."

The news footage of the attack in Kazakhstan had been seen by every person in the complex. Jack and the others knew immediately that it was tied in somehow to James McCabe and whoever paid for his services. Thus far the only thing the Event Group could do was talk the FBI and Interpol into issuing a warrant for the former Delta colonel's arrest, and even then he would only be wanted for questioning about his role in Ecuador. That country had already issued its findings and nowhere was there a mention of Colonel McCabe in their initial report. Jack, Carl, Ryan, and Mendenhall, however, had been given a few pages apiece inside the file that the State Department received from South America on their status as fugitives.

As for the Russian attack, intelligence sources inside an angry Kazakhstan had traced a cell phone found at the site to a group called the Egyptian Islamic Jihad, known to have close ties with al Qaeda. Thus far the public had not been told of the terrorist cell's involvement. They didn't want to scare off the man who once ran the cell, Azim Quaida, known to Jack and antiterrorist organizations as the Mechanic. Collins, as well as many Western intelligence officials, didn't believe this organization could pull off such a dramatic and destructive act as had occurred at Baikonur.

"Here's something for you, Colonel," the corporal said, as he used a pair of tweezers to pull a small chip from its soldered position on the small circuit board. "This here is a chip designed by Hiroki Limited. It only has one use and that's as a link between it and a Tetra Global Positioning satellite owned by that company."

"That means this bomb could have been used as a tracking device after it failed?" Everett asked, tossing a pencil onto his desk.

"Yes, sir, its original task was to allow the detonation signal to reach this unit from anywhere around the world, as long as it was in range of the Tetra satellite. However, it could just as easily be used to track the unit if it wasn't destroyed. So basically they had the option of destroying the plane or following it."

Collins shook his head. He removed the small Tetra chip from the Marine corporal's fingers and looked at it. Then he handed the silicon chip back and closed his eyes.

"Thanks, Espinoza, you can return to your duties, and take that thing with you. See if you can get a spectrum analysis on the C-4. Maybe we can come up with a batch number for a trace."

"Yes, sir," the corporal said, gathering his tools and the makings of the bomb. He left the office.

"So, the assholes may know where we are," Everett said. He stood and reached for the door to the office, closing it.

"At least where our base of operations is located," Jack said with a frustrated look. "All they know thus far is that Niles and his team landed at Nellis. I don't think that's a problem, but if it's McCabe and his people they know now that Niles is linked with us, and *that* could be a problem. In the art of war there are very few coincidences. Our flight plan was filed from Nellis and that's where the tracking device on Niles aircraft led."

Everett, Mendenhall, and Ryan were silent as the colonel started talking through what they had learned.

"We can't learn anything here. And we're only in the way of Niles and his team as they carry out the president's orders. Pete has run into a dead end as far as McCabe goes. His last known whereabouts were Los Angeles six years ago. He has no financial statements, no IRS records after his military days, and no passport, at least one with his real identity on it." Jack sat down hard on the desktop. "The answers lie in Germany."

"Niles has suspended that end of the investigation. The president is trying to find a political solution. As long as there's a chance that we can get into the excavation legally, that's what they want to try."

Collins turned and faced Everett. "If what we think is down there is there, and all of this Flash Gordon stuff fails, there could be a race between us and other countries to get to Ecuador. That's when the shooting will really start."

"I think the shooting's already started," Ryan said, probing gently at the bandage covering his nose. "Just ask the Russians."

"I think you're right there, Lieutenant." Jack stood once more and paced. "It's got to be McCabe behind this. And his paymaster, whoever that is—we have to go to Germany."

The three men from the Security Department watched as Jack stood and left the office.

"I think we'd better brush up on our German, because I've seen that look before," Everett said as he too stood.

"Where are you going, Captain?" Mendenhall asked.

"Where else?" he said, smiling. "To pack."

Jack was waiting for the elevator so he could track Niles down in the Engineering Department on Level 35 when he was tapped on the shoulder. He turned and saw Sarah standing there with her arms full of books, smiling up at him.

"Hi, short stuff," he said as he saw several men and women passing by in the large hallway on Level 7, enough that any more intimate contact was out of the question.

"Colonel Collins," Sarah said formally.

"What's all this?" he asked, waving his hand at the armload of thick books.

Sarah didn't answer at first and actually lowered her eyes before speaking.

"They're nothing, geological stuff, far beneath your pay grade."

Jack saw the look that said I can't talk about it, and was about to comment on her shortened answer when the elevator arrived with a gentle air-assisted swoosh. He stepped back and allowed Sarah to enter first, and then he followed. A man in a white coat stepped up but saw the look on Jack's face and the simple tilt of his head that suggested he should probably catch the next elevator. The doors closed.

"Level, please?" the computerized Europa asked in her Marilyn Monroe voice.

"Thirty-five," Jack said, not caring what level Sarah needed. "Okay, what gives? You, Niles, and Virginia have been cooped up in the science departments for four straight days while the rest of us have been cooling our heels."

Sarah watched the LED numbers beside the elevator doors descend as the air-cushioned ride accelerated.

"Europa, can you stop here please and secure the elevator?" Sarah asked, looking at Collins.

"Please state emergency," Europa said, as the elevator came to an abrupt but gentle stop.

"No emergency," Sarah said, as she took a deep breath and then went to her tiptoes. She gave Jack a deep, long kiss, so hard that neither noticed three of her books fall to the carpeted elevator floor. She pulled back and looked at him for the longest time. "We're trying to get a handle on this mineral, but so far we're having no luck at all. This afternoon we finally got a linkup with Jet Propulsion Lab and a chance to watch as they tried to bring the rover *John* back online. They're hoping we can view the devastation inside Shackleton."

"That's not all there is. I know you, Lieutenant, and as nice as your kisses are, I'm not accepting the bribe for my silence. Now what's going on?"

"Have Will and Jason received their orders yet?" she asked, reaching down to retrieve her fallen books. That was when Jack noticed a large manila-colored book that had nothing to do with geology: the NASA and United States Air Force training manual for space operations.

"What orders?" he asked, his eyes finally leaving the manual and locking on Sarah's.

"All I know is that Ryan and Mendenhall are being assigned to my team. Nothing more than that."

"Why do you need a security element in a lab?" he asked. His eyes bore so deeply into her own that Sarah had to turn away.

"Jack, I love you, and you know that, but I'm also an officer in the Army, just like you. You follow orders and so do I."

"Okay, short stuff. Keep your little secret," Collins said as he handed her the last fallen book. It was on the mineral properties of meteorites. "But keep in mind that whatever Niles and the president are cooking up, people are starting to die over this thing."

"Jack, we know that, and I wish I could tell you everything, but I just don't know. I do know you, though, and you can't storm into Niles's office and demand that I be kept safe. Whatever they have planned, if you want me to back away from my job, I'll do it, for you. But it has to be me doing the requesting, not you."

Collins reached out and hit the blinking Level 35 button again, overriding Sarah's request for the car to stop.

"You know I won't do that," he said, his eyes cast down. He turned and smiled at McIntire. She smiled in return. "Not because you're an officer in the Army, but because I love you too and would never ask you not to do your job because of that love."

The elevator came to a stop and Europa announced that they had arrived. As the doors opened Pete Golding was standing there. He looked surprised to see both Jack and Sarah.

"Oh, hello, Colonel," he said, adjusting the thick glasses on his nose.

"Pete," Collins said, stepping out of the car. He looked back at Sarah as Golding stepped inside. He winked as the doors started sliding closed.

Before the door closed, Jack heard Pete say, "I'm glad I ran into you, Sarah. Europa wants your exact measurements. NASA needs them ASAP."

"Damn it," Jack said as he turned and went to find Niles.


Jack finally tracked Niles down in the astrophysics lab on Level 35. When he walked inside he saw that the entire division was present. Most of the technicians and scientists were sitting at computer consoles and the rest were studying virtual reality diagrams projected onto every inch of wall space. Collins saw designs he had seen as a kid from the Apollo program. These were being studied and modified by the people Jack knew as the best in the astrophysics business. He saw Niles in the far corner conferring with Virginia Pollock and when Compton finally noticed Jack standing at the door he nodded once to Virginia and excused himself.

Niles once more looked tired and ragged, his white shirt stained with ink at the front pocket and the slight rim of hair that circled his head uncombed and messy. He smiled as he stepped up and faced Jack.

"I figured you would come looking for me before too long," he said as he removed his glasses and rubbed his eyes. "Jack, the president has more than enough to handle at the moment, Ecuador is really pushing Interpol to get that arrest warrant to the State Department."

Jack remained silent as his eyes moved from Niles toward the far wall, where he saw the projected image of the Ares VII rocket. It was being moved by crawler to an assembly area at what looked like one of the Western Air Force bases. That meant it was either Vandenberg or March. His bet would be the Vandenberg launch facility in Central California.

"What in the hell is going on here, Niles?" he finally asked as a flurry of activity near one of the engineering stations drew his eyes. "I see the president's not taking any chances like the Russians did."

Niles placed his glasses back on and looked at the image of the giant Ares being moved toward the second assembly building at Vandenberg.

"The Chinese are only two weeks away from launch. We've learned from NSA and CIA resources that they have a totally viable system in the Chinese Lunar Exploration Program, or CLEP. They're far more advanced than Western intelligence ever thought possible. They actually have two ready-to-go platforms and are capable of placing twenty men and women on the Moon." Niles turned back to face Jack. "We've also learned that as many as fifteen of those may be Chinese Special Forces personnel, but we're still gathering intel on that."

"What you're saying is they're preparing to introduce armed force into this thing?"

"Yes. At least *I'm* convinced that they are. The president, not so much."

"Are they fully capable?" Jack asked, remembering the books Sarah was carrying.

"The China National Space Administration has every intention of not only recovering the mineral and technology from the surface of the Moon, they intend to hold their ground with a series of launches, possibly creating a permanent or at least rotating presence on the Moon." Niles took Jack by the arm and steered him toward an empty corner of the massive room. "The Chinese have adapted no fewer than six of their heavy-lift Long March launch vehicles for lunar operations. They have the landers and science to back this up. Everyone was caught off guard—again."

"Jesus," Collins muttered.

"In two weeks they plan to launch at least two systems from their Xichang Satellite Launch Center northwest of Xichang City. They really screwed the European Space Agency. They stole a lot of their hardware and software technology for the missions."

"The damn world is going to turn the Moon into an armed camp," Jack said, looking harshly at Niles. "You know what happens when you get a bunch of soldiers together in an intense environment and they all have guns, don't you, Niles?"

Compton rubbed his temples.

"People start shooting each other," Jack said as he shook his head. "Tell the president the priority is on Earth, Niles. We have leads on where to find Columbus right here, so why risk the lives of people by sending them out there?" he asked, gesturing angrily toward the sky.

"Jack, the president is basing his decision on my recommendation, and there are elements that outweigh . . . well, we need to be in on this for reasons I can't go into right now. That's a presidential order—the hanging kind, if disobeyed."

Collins was taken aback. He had never known Niles Compton to take the extreme measure before the practical. The look in the director's eyes was one of determination, and Jack knew he had better not push the issue further, at least not yet. He hoped Niles wasn't feeling power-hungry in a way that would taint his decisions.

"Do you think you're using your influence with the president a little outside the lines of what's proper, Mr. Director?"

Niles looked at Jack and his features were a cross between hurt and anger.

"I guess that's for the president to decide, Colonel," he answered, but he saw that Collins immediately regretted what he had said.

"I'm sorry, Niles," Jack said. He took a step back and rubbed his eyes. "That was uncalled for."

"Jack, what if we don't find Columbus or if we can't get into Ecuador even to search? What's our backup?"

"That's why the president has to allow me and a team to get our asses to Germany."

Compton turned away from Jack and watched the harried activity around him. He smiled to himself and shook his head.

"Jack, Interpol will be on you like hounds. They're taking this murder thing seriously. They want you and Carl pretty bad. The president suspects the Ecuadorians are being pushed by someone."

"Better people than Interpol have wanted my ass before, Niles." Collins watched Compton to see how he reacted to what he said next. "I noticed you didn't include Mendenhall and Ryan in that statement. The last I knew they were with Carl and me in Ecuador."

"You sneaky son of a—!" Compton paused. "What do you know?"

"Nothing, I just observe when I'm down here, that's all." Jack picked up a small electronic device. He looked it over and placed it back on the console.

"Okay, Jason and Will are being reassigned to a team being led by Lieutenant McIntire. That's all I can say for now, Jack. This is a NASA thing, not mine." He took Collins by the arm and looked into his eyes. "I can tell you that what you're worried about is remote. There are two elements, or teams, ahead of hers."

"We can stop all this madness, Niles. Let me and Carl get to Germany before it's too late."

"And what if you're caught and extradited to Ecuador?" Niles asked with a tinge of anger in his voice.

"Well, we'll need to go back there eventually anyway," Collins said with a smirk. "All kidding aside, Niles, we may be able to prevent something really bad from happening. In case you hadn't noticed, we have some very well equipped people out there who aren't all that thrilled about outer space and what it has to offer."

"I know that," Niles said. He mentally surrendered and waved Virginia over to where they were standing.

"Jack," she said, pushing her hands into her lab coat.

Collins nodded and looked at Niles, who had made a decision.

"Virginia, cut the colonel and Captain Everett orders releasing them from duty at the complex. They are on extended leave for the next five days." He looked at Jack.

"Okay," she said, turning to face Collins. "Going fishing again, Jack?" A smirk of her own stretched across her pretty face.

"Yeah, something like that. Look, since we won't have Mendenhall, I need someone who's good with Europa on a mobile terminal. Can you spare anyone?"

Niles lowered his head in thought. He looked at Virginia and then at Collins.

"We're in the planning stages of what we need to do. I have the entire computing staff at my disposal and I have Virginia. That leaves our resident genius Pete Golding free. Take him."

Collins looked from Niles to a surprised Virginia. Neither could hide their shock at the mention of Pete's name.

"I appreciate the offer, but Pete has exactly zero hours in the field. This could get a little dicey."

"I understand that, but with Pete you have a fighting chance of discovering something others would overlook. He's the best, and you need every advantage you can get. He'll dig up a starting point for you. Leave him on the plane if you have to, but take him."

"Okay, Pete it is." Jack knew that they did need someone good. They were going to Germany without really knowing who it was they were looking for. "I also want Doc Ellenshaw. He's down in the Crypto Department doing absolutely nothing, and we just happen to be dealing with something that's not just about the past but may be about our entire history. Ellenshaw irritates Pete to do better. And besides, I like the way the doc thinks out of the box."

The director looked happy that Jack seemed satisfied. Then the happiness fled as Collins faced Niles and Virginia, focusing finally on the director.

"Can I ask a question that you probably won't answer?"

"Of course."

"Why did the president choose you to coordinate something this big when it's obviously out of your area of expertise?"

Niles ignored Jack's question. "You got Charlie and Pete and your orders. Good luck, Colonel." Niles started turning away to get back to the amazing work going on in the science department. Then he stopped and turned back to face Collins. "Colonel, if you get caught, I don't know if we can help you," Compton said. He watched Jack, who had already turned for the door. "And take care of those two professors. I happen to like them."

"Say good-bye to Lieutenant McIntire and tell her she better not do anything stupid while I'm gone."

"Jack, did you hear what I said?" Niles asked. Collins reached the doorway and then turned and looked at both Niles and Virginia.

"Mr. Director, concentrate on the *what if*'s of getting those people back if you have to send them up there. That's a little more unforgiving than being caught by Interpol."

As they watched Collins leave the lab, Niles looked at his deputy director.

"He's got a point, doesn't he?"

"That's one thing I've noticed, Niles," Virginia said, as she watched the door closing behind Jack. "The colonel always has a good point."

## FAITH MINISTRIES, INC., LOS ANGELES, CALIFORNIA

The meeting was as tense as McCabe had ever had with the billionaire head of Faith Ministries.

"I really don't understand your anger," he said to Rawlins. Rawlins's daughter stood by the window without comment and without much expression during the whole meeting. "We have stopped the Russian project dead in its tracks with a minimal expenditure of men and material, and placed the blame on our friend the Mechanic just as planned. He's none the wiser. We now know that this Compton is linked to the intrusion of Colonel Collins and his men down in Ecuador. We have the government of that nation on our side thanks to your bribes, so now we have the upper hand there also."

"The point of my daughter killing this Compton was to send a message to the president, telling him in no uncertain terms that there is a growing groundswell of religious passion he has to deal with." Rawlings spat the words. "Killing his front man would have given him pause. Just look at the thousands of God's people who protest in front of the president's home. He cannot ignore the facts any longer—going into space is not the Lord's will."

"I don't know what world you live in sometimes, but the killing of one man rarely deters a president from doing what he needs to do. My intelligence people have linked the president with Niles Compton. They're old school buddies.

Killing him would have had the opposite effect of what you desired. So please, allow me to conduct the operations as I see fit, or you can go about them alone."

For the first time in the meeting, Rawlins was silenced. McCabe saw him take a breath and then his eyes wandered to Laurel's back. Her arms were crossed and her body stiff.

"Your daughter's desire for excitement, while dangerous, can be assuaged if she wishes. The last remaining man who can pinpoint the burial site for Columbus has been found in Munich and preparations for his elimination are progressing. If Laurel wishes, she can accompany the Mechanic when he goes to Germany to take care of this gentleman."

Both Rawlins and McCabe turned their eyes toward Laurel. She finally turned and looked at McCabe. He saw that the storm in her features had not yet subsided.

"To watch as your little pet terrorist does the wet work?"

"Laurel, you're still learning. Anything more at this time could get a little dangerous," Rawlins said, standing and attempting to hug his elder daughter. She angrily threw his arms off and continued to stare at her now ex-lover McCabe.

The former Army officer finally smiled and stood.

"Okay. I'll send you to meet with the Mechanic and I'll order him to allow you to have your warped fun. Right now he's in California making plans. Your plane leaves for Germany in eight hours."

A smile crossed her face. She looked from McCabe to her father. He wasn't smiling.

"I never imagined you were so dedicated to the Lord that you would offer yourself up as a sacrifice to his cause," he said, placing his hands on her shoulders. He pulled her to him and hugged her. "I pray it's not for the want of blood that you do these things."

She maneuvered her head so she could see McCabe. He saw her smile, her eyes ablaze with passion—not for the Lord but for the thrill she was getting as she realized that she would soon have a man's life in her hands, a life she fully intended to take.

McCabe gathered his papers and headed for the door.

Soon he'd have to distance himself from these nuts.

## JET PROPULSION LABORATORY, PASADENA, CALIFORNIA

They all watched the rover *John* as it used its drill arm and bucket carrier to right itself at the rim.

The camera angle shifted, it seemed to go crazy for a moment and then the picture stabilized. Loud shouts and cheers coursed through the control room as

*John* had pulled off the miracle and righted itself. The view was once again spectacular and the technicians shouted praises to the telemetry team that had come up with the plan to use the complicated appendage system to correct the problem of *John* lying on its side.

Nathan looked to his left and the president nodded his head, mouthing the words, "Great job."

No one but the closest Secret Service agent could see the small laptop in front of the president of the United States, nor the clear picture of Niles Compton as the president spoke to him in hushed tones.

"Okay. Let's get ready to shut *John* down to recharge," Nathan called out, as he waved for his people to sit back at their stations. "He's got to be tired after all of that effort to sit up."

The president was talking into his headset. Then he nodded to no one and placed a hand over the microphone. He leaned over and said a few words to the director of JPL. The man raised his brows and said a few words back to the president, but it seemed the president had said what he had to say and continued looking at the older man without blinking. He just nodded his head in the direction of Nathan.

"Cancel that order," the director called out. "Bring *John* back to the edge of the crater. We need to get a view of the interior."

"Wait a minute, *John* is starving for power. We need a recharge and if we're not careful we could lose him. If he doesn't receive his order in the right amount of time, he could go right over the edge."

The president of the United States fixed Nathan with a calm look, and everyone could see that he was struggling to keep his cool.

"Mr. Nathan, that is an acceptable risk. Now please bring *John* to the rim of the crater," the director of JPL ordered.

"Yes, sir," Nathan answered, not understanding the willingness to risk the only Beatle left on the surface of the Moon. "REMCOM, shut down until we can get as precise a measurement as possible to the crater's rim."

Before the telemetry relay station could answer, the president stood and looked over the room below him.

"Ladies and gentlemen, you have done great work to this point. What I have to say is that I may know a few things you don't. I'm sorry for the risk, but for the moment use your best guess. We just don't have the time for any lengthy calculations. Get me a view of the inside of that crater—now."

All eyes turned from the president to Nathan, who nodded his head. Not that he understood, but he had to follow the orders of the highest-ranking man in the space program.

"Julie, *John*'s your baby. Give it your best guess as to the distance from *John*'s current position to the edge of the crater. Utilize the boom as much as possible and when you've achieved a good view of the interior, shut down the tracks."

The young technician quickly studied the camera view from *John*. She closed her eyes briefly. A minute later, the view changed as *John* panned its lens around. She made a few keyboard punches and then shook her head.

"Estimate is that *John* can only travel thirteen feet, eight inches, before he goes over the side. I recommend . . . er, uh, my best guess would be thirteen feet and then we'll use the boom to get a look inside Shackleton."

Nathan looked over at the president, who had replaced his headphones and was speaking once more to the mysterious person on the other end. Nathan suspected that person was giving the president very bad advice.

"I sure hope you're right, baldy. If looks could kill, some other lucky jerk would be finishing out my term." The president looked around as he waited for Niles to say something.

"We need to know what kind of devastation we have inside that crater. We have to have some idea of the destructive force of that mineral. I wouldn't ask if we didn't have to have every bit of information we can possibly get. It's either that or you're forced to make a judgment call that will send many men and women on a trip they may not come back from."

The president couldn't argue with the call Niles was making him commit to.

"Okay, once more you've got me over a barrel."

All eyes watched as the command finally reached *John* and the rover started rolling. At first it was a herky-jerky movement that caused a lot of concern. They hoped that *John* hadn't blown one or more of the rubber treads off its long arms and wheels. Finally the ride became smooth and, except for the swaying picture from *John*, the rover started following its dangerous orders to advance to the rim of the crater.

Every muscle inside the control room tensed. The president sat as calmly as he could as the Beatle approached the end of forever. He did not feel as calm as he looked. They were risking the only eyes they had on scene, and that risk was asking a lot.

The camera angled up to the star-filled sky as the rover's ascent of the slope commenced. Every person in the room wanted to send a command for *John* to stop right there, but still the Beatle kept climbing the ridge leading to the edge. Finally an audible sigh of relief coursed through the room as *John* came to a stop.

"Yeah!" Nathan called out. Then he looked around and cleared his throat as he tried to regain some of the professional bearing he always displayed. "Uh— apologies everyone. Julie, great job. Now, REMCOM, let's get the president the view he wants."

"Sending the command," a female voice called out.

The president sat and watched. After the minute of communication delay, the camera started to angle down into the crater. The boom had been extended to its full height of ten feet from the body of the Beatle. As the focus of the lens auto-adjusted to take in the view, another gasp arose from the men and women watching. The president stood, momentarily stunned by what he was seeing.

"Damn, Niles, are you seeing this?" the president asked. This time he didn't care if anyone overheard him.

At first there was silence from the Nevada end of the linkup.

"I think it's fair to say our priorities have just been upgraded."

"What do you mean?" the president asked, his eyes glued to the large screen in front of him.

"No matter what, we are a go for the Moon, with as many people and as much equipment as we can get up there. This cannot fall into the hands of any one nation. If at all possible we have to destroy this should a cooperative agreement on the current emergency not be achieved, shattering the Case Blue accords and ending a possible allied deal. We need what's up there desperately, but not until we can get an agreement as to what that technology is to be used against. If it can't be used in conjunction with Case Blue, then the miracle find needs to be destroyed."

The president refused to comment further as Niles said something he wasn't supposed to mention over the airwaves. The secretive aspect of what only one hundred people in the entire world knew about was what was driving everyone to extremes. He wasn't ready to explain what was really happening yet to the American people, much less the world.

On the large screen below was a sight that froze the hearts of everyone.

Sitting in the deepest part of the Shackleton Crater, buried for what could have been a billion years and uncovered by the explosion of the mineral sample, was what looked like an entire base. Some of the upper reaches of the buildings had been destroyed by the blast, but for the most part it had survived the devastation intact. The billion years of lunar soil had been lifted, burned away, or melted, exposing a sight that rivaled any artist's conception of ancient ruins.

The president counted over seventy-five buildings made from a material he couldn't begin to guess at. There was piping running in and out of glass enclosures, buildings with giant doors and loading platforms. The sight was like looking at a future age Moon base, familiar perhaps to some of the most ardent science fiction fans, but terrifying to others with more earthbound imaginations.

"I would say there may be items in that base that many nations would be willing to risk a war over," Niles said. "Or possibly something we may be able to use against a more worthy and deserving foe. Are we agreed on that?"

"Niles, that's enough. Your point is made. I'll speak with the Chinese again, but not another word about our true intentions over the air." The president lowered his eyes and ran a hand through his hair, then relaxed and looked at the view from Shackleton one more time. "Okay, Mr. Director. You are now a go for Operation Dark Star. Confirm?"

"We're way ahead of you," Niles answered. And then the line was disconnected.

The president pulled off his headphones and lay them on the desk, and then he stood and buttoned his jacket. As he did so, the doors to the control room opened and fifteen blue-clad Air Police from the United States Air Force entered the room. As they spread out toward each telemetry station, they started collecting discs and paperwork describing the day's activities from the Moon.

"Once again, ladies and gentlemen, I appreciate everything you've achieved, and want to say thank you for your dedication, but Operation Peregrine has just been militarized." The president saw the shocked civilian faces of everyone in the control room as their work was taken from them. "All this can and will be explained to you after some decisions are made. You are still in control of the Peregrine mission, make no mistake about that." The president felt like Joseph Stalin for the strong-armed way he was doing things. He had never wanted to be the bullying ex-general that most people secretly feared after becoming president.

"Then why is our work being taken? Everything here has to do with Peregrine." Nathan was no longer able to hold his anger in check.

"Because, pretty soon you'll be assisting a manned expedition to the very spot your *John* is now looking at."

"You mean we're going back to the Moon, sir?" Nathan asked, totally taken aback.

"Yes, Mr. Nathan, we are. In force if we have to."

# PART TWO
# INHERIT THE STARS

# 6

The crazed white hair of Charles Hindershot Ellenshaw III was something of a legend at the Event Group. Crazy Charlie, as he was known to the younger members of the Group, had fought for ten years to make his Cryptozoology Department a respected part of the mainstream sciences at the complex. The amazing thing was that he had done just that by proving almost every crazed theory he had about animal life in the past and showing that those theories not only had a foundation in today's science, but that the animal life in question might still exist. However, that was not the reason Jack Collins had insisted Charlie go along. He knew the professor was one of the quickest and sharpest minds at the Event Group, as well as a man who could formulate a theory faster than anyone Jack had ever seen—and all on a minimum of information.

At the moment, Charlie Ellenshaw was having a hard time keeping up with Everett and Collins as he tried to follow them toward the Computer Center. He was juggling an overnight bag and several books on Ecuador and its legends. He had gotten a jump on Jack and his request by learning all he could on the area of interest. He was already considering several theories on the myths and legends of that people from time immemorial. As he dropped three of his books, he ran into the back of the much thicker Captain Everett, who turned and helped Charlie collect his fallen material.

"Take it easy, Doc. We have time. Jack's going in to inform our good Dr. Golding that he's going on his first field assignment."

"Oh, that's marvelous." Charlie stood up, nudging his load upward as he did so with his thin knee. Once upright he tried to fix his glasses, which were askew, but couldn't. Carl rolled his eyes. He reached out and put the professor's glasses on straight. "Look, Captain," Dr. Ellenshaw said, "I just want to thank you and the colonel for allowing me to come along. You don't know how boring it gets when everyone is on an assignment they deem Crypto unqualified to assist in."

Everett patted Ellenshaw on the shoulder. "Doc, you've earned your stripes. We need fast thinkers where we're going." Carl smiled and squeezed the thin man's shoulder. "Besides we may need your gun hand."

"Really?" Ellenshaw said, excitement coursing through his features.

"No, not really. You're going to stay on the plane and assist Pete with Europa."

"Oh," Charlie said, the disappointment clearly showing.

Everett smiled and shook his head. He noticed Jack entering the Computer Sciences Center.

Collins stood at the top of the uppermost tier of the center aisle and tried to find Pete in the mass of humanity. The computer team was spread out everywhere, all of them mixed in with people from Virginia's Nuclear Sciences Division and the Astrophysics Department. Jack finally spied Pete. He was moving from one group to the other and looking forlorn as he listened to ways in which they could get men and women back to the Moon in record-setting time. Collins hustled down the stairs past three hundred desks that sat on differing levels off the center. He finally reached the main floor and walked up behind Dr. Pete Golding, the most brilliant computer man in the business. He watched as Pete examined a design on a large monitor as several men and women stood around.

"This is just an opinion," said Pete, "but in light of the Russian incident, the fuel used in the Apollo program is just too highly volatile for this kind of mission. I mean, someone could sabotage it with a firecracker. It seems—"

Pete stopped talking when several of the engineers turned and faced him. Their looks said they knew how volatile hydrogen and oxygen can be, but at the moment they had no choice but to work with what they had.

Collins tapped Pete on the shoulder. Clearly the computer genius felt embarrassed at stating the obvious to the men and women next to the engineering station.

"Colonel?" Pete said, as he turned and saw it was Jack.

"Feeling left out, Pete?"

"It seems everyone is dead set on rushing this thing—and you know what that means? It means a lot of people could get killed because someone forgot to dot an 'i' or cross a 't.'"

That statement summed up was what was on the colonel's mind. That was why the mission he and Everett were about to undertake was so important. Maybe they could save the lives of the men and women who were destined to be shot into space on very hurriedly made plans. In particular, there were three people he was most worried about.

"How would you like to get the hell out of here, Doc?"

"Out? You mean, like outside?" Pete looked a little shocked at any suggestion of going out in the sunlight.

"Yeah, Doc. Out, like to Germany. I need you on a field team, and I need what you can do with Europa. We need—"

Pete Golding turned on his heel and started for the risers.

"Hey, where are you going?" Jack called after him.

"To get my overnight bag before you change your mind," Pete called back.

Jack shook his head and followed Golding upward into the highest tier of the Computer Center.

"They've got to get you people out more," Collins mumbled as he caught up with Pete.


Ten minutes later, Jack and Carl had their black duffel bags packed with almost everything they would need overseas, including new passports and all their operations gear. As they waited for the elevator on Level 7, they were spotted from a distance.

"So, are you two off fishing or something?" Sarah asked as she stepped up to Jack. He noticed she was carrying her own duffel bag over her shoulder. She looked at the equipment both he and Everett were carrying.

"We're going to try and stop this insanity," Jack said, and turned to face Sarah. "You people act all excited and privileged about this crap, but I don't feel that way. This project is hurried, and Niles is overlooking the fact that someone out there doesn't want anything going to the Moon. And even if they get there, they may face an armed force of Chinese or someone else."

Everett was a little shocked at the way Jack had delivered his little speech to Sarah. The venom in his voice took both him and Sarah by surprise.

Collins lowered his head and laid down his bag. "I kind of went overboard there, huh?"

Sarah placed her own bag next to Jack's and smiled.

"Well, you weren't shy about saying what was on your mind. You've come a long way, Jack. You didn't use to say that many words in a week."

Collins finally smiled and put his hand on the side of Sarah's face.

"Look, short stuff, use your own common sense with this thing. Personally, I think our director could have chosen any number of geologists for this screwed-up plan of his."

"He needs people he can trust up there, Jack. Besides, it looks like we're the backup plan here. NASA and JPL threw a fit about axing their more experienced teams. They go first on Ares, at least that's the word we're getting."

"Wait," Everett said, looking down at the diminutive McIntire. "They get the new system and you're going on that old relic, Atlas?"

"It probably won't even work," Sarah said with a smile, just as Mendenhall and Ryan walked up with their flight bags slung over their shoulders.

"That's my damn point, the Atlas V is ancient," Everett argued, angrier than even Jack had been a moment before. He looked at Jason Ryan and fixed him with a look that could kill. "And I don't think Mr. Ryan can fly this one. It's not a helicopter or a fighter jet but a million pounds of liquid explosive sitting under his ass. And where in the hell were you, Lieutenant McIntire, when the plane carrying you, Virginia, and the director took off without a preflight check? Were you in a hurry? Oh, by the way, you left Houston with a bomb attached." Carl was actually leaning toward Sarah. "Everyone here is failing to take the right precautions on this thing, and for a bunch of brilliant people, that's just damned stupid!"

Sarah seemed to wilt from his accusation, and the way Everett accused her of negligence made Jason and Mendenhall just as angry.

"We're following orders, just like everyone else," Mendenhall started to say, but he stopped when an angry Collins stared him down.

"At ease, Lieutenant," Collins hissed.

"Hey, wait a minute," Sarah said. "Why are we being attacked? We're only—"

"Following orders, we know," Everett answered for Jack. "But last I heard you can only volunteer for the astronaut corps. And one more thing: There are people out there who would like to blow up every attempt at getting up there, in case you haven't been following the news."

"Oh, you two are ones for the books," Sarah answered with a set jaw and firm stance, taking up the challenge of both Jack and Carl. "Like you don't do crazy stupid stuff all the time!"

"Yeah, and Jason and I always get left behind," Mendenhall said, becoming angry for the first time he could remember where the colonel was concerned. All of the past came flooding back to him, all the times he and Ryan were left on the sidelines as Everett and Collins took all the risks. The funny thing was, this time Mendenhall knew the best bet was to back out of this crazy thing. Being bullied into it was something altogether unacceptable, especially from Colonel Collins.

The small group was being watched and avoided by many men and women in the hallway. The group looked as if it were about to come to blows. Sarah stepped forward, close to Collins's chest with Mendenhall right beside her. Ryan dropped his bag and took an angry step toward Everett, who smiled and waited.

"That's enough!" The voice echoed off the plastic walls from down the hallway.

Everyone stopped talking when the voice sounded. Standing in the carpeted hallway was Niles Compton. He had a look on his face that no one had ever seen before. His clipboard and files were tucked under one arm and his glasses perched on his forehead.

"What in the hell is wrong with you people?" he asked as he approached. "Angry at each other because one group perceives the other is taking the biggest risk?

Colonel, what these three are doing is dangerous. I know because I'm in charge of the attempt to get this madness under control. You're right, Mr. Everett. Space is a voluntary act. I have ordered no one to do anything. Are we clear on that?"

Both Everett and Jack looked away, still angry, but far more embarrassed than they had ever been.

"Now, I think you two have a long-range aircraft waiting for you at Nellis. I'd suggest you get on it and try to find something that will make going to the Moon a moot point." Niles started to walk past the stunned group of five but stopped when he saw that no one was moving. "I said, now!"

Sarah swallowed and reached for her bag, as did Mendenhall and Ryan. Jack stayed her hand and tried to smile. Everett just held out his hand to Ryan and looked him in the eye.

"Good luck, flyboy," he said, shaking Jason's hand. Everett then held out his hand for Mendenhall. "And watch after Will. He doesn't do too well flying."

Collins pulled Sarah off to the side.

"I don't know what the hell is running through my head anymore, so all I'll say is go and do your geology thing, short stuff. I'll be here waiting for you. Good luck."

Sarah smiled and looked around. Then she went to her tiptoes and kissed Jack.

"You too, jackass." She gave him a small smile.

Jack looked at Will and Jason. He shook his head. He knew they were only doing what he had trained them to do and no one could be more proud of two young men. He shook each of their hands, and then the two groups separated after having gone through the first harsh words exchanged between any of them. Jack and Everett entered the elevator and watched as Ryan, Mendenhall, and Sarah turned and smiled. The doors closed and that was when Jack looked at Everett.

"That, Mr. Everett, could have been handled a little better."

"We are a couple of asses, aren't we?" Everett said, smiling at the closed elevator doors.

"And the fact that we're asses amuses you?" Collins asked.

Everett set his bag down, then turned and looked at Jack, the smile still on his face.

"I really thought Ryan was going to kick my ass there for a minute."

They both laughed as the elevator took them up to Level 1. The smiles didn't last long as each of them thought about their friends and the mission they had been chosen for.

The two officers knew that the fates of Will, Jason, and Sarah, along with many others, could very well be in their hands, and at the moment they didn't know if they could help them at all.

For one of the first times in Collins's memory, things were happening faster than he had the ability to keep up with and that was what he hated above all else.

"Jack?"

"Yeah," he said, as the doors opened.

"You know the main reason we were so angry back there?"

Jack threw his duffel bag over his shoulder and stepped out of the elevator.

"Yeah, I know. It's because we're too damn old to do what they're doing."


*The New York Times*

It has been widely reported that Russian commandos stormed several locations today in the Republic of Georgia, seeking out extremists in connection with the devastating attack in Kazakhstan at the Baikonur Cosmodrome. The terrorist cells that were attacked had long been known for their ties to Muslim extremist groups, including al Qaeda, where Russian authorities claim the plan had originated.

Russian officials have not commented as of today about the link between Georgia and the Middle Eastern terrorist cells they claim to be responsible for the attack. There was no word on casualties in the seven separate military raids.

In a related story, Chinese officials have been silent about the reports coming out of Beijing regarding large-scale protests by Christians, Muslims, and Buddhists in the wake of the Russian attack. It has been confirmed, however, that more than a thousand people have been detained by the state for illegal assembly and seven have been arrested for unspecified crimes against the state. Many slogans have begun to appear in graffiti across this city, some about the corrupt attempt to reach the Moon by this government. The fervor of these protests has not been seen in China since the Tiananmen Square incident two decades ago. Thus far, the People's Republic has had no official comment about breakaway religion and their concerns about Chinese missions to the Moon and their true intent. Other nations are starting to report large protest demonstrations concerning the expenditure of massive amounts of money and religious ignorance of the space programs involved. Many private think tanks wonder about the cost and the danger involved in such a venture.


## EVENT GROUP COMPLEX,
## NELLIS AIR FORCE BASE, NEVADA,
## 4 HOURS LATER

The conference room was full.

The hookup was a five-way link among the Event Group at Nellis, the White House Situation Room, the Pentagon Space Command, NASA, and the Jet Propulsion Lab in Pasadena.

"Ladies and gentlemen, for those of you who have never met him, this is Dr. Niles Compton," said the president. "He heads a private concern here in Washington that deals with event planning and execution. I have given him the difficult task of analyzing and planning for our response to the events that have occurred on the Moon. I believe he and his team are prepared to outline what our response should be. Dr. Compton, you may begin."

"The mission is called Operation Dark Star," Niles told the group "It is a multilevel plan for getting not one, but two complete teams to the surface of the Moon within two weeks, with one emergency crew and their launch platform as a backup."

Niles saw that the in-house camera systems were registering the shock on the faces of everyone who heard the launch goals. He kept speaking.

"An Ares I and an Ares V, experimental first-stage systems intended for use in the now canceled Constellation Moon program, have already been shipped in sections from their Minnesota facility. Since the emergency on the lunar surface, over two hundred thousand employees from various companies, such as Alliant Techsystems Inc., manufacturer of the Ares system, and Boeing, the contractor selected for the crew module and all upper stage systems for the Ares, have been at work since the systems were chosen. The third and final system, used as an emergency backup, is the Atlas V platform. It has been warehoused in Florida since the Apollo program cancellation in the seventies. All of these systems are viable and on their way to assembly points at Cape Canaveral and Vandenberg Air Force Base in California. We *will* launch in two weeks."

The various rooms exploded with naysayers protesting that the goal was impossible. Again Niles took a deep breath and waited. Not until the president asked for calm did the commotion finally cease.

"In the matter of the crew capsules, we are axing them from the systems. We will shuttle the crews to the International Space Station via three separate shuttle launches from the Cape and from Vandenberg. This action will save payload weight and expedite the systems for readiness."

"NASA here, Doctor. I know you've been working with many of my younger, far more dream-oriented quality and design engineers, but may I ask, since most of us have not been informed, just what are you using the saved payload weight for?" The director of NASA was clearly irked beyond measure that he had been cut out of the loop as far as planning went.

"First off, let me apologize to each and every person hearing of this for the first time, but the president and I felt that we needed new thinking here. That's why we asked some of the younger engineers to assist. I must also add that they came through with flying colors and devised a viable plan in a difficult area of engineering. As for your question, we are saving the weight because of the larger lander we are using on all three of the systems. We had to cut the crew module and expand a new version of the Orion crew capsule to accommodate five astronauts and seven United States Army Special Forces personnel for each platform within Dark Star. That's a total of thirty-six crewmen if all three sections of Dark Star are needed."

Again, the anticipated eruption, this time over the prospect of militarizing outer space by sending armed troops to Moon.

Niles and a few of his assistants began showing the systems that they had developed with the assistance of over a thousand companies. The 3-D renderings of the Orion crew module made it look like a five-deck version of the Apollo crew system. The Altair lunar lander, the new version of the Lunar Excursion Module, was equipped to carry as many as twelve astronauts to the surface of the Moon and return them all safely to the orbiting Orion. The Altair was significantly different from the originally planned module. That one had only carried four astronauts. The new version had been expanded to a multi-deck system capable of sustaining its crew for a full week in the harsh lunar environment.

The workers at Boeing and other specialty plants across the nation had started construction and expansion on the mock-up versions of all three systems the first day that Niles had come up with the plan, and he found himself responsible for the expenditure of over $93.5 billion that the president would never be able to hide from Congress. That number would surely double as it grew closer to go time.

The president waited for calm and then he forced the issue.

"This meeting was not called to argue the validity of the plan, ladies and gentlemen. It was called to consult and advise only. We are returning to the Moon. The individual space programs will have to meet and face a new era of cooperation due to information I cannot share with you here today." He nodded. "Yes, ladies and gentlemen. We are going back to the Moon!"


## THE WHITE HOUSE, WASHINGTON, D.C.

The press room was packed.

The word "Moon" was on every reporter's lips.

Eventually, the White House press secretary walked to the podium and the crowded room fell silent.

"The president has a brief announcement and presentation. He will not, I repeat, not be taking questions afterward."

"Ladies and gentlemen, the president of the United States."

The president slowly walked in from the left and went directly to the podium, not nodding or greeting anyone on the way as was his custom. His tall frame was firm and his eyes serious as he placed his prepared statement in front of him.

"Good afternoon. As events have unfolded on the surface of the Moon, it has taken this government many days to assess the situation and make the decision that I am here to announce tonight. Millions of years ago, our Moon and possibly our own world were visited by humanoid beings not much different from us."

The press corps started writing furiously and television cameras rolled to catch every nuance of the president's bearing.

"With the exception of a few minor details, these people were the same as us in almost every way. They obviously had our spirit of adventure and exploration, the same qualities that have driven our own species to great heights. The most amazing aspect of this find on the surface of the Moon is that the humanoid remains discovered inside of Shackleton Crater have been determined to be as much as seven hundred million years old."

With that announcement, the press room erupted. Many of the senior members had never seen this kind of excitement, or even pure astonishment, in the White House. The room quieted as an assistant press secretary stepped forward and removed the linen from the first picture. The president remained where he was.

"I am here today to clear up some misconceptions about what has transpired on the Moon and to deny any wrongdoing by the United States in the explosion that rocked Shackleton Crater last week. I will also announce preparations for the return of this country to the surface of the Moon and the reasons behind it. First, I would like to make a brief statement concerning efforts currently underway in other nations for going to the Moon. These attempts will not be based on any exploratory effort. The fact is, there's a race on to recover not only alien military technology from seven hundred million years ago but to recover something perhaps even more important, something that will make nuclear fission outdated—a mineral that could escalate the race for far more destructive weapons than we currently possess. The United States will not allow any substance indigenous to the lunar world to be brought back from the Moon."

The statement was as close as the president could come to making a military threat.


## PASADENA, CALIFORNIA

Joe Horn, a quiet family man from Eugene, Oregon, waited patiently outside the well-maintained house in the Pasadena suburb of Monrovia. The radio was on and he listened to the president's address streaming live from Washington, meaning the west coast of the United States was just waking to the news that America was now in a dead-on race to the Moon. This was a mission meant to undercut the most basic statement of the Holy Bible, that man was created by God Almighty. Now the world was in a rush to prove that it wasn't God who accomplished this miracle, but visitors to whom most of the scientific world would kneel and give their allegiance—the new Golden Calf of the heretic.

Mr. Horn, a man taken to the heights of fervor in the name of God, sat stoically and waited. He watched patiently for the person he had come to see, the leader of the zealots who had been on television day and night for the past two weeks with their little mechanicians of science. He had asked his Baptist minister yesterday for guidance before his long drive down the coast. He had been told that the discovery on the Moon meant nothing, that the faith of all religions should not be shaken by the miracle that was currently taking place, that this discovery only meant that the range of God's miracles was not restricted to just this one solar system.

Horn didn't believe it. The more establishment religions were calling for calm, but Joe wasn't interested in being calm. The word of Rev. Samuel Rawlins was starting to reach the ears of the true followers of the Lord. He was calling for all men and women of the true faith to take up the cause of stopping these blasphemers before they could deface the word of God. Now Joe was here to strike the first blow for Rawlins, as he knew the voice coming over the airwaves had spoken only to him when it called for the righteous to rise up.

Joe Horn sat up straighter in his old, battered pickup truck as the man he had been waiting for stepped out onto his front porch with briefcase in hand.

Joe's heart started pounding, threatening to break free from his chest as he watched the man kiss his wife good-bye and then pick his small daughter up and hug her. He watched as the man set his daughter down on the porch and waved to both. As the man approached his Hyundai, Joe stepped from his pickup and strode across the street.

"Mr. Nathan? Mr. Stan Nathan?"

The mission leader from Jet Propulsion Lab turned and saw an older man walk toward him from across the street. He was wearing farmer's overalls and had a green baseball style cap on. His smile was broad and friendly. When he had called out his name, he saw out of the corner of his eye that his wife had hesitated closing the door and stood with her daughter in her arms, wondering why her husband was being approached. Two other neighbors of Nathan's were heading for work and paid the old man no attention as they went to their own cars.

"Yes, I'm Dr. Nathan," he said, placing his left hand on his car's door handle. His eyes widened when he saw the man reach into the large pocket in the front of his overalls.

Joe Horn reached inside and came out with a very old .38 Police Special. He started shooting as he ran straight at the engineer. The first two bullets struck the door and a third the driver's side window as Nathan reacted quickly, ducking and throwing his briefcase up for what little protection it would provide. Joe Horn stopped shooting so he could take aim more carefully. He hadn't thought to bring more bullets than the six he had chambered in his father's gun, which had lain upon a shelf in his bedroom closet for his entire forty-year marriage.

Stan Nathan lost his balance and fell backward as the realization of what was transpiring hit him full force. He thought he heard his wife scream, but he couldn't be sure. He heard a car start and as he fell on his backside he thought he heard the backfiring of another car. That was when he felt the first sting of being shot.

Horn had taken several strides toward the fallen engineer and now stood within five feet. He placed a trembling hand on the .38, aimed, and fired.

"We cannot allow the blasphemers to spit in the eye of God!" he cried out. He fired twice more, finally hearing the hammer hit on nothing but an empty shell casing.

The last two bullets were more than enough to do the job. The fifth round had caught the aerospace engineer in the side of the head after careening off a large Texas Instruments calculator inside his briefcase. The sixth and final bullet hit him directly in the heart.

Mrs. Nathan screamed again as she watched her husband die in front of her. The one neighbor who had started his car heard the shots but had reacted far too slowly to stop the inevitable. When he saw the assassin standing close over his neighbor, the man threw his car in reverse and peeled rubber on his way out of the driveway. He was under the impression that the maniac would soon turn his attentions to the woman and her child. The car bounced as it careened into the roadway and then it bounced again over Stan Nathan's driveway. Before the neighbor fully realized what he was doing, the rear bumper struck Joe Horn and sent him flying into the shrubbery Stan had planted when he and his young wife had moved into this, their first home, years before. The neighbor knew he had hit the killer of his friend hard enough, so he just sat there after bringing the car to a stop on the manicured front lawn. He was shaking badly as he heard Nathan's wife screaming and his daughter crying.

## TEMPELHOF INTERNATIONAL AIRPORT, BERLIN, GERMANY

The U.S. Air Force C-22B transport aircraft sat next to the American consulate hangar at Berlin's busiest airport. The aircraft was on loan to Department 5656 from the U.S. Air Force, but to Jack Collins's frustration it had become nothing more than a large mobile hotel. They hadn't moved or disembarked since their arrival in Germany.

Jack sat in one of the large seats near the back of the aircraft while Carl was in the plane's galley making them lunch. The plane and its occupants had been sitting at Tempelhof for the past sixteen hours while Pete Golding, with the assistance of Charles Hindershot Ellenshaw III, stumbled through the elusive Columbus files that Europa had been able to uncover from German and Allied reports and documents. So far they'd hit a stone wall, and it was driving Jack crazy, especially knowing that Sarah, Mendenhall, and Ryan had flown out of

Nellis bound for Houston and the training regimen that had been set up for them.

Everett cleared his throat and Jack opened his eyes. He heard the sound of Ellenshaw and Golding arguing over some fine point or the other from their station at the midway point of the aircraft. Collins shook his head and finally focused on Everett.

"It's rough waiting for something to break, I know."

"Yeah, so how do you handle it?" Jack asked as he sat up and rubbed his hands over his face.

"I eat," he said, shoving a sandwich toward Jack.

Collins shook his head and accepted the offering. "What about Pete and Charlie. Are they hungry?"

"I offered them something when I took the flight crew some food. All they did was look at me as though I was asking if they'd like to dance. I think they're out to prove their worth to you. They're just grateful to be asked along on one of Colonel Collins's excellent adventures."

Jack took a large bite out of the sandwich. He chewed twice and then stopped. The look on his face was one of abject horror as he spit the single bite into a napkin.

"What the hell is this?" he asked, looking at the sandwich in his hand.

"Sardines, tortilla chips, and cheddar cheese," Everett answered, taking a bite of his own concoction.

Collins didn't say anything. He gently lay the sandwich down as though it were in danger of exploding. He took a long drink from his bottled water, his eyes never leaving Carl's.

"Hmm, look at this," Everett said, laying his own sandwich down and pulling the television monitor around for Collins to see. On the screen, it looked as though several thousand people had gathered in what the caption was telling them was Rio de Janeiro. Bottles, rocks, and other objects were being hurled toward a police barricade surrounding government buildings. The scene switched to a view of Los Angeles where the same sort of rioting and unrest was taking place. Then there was another scene, this one in London. Everett reached over and turned up the sound on the television:

"*. . . the unrest has been repeated in countries the world over as religious fundamentalist groups have organized to halt the missions to the Moon, where they feel their beliefs will be undermined by the significance of humanlike remains discovered there.*" The scene again switched. This time the caption at the bottom was Los Angeles. "*Clearly the leader of this discourse is the Reverend Samuel Rawlins. His Faith Ministries has been at the forefront of this movement that has spread so quickly that it caught most government law enforcement agencies totally unaware. Reverend Rawlins, the leader of the largest privately funded evangelical organization in the world, is calling for civil disobedience to halt the advancement of what he calls a declaration of war on organized religion. The Reverend Rawlins has been rebuked by the pope and the*

*World Evangelical Council, which he has pulled away from in the past month, declaring his own . . ."*

"Who is this nut?" Everett asked.

Jack sat silently and watched the scenes of rioting unfold across the screen. The BBC reporter signed off. The bumper for the next segment showed a picture of a tall man with silver hair pounding a golden pulpit and looking for all the world like someone who took lessons from Adolf Hitler himself.

"I don't know, but someone better start taking him seriously, especially after the murder of the Jet Propulsion engineer this morning," Jack said. He reached out and shut off the view of the Reverend Samuel Rawlins.

"Well, security will be tight from here on out," said Everett.

"Colonel, we may have something," Charlie Ellenshaw said, leaning over Jack's seat. As the professor was getting ready to turn away, his nose wrinkled and he looked down at the tray in front of Collins and Everett. "What is that smell?" he asked.

"Lunch. You want some?" Everett asked.

"Not on a bet," Ellenshaw said in disgust. Jack and Carl walked past him toward the communication shack. Charlie was about to turn away, but instead looked around to see if anyone was watching. Then he reached down and took the remains of Jack's lunch. He took a bite. His eyes widened and he made a face, then he chewed and nodded. "Not bad," he said to himself, turning to follow the two officers with his newly acquired lunch in hand.

Collins peered into the large communications area and saw Pete Golding sitting in front of a large monitor. He was examining an old document that Europa had brought up on the screen.

"What have you got, Pete?" Jack asked anxiously.

"Ah, Colonel. Please have a seat," Pete said. He pulled one of the rolling chairs out for Jack. "This may be what you would call a long shot, but Europa believes the men here are definitely connected."

Jack sat as Everett and Ellenshaw also took seats.

"As you see, we have General Heinz Goetz. I believe you said he was the antagonist of Senator Lee."

"Yes, he was involved in Operation Columbus."

"Well, I'm sure it will surprise no one that our dear general was a confidant of none other than Heinrich Himmler himself."

"Oh, Mr. Wonderful," Everett said, as Europa brought up a picture from the war years showing Goetz and Himmler standing together outside one of the smaller buildings at Wolf's Lair, Hitler's Eastern Front headquarters in Poland.

"Goetz was what you would call a special projects coordinator for Himmler."

Jack looked at Pete. "Special? You mean beyond the horrible historical connotations that word brings to mind?"

"Yes, Goetz had nothing to do with the Final Solution. His talents were more appropriate for the protection of projects like the Vengeance rocket program at

Peenemünde. It says nothing, however, about his participating in anything called Operation Columbus."

Jack studied the picture of the small, heavyset general. He knew that it was his old boss, Garrison Lee, and Alice's first husband, Ben, who had dispatched the man from the world of the living.

"But there's this," Pete said. He ordered Europa to bring up a series of pictures of General Goetz. The photos had been taken at various places around the Third Reich and Russia. "Are you seeing what we saw, Colonel?" Pete asked. He turned around and looked at Ellenshaw and what he was eating. He made a sour face and turned back to the screen.

"This man right here," Jack said, pointing to a small, bookish-looking officer in an SS uniform. "He's the common denominator in every photo."

"Very observant, Colonel. His name is Joss Zinsser, a corporal. We suspected he might be an assistant to Goetz or possibly a secretary. We cross-referenced the corporal's name against the report filed by the FBI field office from the site where they found the empty train. While the bodies of Goetz and several others were positively identified, there was no mention of our little corporal. It seems our friend Zinsser escaped into the night, you might say."

"And?" Jack asked.

"He disappeared after the war. He was finally captured with false papers by the British in 1947. He was convicted of assisting in the war crimes of General Goetz and was sentenced to twenty years. He was sent to Spandau Prison and released in 1956 after serving eight years of his sentence. He was a low-priority prisoner and very much ignored by the Western media at the time."

"Okay, anything else?" Collins asked. He nodded at Everett and gestured for him to get organized. Carl immediately turned and disappeared.

"Yes, there is," Pete said. He turned and spoke to Europa. "Please bring up the cell allocations for Spandau Prison in the years 1948 thru 1956."

As Jack watched, several frames flashed before his eyes. Cell assignments started scrolling down until Europa locked on cell number 117. There was the name Joss Zinsser. However, it was the second name that caught his attention, the name of the man's neighbor for almost eight years.

"Albert Speer," Jack said, nodding.

"Exactly, Colonel. Unless you believe in happenstance, I would say that these two men who shared breathing space were the only two left after the war who'd had anything to do with a top secret project known as Operation Columbus."

"Tell me this man is still alive," Collins said, standing and carefully avoiding Ellenshaw and his lunch.

"That he is. He's a spry man of ninety-one years and the best part is that he never left Berlin. He lives with his daughter in a small apartment, 236 Rosa-Luxemburg-Strasse, part of a large apartment complex." Pete handed Jack a slip of paper. "Here are the directions," he said.

"It's a start, Pete. Good job. You and the Doc stay put and we'll be back as soon as we can."

"You mean we don't get to go?" Golding asked, removing his glasses.

"No, you two keep trying to get hold on any other links to Goetz in case this doesn't pan out."

Golding deflated at the prospect of being left behind. He looked at Ellenshaw, who took the seat Jack had just vacated.

"They do this all the time. I never got used to it either," Ellenshaw said. He took another bite of the fast dwindling sandwich.

"Maybe they wouldn't have left us behind if you didn't smell like crap. Just what in hell are you eating?"


The rental car eased slowly past the massive demonstrations. As Carl drove, Jack read the banners. They not only protested the cost of ESA's attempt to land on the Moon but complained that it was a slap directly to the face of God. The two groups, though different in makeup, had the same goal in mind—making the German government pull all funding from the European Space Agency's attempt at a Moon landing.

"With the pope and the other heads of organized religion calling for calm while this mystery is solved, where are all of these fundamentalist movements getting their gas from?" Jack asked. Outside, several men and women slammed their hands and fists against their car.

"In my opinion, most people don't need a leader anymore to show that they're idiots," Everett said. He reached through the car's window and pushed one of the protesters away. The long-haired man dropped his placard, which read in both German and English: "Hoax! America is once again perpetrating the greatest fraud against God!"

As the car slowly moved through the multitude, Jack saw a large group of skinheads gathering on the street corner not far from the center of the throng. He could see immediately that these men and women were here not to demonstrate but to do what they did best—start a riot.

"This could get ugly real fast," he said, pointing to an empty side street. "Rosa-Luxemburg-Strasse is right up there. Let's dump the car down that alley and walk the rest of the way."

Everett saw where Jack was pointing and steered in that direction. Several protesters refused to move, but apparently decided against any action when Everett's eyes bore into them. They gradually moved out of the way.

Everett finally made it to the alley. Both he and Jack got out and returned to the street. The mass of humanity was growing by the thousands and the mood was becoming angrier by the minute. Sirens and the sounds of police bullhorns could be heard further down the street as authorities started ordering the protesters to disperse.

"There," Jack called out over the noise of the chants. Voices had just started calling for a break with the United States and the European Community.

A large set of stairs fronted the apartment complex. The large structure was one of the remaining vestiges of an era long gone in Germany. It was one of the last buildings that had been owned by the Nazi Party and had once been used to house VIPs, but now housed the poorer residents of downtown Berlin, with each of the original apartments cut into three.

They pushed their way through the crowd, drawing angry looks from some very large men with shaved heads. As they made it through the first group, Jack and Carl both saw that a second line of neo-Nazis had formed a cordon at the front entrance. They stood with arms crossed, as though they were guarding the building.

"Did I ever tell you I hate these guys, Jack?" Everett said. They came to a stop ten feet in front of the group of thirty men. Everett reached behind and under his leather jacket and made sure the Beretta nine-millimeter was secured, in case he was jostled on the way in.

"I don't particularly care for them myself, Mr. Everett, and they do seem to be blocking the exact area we need to go." Jack started making his way to the man who looked like he was in charge.

Collins had to reach around a large man with a bandanna across his forehead to get to the first set of door handles, but the man attempted to block him. Jack's hand remained where it was.

*"Möchten Sie Ihre Kugeln wo sie sind?"* he asked the young German, just loud enough that only the man blocking his hand could hear. At the same time Jack allowed his jacket to part enough so that the man could see the gun tucked in his waistband.

Everett watched the man blocking Jack lick his lips and then was amazed when the black-jacketed youth stepped away from the door. He followed Jack inside as the group of Nazis crowded around wondering why their leader relented so easily.

"What in the hell did you say to that guy?" Carl asked as they went for the large staircase.

"I just asked him if he liked his balls where they were."

Everett smiled as they started up to the next floor, taking the stairs three at a time.

"Evidently he did."

As they went up the stairs Jack had the distinct feeling that they were being observed. He slowed to take the stairs one at a time, swiveling his head to look for security cameras. The dilapidated building didn't seem like the type of operation that could afford much security, so he figured it must be a human element watching them. As they gained the second floor and stepped onto the scratched marble that was once a glory to behold, Jack saw the apartment they were seeking—Number 236.

Jack pulled Everett aside. He looked up and down the long hallway, then reached into his jacket and pulled out the nine-millimeter. "We have company," he said as Everett also pulled his weapon out.

"Inside or out?" he asked, going to Jack's left.

"Don't know," he answered. He knocked on the door.

Everett looked in both directions but the hallway was empty. The only sounds were the yells and chants coming from the street below.

"*Ja?*" a female voice answered from the other side of the door.

The voice was that of an older woman. It sounded strange, out of the norm, as if whoever answered was frightened.

"*Wir sind hier, um zu sehen, Herr Zinsser,*" Jack said in German.

There was no immediate answer.

"*Sind Sie die Tochter von Herrn Zinsser?*" he continued, asking if he was speaking to Zinsser's daughter.

"*Ja,*" the voice answered.

Jack heard a shuffling from behind the door.

"*Laßt uns in Ruhe, geh weg!*" the deep voice of a man said loudly.

"What was that?' Everett whispered.

"He said leave them alone and go away."

"Friendly," Everett said. "But that doesn't sound like a ninety-one-year-old man."

Jack leaned closer to the door. He heard a woman softly sobbing. He shook his head as he stood back and examined the door.

"Well, there's no sense in standing on ceremony," Jack said. He raised his right foot and kicked as hard as he could. The door caved in and Jack saw a large man with a shaved head go flying backward with the door covering most of his frame. He entered with his gun held high. Everett, watching Jack's every move, quickly followed through the empty door frame.

The man tried to push the door off himself, but before he could Jack raised his right foot again and brought the heel of his black shoe down into the man's nose, instantly sending the German to dreamland. The man's right hand stuck out from under the smashed door. Jack reached down and retrieved the gun, tossing it to one side without looking. Carl deftly caught it and went to the left of the entranceway. Jack slid by the unconscious man. The old woman had collapsed and was holding her hands over her face.

"Do you speak English?" Jack asked. He bent over and assisted the elderly woman to her feet.

"*Ja,*" she said, slowly wiping away her tears. "Yes," she repeated.

"Your father, is he here?" Jack asked.

The woman started crying and pointed toward the back of the small apartment. Jack handed the woman off to Carl and slowly crept toward one of the two bedrooms. The door on the left was ajar and Collins eased it open with the barrel of the nine-millimeter. As the door opened he went to one knee as quickly as he could and scanned the room with the gun. After a moment he spotted the man they had come to question. Zinsser was lying across his bed still clad in pajamas, with only one slipper on. Jack closed his eyes and rose to his feet.

"Clear," he called out, without much enthusiasm. With his gun still out and pointed at the closet door, he stepped forward. He eased the closet door open. It was empty of everything except the clothing of an old man in retirement. He looked down and saw that Zinsser's throat had been cut deeply, nearly to the back of his spine. Shaking his head, Jack looked deeply into the old man's glazed eyes, then turned and left the bedroom. He checked the daughter's room and found it empty. He returned to the small living room where Carl had just eased the old woman into a large chair.

"She said he was alone. He got in by claiming he was a house handyman. She says he didn't ask for anything, just took Zinsser into the bedroom and killed him. He was about to do the same to Ms. Zinsser here, when we showed up."

Jack stepped forward and grabbed the killer by the collar, lifting him off the floor.

"Okay, wake-up time," Collins said as he shook the man. "Come on. Time to answer a couple of questions."

The man moaned and his eyes fluttered open. His hands came up and went to his shattered nose, where blood was still flowing.

"Come on, let me see," Jack said, as if he were trying to help the man. The young German warily lowered his hands. That was when Jack noticed the freshness of the man's haircut. The tan ended far lower than it would have if he had always had a shaved head.

Everett had to smile when Jack's gun hand came up and smashed into the German's broken nose, sending his bald head backward with a scream of agony. Even the older woman had stopped crying long enough to smile as she saw her father's killer in pain.

"Now," Jack said, shaking the moaning man in black. "That was to get your attention. Who sent you?"

"Fuck off," the man managed to say in English, as blood started flowing at a significant rate, soaking Jack's hand. The gun hand flew again, striking the man in a part of the nose that was still intact, breaking a new section.

"We can do this all day long, Fritz, it's up to you."

"We work for no one. We—"

Again Jack's hand flew up, as though it was his automatic reaction to a lie. The gun butt struck the man right across the bridge of the nose, crushing the bone and gashing the skin to the cartilage. This time the kid's weight was too much for Collins and he let the boy fall backward onto the floor.

Everett, who had just given the daughter his handkerchief, saw something on the wall that made him walk over and take a closer look. As Jack leaned over the phony, reeling neo-Nazi, Carl turned and looked at the daughter.

"Ma'am, who's this man with your father?" he asked, his question drawing Jack's attention away from the gagging man on the floor.

"That is Albert Speer," she said, with sad eyes. "I'm afraid he and my father spent many years together inside Spandau."

"Yes, but that's not who I mean." Carl touched the image of a blond-haired man dressed in the uniform of an American lieutenant colonel. "Who is this?"

"That was one of my father's jailers for a time at the prison. I cannot recall his name at the moment," she answered. She started crying again.

"Jack, you want to leave your dance partner there for a minute and look at this?"

Collins slapped the man on the side of the face.

"Will you excuse me? I'll only be a minute."

The man rolled to his right, clutching his gushing nose. He didn't bother to answer.

"What have you got?"

"Does this guy look familiar to you?" Everett asked. He turned to make sure Zinsser's killer wasn't moving.

Collins saw the picture of the three men and tilted his head.

"He does, but I'll be damned if I can place him." Jack turned to the woman and sat on the armrest of the chair. He kept his gun out of view to keep from frightening her any more than she already was.

"Do you know when this photo was taken?"

"I . . . I . . . don't know. At least I'm not positive of the date. I would think it was around 1947, a year or so after my father was convicted of crimes against humanity." She wiped at her wet eyes. "He really wasn't a criminal, not like the rest of those pigs. He . . . he was just a clerk, nothing more."

"Yes, ma'am, we know, but the man beside—"

That was as far as Jack got. A shout sounded and several men stormed into the room with guns drawn. Jack raised his hands and let the gun slip from his grasp as he recognized the uniforms of the local German police. The five of them were followed by two men in suits. Everett muttered "shit" as the police turned him around and frisked him. Jack endured his own search stoically. Another two officers pulled the killer to his feet.

"Colonel Collins, you are under arrest for entering Germany with false papers, and you are also under arrest for murder in the Republic of Ecuador." The smaller of the two well-dressed men took Jack's wrists and handcuffed him.

"I take it you're Interpol?" he asked as he was turned around.

"We have been informed of your considerable prowess at escaping from custody, and your military accomplishments are valued reading at our offices,

Colonel. So please, don't try any of your tricks. You may find out that you're not faster than a speeding bullet."

"Damn, Jack, you mean you really can't outrun bullets?" Everett smirked as he was led out of the apartment, just behind Zinsser's killer.

"No, and I can't jump buildings in a single bound either, smartass."

"Then I'm afraid we're going to jail, buddy," Everett called back.

Just as Jack was led to the door, the old woman stood and kissed him on the cheek.

"*Danke*," she said, as she was pulled away by two uniformed officers. She looked at Collins with tears running down her cheeks.

"For what it's worth, ma'am, we know your father wasn't anything like those he spent time in jail with."

Jack was pulled away and the woman looked lost as she watched the scene before her, grateful that her own murder had been interrupted by the two Americans who had arrived out of nowhere.

The man was dressed in the uniform of the Deutsches Heer—the fatigues of the German army. He stood at the large window across the way from the apartment building and gazed through binoculars. The woman beside him stepped anxiously from one foot to the other, waiting nervously for the result of the setup. Laurel Rawlins watched the reaction of the bearded Mechanic as he scanned the apartment building across the way. He moved the field glasses to the right and then the left, making sure his people were in place.

"You will see, Ms. Rawlins, why our plan calls for the first domino to be placed in exactly the right position for our plan to succeed. You will learn here today why things must be in a special order to achieve the results you seek."

"If you ask me, we should have killed those men as soon as their aircraft landed at the airport. This elaborate setup is a waste of time."

"No one is asking you," the Mechanic said. He seemed satisfied with the placement of the men and the explosives. "However, Mr. McCabe has asked me to school you on the finer points of the domino theory he has devised." He turned and looked directly at Laurel with his black, penetrating eyes. "The men that we allowed to enter the building would come across one of two results inside the apartment—one, our man there had succeeded in his duty and killed the two occupants, which he had plenty of time to do since we arranged his entry into the apartment at a time we knew the two Americans we were following would enter. Mission one completed. Mr. Zinsser is dead, one hole to Columbus is plugged."

"Which should have happened years ago," Laurel said in exasperation.

"That is not my concern. We were only recently brought into this haphazard operation. You can blame your father for that little oversight, not me. And not Mr. McCabe." The Mechanic turned and scanned the front doors to the apartment building. As he saw the angry crowd start to shove forward toward the police barricade, he smiled. "Number two, we tip Interpol and the local police about our two American friends who just happened to be wanted for murder in Ecuador, thus they arrive and catch them in a very compromising position with one, two, or three dead men inside."

"Again, a waste of time," Laurel countered, trying to anger the Mechanic even further. "These men obviously have high government connections and will undoubtedly be released to their embassy—thus, as I said, a waste of time."

"Your learning curve may not be progressing as fast as Mr. McCabe seemed to think it would, miss." He smiled as he saw the front doors open across the street. The police and plainclothes Interpol agents walked out with the two Americans in tow. They were followed by the handcuffed killer and several other police officers. He nodded.

Down below in the area leading to the apartment building, the men he had paid handsomely started their small deceit. The neo-Nazi skinheads started crowding around the police, the agents, and the two handcuffed Americans. The police started shoving and the crowd below grew wilder as protesters from the street were attracted by the action. The Mechanic lowered his field glasses and looked at the three devices lining the window seal in front of him.

"The second domino to fall, miss." He picked up the first remote detonator. "The police are about to be attacked by your father's words from six thousand miles away. The demonstration below is about to turn ugly." He turned and looked at Laurel. "Now do you see? It's all going to be bundled into one nice package—no witnesses and our Mr. McCabe is eliminating a serious threat to your father's plans by having this Colonel Collins and his friend blown to Allah. And all the while the blame will be placed on the civil unrest in the streets."

"And this will make Germany pull its backing for the space launches by the ESA?" she asked, shaking her head.

"Exactly."

"Too much. This could have been done a lot simpler."

"But it wasn't. Would you like to do the honors?" he asked, offering her the remote device.

Laurel smiled and all doubt about the plan seemed to vanish as the opportunity to kill presented itself.

"What am I detonating?" she asked, swallowing and starting to sweat as she caressed the detonator. The Mechanic watched her and his black brow rose. He knew beyond a doubt that this woman was trouble, and her insanity, not to mention her father's, could very well lead to disaster.

"You are starting a series of detonations. The police will have trouble getting to their vehicles because of the delay that we have paid for. Once in the street, you will press that trigger and five claymore mines will explode in the path of the police, our assassin, and the Americans."

"And several hundred civilians," she said, her eyes alight.

"A necessary sacrifice if we are to deter the German government from supporting the space launch. We have people in France, Japan, and Italy doing the same things as we speak. Your father's words of revolt have spread, as per his plan. The incident with the JPL employee, though unplanned, was a surprise result of your father's inflammatory words."

"My God," Laurel said, as she closed her eyes and stepped toward the window. She opened her eyes again and saw the two large Americans being pulled through the rowdy crowd of protesters. She looked to the right and saw a hundred more Berlin policemen in riot gear trying to push through the crowd, their shields and clubs making a path as people started pushing back. All of a sudden, James McCabe's plan started to open up before her.

"Yes, praise be to Allah," the Mechanic said, as he saw the ecstasy cross Laurel's beautiful face. "I see you are coming to grips with the domino theory."

The woman didn't say anything as her thumb played over the detonator that would cause five U.S.-made claymore mines to explode, sending five thousand ball-bearing-sized missiles flying into the mass of humanity.

"God is great," she whispered.


Down below in the street, Jack and Carl didn't think the angry mob was going to let them get to the police cruisers. The cars were being jostled by the protesters, each being rocked back and forth on its suspension. Suddenly Jack was pushed to the ground along with Everett. When Collins looked up, he saw that the same man he had threatened before entering the apartment building was standing above them. He had a crooked grin on his lips as Collins saw he wasn't alone. The police were there and trying desperately to pull the skinheads away from their prisoners. Jack heard a loud grunt behind him and managed to roll onto his back just as one of the skinheads pulled a large knife from the man who had just killed Joss Zinsser upstairs. The man looked over at Jack and Carl amid the shuffling legs and feet.

"Uh-oh," Carl yelled out loud but to no avail as the policemen were busy trying to keep men and women back from their prisoners.

Suddenly a surge from the crowd pushed the knife-wielding man away and Jack felt himself being lifted from the ground. As he was roughly turned around he saw the smiling face of the man from the front door. He tilted his head as he raised something to chest level. Jack tried to pull away but knew the knife would be faster than him. While police bullhorns shouted orders in German and somewhere in the distance loud popping sounds started sounding that Collins recognized as tear gas canisters exploding, the skinhead thrust forward with the knife.

Just as Jack thought he was about to feel cold steel penetrate his stomach, the man's face writhed and he was yanked backward by someone's arm. Jack took the opportunity to twist free and kick out with his foot, catching the German in the stomach just as he was pulled over backward by the person who had grabbed him. Jack assumed that this was a policeman, but he wasn't about to wait around to confirm it. He turned and tried to find Everett, but the tear gas had started to roll into the crowded and dangerous street.

"Jack, help him!" a voice yelled out, rising above the pandemonium.

Collins turned back around, not seeing who was yelling at him, but he did see the struggle on the ground as the skinhead thrashed away at the man holding him on the ground. The German's body covered Jack's savior so he couldn't see who it was, then the shout from the crowd came again.

"Jack, help him!"

Instead of finding Everett and running, Collins did what he did best. He again raised his foot and brought it down into the Nazi's face, sending him into oblivion and stopping his struggles with the policeman holding him. Jack turned and started looking for Everett again.

"Colonel!" came a voice from the crowd.

"Jack, get the doc!"

Collins turned back and saw the Nazi's body being pushed away. A familiar face looked up as four sets of legs came into view and stepped all over his savior. Then he recognized the crazed hair of Doc Ellenshaw. Jack figured there couldn't be another hairdo like that in the entire world. The frizzy white hair was all over the place and Jack almost panicked when he saw that Ellenshaw was about to be trampled underfoot by the now crazed crowd. He leaned over the prone cryptozoologist.

"Grab my neck, Doc!" he shouted.

Ellenshaw threw his arms around Collins. Jack pulled up and back. His hands were still restrained by the handcuffs, so he had to use another means of rescuing the man who had just rescued him. Soon there was another set of hands pulling on Jack from behind as both men straightened.

"May I suggest we make an exit from this place?"

A totally confused Collins turned and saw the familiar thick glasses of Pete Golding. Jack shook his head and then nodded toward the street.

"That way," he shouted.

The four men started running as fast as the crowd would let them. All around them men and women were shouting, coughing, throwing stones and bottles—one of which clipped Ellenshaw as he held on to Jack's belt.

"The alley!" Collins yelled again, spotting a somewhat safe haven for the moment.

As they pushed and head-butted their way across the street, their bodies seemed to start flying. All motion and sound came to a stop. Jack was pushed from behind by a superheated wave of pressure as the five claymore mines detonated from their hiding places on five separate street lamps lining the street. Ball-bearing-sized pieces of steel exploded into the now panicked crowd of protesters, slicing into skin, muscle, and bone. Jack, Ellenshaw, Everett, and Golding were shoved into the alley and they all fell as one on top of one another. As they hit the cobbled alley floor, the sound and the smell hit them all at the same time. Collins rolled to his back and looked up just in time to see a horrible sight. A cloud of red mist settled into the alley, assisted by the rush of air. He knew by the smell and the sharp report of ricocheting pellets that the protesters had been hit by something similar to antipersonnel mines.

"Oh God, oh God," Golding was saying, as he came upright and felt for the pulse of a woman who came to rest across his legs. "What happened? What do we do? Oh God, oh God—"

Everett shoved his body into Pete's. "Get these cuffs off me," he shouted, his ears ringing harder than he had ever experienced before. Carl was shaking his head as he saw the death in the street.

"Son of a bitch," he said, still unable to hear his own voice. "Jack," Everett shouted, "Jack!"

Ellenshaw was trying desperately to get Jack's handcuffs off with a small jeweler's screwdriver, but he was shaking so badly he couldn't.

"Doc, take your time. Calm down. We need to get out there and help some of these people. Now take a breath."

Ellenshaw did as he was ordered and he finally inserted the small screwdriver into the cuffs. In order to help calm Ellenshaw, Jack half turned and tried to get the professor's mind off the horrible situation all around them.

"What possessed you two to come looking for us?" he asked while trying to see what the doc was doing.

"It was my idea. I'm sorry, Colonel," Ellenshaw said as tears started running down under his wire-rimmed glasses. He used his free hand to swipe at the tears. "I just thought . . . thought—"

"Hey, hey," Jack said, shouting above the noise of people dying around them. "You did real good, Doc, you saved our asses out there." He turned to see a shocked and battered Pete Golding sitting and leaning against the wall of the alley. Everett was trying to calm the computer specialist.

"That's for sure. You can come with us anytime, Pete. You see how much trouble me and Jack always get into?"

Pete didn't respond. He was looking at the dead woman lying in front of him. Everett could see that he was in shock. He looked up at Jack just as the colonel's hands were released from the cuffs. From the street the initial sounds of terror, fear, and pain started collecting into a wail of anguish that was close to driving both scientists mad.

"Jack, get me out of these and let's lend a hand."

As Jack surveyed the situation before him, for the first time in his life he felt truly helpless as the scene of devastation confronted him.

"What is it?" Everett asked, finally gaining his feet. There was blood coursing down from his left ear.

"This was an ambush," Collins said.

Power had been restored to the square as the bodies from the attack were placed along sidewalks and lined against building walls. The protests had ceased as most Germans had come together, waiting for the right moment to start speculating on who could have perpetrated such a cowardly act. Jack, Everett, Ellenshaw, and Golding were exhausted as they leaned against a shattered wall and caught their breath. A public announcement board and video screen flickered to life above them in the square as dusk settled in.

"I think it's time to get out of here, Jack," Everett said. He stepped up to a broken water main and stuck his hands in the spray of water. He ran a soaking hand over his soot-covered face.

Collins shook his head without really looking up.

"I hate leaving here without any answers," he said, taking a deep breath.

"Colonel, may I remind you of the fact that we found you in handcuffs? I'm sure the police will recover much faster from this terror attack than we think. They could come looking for you again. I think we've done about all we can do here to help these people. It's time we look to ourselves."

Jack placed his hand on Professor Ellenshaw's shoulder and nodded. "Okay, Doc, let's go home."

As they started gathering themselves, the large announcement board sprang to life. A public service message flashed across the thirty-foot screen with a warning tone that demanded the attention of those watching. Most people continued their duties in helping the EMS teams who were treating the wounded and attending the dead. Policemen were everywhere as they tried desperately to get evidence of the most dastardly crime in modern German history. Collins wasn't paying any attention to the announcement as he washed his own face in the shattered water main on the battered curb.

"Am I seeing this?" Pete Golding asked from behind Jack.

"Oh, shit," Everett said, tapping Collins on the shoulder. "Keep your face down, Jack, and head back toward the building."

"What now?" he asked. He did as Carl said, keeping his hands over his face.

"Take a quick look and then head down the alley. My German isn't that good, but I think the police are announcing they have a suspect in the terror attack."

As Collins chanced a quick look up at the announcement screen, he was greeted by a 1997 U.S. Army photo of himself taken at Fort Bragg. Beneath the picture it said he was wanted for questioning in the day's events.

"I've always hated that picture," he said. He allowed Everett to pull him deeper into the alley as Golding and Ellenshaw followed, blocking any further view.

"We may be too late, gentlemen," Ellenshaw said, "I think the proper words are, we've been ratted out."

Everett looked up and saw a tall, beautiful blonde pointing them out to blood-soaked and dirty policemen. The officer looked up and Ellenshaw couldn't think of anything to do other than give a quick wave of his hand as he backed into the alley. When the police officer looked closer he was stunned to see four men suddenly sprint down the open alleyway. He gave pursuit, alone and unarmed, shouting for the men to halt.

The blond-haired woman watched the pursuit and then turned to her companion. They both walked away.

"Imagine, all of those mines exploding at once and this man Collins escapes without so much as a scratch," she said, looking into the face of the Mechanic as they walked and tried to avoid the damaged areas of the street and the small puddles of blood. "It seems he's a domino that's hard to topple."

The Mechanic looked up at the video board with the photo of Jack Collins still on it. After seeing Jack and the others on the street he had to react fast, so he contacted McCabe and came up with a quickly thought out alternative. He offered the U.S. Army photo of the colonel to the German authorities.

"Sometimes the domino takes a while to fall, miss, that's all. And I suspect this particular domino we are after will continue his pursuit of the men imprisoned together after the war. That is the key for him and we'll be waiting."

As the two walked away into the gathering night, the sounds of sirens and shouting still filled the air of downtown Berlin.

# 7

## JOHNSON SPACE CENTER,
## HOUSTON, TEXAS

The Lyndon B. Johnson Space Center (JSC) is the National Aeronautics and Space Administration's center for human space flight activities and home to the astronaut corps.

Sarah McIntire, Will Mendenhall, and Jason Ryan had just gone through a battery of tests that would have strained the patience of a saint. Will complained that his right arm and butt cheek were about to fall off from a series of shots they had endured in the accelerated astronaut training phase.

Sarah was so sore she was having a hard time zipping up her blue coveralls. Ryan walked over and helped with the zipper.

"Thanks," she said. "Remind me to send a pipe bomb to Director Compton for doing this to us."

"I'll supply the postage," Ryan said as he slapped Sarah on the back, making her wince.

"All of this with only a five percent chance we'll be going," Mendenhall said. "I mean, we're the backup to the backup, which is backing up the first team." He gingerly sat on the locker room bench beside Sarah. "That means two teams have to fail to make it to the space station in order for us to even suit up."

Sarah wasn't listening. She was watching a group of trainees, several high-ranking officers among them, looking up at a television monitor just inside the lounge. Sarah stood, moving her aching shoulders as she approached the men and women watching.

"What's going on?" she asked.

"Someone just blew the hell out of an anti-Moon demonstration in Berlin. There's a whole bunch of fundamentalists dead," answered a woman who had been chosen for the first flight team of Operation Dark Star. She was a geologist like Sarah, but while not quite as knowledgeable she was a better astronaut.

Sarah watched the taped footage of the aftermath as Jason and Will stepped up behind her.

"This isn't good," Ryan said, looking on as one of the men in the front reached out and turned the volume up:

"*. . . as the crowded streets became overrun with more serious elements of the discontented protesters. It was only moments after the violence broke out that a series of explosions rocked the downtown area of Berlin. The number of devices detonated has not yet been determined.*" The scene switched to the Atlanta studio. "*The police have announced a lead in identifying a man caught on videotape the night before, possibly planting the devices. On the video he is clearly wearing the uniform of a German army officer. The man, seen here in a United States Army photo, has been identified as Colonel Jack Collins. His whereabouts are unknown at this time.*"

Sarah, Will, and Jason couldn't move as they saw the picture of Collins flash onto the screen. The other astronauts watched with growing uneasiness as an American was named as a person that may have been directly responsible for the horrible act they were seeing.

"*. . . the suspect's military history is one of black operations in the Middle East and he has been known to be a rogue, even being brought before the congressional committee investigating failures in the war in Afghanistan.*"

As the men and women cursed the face of Collins, Sarah turned away, wanting to shout at the trainees around her to be quiet, that they didn't know the man like she did. Instead she walked back into the locker room and sat once more on the wooden bench, where she was joined by Mendenhall and Ryan.

"Damn, obviously a frame job if I ever saw one," Ryan said as he sat next to Sarah.

"Yeah, they said he's a suspect, but that he's not in custody." Will placed a hand on Sarah's shoulder.

"Ryan, McIntire, Mendenhall, let's go. You've got six hours of flight simulation scheduled with your flight leader. Let's move it!"

Sarah looked up at the Air Force master sergeant who stood in the doorway of the locker room.

"Come on, the president has just pushed Dark Star up by seventy-two hours because of this maniac's actions in Germany."

Sarah looked as if she were about to attack the sergeant, but Will and Ryan gently placed their hands on her and turned her away.

"Comin', Sarge," Will quickly answered.

Sarah calmed and then tried to smile. "Thanks."

"Well, let's go keep ourselves busy, and hope the colonel and the others get their asses out of Germany without getting them shot completely off."

Sarah looked at Ryan and then nodded.

"Come on, let's go simulate crash-landing on the Moon," Mendenhall joked. "Jason hasn't done that in a few hours. I'm getting to where I like it. It's so much better than the always boring landing upright thing."

As Ryan complained how hard the lunar lander simulators were for the hundredth time that day, Sarah could only think about Collins and wonder just what he had gotten himself into.

"Jack, I swear to God, I can't take my eyes off of you for five damn minutes without you getting into some kind of bullshit!" she hissed as she followed Jason and Will out of the locker room.

## BERLIN, GERMANY

Everett had the policeman's gun. The man was unconscious and lying by the back doorway to a Chinese restaurant. Carl ejected the clip from the nine-millimeter and then ejected the chambered round. He thought briefly about keeping it, but knew the man would probably be in enough trouble for being disarmed by a suspect. Besides, he knew he couldn't use it against law enforcement.

Jack stood beside Carl and nodded, then he reached up and pounded on the back door of the restaurant. It was opened by a startled Chinese man who stood stock-still when he saw the large blond man and the police officer.

"English?" Jack asked.

The small man just shook his head negatively, so Everett eased the cop inside the door and lay him down gently.

"*Die Polizei*," Jack said, as he pulled Carl away from the door. Everett reached out and handed the Chinese man the weapon, then turned and ran into the darkness of the alley.

Jack and Carl reached the end of the long alley and looked out onto a far quieter street. They spied Ellenshaw and Golding, secluded inside a small Audi. In the illumination of the overhead street lamp, they saw Ellenshaw raise his head on the front seat of the car and then duck back down. Jack shook his head at the suspicious way the two scientists were going about trying to steal a car.

Suddenly the motor sprang to life and Ellenshaw sat up. He and Pete exchanged high fives.

"We don't give these guys enough credit," Everett said as he and Jack cautiously and slowly left the alley.

"Good work, guys," Collins said and ducked into the backseat with Everett pulling the two professors out of the way.

"Get in, I'll drive," he said to a stunned Ellenshaw, who instead of arguing ran around to the far side and got in the front seat. His hair was a mess as usual as he looked over at Carl.

"Where's that young policeman?" he asked, looking around the darkened street nervously.

"He went for Chinese," Everett replied as he threw the car in gear and sped off.

"What's the plan?" Golding asked, scanning the dark outside the rear window.

"First off, you two should stop looking like you're on the run," Jack said. He reached out and stilled the turning head of the computer genius.

"Oh, sorry," Pete said. He settled in and closed his eyes. Then a thought struck him. "Did we come away with nothing?"

"Nothing but a familiar face in an old photo," Jack said. "Right now, let's just hope our aircraft hasn't been compromised and that Mr. Everett here can find a back way into Tempelhof."

"Yeah, I think it's time to retreat from Germany," Everett said, taking a corner faster than he wanted to.

"Where to now?" Ellenshaw asked, actually enjoying the intrigue.

"Jack?" Carl looked in the rearview mirror.

"We're not leaving," was Collins's surprise answer.

"Uh, Jack, in case you didn't notice, you're probably the most wanted man in the Western world at the moment." Everett grimaced at the thought of staying.

"Yeah, but we need to get to the records at Spandau."

"We can do that through Europa," Pete said. "And if memory serves, Spandau was demolished in 1987."

"If the plane's been compromised we can't use Europa. We just can't take the chance we'll run into an ambush. Someone gave the authorities my picture and only one name keeps coming into my head."

"Your old friend McCabe?" Carl asked.

"You bet. We need to know who that guy was in the photo at Zinsser's apartment. I have a gut feeling everything here is connected somehow." He looked to his left at Golding. "And you're right, Pete. Spandau was demolished, but the Germans, being as honest about the Nazis as they can to the general public, have a small museum dedicated to it."

"If we're staying, I would feel better with a gun, and preferably not a policeman's weapon."

"Well, we better get some," Collins said in answer to Everett's suggestion. "I know a man here. But first we have to hole up somewhere and get some rest. We'll let my celebrity cool down for a day or two, at least until I can make a few local telephone calls."

"What about this?" Pete said, holding out his cell phone.

Jack watched the buildings of Berlin slide by his darkened window, so Pete could only see Jack's reflection and the set of his features.

"They can trace that signal, Doc. No cell phones."

Golding swallowed and then pulled the phone away from Collins. He nodded his head and then turned and saw his own scared reflection in the glass.

Ellenshaw turned around in the front seat and looked at Pete Golding.

"I told you, Doctor. Now isn't this better than being stuck inside the complex all the time?"

Pete didn't say anything as Everett sped sharply around a corner, almost bringing the vehicle up on two wheels.

For a man who had never left Nevada on a field assignment, Pete Golding was taking the adventure rather stoically, but still wide-eyed and excited, feeling alive for the first time in years as the Audi sped into the night.

## EVENT GROUP COMPLEX, NELLIS AIR FORCE BASE, NEVADA

Niles was examining the Moon rocks that had been couriered over from the National Geographic Society. There were two of them and they had the identical properties of those seen in the video from *Paul* the Beatle on the Moon's surface. The CIA had donated them to the National Geographic Society when they were discovered in their archives back when the CIA went by another name—the OSS. Not knowing what else to do with the stones, they emptied their files of the only specimens that had survived Operation Columbus all those years before.

"As far as our records are concerned, there are only twelve such examples in the world like those. We estimate that of all the meteorites discovered in history, these are the rarest."

"Where are the rest of the meteorites?" the president asked from over two thousand miles away in Washington.

"Several that we know of found their way to China and France after the war. The OSS was sketchy on the details of something called Operation Columbus."

"Well, that kind of sums it up, doesn't it? These two countries know firsthand the properties of the mineral, thus their lust for it and their massive expenditures to get to the Moon to recover more."

Niles was silent as he listened to the president excuse the director of the

CIA. A moment later the president's face came into full view, after the selling job and acting class 101 let out.

"Niles, how is everyone taking to the fact that I advanced the timetable for launch?"

"Everyone here in Houston and Florida is worried that we're lagging in safety precautions, and I agree." Niles held up his hand for the president to see, halting him from saying anything. "However, I also agree with your new timetable and have explained it to the parties involved."

"Things are getting out of hand fast, Niles. The religious fanatics are killing us in the press, and their coordinated antigovernment protests in every city in the world aren't helping matters."

"I don't understand. The mainstream religious communities are lying low on this one. Only the fringe element is rearing its head. Fundamentalism may be creating some strange new bedfellows."

"Speaking of which, have you heard from the colonel?"

"Not a word since he and Captain Everett flew out."

"We've got quite a mess on our hands in Berlin. I hope he knows what he's doing over there. I want you to understand, Niles, that if he's caught we can help him. The German government will assist in getting him out of there quietly, but if he's shot while on the run it will be a purely legal act."

"I assume Jack knows that. If he's staying in place, it's because he has a lead on Columbus and its backers. I just assume if he comes up with something here on earth that will stop us from sending men and women into space, that you're prepared to do something about it."

"Short of war, I'll do anything, Niles."

Compton didn't question the statement. He just looked into the monitor.

"What is it?"

"I was just wondering what the difference was between a shooting war on the Moon and one that starts right here."

The president didn't answer for the briefest of moments. Then he reached out and for a second his hand paused over the off button on his laptop.

"About six billion eight hundred million people—give or take a couple of kids."

Niles smiled as his eyes widened in mock surprise. "You do have your moments of clarity don't you, Mr. President?"

"Once every few years, Mr. Director, I get lucky."

Niles had one of the most important meetings in his life scheduled in just ten minutes.

The U.S. Navy signalman was already preparing the camera for the linkup with Houston, Florida, Jet Propulsion Lab, and Washington. He was about to hand over control of the mission to the more experienced arm of NASA. His coordinating and planning days were now over.

As Virginia Pollock and several others prepared the charts and graphs to be used in the director's final meeting with the space groups, Niles walked to the conference table and waited. He had forced himself in the past week and a half to concentrate on the Moon and how the U.S. could get there, and had pushed out of his mind the situation with Garrison Lee and his final days.

"Director, Alice Hamilton is on line two," his assistant said from the outer office.

Niles hesitated one moment before picking up the phone. He really didn't know how to approach the subject of the senator's health. Everything he thought of saying seemed so shallow.

"Alice, how are you?" he asked, avoiding the main question for as long as he could.

"I'm fine, Niles, and for the moment so is the senator."

Niles closed his eyes and a small smile reached his lips. Leave it to Alice to cut to the chase and place him at ease.

"Good. I've been a little busy here."

"So we've noticed. We also see that Jack has been a little busy too. His face is plastered on every news broadcast from here to China."

"Don't believe everything you hear," Niles said as he placed the phone between his head and shoulder. He pulled the knot on his tie upward.

"We never believe anything we hear, Niles. You know that. Are Jack and Carl all right?" Her voice dropped in volume. Niles suspected she didn't want the senator to overhear.

"Jack and Carl haven't been heard from in forty-eight hours. They also have Ellenshaw and Golding tagging along, so that may be the reason they're a little slow in getting to a phone."

"Jack always takes the strangest people on missions. How about you, Niles? Are you being careful? That assassination in Pasadena caught us by surprise."

"The opposition to the mission is getting stronger and far more organized than should be possible among such diverse groups. If I didn't know any better I would think that it's—"

"Being orchestrated?" Alice said, finishing Niles sentence. "The senator's exact words. He told me to tell you to look to the obvious first."

Compton understood what Alice and Lee were trying to tell him. This was his next project. If one group or a single individual was responsible for the loss of life in Kazakhstan, Berlin, and here in the States, he would find them. Thus far they knew the Saudi-born Mechanic was involved, but the current global operation seemed a stretch for what amounted to a small-time terrorist.

"You take care of yourself, Niles, and I'll let you know when things go bad here. Concentrate on what you need to do. That's why your friend the president chose you to get this thing off the ground. He trusts you and you also just happen to be the smartest man on the planet."

Niles had to chuckle. "Unfortunately, we're dealing with a little more than just this planet."

The line then went dead and Niles hung up.

"We're ready Director Compton," the signalman said. "All interested parties have confirmed audio and visual."

Niles nodded and accepted the recommendations from Virginia. He stepped to the podium, glancing over at the largest of the monitors. Besides the cameras at the Johnson Space Center and JPL, he was hooked into Cape Canaveral and the Pentagon's Space Command, and all of the general contractors for the systems that had been chosen to bring this hurried mission to its final stages. On the center monitor was the Johnson Space Center, and sitting in front of the crowded room of over two hundred men and women was the vice president of the United States, Harold Darby, the technical head of the entire space program.

The Navy signalman pointed to Niles as the others in his conference room went to their seats. He looked at Virginia and her staff that had done so much to get them where they were today, feeling proud of her and all of his people. They fought and succeeded in coming up with a viable plan on the shortest timetable in the history of the space program. They would at least have a fighting chance.

"Good afternoon. We're ready to start the final assembly of the platforms. All I need to do now is step aside and hand Dark Star over to people with far more capable hands than my own." Niles glanced again at the center screen and the stern visage of the vice president. "I have taken a lot of time exploring the facts and personal histories of all personnel involved in every aspect of Dark Star, and I have come to the conclusion that we need to stay in-house, so to speak."

Vice President Darby smiled as he looked around at the men and women at his table.

"Since the senseless murder of Stan Nathan a few days ago, this choice had become even more important. I had to factor in many differing elements and the person that met or exceeded knowledge in every aspect of the platforms to be used is Flight Director Hugh Evans. His knowledge of the Ares system and his experience with the Apollo program preclude anyone else taking command of the mission. Mr. Evans, you may not like it, but congratulations anyway.

"Now, I will allow Hugh to absorb the enormity of what I've placed before him and give him time to decline, a notion that would immediately be rejected by the president, of course. And then we'll cover what the base plan is. For the general contractors and their employees, the president wants me to pass along his sincerest thanks for all of the hard work you have put in."

On the monitor from Houston, Niles saw the seventy-four-year-old Hugh Evans stand and walk toward the back of the room, out of view of the camera.

"Ares I and Ares II are scheduled for heavy load liftoff in seventy-eight hours. The crews will be shuttled to the International Space Station immediately after the two Ares launches. The shuttles *Atlantis* and *Discovery* will launch from Vandenberg Air Force Base, and the shuttle *Endeavour* from the Cape, if that mission becomes necessary because of the failure of one or both of the first launches. We were very lucky that the shuttles' last scheduled missions kept them in fine mechanical shape. Dark Star will be one hell of a note for the shuttle fleet to retire on."

Niles smiled when he heard applause erupting from every view of every venue. He also saw the vice president stand and leave the Johnson Space Center mostly unnoticed by anyone.

"The backup is, of course, the Saturn V launch vehicle. The payload, as with the two Ares rockets, has been expanded to carry the new Lunar Excursion Module and the expanded crew cabin that will eventually double as the crew capsule on the ride to and from the Moon. The Altair Lander has been massively redesigned to carry the necessary men and equipment to and from the lunar surface. Needless to say, ladies and gentlemen, this is where the real danger lies. The Altair system is totally untested—therefore the need for two complete crews and one solid backup in the Atlas. These three expanded crew capacity landers were only prototypes five weeks ago, and the engineering done to complete the systems has just been amazing. The Dark Star mission time will be a record-setting two days to the Moon, with four days there. We'll leave coming home to another timetable."

Niles allowed that to sink in for the general contractors who had not been privy to the time element before today. He braced himself for what was coming.

"At this time, I am ceasing today's communications with all but the military and space elements of Dark Star. For the contractors who have contributed so much manpower and time in bringing these systems, expanded prototype landers, and equipment online, thank you and good-bye."

Three quarters of the monitors went dark inside the Event Group conference room as Niles saw the civilian aspect of the mission vanish. He looked at the Navy signalman.

"Please bring up the astronaut training facility," he said, opening a red-bordered file folder on the podium. He glanced up and looked at the president, who was waiting as patiently as the others.

On one of the monitors, a room full of blue and red clad men and women appeared. They sat patiently with pen and writing tablets. They knew they were about to be briefed on the parameters of the mission ahead. In the back of the astronauts' room, Compton saw his very own people looking at up at his image. For all he knew, this might be the last time he saw the young faces of Sarah, Mendenhall, and Ryan.

"Our mission goals," he said, not looking into the camera, "are to militarily secure the Moon and any artifacts found there. The mission landing area is one mile from Shackleton Crater. NASA personnel will deliver geology specialists and engineers to the surface of the moon. The site will be secured by fourteen United States Special Forces personnel undergoing training in California. If the failure to secure Shackleton is likely, and it looks as if the Chinese will take it intact, the site will be destroyed. I repeat, the site will be destroyed. This act is regardless of any foreign government's presence in or near the crater. None of you will be expected to go into this blindfolded. What follows is top secret information. The European Space Agency and NASA have been cooperating since the emergency began, for reasons I cannot go into now. The base problem here is the Chinese government. The president is attempting to gain cooperation from the People's Republic in this and other matters, but as of this moment that issue is in doubt."

At every location from the Pentagon's Space Command headquarters, to Pasadena, U.S. Air Force personnel started handing out sealed orders to every man and woman assigned to flight control, security, and engineering positions for the mission.

"If, in a military circumstance, the European and American personnel see a viable chance at taking the technology if it falls into Chinese hands, they are to take it regardless of cost. If not, destroy the technology in place. Study the mission parameters, and at this time I will say good-bye and wish each and every man and woman Godspeed."


## BOROUGH OF SPANDAU, BERLIN, GERMANY

Spandau Prison was built in 1876 and demolished in 1987 after the death of its last inmate, Rudolph Hess, Hitler's right-hand man in the early days of the Nazi regime. The old prison was torn down before it could become a shrine to the neo-Nazi movement across the globe. Today there was nothing left to mark the site where the convicted Nazi hierarchy had tended gardens and made paper.

The lone structure still standing was a brick building. The facade was nothing to write home about as it stood stark against the darkness of the night.

"So, how do we get in?" Everett asked.

"We don't. The weapons we asked for are meeting us here, along with an old friend of mine. Right now I think we should step out of the car and let them know we're here."

Everett, Ellenshaw, and Golding were confused as to Jack's methods, but they did as he said. A brief moment later they became even more confused when Collins raised his arms into the air as though surrendering.

Everett did the same and gestured for the two professors to follow suit.

"You want to let us in on what's happening, Jack?" Carl asked quietly, as his eyes scanned the darkness around the building.

Collins didn't answer. Instead, he allowed their guests to do it for him. Several red laser beams pierced the night air and each man standing around the car had three pin-sized red dots targeting their chests.

"Wow, this is really uncomfortable," Everett said as he recognized the lasers for what they were.

Ellenshaw saw the three dots on his jacket and swiped at them like they were bugs.

"Doc, hold still please," Jack said. Ten dark figures stepped from the trees surrounding the lone building.

"Oh, my," Ellenshaw said as he saw the black-clad men.

"I take it we're caught," Pete Golding said. He watched the heavily armed masked men approach them cautiously.

"Easy, Pete. I think these guys may be the result of Jack's phone calls," Carl said as he saw one large man take the lead.

The lone figure stood still as he looked Jack and his men over, then took two steps forward and removed his black hood.

"You know, officially I have orders to hunt you down and place a bunch of bullets into your head and face, maybe one in your ass also."

Jack lowered his hands and smiled. "Oh, I saw you and your unit the moment we drove up," Collins said.

"Bullshit, Jack. We had you cold."

Collins walked forward and held out his hand. The other black-clad commandos lowered their weapons and surrounded the colonel.

"How in the hell are you, Sebastian?" Collins asked, holding out an extended hand. "And thanks for not shooting me in the head and face, and especially my ass."

The two men shook hands and the large German slung his automatic weapon over his shoulder.

"I'm fine, Jack. Better than you, anyway."

"Mr. Everett, meet Major Sebastian Krell of the German army. He's the team leader of the elite counterterrorism force GSG 9. He's an old buddy of mine from the Gulf War."

Krell shook Everett's hand and looked him over.

"I smell U.S. Navy in this man, Jack."

"You don't miss a beat. Mr. Everett here is a SEAL—he comes in handy from time to time."

"I'm impressed with Jack's new friends," he said to Carl.

"As I am with the company you keep," Everett said. He released the man's hand and gestured to the nine commandos around them.

"Ah, I just keep them around for running errands and getting coffee."

Major Krell held out his hand and two of his still masked men stepped forward and handed him two items, a bag and a thick file.

"Here's four nine-millimeter handguns stolen from my daughter's room," Krell said, joking, while handing Everett the black bag. "There are ten clips of ammunition inside as well. And this is what you specifically asked for, Jack. We just went in an hour ago and retrieved them from the museum."

Collins took the offered file and looked up at Sebastian. "Thanks, this will help."

"Your president is a very persuasive man."

"He can be, but I imagine I'll still be in hot water when I get home."

"Who did it, Jack?" Sebastian asked, getting serious for the first time.

"We think James McCabe may be in on it, but we're not sure." He looked at the German commando in all seriousness. "We're still piecing this thing together."

"McCabe? Jesus, I know he's dirt, but something like this?"

"Money makes for a good motive. I suspect that's all it takes with him."

The large German turned and gestured for his men to back away. As they watched, the commando team blended into the darkness and was gone.

"I wasn't going to charge you for the file and the weapons, Jack, but now I am," Sebastian said as he stepped closer to Collins. "I want whoever is responsible for the bombing. No matter what the protesters were doing there, and their reasons, they didn't deserve that. They are still German citizens."

"You got it. If it's McCabe, you can have him. As a matter of fact, there may be something you and your government would have an interest in helping us with in Ecuador."

"Just call us, Jack," Sebastian said, turning around and walking away. "Mr. Everett, watch that guy," he shouted over his shoulder. "Just because he was in on training us doesn't mean he's worth a damn."

Everett smiled and looked over at Collins as he inserted a clip into one of the nine-millimeters.

"I like him, Jack," he said, glancing over at Golding and Ellenshaw. He shook his head when he saw they still had their arms raised. "It's okay, guys. The scary men are all gone."

Ellenshaw and Golding slowly lowered their hands and looked at Everett and Jack.

"Do you two know anyone that leads a normal, dull life?" Pete asked Collins.

"Only you, Pete, only you."


## INCHON INTERNATIONAL AIRPORT, SOUTH KOREA

The hangar was leased to Chan Ri International. The company was a lesser known aircraft manufacturer that specialized in avionics packages for advanced fighter aircraft. The packages were made up of fire control systems and other avionics that were used by the Western powers. Most Asian stock market watchers were a little surprised when Chan Ri stocks suddenly sprang to life after a three-year period when most traders thought the company was on the way out following the introduction by the U.S. of the highly advanced F-22 Raptor, the

new fighter for the twenty-first century that left Chan Ri technology far behind. But somewhere along the way the company had received a massive influx
of capital, and try as they might, agents of the Securities and Exchange Commission could not uncover where the money had come from.

The twenty-five-year-old Grumman F-14 Super Tomcat sat gleaming inside the small hangar as several technicians checked the hard points along the
fuselage of the U.S. Navy fighter jet. As the first of the two weapons was raised
into position just below the starboard hard point, the pilot walked over to make
sure the job was being done right. He placed a gloved hand on the plastic nose
cone of the missile and felt a rush of power course through his hand and then
his entire arm. He rolled his eyes and knew he was coming home again. The
small pilot almost dropped his black-painted helmet onto the floor of the hangar as he felt the euphoria. The South Korean technicians turned and wondered
why this pilot, whom they had just met that morning, was acting so strange.

Former naval aviator Thomas Green finally removed his hand from the
missile and stepped back. He watched the final loading and was satisfied that the
long, heavy weapon was placed properly. He stepped over to the rolling munitions cart and saw the second weapon as it sat gleaming white under the bright
fluorescent lights of the hangar.

Green had been free just thirteen weeks from the maximum security
penitentiary at Huntsville, Texas, where he had served ten years of a twenty-
year sentence for an abortion clinic bombing that had killed three nurses and
the doctor who owned the building. Unfortunately for the former Navy pilot,
he had also killed two of the protesters, his own people, outside the clinic. All
of this had been spawned by a woman he had once called his wife, who had
murdered their unborn baby while he had been deployed to the Persian Gulf in
1991 during the First Gulf War. Since then, Green had found God, and God
had placed the burning sword of righteousness into his hand and told him to
strike. Two powerful swords were being placed on his aircraft at that very moment.

The crated parcels from Raytheon Corporation had been stolen in the
month prior to Green being brought onboard the project. He knew that all he
had to do was pull the trigger and the illegal weapons from the United States
would do the rest. The seeker heads had been changed out in San Diego before
their shipment to South Korea—they were now the largest heat seekers the world
had ever seen.

The two Vought ASM-135 ASAT missiles had gone through extensive testing
at Raytheon in the late eighties, and then when the antisatellite missile treaty was
signed between the United States and the Soviet Union they were crated and
stored at the testing facility, never to see action.

Tommy Green had been offered $3 million for this one mission, with more
money and missions to follow, but after speaking with the financial backer many
times in prison, through the thick glass of the visitor center, Green had decided

he was doing it because that's what the Lord wished him to do. The money had been declined on the promise that he would have the opportunity for all of the missions if they became viable.

A man in a dark pair of slacks and a nice pullover shirt stepped up and slapped Green on the back.

"Well, the Chinese launch in twenty minutes, at 0615," James McCabe said as he looked the pilot over. "You'll taxi at exactly the same time. I am told to tell you good luck, Captain, and that your martyrdom, if it happens, will be the plague that brings down Pharaoh."

"Praise the Lord," Green said as he slid on his black helmet. "I only wish I could call out to the world as the hand of God reaches out for the heathen's rocketry and say, Thou art great!"

McCabe watched the man climb up the ladder and into the cockpit. He shook his head and stepped back. He now knew why so many millions upon millions of deaths had been brought on by religious wars. It was because the true believer was the most dangerous animal of all. He waved his hand one last time as Green looked his way and saluted.

McCabe stepped away as the twin GE turbofans started turning on the old and venerable F-14 Super Tomcat. As the hangar doors rose and the morning sunlight diffused the bright fluorescents inside, McCabe turned and left for the car that would take him to his private jet, where he would fly out before all international airspace was closed—and before the Chinese started looking in earnest for the murderers of their space crews.

"The fireworks are about to begin," McCabe said as he settled into the backseat of the limo. The powerful F-14 Tomcat pulled free of its hangar with two gleaming white claws attached to its sides in the form of the most powerful anti-satellite missiles ever created.

The F-14 received immediate clearance to taxi to runway 3B. The controller watching from the large tower glanced out the window and saw the polished white jet as it sped to the taxi line. The voice on the Tomcat's radio had an American accent, but as the controller adjusted his binoculars he saw for the first time that the American-built aircraft had South Korean military markings on its fuselage and wings. As he pondered the strangeness of the plane's identification, his eyes widened. He saw what was strung along the underbelly of the large naval fighter. Because Inchon International was so close to the North Korean border, it was agreed between North and South that no military aircraft could take off armed as this one obviously was. The South Korean air force was not even allowed to place dummy bombs and missiles on their aircraft, as this was not a military airfield and the North might just mistake the flight as a first strike attempt.

The controller lowered the glasses and reached for the large alarm button on his console. He knew he had to alert the airport security staff and the air force of this attempted military flight. Just as the alarm sounded the controller knew he would be too late even as all controllers calmly told their departing flights to hold at their present locations.

The F-14 Tomcat roaring down the runway was the last to lift into the blue sky.

The ASM-135 ASAT space weapons were about to spread their wings for the first time in actual space combat.

## JIUQUAN SATELLITE LAUNCH CENTER, GOBI DESERT, CHINA

The ten active launch pads at Jiuquan were guarded heavily after the debacle in Kazakhstan. The People's Republic had brought in five hundred specially trained army personnel to oversee the security aspects of the flight center.

Launch pads 1-C and 7-A were active for the historic Chinese flights. This was the first Chinese manned mission intended to reach the lunar surface. Two massive Long March 8s, the second largest rocket system in the world, sat at their launch towers complete with the Zihuang lunar landers. Each Long March had a crew of ten Chinese air force personnel aboard. The mission had been planned so rapidly that the Chinese engineers were still evaluating the return specs for the two-capsule twenty-man flights. Nothing had been assured, not even a successful landing on the Moon.

The three-staged Long March launch system had four solid rocket boosters attached to the mainframe of the rocket. The main system itself had four power-ful Shang-7 engines, almost equal in thrust to the American version from which the engines had been "borrowed" in the late seventies. At T-minus thirty seconds and counting, all four hundred engineers in the nearby control center watched with wide eyes as the elevator system and fuel hoses started popping free of the two giant rockets. Television cameras from China's state-run facili-ties were carrying the launch to over 800 million Chinese on a five-minute de-layed "live" broadcast.

The first rocket and crew to be lifted from the pad was named *Glorious March*. The second was *Magnificent Dragon*. Each was hastily built and each of the twenty-man crews knew that an explosion was more likely that a clean lift-off. But no crew member, even the military personnel who were prepared to do battle if necessary, would have traded places with any other man or woman on Earth. Every rocket had a glorious red band separating each of its three stages, and each band had the golden Chinese stars encircling it, with the stars ulti-mately shooting off toward the next stage in line. Other than that bit of color, each system was ivory white and stood out magnificently against the clear morning sky above the Gobi. Finally, at T-minus ten seconds, the loudspeakers came to life as the crowds of reporters watched on the chilly morning.

"... *ten, nine, eight, seven, six, five, four, three, we have main engine start,*" the

Chinese announcer called from the mission control building as the four main engines fired, sending a tremendous cloud of gases and fire free of the spacecraft. "... *two, one, we have solid booster ignition on all four solid rocket boosters.*"

Every journalist present could hear the excitement in the voice of the announcer as he watched the cloud of hot gases pour out of the engines on launch pad 1-C. The cameras zoomed in as the first movement of the giant rocket became apparent. The extending arms that carried oxygen and fuel to the main engines finally separated and the vehicle started to move. The clock was now running on *Glorious March* as its bulk lifted free of the Earth. Before it cleared the tower's uppermost reaches, the ten-second countdown of *Magnificent Dragon* began. The same sequence sent the main engines to flame as *Glorious March* fully cleared the giant tower. Men and women, engineers from around the world, couldn't help themselves, from Houston to Guiana, to Baikonur Cosmodrome, men and women from every country stood and cheered or pounded their fists as the two Chinese rockets cleared the restraints of Earth's gravity. No one ever wanted to see astronauts die or an attempt at space fail. It was a human weakness to see greatness and cheer it.

The two massive rockets rotated, sending their bulk dangerously close to the stall point as they rolled 15 degrees in the clear sky above the desert. Reporters from the world over were stunned at the power of the Long March launch system as the ground still shook beneath their feet. The *Glorious March* led the way, followed four miles behind by *Magnificent Dragon* as the first stages separated.

The Chinese mission to the Moon had begun.


The F-14 Tomcat climbed at a 45 degree angle. Then, as Green watched with his dark visor down, he saw the bright red and gold plumes of the two launches out of the Gobi. His radio was crackling with warnings from the North Koreans and the Chinese that the Tomcat was in violation of their joint airspace. Green reached out and shut down his communication system. He then pushed the Tomcat's throttle as far forward as it could go, sending JP-4 jet fuel into the exhaust of the nacelles. The exhaust rings expanded and the F-14 was pushed into afterburner. Green pulled the stick straight back into his belly and the Tomcat turned nose up as it started its climb through the Earth's lower atmosphere.

As he climbed, Green raised the small protective cover on his control stick and pushed the blue button. The seeker head in the first ASAT came to life as it started its infrared sweep of the area in front of the F-14. First one and then the other missile locked on its particular target—each of the two Chinese rockets as they climbed for high Earth orbit.

"It's in God's hands now," Green said, as he thumbed the red switch. He closed his eyes and again whispered an almost silent prayer as the first ASM-135

ASAT left its launch rail. With the Tomcat facing straight up into the air, the missile's exhaust streamed back along the clear canopy of the jet, fogging the plastic. The plane was starting to shudder as it fought for altitude against the turbulence created by the giant ASAT, which was now trying desperately to close the gap between it and the second stage of the Long March rockets. The Tomcat's GE engines fought and struggled for air in the high reaches of sky.

As Green switched seeker heads and missiles, he locked on to the *Magnificent Dragon* as it lagged behind the first rocket. He pushed the trigger and waited three seconds as the powerful engine of the ASAT cleared the aircraft. Green immediately pulled away as his starboard engine started to flame out due to a lack of breathable air. Green swung the jet over onto its back and then he rolled and fell into a nose-down dive for the deck. It was at that exact moment that his threat radar illuminated from the west and the east. He was being tracked by air-to-air weapons.

"Thank you, Lord, for this final challenge, this last test of my faith and my allegiance to your cause," he said into his oxygen mask as he saw the eight radar blips on his screen. Chinese and North Korean fighters were trying to prevent him from reaching the Sea of Japan, where his rescue boat was to be waiting for him. Green smiled and switched the control stick selector to guns, as he knew he had no defensive or offensive missiles left. In fact, they had never been loaded. "As I walk into the valley of the shadow of death, I shall fear no evil . . ."

The Tomcat dove straight into the advancing communist fighters as the first ASAT found its target.


The giant first stage separated with a bright flash as the controllers followed the ascending rockets on the long-range telemetry and photo analysis provided by a MiG-31 chase plane. As the fighter climbed on afterburners, its cameras, three still and two video, transmitted a continuous stream of pictures to mission control. Suddenly, a dark object streaked toward the leading Long March just as its first stage separated from the second. All eyes watched as the bright flash of exploding bolts and the ignition of the second stage blurred the picture momentarily, and when it cleared they saw the object and were horrified when they recognized it as a streaking missile. Just as the ASAT's radar and IR seeker head came into the thirty-foot-diameter target range, the missile broke apart and a ten-pound explosive charge detonated, sending out five thousand ball-bearing-sized steel projectiles. The bulk of them struck the empty first stage as it fell back to Earth, but enough fought their way through the disturbed air and heat to connect with the three engines of the second stage. They struck the exhaust bells of the engines and punctured through the fuel lines that provided the combustion chambers the needed oxygen and ~~nitrogen~~ hydrogen mix.

As millions of eyes watched in horror, the second stage simply vanished in a white and red plume of fire. The second and third stages fell apart in the expanding fireball that sent the lunar lander smashing up and into the ten-man compartment of the crew module. The debris expanded even further, slowly spiraling in all directions as the Long March ceased to exist in the blink of an eye.

The witnesses to the tragic happening then noticed another streak of light as it plowed through the remains of the first rocket. A second antisatellite missile shot upward and was on track to strike the *Magnificent Dragon* as the first spent stage went flying past the ASAT. As luck and fate would have it, a fortuitous accident occurred. The remaining fuel of the solid propellant rocket boosters was being spent even though the first stage had separated cleanly. As they spun out of control, falling back toward the Earth, a sudden burst of flame shot from the exhaust nozzle of one of the boosters, catching the ASAT as it flew past. The heat was tremendous and burned through the hard plastic nose cone of its seeker head. With molten circuit boards and damaged processing units, the ASAT exploded before its outer casing could be blown free; thus the ball bearing shrapnel was slowed by 50 percent of its normal velocity. The particles shot up and over the second stage, scraping along the aluminum fuselage and then past the third stage where only five of the steel balls penetrated the outer casing into the lunar lander's protective shell. The rest, over a hundred fragments, hit the crew module, three of them penetrating.

The crewmen reacted fast, even though they had little training in this event, as it had not been foreseen. The three holes threatened to destabilize their environment, and as the second stage fired and separated from the third, the crew managed in spite of the g-forces that threatened to crush them to place three plastic patches against the holes that appeared as if by magic.

The ten-man crew didn't know what had happened either to them or to the *Glorious March*, but they did know that one of their three computer systems was out along with their radar. The communications module was damaged and they were leaking oxygen.

On the ground, multitudes watched as the third stage of the *Magnificent Dragon* reached lower orbit and kept climbing, barely escaping the death that had caught her sister ship. All at once a thousand voices started shouting out their troubles from the various telemetry stations.

The *Magnificent Dragon* had achieved orbit, but no one knew yet if it could stay there, much less continue on to the Moon.


Sixteen miles away, Tommy Green didn't know if his crusade had achieved the desired effect as he scrambled to get the F-14 out of North Korean airspace. There were now ten MiG-31s on his tail and he doubted if escape was in his future, but he suspected it had never been in the plans of his employers. He should have been angry, or disappointed, but he knew he had been given the choice, and God had helped make the decision for him.

With no thought of regret or remorse, Thomas Green, former captain in the United States Navy, and a devout follower of Samuel Rawlins, turned the F-14 Tomcat around and headed straight toward his pursuers. He released the clip on his oxygen mask and started saying the Lord's Prayer as he pointed the Tomcat's nose at the flight leader and opened fire with his rotary cannon. To his surprise, the barrel started its electrically driven spin, but no twenty-millimeter rounds came out of the rotating barrel. Green smiled and shook his head, not feeling betrayed in the least. After all, he thought, the mission parameters were such that his trail could not lead back to McCabe or Rawlins. Their work was far from complete, while his duty to God was.

Green closed his eyes a split second before six Chinese-made Luoyang PL-12 active-radar-guided missiles slammed into his Tomcat, scattering small pieces over the Sea of Japan.

# 8

## BERLIN, GERMANY

The four men listened to the BBC radio broadcast and heard the news just after midnight in Berlin. None of them could believe the audacity and firepower the unseen forces were bringing to bear. Jack and the others knew now that it had to be McCabe behind what was happening. The memory of the crated weapons systems haunted the men as they sat listening to the report on the loss of life involved in the Chinese incident.

"These nuts are serious," Everett said, staring out of the windshield at the darkened street beyond.

"It seems to me that all of these governments would be more than ready to stop this foolishness and cooperate now that people are dying for nothing," Ellenshaw said from the backseat, as he stared without interest at his McDonald's cheeseburger.

"You'd think," Jack said, as he adjusted the small dome light. He had begun reading the file the German commando had delivered to him. "You'll soon learn, Charlie, that once a course of action has been initiated by any government, it's harder to stop than an avalanche." Jack stopped talking when he came across a picture captioned "1947—Spandau." He saw the face he had been looking for. It was a group photo of sixteen American officers lined up in front of the Spandau military prison.

"Here's our boy," Jack said, as he slid the photo out of the file and handed it to Everett.

"That's him, all right, and I'll be damned if he doesn't look as familiar as he did before. He's a lieutenant colonel, I can see that. But I can't see his shoulder patch. The commanding officer of the prison is listed, but his staff isn't."

"Here's the list of the only seven prisoners ever kept there," Collins said, passing the list to Carl, who handed the photo to Golding and Ellenshaw in the backseat. "Notice something odd?"

Everett read the list aloud. "Rudolf Hess, life sentence, died 1987. Walther Funk, life sentence, released 16 May 1957. Erich Raeder, life sentence, released 1955. Albert Speer, twenty-year sentence, released 1966. Baldur von Schirach, twenty-year sentence, released 1966. Konstantin von Neurath received a fifteen-year sentence but was released in 1954. Admiral Karl Dönitz served a ten-year term and was released in 1956." Everett scanned the rest of the original roster and he indeed noticed something. "No mention of our boy Joss Zinsser."

"Quite an omission, don't you think?" Jack asked.

"Well, we know he was there. Why would someone erase his name from the list of prisoners?"

"Simply to make what we're currently attempting that much harder," Collins answered as he turned back and looked at Pete. "We need Europa."

"That means returning to the plane, Jack. That could be a little dangerous, at least until your friend clears the way for us."

"We can't wait. We need to know who this American lieutenant colonel is."

"Well, get me to the plane and we'll take a shot at it," Pete said, looking over at an excited Ellenshaw, who reached out and lightly elbowed Pete.

"You see what I mean. We're in danger constantly with these two, and it only gets better."

Golding gave Ellenshaw a look and a brief smile that never touched any other part of his face. He nodded and looked out of his window as Captain Everett started the car. He saw Charlie Ellenshaw's face reflected in the glass and noted that the rumors about crazy Charlie were accurate—he was indeed crazy.


An hour later Jack stood next to the main gate at Tempelhof International Airport as Everett, Golding, and Ellenshaw watched from the shadows. The private portion of the airport was guarded by what appeared to be military personnel and Collins knew the security situation had changed since the attack in Berlin the day before, necessitating the change in airport status. Jack hissed through his teeth as he realized that, without the use of deadly force against the soldiers, there would be no entering from that area. He turned and ducked back into the shadows of a hangar that lined the fenced-in area.

"Forget about the gate," he said as he approached Everett and the others.

"How about this?" Everett asked, lightly tapping an aluminum building that housed a private aviation company.

Collins looked it over but saw that there was no window or door access on this side of the secured area.

"Not unless we have a blow torch or hacksaw."

"I'm sure the owner would be very put out if you damaged his building," a voice said from the darkness.

Jack relaxed when he recognized Sebastian Krell, who eased out of the shadows of the building next door.

"Damn, you're getting better at that," Collins said.

"I had a good teacher." Krell removed the dark mask and shook Jack's hand. He nodded at the others. "Those are my men at the gate. I told the airport security department we would be running a drill for the next three hours, so I suggest that since you're an hour late you board your aircraft and get the hell out of Berlin before one of my brethren in law enforcement blows your ass back to the States."

Collins slapped Krell on the shoulder. "Hang out awhile until we get airborne?"

"That was the plan." Sebastian looked at all four men. "Now look, you have an authorized aircraft next to your own. We're running a check on it at this time, and we can't just board it, so we don't know who it belongs to."

"Why do you mention that?" Everett asked as he felt for the comfort of the nine-millimeter under his shirt.

"Because, Captain Everett, the aircraft's pilot, like your own, never left the plane after landing two days ago. We can't get a view inside and I neglected to bring our heat-sensing equipment."

"Okay, at least you're giving us a start," Jack said. "Shall we?" he asked the others as he turned for the gate.

"We will cover your team from the tarmac, staying out of sight." Sebastian took Jack's hand and they shook, then Collins went toward the gate. "*Auf Wiedersehen*, old friend."

As the commando team, camouflaged in airport security garb, waved them inside the gate, Jack also felt for his nine-millimeter.

"Pete, Charlie, if anything happens, get the hell out of here and run back to where we left Sebastian."

"But—" Charlie started to say.

"But nothing, get the hell back," Everett answered for Jack.

"All right, but under protest," Ellenshaw said.

As they found the tarmac and the silhouette of their aircraft, Jack slowed and allowed his senses to take hold. He saw the neighboring plane and its darkened interior. Then his eyes switched to their own aircraft. He saw the cockpit cabin lights on but no movement. He figured the plane's Air Force personnel were in the back asleep. They had been ordered to stay put for three days while the ground team was in the city. A six-day supply of food had been stored onboard because Jack had known they might be traveling to more than one continent on this investigation. When he didn't feel any eyes on him other than those of Sebastian and his nine men, Collins waved Everett up the portable stairs. He saw Carl tap on the door with the flat of his hand.

Ellenshaw and Golding were nervously looking around them, even scanning the high control tower a mile and a half distant.

The door opened and Jack relaxed when he saw the United States Air Force captain looking sleepy-eyed and surprised to see Carl.

"Okay, guys, up the stairs, quickly," Jack said, as he continued to study the white-painted aircraft next to their own. As he did he saw one of the window blinds raise about six inches and then lower again. Collins hurriedly took the steps two at a time and then closed and secured the large door. "Captain, warm this thing up and preflight us for London for now."

The sleepy pilot shook his copilot and engineer awake and then turned to Collins and the others, who had shocked them with their bruised and dirty bodies.

"It'll take us thirty minutes, Colonel, and that's rushing it. Without filing the flight plan in person, we're breaking about six hundred different rules."

"We have a friend who will get us clearance. Just get her done, Captain. We don't have much time. In case you didn't notice, we're wanted for mass murder."

The captain turned and with his copilot and engineer entered the cockpit.

Jack ran a hand through his hair and gestured to Everett. "Carl, keep your eye on our mysterious friend next door."

"Aye," he said, as he went to the emergency door behind the cockpit and looked out into the darkness.

"Doc, you and—"

Pete and Ellenshaw had already disappeared into the communications area of the plane, and Golding was already connected to and giving orders to Europa. They had completed the uplink to the secure computer system. Jack went to join them. The lights flickered as the pilot switched over to internal systems. The copilot left the plane to disconnect the ground power source, leaving the door behind him ajar. While the door was not secured, Jack pulled his nine-millimeter and kept it at his side.

"Europa, scan the selected photo from Spandau Prison, Germany, year 1947. The object of investigation is the lieutenant colonel second from the right in the front row of officers."

Jack watched Pete insert the photo from the file into the scanner. His eyes went to the large monitor placed on the aircraft's wall.

"Scanning," Europa said, in her ever-present sexy voice. "Dr. Golding," she replied almost immediately, "there is no record of this lieutenant colonel in the archival accounts at Spandau Prison in the time frame given."

"Damn!" Pete said, as he looked at the blowup of the photo on the screen.

"Europa, can you scan the uniform of the officer in question and find out if there are any identifying insignia or shoulder patches?" Jack asked, leaning closer to the monitor. "In particular, the lapel area of the jacket."

"Yes, Colonel Collins."

Jack watched as Europa started blowing the photo up into larger sections, scrambling and then descrambling the image. It finally locked on the area Jack had interest in.

"I'll be damned," Pete said, as the image cleared. "It was there the whole time. All we needed was a magnifying glass."

Collins saw the silverfish-looking cross on the colonel's left lapel.

"A priest?"

"Europa, is there any record of religious personnel stationed at Spandau?" Jack asked, starting to put a face on his developing theory.

Europa started sending a series of differing faces across the screen, pushing each photo into the upper left corner of the monitor with names and ranks and service country. The only country not represented was the Soviet Union, for obvious reasons. The man in the original photo wasn't among those listed.

"We have two Catholic priests, three Episcopal priests, and five Baptist ministers listed as being assigned Spandau duties in that one year, but still nothing on the man in the photo."

Jack placed his hands on Pete's shoulders as he tried to think. Then he had an idea.

"Europa, Spandau Prison didn't start housing prisoners of war until 1946, but there had to be a transition team stationed at that facility during the trial for preparations for criminal transfer. Is there a list of personnel that interviewed each prisoner before being transferred from Nuremberg?"

Europa only took a second to delve into U.S. Army, British and French forces, and Soviet legal personnel files before a long list appeared.

"Come on Europa, follow along," Pete scolded the system, "please break the list down to American religious personnel or counselors."

Europa didn't respond; it was as if Pete had hurt her feelings as the photos and file names started dropping from the screen. They were left with two pictures, one a captain who was assigned as a Roman Catholic priest and the other a Baptist minister from Gillette, Wyoming, Lieutenant Colonel William T. Rawlins. The pictures from 1947 matched. The reason Rawlins wasn't listed as being stationed at Spandau was because all he had done was examine and interview each prisoner before their arrival at the prison as to their religious needs. He had only been at Spandau for the one day as the prisoners arrived, and that was when the picture of the new staff was taken.

"That name is very familiar," Ellenshaw and Pete said at almost the same time.

"Almost as familiar as the man's face, wouldn't you say?" Jack asked as he leaned over and instead of asking Europa a question, he typed it in with the keyboard.

As Golding and Ellenshaw watched the monitor, a videotaped segment flashed onto the screen and both scientists were amazed at what Jack had figured out before they themselves had even asked the right question.

"Unbelievable," Ellenshaw said.

"You mean to say that the man here, this Samuel Rawlins, the evangelist, is this colonel's son?" Pete asked with incredulity etching his voice.

"Yes," Jack said. "And also the man that is most vociferous and adamant about us not going to the Moon."

"What are you suggesting here, Colonel?" Ellenshaw asked.

Collins sat up straight and watched the soundless image on the monitor as the man on the world stage slammed his fists into the pulpit and screamed about something they couldn't hear, but Jack knew the man's tirade was directed at the president and the men and women attempting the excursion to the lunar surface, and that possibly meant Sarah and his two men. He watched the man as he delivered his words. Pete reached out and was about to turn up the volume but Collins stayed his hand and just watched the gesturing of the Reverend as he spoke.

"I believe we are looking at the man whose father discovered the truth and the whereabouts of Operation Columbus, and passed along not only the secrets of seven hundred million years ago, but also the reason why it was in their best interest to cover it up."

"Wait," Pete said turning around to look at Jack. "You're saying that this man knows where the artifacts from 1945 are buried?"

"No, I'm saying he and his father own the land where the artifacts are buried. And not only that, I believe our good friend McCabe is working for him."

"He is one of the five richest men in the world," Ellenshaw offered.

"A lot to protect if people saw Columbus and its artifacts as an alternative to the Genesis account in the Bible," Collins said as he finally looked away from the silver-haired man on the monitor.

"But, Colonel, religion is all faith-based, that shouldn't have a bearing on what people perceive as threats to their beliefs," Pete countered. "Besides, seven hundred million years ago would have thrown off the evolutionary scale somewhat. I mean, come on, that's a long time before the birth of the dinosaurs to the coming of the mammals."

"Normally, yes, you're right. The more forward-thinking religions are not frightened by new discoveries and theories; after all, they believe that God created everything, even you two."

Ellenshaw nodded his head in agreement but Pete still wasn't convinced.

"Pete, we need to get this to Niles so he can talk to the president. I think the FBI should be brought into this as soon as possible before this maniac attempts another attack."

Pete agreed and was about to send a message through Europa to Niles Compton when Everett called from the front.

"Jack, this doesn't look good, we have company."

Pete, Ellenshaw, and Collins looked out the nearest window and saw men running down the portable staircase attached to the plane next to theirs. Jack cursed just as the aircraft's engines started to whine. He was about to shout toward the cockpit when the first bullets struck the fuselage and the window they were looking through exploded inward, sending glass and plastic into the cabin.

As quickly as the shooting started, it stopped. Everett had sealed the door only to realize that the copilot was still outside.

Jack chanced a peek through one of the windows, then he noticed something that gave him pause as he tried to figure out what was different. The angle of the aircraft had changed. It was a small but perceptible difference.

"Jack, if I didn't know any better—" Everett started to say.

"They shot our tires out on the right side."

Everett looked back from the doorway just as the pilot, hunched over in case they received any more gunfire, duck-walked down the aisle.

"I just shut the engines down, Colonel. We're not going anywhere. We lost the tires on the right side and the nose wheel."

"Take cover," Collins said. "We're not exactly sure who we're dealing with here." He ducked his head into the communications room. "You two, stay down," he said to Golding and Ellenshaw, who had anticipated the order and were already hidden underneath the radio console.

"Jack, we have movement on the left side of the plane. Wait, it looks like Sebastian. Damn, he has his hands up and he's speaking with someone. Crap, I think they're German SWAT."

Collins hunched as low as he could and joined Everett on the left side of the 727. He chanced a quick look and saw that, indeed, Sebastian had his hands raised in the air. His eyes narrowed as he saw the black Nomex uniform and the gold German lettering on the back that said "Polizei."

"Mr. Everett, I think we've been had."

"Colonel Collins, I wholeheartedly agree with your assessment. You think your friend set us up?"

"No, it's not in him. I think he's trying save our lives."

As Jack spoke, Sebastian handed over his automatic weapon and accepted a bullhorn from the police officer. He took a few steps toward the plane and then held the device to his mouth.

"Colonel Collins, I am to inform you that your aircraft has been disabled and that you are surrounded." Sebastian glanced over at the man watching him closely. "The Berlin police are guaranteeing your safety if you and your men exit the aircraft." Sebastian lowered the bullhorn and took another five steps toward the plane. He looked up at the darkened windows. "There's nothing I can do for you now, Jack. Give up and we'll work at getting you out of custody, even if I have to go to the chancellor myself."

Jack cursed under his breath and then glanced back at Golding and Ellenshaw.

"Pete, you and the Doc have exactly thirty seconds to destroy that motherboard in the computer link. Set up a tapeworm or whatever you do, but make sure no one can get into Europa from this end."

"Yes, Colonel," Pete said as he reached up and pulled the laptop down to his level and started typing commands.

"Aren't we going to fight?" Ellenshaw said, with as much bravado as he could muster.

"They're cops, Doc," Collins said, holding out his hand. "We don't shoot cops. Now give me that gun you're trying to hide. These boys will not hesitate to shoot your skinny ass to pieces."

Ellenshaw angrily reached for his nine-millimeter. Then, as if he were letting a favored relative go to his doom, he slid the weapon across the aisle toward Jack.

"Okay, Everett, open that emergency door."

Everett stood, safed his own weapon, and turned the handle to the door, cracking it open. Then he tossed the nine-millimeter out onto the steel steps. Jack tossed him his and Ellenshaw's weapons and Carl tossed his out also.

"Now, Doc, give me Pete's weapon, the one you have on you, before I toss you out on the tarmac." Jack turned and looked at the shocked Ellenshaw.

Charlie angrily safed Pete's weapon and then tossed it to Collins.

"I told you he wouldn't forget," Pete said as he kept typing in commands. "Done, Colonel. The memory is totally clean," Pete said as he lowered the laptop and hit enter.

Jack stood and went to the door. He tossed the last weapon out through the crack as Everett held it open.

"Is the arrest warrant for me only?" Jack called through the door.

"The major here says he has warrants for all of you, even the pilot and copilot. Jack, we'll get you out of this. You have my word."

Collins nodded and Everett held the door open as the colonel stepped outside into the night with hands raised. Everett, Pete, the pilot, engineer, and then Ellenshaw, looking like a crazed old-time gangster, followed.

The Event Group's mission to Germany had been stopped dead in its tracks as the angry Berlin police took the men into custody.

Half a mile away, the Mechanic lowered his glasses and shook his head. He felt that the outcome, while acceptable, was far from an assurance that this American was out of the picture. This man Collins seemed to have nine lives. He watched as the Americans were roughly searched by the police for hidden weapons. While Collins was on the ground, his head turned toward the darkness and the Mechanic was surprised. It was if Collins was staring right at the shadowy position where he stood.

"You do know I am here," the Mechanic whispered to himself. "Don't you, my friend?"

## CHURCH OF THE TRUE FAITH,
## LONG BEACH, CALIFORNIA

"Amen!" declared Reverend Rawlins. "And may the will of God prevail!"

He mopped the sweat from his brow and took a deep breath and turned away from the congregation.

Standing in the wings were his two daughters, the younger of whom came out on cue as the music started playing and the choir began to sing. The older, Laurel, watched her father as he clapped his hands and began ascending to where she stood. He clapped and smiled until he reached her and then accepted his usual towel and glass of sparkling water. He drank deeply as he wiped the sweat from his face and neck.

"So, did you learn anything from your little trip?" he asked softly, hiding his anger at the lack of success in Germany. The death toll should have been much higher, and the man who had been framed for the attack wasn't dead, only under arrest.

"It's not what I learned, it's what I saw," Laurel said. She turned and stepped away from her father.

"And that is?" he asked, giving the empty glass away and accepting the robe as it was placed over his shoulders. He nodded his head to indicate that the young girl who was acting as his valet that night could leave his presence. The music in the cathedral was rising to a deafening crescendo.

Laurel stepped toward her father and tied the belt of his robe tightly around his waist.

"That we are not being aggressive enough. James and his intricate plan will only slow down the attempts at getting to the Moon, not stop them, as was proved today. One of the Chinese missions may still succeed."

"I think two out of three is acceptable." He looked down at his daughter, who was holding his blue eyes with her own. "McCabe is doing exceptionally well, and I would have thought you would have given your lover far more credit."

Laurel turned away and watched her little sister's unbridled enthusiasm as she led the final moments of the worship service.

"We need a far more dramatic statement than shooting down a bunch of rockets that have just as much chance at failure at takeoff as we have of shooting them down."

"What are you getting at?"

"You said it yourself not a few days ago. We need to eliminate the driving force, at least on the American side."

Rawlins smiled for the first time since he had seen the drop in attendance.

"Eliminate the driving force? Even though McCabe said it would be a mistake?"

"He's timid, and what's most important here is the fact that he is not family. Even more important than that—he's not a true believer in our cause. His cause is money and survival, not the sanctity of God's written word. He is a Judas waiting for his reward."

"And how would we achieve such a plan? You forget, daughter, that our motives are somewhat in accordance with McCabe's. We're the real hypocrites here."

"The Mechanic says he has lost faith in his own cause, but I sense he has not. My plan would involve him, a man of devout beliefs but also a man who has come to doubt those around him. A man who now says he is in it for the money like his boss, McCabe."

"You believe he has the will and the desire to see that God prevails here?"

"More than that, he sees this as a chance to right his cause. He will do what I ask." She turned and put her arms around her father. "Chaos will be to our benefit, and it will also place a dear friend in the highest office in the land. At the same time, after the Mechanic has done our bidding, he will continue on as our fall guy."

"And McCabe?" he asked, knowing Laurel's answer long before she voiced it.

"I think as soon as his Houston and Cape Canaveral missions are complete, and the second gallery inside the mine is reopened, we'll allow him to remove any weaponry and technology from the mine. Then he will cease to be an asset to our cause. Just empty baggage that needs to be left on the ground."

Rawlins smiled and felt better about the events of the day, even more so because his sermon had relaxed him and renewed his own enthusiasm about keeping Operation Columbus under wraps until his corporations could cash in on the technologies discovered so long ago.

"Make your plans and include your offer to our friend the Mechanic. Then we'll see if he's a true man of God. Show me something in two days."

## EVENT GROUP COMPLEX, NELLIS AIR FORCE BASE, NEVADA

Niles Compton watched the experiment unfold.

The mineral-encrusted rocks recovered from the CIA vaults were in water and the steam they were producing was actually growing in pressure. The test had been running for thirteen hours with a steady increase of heat emanating from the meteorites.

"They are truly remarkable," Virginia Pollock said as she stood behind the glass with Niles. "If the Chinese and the Russians have samples, they know their capabilities. I suspect that with these small stones alone we could run an entire power generation plant."

"The long-term effects?" Niles asked, watching as the steam inside the clear glass chamber channeled into a small generator.

"We can't know that yet," Virginia said. She watched her boss closely. "What are you thinking?"

Niles turned away from the thick glass separating them from the laboratory and fixed Virginia with a questioning look.

"Meteorites—think about the word, Virginia. They came here as meteorites. That would mean that the space body they once belonged to may not exist today. What if the planetary body they originated from exploded, not because of some interstellar incident, but because this element is so unstable?"

"That would call for too much speculation at this time," she countered, turning back and watching the needle on the power gauge rise by increments.

"You're seeing what I'm seeing. No power source actually gains in intensity after expending as much energy as these stones. They're gaining power, even as we attempt to drain it."

"It could level off, just like our nuclear fuel, at least to a controllable level," Virginia countered.

"As you just said, that calls for too much speculation at this time. I want the experiment terminated for the time being."

"But Niles, we have an opportunity here to—"

"Terminate the experiment, Virginia," Niles said as an assistant stepped through the observation room doorway and handed him a small piece of paper. Niles hesitated while he made sure Virginia understood her orders.

"Very well, we'll start a controlled shutdown," she said, turning for the door.

"Niles." The president spoke from a secure hookup. "I've spoken directly to the German chancellor and he knows the colonel is right in the middle of a frame-up. However, at the moment, with the video evidence and the two claymores found in the U.S. Air Force jet, the chancellor is between a rock and a hard place. He would get crucified if he released the American believed responsible for over a hundred deaths."

"How soon?"

"The FBI says they can probably come up with something to give the *German* chancellor a reason to free him, at least on bail and as a personal favor to me, in three weeks. Captain Everett is being extradited to Ecuador to face his charges there. Even when Collins is released, the Ecuadorians will be there ready to extradite him also. It's a big goddamn mess, Niles."

"I want my two scientists back. Or are they going to charge them too?" Niles asked, his anger at the situation finally cracking his stoic facade.

"They're being released this afternoon. They haven't any evidence against them, although my FBI sources tell me they are far more trouble than either Collins or Everett."

"That I can believe. Has Jack spoken to our envoy in Berlin?"

"He refuses to talk to anyone, other than to pass along a message to you through the embassy. He said to check out the Faith Channel on television tonight. He said all roads lead to the Lord."

Niles looked away from the small camera and thought a moment.

"I hope you know what the hell that means, because as far as I'm concerned these fundamentalist protesters outside my window are just about all the religion I can handle at the moment."

"I haven't the vaguest idea what the colonel means, but I will—"

That was as far as Niles got as a tremendous swaying motion struck his office and alarm bells started jangling. Dust and debris fell from the ceiling and the lights flickered and went out. The overhead fluorescents flashed and then came back on.

"Jesus, I just got this place back together!" Niles shouted as he looked at the camera. "I'll call you back!"

The monitor went dead.

Compton ran out of his office and saw that the false ceiling in the outer office had caved in. His assistants were struggling to free one of their own from the debris.

"Emergency extraction and fire teams to Level 23, Nuclear Sciences Laboratory 211. This is no drill," announced the calming voice of Europa.

"Are you handling this?" Niles asked on his way to the elevators.

The three assistants had just pulled the fourth from the soft ceiling tiles and nodded that they had it under control.

"The elevators automatically shut down, sir!" one of them called out, but Niles entered the rounded doors anyway.

"Europa, Director Override 1 Alpha. Activate Elevator 3, Level 23." he said calmly, placing his entire hand on the security glass next to the door to have it scanned.

"Yes, Director Compton," came the reply as the doors slid closed. "Director Override 1 Alpha accepted." The elevator started moving downward at a dizzying speed.

"Are the emergency teams responding?"

"Security, fire, and rescue teams are currently arriving on station."

Niles leaned against the far wall of the elevator. "Cave-in or explosion?" he asked, already knowing the answer.

"Explosion was detected by a higher than normal rise in laboratory temperature and vibratory analysis. This was confirmed by on-site personnel at 2210 and 13 seconds."

The elevator came to a stop and before the doors opened Niles could hear the alarms and the shouts of rescue workers; he braced himself for the worst. The doors slid open and the car was inundated with smoke and heat. Niles placed a handkerchief to his mouth and nose, and then stepped out into the chaos that was the long, curving hallway. He grabbed the first man he came to, whom he recognized as Sergeant Gomez, a Marine attached to Jack's security department and the on-duty security chief this afternoon.

"Report, Sergeant?" Niles asked, while holding the man's arm.

"Not clear yet, sir. We have a lot of people down and a situation in the lab that's out of control."

"Okay, first off, let's get these damn alarms shut off, so we can hear." The director slapped the sergeant on the back.

Niles turned and made his way to the lab doors, which had been blown off their reinforced hinges. Compton had just left this lab twenty minutes before and now nothing was recognizable. He saw two paramedics working on someone in the observation room, which was still smoldering from the blast. His eyes widened when he saw it was Virginia Pollock. She lay on her back with blood coursing down her face. She was fighting with the men trying to work on her, slapping at the hands that were attempting to give her oxygen. Niles ran to her side and kneeled down.

"What happened?" he asked. He became worried when he saw that Virginia's left eye was severely swollen shut and that she had at least a ten-inch gash along her scalp. Virginia slapped away the oxygen mask and tried to fix on Niles with her good eye.

"Reroute . . . the nuclear core mud to . . . the lab, we . . . have . . . to . . . drown it . . . concrete, through . . . the pipes. Out . . . of . . . control, energy . . . still . . . building." Virginia grabbed Niles by the shirt collar.

"I understand, treat it as a reactor meltdown, correct?" he asked, worried his friend and the assistant director for the Event Group wasn't going to make it.

Virginia could only nod her head once before she passed out. The paramedics lifted her onto a gurney and started on their way to the elevators. Niles watched her for a moment and then stepped into the destroyed lab. He saw men with fire hoses and the complex's engineering corps as they tried to see into the intense burning in the center of the room. As Compton looked on he saw numerous men and women who had been slammed into the walls and furniture by the blast. He found the Corps of Engineers captain who oversaw the Event complex, including its levels and nuclear reactors.

"We're going to a priority scramble of the core reactor on Level 120. We can't operate the system because we have to take the redundant safety equipment off-line there and pump it up here. Start mixing the mud and the concrete. We have to bury this lab before those damn rocks eat their way through to our own power plant. We could end up blowing half of Las Vegas away."

"Yes, treat it as a reactor meltdown," the engineer said loudly. "It will take twenty minutes to reroute the piping."

"Get to it!" Niles said, but the engineer had already left, grabbing some of his people as he did.

Compton looked around and knew this lab would be buried forever in a cocoon of mud and concrete. That was the only way he could think of to cut the oxygen off from the meteorites. As he looked around, he saw the broken bodies. He ran to a young woman pinned under a large lab table. Niles flipped it over but he could see she was far past helping. He fell to his knees and lifted the girl up. He struggled to carry her out of the smoldering lab, cursing his shortsightedness for the disaster that had claimed more of the Event Group staff.

## JOHNSON SPACE CENTER, HOUSTON, TEXAS

Sarah had just finished up with the six geologists who had been chosen for the three flights. They knew what to look for and how to recover samples if they had to, but what was more important, they had learned how *not* to handle the specimens. No water, no oxygen.

Sarah left the classroom sporting the blue coveralls that came complete with the new mission patch on the left shoulder—an eagle holding three rockets in its talons, with the words "Dark Star" emblazoned in gold lettering. Sarah saw Ryan and Mendenhall walking toward her. Ryan looked distraught and Will looked as if he were trying to console him.

"Hey guys, what's up," Sarah asked.

Will stopped and Ryan was so preoccupied he ran into him. Then he looked up and raised his chin in recognition of Sarah.

"Oh, Mr. I-Can-Fly-Anything crashed the lunar lander sim again. He killed us all for the thirtieth time. The thing he doesn't realize is that he's only the backup pilot on a mission that's a backup to two other missions." Will turned to face Ryan. "It just doesn't matter. We won't leave the space station. Can you get that through your head?"

"It's not that," said Ryan. "If those Air Force jocks can land that damn thing, I sure as hell can."

Sarah smiled and slapped Ryan on the back. "They've been at the simulator for the last three years, Jason. You've had less than a week. I think you'll do in a pinch. Besides, Will's right. Our team is third in line. Odds are we get a nice trip to the International Space Station and that's it. A nice view for a few days and then a shuttle ride home."

"Forget it," Ryan said to get a change of subject. "What's the word on the colonel and Mr. Everett?"

Sarah lost her smile. "The last we heard, Jack was in jail in Berlin, Carl is being extradited back to Ecuador, and there's not a damn thing that Niles or the president can do about it."

"Jesus, we're stuck here training for something that will never happen and we lose both our commanding officers in two friendly countries. What in the hell is going on?" Mendenhall said as he turned. "Come on, Jason, we have emergency procedures to run with Captain Harwell."

"How is the captain faring?" Sarah asked about their mission commander.

Will stopped and faced Sarah. "He's a by-the-book stick-in-the-mud."

"But he doesn't crash the lander, that says something for him," Ryan quipped.

Will smiled for the first time since Sarah met them in the hallway.

"Yeah, at least *someone* can fly the damn thing."

"Hey, are we going to get together and watch the ESA launches tonight?" Sarah asked the men.

"If we survive the emergency training, sure," Jason said as they turned and left. Sarah looked at her watch and decided to call the complex to get an update on Jack.

She walked to the security station and asked the airman for the phone. She was notified that her call would be monitored for security reasons and Sarah bit her tongue about what they could do with their eavesdropping, but kept silent and only smiled. She was handed a cordless phone and she watched as the air policeman turned on the recording device. She punched in the number, and then a tone sounded. She tapped in her security code. The phone rang once and Europa came on the line.

"The department you are trying to reach has experienced an emergency situation and is unable to take your call at this time." The phone was disconnected.

Sarah handed the phone back and turned away, biting her lower lip.

Things weren't right in any aspect of their missions, and it seemed as if the fates were working against them.

"Jack, I wish we were all just back at home."

## POLIZEIPRÄSIDIUM (POLICE HEADQUARTERS), BERLIN, GERMANY

The massive headquarters had been built in 1945 and was now the main building for the German Federal Police. Jack was caged on the fifth floor, and thus far had been questioned by the Germans, the Ecuadorians, and Interpol, and that wasn't counting his own embassy. He sat quietly and told them that he had nothing to do with either the bombing in downtown Berlin or the murders of the couple in Ecuador. The military attaché assigned to the embassy in Berlin had been in twice, telling Jack that he shouldn't even have said what he had said; he should have just remained quiet. The attaché told him that it would be all right. The president was working on getting him out of there, but things were a little iffy at the moment. He could tell by the way the man refused to look him in the eye that political pressure on the German government may not be going as well as the attaché was letting on.

At the moment Collins sat on a cold, hard steel bunk and looked at the large hot dog and sauerkraut they had given him for dinner. He took a deep breath and sat the tray on the bed.

He saw a passing guard and called out, "Hey, can I take this food out to the kitchen and get something else?"

The German looked at Jack, not totally understanding what he was asking.

"You, know, maybe go out and get a hamburger or something?"

The guard finally caught on that the American was joking with him. He shook his head and walked away.

"Can I at least watch the space launch?" he called out.

The guard just kept walking. Collins shook his head, feeling helpless. He figured Carl was on his way to Ecuador. The Germans had removed him about eight hours before and he hadn't returned. He was now thinking about Golding and Ellenshaw, hoping they were on their way home with the slim pickings of a report they had pieced together. He was also hoping that the military attaché passed on his cryptic message to the State Department, and that Niles received it. That should start things rolling in the right direction, leading to the good Reverend Rawlins, especially since his Columbus investigation looked to be all but over.

Jack looked around the jail cell and knew that given time and planning he could make a break for freedom, but not without the use of deadly force. He wasn't about to gain the fresh air again by killing policemen who were just doing their jobs.

"Colonel Collins, it is time for your washing." The guard, whom Collins had never seen before, looked frustrated at his English. He looked away and then quickly back through the bars of the jail cell. "It is shower time," the guard finally managed. "Will you please follow me?" he finished, waving down the block as the cell door opened.

Collins stood from his bunk and looked the guard over. The young man was larger than all the others he had seen thus far and was without a weapon of any kind, not even a nightstick like the others wore. Looking the boy over, Jack figured the kid didn't really need one. He was also the first man to use his military title. The guard gestured for Collins to step out.

"Please, Colonel, this way."

Jack did as he was instructed and stepped out of his cell.

"Think I can get a different color jumpsuit? Orange was never really my style."

The kid didn't respond to Jack's joke. He placed a firm hand on his back and easily pushed him forward. They went to an elevator and Collins started to wonder where he was really being taken. He knew there were showers on his block's floor, and from the way the guard acted it was as though he didn't care that he wasn't restrained in even the minimal sense of the word. Jack eyed the large kid again and saw that the uniform he wore was extremely tight-fitting. The cuffs of the blue jacket didn't make it quite to the wrists and the top collar button wasn't fastened underneath the black tie. The guard glanced over at him and Jack smiled, even though he started to get a soldier's sense of impending danger.

As the elevator doors opened, Jack saw that two men were waiting just outside. One was wearing an orange jumpsuit like himself, obviously a guest of the state, and the other man was a guard. The two security men nodded at each other as Jack was led from the elevator. As he walked out he noticed the jail house number on the prisoner's overalls and then Jack really started worrying—the number was the same as his own stenciled number on the left breast. He looked the prisoner over and saw that the man was dark-haired and almost exactly the same height and build as himself. Collins turned and looked at the two men as the elevator doors closed. His guard gave him a gentle shove in the back and he was moved along a long corridor.

The hackles on Jack's neck began to rise as the guard stepped closer in behind him. He reached out and placed a large hand on his right shoulder, stopping him short of a steel door to the right side of the hallway.

"Shower room?" Jack asked watching the kid's eyes.

"Colonel, I . . . was warned that you . . . may try something . . . dangerous to . . . us." The man fought for the right English words." But please, don't . . . not . . . yet?" the guard opened the door and gestured for Jack to enter the room.

As he stepped through the doorway, Jack saw a man with his back to him dressed in all-black clothing. He was eating from a plate. Then his eyes roamed to the back of the room and that was when he saw Pete Golding and Charlie Ellenshaw sitting quietly.

"Colonel," Charlie said, as he stood up along with Pete.

Jack was surprised to see the two scientists, but also worried that they had not been released as he was told they had been. Charlie stopped short of a handshake as the man eating the plate of food turned. Jack smiled finally when he saw Sebastian Krell. The commando put the plate down and stood. He adjusted the automatic weapon slung around his shoulder and looked from Collins to the man who escorted him to the office.

"Thank you. Sergeant. You'd better return that uniform before you bust out of it." The large commando looked at his watch. "We leave here in three minutes." Sebastian turned to face Jack and held out his hand. "Jonathan Dillinger I presume?"

Collins shook his friend's hand and then looked him over. "It's just John, and I hope my situation turns out better than Dillinger's did."

"That's yet to be determined, my friend." The two shook hands.

"What took you so long?" Jack asked, shaking hands with Ellenshaw and Golding.

"We had to wait for the president and the chancellor to come up with this plan. The major here finalized everything but we have very little time before our little ruse is discovered, because you are due to be arraigned in just eight hours. That's when the clock starts running," Pete said as Charlie handed Jack a new set of clothes.

"Your plane has been repaired and is awaiting our team," Sebastian said as he waited for Jack to change.

"Team?"

"It seems my ten men and I have been assigned to you by the chancellor. He doesn't need you caught again inside Germany. He and the president think we may be of service to you in something called Operation Columbus. The chancellor is in the same situation as your president. You see, all the astronauts for the ESA missions were trained in Cologne, and there are eight German scientists aboard the two Ariane rockets to be launched tonight. The fanatics here are charbroiling the chancellor over this. Thus you have us to assist you, even though our space programs are at odds."

Jack buttoned his new shirt and thought about what their next move would be. As he slipped on a windbreaker he looked to the German commando.

"Well, I think there may be more to the chancellor's and the president's motives than meets the eye, but I can't prove anything. Strange bedfellows for strange times, my friend," Jack said, looking at Sebastian. "Our mission is to make all these trips to the Moon a moot point. We need to uncover artifacts found by your government in the thirties and forties. These artifacts and even the mineral can be found right here on Earth. That, I suspect, is why your chancellor and my president have become close friends."

"Okay, I expect you will tell me everything. Where do we start this quest?" Sebastian asked.

"We'll start with, How do you feel about committing another jail break?"

"Well," Sebastian said, smiling, "it beats the hell out of training. Besides, I think I have an affinity for the criminal side of things."

"You know, I've come to the same conclusion about myself and my men," Jack said, slapping the German on the back. "Now, the ESA has men and women ready to die in a hurried mission to the Moon. Your government's listening to mine and now has second thoughts, but can't pull its astronauts without endangering the lives of their fellows. So your government is hedging its bet and going for the answer that is closer to home as well as the one on the Moon. The rest of the ESA is not, because they are not privy to this Operation Columbus intelligence. And where we start is right where Captain Everett has been taken—Ecuador."

Sebastian nodded and then leaned in so only Jack could hear his next words.

"Tell me something if you can, old man. Who are those two strange ducks? Just who the hell do you work for?"

Collins smiled as the sudden change of subject threw him for the briefest second, and then he looked the German commando in the eye.

"Number one, those two guys are among the most brilliant men in the scientific world. And in answer to your second question, you wouldn't believe me if I told you." He looked at Golding and Ellenshaw once again. "But you're right. They're two *very* strange ducks."

Jack and Sebastian walked from the room.

"May I ask where we are off to?" Pete inquired, following Sebastian and Collins through the door.

"Ecuador—Mr. Everett isn't in for a warm welcome there; I thought we may as well kill two birds with one stone. Get my man out of jail and then find out why someone is willing to kill so many people over a bunch of rocks and an old set of bones. That answer lies beneath the ground. And that, dear Professor Golding, is where we are going."

Ellenshaw hesitated a moment and grabbed Pete by the arm as Jack and Sebastian left the small office.

"It only gets better, Pete. You'll never want to stay at the complex again after this."

Golding watched Crazy Charlie leave. He shook his head and then followed.

"I find it is having the opposite effect on me. It makes me never want to get out of bed again."

It took only thirty minutes to get from police headquarters to Tempelhof Airport. While riding in the back of a two-and-a-half-ton Mercedes truck, the ten commandos, plus Jack, Pete, Ellenshaw, and the black ops team of Germans, checked their equipment. The chancellor wasn't going to send them out into the field lacking in firepower.

"I see you plan on running into trouble," Ellenshaw told Sebastian as the leader of the group placed two heavy caliber long-range sniper rifles back into their cases. The German looked up and held Charlie with his gaze for a moment without saying anything. Then he relaxed and sat back against the wooden bench as his other men finished the inventory of their own equipment.

"Dr. Ellenshaw, isn't it?" he finally asked.

Charlie just nodded his head, sending his white hair over his wire-rimmed glasses.

"Over a hundred German citizens were just murdered in the streets of Berlin. My chancellor is in a mood that dictates that we respond in kind to the people responsible. We didn't look for this trouble, but neither shall we run from it." Sebastian looked over at his old friend Collins. "Those days are over. No longer are we to sit out of world policies because of our past. We just saw what happens when we are perceived to be weak."

Jack nodded, not really caring for the ominous tone coming from a man he respected, especially since his words seemed to be directed at the man who assisted in his commando training.

"Ah, we are here," Sebastian said. He took hold of his large bag and then paused in front of Charlie. "Now the question is, Herr Doctor, are you prepared for the trouble we are going to run into or are you just along for the ride?"

Charlie's eyes didn't waver a moment as he returned the German's stare.

"Captain Everett is my friend. I respect him, as I do the colonel. I also have several other friends who are nearing a time when they too shall place their lives on the line if we fail to find out who is responsible and what they are hiding. So in essence—yes, I am prepared to give my life for my friends."

Sebastian handed out his pack to one of his men. Then he looked at Charlie again and nodded his head, not saying anything but making clear that the quirky little professor had given the right answer.

Jack also nodded as he turned and hopped down from the truck.

"Very eloquent, Charles," Pete said, as he stood in the back of the truck.

"Do you agree?" Charlie asked.

"By all means. Couldn't have said it better myself. But I wonder about one thing."

Charlie Ellenshaw stood and followed Pete to the back of the truck. "And that is?"

"Since we are all being brave and, as they say in the military, gung ho, how do we plan on not only breaking Mr. Everett out of jail and taking on the entire Ecuadorian government with fourteen men, but to do all of this in less than twenty-four hours before the U.S. launches the Moon missions?"

Ellenshaw didn't have an answer, so he just pointed out the back of the truck at the figure of the man standing next to the German. Jack Collins was watching the commandos load into the aircraft.

"I don't have an answer for you, Pete, except to say, I'll bet on that man right there."

## ILE DU DIABLE (DEVIL'S ISLAND), EUROPEAN SPACE AGENCY LAUNCH FACILITY, 2 MILES EAST OF KOUROU, FRENCH GUIANA

The three large ships had slipped in unnoticed since most of the French military presence was based on the mainland surrounding the ESA launch facility at Kourou. This is not to say that the French army had not sent out security details in the past three weeks to Devil's Island to make sure there were no intruders setting up camp at the old prison facilities. They had. The last had been a small ten-man French commando team sent there one hour prior to the final countdown of the two Ariane 7 rockets awaiting launch.

The two Ariane rockets were lined up as neatly as the three ships anchored just inside the main harbor at the ominous old prison. The ten-man team had walked unsuspectingly into far more firepower than they could handle. James McCabe shook his head as he looked at the bodies.

"They should have been far more cautious and less arrogant about their abilities," he said as he turned toward the Mechanic. "Are the men we are leaving here all understanding of their orders?"

"I have chosen these men personally. They will do their duty to Allah. They are, as you say, understanding of that duty, and are proud to bring down the infidels' attempt at mocking God. But I am surprised, James, that you find it so easy to send men to their deaths without a moment's hesitation."

McCabe looked the bearded Mechanic over. The man had set up the ambush of the French commandos with the expertise of someone who had far more formal training than he realized. During the brief exchange of gunfire, the Mechanic, with his thirty-man team recently flown in from northern Pakistan, had suffered only two dead and one wounded.

"I have been in the killing and sacrifice business for a long time. You should know that I chased you and your people for many months inside Iraq." McCabe looked at the Mechanic very closely. "You seem to have become more of your old self in the past few days. Are you seeing the light of Allah in your soul once more?" McCabe offered a slight smile.

The tall Mechanic didn't answer the insulting question. He just stepped away from the bodies of the French soldiers and nodded at his men.

"Take your stations and know that Allah is smiling down upon you this night."

The Mechanic was present at the demonstration put on by McCabe and the specialists he had working for Rawlins after the mine had been entered for the first time since the German army had vacated the site. One of the abandoned crates they found had contained one of the ancient weapons from the original German excavation. They had spent six months of hard work trying desperately to reverse-engineer the riflelike weapon, only to fail again and again. Then they had discovered the small satchel of meteorites that had been hidden away over 700 million years before. The properties were soon untangled and then the power source of the ore, or meteorite as the Germans had called it, had been discovered. The light weapon had performed magnificently as its bright blue light pierced solid stone, melting a three-inch steel plate. All of this in just a three-minute test. At the three-minute mark the weapon had burned out. But the source of the design's power had been uncovered and the Mechanic had started having a slow change of heart about the men he was working with. Knowing what his movement could do with that weapon had a profound effect on him.

Too bad they had left the weapon inside the mine, as he would have liked to have shown it to some very special people in Iran, Pakistan, and Afghanistan.

McCabe and the Mechanic watched the fire team as they ran into the old ruins of the reception center where prisoners were once processed for their eventual dispersal into the penal colonies on the different islands. McCabe smiled as the hum of a large generator filled the air as the four launchers were uncovered for the first time since they had been off-loaded. The Lavochkin OKB S-75, better known to NATO as the SA-2 Guideline, was a delightful bonus when McCabe and his men broke into the Raytheon Corporation's storage facility. The Russian-made Guideline was the latest and best version of the venerable surface-to-air missiles commonly known as SAMs. The American company had come into possession of the four weapons during a raid in 2006 on a well-defended warehouse in Taliban-controlled territory in Afghanistan. Once called upon to target B-52s in Vietnam, the Guideline's new mission would be to bring down two Ariane rockets carrying no fewer than twenty men and women. The weapon would be deadly at the short range required. As the nose cones of the four missiles rose above the shattered wall of the old administration buildings, McCabe was satisfied that the men chosen would do as ordered. He nodded and looked at the Mechanic.

"Shall we get out of here before the fireworks start?" he asked, not really expecting an answer. Then he did a double take as he saw something in the former terrorist's eyes he didn't like. He actually looked longingly at the shining white tips of the missiles as they rose into the air, as if he were contemplating staying behind. It didn't take long to have his suspicion confirmed.

"Perhaps they have not had enough training on when to turn on their radars. I think I should—"

"Get on the helicopter. We have little enough time as it is. They can handle it. You trained them on when to light up their radars."

The Mechanic looked from the missiles to his employer. The look told McCabe that the Mechanic was starting to have second thoughts about the way in which he was being rewarded for his duties. He realized there would be no virgins awaiting him in heaven upon his death, only scorn and ridicule from the true believers who had preceded him to the afterlife.

The Mechanic turned and boarded the waiting French-built Gazelle helicopter. With one last look at his unfolding plan, McCabe followed.

As soon as he settled into the backseat of the small helicopter, he put on a set of headphones and leaned forward to speak to the pilot.

"Remember, stay only a few feet off the water as we head east. We cannot be picked up on the ESA radar. They have Mirage fighters all over this area."

The pilot nodded as the twin turbines of the helicopter started their whine.

"Now, get me Los Angeles," he said, tapping on his microphone in a gesture that said he wanted to use the radio. McCabe only waited for a moment when his party was reached.

"The operation will commence in forty-five minutes," he said.

Doubtless with sabotage in the air now, precautions would be made.

But then, end runs around precautions were always part of any game of sabotage!

## EUROPEAN SPACE AGENCY CONTROL CENTRE, TOULOUSE, FRANCE

Philippe Gardenaux was watching the monitors and the telemetry stations. His control center's overall responsibility for the mission would take full effect as soon as the two Ariane missions cleared the two launch towers six thousand miles away in French Guiana. Until then he was a nervous bystander, as the ESA's most ambitious mission to date was only thirty seconds from reality. He had been named over two Germans and one Netherlander for the post of chief of flight operations. As he watched the commencement of the thirty-second countdown in Guiana, he wondered why the cooperation between his agency and the men and women at NASA had suddenly ceased. Even through icy relationships between the United States and other areas of the world, the space programs of both nations had always seemed to be off limits to petty political squabbles. All that had changed, and he suspected it was because of the mineral and the alien weaponry they were going after. He prayed that both nations as well as China would come to their senses.

". . . ten, nine, eight, seven, Ariane 1 has main engine start, four, three, two, Ariane 1 has full ignition start of solid fuel boosters, one, we have separation of restraining bolts and the clock is officially running."

Gardenaux watched at the tremendous power of Ariane 1 scrambled the picture momentarily. He and others switched their view to another monitor that showed the start of the launch from a half mile away. He saw the giant rocket start to lift free of the Earth and start its climb to the sky with its fifty-ton payload and ten astronauts. He watched as the Ariane cleared the top of the tower.

". . . two, we have booster start for Ariane 2," the announcement said from Guiana. "The clock is running."

Gardenaux moved his eyes over to another large monitor and saw the second mission to the Moon start gloriously from pad 3-b in Guiana. Another fantastic eruption of fuel and gases erupted from the tower structure as Ariane 2 started to rise into the sky as though it were chasing Ariane 1 to see which craft could achieve orbit first.

Gardenaux and every European citizen watching the launch clenched their fists and silently or vociferously cheered as the two giant rockets were fully free of the space port.

"Yes, go baby, go!" Gardenaux pushed the two missions into the black South

American sky with just his willpower. Then, as suddenly as the euphoria began it came crashing down as the first missiles were seen rising into that same dark sky as they started their run for the two Ariane mission platforms.

"No, no, no, no!" Gardenaux said, as he stepped out from behind his telemetry station.

"We are a go for roll maneuver on Ariane 1," came the announcement from Guiana.

"They don't even realize what's happening!" the French flight controller shouted.

## EUROPEAN SPACE AGENCY LAUNCH FACILITY, KOUROU, FRENCH GUIANA

The military aspect of the two *Ariane* missions reacted far faster than the scientific end. Four orbiting Mirage IIIs of the French air force streaked into the air a mile back from the first Ariane. The second four were trying desperately to chase Ariane 1 as it streaked to the ten-mile mark in altitude and was gaining fast. They saw the white fire of exhaust from the four SAM as they chased down the heavy beasts of the Ariane 7 like a lion against a wildebeest. The SAMs were locked on target and were relentless as they matched and then surpassed the speed of the French-made systems.

The first Mirage flared its wings as it passed between the first SAM and Ariane 2. The SAM tried to ignore the new radar flash in its seeker head but saw the French-built fighter as an obstacle and tried to swerve to the left as the Mirage placed itself between the climbing Ariane 7 and the SAM. It worked. The SAM clipped the wing of the Mirage and that was enough to send it tumbling thirty feet off course before its damaged brain told the missile to detonate. The Mirage and missile exploded at almost the same time as the second SAM targeted on the Ariane rushed through the falling debris.

The world watched as it merged with the twin set of six solid rocket boosters that encircled the base of the first stage. The SAM exploded only five feet from the outer casing of the solid fuel cells of the boosters, ripping into the thin aluminum and cardboard that lined the interior of the solid propellant boosters. The resulting explosions ripped into the first stage that carried the liquid fuel cells for the main engines of the Ariane 7, detonating the mix as it joined the combustion chambers for the engines. The resulting cataclysm sent the explosive shock wave up and into the second stage, where the fuel tanks were also ignited, and then that explosion in hit the third stage, the one carrying the lunar lander.

The Ariane 7 came apart in a gas cloud as bright as the sun. The power of the blast was felt as far away as San Francisco. Windows shook and pictures fell from walls. The detonation rocked the very sky as the crew capsule carrying the ten men and women evaporated. They never had a chance as the capsule separated from the third stage and was sent hurtling far out into the Pacific Ocean.

The third and fourth SAMs were having a far more difficult time catching their prey. Two Mirage fighters intercepted the third SAM with a heat-seeking missile, a snap shot that connected solidly with the Russian-made SAM, ripping it apart like a large piece of paper. That didn't matter in the end as the fourth SAM found its mark. It wasn't a hit at all, really. It was just a bee sting as the range of the SAM gave out. Sensing its low fuel state and the distance to the target, the SAM exploded fifty feet from the exhaust plume of Ariane 1. The outer casing and not the warhead is what struck all six of the solid rocket boosters, igniting fire plumes from the front, back, and sides of the large solid fuel cells.

Thinking quickly, and only because they were seconds away from an automated program sending out the impulse to separate the first and second stages, the pilot of Ariane 1 flipped the switch, bypassing the programmed separation. They saw the explosion of the rocket boosters. They saw the flash and gas release of the first stage from the second just as the debris from the solid boosters struck the fast-igniting second stage. The shrapnel tore into the lunar lander that was tucked away inside the third stage, but the Ariane continued to rise into the upper reaches of the atmosphere. Trailing far more than just the exhaust plume of the second stage, the mission flew on. With holes punched in the all-important second and third stages, Ariane 1 fought for its life to get into its natural element—space.

As the world watched, a second mission to the Moon was now limping its way along a shallow orbit where it was losing a battle to stay aloft an hour after achieving orbit. The Chinese had repaired their systems, but the ESA mission was now in serious doubt. They had lost ten men and women on Ariane 2, and now if they didn't do some fast patching they would lose everyone on Ariane 1.

The world was now wondering if God truly was angry.


## EVENT GROUP COMPLEX,
## NELLIS AIR FORCE BASE, NEVADA

Niles Compton watched as the doctors worked on Virginia Pollock. Her heart had stopped twice as they struggled to save her life. Three ribs had fractured and punctured both lungs. She was concussed and bleeding heavily inside her chest cavity. Normally she would have been transferred to the Nellis facilities or, if her condition warranted, to the far better facilities in Las Vegas. However, Virginia had run out of time and, luckily for the assistant director of the Event Group, two of the better surgeons in the Southwest had been recruited just after their retirement from Johns Hopkins and the UCLA Medical Center. They were on their first official visit to the complex for their initial orientation;

thus Virginia had the best care possible and she hadn't needed to be moved. Her surgery was being conducted in the medical clinic on Level 9.

Niles watched through the observation glass as the two men worked furiously to get the bleeding stopped.

"Sir?" Event Group Dr. Denise Gilliam said.

Niles cleared his throat and faced his staff doctor.

"Engineering said they have the mineral in total containment. They are now devising a way of getting it out of the complex by the heavy equipment elevator."

Niles just nodded his head without speaking. Denise placed her hand on his shoulder and squeezed.

"She's lucky. So many more weren't. Here's the list of who we lost." She held out a piece of paper.

Niles looked at it and turned away. He watched the two surgeons working on his friend.

"I've made the biggest error in judgment of my career in planning the Moon missions for the president. I'm sending men and women to gather, or stop this material from being recovered, when I just should have recommended a nuclear strike on that crater, no matter what we face in the future." He finally turned and faced Denise. "People are going to die and my arrogance designed it all."

Before Denise could say anything, one of the surgeons opened the sealed door and stepped out while removing his face mask.

"She'll make it. We managed to stop the bleeding, but we have to evacuate her to the surface as soon as we get her sewn up."

Niles swallowed and nodded his head. He found he had lost his voice as he was informed he wouldn't be losing one more person, at least for the rest of the day.

"Thank you, Doctor," Denise Gilliam said for Niles.

Compton turned away and walked a few feet away as the surgeon left the observation room. He put his hands in his pocket and looked up at the monitor, where Europa had placed the view of the events in the Nuclear Sciences Lab. He watched as the engineers and nuclear sciences people, Virginia's men and women, started taking core temperatures to confirm the cooling of the mud and concrete cocoon. As he watched, he found he wasn't seeing the destroyed lab; he was looking at the monitor itself. As Denise became concerned with his stillness, Niles ran from the observation room.

Compton practically sprinted for the elevators as men and women passed by with curious looks on their faces. They had never seen their director walk at even a fast pace before. As the elevator carried him back up to Level 7, his thoughts turned to the note that had been forwarded by Jack through the American embassy in Berlin. When the elevator doors finally opened, Niles ran into his office and past his assistants. Once inside the office he slammed into his seat and hit the intercom.

"Europa, bring up the Faith Channel on broadcast television please."

"Yes, Dr. Compton."

Niles watched the main screen monitor blaze to life and, a moment later, Compton was looking at the Reverend Samuel Rawlins as he treated his congregation to ridicule of the president of the United States and his blatantly obvious attempt at destabilizing the faith of billions across the globe.

As Niles watched, the good Reverend reminded him of the old films of Adolf Hitler as he screamed his manifesto to fanatical countrymen in 1939. As he watched, he thought about the attacks being launched against the efforts around the globe. This man couldn't be responsible; no one man could have that much reach without a government backing him. He had heard that Rawlins was rich beyond easy measurement, but even wealth couldn't provide a madman access to terrorist cells around the globe. They would disdain his American wealth. Niles's thought processes hit a snag as he thought the question over from another point of view. Terrorists around the globe and the fundamentalist wings of certain religions did have a common goal, the retardation of scientific advancement and the eventual withdrawal of anything that didn't match their interpretation of the future—the strict adherence to the Bible or the Koran.

Niles stood from his desk and approached the screen. He watched the white-suited Rawlins as he was joined onstage by a young woman of about sixteen. He introduced her as his younger daughter and swore he would protect her from the community of nonbelievers that threatened her future and the future of all true believers. He screamed for his followers to take action, to take the battle for the Lord to the steps of the White House.

At that moment Niles saw something that really caught his attention. Right in the middle of this tirade a dozen of his followers slowly stood and made their way from their seats. The camera view immediately switched back to Rawlins, who chose not to recognize the rebuke by his congregation, though Niles could see the large man stumble a bit as he hailed the calamity that had just befallen the ESA Moon shots. Instead of the large crowd cheering and applauding or shouting the amens that usually accompanied his outrageous pronouncements, the audience was silent. The Reverend stumbled again but continued with a quick change of tactic.

"These brave men and women of the misguided space organizations of the world were sacrificed in the name of science, in the name of advancing the curse of warfare. These poor souls were ordered to fight the will of God, a will that dictates we stay on the planet he created. His heavens are off limits—off limits to those who refuse to believe in his divine word."

This time Compton heard a smattering of applause, but he knew that for some reason the Reverend had lost the crowd of over two thousand. The director of the TV program was no longer showing congregation shots. The views were locked in on the Reverend and his daughter, who were both looking very uncomfortable. This seemed to infuriate the man on the subject of the president.

"The man who is now preparing to send our men and women, our brave astronauts, to seek the hoax that is being perpetrated just to continue a space program that is and has been a drain on every economy the world over is directed—no, that's not the right word—it's being manipulated by one man, a man who swore there would be no future attempts at landing on the Moon, a man who lied about cutting the budget for this continual drain on the poor of this nation, a man who cares not for the word and warnings of God! This man is the president of the United States!"

Niles made a decision—Jack was telling him that this is what he was uncovering, and that meant that he had found a connection with Columbus to the man he was watching on television.

"Europa, cut the feed," he said as he sat back down at his desk. He immediately hit the intercom. "Jimmy, get me the direct link to the president. No video, just audio."

"Yes, sir," came the answer.

Niles waited and then hit another switch. This time he connected with the Computer Center.

"Yes, sir," came the voice of the man subbing for Pete Golding.

"I want everything you can dig up on Samuel Rawlins, and his corporation, Faith Ministries."

"Sir?" the tech asked.

"I need it ASAP, and get me a link with Colonel Collins. He's in the air on his way to Ecuador."

"Yes, sir."

Niles waited a moment and then his assistant stuck his head through the double oak doors.

"Sir, the president is on his way to Annapolis to watch the Ares mission launch from Vandenberg. He's just now preparing to leave the White House on Marine One."

"Thank you," Compton said, leaning back in his large chair. For some reason that Niles couldn't fathom at the moment, he had a dreadful feeling that he had been too late in heeding Jack's cryptic message from Germany. "Europa, put CNN on the main viewer please."

On the main screen at the center of the room he saw a reporter standing on the back lawn of the White House, just as his friend, the president of the United States, began waving at the onlookers lining the roped-off area. He saw him turn and salute the Marine guard and then bound up the short set of stairs into the helicopter designated Marine One. His wife and daughters weren't traveling with him to Annapolis that day, and for that Niles felt relieved. He reached out and hit the intercom one last time.

"Jimmy, the president will be airborne in just a minute. Give him a moment and then contact him with a 5656 priority message. I have to speak with him."

Niles clicked the intercom off before he received an answer from his outer office. He stood and walked toward the screen again, watching the giant rotors of Marine One start to turn.

## HAPSBURG OFFICE BUILDING, 1 MILE SOUTH OF THE WHITE HOUSE, WASHINGTON, D.C.

Laurel Rawlins watched through binoculars as Marine One started spooling its twin turbine-driven engines. From her vantage point, she could only see the extreme top of the rotor. She moved the glasses to the right and saw two identical helicopters with the exact same paint scheme as Marine One. One came from the direction of Andrews Air Force Base and the other from the east, following the Potomac River. She smiled. That old fool Darby had said in passing one day many years before that the president had not one but three Marine One Sikorsky helicopters that rose into the air at exactly the same moment when the president was utilizing the aircraft—one carrying the head of state, the other two flying as decoys in case someone attempted exactly what she was about to attempt.

Laurel lowered the glasses and reached for the small radio clipped to the inside of her jacket. She felt an adrenaline rush accompanying the action she was about to perform. From the day her high school counselor informed her father that his daughter had a severe problem with authority, she had thought her wealth precluded her from any form of normal social function. She smiled at the memory and lifted the small microphone attached to her coat collar.

"Site one, are you ready?" she asked, the smile lingering on her lips as she actually started shaking with excitement.

"Site one, prepared to lock on to target."

"Site two, are you tracking?" she asked into the microphone.

"Site two is tracking."

"Site three?"

"Three is prepared to do the will of God."

Laurel wanted to laugh at the phrase coming from position three. She wanted to scream that it was *her* will, not God's, that was controlling the fate of the nation today. Instead, she allowed the coat collar to fall back without commenting on the foolishness spouted by site three.

The men had been chosen by the Mechanic and had been taught extensively in the use of the FIM-92 Stinger missile system. The infrared targeting system would lock on to the exhaust of Marine One and send the 10.1 kilogram missile into the proximity of the engine compartment. The Raytheon theft was about to pay off once more.

Just as Laurel was about to start down the winding staircase to the ground floor so she could make a hasty retreat, her cell phone rang and she stopped halfway to the tenth-floor exit.

"What?" she said angrily into the phone.

"My dear, may I ask what it is you are doing?" McCabe said from three thousand miles away. He had just witnessed the culmination of a major portion of his plan and wasn't happy about the failure of the missiles from Devil's Island in not bringing down the first Ariane rocket.

"Doing something that you don't have the balls to do, James. I'm betting heavily that the Americans won't launch tonight, that's what I'm doing. Your plan has failed completely. Now you not only have one but two missions on their way to the Moon."

"Listen to me very carefully, Laurel. The Chinese system will eventually fail. It is far too complicated for a damaged ship to make the trip and land safely. They have a three-day journey and they won't make it. The ESA platform is heavily damaged, so they're also ill-fated. Now stop what it is you are doing because this action will not prevent the United States from following a presidential directive. You are making us all look like amateurs."

"Nonetheless, James, I will do what you are destined to fail at, and I have the man who signs your mercenary checks backing me on this."

McCabe had to think fast. His plans were unraveling and he was bound to be implicated in the actions thus far if Laurel continued to be a rogue element. But if he sent out a warning she would be caught and that would lead directly to her father. McCabe had no illusions that the trail would then lead right to his front door. If so, the plan for framing the Mechanic and his movement would just be a waste of time. McCabe thought of a possible way out.

"I tried," he said as simply as he could. "Do you have a proper escape plan?"

"I'm heading to the street now. I'm taking public transportation to the airport."

"That's good. Then you should tell your shooters to commence lock-on of the target now. I see on television that Marine One is just lifting off."

"James, I was informed that locking on to the target too soon would alert the defensive equipment of not only the presidential helicopter, but the orbiting fighters as well. Just what are you trying to do?"

McCabe now knew who was involved in planning the attack on the president. It could only be the Mechanic, because no one knew the Stinger system as he did. Now he had a confirmation that the Saudi was finally reverting to his old, terrorist ways—or was it something more like avarice?

"Normally that would be true, but you're misinformed, my beauty. You are using the Stinger FIM-101, the newer system that allows lock-on with no tracking flashback from the seeker head. You can lock on early and get the hell out of there, and save your men at the same time. Whoever you're in this with should have explained that to you."

Laurel bit her lower lip.

"Look, you cannot get caught. It would lead directly to your father."

Laurel's vanity overpowered her mistrust of her father's mercenary. She lowered the cell phone and then her hand went to her collar. She raised the microphone to her mouth.

"All stations lock on, now!" she said into the microphone.

Flying at 39,000 feet off the coast of Mexico, James McCabe smiled as he heard the voice in his ear.

"But, miss, we are trained to—"

"Lock on the target, now!" she screamed, sounding like a spoiled child balking at a parental order.

All stations turned on their IR and radar-equipped seeker heads located in the missile itself. The signal was sent through to the microchip inside the handle of the Stinger and the blip appeared as a target that had been acquired. The three Stinger stations placed on the rooftop all called in stating they had acquired the target.

"Now get out of there," McCabe ordered. "Flag a cab about three blocks from the building you're in and don't look back. Meet me in Atlanta. D.C. is going to shut down minutes after the attack."

Laurel listened to McCabe and for the first time she started to get frightened at what she had just ordered. It was like a twelve-year-old getting caught hitting a schoolmate with a sharpened pencil—while the exhilaration was still there, it was nonetheless scary to be caught red-handed.

"But—"

"Get the hell out, now!"

Laurel snapped the phone shut and ran for the stairs.

## U.S. AIR FORCE COMBAT AIR PATROL OVER WASHINGTON, D.C., CALL SIGN—*GUNSLINGER*

The two U.S. Air Force F-22 Raptors were flying at fifteen thousand feet through a cleared corridor dictated by Marine One's flight plan to Annapolis. Their job was to cover the path of the presidential helicopter the entire time it was in the air. This was a new protocol since the attacks on air and space assets in the previous week. The pilots were on a rotating roster and were stationed at Andrews. Their duty was usually one of boredom and routine as they circled well above the commander in chief.

The flight lead was Lieutenant Colonel William "Wild Bill" Lederman, a career officer who was filling in for a pilot who had just received his orders to Afghanistan. He was doing it as a favor so the other man could spend a few more days with his wife and two children. His wingman was Thomas "Hollywood" Henderson, a young first lieutenant who was performing the protection run for only the second time.

The world for both pilots was about to change in dramatic fashion.

## MARINE ONE, 300 FEET OVER WASHINGTON, D.C.

The large Sikorsky gained altitude quickly and its occupants were unaware of what was happening a mile away at an old and decrepit brownstone. Inside the helicopter a communications line buzzed.

"Mr. President, you have a call on the secure line," a Marine corporal said as he leaned into the cabin.

The president of the United States looked over at his national security advisor, who was the only one of his staff accompanying him that evening. He then closed his eyes as the phone rang in the armrest of his seat. He sighed and then snatched up the receiver. He knew it was going to be a long night of nervous tension watching the double launch tonight from Vandenberg. He placed the phone to his ear and heard the scrambling sounds as the Marine communications officer made the connection.

"Yes," he said as he finally received the soft tone telling him the scramble was complete.

"We have a breakthrough from Colonel Collins, and you won't believe it."

The president sat up in his seat when heard the voice of his friend Niles Compton.

"What?" he asked, waving the Marine steward away from his seat.

"Samuel Rawlins, the reverend, the evangelist."

"What about that pain in the ass?"

"We think he may behind all of this," Niles answered.

"I think you've lost your mind. He's an idiot and has been chastised by every religion on the books—they all know he's a fundamentalist fool."

"Jack's reporting that Rawlins's father was a minister at Spandau Prison in 1947, and had access not only to the man they were looking for, this Nazi clerk named Zinsser, but also to Albert Speer. They may have divulged their knowledge of Operation Columbus to Rawlins's father, a lieutenant colonel in the Army at the time. It's all just circumstantial, but given recent events and the Reverend's not so hidden disdain of yourself and the attempt to get to the Moon. I'm sure we have enough to get the FBI out in California to pay him a visit."

The president was thinking. He had never known Niles Compton to run off half-cocked about anything. His guesses were as good as Einstein's theories.

"Okay, I'll order—"

Alarms started sounding inside of Marine One and the communications system was shut down without warning. The president looked up as the giant Sikorsky banked hard to the right and started a nose-down plunge just past the White House grounds. The president dropped the phone and held on as the helicopter's hard maneuver threw him deep into his seat. He heard shouting from up front, but it was controlled as the pilot and copilot started an emergency procedure the president had always heard about but never experienced.

The Marine corporal leaned outward from his seat and looked at the president. The commander in chief saw the worry in the boy's face.

"We've been locked on to with an infrared and radar system. The pilots are attempting to set us down."

The president nodded as Marine One banked in the opposite direction. He was thrown to the right and painfully so, as his ribs dug into the armrest. He managed to look at his national security advisor and saw him cross himself. His lips were moving in prayer.

"Say one for me if you have the time, Tom."

## U.S. AIR FORCE COMBAT AIR PATROL (CAP) OVER WASHINGTON, D.C., CALL SIGN—GUNSLINGER

Lieutenant Colonel Wild Bill Lederman got the call just as his threat receiver told him that he was picking up a sweeping IR targeting of the area surrounding Marine One. His reactions were fast due to his training running the same kind of missions over Afghanistan while protecting attack and personnel helicopters as they flew into hostile territory. He quickly got a fix on the return of the radar and IR signatures and saw that they were emanating from the east at one mile. Without saying anything he rolled the F-22 over and dove for the deck. He just hoped the sky was as clear as his controllers said it was.

As the two F-22s rolled into the city, the lock on Marine One started a steady warbling in the colonel's headphones. He glanced to his right as houses began to become large in his windscreen and vapor started to stream off his wingtips. He saw Marine One start firing off chaff and flares as the large Sikorsky lost altitude very quickly, giving Lederman hope that this attack would fail. As he thought this, he saw the first two fire trails of the missiles as they left their launchers. He knew immediately that the weapons were Stingers. He had seen enough of them in Afghanistan and Iraq. They had received a security report on the theft at Raytheon and he suspected that these may be from that theft. All of this flashed through his mind in the briefest of seconds.

"Gunslinger Two, this is Lead. Take out those launchers. Take them out now!" he said as calmly as he could, just as the third missile left its tube from the rooftop. "Have you acquired target?"

"Roger, Gunslinger Lead, Two is rolling in," came the quick reply from Hollywood.

As Gunslinger One clicked the communication button on his stick, he rolled to the right, away from his wingman just as the first missile suddenly started falling from the sky. The exhaust trail stopped and the missile went down into the office buildings below. The second and third missiles still came on. The F-22 watched as they closed on Marine One. The chaff—little pieces of aluminum foil—and the flares being ejected from the tail boom of the Sikorsky were an attempt to get the Stingers to lock on to a false target, but the colonel knew that the advanced Stinger systems Raytheon produced were programmed to avoid the countermeasures and blast through to the real target.

He decided he had little choice. He turned as hard as he could while at the same time throwing the twin Pratt & Whitney F119-PW-100 turbofans into afterburner. The Lockheed jet responded faster than any fighter in the world could have. It streaked toward the lead missile, trying desperately to head it off.

As the flight lead was in the process of intercepting the assault on Marine One, his wingman locked on to the rooftop of the building. He saw a team of six men attempting to run for cover as his F-22 shot through the sky toward them. Long before their missiles came into proximity of the Sikorsky, the CAP found the weapons personnel. The piper on the heads-up display turned red as the small circle sought the first and second man in line. At the same time as the fleeing men were targeted, Hollywood made the call to his controller saying he was locked, but locked in a civilian neighborhood. He was given the all clear to engage the targets.

The Raptor screamed toward the rooftop and before the men knew they had company there was the short "buruppp" of the twenty-millimeter Gatling gun. The tracers streaked toward the first two men in the line trying to reach the rooftop exit. The explosive rounds struck and tore the two men to pieces. Hollywood touched the trigger one last time for exactly a half a second. The short time span of pressure sent 306 rounds toward the remaining men. The twenty-millimeter shells ripped into the tarpaper roof and then tracked the four men and their suspected path. The men joined their first two comrades in a shower of misted blood and flying flesh.

The F-22 climbed at the last moment, sending debris and gravel from the old rooftops surrounding the attack area. The Raptor climbed back into the evening sky.

*Gunslinger* knew that one of the missiles was going to get through no matter what he did. There was no time for thought and no time for a quick prayer. He jigged at the last minute and caught the first warhead fifteen hundred feet from Marine One. The Stinger caught the Raptor in the right wing and blew ten feet of the composite material free of the fuselage. Just as the impact occurred, Colonel Lederman called a Mayday and reached for the ejection handle over his head. The Raptor rolled to the left at a severe angle and then the fuel lines running from the composite wing that was no longer there ignited the aircraft into a fireball. The Lockheed-built plane came apart in view of Marine One and directly in the path of the third and final Stinger missile.

The Stinger actually struck the disintegrating body and ejection seat of Lieutenant Colonel Lederman as it passed through the cloud of burning debris. It ignored the last of the Sikorsky's chaff and flares and then detonated three feet from the helicopter's engine compartment. The warhead was a 3 kilogram penetrating hit-to-kill warhead type that sent shrapnel out in a perfect arc that punched holes into not only the turbine-driven engines but the composite rotor blades of the helicopter as well. The fifth rotor wobbled for the briefest moment and then it too disintegrated as the helicopter fell from the sky.

It had been hit at an altitude of only eighty feet, but instead of auto-rotating when the loss of engine power dictated, Marine One came straight down and struck the street a quarter mile from the White House. Police helicopters were close by and their powerful spotlights illuminated the scene from almost two hundred feet away. The large Sikorsky struck the street and slid almost sixty feet into a median in the center of a wide thoroughfare. It hit the concrete rise and bounced, sending the green and white Marine One back into the air before it slammed down on its side sending the remaining rotors flying in all directions. Three cars were struck and the heavy aircraft spun them around into each other as the aluminum started to spark from the friction of the roadway.

The police helicopters never hesitated. They dove for the tragic scene below without regard to the power lines that crisscrossed the area. Motorists, seeing what had happened, snapped out of their paralysis faster than anyone could have believed as many rushed from cars and houses, office buildings and fast food restaurants. They all ran for the burning Marine One.

Most of the tragedy was caught live on CNN. All but the final result was broadcast live all around the world along with the frantic calls of the police helicopters.

"Marine One is down!"

The panicked rescuers were trying desperately to get inside as a U.S. Army Black Hawk helicopter sat down hard on the street beside the burning wreckage.

One of the only people who had not witnessed the attempted assassination of the president of the United States was climbing into a cab she had finally managed to flag down six blocks from the launch point of the Stingers.

Laurel Rawlins had the shakes, but the smile was still etched across her face. She knew her father would be proud and he would look on her favorably as a worthy successor to his vast fortune. She would take up the mantle of God's messenger, only her message would be quite different from her father's. Hers would be one of hope, and reconciliation.

She knew that this could only come about if all traces of Operation Columbus were removed from the mines, something her grandfather should have done many years before, and her father when he learned of the excavation many years after.

Her next target would be in Ecuador, and she knew her father may not approve, but by that time his approval might not be as important as it once was. She had to get that technology from the buried second gallery where it was suspected the real wealth was buried. She knew from her father and grandfather that the Germans, for reasons unknown, had sealed that portion of the mine and never gone back in. Her father explained once that they had been spooked by something inside, and if the German army was afraid of its contents, Laurel Rawlins knew she had to have it.

The driver looked at the pretty face of the woman in his backseat and wondered why her smile actually broadened as the cab turned off to National Airport.


For a full hour, reports of the assassination attempt filled every television screen across the land. Americans didn't know if the president was alive or dead. The presidential physician was on duty at Georgetown Medical Center and so the U.S. Army Black Hawk helicopter was diverted there instead of to Walter Reed. A thousand reporters waited outside for word on the president's condition.


# 9

## KENNEDY SPACE CENTER, CAPE CANAVERAL, FLORIDA

It was only four hours before Sarah, Will, and Jason were due to suit up. Their flight commander was an Air Force colonel by the name of Arthur Kendal, in command not only of the three Event Group personnel, but of the six other men who had been assigned to the backup crew of the Atlas platform, and he was anxious to see if his crew would become a viable part of America's return to space.

The crew would be lifted into the sky and delivered to the International Space Station by the Space Shuttle *Atlantis* if their mission became necessary. While they waited at the dinner table where they had been served a steak, Sarah watched one of the three monitors inside the cafeteria. One was on CNN and the others were static views of the launch pads out west at Vandenberg and in Florida at the Cape, where the giant Atlas stood like an ancient monolith, waiting to see if it would be called upon to serve America one last time.

The two Ares systems were ready at Vandenberg in California. Their two crews of ten would be lifted into orbit and delivered to the space station by the shuttles *Endeavour* and *Discovery*. All eyes were watching CNN for news out of Washington. For Sarah, Mendenhall, and Ryan, the news had hit particularly hard because they knew the man who had just been shot from the sky and they also knew that the president's best friend in the entire world was their very own boss, Niles Compton. As they watched, the coverage broke away from the hospital to the CNN news desk in Atlanta.

*"This just in. The FBI has issued a statement detailing the arrest warrants for James McCabe, a former U.S. Army Lieutenant colonel, wanted in the questioning of not only the event tonight in Washington, but for the explosions in Berlin, Germany, that claimed 107 lives, and the attack in French Guiana that claimed another thirty. McCabe has been under investigation for several days now and is known to have ties to fundamentalist movements around the world. The FBI has refused to answer questions about how they came to their conclusions about McCabe, stating only that they have substantial evidence of his involvement."*

Sarah studied the picture of McCabe, an ordinary-looking man who appeared to be an accountant and not a former Special Operations officer in the same army in which she was serving. She looked over at Ryan and Mendenhall, who, like herself, had not eaten anything since they sat down.

"I wonder if Jack had something to do with the FBI getting this information."

Ryan knew none of them had been informed as to what the colonel was up to. They hadn't heard anything about him or Everett since their arrest in Berlin. He reached out and took Sarah's hand.

"I wouldn't be surprised a bit. But for right now, even though it's a long shot, we better start getting our heads on straight. We're looking at a shuttle launch in just four hours."

"I hope those missions out west get a good start, I really don't care for the idea of all those air miles." Mendenhall was trying his best to shake out some of the tension in the room.

"*Dark Star 3*, it's time to report to briefing and dress out."

The mission coordinator nodded his head as ten faces looked up at him standing in the doorway. Each man and woman was left for a moment with their private thoughts about what could possibly be facing them. The spell of silence was broken when mission commander Kendal rose from his chair and looked around the room at his nine people.

"I guess there's no really good time for speeches. The crash course training we all went through has shown me your capabilities, either in the air or on the lunar surface. You may have noticed I used the terminology indicating we will be a go for launch. All of you from this moment forward should assume we *are* going. The systems used for all three launches are experimental, and as you know nothing in real life ever plays out like a Hollywood script—there will be failures. Therefore, we will be launching simultaneously with our platform,

*Dark Star 3*. Now, let's get our game faces on and move out to briefing. Regardless of the fate of our commander in chief, I am informed by Houston that we are a definite go for mission launch."

## EVENT GROUP COMPLEX,
## NELLIS AIR FORCE BASE, NEVADA

Niles Compton was alone with his thoughts. The staff of the Event Group made sure the director was left that way for as long as he wanted. After Niles had issued his report to the FBI and the National Security Agency concerning what they had discovered about the dealings of James McCabe and Samuel Rawlins, Niles had retreated to his office and had not come out for three hours. For the time being he was looking through the very thin file compiled by Europa on the personages of Lieutenant Colonel James McCabe and the Reverend Samuel Rawlins. As much as Niles was worried about the fate of his best friend the president, his mind was still unable to wade through that worry. He was reading everything he could on the activities of the two men suspected of being behind the recent terrorist activity.

Compton reached for a cup of coffee that was an hour old as he wondered about the reasoning behind the delay concerning the questioning of Rawlins. He knew there was no direct evidence of his involvement outside of what Jack had uncovered in Germany and he knew that theory alone wasn't even a cold gun, much less a smoking one, but still it was certain in Niles's thinking that it did warrant at least talking to the arrogant bastard. That alone might persuade him to cease whatever illegal activities he had planned. Thus far only McCabe had been listed as a suspect. Niles took a drink of the cold coffee and grimaced, then placed the cup and the file down in frustration over his inability to call and check on the status of the president. His phone buzzed as one of his assistants called from the outer office. Niles swallowed and tried his best to check his nerves, then he reached for the intercom.

"Yes," he said.

"Sir, Alice Hamilton is on line one."

"Thank you," Niles said and picked up the phone. "Alice, is the senator all right?"

"Niles, with all that's going on right now, it's thoughtful of you to ask—and, yes, he's doing as well as can be expected. That's why I'm calling at such a horrible time. He wanted me to say he was sorry, as I am, about what happened. We know you and the president are close."

"Thank you, but I wish you wouldn't worry about me. You have more than enough to occupy your mind right now. Take care of him, I just couldn't face—" Niles started to say the deaths of two dear friends at one time, but checked himself. "—well, you know."

"I do, and we will. One thing I want to ask of you before I let you go. I know you have more of a full plate than ever before, especially with the space launch tonight on both coasts, but could you let us know where Jack is?"

"Jack? Why, he's in Ecuador. I think you know where."

"That's what Garrison suspected."

"Hey, wait a minute, he's not thinking anything foolish is he? I mean, even using what little strength he has thinking about helping the colonel, well, it's out of the question. You tell him I said to stop thinking for once in his life and rest."

"You, more than anyone, know better than that. That would be like telling the current director of the Event Group to stop, slow down, and relax, especially with people he commands standing on dangerous ground or heading into harm's way."

For the first time in hours, Niles had to smile. His lips trembled as he placed a hand on his forehead and rubbed. He took the briefest of moments to gather his composure until he found he could trust his voice again.

"Okay, Jack's with a German commando team in Ecuador. He's in the process of getting Captain Everett out of jail, and then he will continue his mission to find what Columbus is truly all about."

"Thank you, dear. Now you go do that magic stuff you always do so well."

"Listen, Alice, you take care of that—"

Compton found he was speaking to an empty line as Alice had hung up. He placed the phone alongside his head and lowered his eyes to the desktop. He was about to hang the phone up when the intercom buzzed again, making him jump. He wanted to throw the phone across the room.

"Yes," he said, far louder than he intended to.

"Sir, priority video communication."

"What?" he said, shocked, as the only priority VIDCOM would come from the president. He slammed the phone down and hit a switch on his desktop. The video monitor slid out of the mahogany top. The screen went from blue to the presidential seal. Niles swallowed and then stood so fast that his chair slid back and slammed into the wall. The next face he saw was bandaged on the left side, and there was a swelling to his jaw and his left eye was blackened and nearly swollen shut—but it was the president of the United States staring at him.

"You look like you've seen a ghost."

Niles looked away for the briefest of moments. He then smiled and with his eyes welling up he faced his old friend.

"I'm still not sure I'm not seeing a ghost. It looks like you've been cruising South Beach after midnight."

The president laughed and then stopped as suddenly as he started. "Ouch, don't make me laugh. The doctor says I have a hairline fracture of the jaw."

Niles did laugh. "That will undoubtedly make the first lady extremely happy."

"She is. Now listen, baldy, I haven't a lot of time. It seems they all want to parade me in front of the hospital window to prove I'm not among the deceased. Collins, is he all right and in Ecuador?"

"Yes, sir, he is on the ground and they're cooking something up to get Captain Everett. Then they plan on getting into that old mine."

"It doesn't look like it will be in time to stop these space shots. We have to go through with this because we can't allow anything from the surface of the Moon to fall into China's hands, or at least the current Chinese government. The Western powers need the technology up there. Niles, as a friend, tell me we're not sending these people off on a mission that's doomed from the start."

Niles paused and then looked deeply into the small monitor.

"The best engineers in the world say this mission has a better than seventy percent chance of succeeding. The variables, however, have changed since the planning stages. In case you hadn't noticed, there are some individuals out there with a different agenda."

The president touched the side of his head and jaw. "I have come to that realization, ass."

"I'm positive this maniac that's been blasting you on his broadcasts is behind all of these assaults on launches. He's behind the theft of Columbus and the attempt to kill you. He's not going to stop until we stop him. Arrest the son of a bitch. Maybe this McCabe will see that he's not going to be paid for his services and stop before he shoots down more good people."

"Thanks, baldy, I needed to hear it from your mouth. I've already instructed the FBI to take him in. Now go relax and see if we can get some people back to the Moon."

Niles found that all he could do was nod his head. The picture on the screen went back to blue as he removed his glasses. He reached back and retrieved his chair. He sat down hard and placed his hands over his eyes. He sat up and took a deep breath, then made a decision. He would take the president's advice for once. He stood and walked from the office. His mood had shifted dramatically in the past minute as he strode to the elevator. He called out to his four assistants.

"I'll be in Las Vegas. I'm going to watch the space launches with Dr. Pollock. I won't be back tonight. Patch all calls concerning the launch and Colonel Collins through to my cell phone."

The assistants watched their director leave the office and were glad to see the fire back in his eyes and the confidence back in his gait.

## GEORGETOWN UNIVERSITY MEDICAL CENTER, WASHINGTON, D.C.

The phone was brought in while the president was being poked and prodded by three different physicians. Two of them he was sure were not even out of medical school yet. He had already made an appearance at the window, closely hemmed in by no fewer than six Secret Service agents, and then had made a sorrowful call to the families of the agents who had lost their lives in the attack, and to the widow of his national security advisor. Now he was about to do something he never thought he would do—make a plea for sanity to the chairman of the People's Republic of China.

"Mr. Chairman," the president said once the connection had been made. He looked over at the secretary of state, who was listening in with the official interpreter. The secretary waited for the chairman to speak to verify it was truly he on the phone.

The conversation started out in Chinese and then the interpreter translated. The secretary of state nodded his head—it was indeed the seventy-nine-year-old chairman on the other end.

"Mr. President, it is so very good to hear your voice, and to learn that you are safe. You have the wishes of good health from myself and the people of my nation."

"Thank you, Mr. Chairman. It is very kind of you to say and to accept my call at this very late hour."

"Not at all, I was awakened for the spectacular double launch your nation has planned. You can call it a natural curiosity on my part to see if the same evil befalls an American attempt as it has so many others in the past few days."

The president caught the innuendo, one that in political speak fell just short of an accusation. He chose to move forward instead of arguing with the old chairman.

"Mr. Chairman, I have called to express my sincere desire for a more cooperative approach to what has happened on the surface of the Moon. As you have seen, the attacks on all nations attempting this endeavor have met with a force of unknown assailants that will stop at nothing to see that we all fail."

The American interpreter voiced the president's words and then there was a long silence on the other end of the line.

"Mr. President, I see no reason for my nation to be bullied by the West. I am afraid those days are long past. We do not frighten as easily as you may think. Our spacecraft, the *Magnificent Dragon*, is well on its way. Once the landing has been accomplished, I see no reason why we cannot be cooperative in the findings of the mission. However, I must insist that our mission to the lunar surface not be interfered with by any nation, just as your monopoly of space was ignored by my own for so many years."

"Speaking man-to-man, Mr. Chairman, I find the situation had started out wrong. I truly wish for—"

The interpreter looked embarrassed as the leader of the People's Republic cut the president short.

"We have come into intelligence that the West has known about this for quite some time, and throughout the years has refused to share this information and technology with the People's Republic as well as many other nations. The monopoly of this find in Ecuador has been a well-kept secret for far too long, and now you suggest cooperation between us and your allies? Perhaps if you had come to my predecessors many years ago this situation could have been avoided."

"I assure you, the find was kept secret by the Nazi regime, and only recently have the facts come to light. The United States and her allies have nothing but respect for—"

Again, the president was cut off.

"Mr. President, I must reiterate how pleased I am that you are safe after your ordeal of this day. I am sure once the scales have been balanced by the heroic astronauts aboard the *Magnificent Dragon*, we can come to terms with our past on a more equal basis and work for a better future in regard to Case Blue, if that threat is really viable as you claim. Good evening, and may you have very good luck on your launches tonight."

The secretary of state listened and then looked at the president and shook his head.

"The chairman has hung up, sir."

"Goddamn it!" The president slammed the phone down and reached for a glass of water, chasing the three doctors away with a warning look. "Get me Johnson Space Center. Conference it with Kennedy, Vandenberg, and the Cape. We go."

The room was silent as the president swallowed some pain medication. He looked up at the ceiling and came to a decision.

"Get me my pants and jacket. I'm getting out of here."

"Where to?" the secretary of state asked.

"Home. I want to see my wife and kids."

## HARTSFIELD INTERNATIONAL AIRPORT, ATLANTA, GEORGIA

James McCabe was waiting outside in the limousine for Laurel Rawlins. Even though the luxury car had windows you couldn't see through, he felt like every set of eyes that passed the waiting vehicle were peering in at him. The mistake of allowing Jack Collins to live was a haunting reminder that you could not play by any set of rules when doing what he was attempting to do. Now he had been linked to the attacks. After tonight, it was time to disappear. In order to accomplish that he would need the good Reverend's daughter to assure his financial payoff for a job he deemed completed. Then, after this evening's festivities, he would make sure Laurel and the Mechanic understood that no one double-crosses James McCabe.

The door finally opened, and even though McCabe knew it to be Laurel, he found it difficult not to react apprehensively because of his new status as the most wanted man alive—even more wanted than Jack Collins. He found it ironic that the plan he had set in motion with Jack had come full circle to bite him in his hindquarters and now they were both on top of the list as far as desperation went.

Laurel slid into the backseat of the large black Lincoln and the driver sped away. She leaned in to kiss McCabe on the cheek and was surprised when he held his hand in the air, blocking the attempt.

"I think we're well beyond that," he said, turning to face the side window.

"I know you didn't approve of the assassination, but—"

McCabe looked back and simply nodded toward the small television embedded in the front seat of the limousine. There the president of the United States was waving to a crowd of reporters from inside of his hospital room. The tape was now four hours old.

"That's impossible. We had him—"

"Impossible, but nonetheless there he is. And now I have an arrest warrant out for me and your father will be on the run very soon."

Laurel watched the taped segment of the president and she read the caption that he had already returned to the White House to be with his family. She lowered her head and turned away from the television.

"You will remain with me throughout the evening," McCabe said. "After my contract is complete, you will accompany me to Ecuador to consummate my ending to this fiasco. Your father will attempt to meet us there."

"You have to get the remaining technology out of that mine or you can forget about the riches you think you've earned." Laurel reached for her cell phone and opened it.

McCabe took hold of Laurel's wrist. He twisted it until the phone fell free.

"So you recruited my man to assist you in your stupidity." McCabe smiled, then grabbed Laurel's chin and roughly turned her to face him. "Now, my dear, do you know why your assassination attempt failed so miserably?"

Laurel didn't fight the roughness of McCabe's touch. She just allowed her eyes to seek out his and remain fixed as the sickening feeling started in the pit of her stomach.

"Your shooters turned on their seeker heads far too early. They could have launched the Stingers and then brought the software online. When the target became illuminated the Air Force would not have been able to react so swiftly."

"You told them to light up the target, you said—"

"Indeed I did. Do you think killing the president would have had any bearing whatsoever on the plan? It would not. It would have only infuriated the people of this country, which you've managed to do anyway. After I've covered my tracks in Ecuador, I am finished. With money in hand I will depart forever. I suspect I can take care of all my business down south, tie up loose ends, and be on my way. You, my dear, can go for the technology in the second gallery if you wish. Personally I believe it's going to be a little hot there in a few hours." He smiled as he released Laurel's chin and slapped her across the face. Then he slammed a fist into her cheek and pulled her onto the seat. He held her there, staring at her with hate-filled eyes. "And you and your father are two of those loose ends. I think you can make that call now, only we'll change the wording somewhat."

## QUITO, ECUADOR

It had only taken Sebastian Krell two hours to return with three of his men to inform Jack that Everett was being held inside a fortress that was covered by an army of police. Collins took the news like a blow to the solar plexus. He sat in the large aircraft and turned away from the German commando and his gathered men. Charles Hindershot Ellenshaw III reached out and patted Jack on the back.

Pete Golding saw for the first time the closeness of Colonel Collins and his second in command, Carl Everett, and felt he had to do something.

"Major Krell, would it be possible to get me video of the building the captain is being held in?" Pete asked.

The German tuned to Pete and shook his head. "Anything is possible, Professor, but what practical good would a video of the police headquarters be?"

Pete stood from his chair and paced the aisle. He placed his hand to his chin. That was when Charlie Ellenshaw saw that Pete was formulating a plan. He had seen it before when Golding worked with him on a few projects with help from Europa, his baby. When Pete went into planning mode, he was a dynamo.

"To start, I need every exit the building has. I also need to know approximately where Captain Everett is located."

"I can tell you that," Sebastian said, wondering what the tall and very thin Golding was getting at. "He's being held in the detention area in the basement. The security for a country like Ecuador is far beyond what it was a few years ago. There's no rushing the building to break the captain out."

Pete stopped pacing and looked up at the German. "Rush the building? I'm afraid what I'm thinking is far more ambitious than that."

"Okay, Pete, what gives?" Jack asked, as he regained a margin of hope.

"If I can do what I think I can with the help of Europa, I can maybe give the captain a window of about five minutes."

"A five-minute window to do what?" Sebastian asked and looked from Golding to his men. There was a smirk on the commando's face.

"Why, to allow Mr. Everett the time he needs to walk out of that building."

Jack smiled and looked back at Sebastian. He returned his gaze to Pete. "Of course. What were we thinking?"

## FAITH MINISTRIES, INC.,
## LOS ANGELES, CALIFORNIA

The ten-man team of FBI agents from the Los Angeles field office had waited for twenty minutes. The second team had just raided the palatial residence of the Reverend Samuel Rawlins. The Reverend was not at home, meaning the odds placed him at his office. They had to act before anyone informed the evangelist that the FBI had a warrant for his arrest.

The agent in charge of the team nodded his head and the ten men ran to the glassed-in offices of Faith Ministries with guns drawn, identifying themselves as federal agents. The staff of forty office workers stood as one. Some of the women screamed and others panicked at the abruptness of the raid.

"Everyone down, down, get down!" the lead agent called as he ran the forty paces to the large double doors with gold lettering across them. He placed his shoulder on the polished wood as he hit it on the run. He was covered by three other men as he aimed inside the office. He saw immediately that there was no one there. He cursed and stood, holstering his weapon.

"Check the employees," he said to the men who had followed him into the office. "Find out where the Reverend has gone." He stepped around the large ornate desk and saw that the computer was still on. He adjusted the monitor with his wrist, not wanting to place his fingerprints on anything in the office. On the large screen monitor was a live shot of the Vandenberg launch facilities. "Inform Washington that Reverend Rawlins is not here."

The field agent knew that in one hour all air traffic over Los Angeles and the far west side of California was due to be shut down for security reasons for the double-double launches of the shuttles and the Ares platforms, but to his way of thinking that was far too much time.

"Damn it, contact Washington. I need the commercial and private corridors for Los Angeles shut down an hour early. No planes in or out."

As his men started calling on radios, the man in charge of the L.A. field office watched the countdown of the Dark Star mission hit the sixty-minute mark. As the clock went to fifty-nine minutes he had a feeling in his gut that the evangelist had this particular CNN broadcast on for a reason, and he also suspected the Reverend was already in flight out of the state. The suspicion that he was in partnership with this Colonel McCabe was slowly being confirmed. He looked at his wristwatch and saw that it was two P.M. Pacific Time.

On the monitor, the view of Vandenberg Air Force Base showed the Combat Air Patrol as the group of four fighter aircraft shot over the launch pads for the final time before the launch.

"Well, at least they have the launches well covered. I don't think anyone will mess with the Air Force on this one," his second in command said as he safed his weapon and placed the nine-millimeter into its holster.

The lead agent looked at the man and shook his head.

"Yeah, that's what worries me."

"I don't get you."

"They had the same Combat Air Patrol over Washington last night and they still attempted to kill the president."

The two agents were interrupted by a third who walked into the office.

"The director contacted the Pentagon. All air traffic except for military and law enforcement has been shut down from Oregon to Ensenada."

"This goddamn thing is far too large in scope for the Reverend and this Colonel McCabe—someone is backing them, and it's not just your regular bunch of terrorists. This has to be an organized military action."

"Well, preliminary data on the weapons used last night say that the Stingers were definitely from the lot numbers on the manifests of the ones stolen from Raytheon. If they were backed by a government, why go to all the trouble? Why not use that government's military equipment?"

"I don't know, but as I said, this is too large in scope for one man, I don't give a damn how rich he is."

An hour later, the agent's worries would be borne out.

## VANDENBERG AIR FORCE BASE, SANTA MARIA, CALIFORNIA

In the history of space flight, the world had never seen such a sight as was on display at the spaceport at Vandenberg. Rising like the spires of ancient Egypt were four towering behemoths of the modern age. The space shuttles *Endeavour* and *Discovery*, with their liquid fuel tank and double solid rocket boosters, were waiting for their turn at the most historic event in space flight history. The two shuttles were poised to be launched into space after the Ares platforms with the crew capsule and the lunar lander. They would follow only fifteen minutes later, closely tailing the remotely controlled rides of the giant Ares. Then they would meet up at the International Space Station for the linking of the lander and the Dark Star command modules, all safely conducted from the confines of the space station.

At the second site were the Ares V and Ares I launch vehicles, both carrying the Altair Lunar Excursion Modules, designated *Thor 1* and *Achilles 1*. The two cargo-carrying vehicles held not only the landers but also the crew command modules. The total payload minus the weight of the twenty astronauts was estimated to be the largest in space exploration history. If there was to be a failure in the missions, outside of an attack, the complicated delivery would be it. The two rockets sat gleaming in the California sun as their solid rocket motors awaited the command to lift them into space.

The reasoning for launching the Ares first was simple. If one didn't make it, the need for one of the aging shuttles to launch would be a moot point, saving the possible failure of that system and the lives of the shuttle crew and its ten male and female passengers.

The engineering of the remote aspect of the launch of the two Ares had done its job. The rendezvous with the space station would be conducted by sophisticated remote systems from the Jet Propulsion Lab in Pasadena, where the most brilliant men and women in that area of expertise had gathered to finalize the rendezvous. The space shuttles, after they had cleared the Vandenberg towers, were then placed under the command of Hugh Evans and his mission control team in Houston. Then, after the connection and linking of the command modules and Lunar Excursion Modules *Thor* and *Achilles*, Mission Control would take the twenty men and women the rest of the way to the Moon—and hopefully back again.

Operation Dark Star was minutes away from commencing with its most important aspect—the launch of the Ares I and Ares V vehicles.


## JOHNSON SPACE CENTER, HOUSTON, TEXAS

Hugh Evans was sitting at his station watching his men and women far below. These were the new youngsters of the space program, the people who would have the honor of launching into space the last shuttle missions NASA would ever orbit. He glanced at the video of the platforms as they sat majestically awaiting launch at Vandenberg. The helicopter view was stunning and he couldn't help but get goose bumps as the view showed the giant towers of all four platforms. He closed his eyes and gave a small prayer for all involved in the most ambitious program NASA or his country had ever undertaken.

"Hugh, there seems to be a debate about the loading of the liquid hydrogen for the Atlas. The engineers from Canaveral are saying it should be done earlier so they can check for leaks."

Hugh opened his eyes and looked over at a man he had known for years as the telemetry specialist for propulsion, a position the older man had held since the time of *Apollo 11* in 1969. He had been a young man then like himself, a young buck wanting to make his mark in the engineering program at NASA. Now here they were trying to do battle with not only an aging system sitting on launch pad 3-B at the Cape but with the young engineers who didn't like the way the older men did things. Hugh hit the communications button on his console.

"Who am I speaking to?" he asked into his headset.

"This is Jason Cummings, fueling specialist for Apollo," the man said from Cape Canaveral.

"Jason, this is Hugh Evans. Do we have a second backup to the Ares launches besides the Apollo?"

"Uh, no sir, we don't," the young engineer answered, as Hugh looked over at his old friend and shook his head, wondering when people would look at the obvious before committing themselves to a course of action.

"Then if there are fuel leaks on the Apollo, could you fix them in the time frame we have before the mission would be scrubbed and the failure of Dark Star—which by the way is not an option—would have to be contemplated?"

"You know we couldn't, sir, but for safety's sake I suggest—"

"Listen to me very carefully. The safety standards for launches are all well and good, but this is a mission that has to come off. The president believes we have to have people up there and that means that everyone involved with Dark Star has just become expendable, are we clear on that?"

"Yes, sir."

"Then we start pumping $O_2$ and $H_2$ into the Atlas at the appointed time, and that will be exactly thirty minutes after the Ares vehicles are airborne." Evans started to slam his hand down on the COM switch, but then he looked over at the older engineer. He smiled. He reached out and flipped the connection off as easily as a light switch.

"Kids," he said with a large smile. "You would think they were averse to flying by the seat of their pants or something."

The engineer returned to his station as Hugh finally stood.

"Give me a go no go for launch of Ares I and Ares V. Ares I platform?"

"We have a go, Flight."

They went down the list of telemetry stations until all but the shuttle's final go no go questions had been answered. As Hugh looked at the last four command questions on the list, it was the final two that worried him far more than anything else.

"CAPCOM *Dark Star 1*?" he said, looking down at the console and concentrating on the last two questions on the well-thought-out list.

"CAPCOM, *Dark Star 1*—Go—Flight."

"CAPCOM *Dark Star 2*—Go—Flight."

Hugh looked around once the two grounded astronauts from the old shuttle missions called out their telemetry status and his eyes settled on the floor below, at all of the other telemetry stations and technicians that would see the missions through to the Moon. Then he asked the last question of the men who had nothing to do with the flights except for their very protection.

"*Hammer* flight, are you in position and are you a go?" he asked, closing his eyes.

"This is *Hammer* flight one actual, we are orbiting and in position—we are a go."

On one of the large monitors there was an aerial view of four F-22 Raptors as they orbited just above Monterey, California. They were in a position to attempt an intercept of any aircraft or missile that threatened the four flights.

"*Ticonderoga*, are you mission-capable, over?" Hugh asked.

"This is USS *Ticonderoga*. We are at station and we are tracking, and we are a go for intercept," came the reply from the most advanced Aegis missile cruiser in the world.

Hugh nodded his head, never in his life thinking they would need the military in such force for the launching of Americans into space. The world was a different place than it had been only a few weeks before.

"Vandenberg, they're all yours," Hugh said as he sat down. "Godspeed, Dark Star."

## KENNEDY SPACE CENTER, CAPE CANAVERAL, FLORIDA

The environmental suits had not changed much since the mid-seventies. With the exception of computer readouts, a video screen, a three-backup safety and oxygen system, and the input of a virtual reality display for mapping inside the helmet, Sarah felt like she was Buzz Aldrin.

As the twelve astronauts of the first leg of the Florida end of Dark Star prepared for their transport to pad 1-A, they all had thoughts rolling in their heads. They knew they were backups to the backups, but after what the commander of the mission had said earlier, they had all prepared as though they were the last hope of the nation in getting to the moon. The space shuttle *Atlantis* was waiting for its crew to board.

As Sarah was helped to her feet in the bulky suit, she looked over at her friends Jason and Will. She smiled as the helmet was placed on her head and she took what would be her last breath of earthbound air for the foreseeable future. She saw Ryan and Mendenhall do the same. As her eyes roamed over the rest of her crew, she settled for watching the always silent men of the 5th Special Forces Group that had been chosen from a larger group of volunteers for the hazardous mission. Unlike Mendenhall, Ryan, and herself, these men had the confident look of people who followed orders and yet were capable of quick thinking and fast reactions in difficult situations. Sarah knew they were just like Jack. She also knew that these men were going into a hostile environment that was just as deadly as any human foe they could ever face.

"Okay, people, give me a thumbs-up when you're called," said the ground supervisor and environmental specialist, "STS *Atlantis* Commander Johnson?"

The commander pointed his thumb in the air.

"STS pilot Walker?"

Sarah watched each man as they went down the line.

She watched the eyes of Will and Ryan as they waited their turn. Their stiffness in their suits made Sarah love them even more as it reminded her of two small boys in oversized suit and ties awaiting their turn at their first day of school.

"Mission specialist Mendenhall?"

Will raised his right thumb into the air almost too fast, but held it steady as he smiled back at Sarah.

"Lunar lander copilot and mission specialist Ryan?" the technician called, shaking his head as Ryan held up not one but both thumbs, and Sarah could have sworn she heard the muffled words, "We're all going to die."

"Gentlemen and lady," the ground specialist said. "The ground crew wishes you luck and prays you have a safe journey."

As they waited, the circle broke up. Men from the old days of the Apollo program, people who had done the preparation of astronauts in those heady days, swarmed the group of twelve and started shaking their hands and patting them on the back of their oxygen tanks. From the look in their eyes, Sarah could see that each of them would have traded places with anyone of the crew. She felt proud to have been trained by them in their environmental classes and she was happy to have known the men of the old school.

"Crew of *Atlantis*, crew of *Dark Star 3*, man the transport, please."

As the group lined up to leave the prep building, Sarah paused a moment and looked at Will and Ryan.

"Don't say it," Will said. "I wish the colonel and the captain were here too. I would feel safer about having our asses lit on fire and shot off to God-knows-what fate if they were. But—"

"They aren't here," Sarah finished for her friend.

The three Event Group lieutenants smiled and Ryan gestured for Sarah to take the lead toward the end of the twelve-man group.

"Ladies first."

## JOHNSON SPACE CENTER, HOUSTON, TEXAS

Hugh Evans stood as the ten-second countdown for *Dark Star 1* commenced. He closed his eyes for five of those seconds, thinking about Stan Nathan, the man who had been ruthlessly murdered in his own driveway just a week earlier. He opened his eyes and saw the giant Ares V. Then he looked at Ares I in the next monitor. Both platforms were brimming with the mechanics who would send Americans back to the Moon. In the distance he could see *Discovery* and *Endeavour* as they waited like NFL lineman itching to get into the game. The Dark Star mission was about to commence.

"Six, five, we have main engine start, four, three, two, one, we have solid booster start."

Evans watched as the tremendous burst of gases erupted from the giant vent port of the launcher. Through all the trial and error of the now reliable system, Evans still cringed every time an Ares erupted into flame. As he watched he saw the tower stabilizers fall free of the 308-foot-tall Ares I, the lighter of the two systems. The main engine thrust sent a solid plume of white hot gases free of the platform as Ares I started to lift away against the forces of Earth's gravity. Hugh clenched his fist and pounded on his console as the smaller of the two rockets started to accelerate from zero to eight hundred feet a second.

"*Dark Star 1* has cleared the tower, Houston. She's all yours!" came the voice from the controller at Vandenberg.

Evans didn't have to say anything to his people as the engineers started calling out their status and it began appearing across their screens. Hugh Evans calmed himself with some difficulty and then found he was scanning the blue skies around the Ares as it lifted into the sky.

"Stay away, you sons of bitches," he mumbled, expecting at any minute a radar blip that would tell him that the launch was under attack.

Ares I kept climbing, as if daring anyone or anything to interfere with her. She rose majestically, as though propelled by the sheer faith of every man, woman, and child watching. The chase cameras watched the roll of the large Ares as she pointed her nose cone in the right direction for orbit. Then they all cringed as the first stage separated from the second.

Down below, the engineer and representative of Alliant Techsystems, the first stage manufacturer, jumped from his station and threw his fist in the air.

"Yeah!" he yelled. "Was that a perfect performance or what?"

Hugh Evans, instead of telling the man to take his seat, had to smile. How can you reprimand someone whose company had done exactly what you wanted it to do?

As the second stage engines ignited, there was a calm but solid release of tension. Hugh knew that *Dark Star 1* was on the way with lander and orbiter to meet its crew at the International Space Station.

All eyes that were not involved with the telemetry of *Dark Star 1* turned toward launch pad 6-A as the larger, two-booster systems of the Ares V commenced its ten-second countdown. Hugh winced as the main engines of the giant Ares burst to life, straining at the arms that held her at bay. Then the solid boosters ignited. Evans again closed his eyes as the Ares V started its climb.

"Houston, the clock is running." Then, a moment later, "*Dark Star 2* has cleared the tower. Okay, Texas, she's all yours!"

Again, technicians stood and urged the much larger *Dark Star 2* into the sky. She rolled and then started hitting her stride. The plume of exhaust gases could be seen as far away as Los Angeles as she reached altitude, and the million sets of eyes on her watching from the city of San Francisco were glued to the amazing sight as more than a dozen of the old and young pumped their fists in an attempt to get the Ares V into its element.

Hugh and his two teams were watching the first stage fall free of the Ares V when he realized that both remote systems were free of earth's gravity. Hugh sat and calmly informed everyone that they had work to do to get the platforms where they needed to be for rendezvous with the space station. He smiled when he realized how crowded the sky was going to be in just a few more minutes.

## QUITO, ECUADOR

While Jack, Sebastian, and Pete Golding worked on the plan to get Captain Everett out of jail, Charlie Ellenshaw, the two Air Force pilots, and the nine German commandos watched the live launches from California. Charlie stepped into the 727's communications station and nodded his head at Jack, indicating that the two Ares rockets and their payloads had achieved orbit. Collins nodded his head only slightly.

They had been on the ground for three hours. They had a close call when Ecuadorian customs officials came to check out the United States Air Force jet and its personnel, but Europa's forged flight plan and emergency layover due to a faulty relay held up nicely, which was not to say that the empty electronics cabinet didn't get a little cramped down in the avionics compartment for Collins, Golding, and Ellenshaw as they hid from the officials.

"Europa has successfully infiltrated the seventh precinct headquarters, home of not only the Ecuadorian chief of all security forces but also the chief prosecutor's offices. Their computer systems are all tied together. Ecuador is lagging behind somewhat in their prison system and they still do everything by written order. Only the jail in the basement of the building has a closed-loop computer system and it's only linked to the prosecutor's offices above, not to the chief of their security forces. So we can order Captain Everett out of his cell and no one will be the wiser."

"What does that give us?" Sebastian asked.

"Sir, our baby can do many things, but to physically break someone out of jail is not one of them. At some point you and the colonel are going to have to get your hands dirty. I can order the captain to be moved from the cell area to the prosecutor's office five floors above. At some point, probably in the basement or the fifth-floor office of the prosecutor, you two will have to lie in wait and . . . what do you spooky guys say? Oh, yes—bag him. All of this without alerting the large security force inside the building while you're doing so. I would suggest you do it at this point."

Jack leaned over and saw where Pete was pointing. He turned from Europa's blueprint of the headquarters building to face Pete Golding.

"You've lost it, Pete. In case you don't know where your finger is resting, that's the police officers' shower and locker room. You know there would more than likely be people called cops inside?"

"I'm banking on it. Europa can order the systems controlling the plumbing in the building to shut down, leaving the officers' locker room the only viable place for a prisoner to shower before being brought into the prosecutor's office." Golding saw the look Collins and Sebastian were giving him. "Look, it's the only loophole Europa could come up with. Oh, hell, I'll let her explain it." Pete reached out and hit the switch that controlled the supercomputer's voice synthesizer. "Explain your plan to the colonel and major, Europa."

"Yes, Dr. Golding," came the Marilyn Monroe–ish voice from the speaker. Sebastian looked at Jack and Collins rolled his eyes in return. "Two Quito police department uniforms have been secured for you at Authority Clothing, located two blocks west of the station, and may be picked up using your standard police IDs supplied by Dr. Golding. You will then proceed directly to the fifth floor of police headquarters. At that time a command will be sent from the prosecutor's office using the auspices of the Europa system. In that order will be a request from the prosecutor to see prisoner 1962900. The order will include a physical examination for any weapons said prisoner may have secured during his brief stay in his cell. That order will include that the prisoner shower before being brought to the head prosecutor's office. Once the prisoner is inside the shower and locker room, clandestine elements of the mission will secure the prisoner and abscond with his person through emergency exit 29-b, shown on the monitor. Probability is seventy to thirty against success."

"What the hell?" Sebastian asked, looking from the monitor to Jack, who shrugged.

"I guess that's the best she can do," Jack said as he slapped Pete on the back. "You want to get us some IDs, Doc?"

"Already printed and scanned for the security system inside the building." Pete turned and looked at Collins and then Sebastian. "It really is all she could come up with, Colonel. If not for this plan, you would have to storm the building, and with the elements of Interpol inside with over seventy on-duty officers that would be disastrous."

"I didn't say a word," Jack said as he looked over at the German. "Look, why don't you sit this one out. I can go it alone."

Sebastian looked hurt.

"Are you kidding, I wouldn't miss it for the world. Besides, if we pull this off I want you to introduce me to this Europa woman. Deal?"

Jack had a very hard time keeping a straight face, but he managed, as did Golding.

"Deal," was all he said.

"Colonel," Charlie said, as he poked his head into the communications shack. "*Discovery* and *Endeavour* are off. They will achieve orbit in just two minutes."

Everyone could see the relief in Jack's face as the realization that the arrest warrants for McCabe and Rawlins probably staved off another attack.


## JOHNSON SPACE CENTER, HOUSTON TEXAS

Mission Control had just been handed off *Discovery* and *Endeavour* from Vandenberg. They watched and cheered on the *Endeavour*, the last of the two launches, just as the solid rocket boosters separated from the large centerline external fuel tank. *Endeavour* climbed, going to full throttle to reach the unforgiving void of space.

Hugh Evans couldn't remember a more glitch-free launch in his career, much less of four vehicles at almost the same time. The maniacs that put this plan into motion had his respect. The quirky little man who had come up with the outrageous scheme should be the first in line for congratulations. Even the silent boys over at DARPA, who had provided input on splicing all the experimental systems into one mission, had done a job for which they would always be remembered.

"*Endeavour*, this is Houston, you have a clean RSB sep, and are clear for low orbit insertion," CAPCOM said as the blurry, out-of-range image showed the solid rocket boosters falling free of the *Endeavour* and the twelve astronauts she carried. Some were in her command deck, the others in a small pod that had been loaded into her cargo hold. Evans knew that as soon as *Discovery* and *Endeavour* made their low altitude orbit, both shuttles would open their cargo doors to cool off not only the bay itself but the pod carrying the four astronauts that couldn't fit into the current design of the flight module. For the first time men had been sent aloft in the cargo hold of a space shuttle and the environment capsule had performed magnificently. This design idea had come straight from the drafting boards of DARPA and had worked to perfection.

Jet Propulsion Lab in Pasadena was reporting that the remote systems onboard *Dark Star 1* and *Dark Star 2* were functioning at nominal levels. They were now prepared for the command modules to separate from the holds containing the two Altair landers for eventual hookups to both capsules. Then they would remotely rendezvous with the International Space Station for crew pickup. That was when the Moon mission would truly begin.

## MASHHAD, IRAN,
## IO MILES FROM THE BORDER OF KAZAKHSTAN

The small airfield had been constructed in three days with the aid of Iranian engineers. With all evidence of the landing strip designed to disappear in a matter of hours, the plan was to launch the aircraft and then vanish into the mountainous terrain surrounding the small village.

The pilot, an old-time Iranian who had received his training decades before under the regime of the Shah, was ready for a mission that would finally prove his worthiness to the Ayatollah Rahabi and the fanatical president of that country. This would make him a martyr of the state and allow his family the privileges they had for so long been denied since the pilot had fallen from grace when the Shah abdicated so many years before. As he watched the American on the small monitor, he felt shame at what he had to do for the sake of his family. As the ground crew was given the go order, he lowered his head and said a prayer for forgiveness for the evil deed he was about to perpetrate in the name of God and country—even for the sake of his family, the deed may still prove to be too much for his soul.

He nodded his head and the cockpit of the Tomcat—an aircraft left over from the days of the Shah, started to close.

As the F-14 began its rollout from the makeshift cloth hangar, the full Moon struck him as a brilliant reminder of the old days of flying patrol under the Shah. The pilot could feel the weight of the two weapons as they hung from the innermost hard-line points just off the hydraulically controlled wings. The rest of the F-14 had been stripped of anything that would hinder his flight into Kazakhstan. Even the oxygen system had been cut down by 90 percent, and there was no defensive weaponry in the venerable old naval aircraft—even the twenty-millimeter cannon had been removed. In fact, the weight of the two ASATs was double the normal flight load of the Tomcat and there was still some doubt as to whether the aircraft could even gain the altitude needed for launch. The new seeker heads installed by the Iranian military would detect the low-orbiting targets, but it still remained to be seen if the Tomcat could get to the launch point at 65,000 feet. The Tomcat was not designed for the ASM-135 ASAT. It was always launched from the F-15 Eagle and the change had been designed by the best Iranian aerospace people they had.

The Tomcat reached the apron of the hard, earthen-packed runway and was waiting for the go from the radar station thirty-five miles away. The station was monitoring the path of the American shuttles *Endeavour* and *Discovery* as they readied to cross over Russian territory on their way to the rendezvous with the International Space Station.

The secret partner of the ayatollah had been working diligently on the plan for the past ten years and the Reverend had come through by supplying the necessary equipment to the one man who could help bring not only America to its knees but the rest of the world's powers as well. It wasn't this man who was in partnership with Iran; it was his apprentice. After the assault on the shuttles, when no one would be capable of getting the mineral or technology from the surface of the Moon, Iran would take control of the one source left in the universe: the mines in Ecuador.

The Tomcat received the vectoring, precise coordinates, and altitude for the launch of the American-built ASATs, then the pilot was given clearance for take-off. The most complicated interception in history was about to be attempted and, with luck, God's wrath against the Americans would be complete.

The Tomcat's aging GE turbofans lit off at full afterburner as the old airframe tore down the dirt strip. The lumbering fighter held firmly to the ground as the weight of the two ASATs clung to her underbelly. Finally, when it looked as though the pilot would slam Iran's hopes and dreams into the side of the mountain pass, the ground crew watched the tires lift free of the Earth.


The F-14 flew low over the Caspian Sea. As the pilot executed a northerly turn, the red light on his nav-board flashed bright red. The signal was given for the intercept of *Discovery* first and then *Endeavour*.

The pilot said a silent prayer and pushed the throttle to full afterburner, pulling the stick straight back into his stomach. The old fighter fought gravity with all his strength as the Tomcat scratched its way into the dark skies over Kazakhstan.

Normally, the missiles could have been launched at 37,000 feet for any low orbit target such as a communications satellite, but since the shuttles were flying at a higher orbit, they would have to be launched at an incredible 65,000 feet.

The pilot was feeling the effects of the g-forces as the jet fought for its target altitude. The airframe, after so many years of neglect, started shaking and the pilot knew then that it was going to be sorely taxed. As he fought through the 42,000-foot mark, his threat detector announced that he would soon have company. Four MiG 31s were in high-speed pursuit of the venerable Tomcat.

The pilot watched his altimeter roll through its paces. A green warning light flashed as he passed through the 60,000-foot range. He calmly moved his thumb over the selector switch just as the electronic tone in his headphones started making a warbling sound, indicating that his fighter was being painted by enemy radar. Then the tone changed as the MiGs gained weapons lock on the Tomcat. A second later they launched their air-to-air missiles.

The Iranian pilot knew the Russian attack would come too late to stop the launch. He switched the selector over to missiles and the tracking radar in the Tomcat's nose sprang to life with targeting data relayed from the Iranian ground stations. The ayatollah's scientists had successfully intercepted NASA's downrange telemetry signal, which emanated from their radar stations in Kuwait. This gave the seeker heads in the ASATs a perfect vector for the attack. As the pilot watched the relayed information from the ground station, he saw the first blip of the American target aircraft, the *Discovery*. As he reached altitude, the first ASM-135 ASAT was launched automatically. The loss of weight made the F-14 slide to one side as the ASAT left the rail along the right side of the fuselage. Then, a second later, the second ASM-135 ASAT left its rail, its engine flaring to life as the first stage lit off, nearly blinding the Iranian pilot.

As the two ASATs sped on their way, the F-14 turned to meet the oncoming threat of the Russian MiGs and the six missiles heading toward him. Instead of zigzagging to make his fighter hard to detect on the seeker heads of the missiles, the pilot closed his eyes and flew straight on, the g-forces of the dive shaking the overtaxed airframe of the old Grumman. He felt as well as heard a loud snap as one of the streamlined wings lost a restraining bolt along the right fuselage. The pilot smiled as he realized the jet was starting to come apart. The dive was so steep and he was traveling so fast that the g-forces were tearing the aluminum away from the structure. The forces were giving the old pilot tunnel vision as his brain was denied life-giving blood.

The pilot didn't think about his martyrdom. He thought of the family that would now have everything they needed to survive in today's Iran, a land he no longer knew. Then, at that precise moment, the first of six air-to-air missiles detonated in the falling Tomcat's path, sending shrapnel out to meet the disintegrating jet.

A few moments later, the only things left in the sky were orbiting Russian fighters and the falling remains of the F-14.


SST SHUTTLE *DISCOVERY*,
240 MILES ABOVE THE EARTH

*Discovery* was leading the way, followed three hundred miles behind by *Endeavour*. The two shuttles had just opened their cargo doors to cool the interior bay from the massive heat buildup caused by the launch. The crew was starting to settle into the routine of space flight. The mission commander was in the process of explaining to the military personnel how they would proceed once they met up with the International Space Station. He was assuring them that all they needed do was check their small amount of weaponry and stand by for the ride of their lives.

"*Discovery*, Houston, stand by for an emergency OHM burn. Get your people strapped in for evasive maneuvers."

The shuttle pilot didn't stop to ask why. He practically flew to the pilot's side of the spacecraft and prepared to fire his maneuvering jets. He just needed to know which ones and where he would be going.

"*Discovery*, this is Houston. You have an attack heading your way. We believe it to be an ASAT of unknown origin. We are now waiting for the exact targeting data before we move you out of the way. Do you copy, *Discovery*?"

"Everyone strap in, get the cargo doors closed, and prepare for maneuvering."

## JOHNSON SPACE CENTER, HOUSTON, TEXAS

Hugh Evans stood and shouted, knowing at the same moment that no matter what they did, the shuttles would be successfully targeted.

"Get them out of the way!"

With the technicians watching the merging of two ASATs and the two shuttles, they all felt helpless as the ASATs' first stages separated.

"Flight, we have a direct feed of long-range enhanced photog from the ISS."

"Put it on!" Evans said loudly.

As the main view screen on the control room floor switched views, everyone immediately picked out the *Discovery* as she flew in what looked like an upside-down attitude over the blue world below. They also saw the streaking second stage of the first ASM-135 ASAT as it merged with the shuttle. They watched in horror as the warhead struck the cabin between the crew area and the cargo bay. The impact sheared the cabin free of the rest of the shuttle and then they watched as the cabin came apart, sending pieces of composite material and humanity out into space. The harshness of the hit sent electrical currents through to the OHM's maneuvering jets and fuel line. They all erupted at the same moment. The silence of the detonation took every man and woman by surprise, the shock of what they were seeing quickly becoming overwhelming. The explosion became a burst of silent energy as it expanded outward.

"ISS, this is Houston Flight. Give us the track of *Endeavour!*" he said more loudly than he intended.

As the camera shifted to the International Space Station, they saw the second explosion enveloping *Endeavour.* This time the ASAT struck the aft OHM's jets and the fuel tanks housed there. The crew cabin and the newly designed pod for the cargo bay were gone. The wings of *Endeavour* were separated from the shuttle's main body and were floating free of the debris field.

Hugh Evans sat hard into his chair. He had just witnessed the death of two space shuttles and their crews. The twenty men and women of Dark Star were gone in a flash of energy that would haunt everyone who witnessed the tragedy for the remainder of their lives.

Many technicians were still doing their jobs as they tried to trace the attack from its origins. Evans knew he had to get things as far back on track as he could.

"CAPCOM, do we have anything?"

The astronaut manning the crew communications systems tried to raise anyone from the two shuttles. He knew it was official procedure, but he had a hard time swallowing as he tried to get the words out.

"*Discovery, Endeavour,* this is Houston. Do you copy, over," he said as he kept his head low. "*Discovery, Endeavour,* this is Houston. Do you copy, over. Any Dark Star element, do you copy?"

Hugh Evans turned away and looked at the monitor on the far left. The giant Atlas stood poised on the pad as fuel started to flow into her tanks. Evans knew he had to make the call that could possibly send more men and women to their deaths.

"Ground, get the Cape on the horn and advise Kennedy to start the prelaunch countdown for *Dark Star 3*. We are now a go!"

## QUITO, ECUADOR

Major Krell and Collins had secured the uniforms with the forged documents, even managing to send the bill to the president of Ecuador.

Sebastian had learned one thing about black operations from Collins—make a plan, and then stick to it until that plan ceases to be effective. He wasn't surprised when Jack lowered the blue saucer cap as low onto his brow as he could and stepped right into the arms of the largest police force on the Pacific coast of South America. What was amazing to Major Krell was that Jack never hesitated a moment. Sebastian had no choice but to admire the man and follow him in.

The station was crowded and that was to their advantage. The entrance was full of policemen going on duty, and those coming off. The two officers wore an insignia on their collars that announced they were from the second police barracks south of the city, so their being unfamiliar to most should cause little trouble—they hoped.

Jack immediately spied the stairs. The two men had to assume that Europa's falsified orders from the prosecutor's office had gone through as planned. If not, they would be caught waiting just outside a room where several dozen off-duty officers would soon be naked, taking their after-shift showers. That might be a little hard to explain.

As Collins gained the fifth-floor landing he paused at the door. He could hear the sound of men talking, laughing, and fooling around. He looked back at the German major and grimaced as he grabbed the door handle. He opened the door. He and Krell stepped into the hallway just opposite the shower room.

The double doors were propped wide open and Jack could see the entire row of lockers and behind them the showers. He nodded to signal to Sebastian that he should take the right side of the door while Jack took the left. As they moved into place a group of policemen came from what looked like a briefing room down the hall behind the German. They stopped in their tracks and all five seemed to be staring right at Collins and Krell. Jack tried to avoid eye contact with the men as they all continued to stare.

"*Asesinos estadounidenses,*" one of the men said pointing.

Sebastian turned and was about to say something to the men when Jack reached out and took his arm. He turned him to face behind where Jack was standing. He had recognized the words the man had spoken—Murdering Americans.

The footsteps behind them made them both turn and that was when they saw Captain Carl Everett escorted by two men. He was handcuffed and, to the captain's credit, he didn't bat an eye when he saw Jack and Krell in the strange uniforms. He stepped past both Jack and Sebastian as he was led into the showers. The five policemen stopped talking and went on their way, even going as far as to nod their greeting to the American and the German.

"*Pestilente gringo,*" Jack said and they all laughed as they hit the stairwell.

As Everett was unceremoniously shoved into the locker area, he called back with a semi-loud voice, knowing that Jack and Sebastian were the only ones who would understand what he said.

"I heard that," he said using a melodious tone to the words.

"What did you say?" Sebastian asked, wondering why Jack would take a chance at saying anything at all.

"I called him a stinking white man."

"Oh," Krell said, not understanding the colonel's humor in the least.

Collins turned when he saw Everett being told to get out of his yellow jumpsuit. The steam from the showers wasn't what Collins would have preferred, but it would have to do. He stepped inside the locker room. The unsuspecting guards had their attention on Everett as he soaped down. Jack was almost hesitant, but knew he could afford to give these two guards a chance. He tapped the first guard on the shoulder just as he pulled the man's holstered Smith & Wesson Police Special. Sebastian, knowing the drill, was quick to follow.

"*Lo siento, pero este hombre se va,*" Jack said, as he gestured for the two guards to follow him into the break room across the way. Sebastian took his cue and escorted the men, while Collins opened several lockers until he found what he was looking for, an extra-large police uniform that would fit Carl.

Sebastian came back a moment later and Jack eyed him. "What did you do with our friends?" he asked, worrying that Krell was too calm.

"They're locked up in the pantry." Sebastian looked into the shower and then back at Collins. "I have to learn Spanish. What did you say that time when you took the guards?"

"I said that I'm sorry, but this man is leaving."

Again Sebastian was impressed by the simple way Collins had of handling an awkward situation.

Jack winked and then walked into the shower room.

"Hey, swabby, it's time to trip the light fantastic."

Everett turned and caught the clothes Jack tossed him.

"How long were you standing there watching me shower before you said something?" Everett asked as he quickly dried himself.

"Long enough to know I'll be happy with Sarah for a very long time," Collins answered.

"Liar, you know you liked what you saw."

Europa's escape plan fell apart the moment they hit the stairwell leading to the first-floor exit they had planned to use. Not knowing where all of the police officers were inside the station had been Europa's major difficulty in devising the planned escape. As it turned out, it was the fraternization of a male Quito police officer and his female partner that sent the plan spiraling in a direction they hadn't counted on.

As they went down the third-floor stairwell, the couple was hidden away under the staircase. Jack saw them just as they passed. Everett was recognized immediately and while Sebastian reacted quickly by grabbing the male officer, the uniformed woman slipped past and was through the third-floor doorway before anyone could stop her.

"Damn!" Sebastian said as he held the frightened officer in his powerful grip. " "I think this is bad, Jack." He looked at the smaller police officer as if he were contemplating the man's fate.

"Well, let him go. We can't kill him for liking his partner too much," Collins said and removed the Smith & Wesson revolver and pointed it at the officer. "*Vámanos,*" Jack said as he waved the gun at the policeman, who took the hint and shook free of the much larger Sebastian before he ran for the door.

Collins didn't hesitate as he turned and continued down the stairs with Sebastian and Everett close behind. They hadn't made it to the first floor when the warning bells started inside the building, and just as the three men reached the door Collins heard the loud "clack" as the doors locked automatically. Jack came skidding to a stop.

"Jack, I really don't want to finish that shower."

"Can't blame you. Sebastian, I hope you brought that little item with you."

The German was already pulling out the quarter-pound charge of C-4. He tore off a small bundle and wadded the claylike material into a ball. Then he slapped it against the door and the lock, just to the right of the push bar. He pulled his own revolver and gestured for Jack and Carl to take cover under the stairs.

"Excuse me, gentlemen," he said, as he placed his large frame half in and half out of the stairwell. He aimed and then pulled the trigger. The bullet struck the

C-4, which detonated, producing a loud bang that almost deafened them. The door flew off its considerable hinges and Sebastian was the first one through, followed by the two Americans.

"Think you used enough there?" Jack said, running past Sebastian and into the long alley to the rear of the station.

"I thought it was adequate," Krell said. Everett gave the German a stern look.

The three men ran down the alley, shedding police jackets as they went. They heard the sirens and the pounding of feet behind them as the alley started to fill with policemen. Bullets began flying, echoing off the brick walls.

They reached the end of the alley and had the choice to go right or left. Jack chose right, as it would lead them north, where traffic in the city was heavier. He figured if they failed to escape it would be harder for the police to shoot them in the midst of a crowd. But he realized that he had been wrong before when judging police reactions.

As they made the turn onto the main street, one round narrowly missed Everett as he skidded around the corner. Just as he made the turn behind the German, he glanced to his left and saw that the street on that end was full of screeching police vehicles.

"We've had it, Jack," he called out loudly from the end of the three-man line.

As they neared the street, Jack's hopes of escape faded. An Audi patrol car skidded to a halt, blocking their path. As Collins stopped, wanting to turn and see if there was something he'd missed, the rear window of the police cruiser lowered and a skinny arm started waving them forward. All three men were caught off guard, as this was not the reception they had expected. Jack reacted first by running in that direction, soon followed by Everett and then Sebastian. As Collins neared the car, the rear door was thrown open and he jumped into the lap of someone who grunted as his weight collided with him. Everett soon followed and Sebastian after that. The patrol car burned rubber just as the side window shattered from a bullet. Then they heard several loud clunking noises as the trunk was struck.

"Jesus, those guys are serious," Everett said as he tried to push Sebastian off him.

"Jack, if you don't mind, your head is about to break one of my ribs, and I only have so many of them," announced a familiar voice.

Collins looked up and could not believe what he was seeing. Scrunched up against the door of the car was none other than Senator Garrison Lee. As his eyes widened he sat up quickly and looked up front at the driver. She was small and could barely see over the steering wheel. The woman turned sharply onto the broad avenue.

"Where to, Jack?" Alice Hamilton asked, as she fought to control the car. They skidded around the corner.

"What are you two doing here?" Jack asked. He slid in between the open

Plexiglas enclosure and into the front passenger seat. He just stared at Alice, unable to form any more words.

"Well, I can pull over and give you the long version of what that old man back there is thinking, or I can give you the short version on our way to wherever we need to be. Which will it be?" she asked as she threw the car around another corner.

"The short version on the way out of the city—that way," Jack said, pointing to a side street.

Jack momentarily allowed the tension in his body to ease. He turned and looked at Lee. He could see that the senator was in a lot of pain as he popped two small tablets into his mouth. Then the old man looked at Jack with his one good eye.

"Don't look at me like that, Colonel. I'm not dead yet."

"No? The last time I saw you, you were well on your way. Now what in the hell are you doing here?"

Lee seemed to relax as he leaned forward and looked at Sebastian, who was busy looking out the window as police sirens wailed from every direction.

"Who is this?" Lee asked, getting the German's attention.

"I am Major Sebastian Krell, here under orders of my chancellor."

"Senator Lee, this is the man responsible for getting me out of Germany. He's German Special Forces," Jack explained.

They were all tossed to the left as Alice threw the car around another corner to avoid a passing police car.

"Damn, woman, I'd like to spend the time I have left getting to that godforsaken mine and finding out what this is all about," Lee said, grimacing in pain.

"Shut up, old man. I'm not talking to you at the moment."

Sebastian threw Jack a look and pursed his lips as if he was going to whistle. He turned away, knowing that the old woman in the front seat was truly angry and probably wouldn't understand his surprised demeanor.

"Don't mind her. She's in a little bit of a snit because she thought I was just going to go out like an old fool, lying in bed so she can have final control over me after all these years."

"I told you to be quiet," Alice said as she turned onto a road with houses lining both sides.

"I can see this is going to be a fun ride," Everett said, turning to face the front windshield.

"I don't really care to hear anything from you or Jack either."

Alice floored the police cruiser and the car shot off.

# 10

As the twelve-man crew sat at their stations inside the shuttle *Atlantis* waiting for the tower crew to break out the wrenches to free them, thereby ending the mission of *Dark Star 3*, a flurry of activity started around them that sent the astronauts into a quandary. They had been informed in the previous two hours that both Ares platforms had performed magnificently and that *Discovery* and *Endeavour* had achieved low Earth orbit on their way to rendezvous with the International Space Station. That was the last information that had been passed on to them.

For Sarah, Ryan, and Mendenhall, located in the crew pod in the cargo hold, they were wondering if they had been forgotten. They had been hanging in their seats with their backs against the pod bulkhead facing straight down for two hours and they were starting to feel light-headed. Mendenhall was being driven crazy by the sweat that dripped from his nose and collected against the clear faceplate of his helmet. He shook his head and then they felt the movement of the shuttle. An extremely loud rushing noise reached their ears.

"Jesus," Sarah said, turning as far as she could to the center of the three seats. "They're beginning to fuel the main tank."

"No, they would have said something to us," Ryan said as he returned Sarah's worried look.

"*Atlantis*, CAPCOM, we are a go for launch. Stand by for a message from the president."

When the announcement came through the speakers in their helmets, all three froze as they thought at the same time that this wasn't a good thing.

"Crew of *Atlantis* and *Dark Star 3*, it is with a heavy heart that I pass on to you the following information. At 1740 hours Eastern Daylight Time, the shuttles *Endeavour* and *Discovery* were destroyed in low Earth orbit by an unknown enemy. There were no survivors. I made the call to inform you myself, as it is my decision that you be sent into space as per the backup plan. *Dark Star 3* is now the United States's only hope of stopping the foolishness that has brought nations to the brink of armed conflict. While we are near to discovering the identities of those responsible for these horrific acts, including the assault on this office, I fear we cannot wait for an outcome we would like before risking your lives. You know what needs to be done, and I am sure you will all do your duty. May God bless you. I and the American people wish you God-speed, *Atlantis*."

A tone sounded, indicating that the president was done.

"Okay, people, we have completed fueling procedures and we are now in a five-minute countdown. *Atlantis* will launch at 2010 hours, immediately after the Saturn is in low orbit. We will not follow *Discovery* and *Endeavour*. We will be maneuvering at every opportunity once we have cleared the atmosphere. I have informed our shuttle flight team that they will all be fired if we don't make it. Good luck, and I'll see you at the space station."

Sara, Will, and Jason listened to Colonel Kendal and they could all hear the worry in his voice despite his bravado. Whoever was responsible for the attacks had equipment that was meant to do the job.

Sarah heard Ryan mumbling to himself.

"What is it?" she asked.

"Huh? Oh, I was just thinking about the Altair Lander."

"What, you mean *Yorktown*?" she asked. "What about it?"

Jason tried his best to turn his head toward Sarah.

"She's one heavy piece of equipment and she doesn't have any wings."

"Do you know what a long shot it is that you'll have to pilot her?" Sarah said, trying to calm Ryan down.

"It seems lately that betting on long shots is starting to pay off."

"Quit worrying," Will chimed in as he tried in vain to get the sweat off the tip of his nose. "We'll probably be blown to bits long before reaching the Moon."

Both Sarah and Ryan leaned as far forward as their straps would allow and tried to see Mendenhall. It was Sarah who finally said it.

"Your optimism is so inspiring, Will."


All eyes were on the ancient Saturn V as it sat waiting for the electronic signal that would send it one more time into the heavens. The liquid hydrogen collected on its aluminum outer skin and fell free when too much gathered in one spot. The ground crew had been told stories of the rocket's power, but none there had witnessed the event before. Only Hugh Evans in Houston and a few of the old-timers were aware of what was about to happen.

The viewing stands were full of military personnel who wanted nothing more than to join the mission themselves. As their eyes scanned the skies they heard but could not see the four squadrons of naval and Air Force jet fighters in the skies above the Cape. Two miles out to sea were two carrier battle groups ordered in by the president. The carriers *Eisenhower* and *Roosevelt* had their fighter wings on close alert. They had orders to shoot anything out of the sky within a hundred miles of Kennedy. The Navy had the duty of striking any vessel that produced a radar signal within attack range of the space center. All shipping and private boats were ordered to anchor at least five miles from shore.

Anything moving after the ten-minute mark of the countdown would be attacked without warning. The president was doing everything possible to protect this last-chance launch.

The four-man team had been trained by the Mechanic himself. They had been certified as expert divers and had the Stinger system down to a science. There would be no waiting for either the Saturn V or the shuttle *Atlantis* to reach orbit. They would each be attacked at the Cape. The Saturn would be attacked just after the first stage separation and the shuttle just as the solid booster rockets ignited. The strike would be carried out simultaneously from four different launchers.

The four men, all former members of al Qaeda, had trained in South America and had actually been the standby team for the mission against the European Space Agency launch. As soon as that mission had been completed, the Mechanic had them transported to a Panamanian freighter ten miles off the coast of Florida. Once the freighter came within five miles of the coast, the men and their equipment had been eased into the warm waters and they swam the rest of the way in. They had almost been discovered by a circling Apache helicopter gunship, but they evaded the infrared fix by diving deep. They had been onshore for the past ten minutes. Each man knew what had happened to the previous team in South America, but all were willing to give their lives for a success against the Americans.

They had set up in the reeds just beyond the waves at Cocoa Beach. They could see and hear the many American citizens as they watched on their beach towels and their lawn chairs. The men couldn't wait to see and hear their terror at what they were about to witness.

They could all hear the ten-second countdown from five miles away as the announcement blasted through the warm Florida air. The anticipation on the beach was growing. As the countdown proceeded, people began to stand and cheer.

Suddenly, the voice of the Kennedy Space Center announcer went silent. The entire world was blotted out as the Saturn V erupted into a ball of flame that caught even the terrorists off guard. The sight was magnificent. The red and orange fireball splashed free of the confines of the direction chamber just beneath the engines of the great rocket. The ground shook and it was as if everything was frozen in time—a time that went all the way back to the heady days of the Apollo program.

As men and women on the beach yelled in support, some held field glasses to the night sky. They all wondered if the giant rocket was going to lift off at all. Then they got cold chills as the tower stabilizers fell free and the great Atlas V ~Saturn~ started to rise from the Earth. The platform began climbing faster and faster. The exhaust plume lit up the night sky like a false sunrise. Those Americans who had only days before been against the race to the Moon now believed in the cause, believed once more in the power of A~~tlas~~. Saturn

The ship carrying the Altair lander and the largest crew module ever carried into space finally cleared the tower. It rose majestically into the night sky. Many people on the beach jumped up and down as the first stage put out the most power of any rocket in the history of the American space program. All thought of keeping America away from the Moon vanished in the split second it took for Atlas to come to life and make believers of the entire country.

". . . three, we have main engine start of *Atlantis*. Two, one, we have booster ignition and *Atlantis* is a go!" The announcement rang out through loudspeakers and the crowded beach erupted just as the main boosters did. *Atlantis* quickly cleared the tower. The four-man attack element was watching in awe as the American spacecraft rose into the nighttime sky on twin fireballs.

## SPACE SHUTTLE *ATLANTIS* (ORBITER VEHICLE DESIGNATION: OV-104)

Sarah, Will, and Ryan had thought they would be prepared for the liftoff of the shuttle, but they had all been sorely mistaken. At first it was only *Atlantis*'s three main engines that shook the airframe of the giant shuttle. But then the solid booster rockets ignited and they all had the same thought—they were exploding right there on the pad before they could get an inch off the ground.

Will had stopped worrying about how hot he was and was now squeezing his eyes as tightly shut as he could get them. He couldn't understand why Ryan was whooping it up in the middle seat of the three. Sarah was silent as she stared wide-eyed at the far bulkhead of their temporary container. They were shaking, jumping, and then they all felt it. Their stomachs told them they were indeed leaving the ground.

The shuttle shook even more as the true power of the solid boosters started pushing *Atlantis* into the sky. They heard the commands of the shuttle pilot as he calmly called out their status for mission control.

"Open your eyes, Will. You don't want to miss this," Ryan called out.

"Okay, guys, quiet in the main bay. We have work to do up here," said the calm voice of the shuttle commander. "Hang in there. Control, we are a go for roll maneuver."

Sarah managed a quick look over at Ryan and shook her head. Even as far back as they were in the cargo bay, they felt as though they were being shaken to death. They all felt the heat building as the exhaust from the rocket boosters and the three main engines started to penetrate the cargo hold. Sarah remembered the words "experimental crew cabin" as they climbed into the sky.

"Shit," she mumbled, as the g-forces started to hit them.

*Atlantis* was nearing the point of no safe return when the missiles were launched.

"Houston, *Atlantis*, we are throttle up!"

The first stage of A~~tlas~~ *Saturn* exploded outward from the second stage and the engines ignited, sending a rainbow shower of flame and gases into the darkness of the night sky. The separation was seen as far away as Georgia and the Carolinas. The spectacular night show also gave the terrorist element on the beach their cue to act. With no radio communication from the Mechanic directing them, the four-man team stood among the reeds at the edge of Cocoa Beach and turned on the seeker heads in the advanced stingers that had been chosen specially for this operation. The five-pound warhead was propelled by a two-stage experimental system designed by Raytheon for a low-cost strike against an orbiting vehicle. The weight was a total of twenty pounds over the standard Stinger system. The warhead would reach the target at twice the speed of sound once the IR detector locked on to the exhaust plume of both the A~~tlas~~ second stage and *Atlantis*.

The first team, consisting of two men and their launchers, brought their targeting systems up. The IR lock-on had no trouble detecting the large gas plume of the second stage of the A~~tlas~~ V, which carried the crew capsule and the Altair lander. The two men never hesitated as they pulled the trigger on the two weapons. A burst of air sent both missiles out of the tubes; after traveling twenty feet the solid propellant boosters fired and the missiles soared skyward. The heat of the launch and brightness of the flash caught everyone's attention along the beach. Before they could react, the second two-man team launched their own missiles, targeted on *Atlantis*. At the same moment, a bright flare filled the sky as the solid rocket boosters separated from the mainframe of the shuttle. The men immediately dropped their launchers and turned to make their way off the beach to try to blend in with the stunned onlookers who had witnessed the launching of the four missiles. As some watched the streaking missiles climb toward the heavens, others had turned their attention to the men who were even now making their way into the crowd.

## JOHNSON SPACE CENTER, HOUSTON, TEXAS

Hugh Evans watched as the first two missiles climbed toward their target, the second stage of A~~tlas~~. The three blips on the radar screen were merging at an incredible rate. The U.S. Air Force had put a plan in place in the hectic hours after the *Discovery* and *Endeavour* disasters and now that plan was starting to take shape.

Four venerable F-15 Eagles had been flying high-air cover for the double launch. Two were delegated to Atlas, two to *Atlantis*. As Evans stood and watched, he looked over at CAPCOM and shook his head, indicating that he didn't want *Atlantis* to know they were being hunted by two supersonic murderers. *What was the sense in telling them?* he thought. *There would be nothing they could do about it.*

On the high-altitude camera system deployed at the Cape, they saw the momentary bright flash as the Stinger warheads separated from their first stages. Evans knew they were up against superior technology when he saw the second-stage boosters ignite. He lowered his vision and saw the Eagles as they streaked upward at an intercept angle—he saw that the old fighters were climbing almost straight up into the air.

"Go, go, go!" he said loudly, as the rest of the telemetry technicians watched, most in silent prayer as the four missiles rose to assault their targets.

The four F-15Cs climbed at Mach 2.2, far behind Atlas and *Atlantis*. The custom-designed planes had been flown down from their training station in North Carolina and were fitted with a large load of compressed oxygen for their specially tailored mission. There had been four of these aircraft on standby in California. As they climbed to sixty thousand feet, the air became so thin the fighters were in danger of flaming out. Any man in aerospace knew that if the fighters didn't launch their weapons soon, it would be too late.

The four Eagles were equipped with the AIM-120 advanced medium-range, air-to-air missile, better known in naval and Air Force circles as the AMRAAM. The AIM 120-Dm, a solid propellant weapon, is twelve feet long and carries a fragmentation high-explosive warhead. However, the attribute that made it appropriate for this mission was the fact that it didn't need air to breathe. Also, its speed had been clocked at four times the speed of sound. Its seeker head was what is known in the military as a genius weapon. It didn't need the launching aircraft to send the instructions for it to seek out its target. It thought on its own.

As the world watched, the F-15s started to slow as they reached their maximum altitude. Then an amazing thing happened. The four external air-delivery systems attached to the inside of the wings started pumping life-giving air into the General Electric engines on the four fighters. The air expanded and gave the Eagles much needed thrust at high altitude where there was no oxygen. The two lead elements locked their AMRAAMs on to the two streaking Stingers as they neared the ten-mile mark. The two fighters launched simultaneously. Four AMRAAMs were targeted on the two smaller missiles.

An amazing thing happened as the Raytheon AMRAAMs locked on to their sister missiles. Their computer brains knew immediately that they could not hit the targets directly. So they calculated time and distance in a microsecond and then streaked above the faster-moving Stingers. They climbed to a mile above them and three miles behind the high-flying Atlas, simultaneously detonating above the Stingers. Shrapnel from the two AMRAAMs peppered the warheads, sending small pieces of metal in all directions. They struck the warheads, igniting one and severely damaging the other as it fought through the cloud of debris to be incinerated by the rocket engines of the Atlas second stage.

The same attack pattern had been chosen by the computers on the second set of AMRAAMs, but this time only one of the expensive missiles detonated above the Stingers. The second traveled on to meet its target—the space shuttle *Atlantis*.


Hugh Evans thought quickly. The scenario had run a thousand times in his mind and had been discussed with the engineers and flight planners. It had been mapped out with the shuttle commander. The plan was crazy and could end up costing the lives of all twelve astronauts anyway, but he knew now they had no choice as the second Stinger was nearing the streaking *Atlantis*.

"Now!" Evans shouted.

"*Atlantis*, Houston, execute early handoff, now!" CAPCOM said as calmly as he could.

"Houston, *Atlantis*, executing early handoff."

As the long-range cameras gave the ground station a grainy view of events, the explosive bolts holding the giant external tank in place on the belly of *Atlantis* detonated. This happened a full two minutes before it was supposed to; Evans knew they had no choice. They were now deploying the largest and most explosive defensive warhead in history.

The fuel tank broke away and fell right into the path of the Stinger as it was nearing the end of its range. The warhead struck the fiberglass container and detonated. The tank exploded and, as it did, the expanding gases struck *Atlantis*, increasing its speed by over five hundred miles an hour. This pushed the heavy shuttle well beyond its designated flight path, its nose coming dangerously close to flipping, which would have torn the eggshell-like airframe to pieces. The shuttle pilot took a chance and fired the OHM's maneuvering jets on the lowest point on the nose. At first *Atlantis* didn't respond, and then it started to right itself as the explosion of the external fuel tank lessened. Soon *Atlantis* was back on course. It would soon be discovered, however, that the shuttle had suffered three holes that punctured the thin outer skin of the engine mounts and continued through the cargo bay, with one piece of the shrapnel actually shearing away the strap on Ryan's safety harness.

Hugh Evans didn't celebrate because the emergency maneuver had left the shuttle dangerously low. There were also holes punched in the orbiter and three crewmen who were about to burn up if he didn't get those cargo bay doors open to the cold of space. He shook his head and looked over at communications. He nodded as everyone in the room took a deep breath before they started calling out their telemetry statuses.

"Inform *Atlantis* they are a go for low orbit insertion, and tell them to get those three crewmen the hell out of that cargo hold before they burn up."

"*Atlantis*, you are a go for low orbit insertion, and Flight recommends you start your cargo door cycle early to relieve your three crewmen. Get them out of there, over."

"Houston, we are way ahead of you. We can report that the three crewmen are all fine—a little shaken—but in good shape, over."

Hugh Evans reached out and picked up the phone. "Put me through please." He waited until his call was complete. Then he closed his eyes and relaxed for the first time in a month. He opened his eyes as his people started to figure out an adjusted flight plan for the shuttle, which was now on a course to meet up with the Atlas and the International Space Station.

"Mr. Evans, that was some piece of maneuvering," said the voice of the president.

"Thank you, sir, it's not over yet, but we are on our way."

"Excellent. Now, we just received word that that the Russians are preparing to launch once again in two days. So, with the Chinese two days out from the Moon, we need to keep Dark Star on a strict timetable. We still don't know if the Russians are with us, or against us."

"Yes, sir."

"Good job, Hugh, it won't be forgotten."

"I think you need to start with that little bald fella that planned all of this. He's the one that came up with the backup plan."

"He knows how I feel, now get our people to the Moon."

"Yes, sir, the Dark Star mission is on its way."

When four Apache attack helicopters reached the scene of the Stinger launches the crews were amazed to see all four of the suspects in the attack subdued. They were being manhandled by a large crowd of onlookers on Cocoa Beach. The Army warrant officers watched, taking their time as they guided the local police authorities in to stop the lynching that was about to take place.

# PART THREE

# OPERATION COLUMBUS

Come on you stranger, you legend, you martyr, and shine!
You reached for the secret too soon, you cried for the moon.

**—Pink Floyd**

# 11

Niles watched Virginia sleep.

Her eyes fluttered open and her vision fixed on Niles.

"What? Was I slobbering or something?" she asked weakly, as she tried with much difficulty to sit up in bed.

Niles reached out and placed a firm hand on her left shoulder, easing her down onto her pillows.

"Take it easy, and no, you weren't slobbering," he said with a small, worried smile.

Virginia's eyes fixed on the clothing Niles was wearing and then looked up into his eyes. Niles was aware how he looked out of his normally dark suit and tie and figured Virginia would figure it out quickly enough.

"You're going to be running things right from this bed, Virginia. We have nothing going on at the Group that will require anything more than a signature, so you shouldn't have any difficulties. You can have all four of my staff."

"Where are you going?" she asked as she sat up, forcing Niles's restraining hands away.

"I'm going where everyone else seems to be at the moment—Ecuador. Alice and the senator landed there about six hours ago, according to Jack."

"What?" Virginia asked, wincing at the pain that shot from her forehead to the back of her head. "He's not dying fast enough? He has to go to Ecuador?"

"My thoughts exactly," Niles said as he handed her a glass of water. "Anyway, let me catch you up on your plan. Two elements of Dark Star have been destroyed.

We lost the *Endeavour* and the *Discovery*, all hands. *Dark Star 3* is now in geosynchronous orbit over North America and is at the rendezvous point with the space station. The shuttle *Atlantis* was slightly damaged in the attack and has already docked with the ISS." He saw the concern in Virginia's face. "Yes, Sarah, Will, and Jason are fine, as are the rest of the crew. *Atlantis*, on the other hand, will never see the Earth again—she's just too damaged."

"So, we managed to retire the complete shuttle roster in one day," Virginia said, thinking about the twenty-four crewmen lost on *Discovery* and *Endeavour.*

"My plan, my losses," Niles said, then turned and looked away in thought. "The chairman of the People's Republic is still uncooperative, and the *Magnificent Dragon* spacecraft is twenty-four hours away from a landing attempt."

"Are the Chinese personnel still onboard with our plan?" she asked, trying to get Niles to tell her everything.

"Our sources in Beijing, along with the vice chairman, have assured us that the crew understands Earth's plight and is sympathetic to our plan."

"So we don't know," Virginia said as she watched Niles finally turn around.

"We don't know. Won't know until *Dark Star* arrives on the Moon and we find out whether we're welcomed by the Chinese crew or fired upon."

"And if they're welcomed, what will happen in China?"

"A coup—when you say the words, it sounds so simple. But there it is. We're hoping for a coup."

"Why won't the chairman listen to reason? He's had five years to make up his mind. We've given him all of the evidence and information from Matchstick that we have and he still doesn't believe there's a threat. We need that technology, Niles. We're desperate for it. Without it we're a doomed race."

"We may have a chance if the ESA spacecraft makes it. Otherwise, it's all up to *Dark Star.*"

"When are you going to let Jack and the others in on what's really happening?"

"The president has labeled this Black One. No one is to know. I hate it as much as you do, but we're talking about the most guarded secret in human history. The words 'Case Blue'—if any person says them out loud, it will get that person killed."

"We need Jack's thinking on this, or at least the senator's while he's still with us. I've said that since the beginning."

"And I've argued the point since the start and you know it. The president won't budge on this. You, I, the president, and the heads of state of Britain, France, China, and Russia are the only ones who know what's happening. A few others may have guessed, like the Joint Chiefs of Staff, but that's it. It was a brilliant ruse by the president to publicly slash the budgets of NASA, DARPA, and the rest of the space program. That alone should keep the press away from Case Blue for at least a year."

"How are the people taking the Moon shots?" Virginia asked, watching Niles closely.

"The tide has turned for the good there. The polls are saying eighty percent of the people are now backing the space program. That means we'll have a budget to work with after the mission's complete—at least to start with. We won't have to hide so much from the pencil pushers."

"Too bad it took all of those deaths to get the people back."

"It's a shame. Anyway," Niles said, placing a hand to Virginia's cheek, "I'm off to see if we can uncover Columbus. that would go a long way to guaranteeing some kind of defense against what we know is coming."

"Tell Jack, Carl, and the senator what's going on," Virginia said, her eyes pleading with Niles. "It's bad enough that we have Sarah, Will, and Jason up there in the dark. Don't do it to Jack."

Niles removed his hand and turned away, moving toward the door. "Sarah knows. I told her."

"Why just Sarah?" Virginia asked, watching Compton open the door.

"We need to know if that mineral can help us. And she needed to know why we wanted it. An explosive as powerful as nuclear fission with no aftereffects—" He turned one last time to face Virginia. "Besides, any alien technology we may find along with that mineral would be a godsend."

Virginia watched her boss leave and then decided she couldn't stay in bed. She sat up and, on wobbly legs, slowly walked to the door and opened it. She saw Niles stepping into the hallway that led to the bank of elevators. She didn't care if the hospital gown opened all the way in the back as she called out to him.

"You have to tell them, Niles. They're the only ones who have any experience in this. You have to tell them of the increasing probes and attacks. You have to!"

She saw Niles step into the elevator and the doors close. She lowered her head as one of the shift nurses came toward her. Virginia held up her right hand and fixed the young girl with a stern look.

"I don't want any grief from you, young lady. Get me my clothes. I'm going back to work."

As the girl turned to leave, Virginia turned away and went into her room. She sat on the edge of her bed, thinking about the events leading to this rush to the Moon and the reasoning behind it.

"If we don't recover that technology and mineral, Earth and everything on it will die."

## 50 MILES EAST OF QUITO, ECUADOR

Jack was looking straight at Garrison Lee as Alice injected him with a massive dose of morphine to kill his pain. The old man had held up well through their run from the capital city and thus far had handled the overnight stay in the forested area just below the Andes, but now the fare for their little ride was coming due and the senator was a little short.

They were now held up behind some ramshackle buildings off the main road in the foothills. Alice, in her infinite wisdom, had set up a rendezvous with Pete Golding, Charlie Ellenshaw, and the remaining German commandos at the remote location. Thus far the men from the plane were a no-show and the five of them were getting hungry.

"You have something on your mind, Colonel?" Lee asked, as he rolled his shirtsleeve down, flexing his arm as he did so.

"I want to know exactly why you're here," Collins said as he handed Lee a bottle of water.

The former senator from Maine accepted the water with a nod of his head. The fedora he was wearing was tilted at an angle that leaned toward his eye patch.

"Same reason you're here. I want to know what's under this mountain." Lee looked from Jack to Alice. Then his eye fixed on the German. "It was a kind gesture for your chancellor to allow you to assist our boys here."

Sebastian didn't respond, since he felt Lee was baiting him for a reason he couldn't understand. He studied the man a moment and then looked at his companion, the very capable Mrs. Hamilton.

"I follow orders."

"I'm sure you do, son." Lee looked from Krell back over to Jack and then Everett.

"Garrison, are you going to let them in on your suspicions, or are you going to play games all damn day," Alice said, as she placed her small black bag on the backseat of the police cruiser.

"I don't think I have that much explaining to do. I think Jack knows that something in this whole thing stinks to high heaven."

Collins for his part was playing it cool. He did have doubts that people were being straight with him on what was happening, starting with his boss, Niles Compton. However, being the career military man that he was he had learned to swallow his suspicions about superiors and follow orders the best that he could, even though he hated going into a mission with only the smallest of details to assist him. He would let the senator do the talking.

Lee stood and placed a hand on Everett's shoulder, nodding, as if saying he was glad to see him. "For me it all started when I learned that our good friend Niles was placed in charge of organizing the Dark Star missions." He let out a small laugh. He removed his fedora and wiped the sweat from the inside brim using his handkerchief. He then placed the hat back on. "Niles is a genius, we all know that. But outer space, the Moon, and the equipment used to get people there is a little bit out of his field of expertise."

"The president is his friend," Everett volunteered. "He trusts the director. You know, to get it done right."

Lee nodded again and sat on the edge of the police car's backseat, as if standing would be too taxing on his failing system.

"Yes, that's the key word here Mr. Everett—trust. But not in the sense you're using it. When you're out to keep a secret, maybe the largest secret in the history of the planet, you turn to people you trust. Keep that trust localized, within a small circle, if you will, I know. I've been there."

"I'm not getting your meaning," Everett said.

They heard a car coming and Krell stepped out from behind the false front of the old building. He saw an ancient-looking pickup and camper pulling up in front. He saw the crazy-haired Ellenshaw behind the wheel and he relaxed. He leaned back and nodded at Jack.

"It's them."

Collins was relieved they had made it from the airport without being stopped. Once more they were wanted men, being hunted by a very angry, very embarrassed Ecuadorian government.

"Get them under cover as soon as you can, and get that vehicle hidden."

Krell left to get his men settled and find the food that they should have brought with them.

"Back to my meaning, Mr. Everett. There is far more happening than just the recovery of the technology that we believe is here and on the Moon. Why are Sarah and our people on that backup flight?"

"Yes," Jack said beneath his breath. "Why Sarah?"

A voice from behind them said, "Because we needed Sarah on the International Space Station to analyze the mineral if it was recovered. Regardless of the first two Dark Star missions, we needed Sarah on that station as my eyes and ears, as well as for her expertise on the mineral. She'll send back a report the president can trust."

Everyone turned and saw Niles Compton. He was dressed in tan working clothes and his eyes were fixed on Garrison Lee and Alice.

"I should have known you would be getting suspicious. I told the president that you would suspect something," Compton said. He turned to face Jack. "I also told him that you would be figuring things out before too long."

"Can someone tell me what's up?" Everett asked. Just then they were joined by Sebastian, his men, Pete, and then finally, Ellenshaw.

Niles walked over and kneeled down. He looked into Lee's one good eye.

"What are you doing here? You should be at home and in bed." He patted Lee on the knee. He looked from his former boss to Alice, who couldn't hold his gaze for long. She looked down at her feet.

"One last romp around the park," Lee said and looked at Niles. His eye never wavered. "No fool like an old fool."

Niles smiled and straightened. He turned to face Jack and Carl.

"I'm sorry, I never liked keeping things from you and you know that. But this . . . this thing is far beyond my scope. I didn't know what to do or where to turn. So I let the president talk me into secrecy. And I will keep my word on that. Until he gives me the go-ahead, I cannot tell you everything."

The others looked down, as they understood Niles was just following orders.

They could see in his face, his very demeanor, that keeping things from them was driving him close to the edge. Jack for his part watched the man and decided that he would wait to push him on the issue, but he also knew that the closer Sarah and the others got to the surface of the Moon, the more hard pressed he would be not to make Niles talk.

"What are we doing about the people responsible for the attacks?" Jack asked instead.

"The FBI and Interpol have arrest warrants out for your friend McCabe and the Reverend Rawlins. We also know that the good minister has ties with Iran through his ministry and McCabe has his al Qaeda contacts. Thus, we know where some of the manpower came from. The bad news is we can't find them. They caught the attack team at Cape Canaveral, but they aren't talking—three Saudis and one Syrian."

"What's the Pentagon saying about the forces covering Ecuador?" Everett asked.

"That's a major concern and one of the reasons I'm here. The president wants to know what you'll need to get into that mountain. If the mission on the Moon fails, Columbus is our only hope."

"Again, not knowing the full details of the true mission here, I will only venture a guess," Jack said, as he stood and paced inside the old building. "Either we need a full air assault element, maybe the 101st Airborne, or just what we have here. Either not enough or too many. How high a price is the president willing to pay?"

"He'll mortgage the house, Jack. Whatever you call for to get in there, he'll give you. Ecuador is our friend, there is no doubt about that, but the president will burn them down to get at Columbus, and the rest of the world's leaders will stand by and do nothing."

"Just what in hell is that important?" Everett asked. "That we'd kick the hell out of a small country for no reason other than they have something buried here that we want?"

"That's the entire point, Captain," Niles said, almost losing his temper. "We don't just want it, *we need* it."

"Well, we'll see if we can avoid killing a bunch of innocent soldiers and get inside the place the old-fashioned way," Collins said, turning Everett away from Compton. He looked at Sebastian. "What do you say, my German friend. Feel like preventing an invasion of Ecuador?"

"Can we eat first?" Sebastian said, and he and his men laughed.

"What did you bring us to eat, Doc?" Collins asked Ellenshaw.

"Beans and rice," he said, pushing his glasses back up the bridge of his nose. Jack and the others looked at Crazy Charlie and didn't say a word.

"Hey, it's not like they have a McDonald's on every corner in Ecuador."

## INTERNATIONAL SPACE STATION,
## UNITED STATES LABORATORY SECTION,
## CODE-NAMED DESTINY

Will and Jason eased themselves in through the five-foot round hatch. It had been several hours since they had not felt the free-falling weightless phenomenon known as the "floats." The condition is relatively short-lived and the stomach usually falls back into its normal pattern after some time in the weightless world of space. As they entered the American laboratory named Destiny, they saw that Sarah was busy working with something she had carried in a small case the entire time they had been away from the Event Group complex.

"The colonel says we're as ready as we're ever going to be."

Sarah looked up without really seeing Mendenhall.

"Hey, you with us?" he asked, looking from Sarah and then back to Ryan, shrugging his shoulders.

"He says we're ready for that slingshot thing around the Earth," Ryan said, watching her closely. "Hey, wake up," he finally said.

Sarah blinked her eyes and then saw that Ryan was shaking her.

"Oh, sorry," she said finally, smiling. "I was lost there for a minute."

"Playing with rocks will do that to you," Will said as he reached for the meteorite Sarah held in her hand. She pulled it away from him.

"Don't do that," she said, her face etched in seriousness. "We're in an almost pure oxygen environment."

"Hey, that isn't one of those Pop Rocks, is it?" Ryan asked as he floated backward.

"Yes, but unless you get it wet, it's pretty safe. Sorry, Will, but if you had sweat on your hands . . . well, I don't know if it would have set off the chain reaction, but being we're in outer space and all . . ."

Mendenhall looked from the stone in her hands to her face. "Don't worry about it, but we better get moving."

Sarah closed her eyes and nodded. "Right, the old slingshot-around-the-Earth thing. Can't wait." She placed the meteorite back into its Styrofoam-encased box and then placed it in her jumpsuit. She pulled her Velcro-covered feet free of the floor.

"What were you thinking when we floated in here? It was like you were in another world," Ryan asked, following Sarah out of the laboratory.

"The mineral—we're overlooking something fundamental here and for the life of me I can't figure out what it is."

"Well, you've got two days to figure it out. The colonel has decided on a straight-in approach to the Moon, following the same path as Astral. One orbit and then bam, we hit the surface."

Mendenhall nudged Ryan. "What do you mean, bam?"

"You know, land," Ryan said with a wink.

"Have you heard anything about the Chinese?"

"Eighteen hours till they land," Ryan said, as he slowed and waited for Will to slide by him in the companionway.

"Jesus, we're so far behind," Sarah said as she pulled herself into the exercise module where the rest of the crew was waiting.

"Next time I'll just close up that hatch and leave you three here," Colonel Kendal said as he stood poised beside a map of Shackleton Crater.

"Apologies, I was making some last-minute spectrographs on the mineral."

"No excuse. When I call a meeting that means come running." Kendal's demeanor softened and he shook his head. "Now, with the docking procedures completed, and *Altair* joined with the *Dark Star 3* crew module and capsule, we're finally ready. You've all had a great meal of MREs, freeze-dried though they are, so we'll leave now while we have a favorable launch window. In two days we'll be where we want to be. Sergeant, are your men ready for whatever we may run into?"

"I believe so, sir. The Chinese, if it comes down to it, can't be that much more prepared than ourselves. Loaded onboard the Altair we have ten compressed-air M-39 rocket-assisted projectile weapons. We are not carrying any explosive ordnance due to the instability of the mineral. Intelligence reports state that the Chinese forces, like the ESA team and the Russians, if they ever get there, will be armed with basically the same weapons."

Sarah thought the Special Forces sergeant looked extremely young. But then again so did Will Mendenhall. She half smiled at Will when he gave her a sad look.

"That makes the odds pretty much even if the Chinese turn out to be unfriendly. Well, we do have one advantage. The Chinese have made their own mistakes. They cannot adjust their orbit because of fuel loss. So that means they have to land over a hundred miles from Shackleton. That gives us a fighting chance at getting there first. Ladies and gentlemen, we are going to land two hundred feet from the edge of Shackleton. Dangerous, but I think my copilot, Mr. Ryan, and I can do it."

Ryan looked over at Will and Sarah and then smiled broadly. They knew that look as the *we're all going to die* look from years past.

"Okay, the Russians have their systems back online, but they won't be able to launch for another twenty-four hours. So, that leaves us the damaged *Astral* lander of the European Space Agency, and the *Magnificent Dragon* to contend with. I believe our *Altair* is the best craft running this little race. I know we can do this. So, let's go to the Moon."

As the flight team started to file out toward the docking collar, Sarah floated aside to let men and women pass her. She started thinking. She felt the small box with the meteorite inside and then she looked out of the small porthole. The Earth was there, and she could even see South America. She said a prayer for Jack, Carl, and the others. Still, the thought of the small rock she carried bothered her. The keyword she knew was "meteorite." She said it over and over again. Then, Will Mendenhall pulled on her sleeve.

"Hey, you want to get left behind?" he asked.

Sarah didn't say anything. She just floated by Will and into the sleeve that connected the ISS with the crew module of *Dark Star*.

"I was hoping you were going to say yes, because I would have stayed with you."

Will watched as Sarah went inside. He grimaced at the thought of leaving for the Moon.

"Nobody ever listens to me."

## AMBASSADOR HOTEL, QUITO, ECUADOR

The hotel was virtually a fortress as the security element of Faith Ministries moved in. All sixteen floors were occupied by men paid half of what they were owed. Five hundred mercenaries from every continent on the globe had been assembled to augment the security force already in place. The Ecuadorian Armed Forces were still on the fence about falling in line. The president of the United States was bringing pressure to bear on the leaders of the small country through the Organization of American States to open up the mine for general inspection. Since the mine was privately owned by a German firm and another firm registered as an Ecuadorian mining concern, the legalities were such that Ecuador could debate the problem for years and still not come to a final legal determination of the rights of the owners. Little did anyone know the owners were inside the hotel and weren't about to give up any of their rights of possession.

Samuel Rawlins, replete with white scarf, jungle boots, and tan working clothes designed for him by a prestigious tailor in New York, paced the large suite on the topmost floor of the Ambassador. He knew the time would come when he had to relinquish all his holdings, including Faith Ministries; he just never thought it would happen so suddenly. After seventy years of hiding the artifacts from the world, all of his work and all of his father's work before him had unraveled so fast that he was having a hard time believing it had happened at all.

Former Special Forces Colonel James McCabe sat on the large couch and picked some nonexistent lint from his pants. He looked into the corner of the suite and saw the suitcases. They held a new life for him. As of this moment, he was no longer involved with the good Reverend and his scheme to keep mankind in the dark about its past. His job was done, his reward sitting in sixteen different banks around the world. His new uniform was tucked nicely into the brand-new suitcases awaiting him. Bosnia-Herzegovina, a nonextradition country with a deep hatred for the West, was allowing McCabe to take a new post in their government under an assumed name and with a new, surgically altered face. And they were allowing him to keep the $1.2 billion as reward for a job well done. He knew he would leave as soon as a loose thread was snipped away from the fabric of his new life.

"If I had the expertise, I would lead the defense of the mine myself," Rawlins said, as he placed a hand on his daughter's cheek. She covered his with her own and looked up at the ridiculously dressed Reverend. "As it is, I have to bow to the expert."

"If that attack comes at all," Laurel said as her eyes went to McCabe, who raised his brows and smiled.

"Oh, it'll come. It will come just as sure as your death is imminent."

"But the manner of my death will bring martyrdom to my cause," Rawlins said, starting to go off on another tangent. "My two daughters will inherit my wealth, my ideals, and my love of the Lord. Why, they'll—"

"Be dead right alongside you," McCabe said. "Your wealth will be frozen." McCabe stood and walked toward a large window that looked out over the city. "Your church and your industries will be destroyed and dismantled. Your legacy will be disgraced. The country—hell, the world—will not soon forget the murderer of heroes. It seldom ever does."

"And you walk away clean? Is that it?" Laurel asked, looking far more confident than McCabe thought she had a right to.

"Let's just say I walk away. You will not." He turned to face Rawlins and Laurel. He placed his hands in his pants pockets, shaking his head. "It started coming apart when you decided to play assassin, a job you're not very good at. I told you that attacking the president was a mistake, but you decided you knew better than me. No matter the politics of the time, Americans don't care for people who try to kill a sitting president. Your second mistake was trusting in the Mechanic. By triggering his Jihad mentality, you have awakened a dormant desire inside of him to bring down the unbelievers." He smiled and looked directly at Rawlins. "And that includes you. To him you are nothing but a wolf in sheep's clothing, a user of the true believers—one who would kill his own people in the pursuit of placing your faith above that of all others.

"You still control the towel head," Rawlins stated, his anger growing.

"These men here in this hotel, the ones at the mine, they're not my men. They're his." McCabe placed a hand on Laurel's shoulder and squeezed. "Amateurs, that's what you are. Your zeal for protecting your faith against a real truth was never the real issue, just one that you could grasp. For the Mechanic it's the only issue. The discoveries buried in those mines are what will drive him much further than even you could conceive. Bringing Operation Columbus into the light of day may be a casus belli for you to take upon yourself as an affront to your religion, your way of belief, but the Mechanic believes it is a true affront to God. And while you consider yourself a mouthpiece for the Lord, dear Reverend, he believes he is a true messenger of God." He laughed and removed his hand from Laurel's shoulder. "That is why he was so easily recruited by me. He lost his faith when his superiors lacked the willpower to take the fight to the unbelievers. He sought money, but then Laurel got him to thinking again. He despises you and your father so much that you actually made him whole again with your scheming."

"I have him believing that he needs me and our resources," Laurel said with a smirk.

This time McCabe laughed out loud.

"Needs you? My dear you are dealing with a man who was in on the planning for 9/11. Your pretty little face was mere inches away from a cold-blooded killer who ordered the decapitation of women and children for accepting food from American soldiers in Afghanistan. He is the man who has taken over your little plan, a plan that I conceived and made possible." McCabe walked toward the suitcases in the far corner. "And now you'll have to deal with him yourself, Laurel my dear." He picked up two of the suitcases and turned. "Because there is a man on the loose who is relentless in his pursuit of what he thinks is right, and I just gave him something he wants and needs—a warning of your intentions. Colonel Jack Collins is an old acquaintance of mine, and besides wanting to see me again, he would truly love to meet you two and the Mechanic."

"You have betrayed us?" Rawlins said as he stood aghast.

"Betrayed? Yes, I guess I have, but in the end I think we'll all get what we deserve."

Laurel stood and made her way to the door. She paused before opening it for McCabe.

"I suspect we will all get what the Lord has planned for us," she said as she opened the door.

McCabe started to walk forward and then stopped suddenly when he saw who was standing in the doorway. The Mechanic had a pistol leveled at the American. He stepped in and closed the door. His eyes were dull, as though he were going about a task that was necessary but beneath him.

"I guess some of us will get what's deserved far sooner than others," Laurel said as she eased her arm around the Mechanic.

"What is this? Daughter, step away from that man."

McCabe lowered his suitcases and looked from Laurel to the dull-eyed Mechanic. The man had shaved and his clothes were plain. Gone was the white suit and the white shirt. He looked like any Ecuadorian businessman after a day at work, and that was when McCabe knew he hadn't moved fast enough.

"I guess his God wouldn't want you mixing with a true believer," McCabe said, looking from Laurel to Rawlins.

"Reverend, I am taking control of the mines. The Americans will not be allowed to view its contents before my people take what it has to offer for our own aims."

"I hate to say I told you so, but—"

The Mechanic shot McCabe three times in rapid succession. The American took two steps back and then slid down in front of the couch. As he did, Laurel gasped at the suddenness of her former lover's death. Panic gripped her when the Mechanic reached around and removed her arm from him.

"You will never touch me again." He aimed the pistol three feet to his right and then he looked at Laurel, who had stepped back.

"What? I did as you requested. The accounts have been transferred to your banks, you have the money that McCabe was collecting from us, and you have my father's money as well. You owe me everything," Laurel said, looking at the smoking weapon held by the Mechanic.

"I suppose I owe you a debt of gratitude. You have not only awakened in me the true calling for which I was chosen, but also a sense of what the West is about. Your love of killing is not a thing that is warranted through the laws of God, but by the law and the need for money." He leveled the pistol at Laurel. "You and your father are on the right track in dealing with your countrymen, but you must realize that the extreme has not yet been reached. The mine holds the scientific means to lead God's children down their chosen path, the bodies you describe may give rise to doubt in his infinite word of how our world was created, but with the power of the ancient weaponry and a Jihad the likes of which the world has never seen, those untruths shall be destroyed and forgotten. My people will be the guardians of the ancient technology. Your father should have buried the truth long ago, but now it is far too late."

"My father lost his way and tried to gain riches from the assemblage of weaponry in the ruins," said Rawlins. "God, in his infinite wisdom, chose to destroy him, and bury him along with the heresy of that mine. Since his disappearance more than thirty years ago I have made sure that the truth of that place and its contents were well guarded, unseen by the unbelievers. If I had buried it, there are always little men with shovels who would come dig it up. You and McCabe promised me that you could destroy it and at the same time stop more of the technology from being found on the Moon."

"And the mine *will* be destroyed once my people gain the knowledge hidden there. This is a gift from God himself," the Mechanic said in his rediscovered zeal.

The Reverend stepped forward and placed his arm around his equally insane daughter. He pulled her into him and both sets of crazed eyes bore into the Mechanic.

"I would have the world burn before I allow my faith to be crushed by the release of more lies against the word of God."

"Then you will be allowed to witness the start of the final Jihad against the lies of infidels."

Without aiming, the Mechanic pulled the trigger and shot Laurel in the face. Then he shot her once more before she collapsed.

Rawlins stood shocked; his mouth was moving but nothing came out.

"At least the infidels, your countrymen, do not hide their true intent out of fear, but you, Mr. Rawlins, use God to your own ends. This is a sin you will not survive."

Three shots into Rawlins's face and neck sent him hard against the white-painted wall. He slowly slid down onto the floor next to his older daughter. The Mechanic looked at the two bodies in disgust and laid the silenced pistol on the end table near the couch. He picked up the phone and hit one number.

"Prepare the men. I want the mine shut down, and I also want the Americans who are in this country tracked down and killed. The mine shafts and the enclosure will be blasted into oblivion tonight after we remove the weaponry and the other technology."

## THE ANDES, 100 MILES EAST OF QUITO, ECUADOR

Jack didn't like it, but the only men who knew their way around Quito were Pete Golding and Charlie Ellenshaw. Collins had placed Sebastian in overall command of the mission to bring in the two men from Washington who were being sent in by the president. Information was being doled out on a very strict need-to-know basis and that was starting to infuriate Jack.

Since word of the attack on the Atlas and *Dark Star 3* had reached him, he had been champing at the bit to get his team inside the mountain. He had calmed when Niles had passed on word that they now had two days before Sarah and *Dark Star* reached lunar orbit. He knew his reactions and anger at the helpless situation could very well get a lot of people killed; thus he was considering handing over all elements of the advance team to Captain Everett. Then he would have Sebastian take command of any assault elements.

They were now holed up in five small trailers purchased with cash from a small town east of Quito by Director Compton. Several laptops and a satellite receiver had been provided by the U.S. embassy there and now they were in constant communication with Washington and Event Group Center. Most importantly they now had a direct link to Europa. The trailer had been hidden among the thick trees that flourished at the three-thousand-foot mark of the lower Andes. They were well above the mine that held the secrets of Columbus, and the team had thus far only had one close call with a roving patrol of what sounded like German mercenaries. It had taken Jack and Carl over ten minutes to convince Sebastian that he couldn't confront the patrol until they were ready and had permission from the president. That was one of the reasons they had decided to send the German commando off to Quito with Pete and Charlie.

Counting the ten German commandos, Jack could field six men besides himself, and that included the two Air Force pilots who had to abandon the 737 at the airport. Then there were Compton, Charlie, and Pete, not very good odds for facing the small force now guarding the mine's entrance. The colonel figured there were now close to two hundred personnel at the main entrance, and at least another seventy at the waterfall where they had made their earlier escape. One thing was for sure—he suspected that reinforcements would soon arrive as the mission to the Moon neared its objective. If they didn't get a go or receive an infusion of men from the president soon, they would lose the mine and everything in it. That would mean that Sarah and the others would actually have to land on the Moon in an untried and untested lander. Once they were there, they would face another landing team, one that might be hostile. These were the thoughts occupying Jack as he waited for the return of Sebastian, Charlie, and Pete.

Everett stepped up to the tree where Jack was sitting and kneeled down.

"Tough, huh?"

Jack shook his head slightly and tossed the stick that he was holding into the trees.

"You know, the thing of it is, if I'd been asked to volunteer for the Moon, and if I was as young as those three idiots, I would have jumped at the chance," Collins said, shaking his head.

"You and me both." Everett stood and looked around at the towering trees that hid their small camp. "But space is a young man's game. That's why we virtually attacked them before they left the complex. Our jealousy got the better of us, I think."

"It seems like a year since they left for Houston," Jack said as he too stood and looked around. He could see the three visible lookout positions above the mine and the road leading to it. He was satisfied that they were well enough hidden from any helicopter flyovers, so he turned and faced Everett again. "How's the senator?"

"Sleeping. Alice keeps him pretty much doped up. I just can't figure that guy," Carl said as he looked toward the disguised trailer where Garrison Lee was sleeping. "He's not content to spend his last few days at home with the woman he loves. He has to be out here on one last adventure."

Jack smiled for the first time in many hours and kicked at a small pinecone.

"It's unfinished business for him. The Columbus thing from the war, Alice's husband. You know the story." He looked at Everett and held his eyes with his own. "It's also because he, like us, knows we're being kept in the dark about what this is all about."

Everett looked over Jack's shoulder and saw the approach of Niles Compton, who was just leaving the senator's trailer. He came on slow toward the high spot where Jack and Carl stood.

"How's he doing?" Carl asked.

"The same. He's drifting in and out of sleep—dreaming a lot." Niles stepped up to the two larger men and placed his hands in his pockets. "I feel for Alice. She's listening to the senator talking with her dead husband, living his death over and over."

Jack remained quiet. Niles held the information he wanted, but if the director said he was under orders, he was under orders. Niles could tell him he would. The director wasn't one for keeping secrets from his people. If he thought it would cost the lives of his friends and colleagues, he would talk. As it was, he figured Niles understood that whatever he, the president, and Virginia had planned out, it didn't affect the immediate situation.

"Jack, if we had the manpower, could we take the mine and hold it long enough to make a thorough examination and evaluation of its contents?"

"If the people we face are mercenaries only, yes, I think so. But if the Ecuadorians join in, it would take the 101st Airborne to hold them off long enough. There are just not enough details about how large the mine is. The timetable would be all screwed up because of that."

"I've been speaking with the president and he's serious about securing that mine in the next twenty-four hours, by force if necessary. That means invading a friendly government."

"Shit, Niles, there are too many variables in taking an area that we have no intelligence on. We don't know who's really securing that place, or the fervor with which they'll defend it."

"With what these maniacs have accomplished so far, I would say they are willing to go the whole route in either destroying that mine with explosives or fighting off a full-scale attack," Everett said as he heard the approach of a car. He saw a hand appear on the vehicle's roof with its fingers spread. He gestured back that he understood it was a friendly.

"I agree," Jack said, looking from Everett to Niles. "Tell the president we need people in theater and we need them now. We have to have assets here in country, I don't care if they're dishwashers, military attachés, or CIA analysts and typists. It can be someone who works for the U.S. government or an American who just happens to be here on vacation. Get them here with anything they can buy, steal, or borrow. The same goes for any ally we still have who's willing to back our play."

Compton nodded and started to turn away. He stopped suddenly and faced Jack.

"I'll see what I can do. Listen you two, the president was almost killed over this thing, but he also realizes that he's expendable. As a whole, it's something that this planet has never faced before, and Columbus is something that can actually do some good—for everyone, not just us. Please bear with me and try to come up with a plan to take that mine intact." He started walking for the communications trailer. "Because without help, we—and I mean the whole planet here—could very well go under."

"Boy, with all these doomsday hints, Niles just about has me worried," Carl quipped, as he watched Niles hurry down the hill.

Jack watched Niles. He felt the director had meant to come clean about what he knew, but had kept his silence. He turned and looked at Everett.

"I have got to put my fear for Sarah and the others out of my head. We need to get to planning, and if you see me drifting away, kick me in the ass."

Everett smiled and slapped Jack on the back.

"Now that's an order I've waited for. For five damn years."

Jack watched as Sebastian held the door open for two old men. They eased out of the jeep, looking as if they had been thrown into a bag and shaken vigorously. One was a short, balding man, while the other was tall and thin as a rail. Compared to these men, Crazy Charlie was a prime physical specimen. As the two men stretched out their limbs, which still ached from the rough driving of Pete Golding, Jack saw that he and Charlie were starting to look like old pros at running and hiding.

"How did it go?" Carl asked the German as he unslung the short-barreled automatic from the denim shirt he was wearing.

"The capital is closing down. Looks like there are federal troops gathering at the airport. They may be flying in from around the country. Maybe they're antidrug teams that are being recalled. It doesn't look good."

"Anything else?" Jack asked.

"Yes, my friend. We were nearly caught by a small force about six miles from the main road. These men were what you Americans would call *salty*-looking. As we waited for them to pass through the woods heading for the mine, we saw a gathering five hundred strong. The same type, only these guys look like they're ready for anything. Large caliber weaponry, I even saw mortars."

"Jesus, I hate being right," Carl said.

"We have to move soon," Jack said. Then he smiled. "Possession is nine tenths of the law."

"It's the taking possession part I'm worried about," the large German said.

"Hopefully help is on the way, but we may have to move before it arrives." Collins eyed the two strangers walking toward them. "Now, who is this?"

Sebastian stepped out of the way and allowed the two men to step up.

"Colonel Collins?" the smaller of the two men said, holding out his hand. "Jensen Appleby. I'm the director of the agency. This is my colleague from MIT, Franklyn Dubois. He's the chairperson for advanced physics." He took Jack's hand and shook it. "We were ordered by the president to join Dr. Compton here. I believe he wants us to examine something."

Jack released the director's hand and looked at Everett and then Sebastian. He smiled and shook the other man's hand, then faced both. "Do you know what you're looking for out here?"

"Yes, I believe so. Some artifacts that may be comparable to those found on the Moon," Appleby said.

Everett removed a nine-millimeter from his waistband and placed it in the hand of the small bespectacled man from DARPA.

"Almost," Everett said, a small smile creasing his lips. "But you may have to use this before examining those items."

"Oh, dear," the tall, thin man from MIT said, looking at the weapon in Appleby's hand.

"Gentlemen, the man you're looking for is right inside that trailer," Jack said, pointing and at the same time taking Carl's weapon back from Appleby. "He'll explain everything." He turned and tossed the nine-millimeter back to Everett, then gestured for him and Sebastian to follow. "That wasn't nice, Captain," Jack said as they made their way to the third trailer in line.

"No, it wasn't. But maybe the president should think about getting troops in here and stop sending us teachers and professors."

"I agree," Sebastian said, but then he saw Jack's angry countenance. "Then again, I don't know shit and now choose not to speak English."


Six hours had passed since Niles had contacted the president and requested heavy assistance. Since that time Sebastian and his nine commandos had reported more Ecuadorian army personnel arriving at the mine. Thus far it looked as if three companies had been positioned in and around the old excavation. As it looked to the German commando, most of the army personnel were taking up station facing west, downhill toward Quito, defending a front where they thought their main threat would come.

"The president is in constant contact with President DeSilva. He is asking for the removal of Ecuadorian national troops from the area, stating that the mine is a privately owned venture and that Ecuador is not obligated to secure it. Thus far the Ecuadorian military is not budging."

Jack looked at Niles and tossed his pencil down. He angrily looked at his watch.

"*Dark Star 3* is eight hours closer to the Moon than it was the last time we met. We're running out of time. Did the president say anything about reinforcing our position?"

Niles shook his head and tossed his glasses on the map spread out on the table.

"We need at least a hundred more men for this plan to work."

"We should have a minimal amount of help arriving any minute, assets that were already in country. That's all I can tell you, other than that the president has ordered first strike elements of the 101st and 82nd Airborne units into the air. I do know that he has brought several other nations into his secrecy loop, and they may provide some sort of support. But I know you want the Airborne, and the president has approved."

"How long?" Jack asked.

"As far as I know, Jack, they haven't left their home bases yet," Niles answered.

"Any air support at all?" Everett asked.

"There we got lucky. The *Enterprise* battle group is only six hundred miles away from the territorial waters of Ecuador. If the president can figure out the rules of engagement regarding the Ecuadorian military, we should have air cover."

"Well, that's something, if we're fighting anyone other than the home guard," Everett said, just as Sebastian's radio sprang to life.

The German listened and then spoke silently into his radio. He looked at the three men watching him.

"You're not going to believe this," he said, and stepped toward the door of the trailer and opened it. He waved into the darkness and stepped back inside. A knock sounded at the side of the door and an average-sized man in camouflage greasepaint poked his head in the doorway. He looked up at the German standing before him and removed his bush hat.

"Are you Major Krell?" the man asked, in a slow Southern American drawl.

"I am," answered the German.

"My compliments, sir, and compliments to your listening posts in the woods. We stumbled right into them before we knew they were there. They had my men cold."

"And you are?" Krell asked, as he gestured for the man to come in.

"Gunnery Sergeant Alan Pierce, United States embassy security detachment. I have seven men with me with orders from the president and the American ambassador to Ecuador to report to Major Sebastian Krell, and a Colonel Jack Collins."

"And you have found who you are looking for," Sebastian said, turning toward Jack. "I believe this is one of yours."

Collins stepped forward and held out his hand. Instead of taking the outstretched hand, the gunnery sergeant saluted the colonel.

"We're being a little informal here, Gunny. Relax."

The gunnery sergeant lowered the offered salute and shook Jack's hand instead. Then he shook Everett's and Sebastian's hands as they were introduced.

"I take it you're the help we're supposed to get?" Carl asked.

"Well, from the U.S. side, yes sir, at least for the moment. However, we did come across a few more fellas out in the woods two miles north of your camp." Pierce turned and ducked his head through the doorway. Three men stepped forward, all dressed in dark green battle fatigues and all made up just as the Marine was. Their faces were dark with greasepaint and all three looked just as fierce. "Colonel Collins, this is Captain Whitlesey Mark-Patton, of Her Majesty's Special Air Service, currently on detached service to Ecuador for embassy security evaluation."

The British captain raised his hand in a salute and this time Jack returned it.

"Welcome, Captain. A fortunate coincidence that you're right in the country where we need you."

"Well, sir, I'm afraid we're not here in force, as I only have five men with me from my unit, and three Australian army, and two New Zealanders, for a grand total of eleven men. I have been ordered to follow your instructions, and have been given the all-clear to engage forces that have been termed detrimental to Her Majesty's government."

"Thank you. We'll try and put you to good use," Jack said as he turned and faced Everett. He took a deep breath. Then he turned to the other two men who entered the small trailer. They both saluted Collins as they came to attention.

"Okay, gentlemen, that's enough. I think we'll just start out a little less formal." Jack again held out his hand to the first of the two men. "I'm Colonel Jack Collins and this is Captain Carl Everett, U.S. Navy, and Sebastian Krell, German army."

"Sergeant Tashiro Jiimzo, Japanese Self-Defense Forces, stationed as military attaché to Quito. I have four other men with me, sir."

"Sergeant Huynh Nguyen, Vietnam People's Army, reporting on behalf of my government to you. I have ten men accompanying me. We were on duty at our embassy, training security personnel, when the request from your president came through channels."

As the men shook hands, Jack smiled. He had to hand it to the president; he was pulling in some serious favors from friends in other countries.

"Sergeant, Captain—welcome to our little band of invaders. Since this may be all the reinforcements for a while, we'd better get down to planning. It won't be easy. We're outnumbered two hundred to one, with the odds against us growing larger by the minute."

The small Vietnamese sergeant tilted his head when Jack mentioned the numbers. Then he smiled. "The odds are not unheard of, Colonel. It all depends upon the plan."

Jack returned the smile and gestured for the men to have a seat at the map table. He knew the sergeant was schooled on long odds and short hope. That was how he was raised. Right now Jack needed men such as this if what he was planning was going to have a chance of working.

"Gentlemen, our plan is to scare the hell out of an army that's not used to fighting crazy people. So, if I may ask, how much equipment were you able to take out of your embassies?"

The British SAS officer spoke first. "We have ten full-sized G3 assault rifles, 2 G3SG1 sniper rifles, and five G3 KA4 short barrels with collapsible stock, and also five thousand rounds of ammunition."

"All we have is five M-16 automatic weapons with a thousand rounds," Jiimzo said, looking embarrassed.

"The same with us, the New Zealanders and the Australians," Nguyen said. "We have only what we could sneak out of the embassy without being observed by the Ecuadorians."

"Oh, yes, I forgot to mention—ten claymore mines were found in the embassy armory. We liberated them from the politicos," Captain Mark-Patton said with a smile.

Jack looked at the men in front of him. "I'm looking at thirty-six of the best soldiers in the world. Captain Everett, Major Krell, and myself are humbled, to be sure."

"There, there, Colonel. I believe you are selling yourself quite short," Mark-Patton said as he laid his assault weapon on the map-covered table. "I believe you were in on the rescue of that downed Intruder pilot in Iraq in '92 and certain other exploits, including the training of my very own commanding officer on behind-the-lines infiltration. So let's, as you say, be informal here. Yourself, Major Krell, and Captain Everett have more experience than any ten men in this room." The captain reached over and took a field pack. He tossed it toward Everett, who caught it in midair. "Those are BDUs, green and brown. I suspect you would rather go into battle wearing something other than work shirts and Levi's."

Collins looked at Everett and shrugged.

"Okay, gentlemen—again, welcome. Shall we get down to business?"

## DARK STAR 3,
## ALTAIR-FALCON CREW MODULES,
## 98,000 MILES FROM MOON ORBIT

The twelve-man capsule, dubbed *Falcon 1*, was attached nose to nose with the *Altair* lander. The crew module was roomy enough to move around in, but for real exercise the crew had to crawl through to the far more spacious three-decked lunar module.

During their downtime on the voyage, the entire crew, with the exception of the command module pilot, worked on breaking down the large M-39 rocket-assisted projectile weapons designed by DARPA, as well as the short-barreled M-4 carbine, the little sister of the venerable M-16 that each man would carry on any excursion on the lunar surface. There were also four Stinger missile systems and five LAWs armor-piercing rockets that Sarah and Ryan had to learn about. Each of the excursion personnel would also carry a Glock nine-millimeter pistol in a nylon holster.

After six hours of weapons training in breakdown and cleaning, Sarah gave the crew a quick but detailed course on the mineral. Water and air of any kind were forbidden within a dozen yards of the mineral if any was found. Information on the alien weaponry was sparse at best, with only a few grainy pictures of the items they were looking for. Most were rifle-shaped weapons, but Sarah reminded the men present that there could be larger, heavier weaponry that wasn't discovered by the Beatles.

After the meeting broke up, the crew went about eating and exercising. Ryan went forward to speak to the command module pilot and learn about the systems. Sarah had been proud of Jason as he tried to cram everything he could learn in the two-day voyage of *Dark Star 3*. This was a shortened venue for all the training they had to undergo, since it used to take four days to get to the Moon in the old Apollo days, but thanks to the added engine power of the new solid rocket booster engines on the command module, the trip had been cut in half.

Sarah approached Colonel Kendal as he floated onto the exercise bike.

"Any word on the Chinese?"

Kendal started pedaling and looked around to see who was in earshot. Then he placed two small earpieces in his ears and paused over the play button for his iPod.

"The time frame will be right around the time *Altair* lands. We won't know until we're either ambushed or welcomed as an ally. Maybe we can get some chatter from the French, since they land five hours before us, but I don't anticipate getting that lucky."

"The Russians?" Sarah asked, leaning into Kendal.

"Our old friends are a full day and half behind us. They won't get there until the shooting has stopped. Besides, I understand they're having problems onboard their lunar lander *Peter the Great*." The colonel tapped the video monitor next to the lander control station. There was a picture of a large craft that looked similar to their own Altair lander, only more base looking. Below the picture were the Russian words, *Петр Великий Ландр—Peter the Great Lunar Lander.*

"That doesn't help me," Sarah said frowning. "What's wrong with the damn lander now?"

The colonel hit his play button and started pedaling. "I guess they didn't steal the right plans from us back in the eighties," he answered with a wink.

Sarah turned away and bumped into a floating Mendenhall. "What was that all about?" he asked, as turned a complete flip in the air.

"Just more good news about the Russians being a day late and a ruble short."

"Well, let's just hope the Chinese have a good attitude when we land."

Sarah floated past Will and stopped him from spinning before he vomited for the fifth time on the trip.

"That, my friend, is in serious doubt."

*Dark Star 3* was hurtling toward the moon at a record-breaking pace of 35,790 miles per hour. *Altair 1* would attempt to set down in a possible hostile landing zone in exactly nine hours.

The ESA and Russian spacecraft were yet to be heard from.

## THE ANDES,
## 100 MILES EAST OF QUITO, ECUADOR

Niles slammed the headphones down in frustration and was thankful he hadn't been speaking to the president on one of the laptop computers Pete had offered.

"Unbelievable," Charlie said behind the sweating back of Pete Golding. The two men had been steadily poised over a laptop plugged directly into the Europa system, which was being bounced off two satellites. One of these, the Event Group's KH-11 bird code-named Boris and Natasha, had been retasked and was just now coming online for direct aerial views of the mine and the surrounding terrain so Jack could plan his makeshift assault accordingly.

"What is it?" Niles asked as he stood and walked over to the two scientists.

"Europa and our linguistics team have a promising link to the alien alphabet," Pete said and turned the monitor of the laptop enough so Niles could see. "They've been studying the video from the crater—the flag, the lettering on the space suit, the number system on a few of the weapons, and so on. Europa has evaluated the writing and is comparing it with different symbologies that we have here on Earth. She's come to the conclusion that it is a definite cross between a written language and a pictograph system similar to Chinese."

"I don't see how Europa can grasp their language from just a few words."

"Actually, the number system was pretty easy, Niles. She just took every number that we had photographs of and repeated them through her system. As no number was higher than nine, she figured that the system was based on ten. Now, breaking down each number was a little harder. This is where Europa got extremely lucky. It all started with the very first find by the robotic Beatles, the skeleton itself—in particular, the air tank system on the spaceman's backpack. The numbers were taken off and the size of the tanks evaluated by Europa as compared to a similar system of air tanks used by NASA, the U.S. Navy, etc. Europa figured it was twenty gallons or eighty cubic feet of air. She took the symbology for these numbers and deduced that what the writing on the tank said was air capacity of eighty cubic feet, the very same system we use, only it took our strange friends eight letters to spell out the word eighty and three numbers to indicate the numeral 80. The parentheses were easier."

Niles shook his head. "And from this she has decoded their language? That's hard to believe, gentlemen."

"We won't know for sure until we can get more detailed text, but I wouldn't bet against Europa, Mr. Director," Pete said as he pulled the screen back. He looked insulted that Niles had doubted Europa.

"Well, Jack's going to try to get us in the mine as soon as he can. What about the flag and its symbology?"

"The four circles in elliptical form," Charlie said for Pete, who had switched the view on the laptop from the writing program to the picture of the flag and the symbols described by Jack and the senator:

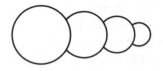

"Europa is very confused, as are most of the best astronomers in the world. She had been monitoring the study of the flag at every university in the world and most of them are of the opinion that it's an elliptical orbit of the alien home world," Charlie said, pointing to the animation of the flag.

"However, Europa does not agree," Pete said, interrupting Charlie. "She seems to believe, and we are arguing with her on this point, that it's a system of neighboring planets—perhaps a series of planets *and* moons. Of course I have asked her to explain and she states that the alignment could be two planets and two moons in the same orbit but on opposite sides of the sun. Personally I think the old girl's guessing. There's nothing remotely like this diagram in the solar system. Not even Saturn or Jupiter has moons that close to their own orbit. As for Europa's theory that those two worlds and their moons could occupy the same orbit, but on opposite sides of the sun—well, we just don't have a precedent for that scenario."

"Simple. It's not our solar system," Niles offered.

"No, sir, I don't believe that's the case. It has to be close to our own system." Pete changed the picture on the screen and they were soon looking at the space-suited skeleton. "Now this is purely speculation on my and Charlie's parts, but the design of this environment suit is not that different from our own—or NASA's, I mean."

"I'm not following, boys," Niles said, keeping his eyes on the monitor.

"Niles, the design of the suit is everything," Charlie said. "It's not that advanced. it would take an advanced civilization to get here from another solar system capable of sustaining life, because it would require that civilization having faster-than-light capability. This suit doesn't demonstrate that kind of scientific and technological development. Okay, it's thin, but it's our theory. These beings have to be from somewhere nearby, not another system in the Milky Way."

"Thin? Gentlemen, this theory is so thin it's transparent. You have absolutely nothing to base this on other than a space suit. And one, I might add, that we know nothing about."

Charlie Ellenshaw lowered his head and looked away. Pete Golding again shook his head and bent back to work. Both men were hurt that Niles wasn't seeing what they were seeing. It was Charlie who refused to go quietly, because he was used to having his ideas and theories ridiculed by others.

"No, wait a minute here. I've been a space buff all of my life. That space suit isn't that advanced. It's common sense to assume that the civilization that designed it is not that far ahead of our own. Let me add, Niles—and the MIT and DARPA chaps can verify this—that we are at least two to three hundred years from even developing a decent theory of faster-than-light space travel and another two or three hundred years away from actually developing it. What's the matter with you? You don't take theory as a valued and viable scientific pattern anymore?"

Niles could see the anger in Ellenshaw's eyes and the hurt in the way Pete refused to look up from the laptop he was working at. He knew he was projecting his own frustrations at the developing situation in space on the two scientists, and he was a fool for doing so. He shook his head and then removed his glasses. He turned and looked at the two men sitting in the corner, discussing the weaponry that the Beatles had sent via facsimile.

"Dr. Appleby, could you step over here and listen to what these men have to say? Apparently I've dropped some IQ points in the last few days. They're speaking a language I can't follow."

Charlie nodded his head and smiled. Pete turned and looked at Niles. He too gave a halfhearted nod, knowing that this was Niles's way of apologizing to the two men. They both knew that he was far more brilliant than either of them, but just wasn't getting the fact that they knew nothing and had to start with theory first. To a man like Niles, that was a killer of rational thought in these pressure-filled times.

Niles turned away and thought about going over to the other trailer. Then he thought better of it and instead stepped out into the cool night air of the Andes. He took a few steps and that was when he saw a tall figure leaning against a tree. He could smell pipe tobacco and noticed a smaller figure in the moonlight standing next to the first. It was Alice Hamilton standing next to Garrison Lee and they were both looking up at the Moon, so Niles decided to let them have their time together, even though he was in the mood to converse with anybody about anything to keep himself from worrying about the fate of Sarah, Mendenhall, and Ryan. He turned away and started to go back inside the trailer.

"No need to leave, Niles my boy. Come and join us," Lee said, half turning and holding a reassuring hand on Alice's shoulder.

Nile turned back toward the couple and walked in their direction. He nodded as two Japanese soldiers walked past. They nodded politely at the small balding man in the tan work clothes and then moved off into the trees.

"Arguing with the boys?" Lee asked, puffing on his pipe. "I know for a fact you won't get anywhere doing that." He looked down at Niles, who had joined him and Alice. "I know because I tried to argue scientific points with you my, dear boy, for almost ten full years. It was like hitting my head against a wall."

"I couldn't have been that frustrating."

"More," Lee said, with Alice nodding in agreement. "And the maddening thing is, just like those two nerd birds in there, you were right more often than I ever admitted."

Niles smiled and looked down at his feet. "I was a little hard on them," he said. "I think they're on to something, but what I need is facts that I can pass along to the president, not more theory."

Lee removed the pipe from his mouth and tapped the bowl against the tree. He then pocketed the pipe and placed his hand on Niles's shoulder.

"The burden of having the president's ear is a large one. I can't help you there, my boy. At least not until you can explain why that mine and its contents, along with the discovery on the Moon, are so damned important to so many people."

Niles looked at Lee. That was when he realized that he and Alice had put their two heads together and had come to a conclusion—they had figured it out. He thought about calling them on it, but decided to let them go on speculating, even if they were right. He didn't want to give his old friend the pleasure of gloating that he was still sharp as a tack even though he was knocking on heaven's door. Even Alice had a nice, smug smile on her lips as she stared into the woods.

"You know, if it weren't for you, our entire civilization would have been totally unprepared for what's coming," Niles said as he turned away from Lee and Alice.

"I don't know what you mean, my boy," Lee said. He turned with the aid of Alice and his ever-present cane.

"Oh, I think you do," Niles said. He returned Lee's crooked grin. "Now, why don't you go in there and spy on Jack for me, then let me know what he plans to do, and then get some rest."

"Oh, I think I know what Jack's plans are, and I wouldn't want to be the mercenaries down there guarding that mine. Have you seen the array of pirates the colonel's got helping him lately?"

Niles laughed and then turned away.

Lee looked down at Alice and she knew by the look that he was in desperate pain. He closed his eyes, then opened them again and smiled.

"I think I'll deny the request to spy on Jack. I think I'd better go lie down, old girl."

Alice just nodded her head, knowing Garrison Lee was fast running out of time.

# 12

The thirty-six men had three pairs of night vision goggles between them. Luckily, they also had two 100-power night scopes for the designated sniper team, one placed at each end of their advance line. The two chosen snipers were a Vietnamese private named An Liang, and an Australian named Johansen. The rules of engagement, or ROE, were to fire only if Jack and Carl gave them the signal: two fingers in the air.

Collins was hoping to have the Ecuadorians leave the facility without a shot being fired. He figured this called for a foolish type of soldier who could walk right up to the gate and explain things to the officer in charge of the security detail camped outside. As for McCabe's men, Jack had no illusions; they were to be eliminated at the outset if he could persuade the Ecuadorians to abandon their posts. That foolish soldier would be himself, and of course Mr. Everett, who would have none of Collins's going alone. Sebastian would be the leader of the assault team if and when the larger force was convinced to leave the area. They knew they couldn't start the fireworks off by killing soldiers of an ally state. That would make what the president was attempting that much harder.

The thirty remaining men were to allow ample time for the security force to leave, then the snipers would take out the gate guards and Sebastian would lead the strike element into the gated compound, where if all went well, they would take the small barracks.

As Collins made sure his sidearm was snapped into its holster, Everett came into the small clearing where they had assembled, only three hundred yards above the mining compound.

"Okay, Jack, the men are in position. I have Pete, Charlie, and Niles standing by. We have a reserve element of ten men, which can be on the move as soon as we gain access."

"Good," Jack said, "Now if we—"

"Wait, Jack, there's more. A listening post on the far side of the camp has picked up a large force five miles away and closing on foot. He can't get an exact count, but they look hostile and they aren't wearing uniforms."

"It can't be McCabe, I mean why would he sneak into his own area? No, this is something else." Jack looked down into the center of the Ecuadorian encampment. All was quiet there. "The listening post is a part of the follow-up element, right?"

Everett nodded his head in the predawn darkness.

"Leave him in place. I want to know all he can see before that force arrives in theater," Jack said, looking at Sebastian.

"Right," he said and held out his hand to Everett and then Collins. "Good luck. I wouldn't want your job."

"Thanks, buddy," Jack said with a smile, and released the German's hand. "Just remember. When we walk up to that gate we won't have a chance to signal, so take it for granted that the mission is on."

Sebastian didn't stick around to answer. He turned and hurried away to distribute what few radios they had to the follow-up element and to the two snipers.

"Well, Mr. Everett, shall we go for a walk?"

"About damn time. I was starting to get bored after my life of crime."

"Me too," Collins said, and turned and started downhill toward the Ecuadorian camp.


"*Alto*," a voice said out of the darkness.

Jack and Carl stopped in the middle of the dirt road only a thousand yards from the front gate.

"*Dos hombres, Estados Unidos*," Jack called out. "*Dos americanos.*"

"Oh, boy, here we go," Everett mumbled, wanting to at least unsnap the holster strap at his side when he heard the sound of men running toward them.

Four men came out of the darkness and shone bright flashlights in their eyes. "Raise your hands, *señor*," the first said, leveling an old M-16.

"You speak good English," Collins said. "We need to see your commanding officer."

"And he would like to see you also, Colonel Collins."

"Uh-oh," Everett said, their plan flying right out the window.

"It seems you have the advantage," Jack said as he considered the clean-shaven officer. He didn't look anything like a local militia man.

"We certainly do have the advantage, Colonel. Now, if you will follow me. You may lower your hands, but please keep them far away from your weapons," the officer said. "Professional courtesy will go only so far."

Jack looked at Everett and then lowered his hands. They both followed the Ecuadorian officer. They walked into the silent camp and were led straight to the largest of the tents that had recently been set up. Jack eyed not only his immediate surroundings but also the main gate, which was now only five hundred yards away. The lighting hadn't been brought to a brighter level, so the alert status at the mine was unchanged. The officer looked at Jack and Everett, then relieved them both of their sidearms.

"Courtesy to a fellow soldier can go only so far."

"I promise not to shoot your commanding officer, son," Jack said, looking at the large air-conditioned tent.

"My commanding officer, *señor*?" The man almost snickered. "Colonel Collins, your actions in my country have earned the highest attention from the highest authority." The officer pulled the tent flap aside and gestured for Everett and Collins to enter.

There were six men inside. One was dressed in civilian clothing, wearing a black sport coat with a white shirt underneath and pressed black pants. He held a large ice-filled glass in his hand, topped off with an amber liquid, and seemed freshly showered. The other five men had a galaxy of stars on their shoulders. They looked upon Jack and Carl with little more than curiosity.

The officer who had escorted them into the tent stepped in front of the two Americans.

"Colonel Collins and Captain Everett, sir. Gentlemen," he said, turning to face Jack and Carl. "May I present to you El Presidente de la República del Ecuador, Rafael Vicente Correa DiSilva."

The president of Ecuador handed one of his generals the drink he was holding. He eyed Everett and Jack in turn.

"You have been very busy men in my country."

"Yes, sir, we seek—"

Delgado held up a hand.

"Did you have designs on attacking this force of men who are bivouacking in their own country, Colonel?"

"Of course not, sir," Collins said, looking shocked at the allegation. "We were merely going to ask the commander here if we could assault that mine and the bad guys guarding it."

The president couldn't resist. He smiled and then looked back at his generals. At first they didn't find anything funny, at least not until the president did. Then they too laughed aloud.

"You were going ask the commander here to leave the area?"

"Yes, we were."

"Tell me, Colonel Collins, all of this trouble you have caused in my capital and the troubles you are accused of in Germany—are you saying you are innocent of these things, and that you are not what you would call a bad guy?"

"Yes, sir, innocent to a certain point. I believe the men responsible for these events are on their way here now, just to the south of this area."

"Is that so?" the president asked, turning to face his generals. "Well, Colonel," he said, glancing at Everett, "and Captain, I have recently had a very long conversation with your president, and he says while you are a man of considerable trouble to him at times, he does not know you as a liar."

"That's nice of him."

"He's also explained some very strange things to me. Let's say he has taken me into his confidence, so to speak. Colonel, we have very strange times coming, which is why I am pulling this detail out of the Andes. You may do as you wish, with the proviso that Colonel Raul DeSouza here accompanies you while you are in my country. I am afraid that is all I can offer, as the mine is legally owned by an American and a German national. As I studied economics at your University of Illinois, I am aware that any assault on these mine shafts would have to prove beyond any doubt that they hold illegal goods or some operation that is hurtful to my nation." He smiled at Jack. "Besides, your president has asked that this operation be kept between him and me, and not to allow any more men into that mine than necessary."

"I wish I could say I understand, but the president has told you far more than us."

"As for the men that you say are coming up from the south, General Santiago here will lead an assault against them to buy you time. There is also further news. Another hundred men are coming from the east, a similar number from the north. We are heavily outnumbered, and my men are lightly armed. They will no doubt meet more firepower than they have on hand. Unfortunately, the rest of my small army is in the cities of my country to guard against the violent protests by various religious factions. We are attempting to get helicopter support, possibly a squadron of Cobra gunships; they are old, but still pack a powerful punch. I am sorry that this is all we have for you, Colonel. Do what you need to do, but please make it fast."

Jack saluted the man in front of him, as did Everett. President DiSilva just smiled a sad smile and nodded, and he and his generals left the tent.

"Well, I guess this was a good news, bad news kind of thing, huh, Jack?"

Collins accepted his nine-millimeter from the Ecuadorian colonel and turned to Everett.

"You know, you're always looking at the dark side of things. I don't know about your attitude lately, Mr. Everett, I think you're getting old, buddy."

"I hope to grow just a little older, Colonel dear."

## EUROPEAN SPACE AGENCY LUNAR LANDER *ASTRAL*, 7 MILES ABOVE LUNAR SURFACE

The *Astral* was named for the corporation that designed her, EADS Astrium in Bremen She was a two-story, three-deck design that had failed in every simulation for the three years she was in development. The lander carried two pilots and eight crewmen, only four of whom were mission specialists; the other four were trained commandos from the elite Commandos Marine of the French navy.

The *Astral* had received severe damage after the attack on the Ariane platforms during launch. One of her four landing gear had been sheared off at the landing pad and was floating free somewhere outside the International Space

Station. Since detaching from the command module, *Bonaparte 1*, the command and control systems had failed twice, and she was now on the third and final backup motherboard for her navigation system. In order to save that last, precious module, the commander, Major Jean Marceau, had ordered the pilots to navigate by directional viewing, meaning they had to rely on map and visual references for landing. They would save the only NAV board on the computer for the all-important rendezvous with the *Bonaparte* when she lifted free of the lunar surface.

As far as the two pilots could tell, they were coming in far too fast and at least 106 miles from the Shackleton landing area. As the *Astral*'s main engine burn flared brightly in the closed circuit television system inside the cabin, all eyes nervously watched the clock as *Astral* was nearing her burn duration—she was fast running out of fuel.

"We must have a faulty gauge, or we're losing fuel somewhere between the tanks and the engine," the copilot said as he vigorously recalculated their consumption by handheld computer. "As near as I can tell we have two minutes of fuel remaining. We're too high and traveling too fast. We have to set her down now, Major."

Marceau turned and ordered all crewmen to get ready for an emergency landing. They secured their helmets and checked their vital systems. The two pilots placed their helmets on in relays as *Astral* halted its forward trajectory and commenced an attitude straight down toward the rocky surface below.

"Major, we have Shackleton in sight at 34.04672 kilometers distant," the copilot reported as calmly as he could.

"Over twenty-one miles distant," Marceau said to himself, as he leaned over and saw the giant crater from two miles up. "We can't help it now. Sit her down. We have some walking ahead of us."

"God, Major, look at that!" the copilot said, gazing out the large command windows on the upper deck.

Marceau saw Shackleton and the damage the explosion had caused. Three quarters of the north wall of the crater was gone. The interior of Shackleton looked scorched and the debris from its interior had spread around the hole like a shotgun blast pattern. The major smiled.

"Some of the interior structures have survived," he said as he looked at the four scientists that were strapped in on the lower deck along with the four commandos. "They must have been built to endure a heavy strike for them to still be standing." As he turned back, he saw that distance and lower altitude had taken the view away from him. *Astral* continued descending.

"One minute of fuel remaining, thirty-two kilometers downrange of landing target. Altitude is ten thousand, descending at three thousand feet per minute." The copilot looked over at his lander pilot. "We're not going to make it."

"Stand by to cut power to main engine. We'll allow *Astral* to free-fall for twenty-two seconds. Then fire everything we have for the final approach."

The copilot's eyes widened as he finally understood the plan for reaching the lunar surface. The last he had heard, there was no such thing as a glide pattern in the airless void of the Moon.

"Stand by . . . stand by . . . shut down!"

The copilot cut the fuel feed to the large main engine, sending the *Astral* into complete silence as she hurtled toward the surface. The pilot and copilot knew that, if the main engine failed to restart, they would impact the Moon's surface at close to two miles a minute, sending pieces of the ESA mission all over the Moon's dusty surface.

Below, all eyes were either closed or looking at the person next to them. There was no sensation of falling, just one of near total silence, with only the blipping and squeaking of the radar to be heard. The copilot was audible through the *Astral*'s communications system.

"Major, we are at two thousand feet. Long-range cameras are picking up rocks in the landing zone. Do we adjust with OHM's rockets?"

"Negative, we don't have the fuel. We just have to hope the rocks aren't that big," the pilot said. He risked a quick look at his younger copilot. "Stand by for main engine ignition. Crew, brace for impact," the pilot ordered calmly. "It's not going to be soft. Remember your emergency egress plan. If we land intact, stand by with purge patches in case there are holes anywhere in the ship."

Marceau knew that this scenario wasn't a viable plan at all. Purge patches were designed in case they were struck in orbit by a small meteorite or debris, creating a small hole in the platform, thus requiring the crew to place small plastic and rubber seals with adhesive backing over the hole to stop any evacuation of the interior environment. Any large breach wasn't covered by the manufacturer's design team. The crew would be either swept from the pressurized cabin or crushed in the impact.

"Three, two, one, fire main engine!" This time the major said it loudly. The command rang throughout *Astral* as the copilot initiated main engine start. The crew heard the blast of fuel as it was purged from the tanks below them. Then they all grimaced as a loud explosion was heard inside of the cabin. The sensation hit them that they were slowing.

"We have main engine start at three hundred feet!"

"Bring main engine and aft OHMs to a full power setting. Burn them until the fuel is exhausted," the major said, as *Astral* hurtled toward the surface.

"Firing six OHMs at attitude zero degrees. We have burn."

With the main engine and OHM attitude jets firing all at once, *Astral* slowed even further. They all knew the small engine bells of the OHM's rockets were not designed for landing, only for maneuvering in space and for small adjustments during the landing cycle.

"Fuel is running out. We just lost the starboard OHMs," the copilot said loudly as *Astral* started vibrating beyond anything they had encountered in simulations. Each crewman who wasn't on the upper command deck was deep in prayer as *Astral* started tilting to the right.

"Shut down all OHM's jets, now!" the major called out. "I'll gimbal the main engine bell to straighten our attitude."

As *Astral* came within a hundred feet of the rock-strewn landing zone, the main engine bell of the lander gimbaled to the right, sending the large craft in that direction and straightening her fall.

"Come on, come on," Marceau said out loud, as he braced for the impact he knew was coming. He looked down and made sure the crew members were strapped in tight as the call came from up above.

"Zero fuel!" the copilot said.

"Brace for impact!" the major called out. He adjusted his feet on the Velcro pads just as he lost sight of the horizon. He hit a small red button on the control under his right hand, sending a signal up to the orbiting command module. "*Bonaparte, Bonaparte, Astral* is going down. I repeat, we are going down!"

"Ten feet, five feet—"

*Astral* hit hard, sending her pad-less landing strut deep into the lunar surface. As she sank to the starboard side, the number four strut struck a large rock, shearing off at the engine housing. Then number two collapsed from the sheer weight of the impact. The lander hit as her main engine bell plunged deep into the lunar dust. *Astral* bounced and then came down again.

Marceau felt something in his back give way and as he reacted to the sudden awareness that he felt no more pain, the main bulkhead gave way and one man was thrown free of the compartment as it opened to the Moon's environment. *Astral* rolled once, twice, and then came to a stop as the second deck partially separated from the first.

As *Astral* stopped its crazily spinning momentum, loose papers and debris were swept out of the compartment. The electrical system was failing, as sparks and smoke started flowing from the environmental control system. To Major Marceau all seemed to be happening in slow motion.

"All crewmen out now. The environmental controls are completely off-line. We have no air. She's bleeding to death and we're on fire," a voice shouted from a strange and cockeyed angle far to their left.

The men started reacting after the shock of the crash. Safety harnesses were released and hands grabbed those too injured to assist in their own egress. Marceau felt hands on him and thought he was finally going to feel the pain of his broken back, but nothing happened as he was finally pulled from his upright seat. He knew then that he was paralyzed from at least the chest down. He turned his head and was relieved he could do even that.

"Survival packs—get the survival packs," he managed to say as he was pulled toward a large breach in *Astral*'s hull.

"We have them, Major, extra oxygen also," one of the French commandos said. He looked shaken but he was in control as he pulled Marceau along by the arm. "The pilot is dead and the copilot has two broken legs."

Marceau felt himself pulled free of the wreckage and he immediately saw the star-filled sky overhead as he was laid next to one of the broken landing struts of *Astral*. As he listened to the rescue of his crew, he knew the ESA mission to the Moon was now officially dead. He only hoped they would be alive long enough to tell someone.

As the surviving men of *Astral* scrambled free and took cover behind the small rim of a crater, they felt as well as saw the bright flash of her tanks as the electrical short ignited the fumes inside. At the same moment, sparks struck the damaged oxygen cylinders bundled underneath the main engine housing. In complete and utter silence, the men of ESA Moon Mission 01 watched *Astral* rise into the airless sky and come apart, peppering the area with debris. It was as though a bomb had exploded. All of their supplies and weapons were gone in a flash of brilliant brightness.

The men of the *Astral* sat for what seemed like an hour, coming to terms with the possibly gruesome fate that awaited them.

"Once everyone is assembled, we start for Shackleton Crater, and hope the Americans have better luck than us," Marceau said, as he felt the coolness of his oxygen flow for the first time. That was when he realized it was the air hitting blood flowing freely from a head wound.

With the survival packs and extra oxygen, they had a total of fifteen hours of life remaining to them.


OVAL OFFICE,
THE WHITE HOUSE,
WASHINGTON, D.C.

The president of the United States slowly placed the phone in its cradle.

The French president had just reported loss of contact with their *Astral* lander. Catastrophic failure was assumed. With the Russians so far behind, that meant possible hostile fire from the Chinese without backup.

His back was still bruised from the attempt on his own life just four days before. He thought about reaching for the intercom once more but pulled his hand back. His eagerness to know what was happening in the People's Republic was gnawing at him but he knew it would be a mistake to push the chairman further.

The intercom gave out a soft tone.

"Yes," he said softly, hoping it wasn't one of the Joint Chiefs calling to tell him what he already knew about the disaster to the ESA mission.

"Mr. President, Wang Zhaoguo, vice chairman of National People's Congress, is on the line from Beijing."

The president sat up, but hesitated before reaching for the phone. He knew this was it, either they had an ally in the overall cause facing the planet or the Chinese mission to the Moon would continue as a hostile force. It all depended on the men Wang represented in the Politburo of the People's Republic.

"Thank you. Please put the vice chairman through." He sighed.

"Mr. Vice Chairman, how are you this evening?" he said when prompted.

"Mr. President, it is indeed good to hear your voice after such a dastardly plot against you," the vice chairman said in very good English.

"Thank you, Mr. Vice Chairman."

"You will excuse me if I make this call as brief as possible."

"I understand," the president said.

"As of this moment, the Politburo is split as to the question of the monumental action of the matter before us. Our generals are also split. As to our action, I am afraid the chairman has become overly suspicious of his closest advisors."

The president knew without asking that the vice chairman was the youngest and most trusted of these advisors to the eighty-one-year-old chairman. If they didn't act, the vice chairman would be caught and executed for treasonous acts against the People's Republic. That would also include every one of the Chinese politicos and military men that had anything to do with going against the authority of the ruling body politic of that country.

"I sincerely hope—"

"Excuse me, Mr. President—as I said, I do not have much time. Our military leaders, while sympathetic to the decision of our best scientists, are still on the fence as far as action against the government is concerned. We will have to take a wait-and-see attitude for the next ten to twelve hours while they decide whether to assist us. Until that time, I am afraid the momentous choice of action or inaction is one that lay with our generals."

"Are you all right, Mr. Vice Chairman?" the president asked.

"No, Mr. President, I am not. I will be arrested in a matter of moments. Thus at this time I wish us all luck. Please pass on to the French president our sincere condolences in regards to their spacecraft. It is always such a hard thing when men of bravery and honor die in the name of our future, is it not?"

"Indeed, sir, it is."

"Mr. President, I hear my escort at this very moment coming to make sure I face my very backward superiors in the next hour. Good luck to us all."

"Mr. Vice Chairman, I wish you—"

"The call is terminated, Mr. President," said a voice over the line.

The president held the phone away from his ear for the longest time. Then he took a deep breath and placed the phone back to his ear.

"Get me an analysis of that conversation as soon as you can. I want background noises and levels of voice stress, ASAP."

"Yes, sir," came the same flat voice.

The president hung and stood to take a look out of the window. As he pulled the drapes back, he saw that the protesters on Pennsylvania Avenue had dwindled to only the most ardent religious fanatics. He shook his head as he watched a few men and women with their signs decrying the race to the Moon. Rain was falling in Washington and that fit his mood to a T as his eyes focused on the damp street outside beyond the steel gate. The mission to the Moon was still a priority and he could not change the parameters of that mission. He could not request that *Altair* change landing areas to assist the ESA crewmen if they were still alive and he was bothered by it. He only hoped any survivors could somehow make their way to the landing zone. For the French president to not even ask about rescue was to his credit. He understood the priorities as they were made clear by the Case Blue scenario.

As he allowed the curtain to fall back into place, blocking his view of the few protesters who braved the rains, he thought about Colonel Jack Collins and his team in Ecuador. He knew he had done all that he could on the political end of things, getting President DeSilva to stand down, but he also knew Jack had an uphill climb ahead of him in securing the mine shaft with the few international soldiers they could get at the last minute. The last call he received from the Event Group in Nevada was that the Ecuador team had company coming their way and there was nothing the national military of Ecuador could do about them other than defend them as a blocking force.

As these thoughts occurred to him, the president got angry. He turned and slammed his hand down on the intercom one more time.

"Get me General Caulfield," he said without preamble into the intercom.

"The chairman of the Joint Chiefs in on the line, sir," a female voice said less than a minute later.

The president picked up the phone and heard the voice of General Maxwell Caulfield, who spoke a small greeting that the president didn't really hear at all.

"General, I want to know what you've come up with to get Colonel Collins and his team some help down in Ecuador."

"Sir, as you know, both the 101st and 82nd Airborne are on their rotation to Afghanistan. The 10th Mountain has just recently returned and is in no shape to go back out. Thus far we have rounded up SEAL teams five and eight, and another unit that was just finishing NATO jump training at Fort Bragg."

"Who are they?" the president asked, while rubbing his temple with his bandaged left hand.

As he heard the general explain, the president's face grew concerned and his eyes closed.

"Is that all we have?"

"I'm afraid so, sir. We are spread out all over the world and this is the fastest group we could get together on such short notice. If we had another twenty-four hours we could get an entire division in there, as that would be the most expedient way to get Collins the help he needs. Believe me, sir, these boys can fight, and they're ready to go."

"Tell me I have a choice."

"Jack will know what to do with them when they arrive, sir. Don't worry about that."

"Get them there as fast as you can, Max."

"They're already in the air with the SEAL teams, sir."

"Okay, Max, I better make a phone call and explain to their president why I'm sending his boys to war without asking permission first. Goddamn it, what a mess."

# 13

## MÜELLER AND SANTIAGO MINING CONCERN, 100 MILES EAST OF QUITO

Jack and Carl ambled along the road toward the front gate as if they were just taking the night air. Collins forced himself to clasp his hands behind his back, like a man on a leisurely stroll.

"Well, I guess this is where I find out if the training we gave the Germans took hold," Collins said, remembering Sebastian's training and how he was easily one of the best he had ever taught.

As they neared the gate, one man, a large fellow in a gray uniform, stepped outside the small shack. Jack was relieved to see anyone there at all, as they obviously hadn't been alerted that the Ecuadorian army had pulled up stakes only forty minutes before.

"*Alto*," said the lone guard as he stepped in front of the gate. Jack could tell that the Spanish word for stop was laced with a thick German accent. It was one of the same guards from five days before.

"Oh, boy," Everett whispered through the side of his face. "That's one of the guys who escorted us into the mine. We're had."

Jack was tempted to raise his fingers in the gesture that would signal the designated sniper to take the guard out, but held off. He wanted the other guard from the shack visible before any action was taken. Jack stopped walking and waved a greeting.

"Hi," he said, his face filling with the largest smile he could ever remember faking.

The large guard didn't say anything as he clicked on a large flashlight and pointed it at Jack and Carl, who averted their eyes from the harsh light.

"Who is it? Those damn Ecuadorian army people again?" The voice came from the guard shack high above. Jack could see a light flash on and a lone figure come to the doorway. The guard was perfectly silhouetted against the light in the shack.

"I know you," the guard said, and reached for his sidearm.

Just as Collins started to raise his right hand into the air, a sound like a bee's buzz passed overhead. A curious look appeared on the guard's face and his hand froze just over the holster carrying his sidearm. The man tensed and slowly fell to his knees, the flashlight rolling free. Everett saw the perfectly round hole in the man's forehead as he tumbled over. The second guard, in the tower above, was standing as if curious why his partner was doing what he was doing. At that moment two silenced sniper rounds caught him in the neck and head. The man fell backward into the guard shack. "Jesus, whoever Krell picked as a sniper is damn good," Carl said as he recovered the AK-47 from the dirt roadway next to the guard's body.

"Yes, they are," Jack said, raising his right hand into the air and pumping his fist twice.

As they moved toward the gate, Jack saw the camouflaged men exit the tree line above the mine. They quietly ran through the open fence and toward the guard housing unit. Jack grimaced as he remembered the kill orders he had given the assault team and he knew Sebastian would be as ruthless a soldier as he had been taught to be. Collins knew he couldn't afford the manpower to watch over any prisoners. The sleeping men should have chosen a better employer than the Reverend Samuel Rawlins and Faith Ministries.

Jack and Carl entered the guard shack, where they saw the large radio. Collins gestured toward the radio and removed the back panel it. He pulled the motherboard for the transmitter. He couldn't destroy the powerful radio; their own communications capabilities were sorely lacking and they might need it. Then Jack pulled two M-16s and several magazines from the wall-mounted rack inside the door. Everett placed the circuit board in his pocket and lay the AK-47 down just as Jack tossed him one of the M-16s. Everett pulled the charging handle back and then chambered a round. He looked at his boss and nodded.

"Shall we get in that mine and see what the hoopla's all about?"

"You bet," Jack said as he stepped from the guard shack.

They both hurried forward as Sebastian appeared from the larger barracks where the guards were housed. He shook his head as Collins and Everett approached.

"Six hostiles accounted for. I think we can safely assume the others are inside the mine or were out preparing a welcome for us."

"Let's assume they're waiting for us in the mine. That way we'll be covered in both cases." Jack turned and made another gesture into the darkness. He waited a moment as the second element came out of the woods with Niles, Pete, Charlie, Appleby, and Franklyn Dubois, the MIT engineer. Jack used a hand signal telling the group to slow their approach. The civilians were closely guarded by the two Air Force pilots from the 727 jet.

"Okay, Sebastian, bring in your snipers and spotters, place them in position to cover us and let's get the first element inside the mine."

Almost as if on cue, the sounds of a firefight were heard from somewhere down the mountain. Collins shook his head at their bad luck. He had hoped the Ecuadorians would have waited before engaging the assault element tracking them. He knew the government men couldn't be blamed for going early, just as he would have been tempted to attack anyone in his country with orders to murder his people.

"Okay, it sounds like our friendly troops have company down the mountain, and by the sound of the heavier caliber weapons, they're most definitely outgunned. Let's move! Sebastian, get elements of our second line in defensive positions outside the entrance to the mine and then join us at the main doors. Place your claymores accordingly and make kill zones for the rest of your front. We have very little to make a stand, so let's make them hesitate before they come on strong. We have to give the president time to play hero. Go, go," Jack said as his onetime student saluted him.

"Yes, sir," Sebastian said, lowering the salute and pointing to three of his men. Then he silently disappeared into the darkness.

"Mr. Everett, let's get the lights in the compound down to a more mood-oriented level, shall we? Let's use the darkness while we have it. And make sure Sebastian and his men have the extra ammo from the guards for the outer defense. They're going to need it."

"You got it, Jack."

Collins watched his friend hurry to do what he was ordered to do. Then he turned to look at Niles Compton, who had joined them from the tree line.

"Director, keep these people in between the assault element and the defensive line. And remind them that there are only good guys in between, so no shooting."

"Right," Niles said as he realized he had never really seen Jack in his element before. He admired the calm way Collins made everyone feel confident in what he was telling them. He turned and made the civilians follow him up the slope where Sebastian had disappeared.

Jack turned just as several bright flashes illuminated the night sky further down the steep slope of the mountain. He didn't flinch as the sound finally reached him. The explosions were large and loud, and he knew that they were antipersonnel missiles. He also knew the Ecuadorian army didn't have any of those when they left the mine. He only hoped the promised Cobra gunships arrived in time to help the poor bastards.

Everett and a three-man team slowly made their way into the mine opening. The gleaming concrete of the gallery had just recently been cleaned after the removal of the stored weaponry that had so thoroughly destroyed much of the world's hope for the Moon shots. The former Navy SEAL knew there were eyes on them as they slipped into the main gallery and took cover. With the lights out, the three men—the Australian and Vietnamese snipers and Carl—used one of the night scopes. Both of his riflemen had ambient-light scopes attached to their rifles. Even with time a factor, Everett knew taking out the remaining guard element was going to take patience.

He placed his two men at opposite ends of the gallery behind old and hardened bagged cement labeled with German markings. The pallets of material had collapsed over time and had been left to rot in the expanse of the main chamber entrance.

Everett clicked the transmit button on the small radio they had confiscated from the guard shack, letting Jack know they were in place. The dangerous part was coming. Even though he was aware that the remaining guards had obviously seen them enter the mine's main doors, he also knew they would take the obvious targets first, meaning the bait that was about to be laid before them— Jack and Sebastian. His two-man sniper teams had to react fast at the first sign of movement from the spiderweb of gridwork above them. He knew this because that's where he would be if he were the ambushing guards.

Jack and Sebastian made a great show of sliding open the steel door that separated the main gallery from the outside world. The door slid loudly on its runners and Jack played a flashlight about at the entrance. The two men stepped inside just as the first rays of sunlight struck the small valley in the Andes. Collins entered the mine with Sebastian following.

As Everett scanned the steel support beams in the upper reaches of the excavation, he pulled back the hammer on his nine-millimeter, knowing he would be the two snipers' only backup if one of them missed or if there were more guards inside than first thought.

As Jack and the German commando entered and started walking toward the giant steel doors that secured the first section of mine from the next, Everett saw movement. With the distraction of the battle raging only five miles distant, Everett concentrated on the gridwork. As he watched, he heard a loud crack from his right. A man briefly stood and then fell forward onto a catwalk. One guard had been dispatched. Then, just as quickly, another guard sprang up not far from where the first had been hidden. As he did he actually managed to get off a round before the second sniper found him. The guard's bullet struck just to Jack's left, pinging off the concrete flooring. Collins and Sebastian dove for cover as the second guard succumbed to a sniper's bullet. Everett could see no more movement.

"Clear?" Jack called out.

The two snipers called out "clear" and stood from their positions of cover. Collins became concerned when Everett didn't stand and call out his all clear. That was when his hackles rose and he knew that they had been premature in calling all safe.

A third guard opened fire with an automatic weapon from high up in the network of shaft support beams. The Australian sniper flew backward as a line of bullets stitched its way across his chest. Jack was slow to react, but Everett wasn't. With five well-placed shots from the nine-millimeter, Carl dropped the third man. His body struck the catwalk and slid over the edge, falling eighty feet to the floor.

"Damn it!" Everett said as he finally stood and ran over to the fallen Australian. He checked the man for any sign of life but found he had died very quickly. "Jack, are you two all right?" he called out from a kneeling position.

Suddenly lights came on in the overhead. The scene was illuminated by the fifty hanging fixtures from above. Everett looked over and saw the small Vietnamese sniper at the lighting control panel. He felt Jack at his side.

"That's my fault. I was in too much of a damned hurry to get in here."

Everett looked up at his boss and stood up.

"We're all moving too damn fast, Jack. Hell, I should have known better. This isn't the last asshole we're going to run into down here, but we don't have time to do a clean sweep, we have to get Niles and the others in here."

"He's right, Colonel. We have to move. From the sounds of things outside, I don't think the Ecuadorians are faring well at all," Sebastian said and nodded his thanks to the Vietnamese sniper, who was watching them. He continued glancing at the gallery support system above them.

Jack nodded and looked around. "Okay, let's get Niles and his science team in here and see what we can see in case we have to make a hasty retreat out of here."

As they moved to get the others, Jack's radio came to life. He snatched it from his belt and listened.

"The lookouts report helicopter support has finally arrived to assist the battle line down the mountain."

"If there's anyone left," Everett said. He moved to get outside and retrieve Niles and his four men.

Jack exited into the dawn's first light and immediately saw the three Cobra gunships three miles away making their first runs on the unseen enemy below. He also saw his thirty-man fire team as they took their positions in case the distant enemy made it through. As he raised his binoculars to his eyes, he saw the first lines of what looked like mercenaries. He scanned the area and then his heart froze as he saw something familiar.

"Mr. Everett, contact the man we have standing by at the radio in the guard shack. Tell him to get the frequency that those Cobras are using. Tell them they are being tracked by antiaircraft missiles.

Before Carl could react, Jack grabbed his arm—it was too late. They all watched in stunned silence as three streaks of white-hot exhaust broke free of the tall trees lining the battlefield below. They shot upward at Mach speed. The first Cobra never knew what hit it. Its entire forward section disappeared in a ball of flame. The second had time at least to terminate its covering run of the ground troops. It tried to pull up as the second radar-guided missile struck just aft of the two-man cockpit, splitting the old attack chopper into two pieces as it fell into the trees near the troops it had been trying to defend. The third Cobra banked hard and was actually able to bring its twenty-millimeter Gatling gun to bear on the third missile team that had shot at it. The Cobra peppered the site with a thousand rounds, sending the shooters into oblivion. As Jack continued to watch, a fourth missile came out of the trees, tracking the third Cobra as it pulled up into the still gray sky of early morning.

"Jink right, go right," Jack hissed between his teeth.

The pilot never saw it coming. By the time the Cobra had gained altitude, the threat receiver was too late in picking up the radar pulse that had locked on to it. The missile slammed into the spinning rotors and sheared the twin blades off the transmission hub. The chopper fell into the trees like a rock. The explosion and black smoke marked their crash site. As Jack scanned the area below, he saw more mercenaries advance through the trees. The remaining Ecuadorians were scattering after seeing their air support vanish in a split second.

"Mr. Everett, take the science team and secure them inside the mine," Jack said as he lowered the field glasses. "We're going to have a lot of company soon."

"Respectfully, Jack, send someone else to baby-sit them, I want to stay on the line."

Collins looked at his friend and shook his head. "If they don't get in there and find something useful soon, this is all going to be for nothing. Don't argue with me, Captain. It's too early in the morning for that. If the worst happens, I'll let you know. Use the escape route we utilized last week and get them the hell down the mountain. Take that idiot German with you. That's all I can spare."

"I heard that," Sebastian said, as he picked up three extra magazines from one of his manned positions.

Everett looked at Collins angrily, and then he looked at the lightening sky above.

"Remind me to thank the president for all of that help he sent."

Jack nodded his head and watched as Niles and the others approached.

"Move these people into the mine," he said, as he shook hands with Niles and Pete.

Charlie Ellenshaw walked up to Jack and held out his hand.

"Colonel, I would very much like to stay and help out," he said, as he pushed his wire-rimmed glasses back up his nose. "They don't need me in there."

"Thanks, Doc, but I disagree. They do need you down in that mine. You have a way of helping that you could never understand."

"I can fight Jack," Crazy Charlie said, looking pleadingly at the colonel.

"I know you can, Doc, but Sarah, Will, and Ryan need that information, and you can help get it. I need you down there," he said, nodding toward the shaft.

"Colonel, the enemy is only a thousand yards away," one of the German commandos called out.

Ellenshaw finally nodded his head of white hair and slowly turned away. Niles looked at Jack and smiled sadly, then he too turned toward the mine's entrance and left.

"Good luck, swabby," Jack called out to Everett, who had stopped to hear what he had to say.

"Letting you do the hero thing is getting real old, Jack. This time you may just get your ass shot off," Carl said as he turned away. "That's going to leave me with an awful lot of paperwork to do back at the complex, and that is not what I signed up for."

The Mechanic was very pleased with the way his men had performed.

As he scanned the small contingent lining the front wall of rocks in front of the mine opening, he had to smile. If he had the time, it would be easy to just stand pat and lob grenades into the rocks above. It would decimate the defense line. However, he knew that eventually the Americans would react.

"Commence the attack. Kill them all, and do it quickly."

As he watched, 256 men advanced through the trees. Then he gestured. Four mortars opened fire. "Take them fast and make sure none escape."

## MILITARY FLIGHT BRAVO TWO-SIX, 1,000 FEET ABOVE, AND 3 MILES NORTH, MÜELLER AND SANTIAGO MINING CONCERN

The lone Air Force C-130J-30 Hercules had flown through the night, refueling once in midair on its long flight from Fort Bragg. The pilot could swear he felt the tops of the trees brush against his underbelly as he hopped over small rises at the base of the Andes. He was sweating while his copilot manipulated the four throttle controls of the venerable old aircraft. As he allowed the yoke to steady, he pushed forward and sent the Hercules into a shallow dive. They had reached the last valley before the drop point. He heard the flight's engineer open the cabin door.

Lieutenant Commander Scott Englehorn USN, team leader for SEAL Team Five and temporary leader for SEAL Team Eight, stepped up in back of the pilot's ejection seat.

"Three minutes to IP, Commander. Tell your boys back there good luck," the Air Force pilot said as he pulled the nose of the Hercules up again in a flurry of motion.

"Hell, besides the other SEAL team, only five of those kids back there speak English, but I'll pass on your sentiment anyway." The SEAL patted the pilot on the shoulder. "Thanks for the lift, Air Force. It was a smooth ride."

"Good luck, Navy," the pilot said again, feeling for the men that he was about to drop into harm's way.

The Navy commander stepped out of the cabin and slid quietly down the small set of stairs. He looked at the four lines of men lined up in the hold of the Hercules. His SEAL teams would be the first out of the aircraft. They would be followed by the one hundred men of the main assault element. This young group was what was passing for soldiers nowadays in Europe. They and their nation had just been accepted into NATO and had been on station in the United States for training at Fort Bragg when they were recruited by the president on a purely voluntary mission. As he scanned the eager faces of the men, he saw they had no fear, a sign that they had never faced combat before. He shook his head, sliding among the lines of men. As he moved, the red light appeared in six different areas of the cargo hold.

"Two minutes—two minutes," he shouted as loud as he could.

He saw the young captain who led the foreign element and the SEAL nodded his head.

"Is Poland ready for this day, Captain?"

"Poland has always been ready, Commander," the young man said. He looked determinedly into the Navy man's eyes just as the commander placed a hand on his shoulder.

"I believe you are, Captain. Shall we go and rescue some people on the ground?"

"Yes, Commander, let's do that."

"One minute," the commander shouted as he took his place at the head of the jump group.

The aircraft cargo master started lowering the giant ramp. The men would jump four abreast at seven hundred feet, an extremely low altitude jump. Their parachutes would barely have enough time to open before the tops of the trees would be at their feet. This is what SEALs were used to doing, but the Polish element was making the low altitude jump for the first time. The Navy just hoped the president knew what he was doing. Not only were his SEALs working with an Army element, they were working with a foreign army to boot. The world was becoming a strange place indeed.

The mortars had damaged the front line defense. Three of the German commandos were down before a single shot had been fired at the enemy. Jack went from station to station to check on the men and was making sure they kept their heads down until they had hard targets to engage.

"Colonel, if we don't take out those mortar positions they can stand off and take us out a group at a time," the lieutenant from Sebastian's command said, just as Collins ducked to avoid a near miss.

Jack felt someone slide into the rock-covered position behind him. He turned and saw the green bush headgear and the crossed swords on the side of the hat. It was Captain Whitlesey Mark-Patton of Her Majesty's SAS. Beside him was Sergeant Tashiro Jiimzo, of the Japanese Self-Defense Forces. Patton nodded his head.

"Colonel, the sergeant and I have an idea, and with the help of our little Vietnamese sniper friend above, I think we can get to those mortar positions without getting our bloody asses shot off."

"Let's hear it," Collins said, and the two men explained what they wanted to do.

"I'll take my SAS element, and have these generous Japanese fellows along for support. Our sniper friend can keep the closest of the attackers at bay as we wheel around them and hit the first of the three positions—that is something they won't be expecting, for us to actually sally forth in an attack."

As a mortar round landed nearby, Jack could only shake his head.

"Well, Captain, I'm not going to sit here and argue with you. Get it done before someone gets a lucky shot in."

The SAS captain started to salute and Jack gave him a look that said in no uncertain terms that they did not have the time. The captain smiled and then pulled the Japanese sergeant along with him. As Collins watched, the SAS captain was using his radio to explain what he needed from the Vietnamese sniper above them.

"This is getting nasty as hell," Jack said to the German beside him. "We need that help the president promised and we need it now."

"Uh, Colonel, you better see this," the German commando said loudly over the din of gunfire and explosions. He pointed behind Jack.

"Damn it to hell!" Collins cursed as he saw what the commando was pointing out.

On a small ridge close to the second level of their defense he saw Alice Hamilton and Senator Garrison Lee as they slowly made their way along, heading for the mine opening. He could see that Lee was having a difficult time as Alice held on to him. Then Collins angrily shook his head as the old one-eyed man pulled free of her helping hand and brought up an ancient .45 caliber Colt automatic, firing three rounds down the hillside. He didn't hit anything; he just looked happy to be shooting at something. Alice slapped at him and they again started toward the mine opening.

"Ballsy old people," the German lieutenant said and turned back toward the front line of attackers.

"Yeah, they're something, all right," Jack hissed.

"Someday you'll have to explain to me and my men just who the hell you and these people are, Colonel."

"Well—" A mortar round detonated not far from their covered position. When Jack looked back up, Alice and Lee had disappeared into the mine opening. "I can tell you this, Lieutenant. That is a real woman and she's helping one of the bravest men I have ever met in my life."

Before the German could say anything, another detonation went off not ten feet from their position. Jack managed to shake off the dirt and rocks. He looked at the mine's gaping maw of an opening.

"Good-bye General Lee," he said as he slipped back down into the hole.


Everett was in front of the science team as they examined the double steel doors that he had seen on their first visit to the mine a week before. They had opened then for the briefest time and Carl knew that the shaft beyond the doors angled downward on a sharp grade. Everyone started looking for the access panel that would open the doors as explosions outside came at a far brisker pace than just a minute before. Everett and Sebastian both were frustrated beyond measure that they weren't where they thought they should be inside the mine. The large German was slamming against crates and other material as he searched for the panel, intentionally taking out his anger on the objects he felt were in his way.

"Here it is," Appleby said. He opened a large steel door embedded in the rock wall. He saw the large switch and the German lettering below it—*Sicherheitstüren*.

"What does it say?" Ellenshaw asked, looking over the DARPA man's shoulder.

"It says security door, Professor," Appleby answered as he eyed Charlie.

"Oh, I guess that's it then," Ellenshaw said in all seriousness.

Appleby used his considerable bulk to throw the large-handled switch. The big steel doors started to separate.

The others heard the whine of electric motors and turned to see the two eight-inch-thick steel doors start to part. Everett raised his M-16 and he and Sebastian slipped through the small opening first. Niles grabbed Ellenshaw's arm as he tried to follow.

"Let them do their job, Professor," Niles said, admonishing Charlie with a stern look.

As the doors finally opened far enough, they hit their stops and the science team found itself facing eighteen feet of open space. Sebastian and Everett looked around with weapons at the ready, but the entire giant area looked empty, with the exception of several large electric cars equipped with flatbeds parked parallel to the descending roadway ahead of them. Placed down the center line of that road was a red-lighted strip of small glass bulbs embedded in the roadway.

"Seems German engineering was as good back then as it is now, eh?"

They all turned to see Garrison Lee leaning heavily against Alice Hamilton. Niles shook his head. He ran over and quickly took Lee's weight off Alice's hands. The woman relaxed and gave Niles a determined look.

"Before you fly off the handle, he has a right to see this, and I for one wasn't going to say no. Are you?" she asked sternly.

Compton deflated. He held his free hand up to Everett before he could admonish the two older people for their foolishness. Niles shook his head and started for one of the electric carts. He placed Garrison in the back and stepped aside as Carl came up. Carl shook his head at the man who stared at him with one good eye. The old man's brow lifted as he waited for the chewing out by the mission commander that he knew was coming. Instead, Everett drew out his nine-millimeter and turned it so that the butt of the weapon was facing the senator.

"You remember how to use one of these, I presume?"

Lee grimaced in pain, but still managed to slide the weapon back so that he could look to make sure a round had been chambered. Then he pulled out his old Colt automatic and held both weapons up so Everett could see.

"I should have given that to Alice so she could shoot your curiosity-driven ass," Carl said. He reached down and patted Lee on the leg.

"Please. She wouldn't have wasted the bullet, Captain. She would have pistol-whipped me with it. You don't know how mean this woman really is."

"Appropriate, I must say," Niles said. He shook his head at the dying Lee.

"Well, Senator Lee, shall we go see what all the fuss was about back when you were a kid?" Everett said, his anger going the way of a wisp of smoke as he realized Lee was about to go on his final adventure.

"By all means, Captain," Lee said, as he dipped his hat in Alice's direction. "My dear Mrs. Hamilton, would you like to ride beside me and prop this old fool up before he falls out?"

Alice smiled and hopped quickly onto the flatbed. She placed her arm through Lee's.

"I would love to."

"I notice you didn't protest my use of the words "old fool," darling."

Instead of answering, Alice just laid her head onto the broad shoulder of the man she had loved all of her adult life.

Everett directed the others to climb into the lead cart. Then Sebastian took another of the carts with Charlie, Appleby, and Franklyn Dubois—the German handed his weapon to Ellenshaw and took the wheel of the second cart.

"Don't shoot me with that," he said to Ellenshaw.


Jack watched the progress of the young SAS captain and his men as they weaved their way through cover that wasn't thick enough to hide a raccoon, much less grown men. As the attack force neared the mortar positions, they began encountering fixed positions placed around the mortar crews. As they went as far as they could without being detected, Jack could hear on the radio as the Englishman gave instructions to the young Vietnamese sniper, who was well hidden on the upper tier of the ridgeline above his own position. As the SAS men and the Japanese soldiers waited, Jack watched as the sniper started tracking targets closest to the attack team.

"Come on, kid. Earn your pay for the month," Collins mumbled while every eye on the ridge watched, hoping the covering mortar fire could be eliminated.

The binoculars in Jack's hands told the story. He saw a group of pit defenders, as they were called by the SAS captain, start to fall. A group of six mercenaries in the first line guarded the mortar pit a hundred yards in front of the position. This was the extreme range of the sniper's very old but very accurate M-14, a weapon the Vietnamese only had experience with from the early days of the Vietnam War, thirty-five years before this particular Vietnamese kid had been born.

Through the field glasses Jack saw Captain Whitlesey Mark-Patton raise his right hand and then he saw the extended fingers close into a fist. The first terrorist defender apparently saw movement to his front and made the mistake of raising his head. The fortuitous movement coincided with Vinh Tram's line of fire. The first round from 1,200 yards caught the man in the top of his head, sending him backward. The next man in line saw his comrade fall and turned to see what the action was about when the second round caught him in the side of his head. Jack couldn't see if it had been a kill shot because the man's black baseball cap flew off and obscured his head until he sank out of sight. The friendly sniper didn't wait to see if the shot had done its work before he fired four more times in rapid succession—hitting every one of his four targets. The nearest he came to missing was when the last man in the defense pit turned to run back to the mortar men he was tasked to guard. The last round caught the man just at the base of the skull and dropped him.

Whitlesey Mark-Patton never hesitated; he and his SAS team, with their tagalong Japanese contingent, ran forward with nothing between them and the mortar. The assault was ruthless. In just five seconds the SAS and Japanese had eliminated the entire mortar crew and then they were up and on to the next, the unguarded center mortar. They hit in the same fashion and then did the same to the third. They stayed long enough to trip fuses in the mortar rounds and drop them into their tubes. A few seconds later the tubes exploded, and then Whitlesey was headed to the next pit as he made his way back.

Jack saw the terrorist element maneuver in behind them, cutting off their retreat as the mortars blew up, outlining their avenue of retreat to the attackers. Whoever was leading these men knew what had happened and moved his chess pieces before Mark-Patton and his men could escape fully.

"Damn it!" Jack said, but even as he spoke the words he saw the men making up the flanking force start to drop.

"I'll be damned," the German next to him said. "That kid is an amazing shot!"

As they watched, the terrorists started dropping one at a time, each man never knowing where the shots were coming from. The young Vietnamese soldier, with the barest minimum of firepower and optical assistance, was making kill shot after kill shot from a distance of over fifteen hundred yards against an enemy partially concealed by trees and brush. Every time one of the enemies drew close to Mark-Patton and his team, that man would fall with one of Tram's bullets in him.

Finally the SAS and Japanese element made it clear of the tree line and rejoined the defense. Captain Whitlesey Mark-Patton joined Jack before he followed his men to the ridge above. All three mortar crews had been eliminated without one attacker lost.

"Remind me to kiss that kid," Captain Mark-Patton said breathlessly as he plopped against Collins.

"Good job, Captain. That should take away one of their shields when they come on," Jack said as he watched the terrorist element start to move forward in earnest.

Mark-Patton was making ready to join his men when he turned back to Collins and smiled.

"If I don't get the chance later, Colonel, tell that kid who saved our asses out there he can bloody well join my team any day."

"Too late, Captain. I'm adopting him," Jack said as he lowered the glasses. He held his hand out and shook with the SAS man.

"Here they come, Colonel," the German lieutenant said, sighting on the first group of mercenaries to break cover.

Jack admired the discipline of the expert soldiers in his defense team. They held their fire without being told as the enemy broke. He also admired the attack strategy of whoever was leading the group of misguided men below. They came on in stages, not presenting a solid front for his men to concentrate fire upon. They came on in staggered waves, zigzagging their way up the hill toward their very limited defense.

Collins raised his M-16 and sighted. He saw one man in front of a group of thirty-five or so and targeted him since he was turning periodically and gesturing. *A sure leader of men*, Jack thought, as he fired the first round from the first line of defenders. The man fell. That was the signal for the defense of Columbus Ridge, as it would be known in many reports afterward, to begin.

The entire firing line opened up against the overwhelming force of terrorists.

As the three carts traveled further into the mine shaft, Everett could see the expense that was thrown into the mine itself. The German engineers had made a futuristic roadway complete with lighting and smooth macadam road. The further down they traveled, the smaller but more brightly lit the tunnel was. All eyes were watching for guards that may have ventured in ahead of them. Carl heard a shot from behind their electric car. When he stopped, he saw Sebastian lecturing Charlie Ellenshaw about weapons safety. Pete was actually smiling from his position in the flatbed behind Ellenshaw. Satisfied they weren't in the midst of an ambush, Everett drove on. Every once in a while he would glance back at the senator and Alice. Lee was leaning heavily against her and unmoving. Alice would place her right hand against his cheek and rub it until Garrison looked up and reassured her he was still among the living. Carl also noticed the medical bag opened at Alice's side. Lee was being plied with plenty of painkillers for his ride into the bowels of the earth.

Suddenly Carl had to slam on the brakes as they came around a large bend in the lighted roadway. He couldn't believe what he was seeing. Before them stood two giant doors, but that wasn't the amazing sight. On both sides of the road were large kiosks, just like the ones you would find in any museum in the world. Decked out in bright red and black streamers covered in dust and dirt were what looked like gift shops. Inside were displayed Nazi flags and pictures of the mine shaft as it was being excavated. Everett shone a flashlight in one of the large plate glass windows and saw what looked like small models of spaceships that he recognized from his childhood.

"Buck Rogers," Alice explained when she saw what Everett had illuminated.

"Ma'am?" Everett said.

"The spaceships are from an old movie serial of the thirties, *Buck Rogers*. Judging from the looks of things, the Nazis had designs on making this a tourist attraction after their triumph in the war."

Carl shook his head as he climbed free of the small cab. He turned the light on the small gift shop and the equally small snack area opposite.

"I swear, when you think this job has topped out in strangeness, something comes along that makes you feel you'll never see the end," Everett said as he was joined by Sebastian and the others.

Sebastian chose to ignore the strange shops around them and looked up at the thick steel doors ahead. He read the words spelled out in German on those doors: *Galerie Ein—Wohnkomplex*.

"What does it say?" Everett asked Sebastian.

"The first line says Gallery One, Living Complex, and the second line says 'No electric carts beyond this point and no one enters without SS escort.'" Sebastian looked over at Everett. "And before you ask, no, I do not qualify as one of those murdering bastards."

"I never said a word, buddy. You're not responsible for those cheery bastards. Shall we open it up and see what's behind door number one?"

Sebastian just nodded his head and looked over at Niles, who had already found the breaker box for the door. The German dipped his head forward, giving the director the go-ahead.

The giant steel doors started to part. As the black breach expanded, they could see nothing but darkness beyond. Sebastian and Everett were struck with a breeze that chilled them as the doors slid apart. They brought their weapons up and waited. The doors stopped; beyond them both men felt like the vastness of space had opened up before them.

"Boss, see if you can find the light switch," Carl said as the two were joined by Lee, Alice, Charlie, Appleby, and the MIT man, Franklyn Dubois.

Niles found the handle with the electrical symbol above it and threw the switch.

Suddenly the gallery beyond the doors flared into a glorious brightness. They were standing on the precipice of a massive stone ledge overlooking a giant cave system.

"This isn't a mine, it's a cave, a natural formation," Ellenshaw said. He stepped forward and looked down at one of the most amazing sights he had ever seen. The others braved the heights and followed Ellenshaw's lead out onto the ledge.

Far below, they saw a pathway that had been dredged out of solid rock leading down to the bowels of the cave system. Thousands of overhead lights had been installed by German workmen over seventy years before. Illuminated by these lights was what looked like the destroyed remains of an ancient city. The buildings were made up of material that looked like plastic, white and dull with dirt and dust. Some of the structures were upright, others crushed beneath stone and other debris that had fallen over the years. They could see that some of the strange material had actually petrified, indicating its age. They could also see very old German heavy equipment that had been used to excavate some of the strange buildings. Tractors, earth movers, and other construction elements littered the three-mile length of the dig.

"Look at those," Niles Compton said as he joined the group looking out over the crushed and battered cave system below.

"What are they?" Appleby asked.

"Petrified trees," Ellenshaw answered for Niles. "Thousands of them."

"This site used to be aboveground, possibly before the formation of the mountains."

The men and Alice looked at Niles as he continued to speculate.

"Millions of years ago these buildings were in the light of day, but a shift in the continental plates and a buckling of the crust created the Andes as continents collided with each other, forming the up-push that sent stone and dirt miles into the air, covering this site, this small village of visitors."

"Visitors?" Alice asked.

"They had to be. Check out those geodesic domes. They look as though they were meant to be temporary structures, just like we would pitch tents in an unknown land. Can't you feel it?"

Everett watched as Niles and the others visualized a group of explorers setting up a base on an inhospitable bit of land doomed to be crushed by the formation of a mountain range, all of this happening nearly a hundred million years before.

"We have to get down there," Niles said, turning to looked at Everett.

"The path is this way," he said. He looked at Lee. "Sebastian, I think we can break the rules your forebears warned of and take the carts down. If that heavy machinery made it, we can too."

"I agree, Captain," Sebastian said without looking at the ailing senator.

Lee was staring at the large and age-tattered streamers that bore the Nazi swastika. The flags and banners hung around the entire circumference of the rounded chamber below. This is what had led to the death of Alice's husband Ben, and Lee for one was determined to find out what that death had been for, what the price was for the death of a good young man.

"For some reason, I think more than a global cataclysm struck this place," Ellenshaw said. The others, save for Everett, made their way back to the electric cars.

"Come on, Doc. Let's get down there," Everett said.

The Mechanic, using field glasses, scanned the ridge in front of the mine and nodded as he took in the defense line of the Americans. The small force had been cut in half by his on-again, off-again assaults. He had witnessed three men go down in the last minute of battle from the front line of defense. As he adjusted the binoculars, he watched another team of his men run forward throwing grenades, only to be cut down by withering fire from the first and second ridgelines before them. Whoever was commanding those men up there had done a masterful job of concentrating fire on the most immediate threat. But time was running out for them. The attrition he was using his men up for was pushing the defense of the mine entrance to its limits.

He turned to the twenty men of his personal security team and told them to make ready to move forward with the special strike teams. He knew the defense line was soon going to falter and he didn't want any remnants falling back into the mine, where they would have to be rooted out later at great expense in men and, more importantly, time. The pests had caused far more casualties than the Mechanic would have liked. They had killed his men at a rate of fifty to one and that was getting a bit expensive. He needed these men for the removal of the artifacts and the weaponry from the mine.

He lowered his field glasses and admonished his men to keep a low profile as they advanced because of the threat of the most amazing sniper he had ever come into contact with. Try as he might, he could not pinpoint where the shooter was, but he was taking a heavy toll on his men. The man must be running low on ammunition, because his rate of fire had slowed, even though targets of opportunity abounded in the tree line.

"Radio the assault teams to make ready for the final push. I want the Americans to be swept clean of that ridge. We are running out of time. We still have a force of close to two hundred—adequate for the job, but not if we hesitate. Tell them that—"

He never got to finish. A withering fire opened up from somewhere behind them. Men who were formed for the final attack were struck by automatic weapons fire and mortars from their rear. As the Mechanic swung around he saw an amazing sight. From the very positions they had held earlier, a large force of men in green camouflage was running and firing—stopping, adjusting their fire, and moving in relays toward his exposed men.

"Impossible!" he shouted. He was being inundated with fire from the attacking force.

His men were being shredded by a Special Operations unit that could not be Ecuadorian. These men were running toward them crazed but with purpose. They were taking aim and laying down a swath of destruction that would soon render his attack moot and assure his defeat. Before he even knew what was hitting him, he froze. Two jets streaked overhead and four explosions rocked the trees where his men were trying to take cover. As he scanned the sky with his glasses he was amazed to see the jet aircraft climb out of their dive and head back into the blue sky.

"F-18 Hornets!" Where did they come from?" he asked no one. Two more Hornets made a low-level strafing run with their twenty-millimeter cannon, decimating a large group of his men who had exposed themselves far in advance of his orders to do so. "Allah be merciful!"

"We have to leave this place or die here," one of his men said as the group of attackers in the rear grew closer.

The Mechanic thought fast. He looked up at the ridgeline where the well-disciplined troops continued to fire instead of celebrating their rescue, and then he looked at the mine opening. He turned to the man on his right.

"Get my men together. Just from my twenty security personnel and the nearest group. Make it no more than ten. We will go to the river and backtrack to the waterfall, then we will enter the mine at that point. That is where the Americans escaped last week and that is where we will go."

As the man followed his orders, the Mechanic looked at the front line on the ridge. He tried to see who was there, determine who was directing the fight, but all he could see was fire coming from that position.

"You have been blessed for the moment, but God will allow me the final victory."

Jack slapped the wounded lieutenant on his shoulder, careful to avoid the still bleeding wound on his leg.

"Well," Jack said, laying his radio down in the pile of expended shell casings, "say hello to elements of the Second Special Polish Parachute Brigade and two teams of U.S. Navy SEALs."

"A grand sight indeed, Colonel. Now where did the air support come from?"

"Compliments of the U.S. Navy, and the *Enterprise* battle group, which finally decided to get into the fight."

"I never thought I would be pulled from the fire by a Polish brigade and the U.S. Navy, Colonel. Remind me to send them a note of thanks."

"I think we better include the president in that. It took him a while, but he came through."

Jack helped the lieutenant to his feet and handed him off to a dirty but smiling German comrade. Collins looked around at the Polish soldiers as they checked the dead and wounded of the attacking element. The parachute brigade had done its job, and was now learning that being nice to terrorists, either unharmed or wounded, was not an easy task.

"Colonel Collins?"

Jack turned and saw a man with thick green greasepaint covering his face. His bush hat was crumpled and only the whites of his eyes stood out.

"That's my name," Jack said, looking at the man and his two companions.

"Compliments of the president, sir. Lieutenant Commander Scott Englehorn, U.S. Navy, relieving you."

Jack ignored the salute from the SEAL and just held out his hand.

The young officer was taken back. He looked uncomfortable at first, and then he smiled as he took the colonel's hand in his own and shook it.

"I think you may have a buddy up there on the ridgeline somewhere. I think that's where I put the Navy, anyway."

The commander looked around and nodded his head. "We heard there were other ball bouncers around these parts."

Jack smiled at the familiar term the SEALs had for each other, referring to a seal balancing a ball on its nose.

"You can tell them how you liked commanding Polish paratroopers."

The lieutenant commander leaned into Jack and whispered, "Sir, those sons of bitches are fighting fools. I'll take them into combat anytime."

"Pass on to them my thanks, Commander. Now I have to get going. Secure the area and please take care of these men. They deserve it. Bring up the Polish company and make sure that mine entrance is secure. Deadly force is authorized without warning—be sure no one gets in."

This time the Navy SEAL did salute and Jack returned it. As he was moving off the line, he looked at his gathered defense team. They were limping down from the upper ridge, assisting their wounded or carrying their dead. They stopped as one and looked at the man who had held them together for an hour and a half of pure hell. Colonel Jack Collins simply nodded his head at his men. For their part, the men stood watching Jack for the longest time, then slowly moved off to the aid station that the SEALs and Polish paratroopers had set up.

Jack turned away, always proud of the way men acted in the toughest of situations. He had started climbing back up toward the mine opening when he ran straight into the Vietnamese sergeant and his lone surviving private—the sniper from the upper ridge. The smaller man laid the now empty and still hot M-14 at Collins's feet and nodded his head. Jack smiled and handed the boy private his M-16.

"Sergeant, can I borrow this man for a few hours. I think I would feel safer with him along."

The Vietnamese sergeant half bowed and interpreted the colonel's request to his man. The kid smiled and nodded his head.

"Private Tram, am I correct?" Jack asked. He gestured for the kid to follow him toward the entrance to the mine.

The private nodded, understanding Jack's small bit of English.

"I think this is the start of a long and fruitful relationship, kid."

# 14

## *DARK STAR* 3, FOUR HOURS FROM ORBIT INSERTION

The command module *Falcon 1*, with attached Altair lander, passed extremely close to the insertion path the ESA spacecraft had traveled just five hours previous. The crew listened as several large and small pieces of insulation from the French-made Astral lander struck their spacecraft. The damage the ESA vehicle had sustained in the recent attacks had been enough to leave a continual debris trail in her wake as she approached the Moon. Every time the spacecraft was peppered with those floating particles, the crew cringed at the thought of the damage they might sustain to the fragile lander and the command module that was the only way home for them.

Sarah was in the umbilical tunnel that connected the two spacecraft when a loud bang was heard aft of the crew module on *Falcon 1*. Mendenhall, who was busy exercising on the bicycle in the lander, saw Sarah stop and tense as a slight rumble was felt throughout both modules.

"That didn't sound good," Mendenhall said. He turned and faced the mission commander. Colonel Kendal reached out from where he had been doing isometric exercises with hand grips and pulled Sarah free of the tunnel. He immediately floated into the large command module.

"He seemed a little worried too," Mendenhall said. He looked over at Ryan, who was drinking a Dr. Pepper from a small Mylar package.

"Attention, we have some red warning lights up here. I want all nonessential crew members to take station inside *Altair* for the time being. Seal all access hatches and go to separate life support until we get a grasp on what's happening."

After the command module's pilot stopped talking, Ryan floated over to the large triangular window at the pilot's station. As his eyes roamed over the exterior face of *Altair*, he saw several large pieces of gold and silver insulation pass by no more than three feet away.

"No wonder the ESA lost contact with their lander," Ryan said, sipping his Dr. Pepper through a straw. "Most of it seems to be floating right into our path. A lot of that debris is insulation from their oxygen and water tanks."

As his eyes stared at the star field and the growing daylight side of the Moon, he lowered the small package of soft drink and hit the VOX communicator at his side.

"Hang on. We have a large chunk of something coming right at us!" he called out, just as the radar threat receiver sounded throughout both craft.

Ryan's words had no sooner left his mouth than part of the European *Astral*'s docking collar slammed into the upper portion of the command module, missing the large pilot's window on *Altair* by a mere foot. The impact sent a shock wave through both spacecraft and sent every crew member scrambling for their environmental equipment in case they had been holed.

"We ran over something in the road," one of the Green Berets said as he strapped himself in the crew chamber below the upper deck of *Altair*.

"And it was a big something too," Will said. He and Sarah put on helmets and connected their environmental suits to the individual computer stations. The connection would automatically update the suits' GPS computers and their oxygen status, as well as the current disposition of all mapping and telemetry connections.

In the command module, Kendal had cleared most of the crew and placed everyone in the *Altair* in case *Falcon 1* lost her air or was in fire danger mode

He hit his own VOX switch and studied the battery situation. Then he examined the eight LED readouts concerning oxygen status and the water tanks housed near the main engine of the command module. In relief he saw that there was no leakage showing on the sensitive gauges.

"Houston, *Falcon 1*, copy?" Kendal said into the small mike attached to his overalls. He half turned when the LEM pilot held out his ENVI suit and helmet. Kendal shook his head and pointed to the LED readouts on the main console. The needles were holding steady. Pressure readings, a major concern, were at their normal PSI.

"Houston, *Falcon 1*, do you copy?"

As he released the transmit switch, he looked at the Navy pilot and nodded. The young pilot and five-year astronaut lowered his hand to the own voice communication switch on his belt.

"Houston, *Falcon 1*—we have sustained an external collision with an unknown object. Do you copy, over?"

Every crew member waited for the answer from the Johnson Space Center, some staring at nothing, others closing their eyes and hoping the dead air was just a fluke in the COMM system.

"Get on the CCT and see if there's any damage to the ST5-3-10 high-gain antenna," Kendal said, knowing they were in for it if what he thought happened had indeed happened. He looked at the gain numbers on the COMM console and saw that the needle was flat-lined at zero transmit, zero receiving.

The lieutenant brought the closed circuit exterior cameras online and found the camera that showed the large high-gain antenna.

"Jesus, skipper," the pilot said, examining the empty frame.

"Damn thing was torn completely off its mountings," Kendal said. The main cable that attached the interior to the antenna was stretched to its limit. "Adjust angle and see if we're lucky enough to be dragging it in our wake."

The camera angle adjusted, and with relief they saw the ST5-3-10 dish dangling straight out from the taut cable.

"Well, we have to go get that damn thing and repair it," the colonel said. He hissed through his teeth.

"I volunteer for the walk," Ryan said, popping his head into the command module.

Kendal turned and saw the eager lander pilot. He shook his head. "Negative, Ryan. You don't have the space walk training."

Ryan floated the rest of the way into the large cabin.

"Excuse me, Colonel, but do you?"

"The lieutenant and I have two hundred simulations on record, and that's two hundred more than you."

Ryan continued to push.

"Look, I'm sitting here like a bump on a log. I have nothing to do other than being a backup to the lieutenant. And, frankly speaking, if something happens to him, we're shit out of luck. We need him in here to land this damn thing. I need to go out there instead of him."

"Sorry, Ryan. I'll make sure nothing happens to Lieutenant Dugan. After all the times you crashed the *Altair* in simulations, believe me, I'll watch him closely. You stand down, son, but thanks for the offer. You stay in here and assist Maggio with the command module. Contact Houston as soon as we have a signal—clear?"

Ryan looked at the module pilot and then at Dugan, the lander pilot. Both men shook their heads at the obvious eagerness of the untrained and dangerous man they had in Ryan.

"Yes, sir, stay with the womenfolk," Jason said sarcastically.

"Good," Kendal said. "Now, get your environmental suit on, you'll be reeling us out of the module's hatch."

Ryan moved to comply and as he did he saw the dirty look from Sarah as he entered the lowest deck of the *Altair*.

"Quit volunteering for things, Jason. Jack will be pissed. You remember what he said about volunteering?"

"Always let someone else do the volunteering, then you can be the smart one when you pull their asses out of the fire," Jason and Will said simultaneously in the most mundane voices they could use.

"Right," Sarah said. She had to smile at the dull voices her two friends used when imitating Jack's dry sense of humor.

Ryan started pulling on his helmet with the assistance of several of the Army personnel. He looked at Will and Sarah as they locked it into place.

"Don't worry, guys. Mr. Redundancy will be safe and sound inside the command module while others take the risk."

As they watched Ryan float back through the umbilical tunnel connecting *Altair* and *Falcon 1*, Sarah couldn't help but think about the bad luck the ship was having and about how Jack was faring back on Earth, which now seemed light-years away.

"Jason worries me sometimes," Will said, frowning through his glass face-plate.

"You guys are all the same," said an angry Sarah McIntire.


Ryan took the copilot's seat to monitor the space walk. The two men were tethered by separate leads in case one fouled. The space packs they each wore were controlled by hydrogen jets in case something went wrong with the tethers. Ryan and Maggio watched through the camera system while the rest of the crew stood by belowdecks on *Altair*, waiting for word from outside the spacecraft. They watched on the CCT system as Dugan and Kendal made their way back along *Falcon* toward the damaged high-gain antenna.

As the spacecraft was traveling in excess of 34,000 miles per hour, the view was disorienting because they looked as if they were standing still. Kendal made sure the tool belt he was carrying was strapped tightly to his suit and gently pushed off from the hatch. Dugan soon followed. The glare of the sun shone brightly off the white-painted aluminum of *Falcon 1* as they eased themselves hand over hand toward the mount that once held the antenna array. As they came up to the severely damaged mount, Kendal held fast as Dugan started to slip his thickly gloved hand around the cable that was the only anchor for the drifting dish. As he attempted to grab hold, Kendal waved him off.

"Secure yourself to the spacecraft," the colonel said over the radio.

"Roger, sorry," Dugan said. He slipped his hook through the base of the mount. When he did, Kendal waved for him to take hold of the cable.

Dugan expected resistance, as if he were pulling something in from deep water. Instead, he was rewarded with the dish actually sliding nicely toward the mount. Kendal studied the panel that housed the recessed radar system. He saw a large dent on the cover and he shook his head inside the large helmet.

"Here's the problem with the radar and why we got such a late collision warning," he said as he started to unscrew the access panel. When he had the cover off, he saw the smashed circuit on the radar's motherboard. "*Falcon* cut the power to the radar through the circuit breaker panel."

Inside *Falcon*, Ryan lifted free of his seat and floated toward the circuit breaker panel for outside systems. He found circuit breaker 1911-b, radar and sonar, and he easily reached out and popped it into the break position.

"Power down," Ryan confirmed to Kendal.

"Roger, pulling the motherboard for the system. Stand by."

Kendal reached down and pulled the damaged board from the access hole. He looked to make sure that Dugan was having no trouble pulling in the dish. Satisfied, he let the damaged circuit board float free. He reached into his bag and pulled the new motherboard from its protective antistatic covering, then slipped it inside just as the damaged telecommunications dish hit the hard body of *Falcon 1*.

"There we go. She looks good, skipper," Dugan said, as he examined the highly complex dish up close. "Cable is in fine shape. A new bolt assembly ought to do the job."

As Kendal connected the small electronics cable to the motherboard, he looked up and nodded his head. Before Dugan could start placing the dish back on its mount, his VOX system came to life.

"Breakers back on, Colonel. We have radar contact bearing 117. It's big and coming right for us," Ryan said, and then hurriedly read off the coordinates. Maggio says you two should move to the bottom side of *Falcon 1*. The object is traveling fast."

Kendal looked at Dugan and gestured for him to put the dish in its place.

"Wire-tie it for now and we'll come back to bolt it into place."

"Roger, skipper," he said. As he reached for a wire-tie in his pouch, the radio came alive again.

"Smaller debris is heading our way in front of the main object!" Ryan called out on VOX. "Thirteen—no, make that fifteen small targets."

As Kendal looked forward, he saw what Ryan was picking up on radar. From his position it looked like an oxygen or water tank that had once been attached to the ESA craft *Astral*. The smaller pieces were part of the landing pad from its missing gear. It had shattered when the *Astral* had separated from its mother ship. Dugan never knew what hit him as the rubberized pad slammed into him at over 34,000 miles per hour. The landing pad and several of its restraining bolts hit Dugan in the backpack and helmet, sending him skidding off the slick skin of *Falcon 1*, pulling his cable tether taught as it sprung like a bow string when he was hit. As Kendal reached for Dugan, he saw the blood inside the lunar lander pilot's helmet as it spread quickly in the oxygen-rich environment. The sight made the colonel lose his grip and Dugan went flying past. Kendal held on tightly to the bulkhead as the rest of the debris slammed into him.

Ryan pushed off from the main breaker panel and went to the aft window of *Falcon*, where he saw Kendal's suit get punctured in three different places. He saw the venting of his suit's atmosphere just as the tether holding Dugan close to the spacecraft snapped. Ryan watched in absolute horror as Dugan slipped out of view and then Kendal, who gagged for air that wasn't there. Jason watched, his eyes widening as Kendal's rubber-coated tether became taut and then snapped as the ESA oxygen tank from *Astral* not only hit the communications array mount but the spot where Kendal had been anchored. The commander quickly flew free of *Falcon 1*. Kendal smashed into the engine bell and the impact sent him spinning crazily off into space.

Ryan continued to stare out of the window in silence. The two men were so far beyond sight that he just stared at the spot where they had been a brief moment before.

"What's happening?" Maggio asked loudly.

Ryan didn't answer. He continued looking out the thick glass of the window.

"Ryan! Come on, man, what's going on?" Maggio called out again.

"They're gone," he finally answered quietly.

"What do you mean, 'They're gone,' Goddamn it?"

Ryan turned toward the command chair angrily.

"What do you think I mean? They're gone, dead, adrift. What do you want me to say?"

Down below, Sarah heard everything that was happening.

"What do we do?" Maggio asked no one in particular.

"We continue with the mission," Sarah said and released her safety harness.

"In case you didn't notice, we just lost the mission commander and the LEM pilot," Maggio called out, wanting to get out from behind the command seat.

Sarah floated up to the top deck and pulled herself into the access tunnel. She appeared a moment later inside the command module.

"You've just been promoted to LEM pilot, Maggio. I'm senior on the project in rank, so I'll be taking command of the excursion team."

Maggio looked at Sarah for the longest time.

"What mission? It's over here, Lieutenant."

"Yeah, well, she's senior above a bunch of junior grades and Army personnel," Ryan said in a calm and steady voice. "If you can get us there, I'll land us, and Sarah will find what it is we came for. Can you get us there?"

Maggio looked from Ryan to Sarah. The two people had been in the program less than a month, but both commanded authority through their voices and demeanor.

"Yes, I can get us there," Maggio said, "But the real question here, flyboy, is whether you can get the personnel down to the lunar surface without killing every mother-lovin' one of us?"

"If not, Lieutenant, you just may end up having an elementary school named after you."

Maggio was silent when confronted with Ryan's confidence.

"You have to admit, Maggio, the idea of a school being named after you is appealing, isn't it?" Sarah eyed the new command module pilot.

"As a matter of fact, a school in El Paso is just waiting to have my name put on it. Yeah, sure. Why not?"

Sarah reached out and pulled a floating Ryan toward her.

"You be the one to tell Mendenhall," she said.

"Hell, I'm asking him to be my copilot."

## MÜELLER AND SANTIAGO MINING CONCERN, 100 MILES EAST OF QUITO

An hour after the last shots fired at the battle for Columbus Hill, Jack and Tram eased themselves off the electric cart while still in front of the double steel doorways. Jack looked over at the gift shop that had never felt a tourist's touch. He wondered if they had planned on Hitler visiting the mine after the war was over, or if reich schoolchildren would have been paraded in and allowed to buy such items as Nazi coffee mugs and pictures of the artifacts discovered inside the mine. Collins shook his head in wonderment at the arrogance he was staring at.

"Come on, smiley. Let's follow along and see if we can find my friends."

Tram had the now reloaded M-14 lying across his arm as he examined the small Buck Rogers spaceship in the window. He turned and looked at Jack with a curious stare.

"'Private' will do, Colonel," he said, with no malice lacing his voice.

"I'll be damned—I didn't think you spoke English. Your sergeant didn't say anything about it."

"I'm sure he wasn't asked," Tram said as he moved toward the large steel doors.

"You actually sound like you spent time at Yale, at the very least," Jack joked.

Tram turned and faced Jack. With a slight tilt of the head, he gestured for him to go through the doors in front of them.

"Actually, Colonel, it was UCLA."

"Hmm," Jack said. He slid by the small Vietnamese soldier and entered the mine.

When both men stood on the precipice overlooking the main gallery of the mine, neither could believe what they were seeing. The immenseness of the excavation was nearly overpowering. They saw the small electric cart far beneath them in front of the damaged and ancient plastic-looking enclosures. He saw the long forgotten roadway paved over either by the Nazis or someone more recently. The gallery was lit up like New York's Grand Central Station and its brightness cast shadows in all directions from where the lights were anchored overhead.

"Well, your English is so good, try describing this in a letter back home," Jack said. He placed his M-16 over his shoulder and started down the steep trail, following the tracks of the electric cart.

"'Amazing' is the word that comes to mind," Tram said as he turned to follow Collins.

The two men couldn't help but be made uneasy by the false interior breeze that caused the tattered remains of the Nazi banners and streamers to sway and ripple in the wind. It was just another glorious day in the land of National Socialism.

"The day we stop running into more surprises left by these people, I think that's the day I'll retire," Jack said, intending for Tram neither to hear nor to answer.

"They were very industrious, but how many men and women did the SS kill to get this mine dug?"

Jack eyed the Vietnamese sniper as he walked. He wondered why it had taken so long for the private to say something. Now he had an opinion about everything.

As they progressed down the steep incline of the man-made ramp, Jack had a feeling he was being watched, but from where he couldn't tell. He heard Tram click the safety off on the old M-14; evidently he was feeling the same thing himself.

Far in back of them, near the steel doors, a pair of eyes was indeed watching. The Mechanic held up his hand. His men were anxious to get free of the exposed roadway. They were soaked from their climb up the waterfall and their entrance through the underground river. They had lost one man, who had drowned when the river had taken its downhill course under rock. They then had to fight to get up the rock wall Collins and Everett and his men had fallen from the previous week.

As the Mechanic watched Jack and his smaller companion walk the inclined trail, he finally gave the order for his men to follow, instructing them that they must do so from a great distance as he suspected more Americans were inside already.

Since his previous visits to the mine had been only cursory, the Mechanic knew he would have to be led to the valuable cache of advanced weaponry that he knew was hidden here. Once that was accomplished, he would return to his native Saudi Arabia and sell the specifications for whatever he found. From McCabe's and Rawlins's descriptions he knew it would be worth heaven itself to his cause.

The Mechanic fell into line and followed his men as he watched the long-ago flags flap in the strange breeze that seemed to come from nowhere.

As Alice and Sebastian gently sat Garrison Lee on a rock outcropping, Niles examined one of the buildings. He tore a flap of skin from the two-story structure that had been pushed in millions of years before by an earth movement that had slammed it askew of its neighbor. The age was such that any material or organics left over after this disaster had long since vanished. As Niles felt the strange material, he was approached by Appleby.

"It's a composite, perhaps nylon, maybe a plastic and nylon weave, but it's really too strong for that," the man from DARPA said. He joined Niles, who handed the piece of material over to Alice and Lee. "It will take a while to learn how some of the materials survived in their original form, while others petrified."

"I can't imagine the violence of the earth that crushed the life out of this place," Ellenshaw said. He moved the M-16 to his shoulder and looked into one of the glassless windows of the damaged enclosure.

Niles looked around and noticed small plaques had been placed in several rocks lining the ancient thoroughfare of crushed and mangled buildings. The words were in German and had been etched in the bronze of the embedded plaques.

"What do they say, Sebastian?" Niles asked the German major, who was examining the stone and its writing.

"Site excavated 16 June 1939. No sign of habitation at this level."

"This level? You mean there's another one under here?" Ellenshaw asked. He rolled down the sleeves of his tan shirt due to the briskness of the false breeze swirling inside the ruins.

"There must be," Appleby said, as he leaned over and picked up something that caught his eye. "Major, what do you make of this?" he asked. He held out a small object. "There's more than one here."

Sebastian Krell took the small item and examined it. He laughed at what he was holding, then looked down and saw several more of the small round objects on the rock-covered ground around his feet.

"It's the base cap, detonation ball, and string for the Model 24 *Stielhand-granate.*"

"I didn't catch that," Ellenshaw said as he reached down to pick up one of the strange objects.

"A hand grenade," Lee said. He tried to make himself comfortable on a large rock as Alice slid the needle full of synthetic morphine into his right arm. "A Potato Masher. I'm sure you've seen them in war movies, Charlie," Lee said with a smile. A horrified look came over Ellenshaw's features and he dropped the small screw cap onto the ground. "But the cap covers are harmless."

"Maybe they used them for blasting purposes," Appleby said.

Sebastian looked around himself and closed his fist over the detonator cap cover.

"Possible, but why? I mean, there are so many adequate explosives, why use such a small device? The Model 24 didn't even have a shrapnel charge."

"The major's right," Lee finished as he rolled down his sleeve and nodded at Alice. "Why use them for blasting? That's too inefficient. Our old friends the Nazis didn't operate that way,"

"A mystery among many," Sebastian said. He looked around the gallery at the taller structures. "These buildings, they remind me of field setups used by the army. Do you agree, Mr. Everett?"

Carl stepped out of the tilted and damaged structure not one person had seen him disappear into when they arrived.

"Yes, they do. It's like these were temporary structures that housed troops until more substantial housing could be erected."

"Is there anything interesting inside the building?" Alice asked as she closed and clasped the small medical bag.

Everett looked over at Alice and the senator as they waited for him to answer. He had a curious look on his face.

"You could say that. The Germans have everything documented and labeled inside. The flooring—which looks to be wood of some kind—is old and petrified, but still intact. There are several of these," he said. He tossed an object toward Alice, who caught it and looked it over before handing it to Lee. "It has the same writing on it that was on the space suit."

Lee looked at what amounted to an ancient can. It was empty of its long-ago contents, but it may have once contained food. Lee hefted it; it was far lighter than its modern-day equivalent.

"Okay, the Germans marked the trash in the garbage," the professor from MIT said. "What does that have to do with anything?"

"That means they were pretty efficient at keeping this dig in pristine condition. Removing nothing from the dwellings, keeping everything as is for scientific study."

Lee saw where Everett was going with this.

"So the Nazis insisted on accountability," Sebastian said, as he took the can from Lee and examined it. "That's true in every red tape society."

"What's missing in there, Captain?" Lee asked. He had begun to feel the pain-relieving effects of the morphine.

"There's nothing. No tables, no chairs, no canned goods stored anywhere. No mess had been created when the cataclysm erupted around them. The closets are empty, the metal containers that held something at one time have nothing in them."

"Are you suggesting that the beings who occupied this settlement weren't here when the Andes started strutting their stuff?" Lee asked. He eased himself up from the rock.

"That's what I'm saying. I looked at some of the plaques in front of the enclosures and they all list what was in them, but they fail to mention one thing."

Lee patted Everett on the shoulder as if to say he was appreciative of his intelligence in the face of all the brainpower currently listening to him.

"No bodies of the enclosure's inhabitants," Garrison finished for Everett.

"Not only that, you'd better go and take a look at the side of the next enclosure," Carl said as he turned and left.

The small group followed, feeling the emptiness of the giant mine far more than they had a few moments before. As Everett stopped, they saw he was gesturing upward at a sight that gave them all pause. Along a hundred feet of the next building's wall, there were slashes in the material that looked as if some giant cat or something worse had attacked the composite material. The groupings of the slashes were in patterns of three. The rips were so long that it was as if whatever created the marks had punctured the material and then dragged great claws down the sides, exposing the interior to the outside elements.

"What in the world could have done that?" Appleby asked as he examined the edges of the ripped-apart and petrified material.

"If you'll notice, most of the buildings are in the same shape. Whatever it was happened before the camp, or whatever it was, was destroyed by the earth movement," said a familiar voice from behind them.

They all turned and saw Jack and the Vietnamese private as they eased themselves down from a long dead lava flow to the base of the building they were looking at.

Everett smiled, visibly relaxing for the first time since he had left the colonel to fight a battle he thought he should have been a part of. Jack was closest to Sebastian so he shook hands with him. He then walked over to Everett and shook his.

"So you made it, I see?" Carl said, relieved that his boss was still among the living.

"The president sent in the cavalry at the last minute—or at least Polish paratroopers."

Everett smiled more broadly. "The times they are a'changin'."

Niles took Jack's hand and then Lee and Alice gave him a hug. Next was Charlie, but Jack held out his hand real fast before Ellenshaw could hug him. Pete smiled and nodded, but inside he was churning in total relief they hadn't lost the colonel.

"You say you're seeing the same kind of damage in other buildings?" Lee asked Jack.

"It looked . . ." Jack hesitated, "Hell, those marks looked . . . methodical to me."

Ellenshaw was staring at the small Vietnamese sniper. He nodded his head toward him as he eased himself around the stern-looking Tram.

"Are you suggesting that the marks didn't occur naturally when the ground erupted underneath these dwellings?"

"Hell, Doc, I don't know," Collins said. "But after all we've been through the past few years, I don't assume anything that looks like that is a natural occurrence. I'm sorry, but those are some sort of claw marks."

"This breeze," Lee said, getting everyone's attention. "It's being generated someplace. I suggest we find out where, and then maybe we can find the place where the Germans found those artifacts."

"Sounds like a plan," Jack said, looking at his watch. "I suggest we start by looking down there," he said, pointing toward the back of the steeply sloping gallery.

"Is there any word on the status of *Dark Star 3*?" Alice asked when she noticed Jack looking at his watch.

Collins looked down as the others started to move away.

"The president said the Johnson Space Center lost all contact with them at 0930."

Alice said nothing. Instead, she just took his arm.

"They still have a visual on it, and it is under power. They've lost telemetry, so that means they're on their own."


It took close to three hours of steady downhill walking to get to the far end of the excavation. Every few feet Jack, Carl, and Sebastian, and even the Vietnamese Tram, looked down and saw expended shell casings and more detonator cap covers for the German grenades. During one rest stop they compared notes. There were several differing calibers of the expended rounds. Everything from 7.62 to 5.56 millimeter casings were found. They had all come to the conclusion that sometime in the forties there had been one hell of a firefight in the excavation.

As the unnatural breeze inside picked up, they began to hear a wailing sound. The noise was unnerving to all in the group. Jack knew it to be air being pushed through a small opening in the rear wall that they were fast approaching, but the eerie sound made him edgy nonetheless.

"It seems we would have learned our lesson by now about places like this," Everett said, slowing to allow Niles, Alice, and the senator to catch up. Bringing up the rear of the group were Sebastian and Tram. Wedged in between were the four scientists, who continually scanned the surrounding rock strata and the support beams of steel that had been installed by the Germans.

"You would think," Jack said, as he examined the dead end of solid stone ahead. "But what do you expect out of a couple of stupid lifers?"

"I hear that," Carl said, as he used the butt of his M-16 to hammer the rock he was leaning against. "Well, that wind is coming from somewhere," he said, "but it's not here."

"Jack, you may want to take a look at this," Niles called out as he eased the senator down once more. The old man was looking like he was pretty near the end and Jack was concerned for him, but knew better than to call an extended halt.

Collins and Everett nimbly hopped from the perch they had taken a quarter of the way up the large wall of rock.

"You know," Everett said, looking back at the spot where they had just been, "the more I look at that, the more I think that was a cave-in or a rock slide of some kind."

"I was thinking the same thing, swabby," Jack said as they approached Niles.

"What is it, Doc? We've hit a dead end here."

"It's back here," Compton said as he turned and entered a small cove of raised stone.

As Jack and Everett followed, Pete, Ellenshaw, Appleby, and the MIT engineer, Dubois, sat next to Alice and Lee. All of them took long pulls of water from clear bottles they had brought with them. The lighting allowed Jack to see that they were all growing tired. As Collins waited for Tram and Sebastian to join them, he remembered to use his radio to check in. So far, every hour on the hour, he had reported to the guard command watching the mine entrance.

"Charlie One actual calling CQ, come in, over."

"Charlie One actual, this is CQ. Captain Mark-Patton, over."

"Roger, radio check," Jack said, barely able to hear the British officer from two and half miles below the surface of the mountain.

"Signal has slipped down to thirty percent, but clear at the moment," Mark-Patton said.

"Roger, talk again in an hour," Jack said, "Charlie One actual out."

Collins placed the radio back on his belt. He came to a complete stop, as did the others. The vibration came upon them out of the ground. It felt mechanical at first, but then they all could feel it in their inner ears and knew it to be sound. The sound and vibration stopped as Jack looked up. The sixty-five-foot electrical cords holding the lamps were swaying—not much, but they were moving. So far the breeze that had them chilled had not been enough to move the thick, rotting wiring of the lighting system installed in the thirties and forties. Collins looked back and saw that the others, Lee included, had felt it too. The whole event lasted the duration of Jack's radio check, and ceased just as he terminated the call.

"That was interesting," Everett said, looking up at the swaying lights.

"Not as interesting as this," Niles said as he gestured to a flat area fronted by a large rock wall. There, lined up in neat rows stretching for a quarter mile to the right and left, and unseen if you stayed on the trail leading to the dead end, were what looked like graves. Each one had a marker, some larger than others.

Collins and Sebastian reached for their large flashlights and shone them on the first few markers. The lighting here was far dimmer than the rest of the excavation, being blocked by a large lava wall created many millions of years before.

"Unknown Soldier." Sebastian read the German words from the first marker. "Waffen SS, 12 December 1944."

Jack shone his light down the first row until it became too weak to carry further.

"Jesus, from what I can see, they were all buried within three days of each other," Everett said, moving further down the line.

"What do you think, Mr. Director? Cave-in?" Jack asked Niles.

"From the looks of that wall of rock, that seems like a safe bet," Niles said. He turned to face Collins. "At least so you would think. Then again, if you're like me and the senator and have been picking up all these expended rounds on the cave floor, you might want to reevaluate that guess."

"So you were looking too," Sebastian said while he scanned more of the grave markers.

"Pretty hard to miss, Major," Niles answered, brushing some of the dust off the stone markers. "They took the time to use machines to etch their service branch and date of death, but no names."

"I estimate over a thousand graves. Four rows," Everett said as he returned to the group. "The markers go all the way to the cave-in, or whatever it is."

Collins walked with Niles toward the dead end of rock and dirt. He reached down and brought one of the fist-sized stones to his face and shone the flashlight on it.

"What is it, Jack?" Niles asked. He raised his head and looked around.

"This isn't rock," he said. He looked up at the massive fall. "It's concrete. And look here—there's a larger piece." Jack kicked at a one-foot-by-two-foot chunk of white concrete.

"Maybe it was just landfill that the Germans threw in here."

"Or maybe this was an entrance to another gallery. The sign back there said we had entered gallery number one, but we haven't come across any others."

"Good point, Jack," Niles said, turning to reevaluate the mass of rock and concrete before him.

"Maybe this will shed some light on your speculation, Colonel Collins," a voice said from behind them.

Jack and Niles turned to see the Vietnamese sniper, Tram, holding a large sample of stone out for them to see. The rock was ancient lava that had darker markings on it. Jack took the sample and turned the light on it.

"Maybe burn marks from the original lava flow," Niles said.

Jack rubbed his thumb over the scorch marks and rubbed the soot between his thumb and fingers. He brought the mixture to his nose. Then he held his fingers out to Tram.

"Smell familiar, Private?" he asked.

Tram sniffed and raised his brows.

"Semtex, or something like it—maybe some sort of dry explosive. Not any kind of plastique."

"Possibly something the German army or Waffen SS would use?"

"I'm not that familiar with World War II explosives, Colonel, so I will rely on your historical expertise," Tram said.

"Handy little fella to have around, isn't he?" Niles said as he watched the Vietnamese soldier head for the opening that led back to the trail.

Jack smiled; "You don't know the half of it, Niles," he answered, tossing the rock toward Carl. "What do you make of that?"

Everett smelled it, then actually tasted it. He looked at Jack.

"Cordite, some kind of explosive," Everett said. He looked up at the blockage. "I guess we know now that the Germans brought this down to block the entrance to something."

"Let's see if we can get in there. Niles. Could you go back and get the senator and Alice to rest as best they can? I'll get a detail down here with food and water and sleeping equipment. Maybe a medic to keep a closer eye on the . . . well, we may need a medic here anyway," Jack said. He turned to face Everett and Sebastian. "Hopefully our Polish friends or SEALs brought some explosives along with them." He looked at his watch. He frowned when he saw that he was past his self-imposed deadline.

"What time do you have, Jack?" Everett asked.

"*Dark Star 3* just entered the Moon's orbit."

The men all became silent as Jack walked over and sat down next to the first grave marker. He lay down his weapon and pulled the radio from his belt. As he pushed the transmit button and was about to make the call, he felt the strange vibration once again coming through the earthen floor. Then, as he lowered the radio, he heard the soft humming sound in his ears. When he released the transmit button, the sound and vibration ceased. Finally, too tired to think clearly, Jack made the call to CQ.

All around the dead end, the members of the search team felt the vibrations and internal sound increase, and actually seemed to move closer from what they knew now was the other side of the cave-in.

Everett, Sebastian, and Tram all looked from the wall of rock to their surroundings. They simultaneously concluded that they would get little sleep while they waited for their supplies to arrive.

"Come on, let's see if there's a back door to this place," Everett said. He took one last look back at a very worried Jack Collins and knew exactly what he was thinking as he spoke to the command element outside.

"Sarah will make it, Jack."

# 15

After the sudden loss of mission commander Kendal and LEM pilot Dugan, the mood had been somber. Sarah and the other technicians, mainly Will Mendenhall, concentrated on devising a makeshift antenna so the lunar excursion team could stay in communication with *Falcon 1* while on the surface. Thus far Will was frustrated by not enough time and too little equipment to work with.

As *Falcon 1* made its first pass over the lunar surface, most of the personnel were snapping pictures and taking video, along with long-range photography of the landing site two miles from Shackleton Crater. On their first and only pass the long-range telephoto lens on *Falcon* took some very detailed photos of the interior of Shackleton. The damage was tremendous, but as Houston had said in their second to last communication, there seemed to be intact structures inside the crater. The photography also picked up what looked like the remains of the ESA LEM *Astral*, lying on its side heavily damaged. The photos and video showed no survivors. Of *Magnificent Dragon*, there was no trace.

As the only mission specialist who'd be aboard *Altair* when they landed, Sarah McIntire was to be the command operative while on the Moon. She took her predicament stoically and knew she had the difficult job of deciding whether to recover the technology if the Chinese excursion team was friendly or destroying the weaponry if they weren't. As for the mineral, she had already decided it was far too powerful and unstable to recover. She had already briefed the team, soldiers included, on her decision.

Sarah slid into the command module with the final landing data for Ryan to enter into the *Altair*'s computer system. Ryan accepted the new coordinates without comment. His mind was strictly on setting the lander down in one piece, never mind landing in a specific area. Sarah could see that the usually boisterous Ryan had been in no mood for anything but self-reflection following his jump in grade to LEM pilot, a position he had so thoroughly failed at back in the Houston simulator. As the third part in a three-part backup plan, he knew none of them was even supposed to be there.

Sarah watched as Ryan took her latest data and eased through the connecting sleeve into *Altair*. She saw Mendenhall bend over a small workstation, trying to keep his soldering iron and small pieces of circuit board from floating away. The module pilot Maggio was assisting, but was mostly trying to stay out of the lieutenant's way.

"How's it going, Will?" she asked, biting her lower lip.

Mendenhall placed his hands on the small workstation table and took a deep breath as he tried to calm himself. Sarah, for her part, held her ground and kept her eyes on the frustrated lieutenant. He finally looked up and shook his head at his friend. She could see him visibly relax.

"Well, for about a ten-second burst, we caught some Russian from somewhere in back of us just a second before orbital insertion. We lost the communication pretty fast, and it was weak to begin with. So I was thinking it was nothing more than weird atmospherics and Maggio and Ryan agreed." He frowned at Sarah. "In other words, it was nothing I did." He let the soldering iron float free and allowed the small circuit board he was attempting to solder follow. "I can't do it. I mean, it's not like running an old antenna wire up to your roof and wrapping aluminum foil around it and hoping for the best."

Sarah free-floated and nodded for Maggio to start his calculations for detachment of the LEM from *Falcon 1.*

"Twenty-one minutes until separation. We're out of time anyway, Will. I was thinking about all the junk we have on the Moon. Can we salvage a dish antenna just for short-range communications with *Falcon*, so we can get rendezvous data and telemetry for our liftoff?"

Mendenhall looked at Sarah and smiled. "That's an awfully optimistic outlook. Liftoff?"

"I guess I picked up bad habits from Jack. You know, always planning for the right outcome, just in case by a fluke it happens that way."

"Yeah, that's not a bad way to do things. Why I remember—"

Sarah watched as Will's words trailed off to nothing as he was struck by a thought.

"What is it?" she asked.

"The Beatles," Mendenhall said. "They all have not only long-range telemetry installed but a high-gain antenna for remote purposes." He looked up at Sarah. "As a matter of fact, their communications may be better than our own, since they don't have the human touch to operate them. They have to do it all by computer. I think we can use one of them to communicate—maybe not with Houston, but *Falcon 1* shouldn't be a problem."

"See what happens when you pull back and think about things?" Sarah said, as she squeezed Will's shoulder.

"Yeah, now why don't you go and see if you can pass the same confidence on to Ryan."

Sarah smiled back at Will. "You know what Jason has to do on a continual basis?"

"What's that?"

"He has to remind himself that he's the best pilot in the world. If he doesn't do that on a regular basis, he crashes in his head. My money's on him when the chips are down."

"Okay, I'll buy that, but maybe you'd better remind him that those chips you're betting are not the house's money."

"I think he knows that, Will."


Twenty minutes later Maggio was the only living soul inside of the command module, *Falcon 1*. The rest of the mission's crew were strapped into their seats on the lower deck of *Altair*, the only exceptions being Mendenhall and Ryan. They were strapped into an upright position on the command deck, both of them poised over the fly-by-wire maneuvering controls of the very much experimental *Altair*. No one had ever landed anything this size on the Moon and Ryan knew all their lives were riding on his skills as a fly-by-the-seat-of-his-pants pilot. He looked over at Will and shook his head.

"Uh, do you want me to give one of those emotional 'Win one for the Gipper' speeches?"

"Maybe a prayer would be more appropriate," Ryan shot back with a smile.

"Coming up on insertion point in five—ready to separate," Maggio said from his command seat eighty-five feet away.

Ryan closed his eyes and reached for the VOX at his side.

"Ladies and gentlemen, please place your seats and tables in the upright—" Ryan cut the small joke short and lowered his head. Ryan not finishing a joke worried Will far more than anything he had seen from Jason.

"Ah, hell, just remember where all your emergency exits are located and where the life rafts are located under your seats. Release time in one minute—stand by."

Mendenhall smiled and nodded. Seeing Ryan not give in to the panic he was feeling was far more comforting than seeing him go silent.

"What are you nodding your head for? You look like one of those dashboard bobble-heads."

Mendenhall's face dropped and he glared at Ryan—sometimes quiet from the man was better than the cocky version.

"Okay, Maggio, don't let in any strangers while we're out. The number for the restaurant we'll be at is on the table and don't let the kids stay up past ten."

"Roger, *Altair*, the house will be here when you return. Good luck," Maggio said. He swallowed the lump in his throat and raised the plastic cover on the release switch that would electrically unscrew the lead that held the two spacecraft together. "Separation in five, four, three, two, one," he said. He pushed the button and was satisfied when it went from a soft blue to a blinking red. He heard the electric motor engage as it automatically unscrewed with a loud whine. Then there was a pop as the two ships came apart. The snapping of the communication systems came as shock, because it was far louder than the simulations back at the

Johnson Space Center. It was so loud that everyone, including the seven Green Berets, thought something else had gone wrong.

Maggio knew it was only his imagination, but he could swear he felt *Falcon 1* become noticeably lighter without Altair riding nose to nose with her. He closed his eyes and hit his transmit switch, even though he knew none of the lunar excursion team could hear him.

"Godspeed. Come back home soon."

Inside the command deck, the absence of the feeling of motion was at first disorienting to both Ryan and his copilot Mendenhall. *Altair* separated cleanly from *Falcon* and seemed to be drifting backward, but Ryan knew their forward momentum was still well in excess of 25,000 miles per hour.

"Will, open fuel pressure valves one and two," Ryan said calmly.

Mendenhall's eyes widened.

"Right there in front of you, buddy. Just like in our practice runs."

Mendenhall remembered. He took a deep breath and threw the two blue-colored switches until the lights flashed green.

"We have green on fuel pressure valves one and two."

Everyone onboard the craft heard the fuel as it rushed through the metal fuel lines.

A young sergeant looked at Sarah. Through her clear visor Sarah winked and the sergeant seemed to relax.

"You've flown with the lieutenant before?" he asked.

"Not now, Sergeant," the Green Beret master sergeant said.

"No, it's okay, Sarge," Sarah said, smiling at the two men. "Yes, I've flown with Jason three times in various aircraft."

"All good outcomes, I assume," the young sergeant said, relief etching his voice.

Sarah couldn't help it. She just couldn't let it slip by without comment, as she knew Carl and Jack relished opportunities like this with their younger charges.

"As a matter of fact, the first time was in a Black Hawk. Jason slammed the helicopter into a large rock and knocked our landing gear off. The second time was in a seaplane. We cracked up on a river in the Canadian wilderness. And the third time was two days later when he crashed a brand-new Sikorsky into a forest. We burst into flames upside down and forty feet off the ground."

The men lining the lower deck of Altair stared at Sarah as if she were joking. She raised her left eyebrow to let them know she was dead serious. She decided to stop toying with the guys.

"He's the best pilot I've ever seen."

Up on the command deck Ryan flexed his fingers and placed them gingerly on the handles that controlled the jets that the OHM used for maneuvering and for flight. He looked at his attitude gauges.

"Stand by for retro burn and trim maneuver," he said easily and confidently.

Ryan knew he had time and space for mistakes up here, but once close to the surface, the mission became a little more unforgiving.

Will watched as Jason pulled slightly back on the right control and twisted the handle at the same time. He heard the satisfying sound of the OHM's jet popping loudly as it threw *Altair* on its back. Ryan hit the left handle to stop the turn maneuver. He checked his navigation and saw that he had fifteen seconds to start the main engine before they bypassed their first option for slowing the craft down enough to get her into the upper reaches of the Moon's gravity. "Will, I need a ten-second burn on the main engine. Remember, all you have to do is hit the main engine start switch. The computer will do the rest."

"Right," Mendenhall said. He waited without breathing.

"Main engine start in three, two, one—burn," Ryan said calmly.

Mendenhall threw the switch and they heard the loudest pop of all as the main engine came to life. Inside *Altair* they could hear the rumble of the exhaust as it exited the confines of the main engine bell below them. They felt the ship slow as the minimal gravity started to take effect.

"Main engine cutoff in two, one, zero," Ryan said. He watched the attitude compass swing north and south on a correct horizontal plane with the surface of the Moon. They were now flying upright, as was the natural order of things.

*Altair* became silent. Each individual's breathing was concealed behind their helmet. The rapid breathing that each feared the others would hear was self-contained, so nobody had to worry about being the only one to have shown fear.

"Standby for main OHM burn for insertion," Ryan said, as he adjusted his feet on the Velcro mat beneath his boots. "Everyone go to internal oxygen at this point, please."

All crew members, the flight team included, unplugged their suits from the *Altair*'s air system. Air conditioning and oxygen would be in self-sustaining mode for the duration of the landing procedure—for obvious reasons, Jason thought.

"Well, I guess we're ready," Will said. He looked at the altimeter as Altair screamed down from high orbit at close to three thousand feet per second.

"This is really going to add to our frequent flyer miles, huh, buddy?" Ryan quipped. He also watched the altimeter. "Stand by for main engine thrust—seventy-five percent power until I say so."

"Ready for main engine start," Will said, his finger poised over the covered switch.

"Keep a close eye on fuel consumption. We only have five minutes of sustainable thrust."

"Five minutes? Oh jeez, I forgot about that."

"Should be plenty of time, unless we run into rocks where they have no right to be. Or craters that have up and moved on us since the photo run an hour ago. Or the shots from the Hubble Telescope last month. We should be fine."

"If you say so," Will said.

"Three, two, one, main engine start at 0120 and thirty-two seconds. Start the clock."

*Altair* slowed its descent and they all felt the craft jerk and shimmy. Outside it was deathly silent as the vacuum of space sucked up sound like a sponge.

Ryan watched the NAV board closely, adjusting trim to the descent easily, trying hard not to overcompensate. He was learning that the simulator back at Houston was tougher to fly than the actual spacecraft.

"Three degrees off center, and three and half minutes of fuel remaining," Will called out louder than he intended. "Altitude is thirty-five thousand feet."

Ryan turned the right-hand handle five degrees to port and adjusted angle. *Altair* at that moment was coming down right on the target mark.

"Uh, we're coming down a little fast," Mendenhall said. He watched the LED readout of the altimeter spiral down by thousands of feet in the wink of an eye. "Thirteen thousand feet."

"Copy, Will. Easy there, big fella," Ryan called out, as he adjusted trim once more.

"Up throttle in five, four, three, two, one—one hundred percent throttle. Burn it, Will, burn it!"

Mendenhall reached over and turned the small red knob that sent the fuel injector to full power as it shot the mixture of hydrogen and oxygen into the mixing hub of the combustion chamber.

Below, on the crew deck, everyone felt the shakes and shimmies of *Altair* as she neared the lunar surface. They all had their eyes closed and were listening intently to the orders Ryan was calling out. Sarah was glad *Altair* was shaking so violently because it covered up her own internal shaking. She was terrified beyond belief.

"Five hundred feet and slowing to a hundred feet a minute," Will called out.

"Stand by to power down to fifty percent thrust."

"Roger," Mendenhall said. He tried to swallow but found his throat didn't work.

"Throttle down," Ryan called.

Will turned the throttle knob. The shaking and loud noises ceased almost immediately. No one onboard knew if that was good or not.

"Throttle set to fifty percent thrust, two minutes of fuel, altitude at three hundred feet."

Ryan turned his throttle to the aft OHM's jets and brought *Altair* level once more after she had drifted.

"Shackleton Crater at three miles." Ryan breathed a sigh of relief when he saw the rim of the giant crater close up for the first time.

Suddenly a warning chime started and three red lights started blinking.

"Goddamn it!" Ryan said between clenched teeth. He started hitting the

hand-controlled throttle on the left side of his upright chair. "I have a continuous thrust coming from the aft OHM's jet. It's pushing us over!"

Mendenhall watched wide-eyed as Ryan tried freeing the stuck thruster.
"Damn it, it's not here. It's the shutoff valve that's stuck open. We're not only
losing our correct attitude, we're burning our fuel too damn fast. We have to
compensate for the roll."

"One minute of fuel, fifty feet to impact," Will announced as calmly as he
could, not wanting to add to what Jason had to deal with.

"Firing starboard OHMs," Ryan said, more to himself than to the crew.

The roll ceased and Ryan was making the correction, but the fuel warning
bells started sounding and the computer started voicing its opinion rather
loudly.

"Pull up, pull up. Obstacle detected in flight path. Pull up, pull up."

"Shut that damn thing up. I hate its voice!" Ryan said, as he adjusted trim
for the last time.

Mendenhall switched the audio warning off. He knew Ryan was thinking
about the nice voice of Europa, the supercomputer back home.

"Thirty feet, twenty feet, ten feet!" Will called out.

"Main engine to seventy-five percent thrust," Ryan said, as he eyed the patch
of lunar surface below. He knew he had neither the time nor the fuel to maneuver to another spot if he saw they were coming down onto a patch of large rocks.

"That's it. Fuel is exhausted," Mendenhall said. He reached out and braced
himself for a hard landing.

Ryan clenched his teeth as he felt the main engine sputter once and then
stop just as three of four landing pads hit the surface of the Moon. He cringed
as *Altair* went motionless, balancing first on three and then on only two landing
gear. The giant *Altair* teetered, nearly rolling over, and then her momentum
shifted and she fell back, her round shape behaving like a teetering beer can.
Then all four landing gear came in contact with the soft surface of the Moon.
Her hydraulic struts impacted and retracted into themselves, and then expanded
once more as the gas was released, easing *Altair* into stillness.

Throughout the ship, there wasn't a sound other than the ticking of the
cooling engine bell far below the main crew cabin.

Ryan looked over at Will, who was staring out of the large triangular windows at the crater two miles away. His eyelids didn't blink and his hand was
turning white from his powerful grip on the handle above his head.

"That was different," Ryan said, and started breathing again.

Mendenhall finally blinked his eyes and slowly looked at Jason.

"Thank you," was all he said.

The small Navy pilot smiled and patted Will on the back.

"Your visor's a little fogged up."

"I don't know how that can be. You have to breathe for it to do that."

Ryan hit his VOX and waited until he was sure of his voice. "Welcome to the Moon," he said.

## SITUATION ROOM, THE WHITE HOUSE, WASHINGTON, D.C.

The president sat in the White House Situation Room sixty feet below the ground floor of the mansion. He sat quietly and listened to the conference call from the Cape and Houston. Hugh Evans was speaking at the moment, and the president realized for the first time that he was drifting even as Evans was doling out the first good news in days, outside of the fact that Jack Collins and his minimal ground forces had achieved success in Ecuador.

"In essence, even though telemetry and communications with *Altair* and *Falcon 1* are down, we have established that *Altair* is safely on the lunar surface. Unfortunately, we have also confirmed through satellite imagery that the catastrophic debris strike on *Falcon* did in fact take the lives of the mission commander and the *Altair* pilot. The loss of Colonel Kendal and pilot Dugan is a very severe setback to the potential success of the mission."

The president sat up and leaned toward the table, his eyes roaming over his national security staff, who were being kept in the dark on the most important matters of this and all the missions to the Moon. The people with knowledge of the president's actions could be counted on one hand.

"Flight Director Evans," the president started slowly. "We can assume that someone has taken control of the mission. Do you have protocol that dictates who that someone is?"

"We have only one conclusion at this time. We believe Lieutenant Sarah McIntire, U.S. Army, is in command, since she is the senior officer onboard *Altair*."

"And it's my understanding the landing had to have been achieved by Navy Lieutenant Ryan, backup pilot for *Altair*?"

"Correct, sir. We have verified the safe landing since the retasking of the Hubble Space Telescope four hours ago."

"Mr. Evans, thank you for your time. Before you go, do you have any contingencies for reestablishing contact with the lunar team or *Falcon 1*?"

"We are trying to bounce signals off various satellites, but there has been no luck thus far. We do have several other plans, but they require the lunar excursion team to use their own initiative as far as acting on them goes. They could reestablish communications through several sources on the lunar surface. As of right now, we are planning for *Dark Star 3* to continue on mission until its conclusion."

"Thank you, Mr. Evans. Please stay near the phone."

"Yes, sir, Mr. President."

The president leaned back in his chair and looked from face to face. The

Situation Room was crowded with stars and men in rolled up shirtsleeves. Not one of them save for the chairman of the Joint Chiefs of Staff, General Maxwell Caulfield, and the president knew the real truth of what was happening. The vice president was officially under FBI investigation for incriminating cell phone calls to the now disgraced and on the run Samuel Rawlins, so the president had officially handed over all NASA and Space Command duties to Caulfield for the duration of the lunar emergency.

"Gentlemen, that will be all for now. General Caulfield, will you stay behind please?"

As the council shuffled out of the late night meeting, General Caulfield moved from his seat at the far end of the large table to a seat closer to the president. He saw the commander in chief reach down and place a small laptop on the table. Caulfield immediately suspected that the little bald man with the tired look and thick glasses was on the other end of the monitor.

"General, we're being joined by my old friend and advisor Niles Compton from Ecuador. You two have met on several occasions, I believe. Niles, I'm taking you off this damn laptop and am going to place you on our main monitor. General, dim the windows, please."

Caulfield hit a button on the console to his front and the windows surrounding the situation room went completely opaque.

Soon the visage of Niles was on the main monitor and he saw the tired and drawn face of the president.

"You look like hell," Niles said from deep inside the Andes.

"Thank you, baldy. Never let an opportunity slide by to make me feel worse than I already do. I may say the same for you, buddy. It doesn't look like mining agrees with you."

"Thanks for the compliment, and no, I hate field work."

"Niles, your three lieutenants have done one hell of a job stepping up like they did. You heard Flight Director Evans on their status."

"I did, but they're one hell of a long way from the finish line. As far as we know they may have people with guns waiting for them before they reach that line."

"I know, I know. There's still no word from the Chinese on their attempt to change the chairman's mind about cooperation."

"I never thought I would see the day when we could convince the Chinese military to cooperate and have to finagle and make deals with the devil to get the civilian government to deal with us. It's nuts," General Caulfield said as he slid the knot in his tie down and unbuttoned the top button of his blue shirt.

"So, there's still nothing from Beijing?" Niles asked, the worry on his face evident.

"Not a damn thing. Their people could be waiting for ours to step foot on the lunar surface and then massacre them. We just don't know."

"Well, we are now in direct contact with our complex, and Colonel Collins is trying to get into the second mine gallery as we speak. Thus far we haven't turned up any useful information outside of a large grouping of graves onsite, as I have explained to you already."

"I do have this from the FBI field team in Ecuador." The president held up a flimsy. The good Reverend Samuel Rawlins and former Army officer James McCabe were found murdered in a Quito hotel room this morning."

"That means whoever led the strike team against Jack and his men has gone rogue from his employer," Niles said and shook his head.

"That's my thinking. Thus far our forces in country haven't turned up any leadership for the assault force. The FBI believes they may have made their way out of Ecuador. Niles, had the colonel considered the need to bring more men inside the mine? Your telling me of those German graves was a little unsettling. If it's security he's worried about, explain that I am giving permission to bring the rest of the SEALs and the British contingent inside. We can control the British through the prime minister."

Niles lowered his head in thought. Then he looked into the camera.

"I have already given Jack that order. We now have forty personnel in the mine. It's not only the mass graves we found—I have a feeling that as aggressive as these maniacs have been, they won't stop at getting back that mine, or at least its contents. And until we know the Chinese intention on the Moon, Operation Columbus is that much more important."

"Agreed," said the president.

"I have one bit of information you may want to have that I've been reluctant to tell you with all these other concerns."

"Go ahead, Niles, while I'm numb inside."

"We had two additions to our ground team here in Ecuador. It seems Garrison Lee and Mrs. Hamilton came along for the ride."

The president stared into the camera and didn't say a word. He lowered his eyes and rubbed his temples.

"I'll bow to whatever you want to do, Niles. If you want them out, I'll order it."

Niles became quiet as he mulled over the question. He looked away for a moment, then removed his glasses and placed them on the table. It was as though he were fighting back some very powerful emotions.

"I think maybe he's earned the right to be anywhere he wants to be. I also think he's earned the right to hear what this whole mess is about."

The president looked away for a moment before looking back at a dirty-faced Niles. He took a drink of water.

"I agree. Leave him and Mrs. Hamilton alone." The president shook his head as he placed the glass of water carefully down on the polished table. "You know, he's a national treasure, Niles. If he wants to go along, you're right. He's earned it."

## OFFICE OF THE CHAIRMAN,
## BEIJING, CHINA

The chairman of the People's Republic of China sat at his large, barren desk and read the latest communications from the Moon mission, *Magnificent Dragon*. He smiled as he read the report that the American spacecraft was down and his men were ready to spring the trap that would ensure that China received the greatest edge in technology the world had ever known. He laid the communiqué down and removed his thick glasses. Then he wiped at them with a silk handkerchief that had his initials embroidered on its corners. The handkerchief and two dozen like it had been a birthday present from the president of the United States upon his last visit to China. Now the chairman only hoped he could repay the gift, only not in the way the president would have liked. The eighty-one-year-old chairman had replaced the thick glasses when his intercom buzzed.

He sat silently without moving to answer. His official title was that of president, just like the American, but he privately ordered his subordinates to call him *Chairman*, a title he vastly preferred to President. Its association with the great Mao was in keeping with his power, he thought. The buzz came again from the intercom.

"Yes," he snapped angrily into the infernal device. He had left instructions with his personal secretary that he not be disturbed.

"The vice chairman of the National People's Congress and General Guo Boxiong, executive vice chairman of the Central Military Commission, are here to see the chairman," said his squeaky-voiced personal assistant.

"Very well. Send them in."

The massive double doors were opened by two Chinese army sergeants. The two men stepped inside the large office and made their way, hats in hand, toward the large and empty desk.

"Vice Chairman Zhaoguo Wang, General Guo, to what do I owe the pleasure?" the fat old man asked as he folded his hands on top of the polished desk.

"The situation on the surface of the Moon, Mr. President," answered Wang.

The chairman looked angrily at the second most powerful man in China. His scowl was meant to send fear into the much smaller, younger man. His use of the title "President" was meant to cause his temper to rise.

"And what would concern you about the mission?"

"We have made our protests well known. And now we are prepared to take our concerns directly to the ruling body of the movement."

"Is that so," he said, as a knock sounded at the doors. He didn't have to answer as his assistant brought in a silver service tea set.

"May I offer you gentlemen some tea?" he asked, not offering them a seat before his desk.

"We are not here for tea. We are here to make you aware of certain . . . changes in policy concerning our military preparedness, and our request for cooperation with the Western powers in regards to the recent events in our seas and the continent of Antarctica."

As the assistant placed a cup in front of the chairman, he glanced up at the two men, and then just as quickly poured the tea. He turned and left the room.

The chairman leaned forward and placed the teacup in both of his aging hands, then blew on its contents.

"So, I assume you have bought into this ridiculous plan of the Americans and their lackeys in Europe, the fear of a fairy tale long gone cold?"

"The evidence they have produced is valid. Our military scientists have verified all aspects of the forwarded documents," Wang said, watching the old man blow on his tea.

"And it is not only the Western powers that have taken the side of the Americans and their warnings, but our allies as well. We are now alone in our contempt of the situation," offered the general. "We must cooperate or chance the annihilation of our species in less than three years." He saw the chairman smile contemptuously. "And that had also been confirmed by our astronomers."

The chairman finally sipped his tea. He shook his head, savoring the rich taste, and then he sipped again.

"You may leave me. The decision has been made. We move on the American spacecraft inside the hour. You may believe the Americans and their Case Blue warnings, but I have lived through their deceit many times before. We have no imminent threat from regions far beyond this planet. Case Blue is a pack of lies. Good day, gentlemen."

The two men stood before the chairman without moving. He put the teacup down and raised his eyebrows, wondering why the men weren't leaving his office.

"I said you may—"

The men didn't react as the chairman suddenly ceased moving. He tilted his head and raised a shaking, liver-spotted right hand to the top button of his tunic. The question on his age-lined face was evident as he tried to make room for more air that seemed to have disappeared.

The vice chairman reached out and gently, methodically pushed down on the intercom button.

"Please summon the doctor to the chairman's office, he seems to be in some distress," Wang said. He let the button pop free, not waiting for the chairman's assistant to reply.

The old man tried to stand, but faltered as he reached out to steady himself. The two men standing before the chairman stepped back to avoid being hit by the liquid. Finally, the old man settled into his large chair and looked up at the general and his vice chairman.

"You have done many great things for the people," Wang said. "It is time for you to rest. We thought retirement the best course. Unfortunately, the Western powers would be hesitant to deal with the People's Republic if you were still alive and angry over your loss of power, so we had to take this to the extreme. It is time we join the league of men who will eventually have to defend this planet from outside forces, and we can't do that by continuing the old ways."

The chairman tried desperately to pop free the topmost button of the tunic. When he found no strength in his fingers, his arms fell to his lap. As they did, the double doors opened and three men ran inside. Two attendants flanked the uniformed army doctor as he hurried to the chairman's side.

"I believe the president is having a heart attack," the general said. He moved to the far side of the room, placing his hands behind his back.

The army doctor felt the neck for a pulse and then the wrist. The chairman's eyes were wide open and staring at nothing.

The general looked to his left as guards came rushing inside.

"Please secure the vice chairman of the People's Party. He is as of now the acting president."

Wang Zhaoguo stood while two of the guards flanked him just as the doctor straightened and faced the men in the room. Then he looked at his watch, noting the time.

"The chairman is dead."


## MOON SITE CODE-NAMED COLUMBUS CIRCLE

Sarah knew they had a long walk ahead of them, and she had one angry LEM pilot on her hands. Since she was now the mission commander, it had been her duty to inform Jason Ryan that he was no longer a part of the excursion team into Shackleton. His fit lasted three minutes as he tried to stomp his feet in anger, but found he couldn't find purchase enough in the zero gravity to throw the tantrum in style. Finally, she calmed him enough to make her case as to why he couldn't come along. He was the only fully trained LEM pilot left, and in order for them to lift off the uppermost decks of *Altair*, they needed Ryan safe and sound aboard the ship.

It had taken the strength of Will Mendenhall to help make Ryan see the light of day. As it was, he sat in the command deck of the LEM and started making his checklist for the eventual liftoff of *Altair* for the rendezvous with *Falcon 1*.

The weapons for the excursion into Shackleton were handed out to the seven Green Berets who made up the lunar surface team, plus Mendenhall and Sarah. One of the deadly devices would be left to Ryan for the defense of *Altair*, in case it was needed. The compressed-air-launched M-39 rocket-assisted projectile weapons were a development of IBC Corporation of Lansing, Michigan. Designed to replace unreliable powder and projectile weapons, including handguns and rifles, the M-39 air-launched a solid kinetic energy shot from its twenty-round magazine, which after it cleared the tungsten barrel became a ballistic assist weapon. A small charge of solid propellant sent the round where it was aimed at six times the speed of sound, allowing the solid metal bullet to penetrate almost anything with up to two inches of armor plate.

Each member of the crew had become adept at targeting the heavy-bore weapon that was equivalent to a .50 caliber steel shot. The stock was solid plastic and the barrel was made of hardened steel designed by Winchester Firearms. The trigger was as large as a household tablespoon and the guard was as large as a jar lid so that a large gloved finger could get access to the trigger. The weapon basically looked like an old-fashioned Henry Repeating Rifle from the Old West, which caused the designers at IBC many a sleepless night after every person on the excursion team laughed at the ancient-looking "modern" weapons they were wielding.

As Sarah looked over her team, she saw Jason poke his head down the access hatch from the command deck. He had his helmet on and was prepared to start placing the first four crewmen into the small airlock on the starboard side of the crew module. He locked eyes with Sarah as he moved past and he nodded his head inside the helmet.

"I'll have the fire in the fireplace nice and hot when you get back, and a warm cup of soup ready."

Sarah returned the smile as Ryan patted each individual on the backpack, a gesture of good luck. He stopped at Mendenhall, who would egress with the first four soldiers.

"Don't let these Green Beret fellas push you around out there," he said as he half smiled at his friend.

Mendenhall didn't say anything in return. He knew Jason was worried about them all and didn't know how to express it any other way than with a snide remark or a joke.

"All right, no company while we're gone—no women, and no booze," Sarah said and stepped to the rear of the line.

"You got it, Ma," Ryan said. He reached out and hit the overly large button for the access port. "First four crewmen of the excursion team, step forward and say status."

"Mendenhall, oxygen good, COM good," Will said, as she slid easily into the compartment.

"Andrews, $O_2$ good, COM good."

"Johnson, $O_2$ good, COM good."

"Martinez, $O_2$ good, COM good."

Ryan looked one last time at each crew member's environmental suit and hit the button again. The door hissed closed on its pneumatic track. As Jason stared through the window, he waited until Mendenhall looked up from the front of the small compartment. The black lieutenant raised his chin inside his helmet in a farewell nod, just as if he were going to see Ryan later for a luncheon date. Ryan nodded and made sure he had a good seal. Then he turned the knob beside the portal and purged the oxygen from the compartment.

"Okay, I want a thumbs-up from each man. Come on," he said, as he watched the four men.

Each gave him a thumbs-up.


Mendenhall watched as the three Green Berets took up station in a triangular position surrounding *Altair*. Will stayed pretty much out of the way as he admired the bleak and barren landscape of a place he never in his wildest imagination thought he would set foot on. He moved his legs and felt the resistance of the low gravity. It was just enough that he could feel it though his suit. The weapon he was holding was so light he could very easily forget that he was carrying it. He tried a small hop and was delighted at the height the small effort achieved. He wanted to tell someone, but he felt uncomfortable saying anything to the soldiers around him. He wished Ryan was here. They would have had something to say to each other.

He turned and watched the second team of four exit the airlock. These were Sampson, Elliott, Tewlewiski, and Demarest. He watched them deploy, further strengthening their perimeter. Sarah soon emerged by herself. Will smiled when she jumped the last three aluminum steps to the lunar surface. She was heard loud and clear when she laughed.

"Sorry, I always wanted to do that."

Sarah saluted and gestured for her team to join her. One by one the men fell into place, two in front of Sarah and Mendenhall, two in back, two on the flanks, and one in the far rear.

The lunar excursion element of *Dark Star 3* started moving toward Shackleton Crater.


## MÜELLER AND SANTIAGO MINING CONCERN, 100 MILES EAST OF QUITO, 2 MILES UNDER ESPOSITO MOUNTAIN

Jack popped his head into the small tent. Alice was sitting in a small chair and smiled when Collins looked at her. The senator was laying quietly on one of the cots his small group of reinforcements had brought in with the rest of their equipment.

"How is he?" Jack asked quietly.

Alice looked from Jack to the sleeping Lee and shook her head negatively, the smile still on her pretty face.

"Answer the colonel, you mean old woman," Lee said, as he raised his head and looked around.

"He's gone as far as he can go," Alice said. She shot Lee a dirty look.

"That's what she says," the senator sniped as he sat up on the cot. "Did you find another way in?"

Jack looked behind himself and entered the tent.

"We have a six-foot opening at the top of the cave-in. It's right beneath an archway built by the Germans."

"Kind of exquisite proof that they brought the roof down on purpose, wouldn't you say?" Lee said, as he slowly lay back down, taking Alice's hand as he did so.

"We'll be running a COM line in for Europa, so you'll know what's happening at all times," Collins said.

"Jack, give me a little time. I can make it up there and come along," Lee said, this time without rising.

"I'm going to answer that the way you would have many years ago—you would be a hindrance and could get people hurt. I have to say no."

Alice lowered her head as Jack turned away toward the tent's opening, wishing he could just run from the enclosure. He swallowed the lump in his throat and reached for the tent pole to steady his hand.

"Colonel, please give me the opportunity to—"

Without turning, Jack closed his eyes and said what it was he had to say. "I admire you more than any man I have ever known or ever will know. You and Alice have . . . have become special in my life, and Sarah's life also. I—"

"Go do what needs to be done. We'll be here when you get back. He'll undoubtedly want a full accounting of what's over there," Alice said as Lee rolled to his right side.

Jack nodded without turning back and left the tent.

Niles Compton was waiting for him as he exited. He saw the look on Jack's face and decided to let his conversation with Alice and Lee go unvoiced. Niles watched Jack angrily snatch up his M-16 and start toward the men who were gathering at the base of the cave-in. Niles hesitated only a moment before scratching on the outside of the tent. Instead of calling out, Alice stepped through the opening.

"How is the senator?" he asked as Alice took a few steps away.

"Disappointed of course, but I suspect you would know that, since you gave Jack the order not to allow him to enter the second gallery."

Niles knew Alice better than anyone other than the senator. He lowered his head as she turned to face him.

"He won't last more than a few more hours."

Niles, like Jack a few minutes before, tried desperately to swallow the lump in his throat.

"I meant to get here before Jack, but Charlie accidentally pulled the pin on a hand grenade and I had to help look for it. I never meant for Jack to be the one to tell the senator. He disagrees with my decision."

"Of course he does, dear. He's a soldier, just like Garrison. Jack's an idealist, whether he wants to admit that or not. You, my dear Niles, are a realist. Jack believes Garrison should be allowed to go out the way he chooses, while you are of the same opinion as Jack. You're afraid of seeing it happen. The colonel, while not wanting it to happen either, is not afraid of that. Thus you differ. But one thing Garrison and I know for sure." She placed a hand on Niles's shoulder and squeezed. "You both care about him beyond measure."

"Thank you," he said, as he placed his hand over hers. "Jack is far stronger than I am when it comes to death, even though the senator would want to go out any other way than the way he is."

Niles started walking away and Alice watched him go. As she turned to re-enter the tent she couldn't help but realize the world was changing fast, and she knew it was time for her and Lee to leave it for what it was to become. Her own end was maybe a few years down the road, but Garrison's was soon, and in the manner he would choose—not her manner, not Niles's nor even Jack's, but his way. She would allow Lee that one and only advantage in their relationship. He would go the way he wanted.

As Jack was on his way to the cave-in, an excited Charlie Ellenshaw came running over.

"Colonel, you've got to see this!"

"Whoa, Charlie, take it easy," he said as he was joined by Sebastian and Carl Everett.

Charlie placed his hands on his knees and tried to get his breathing under control.

"It's over there. Pete and I found a building that was out of place underneath that giant outcropping of rock. It looked like it was originally a German Quonset hut, but some modern scientific equipment was inside."

"Okay, Charlie, lead the way," Jack said, as Ellenshaw turned and they followed.

Just as Ellenshaw said, the Quonset hut was old, but in good shape. As Jack stepped inside he saw Niles, Appleby, Dubois, and Pete Golding standing around a large lab table. Niles stepped back and allowed the three men to see what they had discovered.

"Well, this is what we were looking for," Niles said.

On the table, secured by some stainless steel clamps, was a rifle, but one the likes of which Jack, Everett, and Sebastian had never seen before. It was about three and a half feet long and had a thick barrel of what looked like steel. Just like the pictures from the Moon, there was a crystal installed on the tip. Only this crystal looked to be shattered. The stock of the weapon was broken and was the only thing that told the weapon's very old age, as none of them recognized the material. There was a sighting aperture and what looked like a magazine.

"I suspect this thing here," Appleby said, pointing to the magazine Jack was looking at, "is the power source. It looks like a large battery. This thing must be very heavy."

"Look at this," Ellenshaw said. He was standing in front of a thick rectangle of steel. There was a perfect hole in the center of the plate and it had what looked like a small rivulet of molten material running from it. Jack walked over and looked at the target. He sighted through it and saw that it lined up perfectly with the barrel of the strange weapon.

"Someone got it to work," Jack said and stepped back around the steel plate.

"Yeah, make that past tense. Look at this," Niles said, pointing out the smashed crystal. "It looks like some kind of overload."

"McCabe?" Everett asked.

"Odds are that it was him or someone he'd been working with. It looks as though this may have been the only weapon they found in this gallery. Hell, maybe the Germans originally found the damn thing."

"The thing is, gentlemen, whoever found it got the thing to work." Appleby stepped up next to Jack and looked through the large hole. "And work impressively."

"Colonel?"

They all turned and saw SAS Captain Mark-Patton standing at the open door.

"We've found a way into the second gallery."


As Jack and the other officers went off to get the search element ready for the incursion into the second gallery, Niles, Pete, Ellenshaw, Appleby, and Dubois remained behind in the makeshift lab set up by McCabe and his benefactors. They found no research paperwork on the weapon that had been tested, but they did find small granules of what looked to be the mineral. After removing the power pack from the receiving unit of the weapon, it was Dubois, the MIT engineer, who discovered the ground-up meteorite dust inside. It was blackened and hard to the touch, but to everyone's amazement it was still warm months after testing had been completed.

"The way it's packed inside this sending unit, it's just like a battery," Niles said, as he held the thick magazine-like unit. "These must be conductors of some kind." His index finger probed two copper wires that protruded from the thickened mass of hardened meteorite dust.

"I don't understand how the power is converted to light," Appleby said while examining the receiver where the magazine was inserted.

"You know, hanging out with Colonel Collins and Captain Everett of late, I have had a chance on several occasions to examine our own weaponry. The receiver for the M-16 rifle is basically a port. The real magic is in the ammunition. The gun itself is nothing more than the dumbest of tools. In this case," Ellenshaw said, as he lowered his tall frame to look down the barrel past the smashed crystal, "I would say that this weapon is just as simple as an M-16. It's the power that makes it special. Introduce a heat source or electrical source to the element inside the receiver and allow the material to be trapped inside, and this trigger releases the built-up energy that's dying to get out."

"I'm not following, Charlie," Pete said. He pushed his glasses back up his nose and followed Ellenshaw's example, looking down the barrel.

"Pete, the crystal that you are looking at is nothing but an amplifier and a lens. Together, they create light. Inside the receiver, once you break it down—which, from the shavings on the tabletop, it appears someone actually did—I believe you will find nothing more than a cooling port, and possibly a small light emitter. That is, you will find a lightbulb. A strong one, to be sure, but basically just a long-life lightbulb. Send power to this light source, a lot of power, and then release it to the only open port available, the barrel end of the weapon. It passes through this crystal, where it is amplified in strength just like the reflector plate on an old-fashioned oil lamp, and pow! You have a handheld laser device capable of doing that," he said, pointing to the steel plate hanging from the ceiling.

As Ellenshaw straightened, he felt eyes on him. He looked at Niles, who was shaking his head.

"Can I ask you what the hell hanging out with Jack has done to you?" said Niles. "That's amazing for just a five-minute examination."

Ellenshaw looked embarrassed, not really knowing if Niles was pulling his leg or trying to make a point about concocting a theory without the least bit of proof.

"Actually, I think along the lines of forensic evaluation, as in my field of work there is very rarely any evidence to examine. I guess I have to use my imagination far more than my colleagues here."

"Well, I for one think it's one hell of an accurate theory," Appleby said, looking closely at Niles. "Just who the hell are you people?"


Jack walked up to the area at the base of the cave-in. Several soldiers were removing the last pile of rocks from its base. As the top row was removed, Collins couldn't believe his eyes. Underneath the uppermost portion, about fourteen feet off the gallery floor, was what looked like a lighted sign, long dead, its face smashed by the explosion that had sent the ceiling crashing down. Jack could guess the meaning of the bright red letters, but turned to Sebastian anyway.

"*Galerie—zwei Gar keine Elektronik,*" Sebastian read aloud.

"Well, don't keep us in suspense, Major Krell. What does it say?" Everett asked.

"Gallery Two—absolutely NO electronics," the German said, his own words giving him the chills.

Jack remembered the strange vibrations he and the others felt every time they used their radios.

"Well, then, if that's what it says, I believe we'll heed the warning," Collins said as the men removed the rest of the blockage.

Soon they were staring at a set of double steel doors. Jack examined them closely and became uneasy at the sight.

"Well, the explosions really warped these things. They're battered all to hell," Everett said, running a hand over the steel plate of what looked to be a portal large enough to accommodate a small truck.

"This is worrisome," Jack said, stepping back to take in the full length and width of the doors. Then he stepped forward and ran his hand over the battered material. "All of this damage is from the other side of the doors. Look," he said. His hand rose as his fingers passed over a large indentation.

"Maybe rocks battered it from the other side," Sebastian offered.

"I agree. Whoever handled the detonation to seal this off couldn't control the fall of the ceiling on this side alone," Captain Mark-Patton said.

Collins looked at Everett, who was seeing the same thing as Jack.

"If that's the case, why didn't the detonation cause the same damage to this side of the doors? Just as much rock from the cave-in battered this side, but the steel is so thick that not one single dent in this steel is evident."

Sebastian and several others played their large flashlights over the double doors. Indeed, there weren't any indentations pushed inward from this side—all of the bulges were from gallery number two's side.

"I hate to be the first wimp to point this out," Everett said while shining his light on the large indentations protruding from the steel doors. "But it really looks like something on that side wanted through that door, maybe after the Germans brought down the roof." He looked at Jack. "Call it a hunch."

Jack and Everett had seen things in their time at the Event Group that would have sent your everyday soldiers to a mental ward. They had seen things that went beyond strange, so they had come to respect their hunches about certain discoveries.

Jack studied the dents in the door for the longest time and then turned to Sebastian.

"Major, you have the most complete team here besides the fifteen Polish troops that we brought down into the mine. You and your men will follow me through the doors."

"Uh, no way, Jack," Everett said, stepping up to this boss. "Sebastian will take his men in with me tagging along. You're the leader of this makeshift bunch of pirates. You don't go in first."

"Mr. Everett, I think—"

"I agree with the captain, Jack. you stay behind until the all clear is given," Sebastian said. "That's Assault 101. Remember what you said in your training sessions with us?"

Collins was pinned down by his own words. He just nodded.

"Captain Mark-Patton will form a fast reaction team for backup." Jack turned to the British SAS captain, who agreed. He pointed to his SAS team and to the ten Marines that would back up Sebastian's assault element.

"Okay, don't wait too long. If the gallery is clear, give the call and we'll follow up with the reaction team. We'll wait until both teams are inside before we start the examination of the gallery."

Sebastian and Carl charged their weapons and assembled the German commandos who would make the initial incursion into the second gallery.

"Colonel, the doors are wedged pretty good, but I think if we cut through at the center latch, we can get them to slide open," a Marine combat engineer said. "If there's no major blockage on the far side, I mean."

"Well, Corporal, I think whatever battered the hell out of that door cleared away whatever blockage there might have been," Everett said, and checked his web gear and the extra ammo he was carrying for his M-16.

"Cut through," Jack said. He moved out of the way as they brought in one of the cutting torches they had found in McCabe's warehoused goods.

Collins was joined by Everett as they watched the cutting torch start doing its work on the giant latch holding together the two halves of the steel-plated doors.

"It's obvious McCabe didn't make it into the second gallery. With the treasure that was waiting for him over there, you have to wonder why. Do you think maybe he had a little more complete information than we do about what happened here in 1945?"

Collins watched the cutting torch burn through the steel and chanced a look at Everett. His face told Carl everything.

They heard the latch fall through onto the far side of the doors with a loud clang, and then watched as a group of Marines and Polish soldiers started to tug at opposite ends of the double doors. They parted gradually with a loud screech and grumble. The echo from the far side told Jack and the others that they were facing a vast open space. The men tensed as the doorway opened into a dark chamber beyond. At the base of the doors, a large pile of rocks had been pushed out of the way. Sebastian's assault team was placed strategically to cover the width of the door. Captain Mark-Patton eased Jack out of the way so that his second team had a clear field to cover the German commandos.

"Mr. Everett, you watch your ass," Jack said, as he turned to a Polish lieutenant. "I want a demo team to place charges above the doorway and I want at least three claymores covering that opening."

The Polish lieutenant saluted and walked away to get the equipment. Collins was taking no chances in case the German SS had the right idea in the first place.

"Night vision," Sebastian called out. His remaining six men and Captain Everett lowered night vision goggles over their eyes and then two men at a time entered the darkness beyond the doors.

Jack was champing at the bit as he tensed, waiting for the first signs of trouble. He hated not leading the first team into the second gallery.

"Captain Mark-Patton, take your team in, no night vision."

"Yes, sir," Mark-Patton called out as he made his follow-up team ready at the doors. Then, with a silent wave of his hand, the second element moved in.

As Collins watched he felt someone step up to him. He looked over and saw Private Tram standing there. He nodded toward the opening of the second gallery. Jack shook his head negatively.

"No, we'll wait for the all clear."

"I believe a commander should be in the lead of his troops at all times," Tram said. "Meaning no disrespect, of course."

Jack smiled as he watched the last of the SAS men and Polish soldiers disappear into the blackness of the doorway.

"None taken, Private," he said. "Believe me, I think the same thing. My military philosophy isn't that different from your own."

"Then we shall wait," Tram said cradling the American-made M-14.

"You know, when this is over, I want that weapon back. You're too damn good with it."


## SHACKLETON CRATER, LUNAR SURFACE

Sarah allowed the Green Beret sergeant to ease over the small rise before her. The column of Americans kept silent, not allowing any talking that could lead to a transmission alerting someone unfriendly. As the sergeant peeked over the top of the small ridge only five hundred feet from the crater, he quickly ducked back down and removed the M-39 from his shoulder. He made sure the kinetic energy round was charged and held a hand up to Sarah and the others, indicating they should wait where they were. He crawled back up the small incline and looked over the side once more. He ducked back and waved Sarah up the slope. When she arrived the sergeant slid back down, careful not to snag his white environment suit on a stone. The bulletproof vest on the front and back of his torso made moving that much more difficult. He pointed at his wrist, eying Sarah through the clear visor. He was indicating that she should switch frequencies to suit-to-suit mode. She punched the small LED terminal on her wrist.

"What's up?" she asked.

"We have seven people down there. They look like they're just sitting around. I see at least five expended oxygen bottles and hoses for refilling the environmental tanks on their backs. I think they're ESA, but I can't be sure."

"Our briefing said their suits are white and blue."

"Yes, but maybe the Chinese knew that and changed from red to what the ESA was wearing?"

Sarah bit her lower lip and shook her head inside her helmet. "We have to draw the line somewhere. I mean, that's too damn devious. The Chinese haven't done anything yet to warrant that kind of thinking." Sarah looked at the sergeant. "No, I say we make contact. They may be desperate for help. And we have plenty of air on our sleds." She looked back down the slope at the four large sleds filled with extra bottles of oxygen.

"You're the boss," the sergeant said, nodding.

Sarah eased herself up, switching her COM system to the open frequency used by all nations during spaceflight. She stood momentarily on the top of the ridge and looked down at the seven people below, who seemed to be sitting and resting. She saw two of them move, so they were alive.

"Do you require assistance?" Sarah called from the ridge top.

All seven heads turned at once. They were looking in all directions and a few weapons were raised as most tried to get to their feet.

"Easy, easy. Lieutenant McIntire, U.S. Army. Are you ESA?"

The men below started laughing and patting each other on the backs when they finally spied Sarah and the sergeant looking down on them.

"*Oui*. Captain Philippe Jarneux. I have six men and we are very low on $O_2$. Are you carrying extra?"

"Yes, we have plenty." Sarah bounded easily down the slope. Not wanting to fall and embarrass herself in front of the French, she slid part of the way. She was surrounded by the ESA astronauts as her men came over the ridge with the sleds of supplies. She was being pounded on the back by some very grateful ESA men when Mendenhall stepped up to her.

"I see you've made some new friends," he said as he watched Sarah be the hero. Then, before he knew it, he was being pounded on the pack holding his oxygen. "Hey, hey," he cried, as he was hit so hard he felt his feet lift from the lunar surface. As he watched, the entire U.S. team was being congratulated. The scene was a good one. They had just gained a partner in the exploration of the crater.

Sarah pointed out the four sleds and the containers of oxygen lying on them. Every one of the seven ESA astronauts was down to two hours of $O_2$ in their tanks.

Sarah stepped away and tried to reach *Altair*.

"*Altair 1*, this is Lewis and Clark, do you copy, over," she said, as she checked to make sure she was still on the open frequency.

All she heard was static. She was joined once more by Mendenhall, who looked at his own frequency setting and then at Sarah, with worry on his face.

The French air force captain stepped up and listened in as Sarah tried again.

"*Altair 1*, this is Lewis and Clark, do you copy, over?" Sarah said, trying to keep any worry out of her voice. Upon exiting the *Altair*, their communications had been crystal clear. Now there was nothing but static.

"If I didn't know better, this sounds like the jamming we ran into in Iraq in the first few days of the war," Green Beret Sergeant Martinez said as he tapped his own radio display on his wrist.

"Lieutenant, you were right about the Chinese not being devious enough, but this is more in their line of operation," the sergeant said as he broke away from the smiling and happy ESA men.

Sarah, Mendenhall, and the French commander turned toward the sergeant as they saw him looking up and back at the place where the Americans had just been.

"Oh, shit," Sarah said as she saw a sight that froze her blood.

"Well, I guess the Moon's becoming a very crowded place," Will said. He slowly brought up his weapon, but knew if he made it look too obvious the twelve trained guns would make short work of them.

Lining the top of the ridge were twelve red-clad Chinese soldiers and they had very lethal weapons. They were aimed at the sixteen ESA and NASA personnel, who had just lost their enthusiasm about joining forces.

"This could get real ugly," Sarah said as she raised her hands into the air, the group now surrounded by soldiers of the People's Republic of China.

The Moon was indeed becoming a very crowded place.


## GALLERY NUMBER TWO, MÜELLER AND SANTIAGO MINING CONCERN, 100 MILES EAST OF QUITO NUMBER TWO

Collins and eighty-five men remaining of the Columbus team waited for any indication of trouble. Jack was standing silently fifteen feet from the double doors. Every few minutes he would see movement in the darkness beyond, but it was nothing more than fleeting glimpses of the men. Because of his order, which he had given on a hunch that really made no sense, Collins knew information making its way back to him could take a while. His hunch may be right, or it may be just paranoia, but they hadn't heard or felt any of the mysterious vibrations since the order not to use the radios or anything else electronic. He also knew that the German SS had left this place without emptying it of its technological riches for a reason, and all of this at a time when their armed forces could have used the miracle weapons that were obviously buried in the second gallery.

Jack turned when he felt someone step up behind him and saw the faint lighting from above shining off the glasses of Niles Compton. Collins turned back to the doorway in front of him.

"I wish you would stay back until I get the all clear from Mr. Everett and Sebastian."

"I need to be here, Jack. I—"

"Just when are you going to tell me what the hell is going on, Niles?" Jack turned and faced the director.

Niles took a deep breath and looked around him at the young faces of the soldiers. There were Poles, U.S. Marines, Japanese, Australians, and others who were no more than babies. He felt responsible for bringing them to this awful hole in the ground.

"Jack, there was a time when I wouldn't give a military man the time of day. Not that I didn't respect them. I just didn't think about them." Niles leaned against a large stone and removed his glasses as he spoke low so no one else could hear his words. "Now look at these kids. They never ask why, or what for. They go where their countries say to go and do what their countries say to do."

Jack turned fully and watched Niles stare at the ground. The dim lights hanging from the top of the first gallery cast eerie shadows that made Compton look gaunt and sallow.

"Since I became involved with the Event Group and became responsible for these boys, it's come full circle. I am intimidated to a point that I hate ordering dangerous field missions because I can't stand to lose anyone. These kids expect that their leaders are doing what's right, and that makes them obligated to obey an order, no matter how crazy that order may sound."

"Guilty consciences from a commander, at least from the good ones, will always haunt those that give the orders, Niles. Hell, all those kids out there are good. They depend on smart people like you to give them something to work with when the shit hits the fan. Not necessarily to have everything explained to them up front, but to know that later on in life they won't have to hang their heads in shame for something they were ordered to do."

Niles placed his glasses back on and stepped up to Jack. He placed his hand on the taller man's shoulder and lowered his chin.

"That's what I'm trying to explain to you, Jack. In the past I have always regretted sending my people—you and your men—out into dangerous places where sick people would kill them for a scroll of paper. But this time, Jack, I have no such qualms about sending boys into harm's way." Niles looked up at Collins and the determined look on his face sent a chill down his spine. "Everyone here—you, me, those kids in there and out here—we're all expendable. I can't tell you until the president says to, but believe me that I want you, of all people, to know what's going on here. But I can't tell you. I wanted to tell you that privately when there was no one around but us, so hopefully you could see my frustration at not explaining things. Just suffice it say that we need this technology and we need it fast. Get it. If you have to take a chance at losing all these boys, do it. We have to take what's here, what's on the Moon, and we have to reverse-engineer whatever we uncover. We have a very short time to do it—maybe two years, maybe three, four at the outside."

Jack watched Niles turn away when he heard the other scientists coming over, silently arguing some point or other. Niles placed his hands in his pockets and turned back to face Collins.

"There's a storm coming, Jack, and I don't know if the world will survive it."

Collins turned back to face the front and looked over at the Vietnamese sergeant as he knelt at his position, waiting for the word to advance. The sergeant turned away and said nothing.

"We have company, Colonel," Tram said. He raised the M-14 up slightly, but lowered it when he saw the large American naval officer emerge from the double doors.

Collins stepped forward, relieved to see Carl as he slung his M-16.

"Sebastian is securing the front of the gallery. It's a deep one, vast, too much to cover with only two teams. We found a generator room with old Nazi equipment. We are attempting to get the lights on. You won't believe this, Jack," Everett leaned breathlessly against the same large rock where Niles had been a moment before. Collins chanced a look back at Compton and saw that he was watching him closely. The words the director had spoken were beginning to drive a wedge into his thoughts. Without explaining anything, Niles had let on how desperate they were to recover anything inside. How sending Sarah, Will, and Ryan to the Moon was only a small part of that desperation move. He turned back to face Everett.

"We go in," he said, as he looked at the anxious men around him.

"Jack, I said the gallery isn't secure."

"We can't secure it with only two teams. Let's get what we came for and get the hell out of here."

"You may change your mind when you see what happened in there," Carl shot back, angry that Jack was going against everything he ever taught to his own people about securing an area.

"Sergeant Averill," he said, as he turned to a Marine gunnery sergeant.

"Sir."

"Move the entire company in, take your Marines and link up with Major Krell and Captain Mark-Patton. The use of radios is still forbidden."

"Aye, sir, moving in with the follow-up force."

Collins watched him go and turned to face Everett. "After you, Captain."

Everett removed the M-16 from his shoulder and, with one last look at Collins, followed his orders, running to the front where the eighty-five men were gathering.

"Niles, you and the science team stay close by. If I say get out, don't give me any crap about the needs of the world. Run, is that clear? The sergeant here will be your escort." Collins faced Tram. "You're responsible for them, got that?"

Compton followed as Jack turned and stepped in beside the last of the men to enter Gallery Number Two. Private Tram followed and looked around to make sure his new charges were close by.

The men all entered a large space, and just like before they knew it was vast, just like the first gallery. As they waited to be led into a previously reconnoitered area, they used the most minimal of lights. The flashlights went here and there, highlighting the cave-in, the old German digging equipment, and what Jack thought were bodies.

"Cover your eyes," said a voice from somewhere to their left.

Collins lowered his head and partially closed his eyelids. He heard the powerful generator start up like an old diesel truck. The large motor revved several times and then he heard the discharge of electrical power as it was released. When he saw the blaze of light, Jack raised his head and saw the chamber stretch out before him. His eyes adjusted to the brightness and that was when he saw the first of the bodies.

"God almighty, what happened here?" Pete Golding said. Several of the soldiers leaned down, examining the skeletal remains of several bodies. The bodies wore black German uniforms, with a few gray regular army uniforms mixed in. The remains were in disarray. Some parts lay close to the main body, others were tossed about like they had been mauled by some giant bear.

The lighting hanging from the ceiling above was bright, but in areas of the vast chamber hundreds of old bulbs had been smashed, leaving those areas in near darkness. Jack was looking at the scene before him and didn't even notice Everett talking to him.

"Jack, I think that's what we're looking for," Carl said, looking from the colonel to Niles. "Jack!"

Collins finally blinked and looked at Everett.

"It looks like the SS set up quite an elaborate science section here. Look down there," he said, pointing to a small drop-off.

Collins and the others stepped forward as the eighty-five men spread out into areas that had already been reconnoitered by Sebastian and the first two teams. As they approached the edge, Jack thought they would see another massive drop-off, but was surprised when he saw that the buildings or huts were only thirty-five yards away. There were fifteen large tin buildings sitting side by side. The first in line was the largest, looking like it was capable of housing a large contingent of troops. As he counted he saw that there were some of the strange composite fiber huts left by the ancient travelers, only these were larger than those in the first gallery and for some reason they looked more permanent. They stretched far back into the gallery. Many of them had been destroyed by the earth movement that had buried the entire ten-mile area, which had been here long before the mountains.

"It's a colony," Niles said. He and the others stepped forward for a better look. They could see that the SS had set up a large perimeter around the three-square-mile site and had encompassed the entire area with watch towers and even a barbed wire fence. In the center of the occupied area, just before the stretch of alien buildings began, there was a large concrete blockhouse.

"How many colonists do you estimate, Niles?" Collins asked, as he scanned the area and watched for any sign of trouble from the men who were going from building to building.

"Hard to say, but for the sake of a starting point—two hundred, maybe less," Compton said. He received nods from the four scientists, who were staring in amazement.

"They came all the way here and then the planet killed them anyway," Jack said to no one in particular. He strode forward into the giant cave system.

He saw Major Krell advance toward him. Sebastian saluted, surprised to see Collins had entered with so many men before he had given the all clear.

"Ease up on the military discipline, Major," Jack said, waiting for a report.

"I believe we have counted close to a thousand bodies and that's not including the slave labor pen about a half a mile in that direction," Krell said, pointing. "There are close to five hundred skeletons in there, mostly in the same condition as the soldiers."

Jack finally faced Sebastian and raised his right brow. Sebastian held his hand out toward the colonel, and when Collins raised his hand the major dropped two items into it. One was a Star of David and the other a red circle of material.

"I believe you know what those are?" Sebastian said, straining with the words as he tried to keep his shock and anger in check.

"The Star of David," Jack said, as he looked from the torn and tattered material to the angry eyes of Sebastian. "The red circle is a marker for a Gypsy. That was their labor force in the mines." They were joined by Niles, who took the two items from Jack's hand and looked at them.

"Hard to take. Here we're searching for answers for all mankind and to do it we have to be shown the ugliness of our past."

Sebastian realized that the director said *our* and not the German past. He was silently grateful for that small mercy. His anger over the discovery ebbed.

"Do you have any idea how they all died, besides very violently?" Jack said as he himself finally snapped out of a haze of thought.

"By the looks of the uniforms and the condition of the skeletal remains, I would hazard a guess that they were torn to pieces, smashed into dust and crushed. A few of them maybe even have been stepped upon by something. There are thousands of expended shell casings, evidence of large explosions, and areas of the gallery that look as if hundreds of men died making a last stand toward the far end of the cave system. There are also many remains by the cave-in, of men who looked as though they fought until the roof was brought down, blocking the way of whatever did this. The cruel thing about that site is the fact that fifty or so of those smashed bodies were wearing those patches, so in the end these people fought for their slave masters in an attempt to keep whatever evil that was here confined."

Collins nodded his head at the quickly delivered report from Sebastian, then he stepped forward with the others following closely. Everett stepped up to Jack as he was handed the swatches of material and examined them. When he looked around at the smashed bodies of the men who were used to secure this place, he tossed the old material away and shook his head.

"I guess the Germans shut this place down when they thought all of this would hurt the tourist trade they were hoping for."

As the soldiers followed the German commando, they knew they had just entered a 700-million-year-old mausoleum.


The men had spread out and searched the German huts. Another team spread out into the original colony area. The first real discovery came from Pete Golding, who was examining the body of a German soldier who had died in the seventy-year-old battle. Pete was squatting beside the remains and looking at the smashed and crushed bones when he saw a piece of rotting, red material poking free of a large slice of once molten rock. He stood and pulled as hard as he could. When Charlie Ellenshaw saw what he was doing, he stepped up to assist. Finally, the facing of the large stone gave way and they jumped back when they saw what fell free.

"Good lord," Charlie said, and felt his bladder weaken.

Lying half in and half out of the stone was the space suit everyone had come to know from the pictures from the Moon. The white helmet was smashed and the skull inside crushed. Pete rubbed his hands on his pants. The remains were so old that they had turned to stone and had become a part of the rock that had killed whoever this was. As they looked on, they nearly screamed aloud when Jack and Niles stepped up behind them.

"Why were they wearing suits?" Jack asked. "Do you think their kind may not have been accustomed to this climate?"

"That's puzzled me ever since the senator told us his story," Niles said as he knelt down to examine the upper torso of the body. "I think I'm beginning to understand. When these beings arrived here, the Earth was a young place, as evidenced by the upheaval of the Andes that swallowed them up. But it was also a planet that spewed poisonous vapors everywhere from the planet-wide volcanic activity on what had to have been the supercontinent. During a large eruption, they may have resorted to the use of their environment suits."

Charlie looked over at Niles and wiped sweat from his brow.

"If that is the case, why would these people colonize such a hostile world?" he asked as he looked from face to face.

"Maybe because they weren't colonists in the sense we may understand," Jack said. He looked at the petrified bone smiling back at them through the smashed helmet.

"Meaning?" Pete asked, also staring at the ancient astronaut.

"Meaning maybe they hadn't a choice but to be here," Collins answered.

Before anyone could follow up with another question, they were approached by a young Marine.

"Captain Everett sends his regards. He would like you to join him right over there, sir."

Jack and the others turned and followed the Marine. They stopped when they saw Carl leaning over a body. This one wasn't petrified nor was he wearing a uniform.

"I think we may have found the man of the hour," Everett said. He stood and examined something. Jack walked over and looked down at the remains. They were also skeletal, but not nearly as old as the others. There was a black suit jacket and what caught his attention more than anything was the white collar wrapped through his once purple shirt collar. The head had been smashed to oblivion just above the minister's shoulders.

"I take it this is the Reverend William T. Rawlins, father of Samuel Rawlins, who disappeared many years ago."

Carl tossed Jack the wallet he was holding and nodded.

"Good guess. I imagine the Reverend went into private practice after the war. He had his son, Samuel, and years later curiosity got the better of him," Everett said, looking around nervously.

"He met the same fate as the others," Pete said, looking at the remains but feeling not the least bit sorry for the good Reverend.

"Look at this, Jack," Niles said, as he straightened from the body. He tossed an object over and Collins caught it.

"A radio," Jack said as he examined it.

"It was in his hand."

"He may have been using it when attacked," Jack said and put the ancient walkie-talkie down.

"It looks like your hunch about the vibrations being linked to the electronic radios may be correct," Everett said, looking toward the top of the chamber.

"Gather up the men. I want to talk to them as soon as possible. Warn them that we may be in an extremely hostile situation. Also, pick a four-man team and get them back to the surface. Call in more help. I don't care if it's Ecuadorian National Guard or their soccer team, just get them here."

As the men surrounding Jack listened, they realized that they could sense fear in the colonel's words, and that in turn made them start looking around for anything other than the technology they were seeking.

Something was inside Gallery Number Two with them.

# 16

Three of the Chinese approached cautiously.

It had been hard to control the soldiers as they took up defensive positions on the low side of the sloping area. As Sarah looked around, she knew that the depression they were in wasn't like the rest of the terrain. The Moon had no hills. Sarah mentally slapped herself and brought her thoughts back to the current situation.

The first Chinese astronauts reached the bottom of the depression and stood there. Their gold-tinted visors were down. The first man stood with his legs apart. He had his comrades lower the weapons.

Whew. No shootout.

The lead man stepped forward six tentative steps. He raised his gold visor. Sarah watched him closely. His red space suit was not unlike theirs. Their weapons were simpler, explosive-driven kinetic-energy weapons, but far more compact than DARPA's design.

"Colonel Kendal?" the man asked in passable English.

Sarah stepped forward, her hands still held out.

"The colonel was killed by debris in space. I am Lieutenant Sarah McIntire, U.S. Army."

"You are in command?" the man asked looking over at the others, who were in various positions around the base of the incline. "Do you speak for the ESA contingent also?"

"I am a geologist. I have command of the American unit."

One of the ESA men stood and shouldered his weapon over the large oxygen package on his back.

"I am Captain Philippe Jarneux. We are under the command of our rescue team. Our lander was severely damaged upon touchdown. Thus I offered the lieutenant the services of my command, since she is the only surviving mission specialist."

"I am Major General Kwan Xiang, commander of the People's Republic spacecraft *Magnificent Dragon*." He took a few steps forward. "On orders of our new chairman, and the people of my country, I am to offer you any and all assistance in the mission as outlined by your president to our chief of staff."

Sarah saluted the general. The general returned the salute.

The Chinese force shouldered their weapons and started down the incline. A sigh of relief passed through the allied ranks as they too stood and relaxed, making it much easier to breathe the tanked air.

"General, I bow to your superior rank," Sarah said as she lowered her hand.

"That will not be necessary, Lieutenant, as I doubt very much we will run into a military situation on this floating rock. I believe you are better suited to carry on the mission as commander of the ground teams. We have other work to conclude. We need to create space aboard two spacecraft for the addition of the ESA team."

Sarah nodded, then realized that the general couldn't see her head bob in the large helmet. She just gestured, hoping the general would follow her. As they moved toward the area where the men were, the other eleven Chinese soldiers joined the group of astronauts. Sarah was happy to see men shaking hands and patting one another on their backpacks.

"Lieutenant, I think you'd better see this." Will Mendenhall addressed Sarah by her rank for the benefit of the Chinese general. "Sergeant, show the lieutenant and the general what we're standing on," Will said.

Forty feet away, a French sergeant scraped away some of the lunar dust. When that didn't seem to do the job fast enough, he went to his knees and clumsily started shoveling handfuls of dust into the light gravity. Metal tubing. As her eyes followed the shape under the lunar surface, she could now see what had caused the rise in the moonscape. There was something buried just under the surface.

"You men spread out and follow the line under the surface. Stand as far apart as necessary, until we can figure out the shape of this thing."

As she spoke, the general ordered his men to follow the American lieutenant's instructions. Sarah walked to the center of the circle of men and saw something at her boots. The general saw it at the same time and both bent over to dig. When three of her men came forward to assist, she ordered them back to their line.

"Hold position, Will," she said over her radio, as she and the Chinese officer dug at a rapid pace.

"Be careful not to pierce your gloves, Lieutenant. I wouldn't want to lose you now."

"Yeah, we took the same classes," she said. "Whatever this thing is, it's sitting in an impact area."

They uncovered a hard, silver-looking surface.

"My God," she said as she stood up. "It's round."

The Chinese general staggered as he saw what Sarah was pointing out.

"Oh, shit," Will Mendenhall said. "It's a damned flying saucer, Lieutenant."

The men were silent as they realized that they were standing on wreckage. The round shape made Will's words understandable to everyone.

"There is something here also," a voice said over the radio.

The men turned and saw one of the ESA men waving a short distance away.

They covered the distance in a brisk hundred steps. Another object. This one was elongated, far larger than the round form in the dust. She could see the remains of massive steel-like rails that ran on for six hundred feet. Compartments of some kind? Was the wreckage of this behemoth lying on its side?

The general and several of his men started uncovering something else. When they were finished, they stepped back and became silent as Sarah approached. The Chinese general pointed at the mangled mess that was buried half in and half out of the lunar surface.

"From historic photos I remember seeing the very formidable ships of the world war. If I didn't know any better, Lieutenant, I would say we are looking at a gun turret—a rather large one."

Sarah looked up at the general and then her eyes saw the shape her lineup of men had created. Then she looked down at the bent and protruding barrel of a large bore weapon. She saw the cannon as it disappeared into a housing like a giant gun turret. Long and shaped like an elongated arrowhead.

"General, I think what we're standing on is a warship."

Sarah, the general, and the French colonel stood off to the side as the American and Chinese broke down the four American sleds and the six Chinese transports.

"The mineral is a main concern. It seems all our governments want this item more than anything. They seem to think that it's here on the Moon in some abundance. I for one will not chance the safety of the men here for the sake of bringing back such a dangerous material. We will bring back only samples, along with an estimate of its availability. We'll leave recovering larger quantities for another, better-equipped expedition. Are we agreed on this?"

General Kwan bent at the waist inside his bulky space suit, indicating his agreement with Sarah's proposal, as did Captain Jarneux.

"I suggest that we break into two groups, one to uncover as much of this warship as possible for closer study, the other to continue into the crater to examine the remains of the base," Kwan suggested.

"Agreed," Sarah said, and then looked at the Frenchman.

"Captain," Kwan continued. "may I suggest that you and half of the men remain here and excavate as much of this vessel as you can, while the lieutenant takes the other half and reconnoiters the crater?"

"Yes, I can do that, General."

Sarah hit the COM switch on her wrist.

"Will, bring me four of our men and half the equipment. Make sure we have the magnetometers and Geiger counters. We don't want to run into anything that will contaminate our ride home. Tell Sergeant Andrews he's to be our scout and he will be accompanied by four of General Kwan's men." Sarah looked at Kwan, who nodded inside his helmet.

"Roger," Mendenhall said as he chose the men and started making sure of their supplies.

"A wise precaution, Lieutenant," Kwan said. He turned to his second in command and issued orders for five of his men to get ready to enter Shackleton.

Then, the Moon *moved*.

Sarah saw the dust underneath her shadow jump and then settle back.

"I don't believe we were briefed on the possibility of moonquakes," Jarneux said. He looked around nervously.

"There can't be a moonquake, because there's no seismic activity on the Moon in any form," Sarah said, as she looked to the others for a possible explanation.

"You don't think there could be a power source still active on whatever it is we have uncovered here, do you?" Jarneux asked.

"All I can say is that I doubt very much this thing is active. It's hard to tell its age because there looks to be no deterioration of the metal properties due to the lack of an atmosphere. And since this is no earthly design, unless the colonel here has been hiding a Chinese leap in technology we didn't see coming, I would say it's old. I doubt anything on it could possibly be working."

"I hope you are right, Lieutenant," the French captain said, and went to begin directing the efforts of his men.

Unlike Jack in Ecuador, Sarah didn't connect the use of her electronic communications equipment to the strange vibration. She never even felt the first effects when she tried to contact Jason in *Altair*.

"Will, General Kwan, we should be off," Sarah checked her chronometer. "I would like to send two men back to the *Altair* soon to make contact with Ryan and find out who could be jamming us."

"I wish to send someone back also, Lieutenant, and since our two landers are on the same compass heading, may I suggest a joint effort? It would leave us shorthanded, but I would rather err on the side of caution in this instance," General Kwan said, looking around the area.

Sarah again nodded her head. "Sergeant Tewlewiski," Sarah said over her shortwave. "Join us, please."

The general called over one of the men who was preparing for the short trek into Shackleton. The two men joined them and they were given instructions.

"I suspect we're far beyond secrets here," Sarah said as she looked the two men over, "and since *Altair* is closer, you should replenish your air there before moving on to *Magnificent Dragon*. Regardless, continue to try to raise Ryan as you go. Maybe this jamming will let up."

"Yes, ma'am," the sergeant said as he half bowed to his Chinese travel companion and gestured that they should start out.

"Shall we go, General?" Sarah said.

The Chinese general looked around the airless void, then turned to McIntire. "Yes, Lieutenant, because in all honesty, I would wish to conclude our business here as quickly as possible."


Sergeant Tewlewiski tried to make small talk, but with the two communications systems sounding scratchy at best and the two soldiers unable to speak the same language, he had given up any attempts at conversation as they trudged through the lunar dust toward *Altair*. He knew that the Chinese soldier was a sergeant too and that his name was Chao. He didn't understand the man's first name so Tewlewiski just called him Chao; for everything else he used hand gestures. He would point to his wrist when it was time for Chao to attempt contact with *Magnificent Dragon*. The signal transmission was still being jammed, but by what they didn't know. All of their attempts to raise *Altair* or the Chinese LEM were being made while they were on the move. Like Sarah, the two soldiers never felt the vibrations coming through the lunar dust. After attempting contact, they would simply bound away, actually enjoying the walk toward *Altair* in the light lunar gravity.

Finally Tewlewiski saw the *Altair*, only sixty-five feet away. He saw no movement at the large triangular windows on the upper deck, so he assumed Ryan was either on the crew deck or going through his preflight checklist as ordered by the lieutenant. He pointed his gloved hand almost proudly at the LEM. Chao nodded in the exaggerated way necessary in the bulky environment suits. The sergeant raised his left wrist and pushed the blue button just above the wrist.

"*Altair*, this is ground team, do you copy, over," he called through the embedded microphone in his helmet. He didn't want to surprise Ryan without making a last attempt to contact him. "Come on, Ryan, you got your ears on?" Tewlewiski said, breaking proper radio protocol.

Sergeant Chao grabbed Tewlewiski's wrist and held it still. He raised his right boot from the dust and nodded his head downward.

Tewlewiski didn't understand at first, then he felt it. There was a vibration emanating from the lunar dust. He tilted his head and wondered what it could be. As he went slowly to his knees he felt the same vibration through his gloves, only stronger since the gloves weren't as thick as their boots.

"What the hell is that?" he asked through the COM system.

"This is *Altair*. Is that any way to talk on the radio, you Army puke? You want the FCC to fine us?"

Tewlewiski gave out a yelp as Ryan's signal blasted through loud and clear. Even Sergeant Chao jumped when he heard the call. Tewlewiski rose to his feet with heart racing. Both men started to laugh.

"Damn, Ryan, we've been trying to raise you for the past two hours, over."

"Well, that's funny. I've been trying the same thing with you guys. I was about ready to suit up and come out there looking for you. I do have some more bad news. The Russian command module went off the air. It seems they may have COM problems too. Or maybe they lost the whole shebang, I don't know. I could hear them one minute and nothing the next. We can still receive from time to time, depending on the orbits of COM satellites, but we can't broadcast. So it looks like the Russians are out of the ball game altogether." There was a pause as Jason climbed onto the command deck. "Hey, I see you brought a friend with you."

Tewlewiski looked over at Chao, who was not looking at him in return. He was staring down at the surface of the Moon and not moving. Then the American understood why, the vibration had increased to the point it felt as if a bus were passing by just underneath the surface.

"Hey Ryan, do you feel anything?"

"Yes, dear, I feel lonely out here all by myself."

"Nut, that's not what I mean. There's a vibration that keeps—"

Suddenly the ground between the two men erupted skyward, sending Sergeant Chao flying through the airless space to land twenty feet away. As the ground sprayed upward in the thirty-yard arc, a massive shape seemed to rise above Tewlewiski.

"Jesus, what the hell was that?" Ryan called out, as he gripped the triple window pane on the command deck of *Altair*. Then he became silent as he saw for the first time just what was standing over Tewlewiski. "Oh, shit, get the hell out of there!" Ryan called out.

The American finally raised his helmeted head and saw what was looking down at him. The machine stood just shy of twenty feet tall. He could see the stainless steel gears spinning and grinding inside its humanoid frame. The torso was thick and covered in armor plate. The arms looked as though they were made from six different lengths of thick hardened steel, culminating in a hand with three sharpened fingers. The head was rounded and there was no mouth, only two giant red eyes that rotated left and right as they took in Tewlewiski. As the sergeant watched in shock, he saw two more arms exit the armored torso. The thick left leg lifted and took a step toward the sergeant.

"Oh, shit, Ryan, tell me you're seeing this?"

"Tewlewiski, just get the hell out of there!" Ryan called out.

The giant mechanical monstrosity tilted its rounded head and swiveled to the right. The neck elongated and spiraled outward toward the spot where Sergeant Chao had landed. He was attempting to rise to his feet when he saw what was confronting him. Chao hesitated as he gained his knees. As if in a slow-motion dream he tried to remove the weapon from his back, but the strap caught on his oxygen container. The beast's eyes rotated; it was following what Chao was doing. Its neck retracted into its body. The mechanical monstrosity took two steps backward and halted. Tewlewiski froze, but the Chinese sergeant didn't. He finally maneuvered the kinetic weapon from his back and without aiming he fired it three times, launching the faster-than-sound bolts of tungsten steel toward the beast. The first two rounds slammed into the steel plate of the torso; the third hit a shoulder blade that was nothing more than hardened plate. The machine rose and waggled as if it were a man who had accidentally hit himself on the thumb with a hammer. A solar panel rose from the area under the plate and then vanished again almost as quickly. The beast turned its eyes toward Chao. It moved faster than either man could believe. It reached Chao in three giant steps and picked him up. While holding the sergeant in one hand, the beast swiped at Tewlewiski with the other. He managed to duck, but the Army sergeant knew he'd be dead in a moment anyway as he felt the sharpened steel fingertips penetrate his suit at the waist. He cursed just as several kinetic energy rounds struck the metal giant in the back.

Chao was firing a continuous stream of tungsten rounds at the mechanical beast and he could see the giant flinch as the half pound missiles struck its back. It was as if the rounds were causing it pain.

"The solar panels on its back, can you hit them?" Ryan called as he scrambled inside the command deck on *Altair*.

The Chinese sergeant took aim and fired again. The beast turned its full attention on the struggling Tewlewiski. Chao heard the desperate sounds coming from the American's COM system and knew the sergeant was being squeezed to death. Chao kept up the steady stream of rounds, trying to aim for the spot where the double blades of steel covered the solar panels that Ryan must believe was its power source. Except for the loud pinging coming through the Chinese radio system, the small battle was as silent as the grave.

Finally it was if the beast had had enough of the game. It turned partially toward Chao and smashed the American astronaut with its free hand. The two steel claws slammed into the helmet and smashed it flat.

"No!" Chao shouted, as he advanced. The robotic killer turned toward him. It charged, but the sergeant held his ground. The beast jumped. Chao kept up the fire even as the beast came down on him, pounding his crushed body into the soft soil.

Ryan stared through the triangular window with the environmental suit only up to his waist.

The mechanical assassin straightened, its steel foot still firmly planted on the body of Chinese soldier. Its head rotated left and then right, and then went completely around in a circle. It seemed to look straight at Ryan, but paid him no attention. Then the robot simply fell over into the dust, curling into a large ball. It started to roll like tumbleweed in the direction of Shackleton Crater.

GALLERY NUMBER TWO,
MÜELLER AND SANTIAGO MINING CONCERN,
100 MILES EAST OF QUITO

Alice Hamilton watched Garrison Lee as he mumbled in his drug-induced sleep. She had been against his traveling, but she knew that arguing with him would have been as useless as shouting at a brick wall.

She was sitting on a small camp chair in the darkened tent next to his cot. She reached out and took his hand and squeezed it. He stopped mumbling and settled down. She heard him call out her name softly and then his face relaxed. She reached up with her free hand and wiped a tear away that had slid down her cheek. Alice had never been one to cry, even when sorrow was bursting to break free of her soul.

She took a deep breath and reached over to retrieve his old brown fedora. She looked it over and sighed. She always wondered why he insisted on wearing that particular one. She was getting ready to place it back at the foot of the cot when she heard men outside of the tent. She looked at Lee for the briefest moment to make sure he had indeed settled into a deeper sleep, and then she eased her hand out of his. She stood and made her way to the tent flap.

Outside, underneath the hanging lights of the first gallery, Alice saw four men talking to three of Jack's people that he had left behind after the main force had advanced. She overheard part of the conversation and stepped out of the tent.

"Excuse me, did you say that Colonel Collins has sent you to bring in more men?"

One of the soldiers, a Special Forces sergeant, saw Alice and nodded his head.

"Uh, yes, ma'am. He wants a backup force brought into gallery number two."

"Has the colonel found something?" she asked, hoping for any information that would take her mind off Garrison.

"So far, ma'am, all I've seen are skeletons—Nazi skeletons, close to a thousand or so. If you'll excuse me, ma'am, we'd better get—"

That was as far as the sergeant got before the bullets cut him down. The six men with him didn't even have time to bring their weapons up before fifty silenced bullets struck them down as well. Alice barely escaped being hit as one of the bullets slammed into the tent pole where she had placed her hand. As she ran to the closest of the fallen men, a hand reached out and took her by the arm.

"I'm sure he is far beyond the need for your attention, madam."

Alice looked up into the dark eyes of the Mechanic.

She had seen the dossier on him that the FBI had sent Jack. She easily recognized the eyes. The beard was gone and the hair was longer than he wore during his insurgent days in Iraq, but it was the Mechanic.

"Azim Quaida, the Mechanic. Which do you want to be called, young man?" Alice asked. Her gray eyes never left the dark countenance staring at her.

"You know me and yet I do not know you. CIA?" he asked and released her hand.

"You've become very popular lately in my country," she said.

"Yes, I imagine I have. The people responsible for that popularity are no longer in a position to use men such as myself."

Alice didn't say anything but tried to block the man's path as he stepped to the tent flap to enter. He easily moved her to the side. He saw Lee lying on the cot with a blanket pulled nearly to his chin. The Mechanic looked from the old man to the woman who now stood next to him. By the look in the older woman's eyes, the Mechanic knew that if she had been armed she most definitely would have attempted something stupid.

"I believe I saw you and this man enter the mine during the battle outside. Who are you and why are you here?"

Alice neither moved nor spoke.

"Madam, know that while I don't particularly like women, I also wish them no harm. However, I have on occasion killed many of them. I shall have no qualms about ending your life."

"Why don't you save your questions for the colonel? He's in there," she said. She tilted her head to the left, indicating Gallery Number Two.

"Ah, the very resourceful Colonel Collins. You know him on a personal level?"

Alice again didn't answer.

"You have said nothing, but have answered me nonetheless, madam. I suspect this old man knows him also, and that you may be close to him in some way. Therefore, you will be what is known as a bargaining chip."

"And you think Jack's going to deal away whatever you want for two old farts like us?"

"For a mere weapon or two from the excavation, yes, he should have no possible argument." He turned and raised a flashlight, clicking it on and off twice. "If not, he risks the chance of me killing you and sending the entire cave system tumbling down around them all. And then we all lose. Yes, he will trade, I believe."

An explosion rocked the gallery. In the distance Alice heard the crashing of rocks and a rumbling beneath her feet.

"Please, don't be alarmed. We just made sure that the front door closed behind us."

The Mechanic gestured for his men to assemble. He took Alice by the arm and pulled her toward the back of the chamber, his men falling into step behind them.


Lee mumbled in his sleep, his good eye opening.

He didn't know what had awakened him, but he felt the last trembling of the earth as it passed through the legs of the cot. He raised his head and felt the cotton in his mouth from the painkillers. He smacked his lips and that was when he thought he heard voices. He tilted his head and listened, but no one spoke again. He tried to sit up but found that his back wouldn't work the way it should. So he threw his left leg over the side of the cot and moved his right leg over after it. He tapped the ground with his boot and tried to move again. This time he sat up until he could rest his weight on his left elbow. He looked around in the semidarkness of the tent. Alice was gone and that helped him get his thoughts into some sort of order. He finally sat up and saw his hat where one of his feet had knocked it to the floor. To Lee it looked as though it had landed a hundred miles away. He shook his head and closed his good eye. He tried to stand. He pushed upward with one hand and swiveled his hips until he felt his feet under him. Then he pushed with both hands against his knees and he was up.

"Well, that wasn't so bad for a zombie," he said to himself. "Now I know why they walk so slow in those movies. It damn well hurts."

Lee turned shakily and eased the flap aside. He ducked his head back into the tent as the last of the terrorist force vanished through the old composite buildings left by the Visitors.

"What the hell is going on? I take a nap and everything falls to pieces. Where the hell is that old girl?" he asked himself, chancing another look outside. As he finally located the head of the force, Lee saw Alice in the front quarter of the men. She was being pulled along roughly toward the falls where Jack and his men had found the opening.

"Goddamn it," he hissed. His brow furrowed and his lips set into a straight line.

Garrison Lee turned and looked back into the interior of the tent. He spied his cane and took hold of it. He reached down without feeling any of the previous pain or stiffness, snatched up the fedora, and placed it on his gray head. He stepped out of the tent and saw that the men, with Alice in tow, had vanished into the opening of the next gallery. When he finally looked away he saw the bodies of the men that the Mechanic had just killed. Lee closed his good eye and shook his head. Then something happened that he hadn't experienced in some time—he became furious, murderously so. He opened his eye and looked at the cane in his hand. He angrily tossed it away and reached down to retrieve one of the fallen soldiers' weapons. It was an Ingram submachine gun. Lee hefted it and liked the weight of it. He reached down and tore free the ammunition belt. It contained a pouch full of ammo clips for the weapon.

"I'm sorry, young man, but in return for the loan of your weapon I'll kill the son of a bitch who killed you."

Collins stood before the cement blockhouse and watched Captain Everett and Major Sebastian Krell enter. He could see the darkened and barred windows flare to life with light, which illuminated still more torn and tattered flags emblazoned with swastikas. The large eagle, symbol of the state, stretched across the opening of the blockhouse and Jack felt anger for what the Germans had done here. As he thought about the situation his eyes never left the windows. He was just dawdling along and totally cut off from any information on the fate of *Dark Star*. It was starting to drag down his ability to think clearly. Carl was forcing him to do things more in line with the book, reminding him that there were a bunch of young soldiers in here who depended on him.

Jack watched as Everett cleared the large blockhouse. He was coming to the conclusion that he would have to turn over command to Everett or Sebastian, because he was starting to take shortcuts, and shortcuts got men killed. Finally, Everett stepped to the large door.

"All clear, Jack," he said. He nodded his head, indicating that he believed they had found just what they had come to Ecuador to find. "Mr. Director, you'd better bring in your equipment."

Niles closed his eyes and thanked God that they had finally found something that would make all this death not as meaningless as it otherwise would have been. He gestured to the twenty soldiers who were carrying their cases, including a large computer for Pete.

"Are you coming, Jack?" Niles asked.

Collins acted as though he hadn't heard Niles. This was the second time the director had noticed that Jack had wandered away in his mind.

Finally Niles slapped Collins on the shoulder and faced him.

"Colonel, are you with us?"

Jack nodded his head and, without saying a word, stepped past Niles and the men carrying the equipment. He went into the blockhouse.

Compton watched until he vanished and then turned to see Ellenshaw looking at him.

"Charlie, lend a hand and let's get this thing over with."

"Didn't you feel that?" he asked, not even hearing Niles.

"What?"

"It felt like, I don't know, a deep rumble, like an explosion."

"Just help with this equipment, Charlie," Niles said as he followed Jack inside the concrete laboratory.

Niles stood beside Jack and saw the technologically advanced weapons sitting in what looked like a large gun rack. There had to be close to a hundred of them. They were all intact and despite being covered in dust looked brand-new. Around the large room there were workstations, a much more elaborate setup than in the first gallery's lab. There were film projectors and screens. There was what appeared to be discs of some kind, lined up and protected by clear plastic. There was a whole row of hanging alien environment suits, complete with helmets protected from the passage of time by the very plasticlike material they were made from. On the far concrete wall was a flag, and it was this that

Jack and the others were staring at. It was blue, and it had the four circle emblem just like the one the senator had drawn for them in his dining room. The
circles were blue, red, white, and gray. The flag was trimmed with gold tassels
and it had a golden triangle in the upper left-hand corner.

"Wow," a voice said from behind them.

Charlie Ellenshaw and Pete Golding entered the laboratory and set down the
large case they had been struggling with. Appleby and Dubois followed them in
and they too were kids seeing Disneyland for the first time.

"Amazing, simply amazing," Appleby said as he saw the stored weapons of
these ancient Visitors to the planet.

"Oh," Ellenshaw said. He advanced into the room and found himself staring
at a globe. It was large, about ten feet in diameter, and the Germans had covered
it with a sheet of plastic. With Pete's help, Ellenshaw pulled the sheet of thick
plastic from the large globe. Both men stared at the unfamiliar terrain of a world
that wasn't theirs. "A green ocean, almost like our own. And look at the continents. They're much smaller than ours and there are only—" Charlie slowly
spun the globe. "—three large ones compared to our seven."

Pete stepped back and looked at the ocean-covered world. He tilted his head
and almost ran to the crate that he and Charlie had just wrestled inside. He
pulled out his laptop. Before Jack could stop him, he opened the lid and turned it
on. Collins, Niles, Sebastian, and Everett froze. They felt a momentary vibration, sharp and hard, which vanished far faster than the vibrations that had preceded it.

"Doc, you take it easy. Don't make sudden moves like that."

Golding ignored him. He was busy attaching what looked to be a camera to
the laptop. He ran out a line and placed the small camera on the tabletop facing
the globe.

"Did I ever tell you my big hobby when I was a kid, Niles?"

"No, Pete, you didn't."

Charlie Ellenshaw watched Pete move around like a bug on a hotplate. He
smiled as he saw the enthusiasm in the computer man's face.

"Well, it was astronomy. Mostly kid stuff. My parents bought me telescopes.
I sent letters to NASA asking for pictures, things like that. Well, I had one set
of pictures that amazed me and I used to stare at them for days on end."

"You go, Pete," Charlie said. He loved the way Golding had become excited.
Ellenshaw knew that feeling of discovery and wanted Pete to take it all in.

Jack, Everett, Sebastian, and Niles turned and looked at Charlie, who smiled
timidly.

"Europa, are you online?" he asked the laptop.

"Yes, Dr. Golding," Europa answered in her sexy voice.

Appleby, the director, looked over at the MIT professor and raised his
brows as the computer spoke in her Marilyn Monroe voice.

"Europa, do you see the planet's representation in your camera lens?"

"Yes."

"Do you recognize the surface features of the planet represented?"

Europa was silent for a moment. Pete looked up at the faces staring at him.

"Yes, Doctor."

Pete stepped up to the large globe and pointed to a raised area mostly covered with snow. The mountain towered from the center of one of the landmasses.

"Europa, according to your records from NASA and the Hubble Space Telescope, what is the name of this mountain?"

"It is actually a volcano, Olympus Mons. Mons means mountain. It is the highest known mountain in the solar system."

Oh, my God," Appleby said as he stepped toward the globe and saw what Pete had noticed right off.

"Olympus Mons is calculated to be 373 miles across at its base and eighteen miles high," Europa added, as if she were bragging about her knowledge.

Pete spun the globe and pointed at another mountain.

"In relation to the polar north and south, what mountain would you say this is?"

"Tharsis Montes, actually a mountain range consisting of three extinct volcanoes, located south of the previously mentioned Olympus Mons."

"I can't believe it," Niles said, finally understanding what Europa, Pete, and Appleby saw.

"Do you mind letting us humans in on what you're looking at?" Everett asked, angry that they were being left out of the thought process. The room remained quiet.

"Europa, what is the name of the planet you are currently examining?" Jack asked, showing that he had no patience for the amazement in the scientists' faces.

"Mars."

Jack was stunned. He leaned against the edge of the large table. He looked over at Everett and Sebastian and saw in their faces that they were just as stunned as he was.

"Look at the oceans," Ellenshaw said. He joined Pete and placed a hand on his shoulder. They all stared at the world known to them their entire lives as the red planet, only now learning that it had once been beautiful and filled with green vegetation and gorgeous oceans.

"Niles, are you going to say that this is where our Visitors came from?" Everett asked, as everyone else remained silent.

"I'm not saying anything, Carl. Nothing at all."

Ellenshaw saw something sitting in the corner. It was larger than the globe of Mars and was also covered in plastic. Charlie kicked a swastika-embossed flag out of the way and struggled with the thick plastic. He pulled on the tarp, assisted by Everett and Sebastian. As the plastic fell free they were stunned to see three more globes.

Jack looked at Compton and they both thought the same thing at the same time. Niles pulled the first and largest globe away from the wall.

"Earth," Appleby volunteered. "Before the continents separated."

The globe was mostly blue, totally covered in water except for the one and only landmass on one side of the world.

"The Pangaea supercontinent," Niles said, looking from the globe to Jack. "Earth, about seven hundred million years ago."

Collins pulled the third and fourth globes over. They looked almost alike. Both were dead-looking worlds. One, Jack saw, was the Earth's Moon. The other was larger and far darker in color. Jack examined the globes and found holes in each. He asked Carl for help and together they pulled the Earth and Mars globes over. Jack reached out and removed a thin rod that had been attached to the large moon. He reattached it to a hole in the Earth globe. He tried the same with a rod from the smaller moon, but the rod wouldn't fit into the hole on the other side of Earth. So he raised the metal bar on the smaller moon and the steel slipped in, where it locked. Then he tried the steel rod from the larger moon. It connected nicely to the small moon.

"What the hell?" Sebastian said, as everyone in the room stepped closer, curious what Jack was doing.

Collins went to his knees once all the rods were connected and found what he was looking for.

"I've always been a wiz at stuff like Rubik's Cubes and Chinese-box puzzles." He flipped a small switch at the base that held the large Earth globe off the floor.

Mouths fell open and everyone stopped breathing as the Earth rose off the floor by three feet, supported by its large metal arm. Then Mars lifted by two feet, the small moon by seven feet, and finally the largest moon by five feet. As they all watched, the ancient globes started turning in an orbital pattern. First the Earth, then Mars opposite it, then the small moon around the Earth, and finally the large moon next to Mars.

Sebastian, Ellenshaw, and Pete had to step out of the way as the worlds began their orbital turn. The rods ran around a small track at the equators of each world and the orbital patterns matched the turning of the largest—Earth.

"Holy cow," Ellenshaw said as he watched the spinning worlds.

"The Earth had three moons, and Mars, the largest moon, was inhabited," Pete said. He removed his glasses and watched the amazing show in front of him.

Niles faced Jack and smiled. "You never cease to amaze me, Jack."

"That part was easy. Pete was the one who recognized Mars for what it was."

"Mars was a moon of Earth. Unbelievable," Sebastian said.

"Now, what the hell happened to the solar system that eliminated the large moon and sent Mars off to a new orbit thirty-four million miles distant? What could have done that?" the professor from MIT, Dubois, asked.

"What do you make of these?" Ellenshaw asked. He handed Pete one of the two-inch-diameter discs. "Looks like a little CD."

Pete looked it over. "That is more than likely exactly what it is," he said. He picked up another and looked it over. "I doubt it's German-made. I don't think the Nazis were that advanced."

"It wouldn't surprise me a bit. I've seen too much strange stuff," Everett said, also picking up one of the plastic-looking discs.

Sebastian looked over at Everett and then at Jack.

"Colonel, someday you will have to tell me just who the hell you really work for."

Pete took the disc he was holding and went to the laptop.

"Europa has a two-inch data slot for discs not unlike this one," he said. He pushed a button on the laptop and a small drawer popped free of the body of the computer. Pete inserted the alien disc and closed the bay.

"Europa, can you read the formatting of the inserted disc?"

"No," came the immediate answer.

"Wow, she sounds like she doesn't even like having it in her," Charlie said, smiling. The smile dimmed as he noticed that no one else was amused by his joke.

"Europa, can you ask the disc to assist in formatting itself to your system?"

"Attempting communication with known language acquired through recent NASA photography."

"At least they're talking. That's something," Charlie said, once again looking around the room and once again getting stares from everyone. "I'm here all week."

Suddenly, as they watched, the monitor on the laptop flashed white, then went blank.

"Adjusting video quality," Europa said. "Cross-referencing alien alphabet. Cross-referencing alien numerical value to thirty-six-word alphabet."

The monitor flashed once more and a picture materialized that was a cross between an old-fashioned sepia-toned photo and a very old 35-millimeter film. The picture was scratchy and faded in large areas. Numbers appeared on the monitor, flashed twice, and then vanished. They were now looking at a man not very much different from themselves as he gazed into what must have been a camera. His hair was long and very blond. They could see that his eyes were somewhat larger than their own. As the humanoid placed his hands on the desk he was sitting at, they saw that his fingers were longer than theirs. His cheekbones rode high on the front of the face and his ears were smaller.

"Damn near a match of our own physique, wouldn't you say?" Niles asked. He moved to get a better view of the monitor.

The man was speaking, and Europa was picking up the strange language, trying to reproduce it in type on the screen. Only a few letters appeared, with extensive gaps in the text.

"Europa, what is the percentage of spoken language you are able to translate?" Pete asked.

"Seven percent, Dr. Golding."

"Can you hypothesize written phonics to make a comprehensible sentence from the words you understand?"

"You wish me to guess, Doctor?"

"Yes, Europa, guess."

The disc started over and flashed again. Then the recording began once more with the numbers 26779.0012 on the computer screen.

"Do you suppose that's a disc number or maybe a date?" Dubois asked.

"Those are as good guesses as any," Appleby said.

"Look at the lettering above the pocket on this person's shirt," Everett said as he pointed it out to the others. "It looks like Chinese characters, Cyrillic letters, and Egyptian hieroglyphics combined."

Pete froze the playback.

"Europa, give us your best guess as to the lettering in quadrant 114.2," Pete asked, referring to the grid coordinates on the monitor that Europa had placed over the picture.

"Computing," she said. "'Gideon' is the closest match to any of the referenced letters in my database."

"Gideon," Jack repeated. "Look at his sleeve. That looks like a rank, possibly a military insignia."

They all saw the strange birdlike emblem with three vertical stripes passing underneath.

"I think you have something there, boss," Everett said, "Maybe a full-bird colonel, er, Colonel."

Pete pushed the play button again.

"We . . . one . . . and . . . disc number 117899.'

Ellenshaw ran his fingers through the pile of two-inch discs. He suddenly stopped and pulled one from the pile, holding it up to his glasses. He looked from the disc in his hand to the monitor as the recording continued. He looked around the room, not really knowing what it was he was looking for. His eyes fell on a piece of equipment he had never seen before. It wasn't German, and it looked as if it had a lens. He walked over and examined it.

"We're not going to get anything from this thing, Doc," Jack said with disappointment. "One in twenty words with Europa even guessing at that one. It's not scientific."

"I agree with Jack. We now know that these people were more like us than we previously thought," Niles said. "That will have to be enough for now."

"Look at this," Ellenshaw said from the far corner of the lab. "I found this disc. It has the very same numbers that appeared on the screen a moment ago. I suspect that the person speaking was referencing this disc, or maybe just talking about it." Charlie was playing with something the others couldn't see.

Niles, curious what the cryptozoologist was up to, walked over and saw the thick power cables running from a boxlike machine no larger than a shoe box to a wall socket. The cords were twisted with what looked like very old-fashioned electrical wire. He figured the German scientists had rigged a power supply of some kind. As Niles watched, he saw Charlie insert something into the little black box with the glass eye and grab the power cable.

"Charles, no!" Niles yelled, but he was too late and Ellenshaw was too curious and determined.

Suddenly the lights went out and even Europa shut down as all the energy in the room was snatched away by the power cord running to the small black box. As the men went stock-still, the glass eye on the small box activated and the room exploded with light and color. A large depiction of the Earth, 700 million years before the present, appeared as a massive hologram, spinning on its axis. The scene was peaceful and serene.

"What the hell is that?" Appleby asked as he backed away from the giant hologram. "Is that a real view of the Earth back then?"

"Look at the cloud formations. They're moving," Pete said. He stepped closer and as he did so the view of the Earth shrank. There was another flash of brightness and the Earth's largest moon appeared—Mars, almost opposite the Earth on the far side of the sun, but in exactly the same orbit.

The men all jumped as Europa beeped and came back online, apologizing for her loss of signal. The men turned away from the small laptop and looked at Mars as it had been 700 million years before they were born.

"It's absolutely beautiful," Ellenshaw said as he moved away from the far wall.

Suddenly the two moons appeared. The larger one looked to be about 300,000 miles from the rotating sphere of Mars and maybe 600,000 miles from the Earth and the moon they all knew. Names appeared below them as a special effects overlay produced by the alien technology.

"Europa, utilize your camera system and view the projected hologram. Translate the names under the orbiting planet to the best of your ability."

"Complying," she said.

They all watched the recorded worlds as they spun on their very strange and unfamiliar orbits. All were amazed and no one could speak or take their eyes off the fantastic scene before them.

"I have an approximation of the terminology listed on the hologram, Dr. Golding."

"Go ahead," Pete said.

"The planet suspected as being Earth is named Tarrafarr. The planet known as Mars is listed as Polomatan. The small moon is Nomtoo and the large moon is listed as Ophillias, or a close approximation of those words."

As they watched, they were shocked to see small ships orbiting the planets. The most activity was around Mars, while nothing was in orbit around the volcanically active Earth. But by far the most traffic was around the large moon,

Ophillias. They were all watching closely when suddenly the realness of the hologram took on a whole new meaning. The view slowed to one eighth speed and everyone in the room ducked when Ophillias exploded. The action was sudden and terrible. The planetoid shattered as though it had detonated from the inside. The debris shot out in a wide arc, taking everything with it as it traveled. Ships and space stations were swept away in the onrush of mountain-sized pieces of Ophillias. Then they all watched in horror as the debris reached Mars. The remains of the shattered moon hit Mars like a shotgun blast, scouring its surface clean of every feature. The oceans were ripped from their beds and the poles shifted as the planet was pushed from its orbit and flung into deep space.

"Oh, God," Ellenshaw said, as if they had just witnessed the real-time deaths of billions of people.

The mauling of the solar system continued as the debris from the exploding world hit the small moon and the violent impact shifted it closer to Earth. Their own home world took the next hit. The supercontinent was smashed by pieces of Ophillias. It started to burn. Volcanoes erupted and the planet became a shining ball of gas as the clouds were pulled away and the atmosphere filled with poison.

When the picture settled they saw the new alignment of the solar system. Mars was now the fourth planet from the sun and Earth was still the third, only it was now much closer to the sun. Two large chunks of Ophillias were still intact. They orbited around the newly murdered world of Mars as its new moons, Phobos and Deimos.

The room was silent as the hologram ended. Niles reached out and unplugged the small machine. He shook his head as he realized that they had just witnessed the most catastrophic event in the history of their solar system—all in actual footage.

"I now believe our alien visitors had no choice but to immigrate here," Niles said.

"But what happened to them?" Charlie asked as he took off his glasses and wiped them on his dirty shirt.

"They came to a hostile world. By the looks of their colony, I don't think they made it," Niles said. He looked at the large globes once more. "But there very well could have been a few who did survive. We're just too close genetically to them to ignore. It may take years to understand, but we are linked somehow, someway."

Jack was about to ask a question when a shockwave struck the blockhouse. It rocked the interior and men fell to the floor for cover thinking it was an earthquake. Only Jack, Everett, and Sebastian knew that it wasn't.

"Get out of here and take cover," Jack yelled as loudly as he could.

As the men started to move, they heard the crackle of small arms fire and then another explosion rocked Gallery Number Two.

## JOHNSON SPACE CENTER, HOUSTON, TEXAS

Hugh Evans was dozing at his station.

He had been awake for seventy-eight straight hours and refused to leave mission control. His relief would sit in a chair next to him and coordinate efforts with Jet Propulsion Lab in getting signals from the Beatle *John* and correlating the data against what little telemetry could find its way through regarding *Altair*. Thus far they were concluding that *Altair* had reached the surface of the Moon but there had been no word on whether the crew was still alive.

It had been twelve hours since the president announced through a joint communiqué that the Chinese space program was now cooperating with the ESA and NASA teams. This had come as a gesture of goodwill after the sudden death of their great leader, who had suffered a severe heart attack while sitting at his desk. The disturbing factor in all of this was that all three space programs—the ESA, NASA, and the China National Space Administration—had not one single scrap of evidence that there were live members of any crew on the lunar surface. All communication, including telemetry, from all three platforms, had ceased. The Chinese could only verify that their *Magnificent Dragon* had achieved orbit and its LEM had reached the surface. Just after the news had been relayed to the Chinese crew that cooperation between the powers had been achieved, communication with the orbiting crew module and the lunar lander had ceased.

Hugh Evans had heard speculation around mission control and the gist of it was that there were ten-to-one odds in favor of all the crews being lost. They would never say that to Evans himself, but the talk was there regardless. The mission thus far had not only lost contact with all elements on and orbiting the Moon, but information had been received through the gossip corridor that the vice president of the United States and executor of the American space program had been placed under house arrest by the FBI. He was more than likely going to be charged for his involvement with Samuel Rawlins, which would implicate the vice president in the assassination attempt on the president. Hugh could only wonder what else could possibly go wrong with Dark Star and the other missions that had been sent to the Moon.

Someone nudged Evans on the arm and he opened his eyes. He was staring at a cup of coffee held by the oncoming CAPCOM specialist.

"Figured since Mohammed wouldn't come to the mountain-grown coffee, the coffee would come to Mohammed."

Evans smiled for the first time in days and sat up in his chair. His eyes felt like there was sand lodged in them. He rubbed them until they were flaming red.

"Thanks," he said, accepting the white cup. As he did so, he saw the NASA logo on its side and wondered if the program would be extinct after the debacle of the Dark Star missions. Sipping the black coffee, he could only speculate if he was presiding over the extinct dinosaur that was now the space program.

To be so close and to lose the last of the LEMs had been a shock to him and everyone at mission control. The presidential calls to the center asking for any update were the worst. He had spoken to the president twice, offering his latest version of the same information, only to feel the president deflate even further after his pat answer.

"What was that?" a technician called out from the fifty rows of telemetry stations.

Evans glanced up at the large center screen. The picture was still being re-layed by the Beatle *John* and the camera view hadn't changed. Evans went back to drinking his coffee.

"There it is again. Could someone tell me just what the hell it is? Flight, we have a shadow that has passed over *John*'s lens twice now."

Evans grimaced at the coffee in his cup and placed it on his console. He ad-justed his headphones and microphone, and then stood up, hearing his bones cracking as he did. He looked down and let his anger show for the first time that day.

"Who is speaking to me?" he asked. "When someone has something to re-port, it would be helpful if I knew who I was talking to."

A young man in row nineteen of mission control stood and looked back at the mission flight controller. Evans was staring down from his high perch with his hands on his hips.

"Sorry, Flight, this is telemetry from *John* coming in from JPL. We're get-ting shadows around the peripherals of the rover's camera."

Evans rubbed his eyes and focused on the young kid, who was connected directly to JPL through a computer link.

"Just what the hell does that mean?" he asked.

"I think we have movement around *John*."

Evans looked up at the picture streaming from outside Shackleton Crater. Neither the camera angle nor the rover had moved in days. The picture was still fixed on the center of the interior, showing the devastation after the explosion. As he watched, he saw nothing out of the ordinary.

"What is JPL saying?" Evans asked.

"Whoever is on duty missed it. I guess I'm the only one who saw it," the young engineer said, looking timid.

Evans nodded his head and fixed the technician with his tired eyes.

"That's okay, son. You report anything you see. You never know." Evans started to sit down and that was when he saw it. He froze halfway to his chair. The rover had moved. "Jesus, has anyone issued a command to *John* to change positions?" he asked. The heads of three hundred men and women looked up as they wondered what Evans was talking about.

On the main view screen, *John* began to vibrate and the camera angle went off kilter.

"Good God, we have movement of the rover! It could be slipping down the slope of the crater."

"No, no," Evans shouted, as he watched the camera view go further askew. "Not now, not now!"

"Wait a minute. JPL is reporting that it's not *John* that's moving, it's the camera's boom arm."

Everybody in mission control stood as one. The camera angle steadied and the smiling face of a helmeted astronaut came into view, waving a greeting.

An eruption of noise sounded in the aisles of mission control as they recognized the smiling face. It was Sarah McIntire.

"It's the lieutenant. They made it!" someone shouted from their station.

"Calm, people, calm," Evans said, as coolly as he could manage. He wanted to jump up and scream himself. He looked over at CAPCOM, who was staring back at Evans and using a handkerchief to wipe at his eyes. Hugh nodded and placed his hands on his hips once more.

On the screen the small geologist held a finger up as the camera angle jostled and then steadied. McIntire disappeared from view and the camera showed several space-suited bodies moving around near the rover. Some wore the distinctive environmental suits of the ESA, and some the white with red trim of NASA, and still others had the solid red-colored suits of the Chinese. Another loud cheer erupted from the floor, and this time Evans himself pumped a fist.

Suddenly a loud crackle from CAPCOM was heard through the speakers lining the walls of the center. Evans looked over at the CAPCOM station and saw his technicians frantically adjusting the sound quality. Just as Evans looked back, McIntire appeared again, this time trailing a long cord from her backpack.

"Hous . . . this is . . . copy, over?"

Evans tried to still his racing heart. He realized McIntire had tied into *John*'s transmitter and was attempting to broadcast by bouncing the signal off *John*'s parent craft, *Peregrine*. He wanted to reach out through the 244,000 miles and hug the smart little woman.

"Damn it, CAPCOM, clean that up. This I want to hear!" Evans said. For the first time he had emotion exploding from his voice. As he watched, CAPCOM nodded and stared at the main viewing screen.

"Houston, this is *Dark Star 3*, do you copy, over?" Sarah said from the Moon.

"*Dark Star*, this is Houston, we read you loud and clear. Welcome back to the world of the living."

"Thank you, Houston. It's good to be back. I am pleased to report that the *Eagle* has landed." Sarah smiled and then laughed. "I've always dreamed of saying that."

Evans plopped down into his chair just as the control room exploded with cheers and applause. Hugh felt around in his pockets and then a hand appeared in front of him. It was the young technician from JPL. He was holding a handkerchief out for the flight controller. Evans accepted it and wiped his eyes. He nodded his head as he reached for the phone that had been tied in earlier. He only had to wait a second after picking it up before the call was answered.

"Mr. President, Lieutenant McIntire has just reported from Shackleton Crater. *Dark Star* is on the Moon and the joint teams, including China, are moving into the crater's interior."

There was silence on the other end for the longest stretch Evans had ever endured. Then the president was heard clearing his throat and sniffing.

"Thank you, Mr. Evans—thank you."

As the line went dead, Hugh Evans looked up with phone still in his hand and all he saw was the smiling face of Sarah McIntire behind her helmet's glass visor. The little geologist was the new love of his life.

Behind Sarah, Evans could see the joint lunar team moving slowly down the explosion-wracked sides of Shackleton Crater.


## SHACKLETON CRATER,
## LUNAR SURFACE

The first thing Sarah saw was several large chunks of the mineral. She had no idea if they had been there before the explosion or if they were thrown free of the complex below. She examined one of them up close, and then let it slip from her gloved hand as she noticed for the first time the complex below in the crater's center. She was amazed at the sight as she took in what was once an underground bunker. The explosion had not only removed the top sixty feet of accumulated lunar dust, it had shattered several of the buildings' roofs. Inside one she saw what looked like tracked transports of some kind, complete with large tanks and other big pieces of equipment.

"It makes one rethink the small problems we on Earth share, does it not?"

Sarah was torn from her thoughts by General Kwan, who had stepped up beside her without her noticing. Sarah looked from the general to the complex below.

"Sometimes we create those problems for lack of something better to do, it seems."

"Well put, Lieutenant. You and I are the same sort of soldier, I believe. Someday maybe my superiors will allow me access to their thinking about why this project could not take a more cautious approach and a time frame more amenable to safety. I have lost many good men who wanted nothing more than to ride a rocket into space."

"Well, we won't find out anything they need to know up here," Sarah said, as she spied Will Mendenhall bouncing toward her. "I believe my escort is here, General. Would you care to join us?"

"It would be an honor."

Will bounded to a stop and gestured toward the slope.

"We're rigging safety lines so we can have handholds on the way down. I didn't think it would be such a hot idea sliding down on our asses."

Sarah hit Mendenhall on the shoulder.

"Always thinking of the easy way to do things."

"Hell, I thought that was why everyone was so hot for me to come along on this little picnic," Will said, looking from Sarah to the general. "That is one nice environment suit, General," he said. He returned his gaze to Sarah. "Now why does NASA insist on white-colored space suits where if you fell down no one could see you, while the Chinese use red ones that you can see from fifty miles off?"

Sara rolled her eyes and eased past Mendenhall.

"You'll have to excuse the lieutenant, General. He's been bitching ever since he volunteered for this."

"Volunteered?" Mendenhall protested. He turned to look at Kwan. "That's our army's euphemism for kidnapped."

The general laughed as he turned to follow Sarah.

"In our army also, Lieutenant."

As they approached the twenty secured ropes, Sarah stepped up to Sergeant Andrews, the man she had chosen to command the rest of the Green Berets. He was conferring with the Chinese soldiers who would be a part of his team for the initial descent into the crater.

"Language barrier?" Sarah asked the sergeant.

"Surprisingly, none at all," Andrews answered. He slung his weapon over his shoulder. "It seems they picked troops with English-language training. Maybe they knew something we didn't, huh, Lieutenant." He reached down and took one of the secured ropes into his gloved hands.

Sarah didn't answer. She knew the sergeant was more right than he would ever know.

The sergeant raised his right hand and then lowered it. At the same moment three other Americans and five Chinese soldiers eased themselves off the edge of the crater, proceeding hand over hand down the treacherous slope.

Sarah took the time to push a small button on the left side of her helmet. A third visor slid down and covered the clear one she had been using. Will followed suit. Sarah immediately saw the difference as she used the Optical Range Enhancer for the first time. The ORE was designed like a set of binoculars, only it had one solid lens instead of two. Sarah shook her head as she became a little dizzy using it for the first time. Nonetheless, a better picture emerged than before. The damage to the bunker system was more extensive that she had first thought. The material the bunkers were made of looked more like Styrofoam than anything else. She figured the walls and roofs of the buildings were plastic of a type she could not imagine.

"Look," Will said, touching Sarah's arm through her suit.

Sarah looked down to where Will was pointing. They were outside the bunker system and had been uncovered by the mineral's detonation. She counted sixteen skeletons, some half buried, others scoured clean of lunar dust. None of them wore space suits.

"Another mystery," General Kwan said as he looked through his own amazing piece of equipment. It was a boxlike device that was actually a camera. The general placed his entire visor into the slot in the back and saw a digitally enhanced view of whatever he was looking at. "Why would these . . . these persons be caught out in the airless environment?"

"I have a feeling it will take more than one trip to the Moon to find out exactly what the hell happened here. A buried bunker complex, a crashed warship, bodies everywhere? Something happened here that we may never understand," Sarah said. She switched her view to Sergeant Andrews and his team. They were nearing the bottom.

General Kwan lowered his viewing device and ordered the remaining men to take up covering stations at the crater's rim.

"Why didn't I think of that," Sarah said angrily.

"Don't feel bad, Lieutenant. I failed to think of it until I saw those bodies down there," the general said, and made sure the men were placed accordingly. "Sergeant Andrews, please cover this northern area on your first walkthrough. That will be the extent over which we can give you covering fire."

Sarah looked at General Kwan, expecting him to justify his dire warning to the sergeant, but he just looked at her, explaining nothing. She looked at Will and he frowned, not liking the feeling he was getting as the men on the ropes neared the bottom of the crater.

"Yes, sir. Northern area only," Andrews said. He allowed the rope to fall free of his hands and jumped the last two feet to the crater's floor. "I will send two men at a time into the buildings with roofs. The rest will cover from the door and in open sight of the rim. That way no one is out of view except for the entrance team, and we will cover them."

"Excellent, Sergeant."

Sarah watched as the rest of the first team hit the bottom. They all removed their weapons from their backs and divided up into two-man teams.

Sarah couldn't help but get nervous as the leading two men entered the first of what had apparently once been underground bunkers.

"Well, we didn't get dressed up for nothing."

Both General Kwan and Sarah looked over at Will Mendenhall, who was checking his own weapon and making sure the air cylinder was charged.

"I'm in favor of getting this done and seeing if the *Altair* can get us the hell back to smog- and traffic-choked freeways."


Over the small rise and a thousand yards north, Captain Philippe Jarneux studied what they had uncovered. He could tell that the ships had impacted with the Moon at very high velocity. He had seen aircraft impact craters many times in his flying days, but never had he seen anything so utterly buried by a blunt-force, high-velocity impact. Still, it was a tribute to whoever designed the craft that the bulk of it had not been obliterated.

Jarneux, after examining the saucer, stood on an exposed superstructure of the second massive warship. They had found evidence of another turret forward of the exposed section. He wondered if there had been still more aft of where he was standing. The men of the ESA expedition seemed to relish their work uncovering such a prize. Whatever powered the great ship and her weapons systems would fit nicely into the ESA plans for uncovering the wealth of technology they had come for. As he looked at the three-barreled turret, he saw the two surviving six-foot-diameter crystals at their mouths. The crystals alone would be worth a ton of diamonds back on Earth.

"Captain, we have uncovered something you may want to look at," one of his men said over the radio link.

Jarneux jumped easily from the exposed superstructure and saw the man who had spoken. He was waving and was about thirty feet away from the leading edge of the crashed ship. Jarneux hopped the twenty yards to the group of two men, who had uncovered something shiny and oblong. He stopped and looked down to see a cylinder. It was covered in a strange swirling design and looked to be made out of something resembling copper. It was fifteen feet long and half again as wide. Its oblong shape tapered at both ends. Jarneux saw thirty or so smashed and cracked lights on the surface and what looked like a small television screen in the center. There was a large gash running the entire length of the object, and it appeared to have been destroyed during or soon after the impact of the two ships.

"A container of some kind?" Jarneux asked aloud.

"Maybe, or maybe it's a shell for one of those weapons," the man on his knees said.

Jarneux looked from the copper cylinder back to the raised third gun of the turret over their heads.

"I don't think so, it's far too big, and I believe the other is some form of light weapon. This is something entirely different. Do you have your digital camera?"

"Yes, sir," the man standing said. He reached for a large pouch on his belt and brought out a small portable digital camcorder. He pointed it at the cylinder and started filming.

Suddenly an aperture opened and a small antenna-like device popped free of the pod. It started spinning rapidly, like a turning radar dish. It stopped and then started again. A few sparks shot out of the damaged section of the cylinder, but then stopped. Several of the lights flashed on and off. The man with the camera stopped filming and stepped back. He lowered the camera and at the same moment the small dish antenna stopped turning.

Jarneux looked from the copper cylinder to the man holding the camera. The thought struck him that the device inside the copper pod had been activated when it detected the digital device filming it.

"Aim the camera at the cylinder and push the record button," he said. He stepped closer to the copper pod and lifted the man who was kneeling there to his feet.

As the second man complied, the dish antenna started turning once more. It stopped, sparked, and started again.

"Stop. That is sufficient," Jarneux said, as he backed away a step.

The three men stared at the dish as it continued to turn.

"Have you stopped filming?" the captain asked.

"Yes, sir," the man said, worry tinting his voice.

At that moment the dish stopped turning and it seemed to have come to a standstill with the open face toward the man with the camera.

"Move the camera to the left," Jarneux said, watching the cylinder closely.

The second man moved the camera and the dish moved with it. It stopped when the man's arm ceased moving.

"It's tracking the digital output of the camera," Jarneux said as he backed away from the cylinder. He reached for his left wrist and switched frequencies on his shortwave, utilizing the digital feature of his COM unit instead of the short-range radio of his man-to-man communication. He caught himself as he realized the digital output would be the same as the camera. He grimaced at the thought that he had almost made a mistake with this unknown device.

As he thought this, all three men jumped. The cylinder cracked open about a foot with an explosive force that shocked them and made one of the men fall backward. As the captain watched in fascination, a long, three-rod assembly popped free. It was about eight feet in length and unfolded before their eyes between the top of the cylinder and the bottom. Then they watched as the thing that resembled a crane's tower slowly lay down in the lunar dust.

"It's damaged, whatever it is. It must have—"

"Captain, look," the man who had fallen said, his eyes fixed on the appendage.

Jarneux was speechless as he saw the very end of the arm open up and the three large fingers unfold, tick once, and come to a stop. They were looking at a hand large enough to cover their entire helmeted heads.

"My God, what the hell is this thing?" Jarneux asked aloud.

Suddenly, three feet away and without making a sound, two copper cylinders exploded outward from the dust. Their lids immediately flew open, and to the terror of the three men they weren't damaged like the first. As they watched in fascination, first one and then the other device unfolded itself from its egg-like cylinder. They rose into the air. The legs made fast their footing and then the torso started to expand. The arms unfolded from the main trunk, and the head slowly rose from a hiding place deep inside the shiny metal structure.

Jarneux watched as the two manlike robots rose into the air. They were at least twenty feet in height and looked as if they were made of chromed steel. He saw the inner workings through the riblike protection, with gears and cogs turn-ing, and he suspected that if he could hear them they would have a mechanical or loud turbinelike whine as they activated and gained power. He saw a series of glasslike appendages pop free on their backs, briefly shining in the daylight. They reflected like glass and Jarneux realized that the plates were solar panels, rapidly collecting energy. The panels sank back into the bodies of the mechanical giants and were covered by what looked like shoulder blades. The two mammoth beasts stood stock-still as first one and then the other started turning their heads, exam-ining their surroundings.

Jarneux eased his right hand over to his left wrist and decided he had to risk communication with the Shackleton team.

"To anyone listening, this is Jarneux. We have uncovered something me-chanical at the first site. I believe they are hostile."

The closest mechanism moved its head toward Jarneux, who took both of his companions by the arms and started pulling them backward.

They watched as the devices stood their ground. The heads swiveled and looked at the three men, then turned and continued to scan the area. The gi-ants stood with massive legs spread and arms half turned up at the elbow. Their construction design was a steel rod system that looked as if it could take serious punishment. Their electrical systems were buried deep inside the cagelike rods, like the life-giving veins of a living creature. They could see no discernible weaponry on the structures, but the powerful claws and thick limbs suggested that they didn't need any weapons other than their mechanized hands.

"My God!" a voice said through their COM system.

Jarneux slowly turned and saw the rest of his team as they stood on the super-structure of the downed spaceship. They were staring at the amazing sight in front of them and were frozen in awe at the two mechanical giants. The captain raised his right hand, intimating that the men should not move or make any threatening gestures. The two robots remained still. They were producing a small vibration that the men could feel through their thick boots. The robot on the left turned slightly and they saw a parabolic dish pop free from the shoulder area. It immediately started turning. The men felt a slight pressure in their ears as a sound wave passed through their helmets and into their heads. The dish stopped turning and folded back into the shoulder. The robot remained still after that.

"Attention, we will slowly start making our way to the crater," said Jarneux.

We will not fire unless attacked. I want everyone to be clear on that. Now slowly turn and start walking."

As the six men on the superstructure and the three below on the lunar surface turned, they stopped dead in their tracks. They were face-to-face with a third mechanical giant. It stood just thirty feet south of the crash site and was silently watching the scene in front of it. Every man saw the beast stand like a predator eyeing its prey. Jarneux realized then that the first two mechanisms had been waiting for the third to block their retreat. They were surrounded. The three menacing mechanicians just stared at the nine survivors of the ESA LEM *Astral*. The machines were not moving, but looked aggressive nonetheless. The colonel once more made sure his frequency was correct.

"Shackleton team, this is Captain Jarneux. We are about to be attacked by a mechanical force of unknown origin. We will attempt to escape and join—"

At that moment the third giant sprang into motion. It took six long strides and slapped the first man it came to off the superstructure of the crashed ship. It hit the man so hard that his helmet was ripped from his head. His body flew off through the Moon's light gravity. The men all broke as one, each one of them jumping and bounding away.

Jarneux, instead of running, pushed his two companions away and removed his weapon from his back. He sighted his rifle on the first robot on his left and fired his weapon on full automatic. The ESA weapon used a combustible mix of gas and gunpowder that sent an explosive .50 caliber round out at supersonic speed. The round would explode on contact. Several of the explosive shells hit the first robot in the chest, making it take three large steps backward, but then it righted itself and followed its companion forward. Jarneux aimed at the head area of the same beast and fired another long stream of rounds into the airless void. They struck its thick neck and face, but it kept coming on, shrugging the powerful rounds off as if they were mere blows from the captain's fists.

"All personnel fall back, fall back to the crater," he yelled as he fired again at the oncoming menace.

The next set of rounds exploded at the giant's feet, taking out large chunks of Moon dust. The void in the surface tripped up the mechanical giant and it staggered, falling face-first into the dust. The captain aimed at the second robot, which had veered to its left in an attempt to strike at the men above. As he aimed, he was grabbed from behind by the third giant. Jarneux was raised to a height at which he was face-to-face with the thing. The captain could see the inner workings of the beast. Its brain looked like a turning gyroscope deep inside its head. He tried his best to get the rifle aimed, but found that his arm had been broken when the robot had picked him up from the surface. Several of his men had stopped in midflight to turn and fire at the giant, but their rounds were just as useless as Jarneux's had been.

Jarneux looked deep into the mechanical beast's red, glowing eyes. He saw the thickness of the glass lens and the brightness of the programming behind it.

The orb glowed from the deep interior, and he knew that this thing had been programmed many millions of years ago to kill anything it encountered. This unthinking giant was man's worst nightmare come true—a beast that wouldn't stop until its programmed goals had been fulfilled. The damnable things had lain in wait for millions upon millions of years for just this opportunity.

As it brought Jarneux forward, the giant seemed to be studying him. It appeared to realize something as it tilted its large steel-encased head. It was as if it were scanning him to confirm his face, body, or uniform.

The French captain became angry at his obvious fate and lashed out at the glowing right eye with his good arm. The gloved fist struck the beast and it didn't even flinch. It remained still and staring. Jarneux struck it again. This time the giant started to squeeze the small human. The captain felt his ribs collapse first and then a scream that only he could hear burst out of his lungs as the giant brought him closer to its eyes.

The last thing Jarneux saw was what appeared to be a satisfied glint in the red eyes. Then he realized that it was his own reflection he was seeing, and that it was wide-eyed and screaming.


Sarah watched the men below as they entered the first structure. It was covered by a roof, so she tensed when the two-man team entered.

As she watched, her COM system sprang to life and the voice of the French colonel burst through her speakers in her helmet. She jumped at the loudness of the transmission.

"Did you understand that?" she asked, turning to face General Kwan and Will Mendenhall.

"Something about an attack," Will said, as he turned and looked to the north, where they had left the first team. "Think it's the Russians?" he asked.

"No, the Russians are a day out. And besides, they're a part of the Arizona treaty and are acceptable to Case Blue. And—"

The two men—Mendenhall and Kwan—looked at Sarah when she stopped talking. She bit her lip, knowing she had said too much, but that was something she would have to answer for later. Right now she knew she had an unseen problem on her hands.

"You men, cover the north. We may have an unknown element breaking through the first team perimeter."

Sarah swallowed as she watched the men covering the crater floor bring their weapons to bear in the direction of the crashed warship. Will Mendenhall rechecked his kinetic weapon and watched with wide eyes. The general went to one knee and aimed his own shorter version of the same rifle at a spot that covered the top of the small ridgeline.

"All of a sudden this place has gotten damn crowded. Who else could be here on the Moon that we don't know about?" Mendenhall asked.

Sarah was breathing way too hard. She had to force herself to calm down as she scanned the area to the north.

"Do you feel it?" she asked, without looking at the two men on either side of her.

"Yes, something is coming this way," Kwan said as he sighted his weapon.

"Jesus, what is it?" Will asked. He too went to one knee for a steadier aim.

As they all watched, the advance team inside the crater babbled excitedly about something, but no one was listening. Sarah moved her weight from one foot to the other as she strained her eyes to see what was coming at them. That was when the first few ESA team members broke from the ridge, bounding and hopping, using the light gravity to speed away from something. Sarah counted only three, plus one straggler.

"Jesus," she mumbled.

"Easy men, easy," General Kwan said. "Aim carefully and cover these men."

As they watched the men scramble toward them they all froze. That was when the first of the three giants made its appearance. Several of the men who were supposed to be covering the retreating ESA men stood and lowered their weapons when they saw what was chasing the men.

"Remain in your positions!" Kwan called out.

The mechanical giants stopped and surveyed the situation along the rim of the crater. They seemed to be scanning for threats. The general saw what amounted to giant Erector Sets standing and looking down on the smaller humans they confronted.

The first of the ESA men stumbled and fell three feet in front of Sarah, Mendenhall, and Kwan. She stepped forward and pulled the man encased in his bulky suit upward.

"Where's Captain Jarneux?" she asked.

"Dead. We're all that's left. These things came from the wreckage near the downed craft. They're killers."

Sarah pushed the man to the side just as General Kwan opened fire from his kneeling position. Sarah flinched as the first kinetic rounds left the barrels of several men at once. The hardened rounds struck the metal monsters in several places and the men who fired saw their spiked bulletlike bolts bounce off, causing no discernible damage.

"We may be outgunned here," Will said. He fired a burst of three rounds toward the head of the leading robot. The rounds struck, forcing the giant's head back. It shook off the assault and started forward again, with the other two also moving.

As General Kwan and the others opened up with a withering fire at the oncoming assault, Sarah reached took the general by the shoulder. He finally looked at her.

"I think we'd better get to cover," she said.

The general looked around and saw that there was only one place to go.

"Yes, that is a good suggestion, Lieutenant," Kwan answered, and turned Sarah around to face the open crater of Shackleton. "Lead the way."

Sarah didn't hesitate, nor did she take one of the dangling ropes. She hopped into the crater and started sliding down its steep incline, falling faster and faster as the others started sliding down the edges behind her.

Will Mendenhall and General Kwan continued to fire their kinetic rounds at the three brutes coming straight at them on a run. When they saw that no damage was being inflicted, they turned and leaped into the dark void of the crater.

After several commands were shouted through their COM systems, the ground team looked up and saw a terrifying sight. They had progressed down the dangerous and very steep slope being cautious for safety reasons, but now they were witnessing a full-fledged retreat from the crater's rim. Men in bulky suits were sliding on their backs and even a few on their stomachs. Some were in danger of ripping the vital life-sustaining material of their suits as they crashed, crawled, and hopped down the crater's side. The men had started running from the confined spaces of the bunkers when they all came to a dead stop as the first of the giant robots made its appearance at the rim. The men froze as they saw for the first time what had forced the men to flee.

The men were in desperate flight to get to cover as the first of the three robots jumped into the crater. It didn't hit the slope on its way down. It landed on Shackleton's floor well ahead of the retreating astronauts.

# 17

## GALLERY NUMBER TWO,
## MÜELLER AND SANTIAGO MINING CONCERN,
## 100 MILES EAST OF QUITO

The mine forces learned the hard way that they had failed to destroy one of the mortar tubes. Jack, Everett, Sebastian, and the scientists ran from the blockhouse into a murderous crossfire. An erratic defense had been mounted, but Jack was sure that whoever was firing on them was going to concentrate on one pocket of resistance at a time.

"I don't see 'em, Jack," Everett called out. He dared to raise his head. Just as he ducked back, a series of bullets stitched the hardened lava of the ridge, sending chips flying in all directions.

Collins turned slightly to make sure the five scientists were keeping low. He knew he had to get them away from the German blockhouse, which was an easy target for the mortar team.

"Well, we sure as hell can't stay here. Whoever it is has the advantage of an elevated position," Jack said. He rose and fired toward the sound of the mortar tube discharging. He ducked back. "Sebastian, we have to get a fire team organized and do it fast."

"I have men over in the next series of buildings, assuming they're still alive."

Before Jack could say more, the German commando turned and ran to the right in search of men he could corral.

"Mr. Everett, we have to ditch these guys," Jack said, nodding toward Niles and the others.

Charlie Ellenshaw crawled forward with his M-16 and looked straight at Jack.

"I heard that, Colonel. You're not leaving me with these guys."

"Yes I am, Charlie. You're going to keep them together and defend them with your little gun—that's an order."

Ellenshaw frowned and then ducked his head when gunfire erupted, closer than before.

"Whoever these assholes are, they're aggressive," Everett said. He popped up and returned fire. "Charlie, get your ass back to Niles. Get them to the far side of the blockhouse and hunker down low along the strongest part—that would be its base. Do not go inside," Everett said. "We'll cover you the best we can."

Ellenshaw finally nodded.

"Ready, Jack?" Everett shouted.

Collins nodded.

As one, Jack and Carl rose up and started firing. To their shock they saw ten men running at them, firing their weapons. They had gotten far closer than either man realized before they made up their makeshift plan for getting Niles and the others to safety. Jack knew immediately that their attackers would be on them soon. Still, he and Carl placed a withering fire on the ten men as they zigzagged through the ancient colony buildings. As Everett's M-16 hammered on an empty receiver, Collins knew that was it. As he aimed at the five men who were only six feet from their hidden position, three of them fell almost immediately. Not waiting for another miracle, Jack opened up on the last two. He missed the second as the man screamed and made the last push for their position. As Collins aimed, the man suddenly straightened and fell to the left, unmoving. Jack turned and slid back down under cover.

"Damn, that guy is downright handy," Everett said, slamming another thirty-round magazine into his weapon.

Collins looked around and saw Vietnamese Private Tram as he quickly slipped another magazine into the old M-14. He looked around and pointed at Jack and Everett, then moved to another position.

"Yeah, I'd pick him for my kickball team any day," Jack said, as a mortar round landed fifty yards to their front.

"These guys are serious, Jack," Carl said, joining them.

The gallery became deathly silent except for the men firing sporadically from various defensive positions. Soon even these shooters stopped and listened.

"Colonel Collins, I assume I have your attention."

Jack looked over at Carl and raised his brows.

"If it's the cops, I'm going to be seriously pissed off," he said, trying his best to figure out who was speaking through the bullhorn. The voice echoed off the giant cavern walls that housed the buried colony.

"You could have called me on your cell phone if that's all you wanted," Collins yelled, at the same time looking to make sure that Ellenshaw had the others hidden as best he could. Then he silently cursed as he saw the scientists do exactly what he had ordered them not to do—turn and enter the blockhouse once more. "You know, after this we're going to have to get a new director, because I'm going to kill this one!"

Everett turned and saw what Jack was talking about. He cursed as well.

"Colonel, a few well-chosen words and a small exchange, and then we will leave you to your task here. We wish you well in your endeavors."

"What the hell is this?" Everett whispered.

"You have the stage, for the moment at least," Collins called out over the lip of the ancient lava flow.

"We want a few items from that blockhouse, and then we will leave you to do your country's dirty business."

"What could be in there that you would want?"

"Colonel, I have heard of you, and because of your duty in Iraq and Afghanistan you have most assuredly heard of me. I am Azim Quaida."

Jack looked at Everett and shook his head. Carl also knew the name also knew that the man speaking was a formidable commander of men—especially when he didn't care who lived or died.

"I thought you had turned to the money end of your business," Jack called out. "Made crazy new friends in California—good, honest, hardworking church folk."

"Ah, the Reverend Rawlins. He and I had a small falling-out. As did I and an old friend of yours. You can say I saved you the trouble of tracking down and killing James McCabe."

Jack took a deep breath and hoped that Sebastian was utilizing this break to get a fix on the mortar.

"Okay, for that I'm grateful, enough so that if you turn around and leave right now, I promise that we'll finish our business another day. What do you say, Mechanic?"

There was a momentary silence as Jack's insult sank into the Saudi's thoughts.

"Colonel, to show you I have more cards than you do in this game, I have someone who would like to speak to you."

Jack closed his eyes and cursed himself. He knew without thinking what the Mechanic was referring to.

"Jack, if you trade me for anything in this gallery, I'll shoot you myself!"

"Damn it," Collins said. He finally looked up at Everett, who slid down the lava wall next to the colonel as he recognized Alice's voice.

"This is a brave if difficult woman, Colonel. It would be a shame for her to die this day. Even though she is a woman who needs to be beaten on a regular basis, I'm sure she's dear to someone. Come and take this black-hearted woman from my hands."

"That son of a bitch doesn't know the half of it," Jack said, Alice being one of the most difficult women he had ever known. He closed his eyes to think. He partially raised his head and found Tram. He signaled to the sniper by raising his chin in a quick motion. Tram knew immediately what the colonel wanted to know. The small private shook his head, telling Jack that he did not have a shot. Collins turned back.

"The senator, is he alive?" Jack asked, fighting for time on Sebastian's behalf.

There was no answer.

"Damn it, Sebastian, find them," he said beneath his breath.

"Colonel, no more talk. I see your rather large friend, who I recognize from Germany. Tell him to stop or you can collect Mrs. Hamilton at the bottom of this rise."

Jack assumed Sebastian had heard .

"All right, what do you want?"

"Just five of the weapons inside the blockhouse. Then you can have Mrs. Hamilton and we'll leave. That is as simple as it can get, Colonel."

"Deal."

Everett looked at Jack and slowly nodded his head. It was an exchange that was well worth it.

"Good, Colonel, good. Now I am going to send Mrs. Hamilton out in five minutes with a transponder beacon and a tracking locator. If the exchange is interfered with I will have the woman pinpointed by mortar fire. You will not find enough of her to bury." The echo rebounded several times.

"Okay, five minutes. I will be making the exchange."

Suddenly the strange vibration started again. None of them noticed as Collins rose and ran to the blockhouse, followed by Everett and Tram. As they entered, Jack saw the five scientists working frantically around the table.

There was a line connecting the weapon to Europa.

"I'll speak to all of you later about the dangers of not following a field commander's orders."

Niles looked up with sweat running down his face. He fixed Jack with his thick glasses and nodded his head to indicate that he understood. He watched as the colonel removed five of the light weapons from the rack.

"I heard. Get Alice back, Jack, and hopefully we can have you some help soon," Niles said. He bent back over the large tabletop just as Appleby cursed and slammed a pair of needle-nosed pliers against the wall.

"Jack, I don't know if you've noticed, but that damn vibration has started again," Pete said. "Europa says that it's not geological. There's a mechanical pattern."

Collins nodded. His arms full of alien weaponry, he dashed through the door.

As Collins and Everett stepped out from the side of the blockhouse, the earth trembled.

"Okay, what now?" Everett asked.

That was when the roof of the giant cavern opened.

Two copper capsules fell into the center of the long dead colony.

The civil war that began more than 700 million years before was about to conclude.

Garrison Lee stumbled and almost fell as he entered Gallery Two. He heard the detonations of the mortar rounds and knew the men who had taken Alice were somewhere on the high rubble ahead of him. He also knew that the men had spread out in a semicircle and were laying down a withering fire on Jack and his men.

As he tried to catch his breath, Lee felt dizzy and started coughing. He could feel the stickiness of his own blood when he placed his hand over his mouth. He began to feel better after the coughing spell had ended. He removed the old fedora and wiped the sweat from his brow. The Ingram submachine gun was feeling quite a bit heavier than it had only minutes before. As he looked around at the hanging lights in the high-ceilinged gallery, the shooting and explosions finally stopped. He leaned against the rubble and listened, placing his hat back on his head. There was someone speaking through a bullhorn, but try as he might he couldn't catch the words. The echo confused them and bounced them around the chamber.

Lee looked up toward the upper reaches of the rubble and saw that it would be impossible for him to climb. He shook his head in frustration and cursed his failing body. Alice was up on the precipice and there was nothing he could do about it. Garrison checked the thirty-round magazine in the Ingram for the fourth time and made a decision. He placed one boot on the rubble and carefully moved the other next to it. He felt the rubble, formed by an explosion seventy years before, shift under his weight, but still he persisted in moving his right foot up. The rocks and rubble gave way and he fell to his knees. He lay down and tried to catch his breath, finally rolling to one side and placing the Ingram's strap over his shoulder. He rested once more and rolled onto his stomach, then forced his knees up and under him. He felt the sharp stones tear away his skin through his pants, but still he pushed.

He glanced upward with his lone eye and saw shadows moving underneath the high hanging lights. Then he heard the bullhorn again. This spurred him forward. Lee set his mouth in a straight line and cursed his dying body one more time, but still he climbed. For every five steps he managed, he would slip back three, but he had never been as determined in his life to overcome the obstacles ahead to get to Alice. She would not be joining him in that final adventure he knew he was going to take that day.

Garrison Lee dug his heels in the mountain of rubble and climbed.

Jack had just stepped from the bunker when the two large objects fell to the gallery floor. As they struck the excavated floor, he realized at that the vibration and these capsules were connected. They hummed loudly and the sound penetrated his inner ear. As he looked upward toward the ridge of debris, he saw several men running about, confused as to what trick he had possibly arranged.

"Jesus, Jack, look at that!" Everett said loudly, as the first of the copper-colored cylinders popped open along the center line.

"Oh, shit," Collins said. He ran forward with his arms full of the ancient weapons and took cover just as the first snaking legs appeared outside the cylinder.

Sebastian, who was huddled with thirty-five men he had gathered for the assault on the mortar position, also saw the cylinders. He sensed the danger inside. He and his men opened fire on the two objects. As the onslaught of automatic weapons fire started striking the hardened cases, the first mechanical giant uncoiled from its shell and started to lift its powerful body. Sebastian and the men closest to the horrible but amazing sight heard the whir and whine of powerful turbines as they spooled upward toward full power. He saw the five-foot-wide and ten-foot-long solar cells pull free from under the back plate armor and face toward the lighting above. Then, just as quickly as they had appeared, they folded over and vanished into their protective armor. Still the whine of their powerful turbines continued to sound.

"What the hell is this now?" Sebastian said, as he aimed and opened fire at the first mechanical giant in line. He tried to focus his fire on the head and face region, where he thought his rounds would hurt the giant most. The bullets from him and the men alongside him bounced off in a shower of sparks.

The first giant rotated its head in a 360 degree circle. The eyes started glowing bright red, as bullets continued to find their mark against its steel-ribbed torso and head. The beast seemed to focus its attention on the area where Sebastian and his men had taken cover. That was when the giant began to move toward them, shaking the cavern. The second mechanical monstrosity turned and concentrated on the fire coming from the opposite side, where the Japanese, Australian, and Polish soldiers had congregated. The entire gallery was alight with tracers.

As the metal monster charged, Sebastian pulled two hand grenades from his vest. He pulled the pin on one and then on another. He used his thumbs to free the handles from the small, round grenades and threw one and then the other in the path of the fast-moving beast. As the giant came on, it placed a large three-toed foot on top of the first grenade as it rolled to a stop. Instead of ducking, Sebastian watched as it exploded. The leg and knee of the metal giant sprang upward and it fell to the left, landing on its side. After only a moment, the giant sprang back to its undamaged legs and continued forward. The second grenade detonated just to its right as it steadied itself. The explosion sent shrapnel into the torso area and ricocheted off the spinning gears and cogs inside, causing not one inch of damage. If anything, it made the beast charge faster.

A hundred yards away, Jack and Carl watched as the first giant reached Sebastian's position. The beast slammed its giant arm and hand into the mass of men. The mechanical horror raised one hand in the air with one of the German commandos in its grasp as the others fired round after glowing round into the beast. The creature then slammed its free hand into the mass of men and brought up another soldier. It slammed the two men together and tossed them away like they were nothing more than garbage.

"We can't stop them, Jack. We need heavier weapons," Everett said. He rose and fired an entire magazine into the back of the giant. Then he slammed home a second magazine and emptied it into the second charging beast, causing it no more harm than the first.

Jack managed a glance upward at the ridge of rubble and saw the men up there in an exposed position. He saw Alice being pushed to the side as the men moved to take better cover, in case the mechanical wonders turned on them. Jack let the alien weaponry fall from his arms and reached for Everett's M-16. He pulled another magazine from his belt and slammed it home. He had seen an opening and he was willing to risk the chance at evening the odds. He aimed and fired upward toward the ridgeline. He caught ten of the men as they moved toward new positions. They had exposed themselves too much and Collins expertly used a full automatic burst to bring them down. Then he tossed the M-16 back to Everett.

"Stay and cover me," Jack said as he rushed forward in the confusion created by the attack of the machines.

Everett watched Jack sprint forward without seeking cover. He had brought up the M-16 when he saw two of the Mechanic's men pop up only thirty feet from Collins. Before Carl could respond to the threat, several rounds echoed close by his right ear. He flinched and saw the two men fly backward as two expertly placed rounds slammed into their heads and faces. That was when Tram slammed into him from behind and took up a covering position next to him. They both started laying heavy gunfire on the upper reaches of the ridge as Jack started climbing rapidly toward the forty-foot summit. Everett reloaded and saw Jack reach for his shoulder holster as he approached a position where Everett could see several heads pop up and then disappear.

"Damn you, Jack. You've pulled this crap once too many times!" Everett said as he fired a three-round burst in a timed manner and hit one of the heads that had reappeared.

Tram looked to his left and nodded at the former Navy SEAL.

"I have my moments," Carl said, and aimed and fired again.

The Vietnamese private reached out and slapped Everett's arm. He was pointing upward at the position where he saw Jack running. That was when Carl saw why Jack was taking the chance that he was. He had seen earlier what he thought was men changing their cover positions, when in actuality he was seeing men relaying mortar rounds to the soldiers firing them. That was where Jack was heading at full speed. Everett realized that not only could he take out the mortar crew, but he could turn the heavy weapon on the monstrosities that were attacking them. That was their only hope and Jack was out to kill two birds with one stone.

"Can you handle things here? I think the colonel needs help," he called to Tram, who only nodded his head and fired twice more with the M-14.

Everett stood and looked for the briefest of moments as the second mechanical robot reached the far firing line of Japanese, Polish, and Australian soldiers. It was at that moment that the men scattered to create more targets for the beast, as it struck their defensive position. All semblance of a fight between them and the terrorist element had vanished as they took on two nightmares from another time and place. Several men tossed hand grenades over their shoulders as they sprinted ahead of the mechanicians.

Everett turned and sprinted after Jack.

Collins pulled his nine-millimeter and hit two men as they rose to shoot at him. He had caught them by surprise and his bullets struck both in the chest.

As Everett watched, his vision bouncing as bad as his feet over the rough rise of stone, he saw one of the men rise once more and fire at Collins's back. He saw Jack stagger and go down.

"Shit!" Everett said, as a round from Tram struck the badly wounded man and dropped him. But the saving shot had come too late for Jack. Everett saw another man rise up where Collins had disappeared after hitting the rocks. Carl fired from the hips and then several more rounds from Tram struck the terrorist simultaneously, dropping him cold.

Carl saw Jack rise once more, stagger forward and then fall. For Everett, all semblance of reality was vanishing fast as he realized Jack was done for.

Niles rubbed a hand over his balding head. He had just returned from outside, where he had witnessed the new problem they were facing—he had nearly frozen at the site of the mechanical giants that were now chasing, catching, and killing the men defending the gallery. He knew these weren't a technology of Earth origin, so he had to believe they had been left here to either kill the ancient travelers, or they had been left here by those same Visitors, though for what reason Niles didn't know.

Appleby slammed his hand down on the alien weapons in the vise grips. He was frustrated when they couldn't get the coolant tube to open. As he grew more and more frustrated, it was nothing compared to what Pete, Dubois, and Ellenshaw were feeling as they tried desperately to figure out where McCabe and possibly the Germans had failed in making one of the weapons operational.

"Look, I'm telling you based on the damaged weapons we've seen in here that they all overheated, so it must be the liquid hydrogen they were using. Either it was not enough, or our coolant just doesn't work with their technology," Dubois said as he looked angrily at Ellenshaw and Golding.

"I can't believe that. No matter where these beings came from, the liquid nitrogen would still be on their periodic table. It would be just as cold on their world as ours. It's not the coolant but the mineral!" Ellenshaw said forcibly, as Pete nodded his head in agreement.

"You're a freaking cryptozoologist," the MIT professor said to Charlie. He turned and glared at Pete. "And you're a computer expert. I think I know who has a degree of confidence here when it comes to physics, and it's not you two. The coolant is failing!"

"Oh, so we're tossing degrees in everyone's face now," Ellenshaw said as he took a menacing step toward the much smaller Dubois. Pete stepped between the two men and adjusted his glasses.

"May I remind you two that we have men dying out there?"

Charlie nodded and angrily turned away.

"Look, I agree with Charlie here. If you look in the power pack—" Pete held up the large magazine-like power source for the light weapon. "—you can see that McCabe and his scientists, and possibly the Germans also, ground up the mineral, particulate matter and all. Look here. See that? It was so hot that heat turned it to solid carbon. We have to break the mineral down into its base form, separating the energy source." This time Golding held up a small meteorite that had been stored inside a large airtight container. "This strange metal here, see the gold and silverish flecks? We have to break that free from the particulate matter. That way the carbon won't overheat the energy pack, causing the nitrogen not to work. It's our only chance."

"How do you suggest we mill it in time? As you said, we have men dying out there," Dubois countered.

"Oh, for crying out loud!" Ellenshaw said. He snatched the small meteorite from Pete's hand and ran to the worktable. He rummaged through the mess of tools there and found what he was looking for. "You guys at MIT spend too damn much time in the lab. You need to get out more," he said as he brought a hammer high into the air and smashed it down on the meteorite. The small rock shattered. Pete started scrambling on the floor to pick up some of the loose debris. Charlie brought the hammer up again and smashed down with all his strength.

"Okay, I see your point," Dubois said. He too started picking up the metal as it was freed from the rock. "We don't have time to chip away the rest of the particulate."

"It doesn't matter, as long as the percentage of heavy metal is far greater than the percentage of rock. That will allow the nitrogen to cool it better and create the chain reaction. The only problem is, in order to discharge the energy buildup, we have to continuously fire the damn thing or it will blow. That's what we don't have the time to figure out," Ellenshaw said. He grabbed another meteorite and started slamming the hammer into it.

"I think I'd better get out of the lab more often," the MIT professor said.

Niles finally found the access tube for the liquid nitrogen.

"The nitrogen works in two different ways with this weapon," he said. "It's introduced into the power pack as the liquid active agent, and this little induction pump here forces oxygen, or air, into the magazine, thus creating the chain reaction we witnessed on the Moon. Once the buildup is achieved, we only have . . . hell, I don't know how long we have, but we had better target something and shoot, or the damn thing will blow up in our hands."

"I see," Appleby said, finally calming down as the noise of Charlie's hammering echoed inside the blockhouse.

"Or I should say Charlie has only so long to discharge the weapon," Niles finished.

Ellenshaw stopped a hammer blow in midair and looked at Niles with a questioning look on his face.

"Well, you're the one who always wants to shoot something. Here's your chance," Niles said and tossed Pete the empty power magazine.

"Great," Ellenshaw said. He slammed the hammer down one last time, freeing the mineral that would either save them or blow the entire gallery into oblivion.

Either way, the battle for Columbus would soon be coming to an end.

## SHACKLETON CRATER, LUNAR SURFACE

As she bounced into the first room she came to, Sarah saw she had entered an area that had offered the visitors of millions of years before a place to suit up into their environment clothing. There was an airlock, which had been destroyed by the explosion created by the Beatle, and then a large connecting room that looked as if it ran off to connect with labs and other parts of the buried complex. As she watched, a soldier bumped into her. She turned and saw General Kwan as he unloaded a full magazine of bolt-sized kinetic rounds at one of the mechanical giants. She pulled him deeper inside the room with no roof. As she did she saw one of the men, a Chinese soldier, go flying past them more than thirty feet in the air.

Her eyes followed him until he vanished over the exposed roof of the bunker. She kept pulling at Kwan as he reloaded a weapon that was the equivalent of throwing rocks at a tank. Sarah let go for as long as it took to activate her COM system.

"Will, get as many of the men together as you can and get them into the bunker any way possible. Maybe we can find a level here that these things can't squeeze into."

There was no answer for the longest time. She once more took General Kwan by the oxygen pack and pulled him along. She had only gone a few feet when a giant hand crashed down through the strange composite material and crushed the wall nearest them. She looked up as she fell and saw the robot staring down at her and Kwan. They were had. The thing towered over them in the silent vacuum of the Moon's atmosphere. She saw that it had no mouth, no ears, and a head that looked like some kind of buffed or stainless steel. The red eyes were like quartz crystals. It had no numbers or distinguishing marks. The gears inside its body spun, stopped, and spun some more. There were pulsating bladders protected by a series of giant metallic ribs separated by only inches. Even if they had ground-to-air missiles, she didn't know if anything like the BGM-71 TOW system could penetrate the strange alien armor. These things were built to survive, and had done so on this hostile rock for 700 million years. As she tried to get up, the metal beast raised its steel-entwined arm into the air and leaned over the high wall of the first building. Kwan kept firing, aiming for the eyes, as he was thinking that maybe they were some sort of information-gathering device. To Sarah's way of thinking this was right, because robots certainly didn't need eyes for aesthetic purposes. She knew that she and the general were about to be smashed to pieces, but at that moment several dozen kinetic rounds slammed into the steel and threw the robot off balance.

Sarah saw this and pulled on Kwan harder. This time the general didn't need much convincing. They both turned and struggled down a not too wide hallway, one that wasn't accommodating for their bulky suits, and made their way deeper into the alien complex. As she did, she heard Will Mendenhall ordering the survivors of the attack inside from someplace where they had attacked the first robot. Thus far she didn't know the disposition of anyone.

Sarah saw a smaller room off to her right and made for it, closely followed by the general. As Sarah turned she saw through the open roof the robot searching for the small humans who had escaped it. Then something caught its attention and it moved off, smashing the remaining roof off a building further down. As Sarah frantically looked around, trying to find something they could use to fight back with, someone's COM system opened up and she heard a man scream. It was one of her own. She also heard Mendenhall directing fire from somewhere. Sarah had never felt so helpless in her life. The general turned and faced her. Inside his helmet she could see a determined look on his face.

"We have to get to the landing vehicles and leave the Moon. We can do no good here. The mission is over."

Sarah looked at him with shock—*All of this to turn and run?* she thought.

"We have to bring something back," she protested.

"Listen to me. We have the coordinates for the downed ship. That's more than we ever hoped to get. That is heavy weaponry, Lieutenant. We have found what we came for, but if we don't get off the Moon it will be for nothing. We cannot fight these things. We don't have the firepower."

Sarah saw the general's point. If they remained, no one would ever know about the warship in the dust, and no one would know what they needed to fight these things.

"Okay, I'll agree that we have to get off the moon, but how the hell are we going to get past these things?" she countered.

"That, Lieutenant McIntire, is the problem we face."

"How far is your LEM?" she asked. She felt a sharp vibration as one of the two creatures struck somewhere close by. As she ducked, she saw several of the boltlike rounds rip into the wall opposite of their position. She knew then that they still had men close by.

"That is what I was thinking. Our lander is actually closer, as you Americans are fond of saying, as the crow flies. If we follow the valley just to the left of Shackleton, on the east side, we would have cover all the way to *Magnificent Dragon*. If I could get half of the men into that small valley and follow the terrain, not exposing ourselves to these creatures, we may make it all the way to our LEM. If we don't use the radio, we have a chance; I don't think they can track us without the use of electronic signals."

"I was thinking the same thing. I believe that's how they hunt. They were probably sent here seeking out human life to destroy. As soon as Mendenhall used his radio rather than his suit-to-suit COM, one of those things attacked."

"Well, that's one theory, and for now I'll accept it, Lieutenant. So now the question is, how do we communicate?"

"Mendenhall to McIntire, where are you?" the voice came over the radio.

Sarah hit her COM switch. "We're in the first set of buildings on the west side. We have a—" Sarah realized too late that she was doing exactly what she had said they couldn't do. Instead of the line-of-sight transmission of a suit-to-suit call, Will had used his radio COM system to contact her. The next sound she heard coming through Will's system was him shooting and she looked up just as hundreds of kinetic rounds flew upward from somewhere to her right.

"Damn!" the general said. "Listen, to all who can hear my voice," he said, taking a chance on using the radio. "Get to the center of this complex. We'll meet there. Now move!"

Kwan angled out of the small room and chanced the hallway that had no roof. Sarah followed and saw one of the metal monsters as it disappeared over the high wall of the building they were in.

"Look!" Sarah said, hitting Kwan of the back. They both stopped, one running into the other as they saw the ramp leading down. At that moment, several men appeared ahead of her. She saw a white-colored NASA suit in the lead. It was Mendenhall and he had several American, European, and Chinese troops with them.

"Look out," Kwan shouted, as a giant three-fingered hand smashed through the wall and knocked Will over. Instead of grabbing Will it grabbed the next man in line. Sarah's eyes widened as she recognized Sergeant Demarest, one of the older Green Berets on the mission. He was lifted out of the bunker and they all watched helplessly as Demarest and the arm vanished. Sarah thanked God the sergeant's COM system was off.

Kwan waved the men ahead of him, indicating that they should go forward down the large ramp that angled downward at a 30 degree angle. He just hoped there were no more nasty surprises waiting for them at the bottom. As the men went, Sarah and the general followed, not knowing if they had found a covered haven beneath the bunker or if they had just found another way to hell.

As they continued heading down into the bowels of the ancient complex, Sarah placed her hand on the strange plasticlike wall. She stopped and felt the movement of the monstrosities above. It felt as though they were tearing the bunker system apart—perhaps trying to dig them out of the rat hole they could be heading into.

"You feel it too, yes?"

Sarah looked up and saw the general looking at her. He had stopped next to her, along with the comforting face of Will Mendenhall.

"They'll dig and dig until they find us. It's like their programming won't allow them to do anything else," she said as she lowered her gloved hand from the wall.

"I'll tell you, whoever built them crazy bastards would have to be related to us somehow, because only our species could ever be so brutal," Mendenhall said, shaking his head inside his helmet.

"I agree, Lieutenant Mendenhall," Kwan said. "But I may venture to add, as long as it was beings like us that built them, it can also be counted on that those same beings can destroy them."

"Unless, like us, they were just dumbass sons-a-bitches," Will countered.

Kwan smiled, continuing down the ramp, following what was left of the three Moon expeditions.

"There again, you may have a point."

As the three fell into line, the helmet lights bounced off of posters, possibly of rules and regulations, in the now familiar alien script. As Sarah looked, the posters began to look like U.S. Army bulletins on the do's and don'ts of surviving in a hostile environment. There were depictions of space-suited men placing a finger to their helmets in a shushing gesture, possibly meaning loose lips sink ships. There were what looked like propaganda scenes on some of them, with flags, and even one that resembled the old World War I Uncle Sam pointing at the reader of the poster, as if saying, "I want you!"

"I'm getting the feeling these people just blew themselves straight to hell," Will said as he tried to look more closely at one of the propaganda posters.

"Look at this one," Sarah said.

Kwan and Will looked at what she was studying as the vibration from above them increased.

On a large and half-torn poster, their helmet lights revealed one very large moon, with what looked like transport ships leaving its surface. Below that was a picture of the mineral.

"Look familiar?" Sarah said, tapping the mineral.

"Looks like they may have been mining it," Kwan said. "Is that our Moon?"

Sarah reached out and pushed the ripped corner back into place. As she did, all of their eyes widened. They saw a much smaller moon in the background of the first. Beside it was the Earth or at least it looked like the Earth. The continents weren't in the right places.

"What the hell is this?" Mendenhall asked.

"My God, they were mining the mineral," Sarah said, "but not from this moon. There was another moon that's no longer there." She reached out and slid up the other corner of the poster. That was when they saw it—another world in the far distance. This one had deep green oceans and red-colored continents.

"What planet is that?" Kwan asked.

"I don't know," Sarah said. "But our hope of finding a source of the mineral on the Moon just went right out the window."

"All the more reason to leave this place as soon as we are able to escape our enemies—which are growing closer as we speak," Kwan said. He turned and started down the ramp once more.

Sarah looked at Will and shook her head and then stepped into line with the general.

Mendenhall wanted to curse as he slapped at the reproduced depiction of the mined moon Ophillias.

"I don't like this moon very much," he said. Then she looked at the second, much larger moon. "Or that one either."

The men ahead had halted. Sarah looked at the altimeter readout on her right sleeve. The small computer screen told her they had traveled a distance of close to a half a mile in a downward attitude. She was starting to think they would find nothing but a basement.

"General, would you and Lieutenant McIntire come up here, please?"

Sarah thought she recognized the voice of Sergeant Stanley Sampson, one of her Green Berets, as she and Kwan, followed by Mendenhall, stepped up to the first man in line. It was Sampson, and he just pointed into a room that held a number of tables along with what looked like a cafeteria serving line.

"Chow's on," the sergeant said, and stepped aside to allow Kwan, Sarah, and Mendenhall to go through first.

"I don't think we want to eat here, Sergeant," Sarah said as her light picked up a pair of bodies in the far corner of the room. There were two large cups sitting in front of a mummified man and woman. They were holding hands across the table and their missing eyes seemed to be locked on each other.

"They must have come down here to die," Sarah said, unable to remove her eyes from the long lost couple.

"Die of what?" Mendenhall said. The couple was having the opposite effect on him as on Sarah.

General Kwan stepped forward and reached for something. Sarah flinched, hoping he wasn't going to disturb the couple. The woman had red hair and the man black. Their hands may have been locked together for millions upon millions of years, and Sarah felt they had no right to disturb their remains. Instead, Kwan turned and tossed a small object to Sarah, who had plenty of time to catch it in the nonatmosphere. She looked at the bottle and then handed it off to Will. It was empty, but all three of their imaginations could figure out that the couple had long ago taken a way out that was more to their own choosing. Sarah wondered how they could have become so desperate.

"Sir, we found something down here," a Frenchman said as he scrambled into the doorway.

As Sarah turned, Will handed her the small bottle and fixed his eyes in the same direction as hers. The unspoken communication was such that they both knew they didn't want to go out that way, or any other way that involved dying on the Moon. Sarah placed a gloved hand on Will's shoulder and then moved away back to the long ramp outside. She followed the rest of the men and that was when she saw that they had come to the end of the wide ramp. There was a double set of doors and she followed the men through them. As she stood there, Sarah couldn't believe her eyes. Lined up as though at an Army motor pool were vehicles—eight of them, ranging from small dune-buggy-type cars to three large transports with rounded bubbled cabs. All the vehicles had oversized tires; two of them were tracked. Several also had large cranes and derricks attached. They were facing toward what she thought was a dead end, but when she examined it closer she saw that it was actually a fifty-foot-wide roll-up door, sealed against the harsh external environment.

"Look at this," one of the ESA men said, tapping a large glass or plastic container. Inside the vessel they saw about a hundred gallons of frozen water. There was thick piping running from the tank into a large pump, and then through the metal flooring into the lunar surface. The ancient lunar explorers had discovered the very thing NASA was looking for in Shackleton Crater—water. There must be an underground supply of ice. Somehow the visitors had found a way to melt it and pump it to the surface.

"Now this is what I call a neighborhood garage—cars, water, and tools. Now all we need are two-week-old hot dogs, overpriced gas, and a Big Gulp machine." Will smiled and walked over to the first dune-buggy-type vehicle and looked in its interior at the unfamiliar gears and levers.

Sarah stepped up behind Will and tapped him on the shoulder as she looked at the strange shifters and dials.

"Well, I hope you can drive a stick and drink your Big Gulp at the same time, Mr. Wizard."

General Kwan turned away from examining the interior of one of the heavier tracked vehicles as some of the men chuckled, a very strange sound considering their predicament.

"Excuse me, but what is this Big Gulp you speak of?"


GALLERY NUMBER TWO,
MÜELLER AND SANTIAGO MINING CONCERN,
100 MILES EAST OF QUITO

Tram was actually zigzagging his way upward to the spot where Collins had fallen a few steps ahead of Everett. Down below, the giant robots were starting to root out the soldiers faster by the minute. They were tearing into solid rock and ancient lava to get at their hiding places. The noise of the attack along with the wiring and whine of the transformers and turbines echoed loudly in the large gallery. The screams and gunshots from their men were even louder.

Tram made it to the spot where Jack had been hit and gone down. As both men ducked and took cover, they were stunned to see that Jack wasn't there. Everett looked around the area and placed his hand on a darkened spot near the rock wall. He lifted his hand and saw that it was blood.

"Damn it, Jack, where the hell did you go?" Carl asked as three explosions rocked the gallery below. As he looked up he saw that instead of the terrorists assisting the soldiers below by firing on the metal monstrosities, they were actually firing into the retreating soldiers.

"Sons of bitches," Everett said, as he vaulted over Tram and continued climbing. The Vietnamese private waited a split second and then went in another direction.

Everett knew Jack was heading for the mortar pit. The problem was that they didn't exactly know where it was on the high wall overlooking the gallery below. They hadn't been shot at yet, so after Jack was hit they must have detoured their firing to another spot.

Everett knew that they and their men below were running desperately short of time.

---

The Mechanic made sure Alice was secure on the rocky incline and he raised his radio. A few minutes before he had seen several men run headlong into the blockhouse three hundred yards away.

"Place three rounds of HE into that blockhouse. There are men holing up in there."

The Mechanic was getting ready to turn and face Alice once more when he saw a sight that froze him to the spot. There was a man approaching the mortar pit from above. He raised his radio, but knew the warning would come too late. He sent forward a squad of men, ordering them to kill that man and make sure they didn't damage the mortar. He cursed himself for underestimating this American colonel.

He reached down and pulled Alice to her feet. For her part, she didn't resist or try to twist away. The Mechanic saw the knowing smile on her face.

"Having problems down below?" she asked. "The colonel can be rather a pain in the ass, can't he?"

The Mechanic shook Alice by the arm, making her wince but not cry out.

"The rest of you, we will change our position in case this American gets lucky. I want ten of you to get to the blockhouse by any means and kill everyone inside. Then bring me back the weapons. We will meet you at the gallery that leads to the underground river. Hurry, our transport is waiting." He looked down at Alice. "I hope you can swim, old one. If not, you will remain with your friends forever in this underground hell."

"Those metal monsters down there have more honor than you," Alice said as she was pulled along the ridge.

"Then you will not mind spending your last minutes with them."


Jack saw the three ammunition runners, two mortar men, and three guards—eight men altogether. He ducked his head back below the rocks where he had hidden himself. He checked his ammunition clip. He had seven nine-millimeter rounds. He then removed his KA-BAR knife from its sheath. He winced as he felt the broken rib where the bullet had lodged. He used his wrist to check the wound and knew he was bleeding heavily. He looked up and saw the two metal giants tearing into the hiding place where Sebastian had managed to lead most of the men.

Collins knew he was slowly bleeding to death, as the blood was flowing far too quickly from a wound he hadn't initially thought that serious. He knew the bullet must have clipped an artery. He grimaced at his bad luck at not seeing the sniper guarding the mortar pit before it was too late. He shot the man who had shot him, but only after he had run headlong into his position, a move that had taken them both by surprise.

As he took the rocks one loose step at a time, another hollow thump sounded from below. Jack stopped and saw the mortar round arc into the cavern's interior, where it nearly clipped the stalactites far above and then sailed downward. It landed mere feet from Sebastian's entrenched troops. He even saw the first massive robot recoil from the explosion. Then, as if nothing had happened, the machine started digging, tossing large stones that appeared to weigh in excess of three tons out of its way. It recommenced pulling and prying at the stone and the long dead lava flow, trying to get at the troops.

"By God, that's enough," Jack hissed, and then jumped the last ten feet, landing in the mortar pit that had been dug into the rubble on the side of the gallery wall.

In the split second before he hit the side of the gallery, Jack shot the man, who had just dropped a mortar round into the large tube.

Collins had hit too hard. He momentarily lost sight of the mortar crew as he slammed into the rocks and then fell onto his chest and face. He hurriedly brought up his nine-millimeter and fired at the man adjusting the sighting of the mortar tube. The bullet caught the man in the side, spinning him into the rock wall. Jack knew he had slowed his reactions down with a hastily planned jump from above. He tried to struggle into some semblance of a firing position. A bullet clipped his left arm just above the elbow and another missed his head by a mere inch. He brought the nine-millimeter around and shot the first thing he saw. It just happened to be the two men carrying the M224 sixty-millimeter lightweight mortar rounds to the pit from a place where they had stored cases of projectiles. The first bullet hit the lead man in the chest, knocking him back into the second. Both of them dropped the rounds they were carrying. Jack aimed quickly and shot the second man as he hit the rock wall beside him. Both had been taken off guard by Jack's makeshift assault.

Collins had no time to catch his breath. He felt a presence behind him. It was one of the pit guards and spun at the last moment, bringing the gun up. He was far too late, as the man anticipated his move and slammed the barrel of his AK-47 against Jack's wrist, breaking the bone and spinning Collins to his right. As he spun, he brought the knife in his left hand to bear and caught the terrorist by surprise just as he thought he had caught the American. The knife sliced cleanly through the man's throat, forcing his hands up. As Jack arrested the momentum of the blow to his wrist, he recovered quickly, before the dying man could get a lucky shot off out of reflex. He thrust with the knife one last time and caught the man before he could figure out that he had been killed. The Russian-made weapon fell to the rocky path the man had used. Jack slammed into the wall and turned, thinking he might catch his breath, only to see the ten men that the Mechanic had dispatched coming down the rock incline directly toward the pit.

As Jack went on both of his knees to retrieve the dropped nine-millimeter, he had to use his left hand for the remaining six bullets. That was when he saw the third ammunition carrier, followed by the last two guards. He fired with his shaky left hand and hit the most dangerous targets, the two guards, first. One of the bullets hit the lead guard in the face, slamming him against the ammunition carrier. The second bullet hit the ammunition carrier by mistake, allowing the trailing guard to take aim at the surprise attack by Collins. The guard saw his chance and pressed the trigger.

Jack flinched as he realized he had made a mistake. He should have been more deliberate in his aiming. He waited. The bullet never came. The man just stood there, unmoving. Then he saw the terrorist slowly fall forward. Jack shook his head as he saw Carl Everett standing behind the man with his own knife. He had dropped down right behind the trailing man and killed him as he aimed his weapon.

"It took you long enough," Jack said, then went down to both knees.

Everett took two long strides forward and lifted Collins to his feet.

"Yeah, well, if I had a commanding officer who explained a plan before he acted on it, I would have been here sooner." Everett helped Jack to a small rock and set him down. Collins slapped at his hands and pushed them away. He pointed.

"More men coming," he said, as he grew light-headed.

Everett pulled Jack's shirt open, tearing free the buttons as he tried to see how bad the wound was. He cursed when he saw how fast the blood was flowing.

"Don't worry about them. We have to get this blood stopped."

Collins again tried to push Everett's hands away. He looked up at the ten men, who were sliding and stopping and then sliding again as they tried to get close enough to kill them both. That was when Jack realized that the men weren't slipping and sliding down the hill—they were falling and scrambling for cover. Rounds were fired from somewhere, bringing the men down. One at a time they were hit and then slid down the incline, never to move once they came to rest. He shook his head as the last four men turned on their heels and started to run back the way they had come. Then he saw dust and dirt fly from the men's backs, as bullet after bullet hit their mark, quickly ending their retreat.

"Tram again," Jack said as he finally let Carl work on him.

Everett tore his own shirt at the bottom and created a makeshift pressure bandage. He tied it as tightly as he could, sending a shockwave of agony through Jack's body. He knotted it off.

"Yeah, at first I thought I left the little bastard behind, but then I realized that he had taken a liking to you and figured he would show up sooner or later. Now we have to get you to a medic. This bandage won't hold."

"No, get that tube adjusted. We have six rounds of HE right here. We have to get those things away from Sebastian and the men."

Everett knew that Jack was right. He took a quick look down below just as the first of the two robots dug a man out of his hiding place and tossed him into the air like he was so much refuse. The man hit the floor and the second mechanical killer raised a large steel foot, bringing it down on the Polish soldier. Everett nodded his head in anger. "Right," he said, helping Jack back to the mortar tube.

He put Jack down and reached for a round from the hands of the nearest dead man. That was when he felt hands shove him away from the large caliber round. He looked up and saw Tram. He laid down his M-14 and gestured for Everett to do the aiming of the mortar. The Vietnamese reached down and hefted the first round into his arms, then approached the tube.

"Handy fella, isn't he?" Jack hissed as he held his side. Before Carl could nod he saw blood oozing out between Collins's fingers. As he bent to adjust the tube, he saw Jack try to stand.

"Sit down, Jack. You're bleeding to death!"

"Have . . . to get . . . Alice," Collins said, as his head started to spin.

"Don't worry about Alice. That asshole's not going to hurt her as long as he has a chance of using her. Now stay down or I'll tie you up!"

Tram brought the round to the tube as Everett made the last adjustment. He turned and saw that Jack wasn't going anywhere. He had fallen back to the floor, cursing his weakening body.

"Adjusting for HE, ready?" He looked at Tram.

The Vietnamese held the round poised above the tube.

"Drop!"

Tram allowed the round to slide through his fingers and into the tube. He ducked away as the high explosive round thumped into the firing pin at the tube's base. With a loud *whump*, the round left the tube. Carl watched and waited, hoping he had remembered how to adjust the sighting correctly.

The round flew out and up. The whistle of the flight could be heard over the destructive digging of the mechanical assassins below. Everett and Tram watched as their quickly adjusted attempt struck just behind the second robot. The round tore a massive chunk out of the gallery floor and the robot fell backward, flailing its giant arms as it tried to regain balance. It disappeared in the flash and debris from the explosion.

"Yes!" Everett said, as he slapped Tram on the shoulder. The Vietnamese didn't return the congratulations but only pointed.

The robot was starting to get up from the spot where the floor had given way to the detonation of the mortar round. First it went to its hands and knees, and then it regained its footing and stood. It looked around as if it knew it had been sucker-punched.

Everett gestured for Tram to reload.

The small private turned and went for another round as Carl adjusted the angle again. Tram held the second round over the tube's aperture.

"Drop!"

The round *whump*ed out of the tube and went on its way. The whistle told Everett that this one would be right on. The round caught the second robot squarely in the chest as it finally regained its footing after the first blast. The HE round detonated and blew the robot backward into the first. They both went down hard.

As suddenly as the two hit the rocky ground, they were back up again.

"This isn't working, Jack. I don't know what these things are made of, but we're not harming them. That's a tough battle chassis."

Jack strained to see over the rocks that were protecting their position. As he did so he saw the first robot stand up and start looking around. Then he saw the strangest thing imaginable. Lasers protruded out of a cavity in its head and began rotating. They seemed to lock on to something, expanding into something that resembled the spokes of a wheel. Then the rotation ceased and the single green laser began tracking the heated arc of the expended round. Jack could actually see the laser start to whip back and forth, creating a haze of light that tracked the arc of the round from its origin.

"Oh, oh," Jack said, as Everett saw the same thing. He didn't hesitate.

"Drop!"

Another round flew from the tube and arced toward the two robots. The round landed right on top of the second mechanical beast and exploded between its neck and shoulder. The force of the blast knocked the robot from its feet and sent the second machine face forward, where it smashed into the hiding places of their soldiers. But even through the smoke and debris they saw both of them rise out of the smoke and fix their positions high up on the gallery wall. They both started forward at the same moment after locking in on the arc of the second round.

"I think we may have a problem," Everett said. He watched far below as the robots not only started coming at them, but began running up the slope, making loud banging noises as their steel feet came into contact with each step. Everett raised his radio.

"Sebastian, get our people out of there!"

Carl didn't wait for a response. He let the radio slip from his hands and reached for Jack as the robots hit the slope of the gallery wall running. He figured they had two minutes left.

"Come on, Jack. Time to skedaddle," he said as he lifted Collins up.

"Put me down and get the hell out of here. Get Alice if you can," he hissed.

"Ain't happenin' this time and there's not a whole lot you can do about it. We'll get Alice together."

With the help of Tram, they lifted Jack up and started to scramble up the slope. They felt the vibrations of the robots as they used both arms and legs to scrabble up the slope. They were focused on one thing, the area that had attacked them. Carl knew they would be caught in about a minute.

"Sit me down," Jack said through clenched teeth as a thunder of small arms fire erupted from below. "That damn Sebastian follows orders and so will you."

Down below the hundred remaining men opened fire on the advancing robots. Their fire was accurate, but it was like watching pebbles bounce off tank armor. The robots paid the men below no mind as they advanced on the more serious threat of the mortar.

Everett turned to Tram.

"Get out of here, son. You've done real well today—now it's time for you to go."

Tram looked at Everett as if he had gone mad. Instead of replying, he reached behind him and unslung the M-14. With his eyes still locked on the captain, he inserted a twenty-round magazine into the old rifle. With deliberate slowness, he raised the M-14 sniper rifle and started firing slowly and deliberately at the first robot in line. The mechanical menace was only fifty yards away.

"Jack, I don't think these men respect our rank," Everett said. He kneeled beside Jack and waited.

"That's what you get when you set an example like that. By the way," Jack hissed, "you're fired, Mr. Everett."

"That's a nice reward for trying to save you."

"That's the reward for not saving me."

Everett turned back and his smile was brief as he saw the lead robot nearing their fragile targets. He watched as the first stepped onto the mortar tube, crushing it like it was a straw, and then continued on up the rocky slope to the real threat—the men who had used the weapon.

Everett reached out and removed his nine-millimeter from its holster. He raised it and fired.

The flash of the light made everyone in the gallery look away. The momentary brilliance of the blue light was followed by a loud buzz, as if a thousand saws had bitten into the same piece of wood at the same moment. There was a sudden smell of ozone as a beam of light reached out and hit the leading robot in the left leg just as it was seeking purchase against the slippery slope of the incline. Then another flash of light struck the robot as it slipped partially backward from its original position. Everett just stared at the barrel of his nine-millimeter, which was when he saw what was happening below at the bunkhouse. Appleby, Pete, Niles, Dubois, and Charlie Ellenshaw were standing and pointing up toward their position. Ellenshaw was aiming one of the alien weapons from the rack. As Everett watched, he fired on the trailing robot. The beam sliced both of its legs off and Everett saw it fall. Then he smiled as he saw Ellenshaw jumping up and down and pointing at his perfect shot. The others were jumping also, slapping Ellenshaw on the back.

"You're not going to believe this one, Jack," he said.

Collins wasn't going to answer. He had closed his eyes and that was when Everett saw that the blood had soaked the bandage. He grabbed Jack in his arms, and with Tram leading the way didn't wait for Ellenshaw and the others to stop their firing. As the laser weapon discharged again, Everett smelled the molten steel of the monsters as the intense heat melted their huge metallic frames. The thick blue beam arced out and sliced the arms off the first as it tried to right itself. Then another shot creased the giant's head, separating it from the rest of the body. Everett heard the turbine inside its massive chest start to run down.

Another shot took the second creature out as cleanly as the first. Then Charlie turned the weapon on the men the Mechanic had sent down the slope toward the blockhouse. The single shot brought them all down, most of them in pieces. As Everett, Tram, and Jack neared the bottom of the sloping gallery wall, there was a burst of light and the sound of a small explosion. When they hit the bottom, Carl saw Sebastian and his men emerge from positions where they had been firing on the metal monsters. They looked as though they were in shock. Carl looked over at the scientists as they finished rolling Charlie Ellenshaw around on the gallery floor in an attempt to smother the fire that had engulfed him after the last shot. There were shouts of anger and happiness coming from the group as Ellenshaw sat up and looked around, the remains of the alien weapon in his hands. His long, stringy, white hair was singed, a mess of electrostatic complications as he sat on his butt, not really sure what had happened to him. Carl approached the men at the same moment Sebastian and his troops arrived.

"What happened?" Everett asked, as two medics started looking Jack over.

"I told him that the mineral was still too unrefined, but Wild Bill here had to keep pressing his luck," Niles said as he walked over and looked at Collins. "Jesus, get him inside." The medics tried to pry Jack away from Everett. Collins reached out and grabbed Carl, anchoring himself.

"Alice," he said, as he was finally pulled away.

"Now we go and get her, Jack." Everett watched them take Collins inside and then turned to Sebastian and Tram. "We have one more thing to do."

The three men sprinted back up the slope, toward a showdown with the man who was holding their friend hostage.

The Mechanic ordered the last of his men to hold off the advancing troops, who were led by the large commando he had seen in Germany. He had witnessed the power of the alien technology and knew he had to secure at least one of the weapons for reverse-engineering, to use in the great Jihad against the unbelievers.

He pushed Alice Hamilton toward one of his men and ordered him to guard her, as they still had need for her services. Then he wrote out a note in English requesting a meeting with Colonel Collins. He shoved it into the man's hand and pushed him in the direction of the Americans. With a glance down at the shattered scene below, the Mechanic could see the devastation wrought by the alien weaponry, even as he remained stunned at the destructive power of the giant robotic monsters. In a span of five seconds the tables had been turned by just one of the weapons. He nodded his head—yes, he thought, the weapon was truly a gift from Allah to the true believers. McCabe and Rawlins had been such fools thinking they could just sell off the magnificent gift from the heavens.

———

Everett was moving at a full run toward the spot where he thought the Mechanic had last been. Sebastian and Tram were having a difficult time keeping up with the large Navy SEAL as he bounded up and over rocks to reach the top of the slope.

As he approached the Mechanic's last known whereabouts, he saw movement ahead. He steeled himself behind a large rock outcropping and waved Sebastian and Tram to a stop. Ahead he saw one of the Mechanic's men moving slowly and cautiously down the slope. Everett stood and pointed his nine-millimeter at him. The shadows cast by the lighting from above showed that the man didn't fear the death that was facing him. Everett had seen this many times before in the men he had faced during the Gulf War and after. A true believer. The man had a rifle, but it was slung over one shoulder. Then he saw the man raise his left hand into the air. With the other he held something out toward Everett. Carl stepped forward, as did Sebastian and Tram. Everett opened the folded note and read.

"Trade, one Alice Hamilton for one alien weapon," he read aloud.

Sebastian stared at the man who had delivered the ultimatum. The man glared at the three men with contempt etched across his harsh features.

"What are your orders for after you deliver this?" Everett asked.

"To return with an answer," the man said with vehemence coloring his broken English.

Everett raised his nine-millimeter and shot the man in the head. He dropped like a weighted bag onto the rocks.

"I like the way you negotiate, Captain," Sebastian said as he kicked the terrorist over with his boot.

"The conversation sort of dried up. Besides, we don't reward people who kidnap friends of ours." He looked over at Sebastian and then at Tram. "Do we, Private?"

Tram only nodded and gestured upward with his hand. Everett nodded back, then turned and ran, retracing the dead man's steps.

Carl, Sebastian, and Tram had gone about a hundred yards when they saw the top of the ridge and the end of the gallery. Everett smelled water and suspected the Mechanic had gained access to the gallery from the very place he and the others had escaped two weeks before. He knew that if they didn't stop the Mechanic here and now, no one else would stop him. They had no men covering this access point to the mines. The Mechanic would escape justice for the crimes he had committed. He decided to take his chance now and stop him.

"By all means, keep coming forward," a voice said from above.

Carl stopped and Sebastian almost ran into him. Tram was nowhere in sight.

"I want the German to turn back down the slope and be back here in five minutes with two of the weapons from the blockhouse. If he has not made it back by that time, your Mrs. Hamilton will see Paradise this day."

Everett saw the Mechanic as he looked out from behind a wall of stone over the small alcove leading to the underground river. Then he saw a line of about twenty men as they watched from a place of concealment. He took no shots at any of them. Their only hope was Tram and his sniper rifle.

"Deal. Let Mrs. Hamilton go and I will honor Colonel Collins's word to you," Carl said, hoping to buy Tram time.

He heard several shouts followed automatic weapons fire on the trail above them. As Carl ducked back into the rocks he heard the familiar sound of Tram's M-14 opening up. Everett grimaced and cursed, knowing that Tram had been discovered. The M-14 was silenced as the small private realized his one shot at surprise had been lost.

"You astound me in your arrogance, Captain. Now just to be clear as to my intent, I will have the man who thought he could outflank me shot."

He heard commands given and then more automatic fire erupted from above. As Carl swung around, he and Sebastian saw the Vietnamese private fall from the outcropping he had been hiding behind. They watched as his body hit the rocks ten feet below. Everett closed his eyes and wondered how many people would have to die over this.

"I am waiting, Captain. You have lost your best asset. Everyone else has to come up here facing entrenched positions—he was your last hope for diversion."

Just as Everett was about to acquiesce to the command, another long burst of automatic weapons fire opened up from above. But this time it wasn't directed at them or anyone below. It was coming from the Mechanic's left. The rounds hit his men with deadly accuracy and dropped them like turkeys in a line. The Mechanic's eyes widened and he pulled Alice in front of him as the last two men dropped at his feet. He had no idea how his men could have been outflanked. The hundred soldiers far below in the gallery couldn't have come up the slope without being discovered. He placed a gun to Alice's head. She didn't fight. She knew all along who it was that lay in ambush, waiting for the terrorist. It was someone the Mechanic could never outthink, and someone Alice had known would be there from the moment she was taken.

As they both watched the trail ahead of them, Garrison Lee stepped out of the shadows. His Ingram submachine gun was still smoking as he stood his ground in front of the Mechanic. Alice could see the spark of life in the old man's one good eye. The other, covered with the eye patch, was just below the old battered fedora. The senator said nothing as he took in the scene before him. Alice could see the sweat running down Lee's face.

"You are the dead man I saw in the tent," the Mechanic said. He tightened his grip on Alice.

"I knew you would come for me, you stubborn old bastard." Alice looked at the man she had loved for well over seventy years.

"You didn't think I would miss this, did you, old girl?" Lee looked at the

Ingram in his hands and saw that the bolt was locked back, meaning the gun was empty. He raised his eyes and then tossed the weapon away.

"Raise your hands, old man," the Mechanic said, pointing his automatic in Lee's direction.

Instead of complying, Lee slowly sat down on a large rock. He removed his hat and wiped sweat from his brow.

"Will you excuse me if I tell you to go to hell?" Garrison said. He leaned over and tried to catch his breath. "It took everything I had to get here and see this young lady once more. Sorry, old girl, but that's all I had."

Alice felt the sting of warm tears clouding her eyes.

"It was more than enough, Garrison. I love you for trying so hard. I knew you would."

Lee just chuckled as he tried to straighten up.

"She will be the last thing you do see, old man."

Lee finally looked up at the man who held the woman he loved.

"Young man," he said. He brought the old fedora up to knee level. "Better men than you have been saying that for many years. I find you and your kind far more despicable than you will ever know." Lee took a deep breath, and knew by the sound that he had ruptured something deep in his chest. He continued walking anyway, to give Everett more time to get there in case he faltered. "You take what is good in something and twist it with your love of killing, when you know deep down inside that the way of murder is not the true way. I find you most distasteful."

"Then I will show you mercy and relieve you of your life and your concerns for my ways. And then I will blow this woman's brains all over your dead body when I am finished."

"You're finished right now," Lee said as his fedora exploded. The 45 automatic Lee had used in the war fired twice. He hoped Everett was prepared to move. The first bullet hit the Mechanic in the shoulder, barely missing Alice's head. The impact allowed Alice to twist away as the second bullet hit the Mechanic's right forearm, sending his gun hand away from her.

The Mechanic, shocked, heard for only a moment the shots coming from behind him as four nine-millimeter bullets slammed into the back of his head, throwing him forward onto the trail. Everett ran up with Sebastian close behind.

As Alice ran toward a sitting Garrison Lee, she saw him toss the ruined fedora away and then stare at her as she came to him and took his large, thin frame into her arms. She collapsed against him and he held her.

"I ruined my damn hat," he said, as he placed his arms around her for the first time with anyone watching. He squeezed her as she cried. "There, there, knock it off. You'll embarrass us in front of the German."

As Everett and Sebastian took in the scene in front of them, they failed to notice a man that Lee had only grazed rise to his feet and take aim at Alice and Lee. Carl, unable to react in time, shouted loudly in fear and frustration as the terrorist aimed. Suddenly, a single shot echoed loudly in the now still gallery. The terrorist spun away and fell down the slope, dead.

"I'll be damned," Sebastian said.

A hundred yards down the slope he and Everett could see Tram, bloodied and dirty from his fall and with more than one bullet in his body, lower the pistol he had used and then, exhausted, turn and sit down.

"I guess he can shoot anything," Sebastian said. He looked at Everett. "I'll flip a coin with you to see who gets to take him home."

Everett smiled and then moved off to tend to Lee. "You'll have to ask Jack. I think he's already claimed him."

Lee held Alice. They both were content. Alice could feel Lee's heart through his shirt and knew it was fighting a losing battle. She finally looked up as she noticed Everett standing over them.

"I think your hat's had it, Senator," Everett said, and reached down and pulled Alice to her feet.

"Funny, that was the one thing I was going to give you in my will," Lee said as he tried but failed to look up at Carl.

"We have medics on the way," he said as he held Alice. "They'll take a look at you, sir."

"They'll look, but that's all they'll do. How is Jack?"

Everett's silence was enough for Garrison Lee.

Alice turned and watched as Lee lay back against the large rock. With his good eye he fixed her with that look that said everything without his having to say a word. She pulled away from Everett and went to Garrison. She sat with him for a while.

The battle for Columbus was over—at least on Earth.

# 18

SHACKLETON CRATER,
LUNAR SURFACE

"Look, all we have to do is get these vehicles into the sunlight," Sarah said as they examined the large solar panels on the tops of all the vehicles. "These damn things look like they'll run almost immediately without a charge once the light hits them."

Kwan was looking at the large roll-up gate that separated the storage area from the outside environment. He shook his head inside his helmet as he turned to face the others.

"That is just one of the problems facing us, Lieutenant. I fear once this gate is open we'll be faced with the task of getting at least two of these vehicles up the slope of the crater—an impossible task for so few men without tackle and block."

Sarah slammed her hand down on the smaller of the vehicles. "We're not getting any breaks here," she said.

"I see no point in arguing," Mendenhall said, looking for a release point on the large steel gate. "We have to use this gate for our escape, anyway. Let's get it open and make a run for it. I'd rather die out there than be caught in here like rats."

"Will's right. Let's get out of here," Sarah said as she looked at her oxygen readout. "We're all running low on O$_2$."

Several of the men followed Mendenhall's lead and started searching. They soon found the simple magnetic lock attached to a large handle that would free the gate. Will pulled the lever down and soon the bottom came loose from the lining of the ancient frame. As six men lifted the gate, they half expected a ton of Moon dust to avalanche inside, but instead they found themselves looking into a large black area. Will allowed his helmet light to penetrate the darkness beyond.

"We have a tunnel," he called out.

Sarah looked down the long, upward-sloping shaft. The roadway was lined with what looked like aluminum plating. It was then that the idea struck her.

"Of course. The visitors wouldn't have had a road that led up and out of the crater. They would have built a road that angled out far beyond. There must be a door at the other end of this."

Kwan stepped forward and saw immediately what Sarah was talking about. A plan began forming in his head.

"Yes, I see your point. We need at least two of the lighter vehicles, because we can't push anything heavier. We can crowd onto them once we've pushed them out of the opening. If there is a gate at the far end, we will have a fighting chance—one vehicle aimed for the *Magnificent Dragon*, the other for *Altair*."

"It's worth a try," Mendenhall said, and he and the others raced around to free the chains holding two of the smaller electric vehicles in place.

The sound of the robots' destructive approach was getting terrifyingly louder. Sarah stepped to the large doorway and looked back up the way they had come. She saw the giant arms of the mechanicians as they pivoted like buzz saws, tearing away the composite material that made up the base. They were only fifty feet away. She turned and ran back inside to assist the remaining twelve men as they started pushing the vehicles free of what had been their home for the past 700 million years.

As they rolled the vehicles out and into the tunnel, they saw the ceiling rip away and sunlight fill the underground chamber. While pushing, they saw the shadow of the first robot swipe at the retreating men. The three-fingered hand missed the last car and slammed into an acetylene-type torch system, knocking it free of its restraining chain. The first robot stepped near it and planted its feet in an attempt to slam its massive hand into the last car, which had caught its wheels on the jamb of the large door that had been used as an environment shield. Sarah, at the rear end of the car, saw something that made her want to shout. Far above the two robots was a figure aiming a weapon down into the subbasement of the bunker. She saw the American space suit and knew immediately who it was and just what he was aiming the kinetic weapon at.

As she pushed the other away from the back of the vehicle, Jason Ryan fired his rifle. The bolt struck the first of the acetylene tanks and passed through it into the second tank. The resulting explosion knocked the vehicle free of the jamb and sent it careening down the tunnel. The robot nearest to the detonation was taken out at the legs. Pieces of the steel-encased leg and wiring from within went flying. One chunk hit Sarah directly in the visor and she saw the spiderweb crack as it raced across the glass. She closed her eyes in anticipation of a horrible death. But instead the crack halted just as someone was pulling her to her feet. As she fought to look back she saw Ryan disappear. The second mechanical giant stepped over the remains of the first and started tearing furiously at the ceiling of the vehicle garage.

"If I didn't know better, I would say that thing was pissed off," Mendenhall said as he pulled Sarah to the vehicle that had come to rest against the far wall after the explosion. "Who saved our asses?"

"Jason," she said as she struggled to hit her COM link.

"Jason, we'll meet you at *Altair*, do you copy?" She screamed even though she didn't need to.

Mendenhall didn't give her time to try again. He placed her where she needed to be and turned the large toggle lever that straightened out the vehicle's large wheels. Then he waved to tell the six men and Sarah that they should start pushing. Soon they had the vehicle moving at a pretty good clip.

The tearing noises filtered through their speaker systems as the second robot continued its frenzied search far in back of them. Soon they saw light up ahead as the end of the long tunnel came closer. They saw Kwan and his men as they pushed the far outer door open. Then they pushed the first vehicle out into the open sunlight. Sarah and the others maneuvered the vehicle into a spot right beside the first. The men immediately collapsed as the car came to rest.

"It . . . would . . . have . . . been nice . . . if we . . . could have . . . just popped . . . the clutch," Sarah said, trying to catch her breath.

"Uh-oh," one of the ESA astronauts said. Everyone turned toward the spot where he was looking. They saw the small Beatle *John*. Right beside it a giant hand had reached out of the crater and taken hold of the rim. The robot started to pull its massive chromed body free of the interior. Once it gained a foothold, it looked around as though gathering its bearings. Then, as its horrid red eyes turned their way, the head locked into position. It began coming toward them at a determined gait.

"I think it's *really* pissed," Will said, as he jumped into the driver's seat and looked at the gauges. Every one of them appeared to be flatlined at zero. Either that or their screens were blank. "We have a problem here," he said.

Sarah looked into the interior. The charging footsteps of the robot could be felt through the soles of their boots.

"Is there a key?" she asked. She made sure the solar panels were deployed at the correct angle toward the distant sun.

As Mendenhall shook his head at the dumb question, he saw the key placed on the side of the steering toggle. Mendenhall turned it. The panel in front of him came to life. Several of the gauges flew over into the green as the sun's merciful rays hit the solar panels and generated the energy the car needed.

"Everyone in. I think this thing may work," Will said loudly as he looked around wildly for the charging robot.

Just as Sarah was about to climb inside the crowded car, she saw the large piece of mineral on the lunar surface. For no reason she could think of, she reached down and picked it up, and then she piled into the front seat.

"Anytime," she said to Mendenhall.

Will pushed the steering toggle forward, hoping beyond hope that it also served as a throttle. His short prayer was answered as the machine shot forward. Soon they had caught up with Kwan and his men as they raced across the lunar landscape.

"Oh, shit," Sarah said, as she turned and saw how close the robot was. It had covered a half a mile in as little as the time it took to get the car moving and had nearly caught up with Kwan. The robot covered the last ten feet by diving forward in an attempt to catch the vehicle. The men on the back hugged the metal frame of the car as the three fingers of the giant missed them by inches. The mechanical giant hit the lunar surface and rolled as its momentum carried it over and over across the pitted world.

"What was that?" Will asked as the vehicle jumped a foot from the impact.

"You don't want to know," Sarah said, gripping the rock.

"Hey, what do you have that for?" Mendenhall asked. His eyes locked momentarily on the meteorite that she clutched in her gloved hands.

Sarah didn't answer. Instead, she pointed to the left of the racing vehicle.

"Crap, look!" she said.

On the far left, about three hundred yards away, they saw Jason Ryan as he tried his best to negotiate the light gravity of the Moon. He was bouncing as he tried to hurry back to *Altair*.

Mendenhall went off course just as the struggling robot gained its feet. The giant head swiveled and it caught sight of its target. Then it saw the man the target was racing for. It started running toward a rendezvous with both. Just as the vehicle approached, Jason saw the robot charging. He leaped into the air and prayed that he had timed his jump well. As the car approached, Sarah stood up, dropping the mineral into the floor of the vehicle. She reached out and Jason actually bounced off the steel hood of the car. He then bounded and almost flew past Sarah's outstretched hand as well as the other reaching arms of the men who tried desperately to secure him. Finally Jason snagged on to the large roll bar and fell into the back of the vehicle. He struggled to sit up in the bulky suit.

"Holy bouncing ball, Batman," he said as he slapped Will on his oxygen pack.

"I hope you can lift off at a moment's notice, because in case you haven't noticed we have the landlord of this place right on our ass."

Jason turned and looked at the robot, which had switched course and was again trailing them at a fantastic speed.

Sarah leaned forward and caught sight of the first vehicle with General Kwan and the remnants of the Chinese Special Forces team. They also had three of the ESA men aboard. They had actually slowed so they could turn in case the worst happened when the mechanized killer made its leap. Now they were off and running again. That was when Sarah realized that the game would be played in their court. The general and his team would make it to *Magnificent Dragon* and word would reach home that the only thing they found that may help their future cause was buried outside the crater, not inside.

"Okay, Will, everything depends on you," she said through her COM system. "Jason, how badly will an immediate liftoff screw up the rendezvous with *Falcon*?"

"We can adjust for that once we're up. It may take a while but we'll manage. The Chinese may have it worse since their command vehicle just passes overhead. *Falcon* is due in forty minutes. We may just make it."

The lunar rover shot over a small rise and that was when they saw the tall structure that was *Altair*. The ladder looked inviting, but Sarah knew they couldn't even approach it until they lost the murderous automaton pursuing them.

"We need a plan," she said as Will swerved the vehicle around a small crater. "We know we can't shoot it out with this thing, so as soon as we dip down into the lowland in front of *Altair*, you have to get out and make a run for it. I'll lead the damn thing off and then join you after I trip him up somehow."

"Oh, that ain't happening, buddy boy. There's no way I'm jumping ship when you try this stupid plan," Ryan said as he saw that the robot had gained on them.

"Look, you most of all have to get inside *Altair* and fire that thing up. Don't wait for me. I'll make it," Mendenhall countered, looking at the grated floor of the lunar rover. The meteorite was still there next to Sarah's booted feet. He swallowed and looked at Sarah. She saw the look on his face and turned away.

Will cut the control toggle sharply and the vehicle turned to the left, leading away from the lander. When the robot changed direction to follow, he again tilted the toggle to the right. The vehicle responded. Then he steered for the crater closest to the lander. He made it to the far side and stopped.

"Everyone out!" he said, as the men hanging on to the back jumped free.

"No, you can't beat this thing!" Ryan said, tightly clutching the roll bar.

"Get out, Jason. That's an order." Sarah turned to face Will. She ripped at a large, bloated patch at her shoulder and tore it free of her environment suit. As she did, small droplets of water were freed and fell gently to her lap. As Ryan jumped free of the vehicle with a loud curse, he was grabbed by the four others and hustled away, though he still strained to look back at Mendenhall.

"I saw your interest in the meteorite. Use this and the $O_2$ transfer tube from your backpack. That will give you the reaction I think you're looking for."

Mendenhall reached out and took the water pack. Then he looked at Sarah, who couldn't wipe away the tear that was rolling down her cheek.

"Take care of that Navy guy. He's a real dick when it comes to blaming someone when the right result isn't achieved."

"I will," she said, taking his gloved hand into her own smaller ones.

"Tell the colonel that I said this was his final test. Ask him if I passed. If not, tell him I think he needs to relax a little on the grades."

Sarah just nodded as she stepped from the vehicle. She reached in and took the small meteorite, tossing it to Mendenhall.

"See ya, Will," she said with a choked voice.

"Not if I see you first."

Sarah stepped back as Will Mendenhall shot out from behind the crater. He sped to the right when he saw how close the robot was.

Sarah watched for a split second and then started bounding for *Altair* fifty yards away.

Will came close to panicking when he saw that the robot didn't change course. It went after the men on foot instead of turning and following the vehicle. He turned the rover sharply to the left, bringing it up on two wheels and nearly tipping it over. The vehicle shot forward as soon as the tires gripped the dust. He steered straight for the robot, which had targeted as its first victim the bouncing Sarah as she made her way toward the rest of the men. It took a few seconds for the alien rover to cover the distance. Will braced himself as the front end of the vehicle slammed into the giant's foot. The robot stumbled, fell to one side, and rolled. Mendenhall bounced over one of its legs and felt a serious blow to the chassis of the solar-powered car. He could feel a harsh grinding through the seat as he pushed the rover to the right. He chanced a look back and saw the robot rise its feet with a look at *Altair* and the men climbing its ladder. It was as if the robot were memorizing its location. Then it turned and sprinted toward the slowly retreating Will and the damaged lunar rover.

"Well, this was a good idea," Will muttered, as he reached behind himself and pulled free the line for transferring emergency $O_2$ from one tank to another. Then he gripped the meteorite and the water bag. He started to knead the plastic-lined nylon. The water inside felt a bit slushy from the zero-degree temperature. He placed the meteorite on the passenger's seat and tore open the water bag, and then tugged on the stitch-covered air hose. Just as he poured the water onto the rock, the robot slammed its large fist down and into the back of the rover.

Sarah was the last through the air lock. She closed and secured the hatch and was rewarded with a green light and the sight of the others getting into their seats. Ryan disappeared up the ladder to the command deck. Sarah passed the other men as they silently strapped themselves in. She then climbed the ladder and poked her head into the command deck. Ryan was prepping *Altair* for the launch sequence that would send them back into space.

"Jason?"

"Stay with the others, Lieutenant. I don't need you here."

Sarah closed her eyes at Ryan's hurtful words. She moved slowly down the ladder and to her chair. Without being aware of what she was doing, she reached out and strapped herself in. All the while she couldn't hold her grief as she looked from face to face of the men that Will Mendenhall had saved.

Will felt the rover flip upward. He didn't realize at first what had happened. He knew he was airborne for the briefest of moments before the rover came crashing back to the lunar surface. He was upside down and felt like his back had been busted in two. Then he started to feel his legs and arms and knew that he wasn't dead yet. He did, however, see the killer machine standing over the smashed rover, as if examining its downed prey.

"Yeah, keep looking, asshole," Will said as he found the oxygen line and pulled on it just as the robot spotted him in the upside-down wreckage. It had just started to reach for him when Mendenhall applied the $O_2$ to the wet meteorite. He dropped the rock and tried to scramble out into the open. As he fell to the rover's ceiling, he momentarily wedged himself in tight between the two front seats.

"Shit," he cursed. He felt the shaking of the vehicle as the giant reached for him. As the three fingers closed around his right leg, the robot's attention was snatched away by a bright, momentary flash that filled the airless void. Will closed his eyes as he realized that his plan had worked. His friends were free from this nightmare world. As the robot watched, the two upper decks of *Altair* separated from the first and shot upward like a bullet in a soundless chamber. Will saw a brief image of metal skin as Ryan blasted *Altair* free of the Moon's hold on it.

As he watched *Altair* rise into the black sky, he realized his leg wasn't being held by the robot. He chanced a quick look to his right and saw that the meteorite was starting to glow a silverish color. He thought about lying there and going up with the chain reaction, but decided that he would rather find some other horrible way to die. Mendenhall began to crawl as fast as he could. He made it clear of the wreckage and turned over onto his back just as the giant metal beast lifted the rover from the lunar surface. Mendenhall could see the chain reaction beginning as the mineral continued to grow hotter.

"Jesus," he said, and turned over onto his stomach and found himself on the rim of Shackleton's sister crater, Andromeda. He looked over the edge of the deep hole in the ground and made his decision—the robot could die alone.

The beast saw Will stand up. It lowered the damaged rover and as it did, the small meteorite fell free of the vehicle and landed in the lunar dust at its feet. Mendenhall saw the small flamelike glow and made the leap outward into space. Very soon the limited gravity grabbed hold and he started heading down. Almost at the halfway point in his descent the chain reaction reached its critical stage. The explosion from high above pushed Will with dramatic force toward the opposite wall of the crater. He hit with such force that he felt his right leg snap in two. He screamed and then he landed, sliding down the crater wall. When his slide toward the bottom stopped, he opened his eyes and looked at the star field above him. He was glad he had saved the *Altair*, and Jason and Sarah. He knew that they would never be able to speak of Will Mendenhall again without choking up.

Will smiled through the pain of his broken leg.

"Yes," he said aloud as he lay on the side of Andromeda.

He would like that very much.

## JOHNSON SPACE CENTER, HOUSTON, TEXAS

Hugh Evans was once more sitting with his red eyes glued to the main viewing screen. It had been an hour since the remote telemetry team had ordered *John* away from the crater after six separate observatories around the world saw one large blast on the surface of the Moon preceded by two smaller ones. He feared the worst as *John* the Beatle moved northwest from Shackleton in an attempt to verify if *Altair*'s landing site was still there, or if had lifted off as they hoped. What worried them at NASA far more than anything was the newly formed crater that *John* had had to bypass as it struggled to reach the landing site. They surmised that there had been another large detonation on the surface not a hundred yards from where *Altair* once sat.

As Evans watched he must have missed something, because the others in mission control gave out a collective cheer as the view of the landing area came into focus in *John*'s camera eye. There, turned over and crushed on one side, were the four landing struts of *Altair*. They were sticking up at an angle. Hugh wanted to ask them what they were cheering about when he finally saw. The command and crew decks of *Altair* were gone. They hadn't been there when the landing package had been knocked over by the huge explosion.

"Long-range radar, I want a tight scan of anything in orbit around the Moon. Get me evidence that *Altair* and *Magnificent Dragon* are both in the sky."

Mission control jumped back into action. *John* was turned around to study the effects of the explosion. The Beatle came close to the rim of Andromeda as it made a wide turn. That was when someone on the floor shouted.

Evans looked up and saw what the camera had picked up.

"REMCON, stop *John*!"

The remote kept traveling and it took two minutes for the rover to make it back to where it was due to the time delay. By that time they were all standing, as a full-view shot of a space suit came into view. As they watched the main view screen, the man inside that suit rolled over. He saw *John* looking at him and waved his hand, and then lay down again.

"My God, someone was stranded on the Moon," a tech said.

Hugh Evans slammed his pencil onto his console.

"That man is alive and we're going to keep him that way until we know for sure if he's stranded."

"The only hope we have is to get him air, and hope the Russians make a successful landing," CAPCOM said from below.

"Yeah, we need that, and we also need the luck that we haven't had for the past two weeks! Now let's start with problem one, how to get *John* to give this man some oxygen."

On the main view screen, little *John* the Beatle turned away and started its own rescue operation.

Hugh Evans was damned he was going to lose one more man on this godforsaken mission.


## QUITO, ECUADOR

The turmoil was just settling down.

The American aircraft had requested permission to land three hours before.

The blue-on-blue aircraft.

The president of Ecuador had raced from his home and the armed forces were placed on alert, watching the aircraft as the last of the surviving German and Polish commandos, the Australian, Japanese, New Zealand, and Vietnamese embassy guards, were escorted by the American Secret Service agents on board. The only surviving member of the Vietnamese soldiers refused to give up an old and battered M-14. With the intervention of Captain Everett and a few very angry soldiers, it was decided that the man known as Tram could board the aircraft as long as he carried no ammunition with him. After all, they were boarding the most secure aircraft in the world—Air Force One.

The president personally greeted each soldier as they settled into the comfortable seats. They were given appetizers and for the first time in forty-eight hours the soldiers had no fear of being shot at or terrorized by machines that were supposed to have stopped operating more than 700 million years before.

The president finally made it to the forward portion of Air Force One. He saw the man he was looking for as he sipped on a bottle of water outside the main conference room, where a makeshift medical clinic had been set up. The Air Force had wanted a C-130 Hercules to bring the troops back to American soil, but the president wasn't about to be denied the chance to thank every man individually for his sacrifice before their governments snatched them away for debriefing. Niles Compton saw his old friend and nodded.

"Good to see you, baldy," the president said, and took both of Niles's hands into his own, spilling the water he was holding as he shook hands vigorously.

"You too."

"How's Jack?"

"It was touch-and-go for a while, but it looks better than it did. I think he's going to ask for a raise after this."

The president nodded and gestured toward the conference room. On the way he shook hands with Pete Golding, who never wanted to venture outside the Event Group complex again. Then he shook hands with Appleby and Dubois, and then finally with Charlie Ellenshaw. He thanked them all and followed Niles into the conference room.

Colonel Jack Collins was sitting up on the bed with several other wounded men around him. The most severely wounded had been taken to four hospitals in the Quito area with a guarantee of protection from the Ecuadorian government. Collins was arguing with Everett and Sebastian about something and they were having a hard time helping the doctor keep Jack on the gurney. They all stopped when the president stepped inside. Jack could see that the man was still shaken from his brush with death aboard Marine One. He was white and his hands were still bandaged.

"What's this all about?" the president asked, standing in the doorway. Then he reached out and took Everett's hand. "It's good to see you made it, Captain."

"Mr. President," Carl said. Then he stepped aside and introduced Sebastian Krell.

"I've heard a lot about you, Major," the president said as he shook the German commando's hand. "I understand you think these two are a bad influence on you and your men."

"They are, sir," Sebastian said, shooting a glance at Collins.

"I think your own chancellor wants a few words with you. Something about a promotion, I believe—probably for breaking people out of jails."

Sebastian smiled and stepped back.

"Colonel Collins, I take it you don't like my aircraft," the president said as he held out his hand. He saw the still bleeding bandage Jack was sporting after the surgeon had removed the bullet and part of his fourth rib. He had a liter of blood dripping from an IV.

"No, sir," Jack said, taking the president's hand and shaking it weakly. "It's just that I don't like to be told I can't do something I'm capable of doing."

"And that is?"

"I want to see Alice and the senator."

The president released Jack's hand and looked from the colonel to Niles. The sound of Air Force One spooling up its engines reverberated throughout the aircraft.

"Then you'd better hurry. The pilots are particular when it comes to people fastening their seat belts around here. Captain Everett, Niles, assist the colonel to his feet and show him into the bedroom, please."

Jack saw the look the president gave Niles. He turned away as Everett helped Jack off the gurney. It was a short walk across the hall to the presidential sleeping quarters. Niles reached out and tapped lightly on the door. Alice told them to come inside.

When the door opened, Jack saw the senator stretched out on the large bed. Alice was sitting beside him with her feet tucked under her legs. She had a hand on Lee's and she smiled when she looked up and saw Collins.

"Thank God you made it, Jack," she said.

Jack cleared his throat as he looked from Alice to the senator.

"How's he doing?" he finally managed.

Alice reached over and brushed some of Lee's silver hair off his forehead.

"He died twenty minutes ago, Jack. Niles and I were with him."

Collins felt his heart fall for the woman he was now looking at.

"I . . . I . . ."

Alice stood and walked over to Collins. She reached up and kissed him on the cheek.

"He said to tell you and Mr. Everett, and that little girl Sarah, that he said good-bye."

Jack lowered his head and Everett closed his eyes. Niles turned and opened the door with tears in his eyes and allowed Jack and Carl to leave. He looked at Alice and she shook her head.

"Now, you know that kind of display would only get you yelled at," she said as she wiped a tear from Niles face.

"Yes, it would. But not anymore." Niles turned and left the presidential bedroom.

Air Force One started rolling soon after, taking the body of Senator Garrison Lee home for the last time.

# EPILOGUE
# GENESIS ACCORDING TO COLUMBUS

The room looked like a hospital ward. Charlie Ellenshaw was sporting a cast from the backfire explosion of the alien weapon on its last discharge. Virginia Pollock had pulled through her surgery with flying colors and she had even learned from Niles that there would be no delay in getting her labs repaired. Jack, still sore and bandaged, sat at his usual spot, with Everett next to him. The guest of honor was at the head of the conference table next to his friend, the president of the United States. Niles Compton sat next to him. The room had been silent since everyone had sat down.

"Before we get started, I have something I want to present to this group." The president nodded his head toward the double doors and a Navy signalman opened them. When Jack saw who it was, he closed his eyes and then blinked. Everett patted his forearm in support.

Sarah McIntire and Jason Ryan walked into the room and everyone with the exception of Collins rose and applauded. Sarah accepted their congratulations as her eyes found Jack. Ryan only half smiled, then stopped and looked almost angry. Sarah finally broke away and walked over to Jack. She took his hand quickly and squeezed. Then she turned and sat in a chair next to him. Ryan sat across from them, still not smiling.

"Welcome home. They just touched down three hours ago after transferring to the *Atlantis*. I suppose you've both had it with space travel?"

Ryan said nothing, just staring straight ahead. Sarah politely smiled as she leaned over and whispered to Jack, "I'm sorry about Will, Jack. My heart is breaking."

"Is that what's gotten into Ryan?" Jack inquired.

"Yes," she said as she saw the strange smile cross his lips.

"Well, he damn well better get over it soon."

"Jack, that was his best friend, I think—"

"Excuse me, Lieutenant McIntire. Is there a problem?" the president asked from the head of the table.

"Not at all sir," she answered and then looked back at Jack, who only raised his right brow. He had that old "What?" look on his face.

"Go ahead, Niles," the president said.

"If I may have your attention, this was picked up by Europa not five hours ago. It's a live stream from Russian television that she hijacked and beamed to us." Niles punched a button and the monitors around the table burst to life.

Jack looked from Sarah to Jason Ryan, who still stared down at the conference table.

"Mr. Ryan, I believe the director wants your attention," Jack said, his stark eyes drilling into Jason.

Ryan finally looked up and fixed his eyes on the monitor in front of him.

On the screen, there was a vast plain of empty tundra. Everyone watched, confused because nothing in particular was happening. Then the angle of the camera changed in time to see five parachutes as they deployed to slow down the Russian space capsule. They watched it as it spent almost four minutes floating down to Earth. Collins watched Ryan as the capsule's door was blown free and Russian ground crew crowded around and started using wrenches to free the hatch covers. Then the Russian cosmonauts started emerging from inside. After all the trouble getting a Russian spacecraft into the air, they were now returning with what was being called the only successful mission to the Moon since *Apollo 17*.

It was Sarah who saw him first. Jack watched as Ryan's eyes widened. Standing in the doorway was none other than Will Mendenhall. A loud cheer went up as each person around the table saw Will and the white cast on his leg.

"What in the hell is he carrying?" Everett asked.

Niles laughed and spoke up as he watched Mendenhall wave to the cameras and the Russian people.

"It's the upper section of *John*, the Beatle. He told the Russians he wouldn't leave without it."

"The Beatle kept Mendenhall alive for the eight hours it took the Russians to find him. Luckily, he was near the path that led to Shackleton. *John* kept running oxygen to him after the remote removed the bottles from some of our dead soldiers." Niles turned the monitors off as Will was helped out of the capsule by very exuberant Russians.

Jason finally looked up at Sarah and smiled at her. He sniffed and then straightened out his facial features before anyone could see that he was choked up. Everett and Collins smiled and turned away. Sarah took Jack's hand.

"Asshole, you knew all along."

The president now spoke. "I suppose it's time Niles and I came clean as to what this has all been about. We have had some of the best minds in the world working on the Columbus site and we have some answers in that area. Niles?"

Niles Compton once more turned on the monitors and the lights dimmed.

"Thanks to many linguists and mathematicians around the world, we have figured out enough of the Visitors' language that we can be pretty certain what they're saying. Through a diary of sorts, a story unfolded that could very well be a precursor to our own civilization." On the screen a large picture of Mars came into view. There were oceans and brown continents on its face. "This is where they came from—Mars, once a moon of our own Earth and an extremely close one at that. There were two other moons, one revolving around the hostile and unsettled Earth at the time and the other, Ophillias, around Mars. It's now known that this ancient world of Mars was attacked, not once but several times." Niles looked around the table, catching Jack's attention. "The final attack was by the perpetrators of the war, not just their mechanical or carbon-based mercenaries. The war was long and in the end catastrophic for Mars and the rest of the neighboring bodies. To stop the invaders, they chose suicide over surrender; thus they exploded Ophillias as a last desperate attempt at stopping their enemy. Only a few chosen men and women would be able to survive on our current Moon to continue their race."

"Only to have our young planet kill them," the president said.

"Yes," Niles said. "But they also brought animal life from their home world of Mars. They also brought another sample of their home world with them—their DNA. Yes, we are directly linked to them. We don't know how yet, but tests have confirmed there is too little difference to say we're not kin. There you have it. They were here and we wanted the technology our ancestors brought with them."

"And we had people die for that?" Charlie Ellenshaw asked.

Niles deferred to the president, who stood and faced the room.

"The secrecy was my idea. We cannot and still cannot have any of this leaked to the press. Only Niles, Virginia, Lieutenant McIntire, out of necessity, and the United Nations Security Council and our closest allies know what is really happening. If it got out there would be worldwide panic and we wouldn't be able to prepare for it the way we could otherwise."

The president paused and paced a few feet away from the table as Niles flipped another switch, this one controlling Europa.

"Five years ago, we had an incident in Arizona. I'm sure you know of which incident I speak—the incident with the Grays. Well, they're here, and they have been for some time." The president nodded again at Niles and he told Europa to run the image. "One thing no one knows is how we knew about the Moon in the first place. The water expedition was a fake; we knew there was something there, thanks to an old friend."

"Matchstick," Jack said aloud.

"Correct, Colonel. Mahjtic is the one who told of an ancient battle on our Moon, and he also gave us an early heads-up that the Grays were coming. Niles, continue if you would."

On the monitors there was a large picture of what looked to be a round shape under ice.

"This was taken two years ago in Antarctica after Matchstick told us about the dreams he was having. Very clairvoyant he is." The image was enhanced. It was the same design as the three ships that had crashed in Roswell, New Mexico, and at Chato's Crawl, Arizona, and the one that had crashed on the Moon over 700 million years before. "When a recon team was sent in, the craft was gone. This invasion of our airspace has been happening for quite some time and is escalating."

"At last count we have 111 visual confirmations of overflights at our and other nation's military installations," Niles said, watching the reactions of his people.

"That's why we need to leapfrog our technology, and Matchstick knew where that technology was—the Moon. I have something else to show you."

Niles switched the view on the screen.

"This was taken from the Hubble Telescope and has since been classified. You and the heads of state of the nations involved in our defense are the only ones to know of this photo's existence," the president said.

In the enhanced picture they saw an amazing sight.

"What you're looking at is the Triangulum Galaxy, a spiral galaxy coded M-33. The picture was taken and enhanced using a classified ability of the Hubble. The galaxy is our closest neighbor." Niles switched pictures.

Everyone in the room was confused as to just what they were looking at. There were hundreds of thousands of small dots appearing on the front half of the galaxy. Niles hit another button and the reality of what they were looking at became crystal clear.

"Those are ships—saucers," Pete Golding said as he stood from his chair.

"Correct, Dr. Golding, they are. Our astronomers tell us that they could be here in less than six years at sub–light speed, faster if they use the wormhole gates we discovered five years ago. The ships that have been appearing recently have not been using these gates. They came from a long way off." The president let his pen slip and fall to the tabletop.

"Thus, the Dark Star operation instigated by Case Blue—our little green friend," Niles picked up. "A prelude to what the president has now code-named Case Blue, so that if any nation or government agency links Matchstick to the name, we can deny it. The Case Blue scenario now entails the defense of Earth against a full-scale invasion."

Stunned silence enveloped the room. It was Jack who asked the obvious question.

"What are our orders?"

"No orders, Colonel. You are to continue your duties here. Others are working on this; your Group has done enough. When needed more directly, you will be notified. I must stress that you need to keep all this in this conference room. The leaders of the world are now cooperating in finding a way to fend off an invasion if it comes, hopefully utilizing some of the technology our ancestors left for us and Matchstick dreamed about."

"That's all we have for now," Niles said, and closed the link with Europa.

Collins looked at Everett.

"The damn worst-case scenario has just been handed over to a group of people who can't even agree on how to feed a small country like Somalia without screwing it up."

"Yeah," Everett said, "and then we'll be asked to get our asses shot off when everything goes to shit."

"Such is the way of the world," Sarah said, and then finally greeted Jack with a kiss after everyone had left the conference room but Everett, who ducked out when he saw the two together.

"Welcome home, short stuff."

"Believe me, I'm never leaving it again."


Jack, Sarah, Everett, Mendenhall—jet lag and all—Ryan, Virginia, Charlie Ellenshaw, Pete Golding, and Niles stood around the open grave as the minister gave Lee his final farewell while Alice just stared straight ahead. They were still silent as the minister walked away.

"You know, he deserves more than this," Niles said. "The president couldn't even make an appearance because of secrecy. I mean, what the senator did in the war years, and what he did with the Group—"

All eyes went to Niles as he held on to Alice's hand and arm with his own.

"If only the people of this country could know what he did in their name, I think—"

"Now, now, let's not get carried away, Niles dear. Garrison wasn't after praise or adoration. If that was what he wanted he would have done something else with his life."

"What was the senator really after, Alice?" Jack asked as he placed an arm around Sarah.

At first none of them thought Alice was going to answer. She raised her head toward the blue sky.

"I guess he was after what we all are in the end. Peace. The truth maybe. An honesty that is very rare in everyone nowadays." She looked at the faces around her as she eased the brand-new fedora onto the casket below the ground. She smiled again. "He sold everyone here on how important the Group was and made sure every one of you was a believer—a believer in finding that truth he always sought."

They all looked around, trying to keep their emotions in check. It was Carl Everett who broke the ice. He walked up to Alice and held out his arm.

"Would you care to join me for a drink, young lady, so we can toast an American icon?"

Alice smiled. She looked at Niles and patted his hand and then she took Everett's strong arm. He was dressed in his Navy summer whites and looked the part of the masculine man that he was.

"I never turn down the Navy, Captain. Hell, if that old man hadn't hung around so long, I would have been in San Diego waiting for the fleet to come in."

They laughed as Everett escorted Alice from Lee's burial site. As they filed away, Jack and Sarah stayed behind. Collins watched Alice laughing at some-one's small joke when she turned and looked back at the grave one last time. Jack saw the sorrow etched in her eyes and knew that no matter how she hid it, the death of Garrison Lee was the death of her very world.

"Hey, are you awake, Colonel?" Sarah asked.

"Sure," he said as he finally smiled.

"You wanna go drink with our friends?"

"You bet. But they're your friends, not mine; I don't like any of them except Alice."

Sarah shook her head at the feeble way Jack pretended he hadn't been af-fected by Lee's passing. But looking at Jack, she knew that Lee may not have passed on at all. As long as Colonel Jack Collins was breathing, some of Garrison Lee was still with them.

Sarah pulled Jack along, in a hurry to catch up with their friends of the Event Group.

On a small hilltop overlooking the grave and surrounded by two dozen plainclothes security men, a small being watched from the arms of his old friend Gus Tilly.

Matchstick had stopped having his dreams, but now he knew as he looked down upon the resting place of Garrison Lee that Earth's chances of survival had just been lessened by the loss of this single man.

War was close at hand and there was little the world could do to stop it.

# GOOD NATURED

# GOOD NATURED

The Origins of
Right and Wrong in
Humans and Other Animals

Frans de Waal

Harvard University Press
Cambridge, Massachusetts • London, England

*Library of Congress Cataloging-in-Publication Data*
Waal, F. B. M. de (Frans B. M.), 1948–
Good natured : the origins of right and wrong in humans
and other animals / Frans de Waal.
p.  cm.
Includes bibliographical references and index.
ISBN 0-674-35660-8 (alk. paper)
1. Ethics, Evolutionary.  2. Animal behavior.
3. Human behavior.
4. Ethics.  I. Title.
BJ1335.W33  1996
599'.052'4—dc20      95-46032

Second printing, 1996

à ma Cattie

# CONTENTS

# PROLOGUE

In addition to being human, we pride ourselves on being *humane*. What a brilliant way of establishing morality as the hallmark of human nature—by adopting our species name for charitable tendencies! Animals obviously cannot be human; could they ever be humane?

If this seems an almost-rhetorical question, consider the dilemma for biologists—or anyone else adopting an evolutionary perspective. They would argue that there must at some level be continuity between the behavior of humans and that of other primates. No domain, not even our celebrated morality, can be excluded from this assumption.

Not that biologists have an easy time explaining morality. Actually, there are so many problems with it that many would not go near the subject, and I may be considered foolish for stepping into this morass. For one thing, inasmuch as moral rule represents the power of the community over the individual, it poses a profound challenge to evolutionary theory. Darwinism tells us that traits evolve because their bearers are better off with them than without them. Why then, are collective interests and self-sacrifice valued so highly in our moral systems?

Debate of this issue dates back a hundred years, to 1893 when

Thomas Henry Huxley gave a lecture on "Evolution and Ethics" to a packed auditorium in Oxford, England. Viewing nature as nasty and indifferent, he depicted morality as the sword forged by *Homo sapiens* to slay the dragon of its animal past. Even if the laws of the physical world—the cosmic process—are unalterable, their impact on human existence can be softened and modified. "The ethical progress of society depends, not on imitating the cosmic process, still less in running away from it, but in combating it."[1]

By viewing morality as the antithesis of human nature, Huxley deftly pushed the question of its origin outside the biological realm. After all, if moral conduct is a human invention—a veneer beneath which we have remained as amoral or immoral as any other form of life—there is little need for an evolutionary account. That this position is still very much with us is illustrated by the startling statement of George Williams, a contemporary evolutionary biologist: "I account for morality as an accidental capability produced, in its boundless stupidity, by a biological process that is normally opposed to the expression of such a capability."[2]

In this view, human kindness is not really part of the larger scheme of nature: it is either a cultural counterforce or a dumb mistake of Mother Nature. Needless to say, this view is extraordinarily pessimistic, enough to give goose bumps to anyone with faith in the depth of our moral sense. It also leaves unexplained where the human species can possibly find the strength and ingenuity to battle an enemy as formidable as its own nature.

Several years after Huxley's lecture, the American philosopher John Dewey wrote a little-known critical rejoinder. Huxley had compared the relation between ethics and human nature to that between gardener and garden, where the gardener struggles continuously to keep things in order. Dewey turned the metaphor around, saying that gardeners work as much *with* nature as against it. Whereas Huxley's gardener seeks to be in control and root out whatever he dislikes, Dewey's is what we would today call an organic grower. The successful gardener, Dewey pointed out, creates conditions and introduces plant species that may not be normal for this particular plot of land "but fall within the wont and use of nature as a whole."[3]

I come down firmly on Dewey's side. Given the universality of moral systems, the tendency to develop and enforce them must be an integral part of human nature. A society lacking notions of right and wrong is about the worst thing we can imagine—if we can imagine it at all. Since we are moral beings to the core, any theory of human behavior that does not take morality 100 percent seriously is bound to fall by the wayside. Unwilling to accept this fate for evolutionary theory, I have set myself the task of seeing if some of the building blocks of morality are recognizable in other animals.

Although I share the curiosity of evolutionary biologists about *how* morality might have evolved, the chief question that will occupy us here is *whence* it came. Thus, after due attention in this book's first chapter to theories of evolutionary ethics, I will move on to more practical matters. Do animals show behavior that parallels the benevolence as well as the rules and regulations of human moral conduct? If so, what motivates them to act this way? And do they realize how their behavior affects others? With questions such as these, the book carries the stamp of the growing field of *cognitive ethology:* it looks at animals as knowing, wanting, and calculating beings.

As an ethologist specialized in primatology, I naturally turn most often to the order of animals to which we ourselves belong. Yet behavior relevant to my thesis is not limited to the primates; I include other animals whenever my knowledge permits. All the same, I cannot deny that primates are of special interest. Our ancestors more than likely possessed many of the behavioral tendencies currently found in macaques, baboons, gorillas, chimpanzees, and so on. While human ethics are designed to counteract some of these tendencies, in doing so they probably employ some of the others—thus fighting nature with nature, as Dewey proposed.

Because my goal is to make recent developments in the study of animal behavior accessible to a general audience, I draw heavily on personal experience. Interacting with animals on a daily basis, knowing each of them individually, I tend to think in terms of what I have seen happen among them. I am fond of anecdotes, particularly those that capture in a nutshell social dynamics that would take a thousand words to explain. For the same reason, this book is liberally illustrated with photographs (which, unless otherwise specified, are mine).

At the same time, vignettes do not constitute scientific proof. They tease the imagination and sometimes hint at striking capacities, yet cannot demonstrate them. Only repeated observations and solid data allow us to compare alternative hypotheses and arrive at firm conclusions. The study of animal behavior is conducted as much behind the computer as at the observation site. Over the years, my students and I have recorded large amounts of systematic data on group-living primates, mostly in outdoor enclosures at zoos and research institutions. In addition, a host of colleagues have been assiduously working

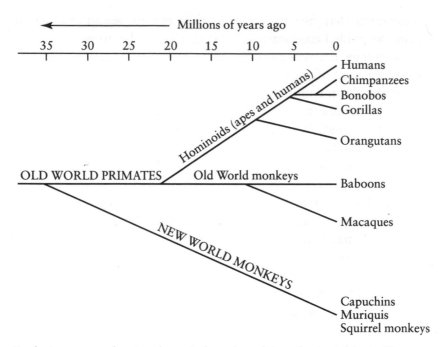

Evolutionary tree showing the main branches of the primate order: the New World monkeys, the Old World monkeys, and the hominoid lineage that produced our own species. This diagram reflects recent advances in DNA analysis that place the African apes (gorillas, chimpanzees, and bonobos) much closer to humans than previously thought.

on related issues, both in the laboratory and in the field. In an attempt to integrate these approaches, at least half of the material presented herein concerns research by others.

Because my writing alternates between stories, theories, and hard-won data, it risks blurring the line between fact and speculation. To help readers distinguish between the two and explore certain topics at greater length, the book includes technical notes as well as an extensive bibliography. Although by no means exhaustive, this additional material makes clear that rigorous scientific methods can be and are being applied to some of the questions at hand.

Western science seems to be moving away from a tidy, mechanistic worldview. Aware that the universe is not necessarily organized along logically consistent lines, scientists are—ever so reluctantly—beginning to allow contradictions. Physicists are getting used to the idea that energy may be looked at as waves but also as particles, and economists that free-market economies can be beaten at their own game by guided economies such as that of the Japanese.

In biology, the very same principle of natural selection that mercilessly plays off life forms and individuals against one another has led to symbiosis and mutualism among different organisms, to sensitivity of one individual to the needs of another, and to joint action toward a common goal. We are facing the profound paradox that genetic self-advancement at the expense of others—which is the basic thrust of evolution—has given rise to remarkable capacities for caring and sympathy.

This book tries to keep such conflicting thoughts simultaneously aloft. The one is not easily reduced to the other, although attempts have been made, most prominently the proposition that deep down, concern for others always remains selfish. By denying the existence of genuine kindness, however, these theories miss out on the greater truth emerging from a juxtaposition of genetic self-interest and the intense sociality and conviviality of many animals, including ourselves.

Instead of human nature's being either fundamentally brutish or fundamentally noble, it is both—a more complex picture perhaps, but an infinitely more inspiring one.

# 1

# DARWINIAN DILEMMAS

Be warned that if you wish, as I do, to build a society in which individuals cooperate generously and unselfishly towards a common good, you can expect little help from biological nature. Let us try to *teach* generosity and altruism, because we are born selfish.

Richard Dawkins[1]

Why should our nastiness be the baggage of an apish past and our kindness uniquely human? Why should we not seek continuity with other animals for our 'noble' traits as well?

Stephen Jay Gould[2]

Famous in her country as the star of several nature documentaries, Mozu looks like any other Japanese monkey except for missing hands and feet and an arresting countenance that appears to reflect lifelong suffering. She roams the Shiga Heights of the Japanese Alps on stumpy limbs, desperately trying to keep up with more than two hundred healthy group mates. Her congenital malformations have been attributed to pesticides.

When I first visited Jigokudani Park in 1990, Mozu was already eighteen years old—past prime for a female macaque. She had successfully raised five offspring, none of whom showed abnormalities. Given the extended period of nursing and dependency of primate young, no one would have dared to predict such a feat for a female who must crawl over the ground, even in midwinter, to stay with the rest. While the others jump from tree to tree to avoid the ice and snow covering the forest floor, Mozu slips and slides through shoulder-high snow with an infant on her back.

One thing that the monkeys in Jigokudani Park have in their favor is hot-water springs, in which they temporarily escape from the glacial temperatures, grooming one another amid clouds of steam. Another factor that makes life easier is food provisioning. Modest amounts of soybeans and apples are distributed twice daily at the park. Caretakers say they give Mozu extra food and protect her when she encounters competition from other monkeys. They try to make up for the trouble she has obtaining food, yet stress that Mozu does not dally at the feeding site. She is really part of the troop. Like the rest, she spends most of her time in the mountain forest, away from people.

## Survival of the Unfittest

My first reaction to Mozu was one of awe: "What a will to live!" The connection with morality came later, when I heard how much paleontologists were making of the occasional survival into adulthood of Neanderthals and early humans afflicted with dwarfism, paralysis of the limbs, or inability to chew. With exotic names such as Shanidar I, Romito 2, the Windover Boy, and the Old Man of La Chapelle-Aux-Saints, the fossil remains of a handful of cripples were taken to mean that our ancestors supported individuals who could contribute little to the community. Survival of the weak, the handicapped, the mentally retarded, and others who must have posed a burden was depicted as the first appearance on the evolutionary scene of compassion and moral decency. Cavemen turned out to be communitarians under the skin.

Accepting this logic, should we not also include Mozu's survival as an example of moral decency? One might counter that the artificial food provisioning at Jigokudani Park disqualifies her, since we do not know if she would have made it without the extra food. Moreover, if active community support is our criterion, Mozu can be eliminated right away because there is no shred of evidence that other monkeys have ever gone out of their way to assist her in her monumental struggle for existence.

Exactly the same arguments have been raised against the Shanidars and Romitos of the human fossil record. According to K. A. Dettwyler, an anthropologist, it is possible that these individuals lived in rich environments in which the sharing of resources with a few impaired community members posed no problem. In return, the handicapped individuals may have made themselves useful by collecting firewood, baby-sitting, or cooking. Dettwyler also argues that there is a wide gap between mere survival and being treated well. She describes cultures in which mentally retarded people are stoned, beaten, and jeered at for public amusement, or in which people afflicted with polio do not receive any special consideration ("adult women crawled on hands and knees with children tied to their backs").[3] As for Western society, we need only think of the filthy asylums of the not-too-distant past, and the chained existence of the insane, to realize that survival does not necessarily imply humane conditions.

Without knowing the precise similarities and differences between Mozu and the human fossils, I do not think these fossils prove moral decency any more than does Mozu's survival. Only a relatively tolerant attitude toward the handicapped can be inferred in both cases. Mozu is certainly well accepted by her group mates, a fact that may have contributed to her survival. If what happened in 1991 is any measure, Mozu may even enjoy a special level of tolerance.

In the spring of that year, the troop of monkeys at Jigokudani had grown so large that it split in half. As usual during fissioning, the dividing line followed the backbone of macaque society, the matrilineal hierarchy (female kin are closely bonded and united in their battles with nonkin, the result being a social order based on matrilineal descent). One piece of the troop consisted of a few dominant matriarchs and their families; the other included subordinate matriarchs and their families. Being of low rank, Mozu and her offspring ended up in the second division.

According to Ichirou Tanaka, a Japanese primatologist who has worked at the park for years, the fission posed a serious problem for Mozu. The dominant division began to claim the park's feeding site for itself, aggressively excluding all other monkeys. Faced with this situation, Mozu made a unique decision. Whereas female macaques normally maintain lifelong bonds of kinship, Mozu ignored the ties with her offspring and began making overtures to individuals in the dominant division. Despite occasional attacks on her, she stayed at the periphery, seeking contact with age-peers, females with whom she had grown up nineteen years before. She made repeated attempts to groom them (without fingers, Mozu's rather clumsy grooming still served to initiate contact). Eventually her peers began to accept her presence, and to return Mozu's grooming. Mozu is now well integrated into the dominant troop, once again enjoying the feeding site, yet having paid for this advantage with permanent separation from her kin.

In no society worthy of the name do the members lack a sense of belonging and a need for acceptance. The ability and the tendency to construct such associations, and to seek security within them, are products of natural selection found in members of species with better survival chances in a group than in solitude. The advantages of group life can be manifold, the most important being increased chances to find food, defense against predators, and strength in numbers against competitors. For example, it may be of critical importance during a drought to have older individuals around who can lead the group to an almost-forgotten waterhole. Or, during periods of heavy predation all eyes and ears count, especially in combination with an effective warning system. Each member contributes to and benefits from the group, although not necessarily equally or at the same time.

Mozu's case teaches us that even though primate groups are based on such give-and-take contracts, there is room for individuals with little value when it comes to cooperation. The cost to the others may be negligible, but their inclusion is remarkable, given the realistic alternative of ostracism.

Noting that Japanese monkeys can be quite aggressive, at times demonstrating what he calls murderous intent, Jeffrey Kurland described the following concerted action against a particular matriline at a site far from Jigokudani.

A female of the top matriline started a fight with a low-ranking female named Faza-71. The attacker and her supporters (a sister, a brother, and a niece) made so much noise that the alpha male (the troop's most dominant male) was attracted to the scene. By the time he arrived, Faza-71 was high in a tree, a position from which she was forced to jump 10 meters to the ground when the male climbed up and cuffed her. Fleeing from her pursuers, Faza-71 saw no escape other than an icy, fast-streaming river. Her attackers wisely stayed on land, but for a long time prevented the frantically swimming Faza-71 from coming back on the riverbank. In the meantime Faza-71's family, powerless to help, fled over a dam across the river.

But for a small pile of sand under a chilly waterfall, Faza-71 would have drowned. Bleeding and apparently in shock, she waited to join her family until the attackers had dispersed. The entire encounter lasted less than half an hour; but it took more than a week for Faza's matriline to rejoin the troop, and many months for them to relax in the presence of the dominant matriline.[4]

## Biologicizing Morality

Social inclusion is absolutely central to human morality, commonly cast in terms of how we should or should not behave in order to be valued as members of society. Immoral conduct makes us outcasts, either here and now or—in the beliefs of some people—when we are turned away from the gates of heaven. Universally, human communities are moral communities; a morally neutral existence is as impossible for us as a completely solitary existence. As summed up by Mary Midgley, a philosopher, "Getting right outside morality would be rather like getting outside the atmosphere."[5] Human morality may indeed be an extension of general primate patterns of social integration, and of the adjustment required of each member in order to fit in. If so, the broadest definition of this book's theme would be as an investigation into how the social environment shapes and constrains individual behavior.

No doubt some philosophers regard morality as entirely theirs. The claim may be justifiable with regard to the "high end" of morality: abstract moral rules can be studied and debated like mathematics, almost divorced from their application in the real world. According to child psychologists, however, moral reasoning is constructed upon much simpler foundations, such as fear of punishment and a desire to conform. In general, human moral development moves from the social to the personal, from a concern about one's standing in the group to an autonomous conscience. While the early stages hardly seem out of reach of nonhuman animals, it is impossible to determine how close they get to the more rational, Kantian levels. Reliable nonverbal signs of thought in humans do not exist, and the indicators that we sometimes do use (staring into the distance, scratching the head, resting the chin on a fist) are commonly observed in anthropoids. Would an extraterrestrial observer ever be able to discern that humans ponder moral dilemmas, and if so, what would keep that observer from arriving at the same conclusion for apes?

Biologists take the back door to the same building that social scientists and philosophers, with their fondness for high-flung notions, enter through the front door. When the Harvard sociobiologist E. O. Wilson twenty years ago proclaimed that "the time has come for ethics to be removed temporarily from the hands of philosophers and biologicized,"[6] he formulated the same idea a bit more provocatively. My own feeling is that instead of complete reliance on biology, the best way to generate fresh air is simultaneously to open both front and back doors. Biologists look at things in a rather functional light; we always wonder about the utility of a trait, on the assumption that it would not be there if it did not serve some purpose. Successful traits contribute to "fitness," a term that expresses how well adapted (fitted) an individual is to its environment. Still, emphasis on fitness has its limitations. These are easily recognized when paleontologists hold up the fossil remains of an ancestor who could barely walk, declaring it a defining moment in human prehistory when the unfit began to survive.

To understand the depth of these limitations, one need only realize the influence of Thomas Malthus' essay on population growth that appeared at the beginning of the nineteenth century. His thesis was that populations tend to outgrow their food supply and are cut back automatically by increased mortality. The idea of competition within the *same* species over the *same* resources had immediate appeal to Charles Darwin, who read Malthus; it helped bring his Struggle for Existence principle into focus.

Sadly, with these valuable insights came the burden of Malthus' political views. Any help one gives the poor permits them to survive and propagate, hence negates the natural process according to which these unfortunates are supposed to die off. Malthus went so far as to claim that if there is one right that man clearly does *not* possess, it is the right to subsistence that he himself is unable to purchase with his labor.[7]

Although Darwin appears to have struggled more with the moral implications of these ideas than most of his contemporaries, he could not prevent his theory from being incorporated into a closed system of thought in which there was little room for compassion. It was taken to its extreme by Herbert Spencer in a grand synthesis of sociology, political economy, and biology, according to which the pursuit of self-interest, the lifeblood of society, creates progress for the strong at the expense of the inferior. This convenient justification of disproportionate wealth in the hands of a happy few was successfully exported to the New World, where it led John D. Rockefeller to portray the expansion of a large business as "merely the working-out of a law of nature and a law of God."[8]

Given the popular use and abuse of evolutionary theory (comparing Wall Street to a Darwinian jungle, for example), it is not surprising that in the minds of many people natural selection has become synonymous with open, unrestricted competition. How could such a harsh principle ever explain the concern for others and the benevolence encountered in our species? That a reason for such behavior does not follow readily from Darwin's theory should not be held against it. In the same way that birds and airplanes appear to defy the law of gravity yet are fully subjected to it, moral decency may appear to fly in the face of natural selection yet still be one of its many products.

Altruism is not limited to our species. Indeed, its presence in other species, and the theoretical challenge this represents, is what gave rise to *sociobiology*—the contemporary study of animal (including human) behavior from an evolutionary perspective. Aiding others at a cost or risk to oneself is widespread in the animal world. The warning calls of birds allow other birds to escape a predator's talons, but attract attention to the caller. Sterile castes in social insects do little else than serve food to the larvae of their queen or sacrifice themselves in defense of their colony. Assistance by relatives enables a breeding pair of jays to fill more hungry mouths and thus raise more offspring than otherwise possible. Dolphins support injured companions close to the surface in order to keep them from drowning. And so on.

Should not a tendency to endanger one's life for someone else be quickly weeded out by natural selection? It was only in the 1960s and 1970s that satisfactory explanations were proposed. According to one theory, known as *kin selection,* a helping tendency may spread if the help results in increased survival and reproduction of kin. From a genetic perspective it does not really matter whether genes are multiplied through the helper's own reproduction or that of relatives. The second explanation is known as *reciprocal altruism;* that is, helpful acts that are costly in the short run may produce long-term benefits if recipients return the favor. If I rescue a friend who almost drowns, and he rescues me under similar circumstances, both of us are better off than without mutual aid.

Wilson's *Sociobiology: The New Synthesis* summarized the new developments. It is an influential and impressive book predicting that all other behavioral sciences will one day see the light and convert to the creed of sociobiology. Confidence in this future was depicted in an amoebic drawing with pseudopods reaching out to devour other disciplines. Understandably, nonbiologists were piqued by what they saw as an arrogant attempt at annexation; but also within biology, Wilson's book provoked battles. Should Harvard be allowed to lay claim to an entire field? Some scientists preferred to be known as behavioral ecologists rather than sociobiologists, even though their theories were essentially the same. Moreover, like children ashamed of their old folks, sociobiologists were quick to categorize earlier studies of animal behavior as "classical ethology." That way everyone could be sure that ethology was dead and that we were onto something totally new.

Sociobiology represents a giant stride forward; it has forever changed the way biologists think about animal behavior. Precisely because of their power and elegance, however, the new theories have lured some scientists into a gross simplification of genetic effects. Behavior that at first sight does not conform to the framework is regarded as an oddity, even a mistake. This is best illustrated by a single branch of sociobiology, which has gotten so caught up in the Malthusian dog-eat-dog view of the world that it sees no room for moral behavior. Following Huxley, it regards morality as a counterforce, a rebellion against our brutish makeup, rather than as an integrated part of human nature.[9]

## Calvinist Sociobiology

At the Yerkes Regional Primate Research Center, one chimpanzee has been named Atlanta and another Georgia. It is impossible for me to forget where I am, as I see both individuals on a daily basis. I moved to the Star of the South, as the city likes to call itself, to resume my study of the species that surpasses every other when it comes to similarity to our own. My tower office has a large window that overlooks the outdoor enclosure of twenty chimpanzees. The group is as close-knit as any family can be; they are together day and night, and several of the adults were born into the colony. One of these is Georgia, the rascal of the group. Robert Yerkes, a founder of primatology, once declared it "a securely established fact that the chimpanzee is not necessarily utterly selfish."[10] From everything I know about Georgia, she is not the sort of character Yerkes had in mind when he made that declaration six decades ago.

When we provision the colony with freshly cut branches and leaves from the forest around the field station, Georgia is often the first to grab one of the large bundles, and one of the last to share it with anybody else. Even her daughter, Kate, and younger sister, Rita, have trouble getting food. They may roll over the ground, screaming in a pitiful tantrum, but to no avail.

No, Yerkes must have thought of individuals such as Mai, an older high-ranking female, who shares quite readily not only with her children but also with nonrelatives, young and old. Or he may have thought of adult male chimpanzees, most of whom are remarkably generous when it comes to food distribution.

While a distinction between sharing and keeping means a lot in human society, it is sometimes lost in the language of a particular brand of sociobiology that takes the gene as absolute king. Gene-centric sociobiology has managed to reach a wide audience with its message that humans and other animals are entirely selfish. From this standpoint, the only difference between Mai and Georgia is in the *way* they pursue self-interest; whereas Georgia is just plain greedy, Mai shares food so as to make friends or receive return favors in the future. Both think only of themselves. In human terms, this interpretation amounts to the claim that Mother Teresa follows the same basic instinct as any inside trader or thief. A more cynical outlook is hard to come by.

Gene-centric sociobiology looks at survival and reproduction from the point of view of the gene, not the individual. A gene for bringing home food for one's children, for example, will ensure the survival of individuals likely to carry the same gene.[11] As a result, that gene will spread. Taken to its logical extreme, genes favor their own replication; a gene is successful if it produces a trait that in turn promotes the gene (sometimes summed up as "a chicken is an egg's way of making other eggs"). To describe such genetic self-promotion, Richard Dawkins introduced a psychological term in the title of his book, *The Selfish Gene*. Accordingly, what may be a generous act in common language, such as bringing home food, may be selfish from the gene's perspective. With time, the important addition "from the gene's perspective" was often forgotten and was eventually left out. All behavior was selfish, period.

Since genes have neither a self nor the emotions to make them selfish, one would think this phrase is just a metaphor. True, but when repeated often enough, metaphors tend to assume an aura of literal truth. Even though Dawkins cautioned against his own anthropomorphism of the gene, with the passage of time, carriers of selfish genes became selfish by association. Statements such as "we are born selfish" show how some sociobiologists have made the nonexistent emotions of genes into the archetype of true emotional nature. A critical article by Mary Midgley compared the sociobiologists' warnings against their own metaphor to the paternosters of the Mafiosi.

Pushed into a corner by a witty philosopher, Dawkins defended his metaphor by arguing that it was *not* a metaphor. He really meant that genes are selfish, and claimed the right to define selfishness any way he wanted. Still, he borrowed a term from one domain, redefined it in a very narrow sense, then applied it in another domain to which it is completely alien. Such a procedure would be acceptable if the two meanings were kept separate at all times; unfortunately, they merge to the extent that some authors of this genre now imply that if people occasionally think of themselves as unselfish, the poor souls must be deceiving themselves.

It is important to clear up this confusion, and to emphasize once and for all that the selfish gene metaphor says nothing, either directly or indirectly, about motivation, emotion, or intention. Elliott Sober, another philosopher interested in the semantic trappings of sociobiology, proposes a distinction between *vernacular egoism,* our everyday usage of the term, and *evolutionary egoism,* which deals exclusively with genetic self-promotion. A plant, for example, is able to further its genetic interests yet cannot possibly be selfish in the vernacular sense. A chimpanzee or person who shares food with others acts altruistically in the vernacular sense, yet we assume that the behavior came into existence because it served survival and reproduction, hence that it is self-serving in an evolutionary sense.[12]

There is almost no point in discussing the evolution of morality if we let the vernacular sense of our terminology be overshadowed by the evolutionary sense. Human moral judgment always looks for the intention behind behavior. If I lean out of a window on the fifth floor and unknowingly nudge a flowerpot, thereby killing a pedestrian on the sidewalk below, I might be judged awkward or irresponsible, but not murderous. The latter accusation would surely be heard, however, had someone watched me grab the pot and throw it at the person. The effect is the same, but the motives are absolutely crucial. Jury and judge would want to know which emotions I showed, the degree of planning involved, my relationship with the target, and so on. In short, they would want to fathom the psychology behind the act.

These distinctions are largely irrelevant within a sociobiology exclusively interested in the effects of behavior. In such a framework, no different values are attached to intended versus unintended results, self-serving versus other-serving behavior, what we say versus what we mean, or an honest versus a dishonest mistake. Having thus denied themselves the single most important handle on ethical issues, some sociobiologists have given up on explaining morality. William Hamilton, the discoverer of kin selection, has written that "the animal in our nature cannot be regarded as a fit custodian for the values of civilized man," and Dawkins urges us to cultivate pure, disinterested altruism because it does not come naturally. "We, alone on earth, can rebel against the tyranny of the selfish replicators."[13] By thus locating morality outside nature, these scientists have absolved themselves from trying to fit it into their evolutionary perspective.

An even more alarming position was adopted by George Williams in a commentary on Huxley's celebrated "Evolution and Ethics" lecture. Calling nature morally indifferent, as Huxley had done, was not enough for Williams, who preferred "gross immorality" and "moral subversiveness." He went on to demonstrate that "just about every . . . kind of sexual behavior that has been regarded as sinful or unethical can be found abundantly in nature." This conclusion was accompanied by a depressing enumeration of animal murder, rape, and wretchedness.[14]

Can we really pass judgment on other animals any more than we can on the flow of a river or the movement of nuclear particles? Does doing so get us beyond age-old stereotypes such as the hard-working bee, the noble horse, the cruel wolf, and the gluttonous pig? Granted, animals may possess standards of behavior, perhaps even ethical standards. Yet Williams was not measuring their behavior against their own standards, but against those of the culture of which he happens to be part. Since animals failed to meet his criteria, he declared nature, including human nature, our foe. Note, again, how vernacular egoism slips into a statement about the evolutionary process: "The enemy is indeed powerful and persistent, and we need all the help we can get in trying to overcome billions of years of selection for selfishness."[15]

By now, I am sure, the reader must have smelled the perfume Egoïste (an actual Chanel creation) to the point of either conviction or stupefaction. How in the world could a group of scientists come up with such a pale view of the natural universe, of the human race, of the people close to them, and of themselves (because we must assume that their theory knows no exceptions)? Do they not see that, to paraphrase Buddha, wherever there is shadow, there is light?

Underlying their position is a monumental confusion between process and outcome. Even if a diamond owes its beauty to millions of years of crushing pressure, we rarely think of this fact when admiring the gem. So why should we let the ruthlessness of natural selection distract from the wonders it has produced? Humans and other animals have been endowed with a capacity for genuine love, sympathy, and care—a fact that can and will one day be fully reconciled with the idea that genetic self-promotion drives the evolutionary process.

It is not hard to find the origin of the proposed abyss between morality and nature. The conviction is well established outside science. The image of humanity's innate depravity and its struggle to transcend that depravity is quintessentially Calvinist, going back to the doctrine of original sin. Tension between civic order and our bestial ancestry, furthermore, is the centerpiece of Sigmund Freud's *Civilization and Its Discontents*. Freud argues that we need to control and renounce our baser instincts before we can build a modern society. Hence, we are not dealing with a mere biological theory, but with a convergence between religious, psychoanalytical, and evolutionary thought, according to which human life is fundamentally dualistic. We soar somewhere between heaven and earth on a "good" wing—an acquired sense of ethics and justice—and a "bad" wing—a deeply rooted egoism. It is the age-old half-brute, half-angel view of humanity.

It must be rather unsatisfactory, to say the least, for gene-centric sociobiologists to be obliged to exclude one domain from their Theory of Everything. And not a trivial domain, but precisely the one many of us consider to be at the core of being human. Failure to account for morality in terms of genetic selfishness is the logical outcome of such reductionism. If we shrug off attempts to attribute love to hormones or hatred to brain waves—knowing that these attributions are only part of the story—it is good to realize that these are tiny jumps compared with the reduction of human psychology to gene action.

Fortunately, the current pendulum swing is away from such simplifications. It is toward attempts to explain living systems in their entirety, integrating many different levels. In the words of a recent task force of the National Science Foundation, "The biological sciences are moving away from the era of analytical reductionism . . . from taking biological systems apart to see what the pieces are and how they work, to putting the pieces back together to understand how the totality works together."[16]

One does not need to follow this holistic swing all the way to Gaia (the idea that the biosphere acts as a single organism) to agree that the current development indicates greater scientific maturity. In the New and Improved Sociobiology, animals still do everything to survive and reproduce, yet take their circumstances into account so as to choose the best course of action: from "survival machines" they have become "adaptive decision-makers." With so many degrees of freedom added, selfish-gene thinking can now safely be relegated to history as "classical sociobiology."

Have I been kicking a dead horse, then? I do not think so. Gene-centric sociobiology is the type best known to the general public. It is still widespread in certain academic circles, particularly those outside biology that have battled hard within their respective disciplines to stake out and defend an evolutionary approach. Furthermore, as a corollary to the belief in a natural world red in tooth and claw, there remains tremendous resistance, both inside and outside biology, to a terminology acknowledging beauty in the beast.

The sociobiological idiom is almost derisive in its characterization of animals. Given the image of biologists as nature buffs, it may be shocking for outsiders to learn that the current scientific literature routinely depicts animals as "suckers," "grudgers," and "cheaters" who act "spitefully," "greedily," and "murderously." There is really nothing lovable about them! If animals do show tolerance or altruism, these terms are often placed in quotation marks lest their author be judged hopelessly romantic or naive. To avoid an overload of quotation marks, positive inclinations tend to receive negative labels. Preferential treatment of kin, for instance, instead of being called "love for kin," is sometimes known as "nepotism."

As noted by economist Robert Frank (referring to a problem common to the behavioral sciences):

> The flint-eyed researcher fears no greater humiliation than to have called some action altruistic, only to have a more sophisticated colleague later demonstrate that it was self-serving. This fear surely helps account for the extraordinary volume of ink behavioral scientists have spent trying to unearth selfish motives for seemingly self-sacrificing acts.[17]

As a student of chimpanzee behavior, I myself have encountered resistance to the label "reconciliation" for friendly reunions between former adversaries. Actually, I should not have used the word "friendly" either, "affiliative" being the accepted euphemism. More than once I was asked whether the term "reconciliation" was not overly anthropomorphic. Whereas terms related to aggression, violence, and competition never posed the slightest problem, I was supposed to switch to dehumanized language as soon as the affectionate aftermath of a fight was the issue. A reconciliation sealed with a kiss became a "postconflict interaction involving mouth-to-mouth contact."

Barbara Smuts ran into the same resistance when she chose "friendship" as an obvious label for intimate relationships between adult male and female baboons. Can animals really have friends? was the question of colleagues who without blinking accepted that animals have rivals. Given this double standard, I predict that the word "bonding" will soon become taboo as well, even though it was initially coined by ethologists as a neutral reference to emotional attachment. Ironically, the term has since entered common English with precisely the meaning it tried to circumvent, as in "mother-child bond" and "male bonding." It is rapidly becoming too loaded for students of animal behavior.

Animals, particularly those close to us, show an enormous spectrum of emotions and different kinds of relationships. It is only fair to reflect this fact in a broad array of terms. If animals can have enemies they can have friends; if they can cheat they can be honest, and if they can be spiteful they can also be kind and altruistic. Semantic distinctions between animal and human behavior often obscure fundamental similarities; a discussion of morality will be pointless if we allow our language to be distorted by a denial of benign motives and emotions in animals.

An intriguing expression of emotion occurred once when, in the middle of the day, our entire chimpanzee colony unexpectedly gathered around Mai. All the apes were silent, staring closely at Mai's behind, some of them carefully poking a finger at it and then smelling their finger. Mai was standing half upright, with her legs slightly apart, holding one hand between her legs. Remarkably, an attentive older female mimicked Mai by cupping her hand between her own legs in exactly the same fashion.

After approximately ten minutes, Mai tensed, squatted more deeply, and passed a baby, catching it in both hands. The crowd stirred, and Atlanta, Mai's best friend, emerged with a scream, looking around and embracing a couple of other chimpanzees next to her, one of whom uttered a shrill bark. Mai then went to a corner to clean the baby and consumed the afterbirth with gusto. The next day Atlanta defended Mai fiercely in a fight, and during the following weeks she frequently groomed Mai, staring at and gently touching Mai's healthy new son.

This was the very first time I witnessed a chimpanzee birth. I have seen several macaque births, though, and the big difference is that other macaques do not approach the mother. It is hard to tell if they are even interested; there is no obvious excitement or curiosity about the delivery. Positive interest occurs only after the amniotic sac has been removed and the infant has been cleaned. For macaques are extremely attracted to newborns. Our chimpanzees responded much earlier; they seemed as much taken with the process as with its outcome. It is entirely possible that the emotional reaction of Atlanta (who has had quite a few infants of her own) reflected *empathy,* that is, identification with and understanding of what was happening to her friend.[18]

Needless to say, empathy and sympathy are pillars of human morality.

## A Broader View

A climbing orangutan grasps a branch with one hand, holding on tightly until the other hand has found the next branch. Then the roles are reversed, and the first hand releases its grip in order to get hold of another branch. Elias Canetti, in *Crowds and Power,* noticed a connection between the ancient arboreal function of one of our most versatile organs and the universal human ritual of barter and trade: climbing through the trees may have predisposed us for economic exchange, since both activities depend on the careful coordination of grasp and release. With his goods held out in one hand, the tradesman reaches with the other for his partner's goods, mindful not to release anything before his grip on the desired goods is secure. Failure to perform this sequence in the right order or with the right timing may have fatal consequences in the trees in the same way that it may leave the human trader empty-handed. Material exchange has become second nature to us; most of the time we reflect as little on the risks as does a monkey racing through the canopy.

Canetti's is a fascinating parallel, yet there exists of course no causal connection. Otherwise the octopus would be the champion merchant of the animal kingdom, and animals without hands, such as dolphins and bats, would be excluded as possible traders. It is precisely bats, mammals with front limbs transformed into wings, who provide us with some of the first evidence for give-and-take relations in animals. Gruesome as it may sound, vampire bats trade meals by regurgitating blood to one another. At night these bats stealthily lap blood from a small patch of flesh exposed by razor-sharp teeth on a sleeping mammal, such as a horse or cow. With their bellies full, the bats return to the hollow tree in which they spend the day. We know about their blood economy because the bats sometimes share their roost with a scientist who spends hours on his back, legs outside and torso inside an opening at the base of the tree, peering upward to collect behavioral information along with the inevitable bat droppings.

Having tagged his subjects with reflective bands in order to recognize them in the dark, Gerald Wilkinson noticed that mother bats often regurgitate blood to their offspring. While this is not too surprising, the investigator saw other combinations share on twenty-one occasions—mostly individuals who often associated and groomed. There appeared to be a "buddy system" of food exchange, in which two individuals could reverse roles from night to night, depending on how successful each had been in finding blood. Because they are unable to make it through more than two nights in a row without food, it is a matter of life or death for vampire bats to have such buddies. Although the evidence is still meager, Wilkinson believes that these animals enter into social contracts in which each occasionally contributes part of a meal so as to be able to solicit a life-saving return favor during less favorable times.

Petr Kropotkin would have loved these little bats, as they exemplify the evolutionary principle advocated in his famous book *Mutual Aid,* which was first published in 1902. Though bearded and an anarchist, Kropotkin must not be thought of as a wild-eyed zealot. Stephen Jay Gould assures us, "Kropotkin is no crackpot."[19] Born a Russian prince, and very well educated, he was a naturalist and intellectual of great distinction. He was offered the position of secretary to the Imperial Geographical Society in Saint Petersburg, and later, during his exile in England, a chair in geology at Cambridge University. He declined both positions inasmuch as they would have interfered with his political activities, which aimed, according to a comrade, at opposing with an ecstasy of expiation the very injustice of which fate had made him the involuntary beneficiary.

Animals, Kropotkin argued in *Mutual Aid,* need to assist one another in their struggle for existence; a struggle, not so much of each against all, but of masses of organisms against the adversity of their environment. Cooperation is common, as when beavers together dam off a river or when horses form a protective ring against attacking wolves. Kropotkin did not stand alone in his emphasis on sociality and communion among animals: an entire generation of Russian scientists was uncomfortable with the primacy given in evolutionary thought to competition. Daniel Todes, in a fascinating treatise on Russian natural science aptly entitled *Darwin without Malthus,* argued that there may have been geographical reasons for this different outlook.

Whereas Darwin found inspiration in a voyage to rich, abundant tropical regions, Kropotkin at the age of nineteen set out to explore Siberia. Their ideas reflect the contrast between a world where life is easy, resulting in high population densities and intense competition, and one where life is harsh and filled with unpredictable dangers. When discussing evolution, Kropotkin and his compatriots always had their sparsely populated continent in mind, with its rapidly changing weather and extreme seasonality. He described climatic calamities that could render a territory as large as France and Germany combined absolutely impracticable for ruminants, in which horses could be scattered by the wind, and entire herds of cattle could perish under piles of snow.

> [These calamities] made me realize at an early date the overwhelming importance in nature of what Darwin described as "the natural checks to over-multiplication," in comparison to the struggle between individuals of the same species for the means of subsistence, which may go on here and there, to some limited extent, but never attains the importance of the former. Paucity of life, under-population—not over-population—being the distinctive feature of that immense part of the globe which we name Northern Asia, I conceived since then serious doubts as to the reality of that fearful competition for food and life within each species, which was an article of faith with most Darwinists, and, consequently, as to the dominant part which this sort of competition was supposed to play in the evolution of new species.

Kropotkin objected vehemently to the depiction of life as a "continuous free fight" and a "gladiator's show" made popular by the same Huxley who five years later, just before his death, partially reversed and softened his position to introduce morality as humanity's saving grace. Playing down Huxley's competitive principle, Kropotkin instead saw a communal principle at work: cooperation and mutual assistance among animals arose in response to the common enemy. The idea of a common enemy is perhaps the most significant of all of Kropotkin's ideas. In his mind it referred to the hostile environment in which many animals try to exist and multiply.

Kropotkin's analysis had serious flaws, and he sprinkled *Mutual Aid* with highly selective, often dubious examples to make his case. He had a (not so) hidden revolutionary agenda, and read political preferences into nature to the point that he totally overlooked its nasty side. He stated that "in the face of free Nature, the unsociable instincts have no opportunity to develop, and the general result is peace and harmony." Kropotkin, however, was writing in direct response to people who reduced everything in nature to savage, unmitigated combat.[20] Their position too could hardly be considered free from ideological bias. Russian scientists of that period saw the gladiatorial view as a concoction of the British upper class to defend the status quo.

Kropotkin cast his arguments in terms of survival of the group, or the species as a whole. Rejection of this view, known as group selection, marked the rise of sociobiology. Contemporary biologists in general do not believe that behavior evolved for a greater good. They assume that if bats, bees, dolphins, and other animals help one another, there must be benefits for each and every participant or their kin, otherwise the trait would not have spread.[21]

Old ideas never die completely, and group selection has been staging a gradual comeback.[22] It is also good to realize that Kropotkin was in excellent company in his belief that the success of the group matters: Darwin himself leaned toward group selection when tackling the issue of morality. He literally saw one tribe gain advantage over another:

> At all times throughout the world tribes have supplanted other tribes; and as morality is one element in their success, the standard of morality and the number of well-endowed men will thus everywhere tend to rise and increase.[23]

I should not leave the impression that Darwin and Kropotkin were in the same league as thinkers about evolution. Darwin argued his case much more systematically and coherently, and with vastly greater knowledge, than did the Russian naturalist. *Mutual Aid* was no match for Darwin's powerful exposé of the principles of natural selection, and Kropotkin, despite profound disagreements with Darwin's followers, never wavered in his admiration for the master himself.

Mutual aid became a standard ingredient of sociobiology, not through the writings of Kropotkin but because of a single article that presented the concept with such precision and clarity that modern biologists could not ignore it. I still remember the excitement when in 1972, with a number of students at the University of Utrecht, I analyzed Robert Trivers' "Evolution of Reciprocal Altruism." It remains one of my favorite articles. Rather than simplifying the relation between genes and behavior, it pays full attention to the intermediate levels such as emotions and psychological processes. It also distinguishes different types of cooperation based on what each participant puts into and gets out of it. For example, cooperation with immediate rewards does not qualify as reciprocal altruism. If wild dogs together bring down a wildebeest, all hunters benefit at the same time. Similarly, if a dozen pelicans form a semicircle in a shallow lake to herd small fish with their paddling feet, all birds profit when they together scoop up the fish. Because of the instant payoff, this kind of cooperation is widespread.

Reciprocal altruism, on the other hand, costs something before it delivers benefits. It has the following three characteristics:

1. The exchanged acts, while beneficial to the recipient, are costly to the performer.
2. There is a time lag between giving and receiving.
3. Giving is contingent on receiving.

This process is evidently a lot more complicated than simultaneous cooperation. There is, for example, the problem of the first helpful act—a gamble, since not every partner necessarily follows the rules. If I help you move your piano, I cannot be sure that you will do the same for me in the future. Or if one bat shares blood with another, there is no guarantee that the other will return the favor the next day. Reciprocal altruism differs from other patterns of cooperation in that it is fraught with risk, depends on trust, and requires that individuals whose contributions fall short be shunned or punished, lest the whole system collapse.

Reciprocal altruism does not work for individuals who rarely meet or who have trouble keeping track of who has done what for whom: it requires good memories and stable relationships, such as are found in the primates. Monkeys and apes make sharp distinctions between kin and nonkin as well as between enemies and friends. The chief purpose of friendship being mutual support, it is only natural that

Chimpanzee

Bonobo

Baboon

Stump-tailed macaque

Rhesus macaque

Capuchin

The order Primates includes nearly two hundred different species, ranging in size from the 100-gram pygmy marmoset to the 100-kilogram male gorilla. The six nonhuman primates most often referred to in the text are portrayed here. Chimpanzees and bonobos, as apes, belong to the same hominoid branch of the evolutionary tree as our own species; the other four primates depicted here are monkeys. The capuchin is the single New World monkey.

# CLOSENESS

Mammalian societies often are intimate groups in which everyone knows everyone else. Birth and death mark entry to and exit from the system: newborns are the center of attention, and attachments linger long after an individual's demise. The relationship between mother and offspring provides a blueprint for all other affiliations. Handicapped individuals may be fully accepted in the group.

A free-ranging Japanese monkey in Jigokudani Park born without hands and feet. Mozu (portrait on next page) has survived the harsh climate of this mountainous region for two decades.

At the age of three months Azalea, a retarded rhesus female born to an aging mother, showed unusual facial features. At the age of two years—when her peers were already quite independent and enterprising—Azalea was still being carried around and held by older kin—as below by a sister. *(Wisconsin Primate Center)*

A rhesus monkey with cuddly baby features. *(Wisconsin Primate Center)*

A snow-white newborn in its mother's lap, surrounded by other stump-tailed macaques. *(Wisconsin Primate Center)*

The capuchin monkey is sometimes referred to as the South American chimpanzee, even though capuchins and chimpanzees are only distant relatives. The two species share traits such as tool use, large brains, an omnivorous diet, slow development, and long lifespan. According to recent studies, food sharing needs to be added to this list. The photograph shows a mother and infant of the common brown, or tufted, capuchin. *(Yerkes Primate Center)*

Millions of years of selection for mothers who pay close attention to the needs of their offspring have promoted strong nurturing tendencies in mammalian females. A bonobo with her daughter. *(San Diego Zoo)*

Weaning compromises are sometimes worked out between mother and off-spring. One juvenile chimpanzee has developed a habit of "nursing" under her mother's armpit; another, of sucking on his mother's lower lip. *(Yerkes Field Station)*

Chimpanzees have many ways to attract sympathy. An adolescent female persuades her mother to go somewhere. First she whimpers in a plaintive voice, stretching out both hands (facing page). The daughter's face changes when her mother approaches (above, top). The two end up traveling together. *(Yerkes Field Station)*

What is remarkable about these sleeping rhesus monkeys is that they are the alpha female (left) and the lowest-ranking matriarch. Most of the time, hierarchical distance prevents such association. *(Wisconsin Primate Center)*

Rather than treasuring individual autonomy, our primate relatives devote a great deal of time to intimate relationships: a female Japanese monkey grooms a male. *(Jigokudani Park, Japan)*

Fifteen months after having lost her mother, Agatha still regularly returns to the fatal spot to gently turn and feel her mother's skull. *(From* Elephant Memories *by Cynthia Moss; Amboseli National Park, Kenya)*

Robert Trivers' theory of reciprocal altruism, published in 1971, is and will remain the centerpiece of any viable theory of moral evolution. On June 20, 1992, I interviewed Trivers about the history of his ideas at a meeting of the Gruter Institute for Law and Behavioral Research, in Squaw Valley, California.

**Q:** How did you come to write about reciprocal altruism?

**A:** I became aware of Hamilton's paper in 1966 or 1967, which explained altruism among kin. It immediately raised the issue of what other kinds of altruism there might be. Friendship is, I think, as strong an emotion as kinship ties . . . especially in the sort of fractured society that we live in. Naturally, I thought of "you scratch my back—I scratch yours," which is the folk expression for reciprocity.

**Q:** You did not have a lot of animal examples?

**A:** No, I knew about alarm calls in birds and cleaning symbiosis in fish, but none of the animal examples was terribly convincing. I thought coalitions in baboons might be a good candidate, but nobody really knew if they were reciprocal. Then I had a lucky break. I happened to take a course on morality, but the guy who gave it was so confused about the issue that I became more interested in his graduate student, Dennis Krebs, who was writing about what psychologists call "prosocial behavior" [he pulled a disgusted face]. Krebs's paper, which was later published, contained plenty of good examples of human altruism with absolutely no reference to their function or evolution. So all I had to do was reorganize this information along the lines of my ideas.

I was fond of arguing from humans to other creatures, anyway—rather than the opposite—perhaps because I came to biology rather late in life; I did not take a biology course until I was twenty-four.

**Q:** Reading between the lines, I recognize in your paper the same sort of social commitment that led Kropotkin to develop his ideas. . . .

**A:** People keep asking about Kropotkin. You know, I have never read the anthropologists who wrote about reciprocity, and I have never read Kropotkin. [He picked up a tiny ant that walked on the table, and explained how to tell that it was a male.]

But you're right about my political preferences. When I left mathematics and cast about what I was going to do in college, I said [ironic tone], "All right, I'll become a lawyer and fight for civil rights and against poverty!" Someone suggested that I take up U.S. history, but you know at that time, in the early 1960s, their books were entirely self-congratulatory. I ended up in biology.

Because I remained a political liberal, for me, emotionally, to see that just pursuing this scratch-my-back argument would generate rather quickly a reason for justice and fairness was very gratifying, because it was on the other side of the fence of that awful tradition in biology of the right of the strongest.

such relationships develop primarily between individuals with common interests. I know two inseparable females, Ropey and Beatle, in a large group of rhesus macaques that I followed for a decade at the Wisconsin Regional Primate Research Center. They are approximately the same age, and Beatle's family ranks just below Ropey's in the matrilineal hierarchy. I would have sworn they are sisters: they do everything together, often grooming each other, and softly lipsmacking at each other's infants. According to the center's records, however, Ropey and Beatle are totally unrelated.

This friendship typifies a general rule, called the *similarity principle,* which probably has much to do with reciprocal exchange. According to our computer records on hundreds of female-female relationships, female monkeys select friends on the basis of closeness in age and rank. In a macaque society, with its strict hierarchy, females of similar status experience harassment by the same dominants, and need to keep the same subordinates in line. Between females of similar age, important life stages are synchronized: they play together when they are young; they deliver their first offspring at about the same time; their daughters and sons grow up together, as do their grandchildren. With so much in common, it is no wonder that these females gravitate toward each other rather than toward females of different status, or much older or younger in age. The principle is also illustrated by Mozu's successful attempt to connect with females her own age in the dominant subdivision after fissioning of the Jigokudani group,

This is not to say that exceptions do not occur. I still recall the day on which the alpha female of our rhesus group walked up to the lowest-ranking matriarch, presented herself for grooming, and after a long session fell asleep in the midst of this female's family. Alpha was completely out of place as far as status was concerned, with her head serenely resting on the back of the other matriarch while this female's offspring, after much hesitation, huddled against the two in a sleeping cluster that superficially looked like any other.

Such special moments only serve to confirm the rule, which holds for our species as well. Besides age and socioeconomic status, the similarity principle in humans includes political preference, religion, ethnic background, IQ level, education, physical attractiveness, and height. Birds of a feather tend to like and love each other, to the extent that researchers can statistically predict if dating couples will break up or stay together based on how well they match on various dimensions. As in rhesus monkeys, these matching rules probably relate to prospects for cooperation: the more traits and interests one shares with another person, the easier it will be to get along, and the broader the basis for a give-and-take relationship.

That primates, consciously or unconsciously, seek the company of individuals with whom profitable partnerships are possible perhaps sounds too obvious to deserve attention. Not, however, if one considers the tradition in evolutionary biology of pitting the interests of one individual against those of another. Kropotkin's intuitive opposition to an exclusive focus on competition, and Trivers' concrete alternative have yet to sink in fully. Lack of appreciation of the widespread conflux of interests among members of the same species has led respectable biologists to ask the wrong questions. Puzzled by the fact that animals almost never fight to the death, some have felt the need to demonstrate mathematically that there are drawbacks to all-out competition. In doing so, they have zoomed in on the physical risks rather than the social consequences of fighting. The possibility that animals might wage "limited wars" because they know each other, need each other, hence value good relationships, never entered into the equations.

There can be little doubt that in many species the strong can annihilate the weak. In a world of mutual dependency, however, such a move would not be very smart. The real problem is not why aggression is tempered—it needs to be—but how cooperation and competition coexist. How do individuals strike a balance between serving their own interests and operating as a team? How are conflicts resolved without damage to social ties? If these questions (which follow directly from mutual aid as a factor in society) sound familiar, it is because we face them every day at home and at work.

## The Invisible Grasping Organ

As far back as 1714 a Dutch philosopher, Bernard de Mandeville, achieved international fame by exploiting the same shock effect that has since served so many popular authors. In a lengthy poem, *The Fable of the Bees: or, Private Vices, Public Benefits,* he ascribed the loftiest aspects of human life to our vilest qualities, comparing civilization to a beehive in which all individuals happily gratify each other's pride and vanity:

> Thus every part was full of vice
> Yet the whole mass a paradise.[24]

Whereas de Mandeville provided a mere satire, the idea of public blessings derived from the pursuit of self-interest gained respectability when the father of economics, Adam Smith, pronounced self-interest society's guiding principle. In a passage from the *Wealth of Nations,* first published in 1776, Smith saw each individual as being "led by an invisible hand to promote an end which was no part of his intention. Nor is it always the worse for society that it was no part of it. By pursuing his own interest he frequently promotes that of the society more effectually than when he really intends to promote it."[25]

The crux of Smith's famous invisible hand metaphor is that of a gap between intention and consequence; our actions may mean something entirely different in the bigger scheme of things than they do to us individually. Thus, life in the city depends on the professional services of bakers, mechanics, and storekeepers, whereas these people are only carving out a living for themselves and unknowingly are driven to serve the larger whole. To this day, the metaphor is popular with economists: a recent *New Yorker* cartoon showed a gathering of economists kneeling in the grass, hoping for a huge invisible hand to appear in the sky.

Smith's views were complex, however. As a moral philosopher, he knew full well that it would be hard to hold a society together purely on the basis of egoism. Like Huxley, Smith mellowed with age; he consecrated the final years of his life to a revision of *A Theory of Moral Sentiments,* expanding on his earlier belief in unselfish motives. Throughout this work Smith rejected the self-love thesis of de Mandeville, observing in the very first sentence that man possesses capacities "which interest him in the fortune of others, and render their happiness necessary to him, though he derives nothing from it, except the pleasure of seeing it."[26] This passage still stands as one of the most succinct and elegant definitions of human sympathy, a tendency Smith believed present in even the staunchest ruffian.

What makes the invisible hand metaphor so powerful is the idea of simultaneous micro and macro realities: the reality in the mind of each individual is not the same as the reality that emerges when many individuals interact. At one level we do A for reason B, while at another level A serves purpose C. Biologists are familiar with such multilevel thinking. For example, sex serves reproduction, yet animals engage in it without the slightest notion of its function; they are not driven by any desire to reproduce, only by sexual urges (as are humans most of the time). Similarly, members of a species do not need to have the benefits of mutual aid in mind when they help one another; these benefits may be so indirect and delayed in time that they matter only on an evolutionary timescale.

Imagine that you and I are sitting in individual boats adrift in the large swimming pool of an immense cruise ship. The ship has a slow and steady course to the north, but we care only about the direction of our little boats and cannot see beyond the body of water within which we are maneuvering. Even though I decide to head west and you to head south, to the outside observer both of us wind up going north. Since our experiences do not match our eventual destination, we live in separate proximate and ultimate realities.[27]

Intention and consequence need not be independent, however, particularly in our species. Often we have a reasonable understanding of the effects of our actions, especially when these effects are immediately obvious. Thus, it cannot escape us that one function of cooperative behavior is what appears to be its antipode: competition. Is not cooperative competition what team sport and party politics are all about?

In the primate order, the most widespread and best-developed collaboration is alliance formation, defined as two or more individuals banding together to defeat a third. For example, two male chimpanzees team up in order to overthrow the established ruler. The two challengers will swagger shoulder to shoulder in an intimidating manner, with their hair on end, often embracing or mounting each other directly in front of their rival, and of course supporting each other if it comes to an actual confrontation. By doing so for weeks or months on end, they wage a veritable war of nerves that may force the other male out of power. This is one of the most committed forms of animal cooperation that I know, one in which lives are literally at stake. Alpha males rarely go down without a fight.

Idealists such as Kropotkin tend to focus entirely on the agreeable side of cooperation, such as loyalty, trust, and camaraderie, while ignoring the competitive side. Although the Russian naturalist did refer to the role of a common enemy in fostering mutual aid, he conveniently ignored the possibility that the enemy might belong to one's own species. In *The Biology of Moral Systems* the biologist Richard Alexander presents our violent history of group against group and nation against nation as the ultimate reason why we attach so much value to the common good and to ethical conduct.

Alexander points out, however, that conflict between groups cannot be the whole explanation. Ants, for example, engage in terrible warfare on a massive scale, yet no one would argue that they have anything resembling a moral system. Thousands of them may be locked in deadly combat carried out in broad daylight on the sidewalks of our cities, while thousands more are recruited to join the massacre. Within each colony, however, harmony reigns. Ants form colonies of millions of individuals produced by and reproducing through a single female, the queen. With such overlapping reproductive interests, why should they compete with their own colony mates? And without conflicts of interest to be settled, what good would a moral system do?

The second condition for the evolution of morality, then, is conflict *within* the group. Moral systems are produced by tension between individual and collective interests, particularly when entire collectivities compete against one another.

If the need to get along and treat each other decently is indeed rooted in the need to stick together in the face of external threats, it would explain why one of Christianity's most heralded moral principles, the sanctity of life, is interpreted so flexibly, depending on which group, race, or nation the life belongs to. As recently as 1991, a war was declared "clean" and said to have been conducted with "clinical precision" despite the loss of more than a hundred thousand lives! Because the overwhelming majority of the dead in the Gulf War had fallen on the other side, Western media and politicians saw no need to burden our consciences.

Human history furnishes ample evidence that moral principles are oriented to one's own group, and only reluctantly (and never evenhandedly) applied to the outside world. Standing on the medieval walls of a European city, we can readily imagine how tightly life within the walls was regulated and organized, whereas outsiders were only important enough to be doused with boiling oil. There is of course great irony in Alexander's suggestion that the moral underpinnings of the community, on the one hand, and warfare and ethnic strife, on the other, are two sides of the very same coin. In modern times we highly value the first, yet feel embarrassed by the stubborn persistence of the second.

Both conditions for the evolution of morality apply to monkeys and apes. First, many species engage in intergroup conflict, mostly at low intensity but sometimes with extreme brutality. Wild male chimpanzees, for example, may take over a neighboring territory by systematically killing off the males of the other community. Second, while there is no lack of strife and competition within groups, we also know that primates have ways of resolving conflict nonaggressively. Because this was the subject of my previous book, *Peacemaking among Primates,* it is only logical that I investigate morality next. In doing so, I will take the perspective of the animals themselves in their day-to-day social life: their proximate reality. Insofar as the course of the big ship of evolution is concerned, I will rely on the combined ideas of Kropotkin, Trivers, and Alexander.

The one extension I would like to make is what I will call *community concern.* Inasmuch as every member benefits from a unified, cooperative group, one expects them to care about the society they live in and make an effort to improve and strengthen it, similar to the way the spider repairs her web and the beaver maintains the integrity of his dam. Continued infighting, particularly at the top of the hierarchy, may damage everyone's interests; hence the settlement of conflict is not just a matter of the parties involved, it concerns the community as a whole. I do not necessarily mean that animals make sacrifices for their community, but rather that each and every individual has a stake in the quality of the social environment on which its survival depends. In trying to improve this quality for their own purposes, they help many of their group mates at the same time. An example is arbitration and mediation in disputes; it is standard practice in human society—courts of law serve this function—but recognizable in other primates as well.

With their flamboyant orange coats of thick, long hair and their gentle blue faces, golden monkeys are perhaps the most gorgeous primates in the world. In the wild, these rare langurs from China occur in aggregations of up to three hundred or four hundred individuals. Field-workers believe that within these groupings exist many smaller units of a single adult male, several females, and their dependent offspring. As in other primates with one-male units, male golden monkeys are twice the size of females. Even if the male therefore is absolute king, the integrity of his unit probably depends as much on how well the females get along as on his dominance over them.

RenMei Ren, a primatologist at the University of Peking, found that male golden monkeys actively promote peaceful coexistence among their females, intervening in virtually every female altercation. They either break up the flight by dispersing the combatants or prevent further hostilities by taking up a position between them. Occasionally the male will calm tempers by gesturing to both female rivals, turning from one to the other with a friendly facial expression or combing his fingers through the long hair on each female's back. Once, when a male was removed from a captive group for health reasons, Ren noticed excessive violence among the females. The situation improved immediately upon the male's return.

Mediation "from above" by a high-ranking individual is obviously easier than mediation "from below." The principle remains that of a third party promoting good relationships, yet the risks are greater in the latter case because both combatants may take out their tensions on a low-ranking mediator. Nevertheless, such mediation does occur—but as far as we know, only in the chimpanzee. When male chimpanzees fail to reconcile after a confrontation, they sometimes sit a couple of meters apart as if waiting for their opponent to make the first move. The uneasiness between them is obvious from the way they look in all directions—the sky, the grass, their own body—while scrupulously avoiding eye contact with each other. On a previous occasion I described how this deadlock may be broken by a female mediator:

> Especially after serious conflicts between two adult males, the two opponents sometimes were brought together by an adult female. The female approached one of the males, kissed or touched him or presented towards him and then slowly walked towards the other male. If the male followed, he did so very close behind her (often inspecting her genitals) and without looking at the other male. On a few occasions the female looked behind at her follower, and sometimes returned to a male that stayed behind to pull at his arm to make him follow. When the female sat down close to the other male, both males started to groom her and they simply continued grooming after she went off. The only difference being that they groomed each other after this moment, and panted, spluttered, and smacked more frequently and loudly than before the female's departure.[28]

During our studies of the world's largest chimpanzee colony at the Arnhem Zoo in the Netherlands, such mediating behavior was repeatedly observed. It allows male rivals to approach each other without taking any initiative, without making eye contact, and perhaps without losing face. Females in this colony also approached males who were gearing up for a confrontation (male chimpanzees may sit for five or ten minutes with their hair erect, swaying from side to side and hooting, before actually turning against each other) to gently pry open their hands and "confiscate" weapons such as heavy sticks or rocks. If female chimpanzees appear concerned about male relationships, they have excellent reason: males have a tendency to take tensions out on females.

Community concern, then, is expressed in the amelioration of social relationships among others to the intervener's own advantage. This represents a first step toward a system such as human morality that actually elevates community interests above individual interests. Not that the two ever become disconnected—natural selection would never produce such an arrangement—yet the focus may gradually shift away from the individual toward the collective, or rather from egocentric to shared community concerns. Insofar as certain qualities of the social environment benefit large numbers of individuals, it is logical for the participants to encourage each other in shaping the community along these lines. The more developed the system of encouragement, the more important common goals become relative to private ones. Some of this encouragement may take the form of what Alexander has termed *indirect reciprocity:* rather than through a direct exchange of favors between two individuals, as in reciprocal altruism, helpful behavior may pay off via third parties.

Imagine that you have put your life at risk to save little John, who was playing on the railroad tracks. Within hours, the entire village will know what happened because people take careful note of social events around them. Your standing as a fine and trustworthy person will immediately go up one or two notches, which may help your contacts and your business. It is not little John who is doing you a return favor, but the community as a whole. It rewards behavior that improves the quality of life. If all community members keep an eye on how each one of them responds to others in need, they will quickly learn who is likely to help and who is not. Once doing good is appreciated at the group level, it does not need to be rewarded on a tit-for-tat basis to yield benefits.

In a moral community, it matters not just what I do to you and what you do to me, but also what others think of our actions. Perceptions become a major issue. For this reason Adam Smith introduced an imaginary *impartial spectator* capable of evaluating social events with sympathy and understanding. Our actions are mirrored in the eyes of the spectator in the same way that everything we do is reflected in the responses of our group. Theories of moral evolution need to assign a significant role to such outside attention, hence concern themselves with the community level. Although Darwinian at their core, they thus begin to transcend the exclusive focus on the individual by taking as their subject the way conflicts of interest are

Conditions for the evolution of morality:

1. **Group value**     Dependence on the group for finding food or defense against enemies and predators
2. **Mutual aid**       Cooperation and reciprocal exchange within the group
3. **Internal conflict**   Individual members have disparate interests

Given the above conditions, intragroup conflict needs to be resolved through a balancing of individual and collective interests, which can be done at both dyadic and higher levels:

1. **Dyadic level**     One-on-one interaction between individuals, such as direct reciprocation of aid and reconciliation following fights
2. **Higher levels**    Community concern, or care about good relationships between others, expressed in mediated reconciliation, peaceful arbitration of disputes, appreciation of altruistic behavior on a groupwide basis (indirect reciprocity), and encouragement of contributions to the quality of the social environment. (The last two may be limited to human moral systems; the first two are more widespread.)

resolved and societies are constructed. If each individual tries to shape its social environment and receive feedback about how these efforts affect others, society becomes essentially an arena of negotiation and give-and-take.

Our thinking here begins to resemble a *social contract,* getting close to philosophical, psychological, sociological, and anthropological theories of human sociality. While some may regard this as a watering down of the evolutionary approach, it is an inevitable development. Faced with a mountain as intimidating as morality, we either acquire the theoretical gear to climb all the way to the top, or we stay in the foothills with a few simplistic notions.[29]

## Ethology and Ethics

In the 1940s a special label became necessary to distinguish the study of animal behavior in nature from the laboratory experiments of behaviorists on white rats and other domesticated animals. The chosen name was *ethology,* and its most famous representative became the Austrian zoologist Konrad Lorenz. The image of Lorenz being followed by a cohort of honking geese, or calling his tame raven out of the sky, was quite different from that of B. F. Skinner with his hand around the wings of a pigeon, placing the bird in a so-called Skinner box. The distinction was not merely in the personal relation with the subject of study and the way behavioral information was being extracted, but also in the favored explanation—with one school emphasizing instinct, the other learning.

The term "ethology" comes from the Greek *ethos,* which means character, both in the sense of what is characteristic of a person or animal and in the sense of moral qualities. Thus, in seventeenth-century English an ethologist was an actor who portrayed human characters on stage, and in the nineteenth century ethology referred to the science of building character. While it cannot be denied that there are some real characters among contemporary ethologists, the meaning of the word changed when a Frenchman, Isidore Geoffroy-Saint-Hillaire, selected it in 1859 to denote the study of animal behavior in the natural habitat. The term survived in a small circle of French biologists until, almost a century later, it became popular among other continental students of animal behavior. When ethology later reached Great Britain, the term gained its current status in Webster's as "the scientific study of the characteristic behavior patterns of animals" (although most ethologists would probably change "scientific" to "naturalistic").[30]

Early ethology stressed instinct—suggesting purely inborn behavior—yet was by no means blind to other influences. In fact, one of its strongest contributions was the study of imprinting, a learning process. Ducklings and goslings are not born with any detailed knowledge of their species; they acquire information in the first hours of their life. Normally, they do so by watching and following their mother, but they may take cues from any moving object encountered during the sensitive period. In nature, the chance of becoming attached to the wrong kind of object is minimal, but scientists have been able to make birds follow toy trucks and bearded zoologists. Therefore, what is innate in these birds is not so much any precise knowledge of their species, but a tendency to acquire this knowledge at a critical stage in life.

The mind does not start out as a tabula rasa, but rather as a checklist with spaces allotted to particular types of incoming information. Predispositions to learn specific things at specific ages are widespread, the best human example being language acquisition. We are not born with a particular language, but with the capacity to organize rather chaotic information into an orderly linguistic structure. Before the age of seven, we are so incredibly successful at this that our mind seems like a sponge, ready to absorb all sorts of subtleties of the language spoken around us. Whatever we learn later on never compares to the ease of use of our native tongue. I speak from experience: both at home and on the job, I have used two nonnative languages on a daily basis for decades, yet every sentence in these languages still requires a fraction of a second more processing time than my native Dutch. Secondary languages are donned like clothes; only the native tongue feels like skin.[31]

Human morality shares with language that it is far too complex to be learned through trial and error, and far too variable to be genetically programmed. Some cultures permit the killing of newborns, whereas others debate abortion of the unborn. Some cultures disapprove of premarital sex, whereas others encourage it as part of a healthy sexual education. The gravest error of biologists speculating about the origin of morality has been to ignore this variability, and to downplay the learned character of ethical principles.

Possibly we are born, not with any specific social norms, but with a learning agenda that tells us which information to imbibe and how to organize it. We could then figure out, understand, and eventually internalize the moral fabric of our native society. Because a similar learning agenda seems to regulate language acquisition, I will speak of *moral ability* as a parallel to language ability. In a sense, we are imprinted upon a particular moral system through a process that, though hundreds of times more complicated than the imprinting of birds, may be just as effective and lasting. And, as in birds, the outcome may deviate from the norm. A friend of mine attributes the thrill she gets from smuggling to the praise she received as a young girl whenever she managed to stash away food (during World War II she spent years in a Japanese concentration camp). The criminal justice system of course encounters far more serious deviations, and these too can often be traced to lessons received, or not received, during sensitive phases of moral development.[32]

Does this make morality a biological or a cultural phenomenon? There really is no simple answer to this sort of question, which has been compared to asking whether percussive sounds are produced by drummers or by drums. If we have learned anything from the debate

IM, the two-headed snake. (Courtesy of Gordon Burghardt; University of Tennessee)

between ethologists and behaviorists, it is that nature and nurture can be only partially disentangled. The same is true of relatively simple processes, such as the effect of light on plants. If a plant in a sunny spot grows taller than one in the shade, it is not because of either genetics or the environment, but both. True, the size difference is produced by variable light conditions, but it is equally true that light matters the way it does because of the genetic makeup of this particular organism; other plants thrive in the shade and shrivel in the sun. Environmental influences—including human culture—vary with the genetic "substrate" on which they act.

Perhaps a snake named IM is the best analogue to the false dichotomies of the past. This double-headed monstrosity, which I once held in my hands (after having been reassured about its friendly character), lives at the University of Tennessee. Gordon Burghardt, an American ethological psychologist, explained that the left head had been named "Instinct" and the right head "Mind" because of the perennial conflict between these concepts. The two heads of the snake literally fight over prey, each attempting to swallow the mouse or rat and thereby lengthening the ingestion process from minutes to hours. It is a futile battle, since the food ends up nourishing exactly the same body.

Nevertheless, scientists retain a tendency to claim the primacy of one head or the other, and ethologists have been no exception. Virtually every existing moral principle has by now been biologically explained, a dubious genre of literature going back to Ernest Seton's *Natural History of the Ten Commandments,* published in 1907. Other biblical titles have followed, principally in the German language, spelling out how moral principles contribute to survival of the species.[33] If law and religion prohibit the killing of fellow humans, the reasoning goes, it is in order to prevent extinction of the human race. Supported by the then-prevailing opinion that no animal ever lethally attacks a member of its own species, this argument sounded logical enough. But we know now that we are by no means the only murderous species, not even the only "killer ape." In the Arnhem chimpanzee colony, for example, one male was killed and castrated by two others in a fight over sex and power. The steadily growing list of species in which lethal aggression occurs—even if rarely—illustrates the weakness of species-survival arguments.[34]

Much of this literature assumes that the world is waiting for biologists to point out what is Normal and Natural, hence worth being adopted as ideal. Attempts to derive ethical norms from nature are highly problematic, however. Biologists may tell us how things are, perhaps even analyze human nature in intricate detail, yet there is no logical connection between the typical form and frequency of a behavior (a statistical measure of what is "normal") and the value we attach to it (a moral decision). Lorenz came close to confusing the two when he was disappointed that the perfect goose marriage, with the partners faithful unto death, was actually quite rare. But perhaps Lorenz was only titillating his readers with his favorite birds' "shortcomings," because he also gave us his student's wonderful retort: "What do you expect? After all, geese are only human!"[35]

Known as the *naturalistic fallacy,* the problem of deriving norms from nature is very old indeed. It has to do with the impossibility of translating "is" language (how things are) into "ought" language (how things ought to be). In 1739 the philosopher David Hume made these points in *A Treatise of Human Nature:*

> In every system of morality, which I have hitherto met with, I have always remarked that the author proceeds for some time in the ordinary way of reasoning, and establishes the being of God, or makes observations concerning human affairs; when of a sudden I am surprised to find, that instead of the usual copula-

tion of propositions, *is,* and *is not,* I meet with no proposition that is not connected with an *ought,* or an *ought not.* This change is imperceptible; but is, however, of the last consequence. For as this *ought,* or *ought not,* expresses some new relation or affirmation, it is necessary that it should be observed and explained; and at the same time that a reason should be given, for what seems altogether inconceivable, how this new relation can be a deduction from others, which are entirely different from it.[36]

To put the issue of ethics back into ethology in a more successful manner, we need to take note of the chorus of protest against previous attempts. Philosophers tell us that there is an element of rational choice in human morality, psychologists say that there is a learning component, and anthropologists argue that there are few if any universal rules. The distinction between right and wrong is made by people on the basis of how they would like their society to function. It arises from interpersonal negotiation in a particular environment, and derives its sense of obligation and guilt from the internalization of these processes. Moral reasoning is done by *us,* not by natural selection.

At the same time it should be obvious that human morality cannot be infinitely flexible. Of our own design are neither the tools of morality nor the basic needs and desires that form the substance with which it works. Natural tendencies may not amount to moral imperatives, but they do figure in our decision-making. Thus, while some moral rules reinforce species-typical predispositions and others suppress them, none blithely ignore them.[37]

Evolution has produced the requisites for morality: a tendency to develop social norms and enforce them, the capacities of empathy and sympathy, mutual aid and a sense of fairness, the mechanisms of conflict resolution, and so on. Evolution also has produced the unalterable needs and desires of our species: the need of the young for care, a desire for high status, the need to belong to a group, and so forth. How all of these factors are put together to form a moral framework is poorly understood, and current theories of moral evolution are no doubt only part of the answer.

In the remainder of this book, I will investigate the extent to which aspects of morality are recognizable in other animals, and try to illuminate how we may have moved from societies in which things were as they were to societies with a vision of how things ought to be.

# 2

# SYMPATHY

> Any animal whatever, endowed with
> well-marked social instincts, the paren-
> tal and filial affections being here in-
> cluded, would inevitably acquire a
> moral sense or conscience, as soon as
> its intellectual powers had become as
> well developed, or nearly as well devel-
> oped, as in man.
>
> *Charles Darwin*[1]

It is simply unimaginable that fish would come to the rescue of an
unlucky pond mate who is jerked out of the water, that they would
bite the angler's line, or butt their heads against his boat in protest.
We also do not expect them to miss their mate, search around, stop
eating, and waste away. Fish are, well, cold to each other. They
neither groom one another like primates, nor do they mutually lick,
nibble, preen, or chat. I say this without any antifish bias. As a
lifelong aquarium enthusiast, I can watch these animals for hours, yet
I would never recommend them to someone in need of affection.

How different from the warm-blooded animals that took to the sea
eighty million years ago!

## Warm Blood in Cold Waters

Reports of leviathan care and assistance go back to the ancient
Greeks. Dolphins are said to save companions by biting through
harpoon lines or by hauling them out of nets in which they have
gotten entangled. Whales may interpose themselves between a

hunter's boat and an injured conspecific or capsize the boat. In fact, their tendency to come to the defense of victims is so predictable that whalers take advantage of it. Once a pod of sperm whales is sighted, the gunner need only strike one among them. When other pod members encircle the ship, splashing the water with their flukes, or surround the injured whale in a flowerlike formation known as the marguerite, the gunner has no trouble picking them off one by one. Such "sympathy entrapment" would be effective with few other animals.

But am I justified in using the term "sympathy," which after all is a venerated human concept with very special connotations? Let us for the moment simply speak of *succorant behavior,* defined as helping, caregiving, or providing relief to distressed or endangered individuals other than progeny. Thus, the dog staying protectively close to a crying child shows succorance, whereas the same dog responding to the yelps of her puppies shows nurturance. In reviewing the succorant behavior of animals we will pay special attention to characteristics it might share with human sympathy, the most important being empathy—that is, the ability to be vicariously affected by someone else's feelings and situation. Psychologists and philosophers consider this capacity so central that "empathy" has gradually replaced "sympathy," "compassion," "sorrow," and "pity" in much of their writings (I have even seen the famous Stones' song paraphrased as "Empathy for the Devil").

This blurring is unfortunate, for it ignores the distinction between the ability to recognize someone else's pain and the impulse to do something about it. Administering electrical shocks to someone else's genitals or pouring bleach in open wounds, as done by the torturers of our fine race, involves the very same ability of knowing what makes others suffer, yet it is quite the opposite of sympathy. What sets sympathy apart from cruelty, sadism, or plain indifference is that sensitivity to the other's situation goes together with *concern* about him or her. As neatly summed up by the psychologist Lauren Wispé: "The object of empathy is understanding. The object of sympathy is the other person's well-being."[2]

Whether based on empathy or not, animal succorance is the functional equivalent of human sympathy, expected only in species that know strong attachment. I am not speaking here of anonymous aggregations of fish or butterflies, but the individualized bonding, affection, and fellowship of many mammals and birds.

There certainly is no shortage of attachment among whales and dolphins, which may beach themselves collectively because of their reluctance to abandon a distressed group mate, including a disoriented one. Whereas this action is often fatal to an entire herd, James Porter, an American oceanographer, describes a fascinating exception. When in 1976 thirty pseudorcas (false killer whales) had stranded on an island off the coast of Florida, they remained together in shallow water for three entire days until the largest one had died. The twenty-nine healthy whales would have been unable to return to the ocean (hence would have perished with their apparent leader) under normal tidal conditions. But the tidal range happened to be minimal, so that most of the time the whales did have the option of leaving. "Stranding" is the wrong word, therefore; the whales stayed close to shore of their own accord.

With blood exuding from his right ear, the sick male was flanked and protected by fourteen or fifteen whales in a wedge-shaped configuration. The group was noisy, producing an incredible variety of chirps and squeaks. "With some trepidation, but no common sense," as he commented afterward, Porter entered the water to snorkel toward the group. The outermost individual responded by breaking loose and heading menacingly toward him. Instead of attacking, however, the whale lowered its head and slid underneath the scientist, lifting him out of the water and carrying him to the beach. This procedure was repeated three times, after which Porter tried his luck on the other side. There, too, the outermost whale carried him back to land several times. Porter noted that the whales lost interest in him as soon as he took off his snorkel, suggesting that they were showing a rescue response to sounds that perhaps resembled those of a clogged blowhole.[3]

The U.S. Coast Guard was unable to break up the formation or push the pseudorcas offshore: "If separated from the pack a whale would become highly agitated, and no amount of human effort could restrain its returning to the group. As soon as the whales touched each other, however, they became docile and could easily be nudged into deeper water."[4] (The calming effect of body contact extended to humans who, in a typical act of cross-species sympathy, applied suntan oil to whale backs exposed to sun and air.)

Once the large male had died, the formation around him loosened. Breaking ranks, the whales headed for deeper water while uttering high-pitched descending whistles. Autopsy revealed that the male,

6 meters long, had a massive worm infection in his ear. It is possible that parasitic worms impair a whale's echolocation system, hence its feeding efficiency: the victim's stomach proved empty.

While this account by no means solves the mystery of whale strandings, it gives an idea of how extraordinarily attached to each other these creatures are. If attachment and bonding are at the root of succorant behavior, parental care must be its ultimate evolutionary source. As explained by Irenäus Eibl-Eibesfeldt, with the evolution of parental care in birds and mammals came feeding, warming, cleaning, alleviation of distress, and grooming of the young, which in turn led to the development of infantile appeals to trigger these activities. Once tender exchanges between parent and offspring had evolved— with the one asking for and the other providing care—they could be extended to all sorts of other relationships, including those among unrelated adults. Thus, in many birds the female begs for food from her mate with the same gaping mouth and wing shaking as that of a hungry fledgling, while the male demonstrates his caretaking abilities by providing her with a nice tidbit.

Absorption of parental care into adult human relationships is evident from the widespread use of infantile names (such as "baby") for mates and lovers, and the special high-pitched voice that we reserve for both young children and intimate partners. In this context, Eibl-Eibesfeldt mentions the kiss, which probably derives from mouth-to-mouth feeding of masticated food. Kissing without any transfer of food is an almost universal human expression of love and affection, which, according to the ethologist, resembles kiss-feeding "with one partner playing the accepting part by opening the mouth in a babyish fashion and the other partner performing tongue movements as if to pass food."[5] Significantly, chimpanzees both kiss-feed their young and kiss between adults. A close relative of the chimpanzee, the bonobo, even tongue-kisses.

The continuum of nurturance, attachment, and succorance may not be entirely understood; still, it is hard to argue with its existence. It explains why dolphins and whales, perfectly adapted to the same milieu as fish, act totally unlike them when members of their species are in trouble. A long evolutionary history of parental care combined with a high degree of mutual dependence among adults has endowed these sea mammals with a profoundly different attitude toward one another.

## Special Treatment of the Handicapped

For the same reason that whales may fall victim to sympathy entrapment, we humans are vulnerable too. Heini Hediger, the Swiss pioneer of *zoo biology* (the discipline that uses ethology for the improvement of captive conditions), recounts how a lonely gorilla once captured an inexperienced keeper. Having noticed the gorilla desperately struggling to free her arm from the cage bars, the keeper hurried to open her cage and assist in the attempt. The ape, who was not stuck at all, quickly hid behind the door to surprise the keeper. All she did was wrap her arms around him—which, in the case of a gorilla, is guaranteed to restrict a man's movements.

Anecdotes of deception—of which there are many with great apes at the center—tend to be scrutinized for signs of intentionality and planning, yet there is another side to the gorilla's my-arm-got-stuck charade. Hediger comments that the ape must have foreseen the caretaker's humane reaction. The important question arises whether anticipation of helpful behavior to the point of exploitation is possible in a creature devoid of aiding tendencies. In other words, does the setting of a sympathy trap not imply familiarity with the feeling of sympathy?

Perhaps not. Apes may simply learn that one of the many amazing things humans do is take care of distressed individuals, and that this tendency can be used against them. Yet, as we will see, the same tendency exists in other primates, and deception resting on this principle is not limited to human-ape relationships. When in the Arnhem chimpanzee colony the oldest male, Yeroen, had hurt his hand in a fight with an up-and-coming young male, he limped for a week even though the wound seemed superficial. After a while we discovered that Yeroen limped only if he could be seen by his rival. For example, he would walk from a point in front of him to a point behind him, hobbling pitifully at first, only to change to a perfectly normal gait when out of the other male's sight. The possibility that injuries inhibit aggression by rivals may explain Yeroen's attempt to create a false image of pain and suffering.[6]

Primates, including humans, develop succorant tendencies surprisingly early in life, thus contradicting an extensive literature according to which the young are egocentric, mean, even egregiously sinful. This negative view reflects a peculiar assumption about kindness: instead of flowing from the heart—or whatever is taken as the center of emotion—care and sympathy are considered products of the brain.

Because young children lack a high level of cognition and moral understanding, the reasoning goes, there is no way for them to overcome their selfishness. Yet when the psychologist Carolyn Zahn-Waxler visited homes to find out how children respond to family members instructed to feign sadness (sobbing), pain (crying out "ouch"), or distress (coughing and choking), she discovered that children little more than one year of age already comfort others. It is a milestone in their development: an aversive experience in another person draws a concerned response, such as patting, hugging, rubbing the victim's hurt, and so on. Because expressions of sympathy emerge at such an early age in virtually every member of our species, they are as natural an achievement as the first step.

In an attempt to keep the focus on mental processes, Philip Lieberman, an American linguistic anthropologist, interpreted the same result as the first sign of what he chauvinistically labeled "altruism in the higher human sense."[7] Apart from the obvious emotional base, Lieberman emphasized cognition and language, thus ignoring the fact that the actions of one-year-olds far outstrip their verbal abilities. Precisely for this reason Zahn-Waxler has expressed reservations about interviews as a way of gauging empathy and sympathy. With the trouble young children have putting sentiments into words, they may well come across as egocentric when in reality they are already quite caring and protective.

Attention to what children actually do, rather than what they tell interviewers about themselves, is revolutionizing our view of moral development: emotions and actions often seem to come first, rationalizations and justifications later. These insights are also relevant for animal research, which of necessity relies on observation. The same techniques can be applied in both cases, as psychologists unintentionally discovered in their experiments in the household: some pets appeared as upset as the children by the "distress" of a family member, hovering over them or putting their heads in their laps with what looked like great concern. Possibly, then, "altruism in the higher human sense" is not limited to our species.

One day in the rhesus group at the Wisconsin Primate Center, several adult members of the highest-ranking matriline attacked a small juvenile named Fawn, viciously biting their screaming victim from different sides. In typical rhesus fashion, the aggressors regularly turned around to glare at Fawn's mother and sisters, keeping them away from the scene. The fight was so unequal and so severe that I broke it up, shouting at the top of my lungs. (Only a few times a year would we consider such intervention necessary.) Fawn was completely overcome with fear when her attackers finally left. For quite a while she lay on her belly screaming loudly; then she suddenly jumped up and fled. Afterward she sat in a hunched position, looking miserable and exhausted. After two minutes her older sister approached to put an arm around her. When the dazed Fawn failed to respond, her sister gently pushed and pulled at her as if trying to activate her, then embraced her again. The two sisters ended up huddling together while their mother, perhaps in order to avert further problems, groomed the female who had spearheaded the assault.

I must add that comforting acts such as the one by Fawn's sister are rare in a rhesus group. In fact, responses to distressed individuals are most conspicuous in the very young of this species. My assistant, Lesleigh Luttrell, and I would no doubt have missed these instances had we not made a special study of social development. Young infants are easily overlooked; they are tiny, look alike, and seem to matter little in the bigger scheme of things. Our study, however, forced us to recognize individually even the smallest infants, recording their every move. It turned out to be a fascinating experience, because at this early age rhesus monkeys do not yet show the rather intolerant, combative temperament typical of their species.

If one of our little subjects screamed for whatever reason, another infant often hurried over for a brief mount or embrace. An infant might have been threatened or frightened, or might have fallen out of the climbing frame. Most of the time the resulting contact seemed next best to a maternal embrace in terms of calming the infant. Yet whereas a mother's protective and reassuring intentions are rather evident, the same could not be said of the peers. Irresistibly drawn to the distressed infant, other infants showed a strong inclination to make contact, but it was not clear that they had the other's interests in mind.

Once, when an infant had been bitten because it had accidentally landed on a dominant female, it screamed so incessantly that it was soon surrounded by many other infants. I counted eight climbing on top of the poor victim—pushing, pulling, and shoving each other as well as the infant. Obviously the infant's fright was scarcely alleviated; the response seemed blind and automatic, as if the other infants were as distraught as the victim and sought to comfort *themselves* rather than the other.

Although it is hard to know the intentions of animals, we can speculate about them and may one day reach the point of testing one interpretation against another. For a research program into animal empathy, it is not enough to review the highlights of succorant behavior; it is equally important to consider the *absence* of such behavior when it might have been expected. Here are two striking examples from rhesus monkeys.

*Example 1*    Rita broke her arm at the age of seven months, leaving it dangling lifelessly at her side. At first we thought the arm had been disjointed, but x-rays showed it to be fractured. The veterinarian decided not to do anything; bones tend to heal rapidly in young monkeys, and treatment would have required the infant's removal from the group. Remarkably, during the weeks in which Rita could not use her arm, none of the other monkeys seemed to notice her handicap. Juveniles would roughhouse with her as if nothing was the matter, and high-ranking adults would threaten or chase her as they would any other junior nuisance. Even Rita's mother, Ropey, did not in any way alter her behavior; she subjected the infant to exactly the same weaning trauma as other mothers did to Rita's peers.

Rita endured this treatment, and her arm did heal perfectly.

*Example 2*    A giant vertical wheel in the middle of the cage invites all sorts of games, the most spectacular being pubertal males spinning it faster and faster so as to catapult themselves to the cage ceiling, meters above the wheel. I have never seen a device so effective in keeping monkeys occupied and active. As with all such devices, it is not entirely without danger. One day an infant shrieked in panic when its arm caught in the spokes of the wheel while "teenagers" were playing their daredevil games. An adult male resting next to the wheel became so annoyed by the din that he threatened and hit out at the screaming infant each time it passed. Because this male was normally quite tolerant of small infants, the scene suggested his total lack of realization of the infant's predicament.

In the above examples, monkeys faced an acute situation or a temporary change in another's condition. What if an impairment lasts longer than a couple of weeks? In such cases, monkeys do learn to adjust to the other individual in the same way that they learn to take the needs and inabilities of the young into account. I always admire the complete control of adult males at play; with formidable canines, they gnaw and wrestle with juveniles without hurting them in the least. During play with older and stronger partners, on the other hand, monkeys pull no punches; juveniles will jump on an adult male's back and hit him in the face with an energy that would be fatal if it happened the other way around. Primates play one way with the strong, another way with the weak.[8]

Play inhibitions most likely are a product of conditioning. From an early age, monkeys learn that the fun will not last if they are too rough with a younger playmate; the youngster will scream in protest, try to pull away, or worse, the play will be broken up heavy-handedly by a protective mother. These negative consequences shape the behavior of older individuals. The same process of *learned adjustment* may explain why handicapped members of monkey societies are treated differently. Healthy members do not necessarily know what is wrong, but gradually become familiar with the limitations of their less fortunate mates.

Learned adjustment is best contrasted with *cognitive empathy*. that is, the ability to picture oneself in the position of another individual. This is an extension of sensitivity to expressions of emotion but goes quite a bit further. To explain how it works, imagine that a friend has lost both arms in a car accident. Just from seeing his condition, or hearing about it, we will grasp the reduction in physical ability he has undergone. We can imagine what it is like to have no arms, and our capacity for empathy allows us to extrapolate this knowledge to the other's situation. Our friend's dog, by contrast, will need time to learn that there is no point in bringing her master a stick to fetch, or that the familiar pat on the back is being replaced by a foot rub. Dogs are smart enough to get used to such changes, but their accommodation is based on learning rather than understanding. The result may be somewhat the same. But in the first case, differential treatment of the disabled is based on an understanding of their limitations; in the second, on familiarity with their behavior. Needless to say, the dog's learned adjustment is a slower process than cognitive empathy.[9]

Cognitive empathy may not be widespread in the animal kingdom. It occurs in people and perhaps in our closest relatives, the apes, but may be absent in other animals. There are as yet no indications that the special treatment that monkeys accord the handicapped is based on anything other than learned adjustment. The attitude toward Mozu is a case in point: the tolerance toward her probably reflects learning by other monkeys in Jigokudani Park that Mozu is slow and poses no threat. Nothing in their behavior suggests that they realize how or why Mozu differs from them, and what her special needs are.

Below are three further examples of adjustment by monkeys to permanently disabled species members.

*Azalea: an infant with a chromosomal abnormality*   In 1988, a unique rhesus monkey was born at the Wisconsin Primate Center. Azalea had a strange, somewhat vacuous facial expression and was clearly deficient in motor abilities. Her condition, which had come about spontaneously, was detected early on because she happened to be part of our developmental study. Testing showed that she had the extremely rare condition of autosomal trisomy: instead of possessing only pairs of chromosomes, she had one triplet, similar to the chromosomal condition underlying Down syndrome in humans. In a further parallel, Azalea was born to an aging, almost postreproductive female (more than twenty years old) who previously had produced eleven normal offspring.

Running, jumping, and climbing posed major challenges that Azalea achieved at a considerably later age than her peers, and then only incompletely. Her coordination was imperfect, her reaction time slow. She was the only monkey who never learned to walk through the spinning wheel by stepping into it at one point and exiting at another point as she took changes in speed and position into account (the way we learn to step smoothly in and out of a revolving door). If Azalea was "trapped" in the wheel, an elder sister often rescued her by pulling her out. Feeding was another serious problem: instead of holding hard monkey biscuits in her hands and biting off pieces, Azalea licked crumbs from the floor in doglike fashion until the age of five months. She would never have survived in the wild.

Socially, Azalea was aberrant as well. She moved out of her mother's reach for the first time on the thirty-seventh day of life, compared with an average age of thirteen days for her peers. Azalea's mother never showed signs of rejection, yet was not particularly interested in this offspring. Azalea's elder juvenile sister, on the other hand, did pay extra attention, carrying her around well beyond the normal age for such sisterly care and protecting her against other monkeys. If others acted toward Azalea in a manner to which any normal rhesus infant would object, such as pulling out one hair after another during grooming, her sister would interrupt the activity even though Azalea herself uttered not the slightest protest.

Although Azalea's membership in the top matriline offered strong protection, she was at the receiving end in a few serious fights—because of miscalculation. If her mother threatened another monkey, Azalea would join in almost blindly, enthusiastically grunting and lunging at the same individual, however big he or she happened to be. Alliance formation (two parties banding together against another) is common in monkey groups; it often results in large-scale confrontations in which many parties go after one another. On these shifting battlegrounds it is of paramount importance for each monkey to keep track of the positions and movements of all others, friend as well as foe. Inasmuch as this task was totally beyond Azalea's capacities, involvement in her mother's battles often placed her in an uncovered position face to face with an adversary who could seriously harm her. Her opponents rarely hesitated, and one time they literally wiped the floor with her. An adult male dragged her down the stone incline of the enclosure, smashing her head onto the concrete floor. Azalea went into a seizure of several seconds, during which she lost control on one side of her body. She did learn from this incident, though: afterward she kept a wary eye on this particular male, avoiding him even if he showed up only in the distance.

Most of the time, Azalea was exceptionally passive. She rarely played with others; if she did, it was with younger partners, her peers being too fast on their feet and too wild. It is a testimony to the group's complete acceptance of this backward juvenile that others, including nonrelatives, groomed Azalea twice as much as they did her peers.[10]

At the age of thirty-two months, Azalea showed severe convulsions and disorientation (bumping her head into walls) and had to be put down.

*Wania-6672: an infant with a neural disorder*    In 1972 two Canadian primatologists, Linda and Laurence Fedigan, observed an unusual infant born into a population of Japanese macaques in a 44-hectare brushland enclosure in Texas. The infant showed symptoms of cerebral palsy. Having more control over arms than legs, Wania-6672 would hop like a rabbit, swinging both legs simultaneously forward outside his arms. The infant appeared visually impaired: he always sniffed at other monkeys as if to identify them, and regularly collided with bushes and cactus. Another similarity with palsied human children was excessive aggressivity and hyperactivity. Wania-6672 showed extreme hostility toward monkeys grooming his mother, trying at all costs to insert himself between the two parties.

He spent an enormous amount of time following his mother, seeking to nurse, and was often carried and groomed by her. When they were separated Wania-6672 vocalized persistently; he never achieved any degree of independence. Juveniles, particularly females, frequently ran over to cradle and hold him when he gave distress calls.

Group members were thoroughly puzzled by this infant's behavior. Instead of running away when threatened, Wania-6672 would scream and crash aimlessly about. "When confronted with this strange response, most monkeys stopped threatening immediately and many peered at the abnormal infant as if confused by the unusual response."[11] Perhaps because of the lack of appropriate behavior, other monkeys lost interest in trying to teach him the usual rules of conduct; they tended to ignore misbehavior by Wania-6672 that they would never accept from other infants. One time an adult male did nothing when Wania-6672 collided head on with the adult's groin. Another time, the alpha male was being groomed by a female, reclining and dreaming away until the infant began tripping over his feet. The male raised his eyebrows several times—a sign of irritation—then sat up staring at the offender with a full-blown threat face. But he lay down immediately when he saw that it was "only" Wania-6672. Any other infant would have been grabbed by the scruff of its neck and rubbed in the dirt.

*I585-B: a congenitally blind infant*    In 1982 a blind infant was born into a free-ranging population of rhesus monkeys released onto a Caribbean island. Apart from being sightless, the infant appeared perfectly normal: he played, for instance, as much as other infants his age. Compared to his peers, I585-B often broke contact with his mother, thereby placing himself in situations that he could not recognize as dangerous. His mother responded by retrieving and restricting him more than other mothers did with their infants.

In other studies of blind infant monkeys such infants were never left alone, and specific group members stayed with them whenever the group moved.[12] Similarly, I585-B's kinship unit was extremely vigilant and protective, as noted by Catherine Scanlon.

On several occasions, the blind infant was seen in the lower branches of a tree between two and five meters from close kin: the approach of an unrelated animal was observed to result in an unusually high number of threats from one or more of these kin, in particular his mother, his aunts, and his five-year-old male cousin.[13]

Let us not forget that, in theory, learned adjustment can take *two* directions. The first is exploitation, as when healthy monkeys learn to take advantage of the lack of speed, strength, and perception of a disabled group mate. For example, the younger members of the stump-tail monkey group at the Wisconsin Primate Center used to tease Wolf, an old, virtually blind female, by jumping or climbing on her back—a feat they would not have dared before Wolf lost her eyesight.

Among animals who have lived together for a long time, however, such maltreatment is not the rule. What is most striking about adjustment to handicapped monkeys is that it so often takes the opposite form: instead of being torn to pieces or abandoned as a useless community member, the disabled individual receives extra tolerance, vigilance, and care. This pattern applied to Wolf as well: after the deterioration of her eyesight, the group's adult males became extremely protective. Each time human caretakers tried to move the monkeys from the indoor to the outdoor section of the enclosure, adult males would stand guard at the door between the sections, sometimes holding it open, until Wolf had gone through. Interposing themselves between her and the caretakers, they made it quite obvious that Wolf still meant a great deal to them.

Special treatment of the handicapped is probably best regarded as a combination of learned adjustment and strong attachment; it is the attachment that steers the adjustment in a positive, caring direction. Sometimes, however, special treatment occurs when there has been little or no time for learning. For example, monkeys may suddenly increase their vigilance if one among them is injured or incapacitated. When a juvenile in a captive baboon colony had an epileptic seizure, other baboons immediately turned highly protective. An elder brother placed his hand on the disabled juvenile's chest, threatening people who wanted to enter the compound for a closer look. According to Randall Keyes, who reported the incident, this brother normally did not act so protectively.[14]

Such an immediate response to a group mate's vulnerability is not easily explained on the basis of a slow learning process. Perhaps primates follow a hard and fast rule—without too much reflection— that tells them to double their protectiveness as soon as one among them fails to respond to danger. Or they may have learned that individuals who remain immobile at critical moments tend to get into trouble, and they generalize this knowledge to a newly incapacitated group mate. Explanations along these lines may account for the extra protection of the blind infant, Wolf, and the baboon with a seizure.

The alternative would be that they recall their *own* encounters with approaching danger when watching another's lack of response. This possibility would be of the utmost interest, because to understand another's predicament based on one's own experiences would require extrapolation from self to other.

## Responses to Injury and Death

If attachment underlies care and sympathy, the attitude toward dead or dying companions is worth investigating because there is no more poignant evidence for attachment than agony following the final breath of a relative or companion. A well-known example is elephants, who sometimes pick up the ivory or bones of a dead herd member, hold the pieces in their trunks, and pass them around. Some pachyderms return for years to the spot where a relative died, touching and inspecting the relics. Do they miss the other? Do they recall how he or she was during life?

Dereck and Beverly Joubert watched the final hours of an old bull lying in the sands of the Kalahari Desert. Other elephants tried to raise the dying individual by slipping their trunk and tusks underneath him and lifting as hard as they could, some breaking ivory in the effort.

Cynthia Moss, in *Elephant Memories,* describes the response of elephants in Amboseli National Park when a poacher's bullet entered the lungs of a young female, Tina. After the herd had escaped from danger, Tina's knees started to buckle, and the others leaned into her so as to keep her upright. She slipped beneath them nonetheless, and died with a shudder.

Teresia and Trista became frantic and knelt down and tried to lift her up. They worked their tusks under her back and under her head. At one point they succeeded in lifting her into a sitting position but her body flopped back down. Her family tried everything to rouse her, kicking and tusking her, and Tallulah even went off and collected a trunkful of grass and tried to stuff it into her mouth.[15]

Afterward, the others sprinkled earth over the carcass, then went off into the surrounding bushes to break off branches, which they placed over Tina's body. By nightfall the corpse was almost completely covered. When the herd moved off next morning, Teresia was the last one to leave. Facing the others with her back to her dead daughter, she reached behind herself and felt the carcass with her hind foot several times before she very reluctantly moved off.

Monkeys react to the death or disappearance of an attachment figure in a way outwardly similar to human grieving. In the 1960s this process was investigated in the laboratory by Charles Kaufman and Leonard Rosenblum, who separated infant monkeys from their mothers. A *protest phase,* with vigorous calling and searching for the mother, was followed by a *despair phase,* with nonresponsiveness, loss of appetite, slouching posture, and empty gaze. It is unclear, however, if such depressions ever reach the point where monkeys *die* of grief in the way that Jane Goodall described for the wild chimpanzee Flint, who died three weeks after the loss of his mother, the famous Flo. Flint was already eight and a half years old, but had been unusually dependent. In Goodall's words, "His whole world had revolved around Flo, and with her gone life was hollow and meaningless."[16] Autopsy revealed inflammation of Flint's stomach and abdomen. It is indeed possible that his death was caused by a weakened immune system due to depression, yet we cannot rule out the obvious alternative that Flo and Flint had fallen victim to the same disease, and that Flint had merely held out a little longer than his mother.[17]

If the reverse happens, that is, if a mother loses her infant, primates demonstrate their attachment by carrying the corpse around for days until it literally falls apart. Once they have given up the carcass, it usually is hard to recognize signs in female monkeys, other than swollen breasts, of the loss of an infant. Yet some females are restless and seem to look for their offspring. I have known rhesus females who paced and vocalized for an entire day following removal of the cadaver. And Barbara Smuts, an American primatologist, describes in *Sex and Friendship in Baboons* how a wild female baboon named Zandra responded to the loss of her three-month-old infant, Zephyr, who had been severely bitten, most likely by a male baboon.

> For the next several days, I looked for signs of grief in Zandra but could see none. During this time, the troop did not travel

near the spot where the infant had been killed and where she had lost the body. Then one day, about a week after her infant died, the troop passed through the same bushy area. As they drew near, Zandra became extremely agitated. She rushed about as if looking for Zephyr, and then she climbed a tree. When she came to the top, she looked all around and began calling . . . Her searching activities were unmistakable, and she repeated her agitated looking and calling each time the baboons passed through this area for the next few weeks.[18]

Similarly, female chimpanzees commonly wail and whimper, and sometimes burst out screaming after the loss of an offspring. One of the females in the Arnhem colony, confusingly named Gorilla because of a resemblance to the other ape species, would not only whimper and scream, but after each flareup would vigorously rub both eyes with her knuckles exactly like a human child drying tears. Because humans are supposedly the only primates to shed tears when they cry, Gorilla's behavior so surprised me that I requested that her eyes be checked for infection. The veterinarian could not find anything, however, and I must stress that I never actually saw tears.[19]

Seeing the termination of a familiar individual's life, chimpanzees may respond emotionally as if realizing, however vaguely, what death means—or at least that something terrible has befallen the other. In a second incident involving Gorilla a young adult female, Oortje, simply dropped dead. Oortje had been apathetic since delivering, two months earlier, a healthy son whom she rejected. She had started coughing before that time, and her condition had deteriorated despite treatment. Kept indoors because of the winter, the colony had been divided into two groups that could hear but not see each other. At a certain moment one day Jeanne Scheurer, a regular zoo visitor who knew every chimpanzee by name, saw Gorilla intently stare at Oortje, who was sitting on a log. Without apparent reason, Gorilla burst out screaming in an excited, hysterical voice. The screaming was neither aggressive in tone nor accompanied by threat gestures; rather, Gorilla seemed disturbed by something she saw in Oortje's eyes or demeanor. Oortje herself, silent until this point, now feebly screamed back at Gorilla, then tried to lie down, fell off the log, and remained motionless on the floor. All this happened within a minute. Heart massage and an attempt at mouth-to-mouth resuscitation by the caretaker (after having moved the other chimpanzees inside) were in vain. A female in the other hall uttered screams similar in sound to Gorilla's, then every chimpanzee in the building went completely silent. Oortje must have died of heart failure; autopsy showed a massive infection of heart and abdomen.

As mentioned before, one adult male in Arnhem did not survive serious injuries contracted in a fight. After hours of surgery we placed him in one of the night cages, where he died. That evening, when the rest of the colony entered the building, there was absolute silence. The next morning, silence persisted even when the keeper arrived with food (normally a time for tumultuous joy). Vocal activity resumed only after the corpse had been removed from the building.

One early morning in 1968, Geza Teleki followed a small party of wild chimpanzees shortly after they had descended from their sleeping nests. He hurried over to a site from which raucous calling could be heard. Six adult males were wildly charging about, their wraaah calls echoing off the valley walls. Activity was concentrated around a small gully in which the motionless body of a male, Rix, was sprawled among the stones. Although Teleki had not seen the body drop—at the critical moment he had stepped into a safari ant nest—he felt he was witnessing the very first reaction to Rix's neck-breaking fall out of a tree. Several individuals paused to stare at the corpse, after which they redirected their tension by vigorous charging displays away from it, hurling big rocks in all directions. Amid the din chimpanzees were embracing, mounting, touching, and patting one another with big, nervous grins on their faces.

Later on, some chimpanzees spent considerable time staring at the body. One male leaned down from a limb, watched the corpse, then whimpered. Others touched or sniffed Rix's remains. An adolescent female uninterruptedly gazed at the body for *more than an hour,* during which she sat motionless and in complete silence. After three hours of activity around the corpse, one of the older males finally left the clearing, walking downstream along the valley bottom. Others followed one by one, glancing over their shoulder toward Rix as they departed. One male approached the remains, leaned over for a final inspection, then hurried after the others.

When a companion is close to death, chimpanzees act as if they are aware of the pain of this individual, as movingly described six decades ago by Robert Yerkes, who watched a group of juveniles.

Impressive indeed is the thoughtfulness of the ordinarily care-free and irresponsible little chimpanzee for ill or injured companions. In the same cage were a little male and two females, one of the latter mortally ill. She was so ill that much of the time she lay on the floor of the cage in the sunlight, listless and pathetic. There was excellent opportunity to observe the attitude of her lively companions towards this helpless invalid. In all their boisterous play they scrupulously avoided disturbing her, and, in fact, seldom touched her as they climbed, jumped, and ran about the cage. Now and then one or the other would go to her and touch her gently or caress her; or again one of them, fatigued or worsted in some game, would obviously seek refuge and respite by going close to her. In this position, safety from disturbance was assured.

To this, Yerkes adds his interpretation: "A certain solicitude, sympathy, and pity, as well as almost human expression of consideration were thus manifested by these little creatures."[20]

Note that this reading goes well beyond the learned adjustment hypothesis discussed earlier: Yerkes assumes empathy. The same assumption shines through the following account of extraordinary care by Lucy, a chimpanzee in a human family. Maurice Temerlin, an American psychotherapist, analyzed Lucy's every move, personality trait, and sex game from the time she was a baby until she had grown into a 40-kilogram humanized chimpanzee. Lucy was particularly tender with Temerlin's wife, Jane, as described in *Lucy: Growing up Human.*

> If Jane is distressed, Lucy notices it immediately, and attempts to comfort her by putting her arm about her, grooming her, or kissing her. If I am the cause of the distress, for example, if we are arguing, Lucy will attempt to pull us apart or to distract me so that Jane's distress is alleviated. If Jane is sick, Lucy notices it immediately. For example, on every occasion when Jane was ill and vomited, Lucy became very disturbed, running into the bathroom, standing by Jane, comforting her by kissing her and putting her arm around her as she vomited. When Jane was sick in bed Lucy would exhibit tender protectiveness toward her, bringing her food, sharing her own food, or sitting on the edge of the bed attempting to comfort by stroking and grooming her.[21]

It is entirely possible that succorant behavior and sensitivity to the needs of others are better developed in apes than in monkeys. From my experience, the death of an individual to whom they are not closely attached produces a rather unremarkable response in monkeys, and I have never heard of monkeys offering the sort of solicitous attention to indisposed companions described above for chimpanzees. While there may be a real difference between monkeys and apes, our knowledge leaves much to be desired. Monkeys do show many kinds of gentle care, protectiveness, and vigilance toward the sick and injured, and most of the time the similarities with apes are more striking than the differences.

The assumption of higher mental processes in chimpanzees today is so prevalent that widespread mammalian habits, such as the cleaning of wounds, are sometimes interpreted differently depending on whether they are exhibited by a chimpanzee or another animal. Wolfgang Dittus documented how toque macaques in Sri Lanka lick each other's wounds caused by fights, a behavior that is especially important for wounds out of the victim's own reach. Because of the antiviral and antibacterial properties of saliva, cuts as long as 15 centimeters heal quickly and leave virtually no scar. The care is so crucial that one male injured upon emigration to another monkey group, without friends to provide this service, returned to his former group—where his wounds were tended by male peers with whom he had grown up.

Dittus does not speculate about his monkeys' awareness of each other's pain, but Christophe Boesch, describing identical behavior in chimpanzees in Taï National Park, Ivory Coast, takes wound cleaning to mean that his apes "are aware of the needs of the wounded" and demonstrate "empathy for the pain resulting from such wounds."[22] Other chimpanzees lick away blood, carefully remove dirt, and prevent flies from coming near the wounds. They also protect injured individuals, and travel more slowly if these individuals cannot keep up the pace.

Does this indeed prove that chimpanzees have empathy, and, by extension, that monkeys and other injury-cleaning mammals do too? Unfortunately, the tending of wounds per se tells us nothing about the underlying mental processes. A skeptic could argue that it only proves that blood tastes good; indeed, it is not unusual for primates to lick blood off plants or branches splattered during a fight or a birth. I believe there is more to the cleaning of wounds; many hard-to-convey details in the behavior of chimpanzees (the way they approach an injured individual; the concerned look in their eyes; the care they take not to hurt) make me intuitively agree with the views of Yerkes, Temerlin, and Boesch. That such details are less obvious in monkeys does not necessarily mean that they perform the same actions devoid of feelings, or without any understanding of what happened to the victim; monkeys are harder to read because of their greater evolutionary distance from us.

That high levels of care are not restricted to species close to us has already been demonstrated with salient examples from elephants and dolphins; the same applies *within* the primate order. Some ethologists, myself included, would no doubt have thought caring responses to be less developed in prosimians, an ancient branch of the order from which the true simians evolved. In a few languages prosimians are known as *half-monkeys;* they have a reputation for being primitive and unsophisticated compared to monkeys. This image may need correction in light of what Michael Pereira, an American expert on their behavior, described to me as an "absolutely mind-blowing" series of events among ring-tailed lemurs in a forested enclosure at the Duke University Primate Center.

One day a three-month-old infant climbs up an electric fence, receives a jolt to her temple, and falls to the ground in convulsions. The student assistant, Louis Santini, who witnesses the drama, runs off to seek help, and returns to find the infant on the back of her grandmother, who normally *never* carries her. The infant's own mother, who had not been present at the incident, pays no attention and continues to feed in a tree in the distance. The grandmother carries the infant for ten minutes, then drops her off at a quiet spot where the infant sits in a daze.

After another ride on the grandmother's back and continued lack of interest by the mother, the infant is approached by peers, who groom her intensely for several minutes—another highly unusual behavior, as infants rarely groom anyone. Three infants start a round-robin game among themselves near the dazed one, occasionally interrupting their play to take turns briefly grooming the victim. When the group of lemurs moves off, the infant climbs on the back of her mother, who has not been near her for over an hour, and succeeds in riding on her. The mother, known as rather rejective, suddenly sits up to violently shake the infant off her back. The grandmother responds instantly by attacking the mother, which results in the mother's allowing her daughter to remount and stay on for a longer distance. Five minutes later, the group settles down. The infant rests on her mother's ventrum like other infants in the group. She now appears fully recovered (and indeed survives without noticeable damage).

This incident shows that even lemurs immediately recognize when one of them is in trouble and respond appropriately. The victim's peers seemed to notice something wrong with their buddy, and certainly the grandmother went out of her way to offer unusual care, going so far as to discipline her own daughter for not accommodating the injured family member. Could the difference in response between mother and grandmother have had something to do with the fact that only the grandmother had witnessed the mishap? The grandmother's action against her daughter was all the more remarkable because older lemur females almost never meddle in conflicts between daughters and grandchildren. What intrigues me most is that she seemed to teach her daughter how she *ought* to behave; precisely the kind of social pressure viewed in moral terms if seen in humans. Mind-blowing, indeed!

If science has not yet gauged the full depth of the emotional and cognitive life of monkeys and prosimians as expressed in care for distressed individuals, even more remains to be discovered with regard to the apes. Take an observation made repeatedly during reconciliations among both bonobos and chimpanzees, yet never in any monkey species that I have studied with equal intensity: after one individual has attacked and bitten another, he or she may return to inspect the injury inflicted. The aggressor does not accidentally detect the wound, but knows exactly where to look for it. If the bite was aimed at the left foot, the aggressor will without hesitation reach for this foot—not the right foot or an arm—lift and inspect it, then begin cleaning the injury. Such action suggests an understanding of cause and effect and may require the ape to take the other's perspective, as if realizing the impact of his own behavior on someone else.[23]

Chimpanzees also excel at so-called *consolation*. Whereas monkeys do on rare occasions reassure a victim of aggression (witness the incident with Fawn and her sister), such behavior is exceptional. A study of three macaque species by the Italian ethologist Filippo Aureli and his coworkers failed to demonstrate regular care for recent victims of aggression. If anything, others tended to stay away from them, probably because of the risk of further attacks on these same individuals. Quite the contrary happens in the chimpanzee colony at the Yerkes Field Station. Watching the colony from high in a tower with an excellent overview of the compound, research technician Michael Seres enters every observed event directly into a computer. These records show that once the dust has settled after a fight, combatants are often approached by uninvolved bystanders. Typically the bystanders hug and touch them, pat them on the back, or groom them for a while. These contacts are aimed at precisely those individuals expected to be most upset by the preceding event.[24]

The chimpanzee's responsiveness to distress in others goes together with a range of humanlike expressions, unmatched by any other nonhuman primate, to *seek* contact and reassurance. When upset, chimpanzees pout, whimper, yelp, beg with outstretched hand, or impatiently shake both hands so that the other will hurry and provide the calming contact so urgently needed. If all else fails, chimpanzees resort to their ultimate weapon, the *temper tantrum*. They lose control, roll around screaming pathetically, hitting their own head or beating the ground with their fists, regularly checking the effects on the other. Tantrums are commonly thrown by juveniles of three or four years when their mothers' willingness to nurse is on the decline; but fully grown chimpanzees may do so too, for example, when another chimpanzee has refused to share food, or after a confrontation with a major rival has been lost.

I still recall the spectacular tantrums of the old leader of the Arnhem colony, Yeroen, when he was being dethroned by younger and stronger males. He would tumble down the trunk of a tree, as if he could barely hold on, screaming mightily, and begging with outstretched hands to anyone in sight, particularly adult females who could help him chase off his opponent. Walking through the zoo, I could hear Yeroen's pleas for help nearly a kilometer away! Often females or juveniles would go over to Yeroen to place an arm around him and calm him down.

As a final proof of the chimpanzee's sensitivity to the distress of others, compare the total lack of adjustment by Ropey, a rhesus monkey, to her daughter's broken arm, with the following response of a chimpanzee mother. During tensions among adult males in the Arnhem colony, one male picked up a juvenile, Wouter, swinging him furiously above his head and against a wall. The action was not necessarily directed against Wouter himself; chimpanzee males enhance their charging displays with virtually anything that makes noise, and juveniles quickly learn to stay out of their way. Several adult females came to Wouter's rescue, and succeeded in putting an end to the molestation, but Wouter limped for weeks afterward.

Fortunately for him, Wouter's mother did seem to understand that something was wrong. Having a younger brother who was still being nursed, Wouter had gotten used to being second in line for maternal attention. This lesson can be hard to learn, requiring mothers to insist by force. During the time that Wouter was disabled, his mother relaxed the rules: on many occasions she shoved her younger son aside, ignoring his fuss, to make room for and tenderly hold the older sibling.

## Having Broad Nails

For decades students of animal behavior considered it wrong and naive to speak of animals as wanting, intending, feeling, thinking, or expecting beings. Animals just behave; that is all we know, and all we will *ever* know about them.

Curiously, the key to behavior was sought not within but outside the individual. The individual was merely a passive instrument of the environment. Psychologists studied how responses to stimuli increase if rewarded, and biologists analyzed how behavior spreads if it promotes reproduction. The first is a learning process, the second natural selection; the timescales are of course vastly different, yet the role of the environment as final arbiter of the suitability of behavior was the same. With biologists and psychologists quibbling endlessly over whose discipline offered the better explanation, it is hard to believe that they shared so much common ground.

The critical insights of both disciplines steered attention away from the acting agents themselves. If the environment controls behavior, why do we need the individual? Psychologists came up with their infamous black box, which mediates between stimulus and response, yet remains inaccessible to science. Biologists described animals as survival machines and preprogrammed robots, another way of saying that we should not worry too much about what goes on in their heads. The final presentation of the late B. F. Skinner, who firmly kept the lid on the black box, therefore could hardly have been accidental. Addressing fellow psychologists, he compared cognitive psychologists to creationists, thus throwing together the enemies of behaviorism and Darwinism![25]

When evaluating the succorant behavior of animals, we face already so many obstacles relative to the scarcity of data and the design of experiments that we do not need the additional burden of a narrow-minded rejection of the entire problem of cognition. Some biologists will point out that most of the accounts of caregiving discussed earlier—certainly the more striking ones—concern kin. Why not simply view these instances as investments of genetic relatives in one another, and leave them at that? While perfectly valid when it comes to evolutionary explanations, this point has absolutely no bearing on the question at hand. We are concerned here with motivations and intentions. Regardless of how care is being allotted, the caregiver must be sensitive to the situation of the other, feel an urge to assist, and determine which actions are most appropriate under the circumstances.

If Tallulah stuffs grass into the mouth of a dying herd member, if a chimpanzee goes to hug another who has just been beaten up, or if the top male of a monkey group fails to punish a brain-damaged infant for bothering him, we want to know what makes these animals react in this way. How do they perceive the distress or special circumstances of the other? Do they have any idea of how their behavior will affect the other? These questions remain exactly the same whether or not the other is a relative.

Times are changing. Interest in the mental life of animals is regaining respectability. Whereas some scientists propose a gradual shift in this direction, depending on evidence along the way, others are less patient. Believing it unfair to hold a new perspective hostage to the availability of final answers, they advocate a clean break with the Cartesian view of animals as automatons.

This is not to say that all we need to do is "feel as one" with animals without some critical distance, without putting ideas to the test, and without choosing our words carefully. Discussions about animal behavior often boil down to discussions about language. The ethologist inevitably borrows concepts from common language, which is primarily designed for communication about people. Yet the familiarity of these concepts by no means absolves us from the obligation to be specific about what they mean when applied to animals. Anthropomorphism can never replace science.

Take "reconciliation" and "consolation," two blatantly anthropomorphic terms applied to primate behavior. They refer to circumscribed encounters and come with a set of predictions that, if contradicted, should spell the end of their use. For example, reconciliation is defined as a reunion between former opponents shortly after an aggressive conflict between them. If it were found that reconciliations thus defined do not occur, or do nothing to reduce renewed hostility, it would be time to rethink the label. The same argument applies to older, more widely accepted terms, such as "threat," "greeting," "courtship," and "dominance," which have already gone through a process of fine-tuning and critical evaluation, but can still be questioned at any moment.[26]

It is this use of anthropomorphism as a *means* to get at the truth, rather than as an end in itself, that sets its use in science apart from use by the layperson. The ultimate goal of the scientist is emphatically *not* to arrive at the most satisfactory projection of human feelings onto the animal, but rather at testable ideas and replicable observations. Thus, anthropomorphism serves the same exploratory function as that of intuition in all science, from mathematics to medicine. As advocated by Gordon Burghardt:

> What I am calling for is a critical anthropomorphism, and predictive inference that encourages the use of data from many sources (prior experiments, anecdotes, publications, one's thoughts and feelings, neuroscience, imagining being the animal, naturalistic observations . . . et cetera). But however eclectic in origin, the product must be an inference that can be tested or, failing that, can lead to predictions supportable by public data.[27]

But what about the cherished principle of parsimony—the one great bulwark against all this liberal thinking? The problem is that insofar as monkeys and apes are concerned, a profound conflict exists between *two* kinds of parsimony. The first is the traditional canon that tells us not to invoke higher capacities if the phenomenon can be explained with lower ones. This favors simple explanations, such as learned adjustment, over more complex ones, such as cognitive empathy.

The second form of parsimony considers the shared evolutionary background of humans and other primates. It posits that if closely related species act the same, the underlying process probably is the same too. The alternative would be to assume the evolution of divergent processes for similar behavior; a highly uneconomic assumption for organisms with only a few million years of separate evolution. If we normally do not propose different causes for the same behavior in, say, tigers and lions, there is no good reason to do so for humans and chimpanzees, which are genetically as close or closer.

In short, the principle of parsimony has two faces. At the same time that we are supposed to favor low-level over high-level cognitive explanations, we also should not create a double standard according to which shared human and ape behavior is explained differently.

Such "evolutionary parsimony" is a factor especially when both humans and apes exhibit traits not seen in monkeys, and two explanations are proposed where one may do. If accounts of human behavior commonly invoke complex cognitive abilities—and they certainly do—we must carefully consider whether these abilities are perhaps also present in apes. We do not need to jump to conclusions, but the possibility should at least be allowed on the table.

Behind the debate about parsimony towers the much larger issue of humanity's place in nature. To this day, those who see our species as part of the animal kingdom continue to lock horns with those who see us as separate. Even authors with a distinctly evolutionary perspective often cannot resist searching for the one BIG difference, the one trait that sets us apart—whether it is opposable thumbs, toolmaking, cooperative hunting, humor, pure altruism, sexual orgasm, the incest taboo, language, or the anatomy of the larynx. Countless book titles reflect this search: *Man the Tool-Maker, Man the Hunter, The Ethical Animal, Uniquely Human,* and so on.

Claims of human uniqueness go back to the debate between Plato and Diogenes about the most succinct definition of the human species. Plato proposed that humans were the only creatures at once naked and walking on two legs. This definition proved flawed, however, when Diogenes brought a plucked fowl to the lecture room, setting it loose with the words, "Here is Plato's man." From then on the definition included "having broad nails."[28]

In 1784 Johann Wolfgang von Goethe triumphantly announced that he had discovered the cornerstone of humanity: a tiny piece of bone in the human upper jaw known as the *os intermaxillare.* The bone, though present in other mammals including apes, had long been thought absent in us and had therefore been labeled a "primitive" trait by a Dutch anatomist, Petrus Camper. Goethe's bone, as it became known, confirmed our continuity with nature long before Darwin formulated his theory of evolution. It was a slap in the face—the first of many—to people postulating human uniqueness.

Do claims of uniqueness in any way advance science? Are they even scientifically motivated? Until now, all of these claims have either been forgotten, like Camper's, or required qualification, like Plato's. As a separate species, humans do possess distinct traits, yet the overwhelming majority of our anatomical, physiological, and psychological characteristics are part of an ancient heritage. Holding the magnifying glass over a few beauty spots (our distinct traits are invariably judged advanced and superior) is a much less exciting enterprise, it seems to me, than trying to get a good look at the human animal as a whole.

In this broader perspective, peculiarly human traits are juxtaposed with the obvious continuity with the rest of nature. Included are both our most noble traits and the ones of which we are less proud, such as our genocidal and destructive tendencies. Even if we like to blame the latter on our progenitors (as soon as people hack each other to pieces they are said to be "acting like animals") and claim the former for ourselves, it is safe to assume that both run in our extended family.

There is no need to launch probes into space in order to compare ourselves with other intelligent life: there is plenty of intelligent life down here. It is infinitely more suitable to elucidate the working of our minds than those of whatever extraterrestrial forms might exist. In order to explore earthly intelligences, we need breathing room in the study of animal cognition: freedom from traditional constraints that tell us that nothing is there, or that *if* anything is there, we will never be able to catch even a glimpse.

Critics say there is no way to see what goes on inside an animal's head. That is, of course, not literally what cognitive ethologists are trying to do. Rather, they seek to *reconstruct* mental processes in much the way the nuclear physicist "looks inside" the atom by testing predictions based on a model of its structure. Admittedly, the use of anthropomorphism and anecdotal evidence, along with reservations about the principle of parsimony, have created uncertainty and confusion—as well as lively debate.[29] Yet these are only the delivery pains of a much-needed change in the study of animal behavior.

With this in mind, let us return to succorant behavior and the evolution of empathy and sympathy.

## The Social Mirror

Without access to slate or metallic surfaces, and lacking rivers that provide clear reflections, the Biami, a Papuan tribe in New Guinea, were assumed never to have seen their own images. This made them ideal subjects for Edmund Carpenter, a visual anthropologist, out to document people's very first reactions to mirrors.

> They were paralyzed: after their first startled response—covering their mouths and ducking their heads—they stood transfixed, staring at their images, only their stomach muscles betraying

great tension. Like Narcissus, they were left numb, totally fascinated by their own reflections; indeed, the myth of Narcissus
may refer to just this phenomenon. In a matter of days, however,
they groomed themselves openly before mirrors.[30]

Polaroid pictures proved even more puzzling. At first, the Biami
failed to understand: the anthropologist had to teach them how to
read the picture by pointing to the nose, then touching the real nose,
and so on with other parts of the body. With recognition came fear.
The individual in the picture would tremble uncontrollably, turn
away from the photograph, then slip away to a private spot with the
picture firmly pressed against his chest. There he would stare at it,
without moving, for up to twenty minutes. Because of this response,
Carpenter speaks of the "terror of self-awareness." But this stage was
quickly left behind. Within days villagers were happily making movies
of themselves, taking snapshots of each other, listening to themselves
on a tape recorder, and proudly wearing a self-portrait on their
forehead.

Of course, the Biami had not been without self-consciousness before the anthropologist set foot in their village. The only thing that
mirrors and pictures do is bring awareness of oneself into sharper
focus and demonstrate its presence to the outside world. Had these
people not responded with surprise, fear, and fascination, we might
have thought either that they had seen themselves before, or that they
failed to grasp what they saw. The latter is unimaginable, as self-
awareness is at the core of being human. Without it we might as well
be folkloric creatures without souls, such as vampires, who cast no
reflections. Most important, we would be incapable of cognitive empathy, as this requires a distinction between self and other and the
realization that others have selves like us.

No wonder responses to mirrors have attracted the attention of
students of animals as well. While almost all visually oriented mammals initially try to reach or look behind a mirror, only two nonhuman species—chimpanzees and orangutans—seem to understand
that they are seeing themselves. The special status of these apes has
been recognized for a long time. In 1922 Anton Portielje, a Dutch
naturalist, remarked that, whereas monkeys fail to understand the
relation between their reflections and themselves, an orangutan "at-
tentively looks firstly at his mirror image, but then also at his behind
and his crust of bread in a mirror . . . obviously understanding the
use of a mirror."[31]

Similarly, the German gestalt psychologist Wolfgang Köhler in 1925 commented on the lasting interest of chimpanzees in their mirror image; they continue to play with it, making strange faces at themselves and checking reflected objects against the real thing by looking back and forth between the two. Monkeys, in contrast, react with facial expressions that are anything but frivolous: they regard their reflection as another individual, treating it as a stranger of their own sex and species.

Compelling evidence was derived in the 1970s from elegant experiments by Gordon Gallup, an American comparative psychologist. An individual unknowingly received a dot of paint in a specific place, such as above the eyebrow, invisible without a mirror. Guided by their reflection, chimpanzees and orangutans—as well as children more than eighteen months of age—rubbed the painted spot with their hand and inspected the fingers that had touched it, recognizing that the coloring on the reflected image was on their own face. Other primates—and younger children—failed to make this connection. Gallup went on to equate self-recognition with self-awareness, and this in turn with a multitude of sophisticated mental abilities. The list encompassed attribution of intention to others, intentional deception, reconciliation, and empathy. Accordingly, humans and apes have entered a cognitive domain that sets them apart from all other forms of life.[32]

Nevertheless, sharp dividing lines—regardless of whether they place our species in a class by itself or create a slightly more inclusive cognitive elite—are to be treated with reservation. The mirror test provides a rather narrow measure of self-awareness. After all, such awareness may express itself in myriad other kinds of behavior and involve senses other than the visual. What to think of the dog's olfactory distinction between his own urine markings and those of other dogs; the bat's ability to pick out the echoes of its own sounds from among those of other bats, and the monkey's perfect sense of how far its hands, feet, and tail can reach in the surrounding canopy?

Some cognitive psychologists view the self as the interface between an organism and its environment. According to J. J. Gibson, the more complex an organism's interactions with its environment, the better it needs to know itself. This premise applies to the physical environment, but perhaps even more to the social milieu. A macaque or baboon can hardly function without knowing the social position of each group mate, the kinship network, which individuals are likely to side with each other in a fight, the possible reactions of others to particular actions, and so on. How could a monkey ever reach such a grasp of social affairs without knowing its own capacities and limitations, and its own position vis-à-vis others? Understanding one's surroundings equals understanding oneself. In this broader view, some species may reach greater heights of self-knowledge than others, but surely there can be no species without any such knowledge at all.

Similarly, it is hard to imagine empathy as an all-or-nothing phenomenon. Many forms of empathy exist intermediate between the extremes of mere agitation at the distress of others and a full understanding of their predicament. At one end of the spectrum, rhesus infants get upset and seek contact with one another as soon as one of them screams. At the other end, a chimpanzee recalls a wound he has inflicted, and returns to the victim to inspect it.

Human ethics everywhere urge us to adopt someone else's perspective and look at the world through the eyes of others, as in the Golden Rule: *do unto others as you would have them do unto you.* Perhaps the evolution of role-taking, which is a very special capacity indeed, began with rather simple forms. For example, monkeys seem perfectly capable of identification with another monkey. If Azalea's sister interrupts hair plucking of her retarded sibling by another monkey, even though Azalea herself does nothing to draw attention, or if a mother monkey hurries over to stop an approach by her child toward an ill-tempered individual well before anything happens, these actions suggest great sensitivity to potential harm involving others.

It is not hard to see why monkeys would want to avoid harm to themselves, but why would harm to another bother them? Probably they see certain others as extensions of themselves, and the distress of those resonates within them. Known as *emotional contagion,*[33] this mechanism initially operates indiscriminately, yet becomes more selective with age. Monkeys learn to recognize subtle signs of distress, even situations in which distress is merely imminent. They follow closely what happens around them, especially if it involves friends and relatives.

Full-blown role-taking involves quite a bit more, however. The other is recognized not just as an extension of the self, but as a separate entity. Cognitive empathy is the ability to put oneself in the "shoes" of this other entity without losing the distinction between self and other. The American psychologist Martin Hoffman believes that this remarkable capacity grows out of emotional contagion. Being vicariously affected by others may make the child curious about their internal state, and stimulate him to search for cues about the others' feelings. Out of this challenge grows an increased awareness of the self in relation to others.

The same challenge may have occurred in the course of evolution. Perhaps some species evolved social organizations in which it became particularly advantageous to appreciate how companions were doing—not just at an emotional level, but also by imagining their situation. Sharper awareness of the other entailed increased self-awareness. If the mirror test somehow taps into this ability, as Gallup suggests, higher levels of empathy may be limited to humans and apes.

One indication of a relation between the two is that the first signs of cognitive empathy in children appear at about the same time as mirror self-recognition.[34] Another sign is that consolation occurs in a self-recognizing species, the chimpanzee, but apparently not in macaques. Do macaques rarely reassure victims of aggression because they lack the required ability to trade places mentally with them? Signs of distress in others do affect them, but once the fight is over and these indications subside, macaques quickly lose interest.[35]

As so often with regard to gradual processes, the tension between continuity and discontinuity cannot easily be resolved. Even if temperatures change steadily, there is an abrupt change in properties when water turns into ice or steam. Both the gradualist and the believer in fundamental distinctions have a point when considering the evolution of empathy and sympathy. Yes, apes do share our capability for self-recognition in a mirror, but no, this capability does not necessarily mean that humans and apes are the only animals conscious of themselves. And yes, apes do show remarkable empathy, but no, they are not the only animals sensitive to the needs of others. We only need think of the incredible assistance elephants, dolphins, and lemurs offer each other to realize how widespread and well developed these tendencies are. Caring responses go back much further in evolutionary history than the ape-human lineage.

In the last few years, self-awareness and mirror tests have become hot topics of debate. The controversy will no doubt fertilize large areas of the behavioral sciences, as it touches on many issues. Apes can be expected to continue to steal the spotlight, for they may be the only animals other than ourselves to care about how they look in the eyes of others. Apes faced with a mirror inspect hard-to-see body parts such as their teeth and posterior. Female chimpanzees twist their bodies to get a good look at the pink genital swellings that arouse the males. Orangutans place vegetables on their heads to size up the effect. Even without mirrors, apes adorn themselves—albeit with peculiar taste. A chimpanzee will find a dead mouse and carefully place it between her shoulders for the entire day, taking care that it does not fall off, or drape vines around her neck in an act of self-beautification.[36]

Undoubtedly, the interest apes show in themselves relates to the complexity of their social life, in which it probably matters greatly how one is perceived. Like the Biami, apes do not need reflective surfaces to gain self-awareness. They are used to watching themselves in the *social* mirror: the spectators' eyes.


## Lying and Aping Apes

A female guppy courted by two males ends up associating with one of them while another female follows the entire process from an adjacent tank. When this guppy "voyeuse" is introduced to the same males to see which one she likes better, she follows her predecessor's choice. Lee Dugatkin, an American ethologist who conducted these experiments, speculates that female guppies rely on each other's assessments of potential mates. The I-want-what-she-wants principle that Dugatkin found had the power of reversing a female's independent preferences known from earlier tests.

Similarly, two Italian scientists, Graziano Fiorito and Pietro Scotto, trained an octopus to attack either a red or a white ball. After the training another octopus was allowed to watch four demonstrations from an adjoining tank. The spectator closely monitored the actions of the demonstrator with head and eye movements. When the same balls were dropped in the spectator's tank, he attacked the ball of the same color as the first octopus.

What both experiments teach us is that even animals with minuscule brains compared to primates notice how members of their own species relate to the environment. The octopus identified with the other octopus and the female guppy with the other female guppy, both letting their counterpart influence their attitude toward a stimulus.

If *identification* is the ability to feel closer to one object in the environment than another, and to make the situation of the first to some extent one's own, this is a very basic ability indeed. It makes it possible to reach out mentally to others, making them an extension of the self, paying close attention to their situation so as to influence it or gain information from it. Identification underlies both empathy and imitation. The precision with which one individual can copy the behavior of another depends on the degree to which that individual is able to assume the other's point of view (another way of saying that the level of imitation depends on the level of empathy).

The simplest form of imitation is mere behavioral copying without realization of the benefit of the behavior. This is perhaps what guppies and octopi do, and what primates do much of the time as well. The premier copier is no doubt the chimpanzee.[37] Juveniles in the Arnhem Zoo would amuse themselves by walking single file behind a female named Krom, which means "crooked," all with the same pathetic carriage. They also walked around supporting themselves on both wrists—instead of on their knuckles as any self-respecting knuckle-walker is supposed to do—resulting in awkward locomotion similar to that of an adult male in the group whose fingers had been mangled in a fight.

Captive chimpanzees, furthermore, learn from watching people how to use tools such as hammers, screwdrivers, and brooms. That they do not always grasp the utility of the tool was noted by pioneering field-worker Robert Garner as long ago as 1896. Given a saw, his chimpanzee "applied the back of it, because the teeth were too rough, but he gave it the motion . . . He would put the back of it across a stick and saw with the energy of a man on a big salary."[38]

It is widely assumed that primates excel at imitation—so much so that we call it *aping*. Usually we mean more than mere copying. Experts on primate behavior are not in agreement about the more advanced kinds of imitation, however. In its most complete form the imitator adopts the model's perspective and recognizes both the model's goal and his method of bringing this goal closer. Are monkeys or apes aware of the problems others face? Do they understand others' solutions, and can they then apply this knowledge to the same problems? Whereas there is little or no evidence that monkeys do so, some scientists believe apes to be different.

The various technologies of wild chimpanzees, such as nut-cracking with stones or termite fishing with twigs, require fine manual skills that take years to acquire (and adult chimpanzees are said to be far better at them than naive humans). Young chimpanzees seem to watch closely and learn from adults. There are even stories of mothers' correcting their offspring's mistakes, which would amount to active teaching. Unfortunately, these observations are made under uncontrolled conditions, and field-workers have a rather fragmentary picture of their subjects' learning histories. Experimental psychologists who have carefully tested captive chimpanzees are not convinced that such high-level processes take place. They do agree that chimpanzees pick up information from watching others (such as the location where rewards are to be obtained, and the kind of tools that produce them), and that this *helps* them find a solution; yet they believe that ultimately problems are solved by each individual independently.[39]

The imitation controversy pertains to the broader question of whether animals view each other as having intentions, feelings, beliefs, and knowledge. Do they look at each other as sentient beings? This question bears directly on ethics: perceived intentions are the stuff of moral judgment. In our daily lives it matters greatly whether someone hurts us deliberately or accidentally. As soon as children can produce sentences, they begin arguing along these lines, confronting their parents with the difficult decision between the wet child's "He sprayed me on purpose!" and the dry child's "I didn't know he was there!" With praise and blame being meted out on the basis of our reading of other people's intentions, it is important to know if animals recognize knowledge or intention behind the behavior of others.

Pioneering research in this area was conducted in the 1970s by an American experimental psychologist, Emil Menzel, with nine juvenile chimpanzees. He would take one of them out into a large enclosure to show hidden food, or a frightening object such as a stuffed snake or crocodile. Subsequently, he would take the "knower" back to the waiting group and release all of them together. Would the others appreciate the knower's information, and if so, would they develop strategies to exploit it? Would the knower develop counterstrategies? All such behavior might require that chimpanzees know about knowing. Few accounts are more emblematic of the modern approach to social behavior than the following one by Menzel. He describes the attempt of a dominant chimpanzee, Rock, to extrapolate the knowledge of an equally canny subordinate, Belle, and outwit her.

> If Rock was not present, Belle invariably led the group to food and nearly everybody got some. In tests conducted when Rock was present, however, Belle became increasingly slower in her approach to the food. The reason was not hard to detect. As soon as Belle uncovered the food, Rock raced over, kicked or bit her, and took it all.

Belle accordingly stopped uncovering the food if Rock was close. She sat on it until Rock left. Rock, however, soon learned this, and when she sat on one place for more than a few seconds, he came over, shoved her aside, searched her sitting place and got the food.

Belle next stopped going all the way. Rock, however, countered by steadily expanding the area of his search through the grass near where Belle sat. Eventually, Belle sat farther and farther away, waiting until Rock looked in the opposite direction before she moved toward the food at all—and Rock in turn seemed to look away until Belle started to move somewhere. On some occasions Rock started to wander off, only to wheel around suddenly precisely as Belle was about to uncover the food.

In other trials when we hid an extra piece of food about 10 feet away from the large pile, Belle led Rock to the single piece, and while he took it she raced for the pile. When Rock started to ignore the single piece of food to keep his watch on Belle, Belle had temper tantrums.[40]

Could Rock have been so persistent without recognition on his part—conviction, really—that Belle knew something that she did not wish to reveal? This explanation certainly would seem the most tempting, although simpler accounts, based on quick learning and anticipation of the other's actions, cannot be ruled out entirely.

In recent years research on attribution and perspective taking has exploded into experiments on both children and apes. Julie Hadin and Josef Perner showed children a picture series in which a girl puts an escaped rabbit back into its cage, then leaves, after which a boy removes the same rabbit from the cage to take it home. The children are then asked where the girl thinks the pet is, and whether she will be surprised to find it at the boy's home. In order to predict her reaction correctly, the children need to understand that the girl's knowledge and their own knowledge of the whole situation are different. Children begin to make such distinctions only by the age of six years.

Daniel Povinelli tested the attributional capacities of chimpanzees in the laboratory of Sarah Boysen. The location of food was pointed out to the apes by either a person who could have seen where the food was hidden, or by one who lacked this knowledge because his or her head had been covered at the critical moment by a paper bag (evidently, nobody worries about our species' image in the eyes of animal subjects!). Because the chimpanzees reacted differently to the advice from these two sources, they seemed to realize that knowing requires seeing.[41]

Monkeys may not recognize this distinction. Using the tendency of macaques to vocally "announce" food, Dorothy Cheney and Robert Seyfarth measured their perspective-taking abilities. A caretaker placed apple slices in a food bin in full view of a mother and her juvenile offspring. In another arrangement only the mother could see the food arrive because her offspring, although nearby, was hidden behind a partition. Mothers did not call more under the second condition, as they should have had they been sensitive to their offspring's point of view and lack of information.

The difference between chimpanzees and macaques emerging from these experiments has been corroborated by Povinelli in a telling study of role-taking. A chimpanzee was taught to select one of four handles. If she pulled the correct one, both she and a human at the other end of the apparatus would obtain food. The human but not the chimpanzee could see which handle was baited, and the human would point at this handle to assist the chimpanzee. It was a happy arrangement, and the chimpanzee soon learned to act according to the hints of her partner. After a large number of trials the roles were suddenly reversed, with the human now pulling the handles and the chimpanzee seeing the hidden food. Three of the four chimpanzees understood what was expected of them, having grasped the nature of the informant role from mere watching: they began helping their partner select the right lever. Yet when rhesus monkeys were allowed to work with human informants, none of them responded with the same sort of immediate understanding when the tables were turned: they first had to *learn* the new contingencies. It may be that chimpanzees can picture themselves in someone else's position and adopt this individual's role, whereas monkeys cannot.

The final, but perhaps least investigated, sign of higher cognition in chimpanzees is their deceptive nature. True deception—one of those capacities that we employ all the time without taking too much pride in it—can be defined as the deliberate projection, to one's own advantage, of a false image of past behavior, knowledge, or intention. In its most complete sense, it requires awareness of how one's actions come across and what the outside world is likely to read into them.

Chimpanzees may possess such awareness; their deceitful tactics have long been known by people who have raised them at home or worked with them in captivity. Many chimpanzees will, for example,

Instances of spontaneous deception in the Arnhem chimpanzee colony.[42]

**Example 1.**   A chimpanzee's teeth-baring signals nervousness. A grin on a male's face may therefore undermine the effectiveness of his intimidation display.

"The most dramatic instance of self-correction occurred when a male, who was sitting with his back to his challenger, showed a grin upon hearing hooting sounds. He quickly used his fingers to push his lips back over his teeth again. This manipulation occurred three times before the grin ceased to appear. Only then did the male turn around to bluff back at his rival."

**Example 2.**   Among thousands of records of reconciliation, six mention a dramatic shift from friendly to aggressive behavior. All instances followed unsuccessful attempts by an older aggressor to catch a younger victim, and involved unusually harsh punishment once the victim had come within reach.

"Puist, a masculine-looking female, aggressively pursues and almost catches a younger female. The victim screams for a while after her narrow escape, then sits down, panting heavily, and rests. The incident seems forgotten, yet approximately ten minutes later Puist approaches and makes a friendly gesture from a distance: she reaches with an open hand toward the other. The younger female hesitates, then approaches Puist with all the signs of mistrust—frequent stopping, looking around, and a slight grin on her face. Puist persists in her friendly invitation, adding soft pants when the younger female comes close. Soft pants have a particularly friendly meaning; they are often followed by a kiss, the chimpanzee's conciliatory gesture par excellence. Suddenly Puist lunges and grabs the younger female, biting her fiercely before she can free herself."

**Example 3.**   Dandy, the youngest adult male, did not always gain access to food if housed at night with the other adult males. The others would threaten him away.

"After a few months the keeper reported that in the twenty minutes or so between entering the cage and feeding time, Dandy was always unusually playful and often engaged the whole male band in play. Arriving with food, the keeper would find them romping around, piling straw on each other and 'laughing' [hoarse guttural sounds associated with play]. In this relaxed atmosphere Dandy would eat undisturbed, side by side with the others. Apparently Dandy feigned a good mood in order to influence the mood of others to his own advantage."

**Example 4.**   Low-ranking males mate with females at their own peril, as dominant males tend to interrupt such sexual activities. As a consequence, the lower-ranked males often hide in a secret rendez-vous that requires female cooperation.

"This kind of furtive mating is frequently associated with signal suppression and concealment. I can remember the first time I noticed it very vividly indeed, because it was such a comical sight. Dandy and a female were courting each other surreptitiously. Dandy began to make advances to the female, at the same time restlessly looking around to see if any of the other males were watching. Male chimpanzees start their advances by sitting with their legs wide apart revealing their erection. Precisely at the point when Dandy was exhibiting his sexual urge in this way, Luit, one of the older males, unexpectedly came around the corner. Dandy immediately dropped his hands over his penis, concealing it from view."

---

quickly collect a mouthful of water from a faucet in their cage when they see a stranger approaching, then wait with a perfect poker face until they can let the intruder have it. Some are such experts that they trick even people who are thoroughly mindful of the possibility. The ape will stroll around in his cage as if occupied with something else, only to swing around at the right moment when he hears his victim behind him.

The first body of evidence that chimpanzees do the same to one another was put together in 1982 in *Chimpanzee Politics,* based on my observations of the Arnhem colony. With years of macaque watching behind me before I was introduced to chimpanzees, I was totally unprepared for the finesse with which these apes con each other. I saw them wipe undesirable expressions off their face, hide compromising body parts behind their hands, and act totally blind and deaf when another tested their nerves with a noisy intimidation display. It is not hard to see how concern about signals emitted by one's own body relates to self-awareness—these chimpanzees acted quite differently from the puppy chasing its own tail.

What is special about lies is that they rapidly lose effectiveness if employed too frequently. For this reason striking instances of deception can be expected to be rare, and anecdotes are probably all we will ever obtain. Work in this area has been criticized yet there is nothing wrong with unique observations: the fact that human moon landings have been rare does not make their occurrence dubious.

Menzel implied the same when asking: "By the way, does anyone have any experimental evidence for deceit in any human president, king, or dictator? All I have ever seen here is anecdotes."[43]

Admittedly, there is an element of judgment, hence risk of over-interpretation, in anecdotal reports. Skeptics would need to explain, however, why chimpanzees appear to lend themselves more readily than other species to interpretations of deception. Does this fact tell us something about the apes or about the scientists attracted to them? The same interpretations simply do not present themselves with monkeys, as I noticed when I returned to watching macaques—over a hundred of them for a decade—and tried to collect instances of deception. The observer was the same, the desire to interpret (or over-interpret) behavior was undiminished, yet nothing even remotely comparable to what chimpanzees do was to be seen.

Similarly, when two British primatologists, Andrew Whiten and Richard Byrne, invited field-workers and other experts on primate behavior from all over the world to send them instances of spontaneous deception, they compiled 253 accounts, the most striking and complex of which concerned chimpanzees.

Even though further research is obviously needed, reports of special abilities in apes—mirror self-recognition, imitation, expressions of empathy, and intentional deception—are varied enough to suggest that somewhere in evolutionary history an important step was taken. Every piece of evidence in and of itself may not convince, but the simultaneous appearance of a number of indications of higher cognition in a single evolutionary branch is hard to explain without assuming an underlying principle that is absent or less developed in other branches.

## Simian Sympathy

Cognitive evolution does not invent new categories of behavior. It works with, rather than replaces, the ancient emotional infrastructure, transforming it by an ever-greater understanding on the part of the actors. As a species, however, we value intelligence so highly that we tend to think that our reasoning capacities *drive* behavior. We are so skilled at producing convincing rationalizations that we begin to believe in them: the myth of rational man, or woman.

An example of overestimation of our rational nature is the "decision" to carry babies on the left hip. Right-handed mothers point out that it makes perfect sense to do so because they need their right hand to stir pots and fold laundry. Left-handed mothers have an equally compelling reason: obviously, a baby is more securely held in the dominant extremity. The fact is that a large majority of women show a left-side cradling bias regardless of handedness or cultural background. Men do not show the bias—they tend to carry babies on their right arm—but the left bias has also been reported for ape mothers. Because it transcends handedness, cultural, and even species bariers, it is unlikely that the left cradling bias has much to do with the rationalizations offered. One theory is that it is a natural tendency that places the baby closer to the mother's heart.[44]

Similarly, if some scientists believe that empathy is based on language or that helping involves a rational weighing of costs and benefits, they are probably overestimating the power of human reasoning and underestimating the role of emotions and subconscious motivations. The word "empathy" was coined as a translation of *Einfühlung,* a German term that became popular in academic circles early in this century. Inasmuch as *Einfühlung* literally means "feeling into," in the sense of getting inside the feelings of someone else, the German word exquisitely balances the interpersonal and affective sides of the process. In a time in which empathy is discussed largely as a cognitive feat, and in which cognition is often compared to the working of a cold-blooded computer, we should remember that the human mind knows no neat dividing line between thought and feeling. One individual's caring for another depends on a *mosaic* of factors ranging from rational and cognitive to emotive and physiological.

For this reason the question at the heart of this chapter is not so much whether any creatures other than ourselves can feel sympathy based on empathy (too much an all-or-nothing phenomenon), but *which elements* of human sympathy are recognizable in other animals. Fellow-feeling doubtless exists among social animals; what we want to know is the degree to which it resembles that among people. The cognitive dimension of this problem has more to do with the precise channeling of succorant tendencies than with the tendencies themselves. As Philip Mercer, a British philosopher, put it: "There are appropriate and inappropriate ways of helping others, and it seems natural to suppose that the more fully we sympathize with someone the more likely we are to give him the kind of help he needs."[45]

Thus, in aiding a friend, I combine the helping tendency of cooperative animals with a typically human appreciation of my friend's feelings and needs. The forces that propel me into action are the same, but I carry out the mission like a smart missile instead of like a blind rocket. Cognitive empathy is goal directed; it allows me to fine-tune my help to my friend's specific requirements.

One element underlying all caring behavior is mutual attachment. We are not surprised to find that dolphins, elephants, canids, and most primates respond to each other's pain and distress, because the members of these species survive through cooperation in hunting and defense against enemies and predators. The evolution of succorant behavior and bonds of affection is understandable, as every individual's life counts for the rest of the group. In a given species, the urge to help others roughly matches the need for help. A tiger needs no assistance and has absolutely no urge to provide it to others, yet the human primate is rather powerless on his own and therefore enters into elaborate contracts of mutual assistance.

A connection between the level of mutual dependency and succorant behavior is confirmed by invalid care in yet another highly cooperative nonprimate, the dwarf mongoose. A British ethologist, Anne Rasa, followed the final days of a low-ranking adult male dying of chronic kidney disease. The male lived in a captive group consisting of a founding pair and its offspring. Two adjustments took place. First, the sick male was allowed to eat much earlier in the rank order than previously. Instead of being chased away, he could nibble on the same piece of food as his father, the alpha male. Second, the rest of the group changed from sleeping on elevated objects, such as boxes, to sleeping on the floor once the sick male had lost the ability to climb onto the boxes. They stayed in contact with him, grooming him much more than usual. After the male's death, the group slept with the cadaver until its decay made removal necessary.

Following attachment, the next most basic ability involved in empathy is emotional contagion—vicarious arousal by the emotions of others. In its simplest form, there is total identification without discrimination between one's own feelings and those of the other. It is unlikely, for example, that a human newborn crying with the rest of the nursery has any notion that she is responding to feelings that originated with someone else. Rather, she seems hooked up to a communication network of direct lines between individual experiences without relay stations to tell her where the calls originated. Infants seem to "lose" themselves in collectivities of agony, joy, and sleepiness.

Caring behavior, even in the largest-brained species, may further

Increased awareness of self and other ———————————————————————————▶

| | | |
|---|---|---|
| | Emotional contagion | Cognitive empathy |
| Attachment | | Perspective shift |
| | Learned adjustment | Intentional deception |
| Identification | | Attribution |
| | Behavioral copying | True imitation |

Cooperative animals with strong attachments identify with one another and are sensitive to the other's emotions. To be genuinely concerned about another's well-being, however, requires differentiation between self and other. Most likely this cognitive step was taken by the ancestors of humans and apes, although its occurrence in other social animals cannot be excluded.

depend on innate releasers, that is, particular stimuli that almost automatically trigger a response in all members of the species. If I approach a chimpanzee friend with a scab on my arm, her eyes will brighten and focus on my little injury. She will beg for access, and, if I would let her, will open up the wound, all the while tooth-clacking with excitement. I could provide her no greater joy. And if one believes that the notion of "innate releasers" does not apply to humans, think again: I know people with exactly the same skin-peeling itch!

Another standard cue is known as the *Kindchenschema:* infantile traits, such as large eyes and rounded features, melt our hearts as well as those of other animals. No one better understood this than Walt Disney. The result was "cutification" of animals on a massive scale. Add dependency indicators, such as lassitude and a high-pitched voice, and one has the perfect formula to arouse protection and care, and to inhibit behavior normally reserved for older juveniles, such as the rejection of contact or punishment of misconduct. The special treatment enjoyed by Azalea and Wania-6672 may have been based on such characteristics; that is, other group members may never have reached the point of seeing them as the juveniles they were because they retained their babyish appeal.

An example of the prolongation of care in the wild is a capuchin monkey born in the Venezuelan jungle with partially paralyzed legs. The monkey could climb but not jump, and needed to be carried in order to get from tree to tree. According to John Robinson, the group carried the infant more than usual for its age (in capuchins many individuals other than the mother transport infants). The bad news was that the infant consumed normal amounts of food. Having no exercise, it grew big and fat and became more and more of a burden. The group bravely carried this butterball until it was seventeen months old, when it disappeared. No one knows how its life ended; it might have been abandoned by the group or snatched by a bird of prey.

Attachment, emotional identification, and innate responses, combined with potent learning abilities, provide a firm enough basis for elaborate caring behavior, which may sometimes be hard to distinguish from human expressions of sympathy. The latter differ, however, in that we recognize the other's experiences as belonging to the other, which is the only way we can feel genuine concern. A mother who shuts her eyes and grimaces when the doctor is about to stick a needle in her child's arm is anticipating the emotional disturbance of her child, hence of herself, while knowing full well that it is the child, not she, who will feel the pain. Identifying with and caring about another without losing one's own identity is the crux of human sympathy. As we have seen, this requires certain cognitive abilities, the most important one being a well-developed sense of self and the ability to assume another individual's perspective.

Two examples of simian sympathy illustrate the advantage of this ability. They describe succorant behavior of greater complexity and solicitude than found outside the human-ape branch of the primate tree.

*The moat and the chain*    The bonobos at the San Diego Zoo used to live in a grotto-type enclosure separated from the public by a 2-meter-deep dry moat. The moat was accessible to the apes by a chain hanging down into it; they could freely descend and climb up again. In *Peacemaking among Primates,* I described a situation repeatedly observed if the dominant male, Vernon, disappeared into the moat. A younger male, Kalind, would quickly pull up the chain and look down at Vernon with an open-mouthed play face—the ape equivalent of laughing—while slapping the side of the moat. On several occasions the only other adult, Loretta, rushed to the scene to "rescue" her mate by dropping the chain back down and standing guard until Vernon had gotten out. Both Kalind and Loretta seemed to know what purpose the chain served for someone at the bottom of the moat and acted accordingly—the one by teasing, the other by assisting.

*Tired of the tire problem*   The Arnhem chimpanzees spend the winters indoors. Each morning, after cleaning the hall and before releasing the colony, the keeper hoses out all the rubber tires in the enclosure and hangs them one by one on a horizontal log extending from the climbing frame. One day Krom was interested in a tire in which the water had been retained. Unfortunately, this particular tire was at the end of the row, with six or more heavy tires hanging in front of it. Krom pulled and pulled at the one she wanted but could not move it off the log. She pushed the tire backward, but there it hit the climbing frame and could not be removed either. Krom worked in vain on this problem for over ten minutes, ignored by everyone except Otto Adang, my successor in Arnhem, and Jakie, a seven-year-old male chimpanzee to whom Krom used to be the "aunt" (a caretaker other than the mother) when he was younger.

Immediately after Krom gave up and walked away from the scene, Jakie approached. Without hesitation he pushed the tires off the log one by one, as any sensible chimpanzee would, beginning with the front one, followed by the second in the row, and so on. When he reached the last tire, he carefully removed it so that no water was lost and carried the tire straight to his aunt, where he placed it upright in front of her. Krom accepted his present without any special acknowledgment and was already scooping water with her hand when Jakie left.

Inasmuch as cooperation is widespread in the animal kingdom, the tendency to assist a member of one's own species is nothing new or original. Yet the precise *intention* behind it changes as soon as the actor can picture what his assistance means to the other. It is hard to account for Jakie's behavior without assuming that he understood what Krom was after and wished to help her by fetching the tire. Perspective-taking revolutionizes helpful behavior, turning it into *cognitive altruism,* that is, altruism with the other's interests explicitly in mind.

## A World without Compassion

When the chimpanzees in Gombe National Park suffered an epidemic of poliomyelitis, probably contracted from people, the partially paralyzed victims were treated with fear, indifference, and hostility, as if they had ceased to belong to the community. According to Jane

Goodall, Pepe met with the following reaction when he first showed up at camp, his useless arm trailing in the dust.

> [The others] stared for a moment and then, with wide grins of fear, rushed for reassurance to embrace and pat each other, still staring at the unfortunate cripple. Pepe, who obviously had no idea that he himself was the object of their fear, showed an even wider grin of fright as he repeatedly turned to look over his shoulder along the path behind him.[46]

At first, healthy individuals avoided the polio victims because of their odd movements and dragging limbs. Next they directed charging displays at them; then they attacked.[47] Shunning grotesquely deformed individuals may be psychologically understandable (as well as adaptive, given the risk of infection), but it is one of many examples of the absence of compassion and mercy in a species in which at other times these very same qualities seem incipient. Brutal intercommunity violence observed between chimpanzees who in earlier years had peacefully traveled and groomed together, and the chimpanzee habit of tearing limbs and meat from prey animals who are still very much alive, such as a screaming colobus monkey, indicate that whatever inhibitions and sensitivities these apes possess, they are easily over-ruled by other interests.

The attitude toward members of one's own species should of course not be equated with that toward other species. Lack of concern for other species is to be expected, given the virtual absence of attachment. Animals often seem to regard those who belong to another kind as merely ambulant objects. Sue Boinsky reports that when an angry capuchin male in the wild ran out of ammunition while hurling things at her, he simply turned around, grabbed an unsuspecting squirrel monkey who sat nearby, and threw it at her as if it were just another branch. The capuchin, who would never have acted in this way with a member of his own species, clearly could not care less about the shrieking little monkeys with whom he shared the forest. Cruelty to other animals is something that we humans may have begun worrying about; it is a concern without precedent in nature. Hunters judge the hunted by caloric rather than emotional value, and even if other species are not perceived as food, usually nothing is to be gained by investing care in them.[48]

On rare occasions interspecific contact takes a cruel turn. Consider the game in which youngsters entice chickens behind a fence with bread crumbs. When they come within reach, the gullible chickens are hit with a stick or poked in the feathers with a sharp piece of wire. This "tantalus" game, in which the chickens were stupid enough to cooperate, was described by Wolfgang Köhler for his chimpanzees. They played the game for amusement, not to get hold of the fowl, and refined it to the point that one ape would be the baiter and another the hit man. It lends further support to the claim of higher cognition in chimpanzees: in the same way that empathy may lead to sympathy if combined with attachment, it may result in intentional harm if combined with indifference.

We are ready now for a second German term, *Schadenfreude,* which is quite the opposite of *Einfühlung* yet related to it for the same reason that sympathy and sadism are extremes that touch each other. Schadenfreude literally means "harm-joy." When people roll off their chairs laughing because Hardy falls into a barrel filled with glue while Laurel stupidly looks on, or because Chaplin gets slapped in the face by the object of his love, they are enjoying someone else's bad luck. The fact that so many comedians offer their audiences opportunities to express this type of glee indicates a deep-seated human urge to boost our self-esteem through the mishaps of others. We tend to conceal this emotion because in real life we experience it mainly in relation to people whom we do not like. The feeling probably derives from a sense of fairness: it is most predictably aroused if someone gets his comeuppance, as when a pompous or dishonest man loses his fortune. We do not feel Schadenfreude when the home of a poor family burns down, or when a child tumbles down the stairs, for these victims never threatened our self-worth.

Schadenfreude is the exact opposite of sympathy. Instead of sharing the pain of someone else, we get a kick out of it. Some of the most shocking, almost unbelievable, illustrations may be found in *The Mountain People.* Colin Turnbull describes an East African tribe, the Ik, who through starvation deteriorated to the point of dehumanization. All gaiety among the Ik seemed at the expense of others. They would shriek with laughter if someone fell, especially if weak or blind, or if an elder lost his food to roaming teenagers, who would go so far as to pry open the mouths of old people to pull out morsels that they had not yet swallowed. Harm to children was not exempted.

Men would watch a child with eager anticipation as it crawled towards the fire, then burst into gay and happy laughter as it plunged a skinny hand into the coals. Such times were the few times when parental affection showed itself: a mother would glow with pleasure to hear such joy occasioned by her offspring, and pull it tenderly out of the fire.

Turnbull never saw children more than three years old being fed by adults, and he observed that people ate away from their homes so as to avoid having to share the small quantities of food they had. Noting how pointless the quest for morality becomes under such inconceivable stress, and how nothing can be allowed to stand in the way of survival, the anthropologist cynically characterizes morality as "yet another luxury that we find convenient and agreeable and that has become conventional when we can afford it."[49]

What intrigues me most in this depressing account is that when love and sympathy are wiped out by circumstances, apparently it is not mere selfishness that raises its head but an actual delight in the misery of others. Could it be that people derive pleasure from an equalization of fate, regardless of whether it is brought about by an uplifting or downward movement? When we are well off, we root for the underdogs and like to see their lot improve. Yet when we are at the border of starvation ourselves, we are glad to see every bit of misfortune around us, as it confirms that we are not the only ones down and out.[50]

Whereas the possible link between sympathy and fairness has been little investigated, the connection with selfishness has received quite a bit of attention. Much of the philosophical literature, especially in the English-speaking world, has been marked by a juxtaposition of egoism and altruism. Rather than keeping alive the tension between these poles of sociality, there has been a tendency to come down on the side of the one or the other, usually the former. It must be obvious by now that I consider this paradigm rather sterile. The everything-is-egoism position is comparable to the claim that all life on earth is a conversion of sun energy. Both belong to the Great Truths of Science, yet in the same way that the second truth has never prevented us from recognizing the diversity of life, the first should not hold us back from making fundamental distinctions in the domain of motivation.

If I have a table full of food and you knock at my window, starving, I can invite you in and derive satisfaction from your happy face, or I can keep everything for myself and derive satisfaction from my own full belly. In both cases I may be called selfish; yet from your perspective, and that of society at large, it makes quite a difference which kind of self-interest I pursue. Also, the reward that I myself experience is altogether different in the two instances. Whereas most behavior is rewarded by how it affects the actor, acts of sympathy are rewarded by how the actor *imagines* that they affect the recipient. If this is selfishness, it happens to be the only kind that reaches out.

Experiments with human subjects by Robert Weiss and coworkers, in which the incentive for a response was the deliverance of another person from suffering, have confirmed that "the roots of altruistic behavior are so deep that people not only help others, but find it rewarding as well."[51] The fact that satisfying feelings tend to accompany acts of sympathy does not in any way detract from their other-directed nature if the only way to reap these rewards is via the other's well-being. When we calm a crying child, hugging and stroking him, we are not so much reassuring ourselves as we are the other. We monitor the impact of our behavior, and it fills us with immediate pleasure if the child laughs through his tears at a joke or a tickle. If human sympathy is indeed the "inborn and indestructible instinct" that David Hume, Arthur Schopenhauer, Adam Smith, and others, declared it to be, it is only natural that it comes with a built-in compensation in the same way that sex and eating do.[52]

With the feeling of sympathy so ingrained, it is only under the most extreme circumstances, as when people lose all means of subsistence or are packed together and starving in a concentration camp, that it dies. It becomes a thing of the past, a painful memory. An old Ik woman, to whom Turnbull had given some food, suddenly burst into tears because, as she said, it made her long for the "good old days" when people had been kind to one another. This common benevolence nourishes and guides all human morality. Aid to others in need would never be internalized as a duty without the fellow-feeling that drives people to take an interest in one another. Moral sentiments came first; moral principles, second.

Despite Immanuel Kant's opinion that kindness out of duty has greater moral worth than kindness out of temperament, if push comes to shove, sentiments win out. This is what the parable of the Good Samaritan is all about. A half-dead victim by the side of the road is ignored first by a priest, then by a Levite—both religious and ethically conscious men—yet receives care from the third passerby, a Samaritan. The biblical message is to be wary of ethics by the book rather than by the heart: only the Samaritan, a religious outcast, felt compassion.

One of my favorite experiments, by John Darley and Daniel Batson, re-created this situation with American seminary students. The students were sent to another building to give a talk about . . . the

Good Samaritan. While in transit they passed a slumped-over person planted in an alley. The groaning "victim" sat still with eyes closed and head down. Only 40 percent of the budding theologists asked what was wrong and offered assistance. Students who had been urged to make haste helped less than students who had been given lots of time. Indeed, some students hurrying to lecture on the quintessential helping story of our civilization literally stepped over the stranger in need, inadvertently confirming the point of the story.

Altruism is valued so highly precisely because it is costly and subject to all sorts of limitations and conditions. It may be subordinated to other interests or to felt obligations, and it may disappear entirely if unaffordable. In *The Moral Sense* philosopher James Q. Wilson characterizes sympathy as follows:

> It is easily aroused but quickly forgotten; when remembered but not acted upon, its failure to produce action is easily rationalized. We are softened by the sight of one hungry child, but hardened by the sight of thousands.[53]

Human sympathy is not unlimited. It is offered most readily to one's own family and clan, less readily to other members of the community, and most reluctantly, if at all, to outsiders. The same is true of the succorant behavior of animals. The two share not only a cognitive and emotional basis, therefore, but similar constraints on their expression.

Despite its fragility and selectivity, the capacity to care for others is the bedrock of our moral systems. It is the only capacity that does not snugly fit the hedonic cage in which philosophers, psychologists, and biologists have tried to lock the human spirit. One of the principal functions of morality seems to be to protect and nurture this caring capacity, to guide its growth and expand its reach, so that it can effectively balance other human tendencies that need little encouragement.

# COGNITION AND EMPATHY

For primates, as for humans, to most effectively help others, one needs to understand their needs and feelings. To gauge the depth of animal empathy and social intelligence, studies focus on responses to distress, self-awareness, the transmission of information, and the manipulation of social relationships.

In an act of consolation, a juvenile chimpanzee rushes over to embrace Yeroen, who screams after having been defeated in a critical battle over leadership. *(From* Chimpanzee Politics; *Arnhem Zoo)*

Learned adjustment in the context of play. When partners differ in size and strength, as do the adolescent male bonobo and infant here, the older partner needs to restrain himself to keep the game fun for the younger. *(San Diego Zoo)*

Kevin, an adolescent male bonobo, striking a philosophical pose. *(San Diego Zoo)*

A juvenile bonobo (right) showing concern for another. He grabs the arm of his buddy when the latter steps closer to the female on the left. The female presents a potential hazard, as she has been in a bad mood all morning and has chased the first male several times. *(San Diego Zoo)*

Mai (in center with back turned) gives birth while other chimpanzees gather around her. Atlanta, standing at her side, utters a loud scream when the baby drops into Mai's hands. Atlanta's reaction suggests identification with the mother. *(Yerkes Field Station)*

Two rhesus infants only a few months old. The female in front, who has just been molested by an adult, receives a hug from a male peer. In rhesus monkeys, such comforting behavior virtually disappears later in life. A rare exception is the case of Fawn (facing page), who huddles with an older sister (upper left) after having been attacked, while her mother (right) grooms one of the aggressors. *(Wisconsin Primate Center)*

The behavior of this macaque mother may reflect learned adjustment to the needs of her offspring. With an infant clinging to her back, the mother reaches for soybeans scattered into a warm-water spring in a Japanese nature reserve. Park officials say they need to keep first-time mothers out of the water because these females tend to drown their infants when diving for food. Experienced mothers are apparently more careful. *(Jigokudani Park, Japan)*

In studies of free-ranging Japanese macaques, Eishi Tokida presented them with a transparent tube containing a piece of apple. Only a few monkeys learned how to obtain the food with a stick or by rolling a rock through the tube. Other monkeys did not seem to learn from their example. The most successful individual, Tokei, occasionally used her own infants, pushing them into the pipe and retrieving them once they had put their teeth into the food. This photograph, however, shows Tokei (stick in hand) threatening her offspring away with a stare. Having grown too large for use as a live tool, the infant is now seen as competition. *(Jigokudani Park, Japan)*

Ropey, a rhesus monkey, holds her daughter (right) together with the alpha female's son. Perhaps such double-holding serves to promote friendship between the mother's own offspring and desirable peers. *(Wisconsin Primate Center)*

The opposite strategy is for a mother to interrupt contact: a high-ranking female breaks up the play between her daughter (left) and a low-ranking peer. She punishes the play partner, pushing her down roughly. *(Wisconsin Primate Center)*

Young chimpanzees test the social rules of their community by teasing their elders. A juvenile holds a stick behind his back, ready to throw it at a resting adult female. *(Arnhem Zoo)*

Faye, a young chimpanzee involved in studies of cognitive development conducted by Kim Bard at the Yerkes Primate Center, plays with a mirror. In an atypical facial expression, she moves her lower jaw up and down while staring straight at her reflection. It is as if she is exploring the connection between her own movements and those in the mirror. Such games are absent in most other animals, who either ignore their reflection or treat it as a stranger. Faye is close to the age, between twenty-eight and thirty months, at which most chimpanzees in Bard's research pass the mark test of mirror self-recognition.

Self-decoration by a juvenile bonobo, who has draped banana leaves around her shoulders. Afterward, she parades around with the leafy shawl. *(San Diego Zoo)*

Four juvenile chimpanzees nervously inspect a stuffed snake hidden in the grass of their enclosure during one of Emil Menzel's experiments on knowledge transmission. *(Courtesy of Emil Menzel; Tulane Primate Center)*

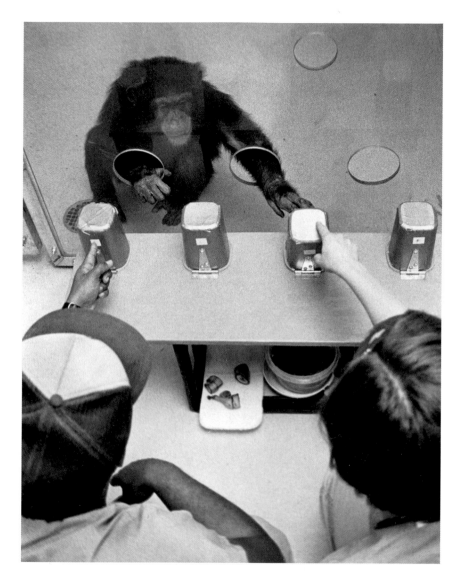

A chimpanzee receives advice from two experimenters about which cup covers food. Only one of the two persons knows; the other was absent or had occluded vision while the food was being hidden. The ape reaches for the cup pointed out by the experimenter on the right, who is indeed the one who knows. Possibly the subject understands that seeing leads to knowing. *(Photograph by Donna Bierschwale; courtesy of New Iberia Research Center)*

During hand-clasp grooming, the two partners hold hands above their heads, grooming each other with their free hand. Chimpanzees at the Yerkes Field Station spontaneously began using this posture a few years ago. Since then, it has spread within the group. The posture, never observed in other captive chimpanzees, is known in only two (geographically separate) wild communities. It thus seems to be a group-specific culturally transmitted behavior.

# 3

# RANK AND ORDER

The overall picture of group organization in these animals [baboons] is of a
sensitive balancing of forces, the balance being achieved by the social learning of individuals in the group from
the time of birth to adulthood, so that
infringements of the group norm are
rare. When they do occur, they may be
severely punished if the victim is
caught.

*Ronald Hall*[1]

One balmy evening, when the keeper called the chimpanzees inside,
two adolescent females refused to enter the building. The rule at
Arnhem Zoo being that *none* of the apes will receive food until *all* of
them have moved from the island into their sleeping quarters, the
chimpanzees actively assist with the rule's enforcement: latecomers
meet with a great deal of hostility from the hungry colony.

When the obstinate teenagers finally entered, more than two hours
late, they were given a separate bedroom so as to prevent reprisals.
This protected them only temporarily, however. The next morning,
out on the island, the entire colony vented its frustration about the
delayed meal by a mass pursuit ending in a physical beating of the
culprits. Needless to say, they were the first to come in that evening.

## A Sense of Social Regularity

That animals follow rules has been known for a long time. Female
mammals, for example, threaten almost anyone or anything that
approaches their young uninvited. They may do so in different ways
or to different degrees, but maternal protection is widespread and

highly predictable. So much so that we may declare it a rule—a *descriptive rule,* to be precise. Because this kind of rule describes typical behavior, it can be applied not only to animate objects, but to inanimate ones as well. For example, we can say that as a rule stones fall when released, whereas helium balloons do not.

Descriptive rules are not particularly interesting from a moral perspective, as they lack the crucial "ought" quality. Stones do not fall to avoid getting into trouble. Only animals and humans follow *prescriptive rules,* rules actively upheld through reward and punishment. With regard to other animals we notice this most readily if the rules are of our own design, such as those that we apply to pets and work animals. Yet the remarkable trainability of certain species, such as sheepdogs and Indian elephants, hints at the possibility of a rule-based order among these animals themselves.

To return to maternal protection, it is easy to see how it would affect the way others approach and treat the young of the species. In a chimpanzee colony, any individual deviating from the mother's standards will either meet with her wrath or find it more difficult in the future to obtain the infant from her. A prescriptive rule is born when members of the group learn to recognize the contingencies between their own behavior and that of the mother and act so as to minimize negative consequences. They learn how to handle the infant without making it scream; to bring it back of their own accord; not to climb to dangerous spots with the infant desperately hanging on, and so on. Such heedfulness is not well developed in juveniles, who still have much to learn about infant behavior and maternal reactions. Thus, when a juvenile carries an infant around, the mother is never far behind. When juveniles reach adolescence, most of them have learned the rules well enough that mothers trust them as baby-sitters.

In the stump-tailed macaque all group members, even the largest males, commonly avoid very young infants who wander about unattended. It is as if they are afraid of getting into trouble. This is also the only species of macaque in which infants have a distinct coat color—much lighter than that of older individuals. It makes them hard to miss in a monkey melee. As soon as a baby is near or on its mother, it attracts extraordinary attention. Mothers are typically surrounded by others who utter special vocalizations, known as staccato grunts, while trying to look closely at the infant's face or inspect its genitals. Do these grunts express endearment? Probably something other than that, because if love and affection were the main motivations we would expect mothers to grunt the most, yet this is not at all the case. For her dissertation research, Kim Bauers recorded hundreds of vocalizations in the stump-tail group at the Wisconsin Primate Center and found that whereas females commonly grunt at each other's babies, they *never* do so at their own offspring.

Bauers found that the shorter the distance between mother and infant, the more likely others will grunt when trying to contact the little one. Even though aimed at the infant, staccato grunts seem intended for the mother as well. Perhaps it is the way members of this species "ask permission" to approach an infant. The fact that mothers themselves do not need such permission would explain the absence of their grunts.

This interpretation is further supported by the appeasing effect of staccato grunts: silent interest in infants is far more often rebuffed by maternal threats and slaps than interest announced by a series of grunts. In other words, directing friendly sounds to an infant forestalls problems with its mother. This may be an acquired social convention; most silent approaches, hence most rebuffs, involve juveniles, who may still be in the process of learning how to overcome maternal protectiveness.

Of even greater interest than rules enforced by individual mothers are rules sanctioned by the community. In the case of the two latecomers in Arnhem, we saw a group response, but the regulation in question was of course put in place by people. Chimpanzees also seem to develop their own rules, however.

Jimoh, the current alpha male of the Yerkes Field Station group, once detected a secret mating between Socko, an adolescent male, and one of Jimoh's favorite females. Socko and the female had wisely disappeared from view, but Jimoh had gone looking for them. Normally, the old male would merely chase off the culprit, but for some reason—perhaps because the female had repeatedly refused to mate with Jimoh himself that day—he this time went full speed after Socko and did not give up. He chased him all around the enclosure—Socko screaming and defecating in fear, Jimoh intent on catching him.

Before he could accomplish his aim, several females close to the scene began to "woaow" bark. This indignant sound is used in protest against aggressors and intruders. At first the callers looked around to see how the rest of the group was reacting; but when others joined in, particularly the top-ranking female, the intensity of their calls quickly increased until literally everyone's voice was part of a deafening chorus. The scattered beginning almost gave the impression that the group was taking a vote. Once the protest had swelled to a chorus, Jimoh broke off his attack with a nervous grin on his face: he got the message. Had he failed to respond, there would no doubt have been concerted female action to end the disturbance.

These are the sorts of moments when we human observers feel most profoundly that there is some moral order upheld by the community. We cannot help but identify with a group that we watch day in and day out, and our own values of order and harmony are so similar that we would have barked along with the chimpanzees if we thought it would have mattered! Whereas some of us are inclined to explain the group's reaction to Jimoh in moral terms, such as "He just went too far," other observers might prefer a more neutral account along the lines of "Chimpanzees sometimes bark in response to aggression." There is one problem with the latter view, however: one never hears woaow barks when a mother punishes her own offspring, or when an adult male controls a tiff among juveniles—even if he uses force in the process. Not every fight triggers these calls. It is a reaction to a very particular kind of disturbance, one that seriously endangers relationships or lives. Thinking in terms of rules and violations may help us come to grips with its relevant features.

Undoubtedly, prescriptive rules and a sense of order derive from a hierarchical organization, one in which the subordinate pays close attention to the dominant. Not that every social rule is necessarily established through coercion and dominance, but prototype rule enforcement comes from above. Without agreement on rank and a certain respect for authority there can be no great sensitivity to social rules, as anyone who has tried to teach simple house rules to a cat will agree. Even if cat lovers fail to see a nonhierarchical nature as a shortcoming—on the contrary!—it does place their pets firmly outside the human moral realm. Evolved as solitary hunters, cats go their own way, indifferent to what the rest of the world thinks of them.

Respect for rules and norms can develop only when the opinions and reactions of others matter. Fear of punishment is important, but not the whole story: the desire to belong to a group, and to fit in, is also involved. According to Lawrence Kohlberg, who pioneered research in this field, these elements are recognizable in the first stages of human moral growth. Development begins with obedience and a wish to stay out of trouble, followed by an orientation toward approval and pleasing others. For the child, it is the adult's approval that is sought; for the adult, it may be that of an omnipotent God infused with absolute moral knowledge. There is obviously more to morality—Kohlberg's scheme counts six stages up to and including an autonomous conscience—yet submission to a higher authority is fundamental. This feature is also less peculiarly human than some of the abilities involved in the later stages: submission to authority is part of a primordial orientation found not only in our fellow primates, but in a host of other animals as well.

It cannot be accidental that obedience and a desire to please are conspicuous traits of man's best friend. That dogs provide almost a caricature of humanity's early moral stages may explain our species' love affair with the canine soul. Most of the time dogs are "good," otherwise we punish them for being "bad" in the hope of changing their behavior. At the same time that dogs are highly sensitive to praise and blame, however, the more advanced stages of human moral development, which emphasize rights and equality, are beyond their comprehension. They think in terms of vertical, not horizontal, arrangements. These animals do not take kindly, for example, to an antiauthoritarian upbringing. Unresolved status disputes provide much of the business of dog therapists. Owners who hate to be masters deprive their pets of the element they need most for psychological stability: a clearly defined social position. Many a dog who cannot be under his owner in the family pack will try to be on top—which, in turn, is bound to undermine the owner's psychological stability!

Dogs inherited their law-and-order mentality from pack-hunting ancestors. In much the way we teach a puppy behavioral rules, dogs and wolves seem to teach their young (see pages 94–95). A hierarchical orientation is by no means limited to the Canidae, however. It is also widespread in the primates, although in their case it is mitigated by a strong tendency to form alliances, that is, a tendency for two or more parties to band together against a third. Alliances usually bolster the position of dominants, but sometimes subordinates jointly stand against higher-ups. The resulting balancing of power, combined with a tendency for reciprocal exchange, produces the beginnings of an orientation to equity, particularly in the chimpanzee.

We can see this orientation when a group is faced with an attractive resource. Will the bosses claim everything for themselves, or will they share? In chimpanzees begging for food is common, and a beggar who is ignored may express frustration by throwing a fit. Temper tantrums are high drama, capable of inducing possessors to relinquish part of their food. The rhesus macaque, in contrast, lives in a society with rather intolerant dominants. From a safe distance the subordinate silently watches the dominant's food consumption. Sharing is absent

Canids have an excellent sense of social rules, which allows for order within the hunting pack and explains their trainability for human purposes. They not only follow rules, they may actively inculcate them in others. Below are examples in which dominant wolves or dogs seem to deliberately wait for or even induce a transgression in order to penalize it.[2]

**Example 1.** Eberhard Trumler describes how a father dog instills obedience, once his offspring have outgrown their puppy license.

"[One day] he 'declares' an old-bone taboo. First, the pups try to get hold of it. Immediately they are severely punished by the father, who grabs the violator by the scruff of his neck, shaking him vigorously. Naturally the victim yelps and, once released, throws himself submissively on his back. Shortly thereafter, however, when the father appears to be busy with something else, the disciplined pup circumspectly sneaks up to the forbidden bone again—only to receive another castigation. This may be repeated several times, and one gets the impression that the pups want to know exactly what kind of response they can expect from the old one. Anyone with a puppy at home will be familiar with such probing of the educator."

**Example 2.** Behavioral modification by a mother wolf is reported in *Of Wolves and Men,* by Barry Lopez.

"A female wolf left four or five pups alone in a rendezvous area in the Brooks Range one morning and set off down a trail away from them. When she was well out of sight, she turned around and lay flat in the path, watching her back trail. After a few moments, a pup who had left the rendezvous area trotted briskly over a rise in the trail and came face to face with her. She gave a low bark. He stopped short, looked about as though preoccupied with something else, then, with a dissembling air, began to edge back the way he had come. His mother escorted him to the rendezvous site and departed again. This time she didn't bother watching her back trail. Apparently the lesson had taken, for all the pups stayed put until she returned that evening."

**Example 3.** The American anthropologist and primatologist Barbara Smuts related another example of apparent rule-teaching seen in her dog, Safi, a mixed sheepherding breed. Safi is older than and dominant over a neighbor dog, an Airedale named Andy, with whom she plays every day in the yard of Smuts's house.

"I threw the ball for them repeatedly. Normally Safi always gets the ball; Andy defers to her even if the ball lands nearest to him. On this occasion the ball bounced in an odd way and landed right at Andy's feet while Safi stood at a distance. He grabbed the ball and brought it back to me. Safi followed with no sign of distress.

"I threw it again, and as usual Safi got it. But instead of returning it to me, as she normally does, she now brought the ball to Andy and dropped it right in front of him, backed off, and waited. Naturally Andy picked it up, at which point Safi pounced on him, pinned him to the ground, and held him with his neck in her mouth, growling softly. Andy immediately dropped the ball and was appropriately submissive. Safi released him and the game continued amicably—except that Andy hasn't been seen since going for the ball. It was as if Safi had intentionally communicated to him 'Thou shalt not pick up my ball!'"

**Example 4.** Early this century, Captain Max von Stephanitz, the greatest authority on the German shepherd dog, explained that there is a lot more to the learning of rules than fear of punishment. Note the distinctly moral perspective von Stephanitz takes when outlining the objectives of training this breed.

"If the dog is too keenly educated without love, then the young dog will be distressed of soul, and his capabilities will not be developed, because the foundation of confidence, which is cheerful trust, has failed. A healthy education will not make a shy broken slave without a will, or a machine working only when asked, but will make him submerge his own wishes to a higher judgment, and become a creature who works freely, and is pleased to be able to work. The education must awaken and develop dormant qualities and abilities, and moderate all excesses, strengthen all weaknesses, and guide all faults in the right direction."

---

in this species, as is begging and protest against monopolization. The contrast can be summarized by saying that rhesus monkeys have different *expectations* than chimpanzees about the distribution of resources. Chimpanzees count on a share; rhesus monkeys do not.

In analogy with the human sense of justice, we may call this a *sense of social regularity*, which I define as follows:

A set of expectations about the way in which oneself (or others) ought to be treated and how resources ought to be divided. Whenever reality deviates from these expectations to one's (or the other's) disadvantage, a negative reaction ensues, most commonly protest by subordinate individuals and punishment by dominant individuals.[3]

The sense of how others should or should not behave is essentially egocentric, although the interests of individuals close to the actor, especially kin, may be taken into account (hence the parenthetical inclusion of others). Note that the expectations have not been specified: they are species typical. Because the expectation, or at least the ideal, of equality is so pronounced in our own species, we perceive the rules among rhesus monkeys as less "fair" than those in our closest relative, the chimpanzee. More important than this human bias, however, is the fact that all species seem to act according to what they can (or have come to) expect from others, thus creating a stable and predictable modus vivendi among themselves.

An obvious problem for the ethologist—and one reason why these issues have not received the attention they deserve—is that expectations are not directly observable. Do animals even have them? We may empirically define an expectation as familiarity with a particular outcome to the degree that a different outcome has an unsettling effect, as reflected in confusion, surprise, or distress. Since O. L. Tinklepaugh's research in the 1920s, we know that a monkey who has learned to find a banana hidden in a particular location will act nonplussed if the banana has been secretly replaced by a mere leaf of lettuce. At first she will leave the lettuce untouched, look around, and inspect the location over and over. She may even turn to the experimenter and shriek at him. Only after a long delay will she "content" herself with the lettuce. How to explain such behavior except as the product of a mismatch between reality and expectation?

A second, even more intractable problem is that of intentionality. I speak without hesitation of social rules from the rule-follower's perspective. When a monkey learns that certain acts always provoke a negative reaction, he will begin to suppress these acts or show them with great circumspection; the monkey can then be said to have submitted to a socially enforced rule. But can we speak of rules from the implementer's perspective? Do animals deliberately teach one another how to behave, or do they just respond to particular situations with frustration, protest, and sometimes violence? I certainly do not wish to exclude the possibility that they purposely impose limits on the behavior of others and carefully monitor the slightest transgression in order to strengthen the rule (the previous boxed examples hint at this possibility in canids), yet I cannot say that the evidence is overwhelming. We do not know if the rules that we recognize in animal behavior, and that we see being enforced, exist *as rules* in the animals' heads. Without experimentation this thesis will be hard to prove. For the moment I qualify terms such as social "rule" and "norm" by adding that they refer to behavioral modification by others regardless of the intentionality of the process.

The only way to estimate a species' sense of social regularity is by paying as much attention to spontaneous social acts as to how these acts are *received* by others. We need to determine which kinds of behavior are accepted and which meet with resistance, protest, or punishment. Here is a brand-new research agenda, one that will reveal differences not only between species, but perhaps also between different groups of the same species.

It will be easy enough to find rules imposed from above, according to which dominants constrain the behavior of subordinates. From the perspective of morality, however, the exciting rules will be those that constrain the behavior of everyone, and emphasize sharing and reciprocity. Before exploring the various possibilities in greater depth, let me give a final example of a negative reaction to another individual's behavior. The incident, first reported in *Chimpanzee Politics*,[4] suggests that the chimpanzee's sense of social regularity is not concerned solely with hierarchical issues, but also with more advanced social arrangements, such as the familiar *One good turn deserves another.*

A high-ranking female, Puist, took the trouble and risk to help her male friend, Luit, chase off a rival, Nikkie. Nikkie, however, had a habit after major confrontations of singling out and cornering allies of his rivals, to punish them. This time Nikkie displayed at Puist shortly after he had been attacked. Puist turned to Luit, stretching out her hand in search of support. But Luit did not lift a finger to protect her. Immediately after Nikkie had left the scene, Puist turned on Luit, barking furiously. She chased him across the enclosure and even pummeled him.

If Puist's fury was in fact the result of Luit's failure to help her after she had helped him, the incident suggests that reciprocity in chimpanzees may be governed by obligations and expectations similar to those in humans.

## The Monkey's Behind

Attributed to Saint Bonaventura, a thirteenth-century theologian, the saying "The higher a monkey climbs, the more you see of its behind" warns of the exposure of character flaws in people free of the usual social constraints. Power creates freedom of action, but often also brings vanity, mercurial mood swings, and constant worry over how long the power will be enjoyed. Reality may merge into fantasy for holders of absolute power; there is nothing to check their will. Few people have the self-discipline to handle this drug. Its trappings are partly due to the admiration and ingratiation received from others. If individuals cannot be powerful themselves, they seek the glow of someone else's power.

When the Great Chief enters a room, all heads turn and discussions come to a halt. We experience the presence of something larger than life. The chief may speak softly, yet everyone listens; he may tell a stale joke, yet everyone laughs; he may make an odd request, yet no one doubts that there must be an excellent reason. Why do we attribute superhuman qualities to such people, and why do we allow them to exploit our feelings of insecurity? Power is not an individual attribute; it is a relational one. For every powerful person there are others supporting that superiority, feeding that ego.

Like any pact, however, the one between dominant and subordinate is fragile. No one is more aware of this than the power holder himself. The more absolute the power, the greater the paranoia. Qin Shihuang, China's first almighty emperor, was so concerned about his safety that he hid all roads leading to his various palaces so that he could come and go unnoticed. More recently, it was discovered that Nicolea Ceausescu, the executed dictator of Rumania, had constructed three levels of labyrinthine tunnels, escape routes, and bunkers stocked with food beneath the Communist Party building on the Boulevard of Socialist Victory in Bucharest.

The vicious circle rotating between the hunger for power and the fear of losing it was summarized by Thomas Hobbes in *Leviathan*:

> I put for a generall inclination of all mankind, a perpetuall and restless desire of Power after power, that ceaseth onely in Death. And the cause of this, is not alwayes that a man hopes for a more intensive delight, than he has already attained to; or that he cannot be content with a moderate power: but because he cannot assure the power and means to live well, which he hath present, without the acquisition of more.[5]

The desire to dictate the behavior of others is such a timeless and universal attribute of our species that it must rank with the sex drive, maternal instinct, and the will to survive in terms of the likelihood of its being part of our biological heritage. It may come as a surprise, therefore, that not all students of animal behavior believe in its existence. Animals do establish dominance orders, and do change ranks via tense confrontations, yet striving for the best positions is not always given the status of a distinct motivation. Some scientists would describe a series of rebellions leading to the overthrow of the alpha animal but painstakingly avoid any implication that the challenger might have set out to achieve this result. The process would be phrased in terms of action, reaction, and outcome, not intention. This view of animals as blind, ignorant actors in their own political dramas is as surprising to me as would be an Olympic athlete who represented her winning of the gold as something that had never even crossed her mind.[6]

The alternative view—at least as old if not older—is that animals deliberately strive to dominate others. In the 1930s Abraham Maslow, an American psychologist who later became famous for his theories about self-actualization, was one of the first to study social dominance in monkeys. He happened to do so in the same small zoo in Madison where I observed macaques decades later. Maslow described the cocky, confident air of dominant monkeys and the slinking cowardice, as he called it, of subordinates. He postulated a *drive for dominance,* in the same breath objecting to the term "submission" as it might imply that subordinates give up any hope of besting their superiors (which according to Maslow they never do). Despite this objection, he was one of the first to speculate about the function of submissive behavior, saying that it placates the dominant by admitting social inferiority.

Subordinate wolves greet those of higher rank by licking the corners of the superior's mouth (similar to the way dogs lick their owner's face), rhesus monkeys present their behind or bare their teeth in a grin, and chimpanzees and humans bow or prostrate themselves. While such displays attest to the extreme importance animals attach to social dominance, their significance was ignored during a period in which hierarchies were analyzed primarily in terms of who-gets-what. The result was such an obsession with the outcome of competition that other aspects fell by the wayside.

The first problem with this approach was that, in some species, who-gets-what is decided as much by social tolerance as by rank. Among chimpanzees, for example, it is not unusual for a female calmly to remove a male's food from his hands even if he tries to prevent deprivation by turning away. Does this interchange suddenly make her dominant over him even if there can be no doubt who would win a fight?

Second, confrontations are won and lost in many ways. To withdraw in a hurry is something quite different from an appeasing display: the first outcome breaks the relationship, the second tries to preserve it. If one sees an alpha wolf with erect, bristling tail surrounded by whining subordinates with their tails between their legs, or a swaggering alpha chimpanzee greeted by groveling subordinates who hurry over to him from great distances, it is evident that these encounters communicate much more than a mere win or loss. Status rituals reveal the deep structure of relationships and express cohesive tendencies as much as hierarchical ones. I will speak of *formal dominance,* to distinguish such external signs of status from everyday contests and their rather variable outcomes.[7]

Changes in formal rank often take place via a series of provocations by the previous subordinate, who may incur defeat and injury before winning any confrontations. A chimpanzee male who used to go out of his way to pay his respects to the boss, bowing all the way and nervously jumping away at the slightest threat gesture, is transformed into a defiant producer of noise and mayhem. He seems to have grown in size, displaying every day a little closer to the dominant, forcing him to pay attention by throwing branches and heavy rocks at him. In the beginning the outcome of these confrontations is rather open ended. Depending on the amount of support each rival receives from the rest of the group, a pattern will emerge, sealing the dominant's fate if it turns out to be in favor of his challenger. In all the processes that I have witnessed, the critical moment is not the first victory for the challenger, but the first time he elicits submission. The former dominant may lose numerous times, flee in panic, end up screaming high in a tree, and so on, but if he refuses to raise the white flag that the species evolved for this purpose, the challenger will not let up. Only when his target formally submits will the challenger change his conduct from aggressive to tolerant. The two rivals will reconcile, and calm will be restored.[8]

How to explain the incredible energy put into rank reversals, the life-endangering risks taken, and the abrupt change in attitude once the other submits, other than as an action-reaction chain *aimed at* forcing the other into recognizing a new order? I am a firm believer that primates (and many other animals as well) are aware of their dominance relationships and share our will to power in the sense that they actively try to improve their positions whenever shifts in alliances or physical abilities permit.

It is even possible that monkeys and apes are aware of more than just their own position relative to others. Robert Seyfarth has demonstrated that wild monkeys of adjacent rank groom one another more than those many positions apart, a finding confirmed by our own research. Seyfarth speculated that monkeys may be so familiar with their rank order that they not only realize who is above or below them, but also by approximately how many rungs on the ladder. This awareness would require an appreciation of rank relations among others.

Another possible indication of hierarchical knowledge is the so-called *double-hold*. Never reported by other students of primate behavor, it may be a local tradition found only (for reasons unknown) in the rhesus monkeys at the Wisconsin Primate Center. There, however, we have seen dozens of females do it hundreds of times.

Typically, a mother with her own infant attached to her belly picks up the straying infant of another female. She then holds the two infants together for a couple of minutes, with both arms wrapped around them as if she has twins, after which she releases the second infant. Obviously, this act by itself does not require any special knowledge. When we began paying more attention, however, we noticed that double-holding is highly selective: nine out of ten times mothers hold their infant with the offspring of females who outrank them. Since the second mother is usually not nearby, the implication is that female monkeys know for each infant in their group whether it is of high or low descent.

Given the general tendency of macaques to try to establish connections with higher-ups in the hierarchy, and given that these connections may pay off in terms of protection or tolerance around resources, the double-hold could be a way of starting this process early. In the same way that siblings develop ties because of their association with the same mother, infants may become close to anyone close to their mother, including peers of other families with whom they have been double-held. Perhaps mothers are "suggesting" upper-class rather than lower-class friends to their offspring. Not that I believe that rhesus monkeys have five-year plans for their young, but there could very well be a long-term benefit from this kind of behavior.

One might counter that it reflects nothing else than attraction to high-ranking infants, and that involvement of the mother's own infant is immaterial. I doubt, however, that this theory explains the high rate of double-holding. Furthermore, a few incidents suggest that the presence of the mother's own infant is not accidental. Our champion double-holder, Ropey, once was approached by an infant making one of his first excursions away from his mother, the alpha female. Ropey gave friendly lipsmacks to the infant, but did not pick him up. Instead, she glanced repeatedly at her youngest daughter, who was playing in another corner of the pen, meters away. Ropey then seemed to make a decision: she dashed away to collect her daughter, brought her back to the alpha's infant, and did a double-hold with the two of them.

The significance monkeys and apes attach to dominance relationships, and their jostling for positions and connections, mean that group life encompasses two conflicting strategies. The first is to probe the social order for weaknesses and look for openings to improve one's standing. Inasmuch as this strategy subverts existing structures and creates chaos, one might regard it as antisocial. Yet from the viewpoint of the parties knocking down the old walls, there is nothing antisocial about it; for them it is pure progress.

The second strategy is a response to the first: conservation of the status quo. Although very much in the interest of the parties with the best positions, the resulting stability also benefits the young and weak, who are the first to suffer in case of all-out war within a group. Hence the potential of a pact between top and bottom in which the lower echelons back the reigning powers, provided these guarantee their security.

Society results from the equilibrium between these contradictory strategies, so each society is more than the sum of its parts. However meticulously we were to test a single organism, we would learn little or nothing about the kind of organization to emerge from the interplay among many of the same organisms. No one doubts that such interplay has its own dynamics, yet much research still focuses on the individual at the expense of the system as a whole. This reductionist bias is revealed in our tendency (mine included) to speak of "dominants" and "subordinates" as if there are two kinds of individuals. Every member of society, however, except the ones at the very top and very bottom, represents both. As pointed out by the novelist and science philosopher Arthur Koestler, "The members of a hierarchy, like the Roman god Janus, all have two faces looking in opposite directions: the face turned towards the subordinate levels is that of a self-contained whole; the face turned upward towards the apex, that of a dependent part."[9]

For the same reason that the pattern of a sweater is lost once it has been pulled apart, social hierarchies cannot be understood by breaking them into their constituent parts. Occupants of top ranks do enjoy privileges—otherwise there would be no need to fight over the positions—yet by definition the top is a small portion of the hierarchy. Therefore, in addition to finding out what is in it for the "dominants," we need to know what is in it for the "subordinates" and consider the organization as a whole. All individuals are embedded in the same social fabric, and must prefer their respective positions to the alternatives of a solitary life or the joining of another group. What would be the point of staying in a group without tolerance and friendship, where one had to look continuously over one's shoulder? Hierarchies distribute not only resources but also social acceptance: the one making them arenas of competition, the other holding them together.

Not surprisingly, given this integrative function, formalized hierarchies are best developed in the most cooperative species. The harmony demonstrated to the outside world by a howling pack of wolves or a hooting and drumming community of chimpanzees is predicated on rank differentiation within. Wolves rely on each other during the hunt, and chimpanzees (at least the males, who are by far the more hierarchical sex) count on the other members for defense against hostile neighbors. The hierarchy regulates internal competition to the point of making a united front possible. The same applies to people. In a classic experiment by the social psychologist Muzafer Sherif, groups of American boys at a summer camp became more hierarchically organized and leadership oriented when pursuing a common goal, such as competition against other groups.

Hierarchies tie individuals together through a conditional proposition along the lines of "*If* you act like this, *then* we will be glad to have you." And its reverse: "*If* you do not act like this, *then* you may get punished or, worse, expelled." Thus, a low-ranking male monkey asks for trouble, so to speak, by mating with a sexually receptive female or attacking any female in the presence of the dominant male. To refrain from such behavior, and to regularly demonstrate low status, is the price he pays for undisturbed group membership. Not that subordinates lead miserable lives; it all depends on the species-typical sense of social regularity. Some species are so mild mannered and affectionate that there is no need to feel sorry for low-ranking individuals. Other species are harsher and stricter, but most of the time some measure of tolerance allows for the full integration of subordinates.[10]

How status agreement opens the door to social acceptance is shown in a nutshell during so-called *assertive reconciliations*. In the chimpanzee, for example, a high-ranking male may approach his opponent after a fight with all hair on end, locking eyes with him. If the other does not budge, another confrontation is inevitable. Most of the time, however, the other bows so as to allow the dominant to move an arm over him. The dominant will turn around immediately afterward to seal the peace with a kiss and an embrace.

Assertive reconciliations are also known in the stump-tailed macaque, in which formal rank is confirmed through a mock bite on the subordinate's wrist. The procedure is never forced on others, and subordinates sometimes approach and wave an arm under the dominant's nose to *invite* one of these inhibited bites.

Rhesus monkeys lack a similar ritual, but Spickles, an alpha male at the Wisconsin Primate Center, developed one of his own. He used it only with other males, both adults and juveniles, after having chased them. Being old and arthritic, Spickles never caught and actually punished any of these males, but as soon as they returned to the ground (they invariably escaped to the ceiling), he would walk up to them in no uncertain manner, firmly hold their head or neck, and briefly gnaw on their cheek before accepting them among the rest of the group. Sometimes the other male would turn away with a submissive grin on his face, but I have never seen one escape the I'll-tell-you-who-is-boss bite of Spickles. They endured it without protest, perhaps because Spickles had subjected them to this idiosyncratic treatment since they were little. As in the stump-tailed macaque, it was a ritualized gesture: not even the slightest injury ever resulted.

Inasmuch as assertive reconciliations require cooperation, they reflect a mutual understanding about relative ranks. Combatants come back together with just enough intimidation by the dominant to affirm his position, yet not so much that it would endanger reunification. It is the familiar link between capitulation and peace wrapped in a single package: the dominant accepts the subordinate, provided the subordinate accepts inferior status and ritual punishment.

Finally, there is the human notion of *deserving* discipline after a conflict or transgression. Not only the offended party may feel the need, but also the offender, who realizes that normalization of the relationship requires crime to be followed by punishment. Although the guilt and shame involved may be uniquely human, the assertive reconciliation of our primate relatives provided the blueprint for this process. Even between people on an equal footing, one party will make reproaches and the other will avert the eyes and apologize for any misdeeds. A temporary dominance-submission relationship is created to restore the balance.

By setting the conditions of social inclusion, the hierarchy has much in common with a moral contract. Perhaps the distinction between acceptable and unacceptable behavior represents a first step toward notions of right and wrong. An authority-based contract, though, is a rather narrow version of morality as we know it. What constitutes acceptable or unacceptable behavior within a hierarchical framework need not overlap with the distinction between right and wrong in society at large. The approval of higher-ups by no means guarantees a clean conscience: grave crimes against humanity have been committed in the name of *Befehl ist Befehl*.

It is also questionable whether, as Kohlberg thought, the earliest stages of moral development can be understood entirely in terms of obedience and conformity. Children of nursery-school age already distinguish rule violations, depending on the impact of the transgressions on others. Two developmental psychologists, Larry Nucci and Elliot Turiel, found that children consider breaking a rule that hurts others (such as stealing or lying) much more serious than a violation of mere etiquette (such as addressing a teacher by the first name or entering the bathroom intended for the opposite sex). Apparently rules that protect other people's interests weigh heavier on a child's mind than mere social conventions.

Even if respect for authority and doing as one has been told have their place in both the evolution and the development of moral capacities, they go only so far in explaining them. These tendencies need to be mixed with others, such as empathy and sympathy, before morality can emerge.

## Guilt and Shame

Imagine that you are a laboratory rat in front of a dozen pieces of food. You pick up one and eat it, do the same with the next piece, and so on. When you reach for the fifth piece, a white-coated giant scares the wits out of you by clapping his hands just above your head. This nerve-racking experience is repeated trial after trial every time you touch item number five. With time, you learn to stop eating after four pieces, however tempting the remaining food may be.

Initially designed to determine the counting abilities of rats, the experiment offers a nice opportunity to look at the persistence of rules. Hank Davis describes it in an article mockingly entitled *Theoretical Note on the Moral Development of Rats*. With a slight variation on the test, he was able to prove that human-imposed rules are not held in very high regard by rats. If the experimenter is out of the room, the animals will typically pause after the fourth piece, stand on their hind legs and sniff the air, after which they happily consume all the food in sight. Davis concludes that by human standards rats are a morally bankrupt species.

The same experiment has not been tried with dogs, but there can be no doubt that these animals act differently. Dogs often obey orders in the absence of the person who trained them. Such uncoupling between behavioral suppression and the negative sanctions that instilled it is known as *internalization* of rules. While some dogs reach near-perfect internalization, even the most trustworthy dog occasionally gives in to his weaker self. After having snatched a piece of meat from the kitchen table, or having destroyed her master's shoe, the dog slinks away—ears in her neck and tail between her legs—even before anyone in the household realizes what has happened. The dog's appearance may actually draw attention to the misdeed; it betrays such awareness that we say the dog is acting "guilty."

Konrad Lorenz wrote about what he called "the animal with a conscience." The zoologist related how one of his dogs, Bully, accidentally bit Lorenz's hand when he tried to break up one of the fiercest dog fights he had ever seen. Even though Lorenz did not reprimand him and immediately tried to reassure and pet him, Bully was so upset by what he had done that he suffered a complete nervous breakdown. For days he was virtually paralyzed, and uninterested in food. He would lie on the rug breathing shallowly, an occasional deep sigh coming from his tormented soul. Anyone who had not seen the incident would have thought he had come down with a deadly disease. For weeks Bully remained extremely subdued.

Lorenz noted that his dog had never bitten a person before, so could not have relied on previous experience to decide that he had done something wrong. Perhaps he had violated a natural taboo on inflicting damage to a superior, which normally (among members of his species) could have the worst imaginable consequences. If so, instead of saying that Bully felt guilty, it might be more appropriate to say that he expected punishment, perhaps even expulsion from the pack.

Having felines and no canids at home, I never see even the slightest trace of "guilt" in my pets. Instead, I have engaged many a dog owner in debates about culpability versus anticipation of punishment, and I

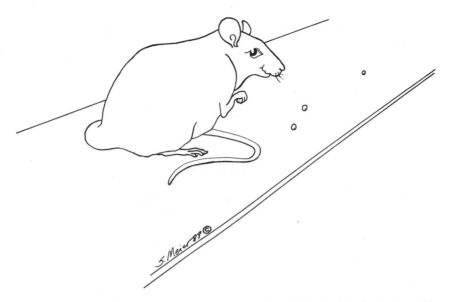

A rat trained to eat no more than a limited number of food pellets helps himself to a contraband pellet as soon as the experimenter has left the room. Unlike humans and some other animals, these rodents do not seem to internalize rules to any great extent. (Drawing by Susan Meier; reprinted by permission of Hank Davis)

feel that the latter offers the better explanation. This view is supported by a test developed by an American animal behavior consultant, Peter Vollmer, to convince owners of mischievous dogs that punishment after the fact does not work.

The procedure is illustrated by the case of Mango, a Siberian husky, who developed a habit of shredding newspapers, magazines, and entire books. Upon returning home, the owner would take Mango to the scene of the crime, whack her on the rump, and loudly lecture her. Because Mango persisted in her bad behavior, acting "guilty" each time her owner entered the house, it was believed that she knew she was doing something wrong but continued nonetheless out of spite over being left alone. This interpretation, however, was not corroborated by the test results.

Vollmer's test consisted simply of the owner *himself,* with Mango out of sight, shredding a few newspapers. After having let the dog back in, the owner left for fifteen minutes. Mango acted just as "guilty" as when she herself had created the mess! The only thing she seemed to understand was:

Evidence + Owner = Trouble.

The behavior of dogs after a transgression is therefore best regarded not as an expression of guilt, but as the typical attitude of a hierarchical species in the presence of a potentially angry dominant: a mixture of submission and appeasement that serves to reduce the probability of attack.[11]

Dog breeds vary greatly in their performance on obedience tasks. In a series of experiments, David Freedman found that, left alone with meat after having been punished for touching it, Shetland sheepdogs will not touch it again, whereas Basenjis start eating as soon as the trainer has left the room. The fact that internalization of rules can be bred into domesticated animals should give pause to anyone skeptical about the possibility of an evolutionary component of morality. Darwin relied heavily on his knowledge of artificial selection to illustrate the power of natural selection. Similarly, we cannot exclude the possibility that a trait subject to artificial selection in dogs has been subject to natural selection in our own species.

We are familiar with all shades of emotion related to internalization, ranging from the simple fear of getting caught to the Dostoevskian complexities of private guilt. For the moment it is unclear— and truly hard to know—if other species experience anything even close to remorse. There is no evidence that dogs ever regret forbidden acts committed away from and unbeknownst to their human masters. Not that this necessarily places them at a vast distance from us. Anticipation of punishment and fear of endangering a valued relationship are not unrelated to guilt. If rules can be internalized to the extent that they are obeyed even if the chance of punishment is minimal, fear of punishment can be internalized to the extent that we feel guilty, hence castigate *ourselves,* even if the offense will never be detected. With increased awareness of exactly what triggers the disapproval of others, and a desire to avoid such reactions even if they are not immediately forthcoming, comes the possibility of feeling culpable about transgressions regardless of who is aware of them.

What about shame? Dictionaries define it as a painful emotion caused by a sense of guilt, disgrace, or impropriety. At its core is an awareness of how one looks in the eyes of others. Could this awareness perhaps apply to Mango? After all, the mess in the house made her look bad regardless of who had caused it. Her embarrassment may seem perfectly logical to us—especially in light of her inability to explain—but it would require capacities that I am not sure we need to assume. It would mean speculation on the dog's part about how her master would take in the situation, and on whom he would blame the misdeed, given the available information. In short, it would require attribution—quite a sophisticated capacity compared to the associative learning that seems to explain her behavior equally well.

The workings of the human conscience are so intricate and rich, with their own axioms and logic, that they will forever keep philosophers, dramatists, poets, and novelists occupied. If guilt derives from the internalization of rules and values, and shame reflects concern about the opinions of others, we are dealing with complex emotions indeed. So complex, in fact, that the term "emotion" docs not do them justice; self-consciousness, perspective-taking, and attribution are also involved. Even the so-called emotivists, who tried to derive morality from sentiment, recognized the need for this cognitive component. Adam Smith imagined that our every thought and deed is monitored by an "impartial spectator," as if we are holding up a mirror to decide how our behavior looks from the outside. Thus, the social environment that shapes conscience in childhood is gradually replaced by a set of internal regulators that mimic its effects. We need wait no longer for the praise and blame of others: we mete them out to ourselves, according to the standards we have made our own.

In my more cynical moments I wonder if we do not overrate the power of internalization. Consider how people throw inhibitions overboard when conditions change, as during war or famine, during political unrest, or when running with a rowdy mob. Many a supposedly upstanding citizen loots, steals, and kills without compunction when there is little chance of getting caught or when resources have become scarce. Even a less dramatic change of circumstances, such as a vacation in a foreign land, may induce people to act in silly or outrageous ways unthinkable in their hometown. Are the members of our species—apart from the occasional saint—really any better than the rats who sniff the air and decide that it is safe to do what once was forbidden? Perhaps guilt and shame are less deeply rooted than we like to think; fear of negative consequences may need to persist, at least at the back of our heads, for our moral reasoning to stay on track. It might be argued, then, that the link between external and internal regulators of behavior is never completely lost.

One of the best-known external regulators in social primates is the effect of high-ranking males on the sex life of low-ranking males. The relation between punishment and behavioral control discussed for dogs, including signs of "guilt," can be observed. As a student working with long-tailed macaques, I followed activities in an outdoor section of their cage connected to the indoor section by a tunnel. Often the alpha male would sit in the tunnel so as to control both sides. As soon as he moved indoors, other males would approach the females outdoors. Normally they would be in deep trouble for doing so, but now they could mate undisturbed. Fear of punishment did not disappear: I have seen low-ranking males act extremely submissive, with wide grins on their faces, if they encountered the alpha male shortly after one of these sneaky copulations—even though alpha could not possibly have known what had happened.[12]

The effect of past behavior on current relations was put to the test by Christopher Coe and Leonard Rosenblum. In one series of experiments, subordinate male macaques were allowed to be with a female while the dominant male looked on from inside a transparent isolation chamber. None of the subordinate males dared to initiate sex under these circumstances. Their attitude changed dramatically, however, in the second test series, in which dominant males were entirely removed. Now the same subordinates felt free to copulate. They also suddenly performed bouncing displays and walked around with their tails proudly in the air, actions characteristic of high-ranking males.

Upon return of the alpha, these subordinate males showed considerably more avoidance and submission than when they had not been with a female. The investigators conclude that "this experiment provides intriguing evidence that animals can incorporate behavioral rules which are associated with their social role and can respond in a manner that acknowledges a perceived violation of the social code."[13]

These kinds of when-the-cat-is-away situations are amusing to watch, as the cat is never far from the minds of the mice. In the rhesus group at the Wisconsin Primate Center, Spickles sometimes seemed to get tired of keeping an eye on five or six restless males during the breeding season. Or perhaps he wanted to warm his old bones in the heated indoor section. At any rate, he would go inside once in a while, sometimes for half an hour at a stretch, leaving the others plenty of opportunities to mate. The beta male, Hulk, was popular with the females and often mated on these occasions. He was so obsessed with Spickles' whereabouts, however, that he was irresistibly drawn to peek inside through a crack in the door. Perhaps Hulk had had unfortunate experiences in which the boss unexpectedly showed up, and he wanted to make sure that alpha was staying put. Inasmuch as rhesus monkeys are multiple-mount ejaculators (several mounts and dismounts are required before the male ejaculates), Hulk would nervously race back and forth a dozen times between his partner and the door before completing a mount series.

These observations suggest that social rules among primates are not simply obeyed in the presence of dominants and forgotten in their absence. If this were true, Hulk would not be checking on Spickles, and low-ranking males would not be overly submissive after their exploits. The responses show that inhibitions are rooted deeply enough that concern about the enforcer's reaction persists in his absence. Admittedly, this is not much of an internalization compared to the near-total behavioral control that can be instilled into animals artificially bred for obedience. It may nevertheless have provided the starting point in the primate lineage for the evolution of a capacity for guilt and shame.

## Unruly Youngsters

How monkeys acquire social rules is largely unknown; study of this topic may produce fascinating parallels to human moral development. Initially, comparisons would of course suffer from a problem pointed out by Davis in his paper on rats, namely that descriptions of human morality tend to be "couched in terms that have limited operational relevance to other species."[14] Perhaps animal research will stimulate psychologists to come up with definitions that do not rely exclusively on verbalized thoughts and feelings but also cover how people behave. What is different about the way we *act* that makes us, and not any other species, moral beings? And if this question is hard to answer, what exactly is the significance of morality? Nothing like a little challenge to bring matters into focus! Similarly, language research on apes has served to sharpen the definition of language, if only because of the desire of linguists to keep their domain free of hairy creatures.

John Finley Scott, a sociologist, sides with biologists by putting the need for a new conceptualization this way in *Internalization of Norms:*

A definition of the norm that applies to all learned social organization, one that can build on interspecific comparisons, will serve sociological theory better than an anthropomorphic concept which imposes purely terminological barriers across an otherwise continuous dimension of activity.[15]

Monkeys do not come into this world with social rules imprinted in their heads. Neonates enjoy a certain *Narrenfreiheit:* like jesters at the court, they live above the law. Young infants may bump into high-ranking adults or approach food that others are interested in without being threatened or chased away as any juvenile would. In our studies of rhesus monkeys, for example, we discovered that infants occupy a better position than their mothers in the group's drinking order because they are allowed to approach the water basin and drink side by side with dominants who do not tolerate the mothers. Adult males accept them better than do high-ranking females, and the youngsters quickly learn to approach the former and not the latter.

Mothers seem aware of these special privileges. Fernando Colmenares observed a female baboon at the Madrid Zoo who held her infant firmly by the tail at feeding time while the infant entered a dominant male's personal space, normally taboo when food is around. The infant was not terribly interested in the food, but played with pieces picked up near the male. The mother, in turn, pulled her offspring toward herself a few times to quickly remove these tidbits for her own consumption. Noticing this, the male threatened her (not the infant), at which the mother presented her behind and kept the food. The infant served as a tool to circumvent the rules.

Infants do not always respond to threats, and perhaps as a result adults exaggerate the signals. Instead of slightly raising the eyebrows and giving them a stare—usually sufficient in the case of a juvenile—they will perform the entire pattern very clearly, with staring eyes, open mouth, ears spread, head bobs, and so on. I have seen adults grasp an infant's head with both hands to threaten it at close range straight into the face. They may have learned to give such "instructional" threats because very young infants often blithely ignore less conspicuous warnings.

With age, the consequences of ignoring threats become more severe. Punishments move from a slap or a firm shake with the hand to mild bites, until one day the infant receives its first serious bite. The time it can get away with murder is forever gone: the young monkey learns which situations and individuals to avoid. The risk of attack differs by species and is perhaps greatest in the rhesus monkey, where infants occasionally lose fingers and toes as a result of punishment. With the cost being so high at such a young age, it is no wonder that this species heeds its hierarchy so carefully.

Like Spickles, Orange, the alpha female of the Wisconsin rhesus

group, developed her own stereotypical punishment. The big difference was that whereas Spickles' gnaw on the cheek was inhibited,
Orange's was a real bite. Curiously, she used it almost exclusively on
infants approximately six months old. At an unexpected moment,
Orange would grab them and clamp her teeth so firmly on their wrist
that she would draw blood. The victim would be upset afterward,
limp for a couple of days, and from then on keep a safe distance and
pay close attention to Orange's movements. What made the deepest
impression was perhaps not even the pain itself, but the fact that no
one had come to help. As all-powerful queen, Orange could do whatever she wanted. During the decade that I followed the group, this
became a highly predictable pattern; few infants escaped the treatment. Thus, each fall (rhesus monkeys are seasonal breeders) we
would see Orange do her wrist-biting (or notice its results) as if she
had determined that it was time to instill fear and order into the new
generation.

There is no single individual from whom infants and juveniles
receive more aggression, however, than their own mother. Usually, of
course, it is of the nondamaging kind, but bites and even injuries do
occur. Irwin Bernstein, a well-known American primatologist, inter-
prets it as *socialization,* in which mothers teach their offspring to
inhibit particular behaviors that may get them into trouble. Even
though maternal aggression may not be to the youngster's immediate
advantage, it promotes the caution and behavioral control required
for survival in a hierarchically structured social environment.

As with the implementation of rules, it is questionable that this
socialization process is intentional. Undoubtedly, the young monkey
learns lessons for life from the corrections received, but adults are not
necessarily teaching them these lessons on purpose. As yet the issue
is unresolved and relates to how well animals understand the effects
of their own behavior. Do they realize that a punitive action may
permanently alter the other's behavior? Do they evaluate the results
and punish harder if previous attempts failed? And why do they
sometimes give up and let things be, as we saw with some of the
handicapped monkeys? Azalea, for example, never achieved a well-
defined rank. Her responses lacked consistency; she often wavered
between threat and retreat. Yet the others simply ignored this behavior. Instead of punishing Azalea for threatening back at them, dominant monkeys would stare at her, perhaps make a brief lunge, then
leave her alone as if she was just not worth wasting energy on.

We also should not assume that social rules are always actively enforced by one party and passively learned by another. The establishment of rules is a dynamic process involving rule-testing and social exploration on the part of the learner.

One technique is *teasing*. Because of the different risks involved if a teaser is caught, this behavior is rare in rhesus, not uncommon in stump-tails and baboons, and ubiquitous in chimpanzees. Youngsters of the last species throw handfuls of dirt or pebbles at their elders, hit them with sticks, splash them with water, jump on their heads when they are dozing, and so on. Much of the time, the individual thus bothered takes it remarkably well, tickles the youngster, or makes a mock chase that turns the whole incident into a game. The individuals who cannot resist a hostile reaction are the ones who are going to be pestered more, as Otto Adang discovered in his study of teasing by young chimpanzees at the Arnhem Zoo.

Adang documented the various teasing techniques, the reactions to them, and how they change with age. At one end of the spectrum are the innocuous little pushes from behind by an infant, who jumps away when the adult turns around. But at the other end are full-blown charging displays of adolescent males seeking to engage females in physical combat. Throwing sand into the faces of those in power is a sure way of provoking a reaction—unpleasant stimuli have this advantage—and learning about one's place in society. Where do I stand, what are my limits? Provocation is also a way of expanding limits by monitoring carefully how others react, and looking for an opening to cow them.

In short, teasing serves to gather information about the social environment, and to investigate authority. Its presence in primate youngsters confirms the importance of knowing the limits set by society.

## The Blushing Primate

Even if rule-learning, rule-testing, internalization, and guiltlike behavior are observable in our closest relatives, it is evident that no species has perfected these processes to the degree that we humans have. Whereas some other animals can be described as conformists—that is, they learn to obey rules—people go well beyond conforming by internalizing not merely the rules but also the values and ideals behind them. In addition, we build such an elaborate network of sanctions that even when the coast seems perfectly clear, transgressions entail serious risks, ranging from gossip by an accidental witness to entanglement in lies. Futhermore, millions of people believe in the watchful eye of an omnipresent God, in retribution after death, and in a connection between moral decay and natural catastrophes. There is no escape: we are subject to both real and imagined pressures to behave in specific ways.

Our extreme susceptibility to social and religious influences is closely tied to the central role of *reputation* in human society. Reputation yields both the stick and the carrot for much of our behavior. Evolutionary biologists, such as Richard Alexander, relate this circumstance to systems of mutual aid that are constructed around trust. Within such systems, partners are selected on the basis of their ability to make commitments. Inasmuch as every act is indicative of future acts by the same person, it pays to watch others closely and learn what to expect from them. This scrutiny in turn produces a definite preoccupation with the social mirror, to the point of causing constant worry about possible loss of face.

If personal reputations varied from day to day, there would be little reason to adhere to social norms. Why not pay lip service to the rules in public but break them whenever convenient? Yet the system does not work this way. Reputations are durable and incredibly fragile: built up over many years, they can be destroyed by a single faux pas. The television evangelist who slept with a secretary is history, as is the political candidate who cheated on his taxes. And imagine the situation of our ancestors, who undoubtedly belonged to the same small community for most of their lives: virtually everything there was to know about them must have been known by virtually everyone.

In order to become a respected member of the community, we need to be almost blindly consistent. To resist every little temptation to stray from the chosen path, we need to believe steadfastly in right and wrong. Only a firm moral conviction ensures behavior that contributes to a lasting reputation of honesty. Indeed, most people reach a point at which the values imbued by society combined with their personal experiences crystallize into a stable pattern of thought and behavior from which they cannot deviate without great personal discomfort. Instead of being led by the reactions of others, or responding to immediate situations, to stay on course they rely on an internal compass, bolstered by strong emotions of guilt and shame.

It is this inner strength that we look for when evaluating a person's trustworthiness; we are experts at detecting the difference between people with an effective compass and those with a defective one.

According to Robert Frank, an American economist who has written extensively about reputation and emotional commitment, it hardly pays to fake generosity or obey rules only in public. People are too astute at distinguishing such a facade from acts that come from deep inside. In *Passions within Reason* Frank explains that people committed to integrity and fairness occasionally pass up opportunities to achieve private gain, yet create other opportunities for themselves that are out of reach of opportunists. For example, an honest man will leave a tip in a restaurant that he does not expect to visit again, whereas the opportunist will see this as a chance to save money. In the short run the honest man loses, but in the long run the convictions dictating his behavior will be recognized and valued, providing him with a passport to partnerships with like-minded people.

And there is more: reputation-building has apparently been so central in our evolutionary past that serious obstacles have been erected for anyone trying to take the unethical route. Painful truths sometimes emerge because of our incomplete control over voice, eyes, and the small arteries of face and neck—exactly the body region where a crimson color best signals guilt and shame.

Blushing is a truly remarkable trait, as Darwin long ago realized: "Blushing is the most peculiar and the most human of all expressions. Monkeys redden from passion, but it would require an overwhelming amount of evidence to make us believe that any animal could blush."[16]

What could be the advantage of signaling shame or embarrassment? Does blushing not seriously handicap us? Quite a few additional assumptions need to be made before this characteristic fits the self-interest models of evolutionary biology, assumptions that include the need to come across as a desirable partner for cooperative ventures—one who can be relied on, thanks to a strong internal compass that makes that person susceptible to guilt and shame. A person who lies without blushing, who never shows remorse, and who grabs every opportunity to bypass the rules just does not strike us as the most appealing friend or colleague. The uniquely human capacity to turn red in the face suggests that at some point in time our ancestors began to gain more from advertising trustworthiness than from fostering opportunism. And what more effective way to do so than by telltale signs beyond their control?[17]

In our analysis we should not confuse evolutionary benefits with actual motives. Because we are unable to change color on command, blushing cannot possibly be part of a calculated strategy to create a favorable impression. People assimilate the values of their society so profoundly and so completely that they are genuinely moved by them. I firmly believe that people can be altruistic and honest without on every occasion thinking of the advantages.

This view of human motives as independent of the evolutionary process that shaped our minds and bodies is, as we have seen, not universal among biologists. Some believe that a self-serving agenda guides human behavior under all circumstances; people who believe otherwise are simply fooling themselves. To this day the sincerity of human feelings continues to be a topic of debate. As recently as 1994 Robert Wright, an American science writer, argued in *The Moral Animal* that humans are potentially but not naturally moral. In Wright's eyes, we are hypocrites living in constant denial of our thoroughly selfish nature.[18]

To give the human conscience a comfortable place within Darwin's theory without reducing human feelings and motives to a complete travesty is one of the greatest challenges to biology today. We are born to absorb rules and values, many of which place community interests above private ones. We have been selected for such profound internalization that these rules and values become literally our own. We have built-in physiological mechanisms that frustrate attempts to cheat. No doubt these capacities evolved because they served a purpose in the highly cooperative and trust-based societies of our ancestors. To believe that this purpose must figure as a conscious or unconscious motive in our minds assumes a direct connection between genetic adaptation and day-to-day decision-making for which there is absolutely no evidence. The same assumption would lead one to claim that if squirrels store nuts in the fall they must know about the deprivations of winter and spring. Squirrels would have gone extinct long ago if such knowledge were required, and people would never have developed a conscience had their minds been preoccupied with the reproductive calculations that fascinate evolutionary biologists.

## Two Genders, Two Moralities?

Like every European boy, I could barely walk when I began to play the world's most popular sport. Before I knew it, along with the fun of chasing the leather, I was receiving important moral lessons. Team sports, with their rules and expectations, are a microcosm of society. Whether one plays on grass or on pavement, the risk of a fall is not nearly as serious as the risk of not knowing how to behave, or not contributing to the team. Most important, it is not the almighty adults who keep an eye on you and on whom you keep an eye; it is your peers and equals!

In the beginning are simple rules about which body parts may touch the ball and what kind of contact with other players is within bounds. Gradually the rules become more complex and precise, until one day an older boy shouts "offside" during a promising offensive—and the most frustrating regulation of all is introduced. In addition to obeying these rules, you learn to uphold expectations and obligations. On the one hand, you are not meant to simply stand around and take it easy. On the other hand, you should not try to outshine your pals. Instead of shooting at the goal from an impossible angle, for instance, you are supposed to pass the ball to a teammate who may end up triumphant. He, in turn, is expected to acknowledge your assistance.

This knowledge is acquired via endless debates about what one did versus what one should have done. And even if the game is not halted for a particular violation, it is made perfectly clear that the disadvantaged team has been generous—a gesture to be recalled as soon as the other team fusses over some minor infraction.

Boys seem to enjoy these legal battles every bit as much as the game itself, as observed in 1972 by Janet Lever in a now-classic study of children's games in Connecticut. Lever found that girls tend to play in smaller groups, and less competitively, than boys. Their games are considerably shorter, partly because girls are not as good as boys at resolving disputes. Based on observations and interviews, Lever contrasted the two sets of attitudes toward disagreement: "Boys were seen quarreling all the time, but not once was a game terminated because of a quarrel, and no game was interrupted for more than seven minutes." In contrast "Most girls claimed that when a quarrel begins, the game breaks up, and little effort is made to resolve the problem."[19]

Following in the footsteps of the famous Swiss developmental psychologist Jean Piaget, who first analyzed the moral lessons derived from rule-bounded games, Lever concluded that boys' games offer better preparation than girls' games for the adjudication of disputes, respect for rules, leadership, and the pursuit of collective goals. With jump rope and hopscotch involving turn-taking rather than contest, and with girls playing in pairs or trios of close friends rather than in larger groups, the typical girls' games seem to serve as a training ground for delicate socioemotional skills. Lever saw these skills as valuable mainly for future dating and marriage, not as part of moral development.

Certainly Carol Gilligan has another interpretation. In *In a Different Voice* the American psychologist claims that female moral commitment is rooted in attachment, intimacy, and responsibility for the other, whereas male commitment is oriented to rights, rules, and authority. For simplicity, let us call these types sympathy-based morality and rule-based morality. Gilligan makes the point that although human morality is based on both rules and sympathy, men and women reach an integration of the two via different routes. For this reason, the sensitivity skills developed in girls' games may be as morally relevant as the boys' experience with conflict resolution and fair play.

Instead of standing in awe before principles higher than themselves, women have a rather down-to-earth approach to the dilemmas of moral judgment presented by researchers. Gilligan asked her subjects how they would resolve an imaginary situation in which the interests of various persons collided. Female subjects wanted to know all sorts of missing details concerning the nature of these hypothetical people—where they lived, how they were interconnected, and so on. They ended up with moral solutions tailored to these people's needs based on the logic of social relationships rather than abstract principles.

Gilligan warns against the excesses of a rule-based morality: "The blind willingness to sacrifice people to truth has always been the danger of an ethics abstracted from life."[20] In a powerful biblical reference, she contrasts Abraham's offering of his son's life to show the strength of his faith with the woman before Solomon who lied about her motherhood in order to save her child. In his wisdom, Solomon knew that only a mother would do such a thing.

In one study on this topic, Kay Johnston asked adolescents to suggest solutions to Aesop's fables, such as the one in which a porcupine, on a cold night, enters a cave occupied by moles. "Would you mind if I shared your home for the winter?" asks the porcupine. The moles consent, but soon come to regret their generosity; the cave is tiny, and the porcupine's quills scratch them at every turn. When they finally find the courage to ask their visitor to leave, the porcupine objects, saying "Oh, no. This place suits me very well."

A majority of the boys who read this fable preferred solutions based on rights ("The porcupine has to go; it's the mole's house" or "Send the porcupine out, since he was the last one there"), whereas most girls preferred mutually agreeable solutions ("Wrap the porcupine in a towel" or "The both of them should try to get together and make the hole bigger"). A fair number of children proposed both kinds of solutions, however, and many were able to switch orientation when asked if there was another way of solving the problem. Even if the two sexes set different priorities, both were capable of following alternative lines of reasoning. This seems to be true to such a degree that many of Gilligan's colleagues have begun to question her dichotomy between male and female moral orientations.[21]

For one thing, it would be quite incorrect to say that men attach little value to expressions of sympathy. Even if men typically favor a rights orientation, we should not forget that rights are often an abstract, regulated form of caring. Rights go hand in hand with duties, hence are concerned with social relationships and responsibilities as well. It is to male philosophers, such as David Hume, Arthur Schopenhauer, and Adam Smith, that sympathy owes its prominent place in moral theory. Conversely, it cannot be said that women are aversive to framing issues in terms of rights, as the last few decades of worldwide stuggle for equity, justice, and fairness ("women's rights") have shown. In other words, the two orientations distinguished by Gilligan are not quite as far apart as they sound.

The centerpiece of the attack on her position, however, is a comprehensive review of research on moral development in more than ten thousand subjects by Lawrence Walker. Failing to find systematic evidence for sex differences in the data collected by a large number of investigators, Walker concludes that "the moral reasoning of males and females is more similar than different."[22]

Walker goes on to admit, however, that the moral development scales used for his analyses say very little about the precise norms and social orientations underlying moral judgment. Could it be, then, that both sides in the debate have a point? The intuitive appeal of Gilligan's distinction between male and female attitudes should give pause to her critics. When an American linguist, Deborah Tannen, in *You Just Don't Understand* classified the conversational styles of men and women in terms of a male preoccupation with autonomy and status and a female preoccupation with intimacy, she touched on very much the same issues. Tannen's position, too, struck a chord. Critics argue that the proposed sex differences represent convenient "stereotypes" that people cannot resist, but it is of course also possible that these ideas have become popular because they reflect some deeper truth about ourselves.

At least one sex difference manifests itself so early—on the very first day of life—that culture can be ruled out as an explanation. Newborn babies cry in response to the sound of another baby's cry. It is not just a matter of noise sensitivity, as babies react more intensely to these sounds than to equally loud computer-simulated cries or animal calls. Their reaction is regarded as an expression of emotional contagion, and thought to provide the underpinnings of empathy. Studies consistently demonstrate higher levels of this kind of emotional contagion in female than in male infants.

At later ages as well, empathy seems more developed in females. On the basis of a wide range of studies, Martin Hoffman concludes that whereas the sexes are equally capable of assessing someone else's feelings, girls and women are more strongly *affected* by the resulting knowledge: "Females may be more apt to imagine that what is happening to the other is happening to them; or, more specifically, to imagine how it would feel if the stimuli impinging on the other were impinging on the self."[23]

It is possible that boys and girls play different games, build different social networks, and develop different moral outlooks because they are born with psychological differences that are subsequently elaborated and modified by the social environment. In this view, culture and education mold gender roles by acting on genetic predispositions. If true, two fundamental questions result. First, Why do people seem to encourage these particular sex differences? Why are girls taught to be sensitive and accommodating, and boys urged to go out and prove themselves in competition with other boys? Is it easier to amplify what is there than to steer social attitudes into a new direction, or are all human societies structured in such a way that it is convenient or necessary to have men and women occupy these particular roles? This question is one for developmental psychologists, sociologists, and anthropologists.[24]

The second question concerns the evolutionary reason for these differences. Why would females be born with a stronger responsiveness to someone else's feelings, and why would males have an orientation toward competition and status? Do such differences make biological sense? The short answer is yes. The long answer is that it is always dangerous to think in typologies, and that we are basically comparing *average* tendencies. Yet these tendencies over the long run may have favored the reproductive success of males, who depend on status to gain access to mates, as well as females, whose offspring would stand no chance at survival without continuous care and attention.

By bringing the issue to this level, we are no longer comparing moral outlooks, but instead basic psychological traits that may have served males and females in the course of evolution.

## Umbilical versus Confrontational Bonds

Even if contemporary society emphasizes the considerable nurturing abilities of men, it cannot be denied that in virtually all primate species females are the primary or only caretakers of the young. Responsibility for a completely helpless and vulnerable member of the species, who depends on you for food, transport, warmth, comfort, and protection, is an obvious starting point for the evolution of sensitivity to the needs of others. The slightest distress call, often barely audible, alerts the mother and causes her to adjust either the infant's position or her own posture so as to allow access to her nipples, stabilize the infant on her belly or back, or remove pressure. Failing to do so may cost the infant's life, as we sadly learned from a deaf chimpanzee who never managed to raise offspring. Despite her fascination with the infants, she would accidentally sit on them without noticing, or deprive them of milk for extended periods without paying attention to their complaints.

Attached with an emotional umbilical cord to her offspring, the primate mother is never free. Her infant may be asleep or nursing when she is ready to move, or she herself may be resting when an infant-crazed, clumsy juvenile female tries to kidnap her little one. Then there is the sheer weight when the offspring grow bigger. It may be fetching to see an infant monkey hold on with hands and feet to its mother's hair, hanging upside down beneath her, yet that infant must be a painful load. Often females risk trouble with their offspring, trying to pry open the clenched little fists; the infant may protest noisily as it has no desire to give up the free ride. Torn between the need to move and the impossibility of leaving their offspring behind, mothers almost always give in and carry the burden.

Even when the young begin to move on their own, mothers need to stay alert in order to protect them against aggression or predation, and to help out when their motor skills fall short. In some arboreal species mothers use their own bodies as bridges, holding on with their feet (or tail) to the branches of one tree and with their hands to those of another. I once saw a muriqui monkey do this high in the canopy of a Brazilian forest. American primatologist Karen Strier has seen many such live bridges, describing them as follows:

> Juveniles screech when their mothers leave them to negotiate difficult tree-crossings alone. Small juveniles are reluctant to fling themselves across wide gaps in the canopy which larger muriquis can swing or leap across with ease. Often in these contexts, mothers respond to their offspring's screeches by using their bodies to form bridges for them to cross, and, in the early stages of weaning, young muriquis take advantage of these opportunities to latch onto their mothers. Later on, however, they run across their mothers' backs without even trying to hitch a ride.[25]

Given that nurturance is essential to raising offspring, and that in nearly two hundred million years of mammalian evolution the need to provide it has applied to each and every mother—from the tiniest mouse to the largest whale—it is no mystery why females of our own species value intimacy, care, and interpersonal commitment. These traits are visible in parenting styles (with maternal love being unconditional and paternal love being more qualified), but also, as Gilligan points out, in the approach to moral issues. Impersonal rights and wrongs are not a top priority of women, who often favor compromises that leave social connections intact.

The moral outlook of men, based on rules and authority, follows directly from a dominance orientation. Wherever men come together—in the military, in secret societies, in religious organizations, in prison, in corporations—hierarchical relations are rapidly established to create an environment in which men seem to work together best. Despite its grounding in competition, the hierarchy is essentially a tool of cooperation and social integration. Picking a fight can actually be a way for men to relate to one another, check each other out, and take a first step toward friendship. This bonding function is alien to most women, who see confrontation as causing rifts. If an open fight does break out, boys and men are more likely to make up afterward, as illustrated by Janet Lever's playground study. Similarly, a Finnish research team found that grudges among girls outlast those among boys,[26] and Tannen reports hostile conversations followed by friendly chats among men:

> To most women, conflict is a threat to connection, to be avoided at all costs. Disputes are preferably settled without direct confrontation. But to many men, conflict is the necessary means by which status is negotiated, so it is to be accepted and may even be sought, embraced, and enjoyed.[27]

In chimpanzees, too, males are the more hierarchical sex and reconcile more readily than females. Females are relatively peaceful, yet if they do engage in open conflict the chances of subsequent repair are low. Unlike males, females avoid confrontation with individuals with whom they enjoy close ties, such as offspring and best friends, whereas they let aggression run its destructive course in case of a fight with a rival. During group formation in captivity, females have been observed to reconcile at higher rates—making peace is well within their abilities—but typically, in well-established groups, it is the males who go through frequent cycles of conflict and reconciliation, who test and confirm their hierarchy while at the same time preserving the unity required against neighboring communities.[28]

Thus, chimpanzees and humans seem to share fundamental sex differences in their orientation toward competition, status, and the preservation of social ties. In both species, however, simple dichotomies should be treated with caution as there is a great deal of plasticity. With the exception of nursing, males are capable of every behavior typical of females, and vice versa. In chimpanzees, for example, males have been known to adopt and care for orphaned juveniles, and females have been known to intimidate others by means of charging displays as impressive as those of males. It all depends on the circumstances. Most of the time, sex differences follow a specific recognizable pattern; yet in an environment that requires different responses, both sexes can and will adjust.[29]

Similarly, in modern society we see households run by single fathers and we see women working their way to the top. It is this culture dependency of sex differences that has lured feminist scholars and social scientists—at least for a time—into thinking that biology is irrelevant, as if the manifest influence of one factor would in any way preclude the influence of another.

Mindful of these complexities, Gilligan softens her position toward the end of her book, arguing that with increasing maturity both sexes move away from the extremes. Women move from the absolute of care, initially defined as not hurting others, to the inclusion of principles of equality and individual rights. Men begin to realize that there are no absolute truths, and that not all people have equal needs. The result is a more qualified judgment and an ethic of generosity. The intertwining of these strands of morality into a single basket is partly a product of men and women learning from each other that there are different angles from which problems can be tackled, and that morality can be reduced neither to a book of rules nor to pure warmth and sympathy.

## Primus inter Pares

If men are such hierarchical creatures, how do we account for what anthropologists call "egalitarian" societies, such as the Navajo Indians, Hottentots, Mbuti pygmies, !Kung San, and Eskimos? Ranging from hunter-gatherers to horticulturalists, many small-scale societies are said to eliminate distinctions—other than those between the sexes, and between parent and child—of wealth, power, and status. The emphasis is on equality and sharing. Since it is entirely possible that our ancestors lived in this fashion for millions of years, could it be that hierarchical relations are less prototypical than assumed?

Status differences are never completely abandoned, however. Instead of having no hierarchy at all, egalitarian societies occupy one end on a spectrum of dominance styles ranging from tolerant to despotic. *Dominance style* refers to the amount of control that high-ranking individuals exercise over low-ranking ones—and vice versa. An egalitarian dominance style is produced by political leverage from below that restrains the top's power and privileges. If our species' sense of social regularity goes by the name of a sense of justice, it is precisely because we possess this equalizing tendency. We sometimes get rid of unpopular power holders, or at least criticize them and let them understand that there are limits to our obedience. Admittedly, there has been little evidence for egality during long periods of history—equity and justice are sometimes thought of as recent innovations—yet the existence of so-called egalitarian societies suggests that the tendency has been with us for quite some time.

Variation in dominance style is obvious even within such a relatively small cultural sample as Western Europe. The inhabitants of some regions have a reputation for being almost militaristically hierarchical, others for maintaining sharp class divisions, and yet others for cutting down to size anyone inclined to self-aggrandizement. There may be ecological explanations. Odd as it may sound, the dislike of the Dutch for aristocracy has been linked to life below sea level. The continuous struggle to keep the country dry created strong common purpose, particularly during the onslaught of storm floods in the fifteenth and sixteenth centuries. Every burgher had to pitch in and carry bags of clay in the middle of the night when a dike was near collapse. Those who put status above duty were in effect disqualified from the benefits. The contempt voiced by a well-known engineer of that period for "the slippers, the tabards, and the fine fur mantles which have no value at the dikes"[30] became so much part of Dutch culture that even today its monarchy shuns pomp and circumstance.[31]

Paralleling this cultural variation, differences in dominance style are recognizable within the primate order. Once again, it was Abraham Maslow who first drew attention to the phenomenon. Publication of his observations was delayed for years because prominent primatologists of his time disagreed with his views. (Maslow alludes to their objections without revealing their exact nature.) Maslow was entirely correct, though, to contrast what he termed the "dominance quality" of chimpanzees and rhesus monkeys. Two more different temperaments can scarcely be found.

In rhesus, Maslow explained, the dominant puts priority rights above all else and is never the least bit shy about punishing a subordinate for liberties taken. The subordinate, in turn, lives in fear. What a difference with the chimpanzee, in which the dominant often acts as friend and protector of the subordinate: they share their food, and a frightened subordinate may run straight into the arms of the dominant. There is also remarkable room for low-status individuals to voice their feelings. With some delight Maslow recounts how a young chimpanzee got so fed up with attempts of the most dominant ape to take her friend away to play that she ended up attacking the big male and hammering him with her fists. The only reaction he showed was to run away laughing (chimpanzees make hoarse laughing sounds during play) as if her audacity amused him! Maslow rightly notes that the same protest by a subordinate rhesus would have cost her dearly.

Maslow's study had serious limitations, however, not least because his chimpanzees were rather young (which may be what the referees of his paper objected to). Yet even the rank order of adult chimpanzees is never as strict and rigid as that of rhesus monkeys. Real and profound differences are glossed over by flat statements that all primates know dominance-subordination relationships.

To appreciate this variability we do not need to compare such distant relatives as rhesus and chimpanzees. Rhesus monkeys are despotic even when compared to some members of their own genus, such as stump-tailed macaques. Stump-tails seem to emphasize harmony over priority rights. Compared to his rhesus counterpart, a dominant stump-tail tolerates quite a bit more, including counter-threats in an argument, and drinking or feeding from the same source shoulder to shoulder with subordinates. Stump-tails also groom one another more and are among the best peacemakers after fights.

According to socioecologists, who look at the natural environment to explain social dispositions, the optimal condition for the evolution of egalitarianism is dependency on cooperation combined with the option to leave the group. The first prerequisite is not unlike the struggle of the Dutch against the ocean: there is nothing like a common enemy to promote unity and tolerance. The need for cooperation may relate to the physical environment, to predators, or to enemy groups of the own species. The second stipulation—freedom to exit—depends on predation risks outside the group and the willingness of neighboring groups to accept new members. If there exist both mutual dependency and realistic opportunities to leave, dominants had better be very "nice" to their companions lest they find themselves without anyone to dominate. The reverse is, of course, equally true: when subordinates have nowhere to go, dominants can exploit and terrorize them with impunity.[32]

Unless, that is, subordinates have a way of joining forces: alliance formation, a characteristic of the primate order, blunts absolute power. Originally, alliances chiefly served the acquisition of dominance, as when female monkeys assisted their younger kin to ascend the social ladder. The same instrument, however, permits lower echelons to rise up against and even overthrow rulers. Such use is already visible in the chimpanzee, in whom cooperation against dominants is not nearly so unusual as in macaques and baboons. Thus, alliances evolved from a means of building and enforcing the hierarchy, to one capable of weakening it.

In egalitarian societies, men intent on commanding others are systematically thwarted in their attempts. The weapons used by their supposed inferiors are ridicule, manipulation of public opinion, and disobedience. The boastful hunter is cut down by jokes about his miserable catch, and the would-be chief who tries to order others around is openly told how amusing his pretensions are. The power of leaders is thus delineated by an alliance from below. Christopher Boehm, an American cultural anthropologist (who later took up research on chimpanzees), studied these leveling mechanisms. He found that leaders who become too proud or bossy, fail to redistribute foods and goods, or close their own deals with outsiders, quickly lose respect and support.[33]

In extreme cases they pay with their lives. A Buraya chief who appropriates the livestock of other men and forces their wives into sexual relations risks being killed, as does a Kaupaku leader who oversteps his prerogatives. Such executions, sometimes secretly arranged, have been reported for ten of the forty-eight cultures reviewed by Boehm. The author goes so far as to speak of a "reversed hierarchy," meaning that leaders are in effect dominated by their followers. Other scientists have objected to this notion on the grounds that it ignores the fact that, however much the hierarchy is leveled, a leader is a leader nonetheless. David Erdal and Andrew Whiten explain: "Since respect is still given to leaders in particular situations, the incipient hierarchy is not really reversed but rather prevented from developing beyond those particular situations where leadership is required."[34]

In other words, egalitarian societies permit certain men to act as leaders because it is harder to survive without any leadership at all than with a limited degree of inequality. One domain in which the need for leadership is most strongly felt is the resolution of intragroup disputes. Instead of having all community members take sides—and make matters worse—what better way to handle the situation than by investing authority in a single individual assigned to enforce the interests of the community by finding fair solutions to disagreements?

Conflict mediation from above is not limited to our species. Irwin Bernstein was the first to describe the *control role* of monkeys: alpha males respond aggressively to external disturbances, such as predators or other groups, but also internal disturbances, such as conflicts within the group. Smothering the latter is achieved through direct interference, often by chasing off the aggressor. There is great variation in the effectiveness of control measures, however. I have known alpha males who could stop a fight by raising an eyebrow or with a single step forward, whereas others only aggravated the situation by getting involved. Competent control requires special skills, such as interceding with just the right amount of force—enough to command respect, yet not so much that everyone would have been better off left alone.

Individual variation in the effectiveness of intervention, combined with the fact that the control role is poorly developed in some commonly studied species, has led to serious reservations about the whole concept. All the same, a few species do exist (stump-tailed monkeys, gorillas, and chimpanzees) for which there can be little doubt that high-ranking individuals consistently and effectively mediate conflicts. The strongest evidence concerns the chimpanzee, whose pacifying interventions have been documented at Gombe National Park by Boehm and in captivity by me. Dominant chimpanzees generally break up fights either by supporting the underdog or through impartial intervention. All hair on end, they may move between two combatants until they stop screaming, scatter them with a charging display, or literally pry locked fighters apart with both hands. Their main objective seems to be to put an end to the hostilities rather than to support one party or the other. The following quotation from *Chimpanzee Politics* illustrates how Luit, within weeks of attaining alpha rank, adopted the control role.

> On one occasion, a quarrel between Mama and Spin got out of hand and ended in biting and fighting. Numerous apes rushed up to the two warring females and joined in the fray. A huge knot of fighting, screaming apes rolled around in the sand, until Luit lept in and literally beat them apart. He did not choose sides in the conflict, like the others; instead anyone who continued to fight received a blow from him. I had never seen him act so impressively before.[35]

What is special about the control role is, first of all, its impartiality. Because my students and I recorded thousands of interventions in Arnhem, we were able to compare them statistically with partner preferences expressed in grooming and association. While most group members favored their relatives, friends, and allies when interfering in a dispute, control males were exceptional in that they placed themselves *above* the conflicting parties.[36] They seemed to interfere on the basis of how best to restore peace rather than how best to help friends. Because control interventions do not seem to be a way of pulling rank, or of helping parties who might return the favor, the chief objective seems to be to get rid of internal disturbances. The same attitude was observed by Boehm in wild chimpanzees:

After successfully damping the conflict, often an individual acting in the pacifying control role withdraws and sits down, or else returns to a prior activity such as feeding, but appears to be ready to intervene again should the conflict resume, while fights are regularly headed off, stopped, or ameliorated when these methods come into play.[37]

The second characteristic of the control role concerns the point that return favors do not seem to be the object. The quickest way to cement profitable alliances obviously would be to support the most powerful players in the group, hence the usual winners of fights. Instead, the control male often interferes in the smallest squabbles among juveniles to protect the younger of the two. In fights among adults, he supports the loser, such as a female attacked by a male— even if this male happens to be his best buddy. He does not seem to be out to please those individuals capable of doing him the greatest return favors. Indeed, a male who operated on this basis would be ineffective as arbitrator and encounter strong resistance.

We observed such resistance when Nikkie, with Yeroen's help, rose to the top in the Arnhem colony. Young and inexperienced, Nikkie favored Yeroen and certain high-ranking females whenever he interceded. Perhaps for this reason, and because of his heavy-handedness, the females did not take kindly to Nikkie's interventions and often mounted coalitions to keep him away from a scene of conflict. Yeroen's interventions, on the other hand, were impartial, controlled, and readily accepted. Within a few months, Nikkie left all control activities to the old male.

I learned from this development not only that the control role can be performed by the second-in-command, but also that the group has a say in who performs it and how. It appears to be one of those social contracts in which one party is constrained by the expectations of the others. As a result, the control role may be regarded as an umbrella shielding the weak against the strong, yet one upheld by the community as a whole. It is as if the group looks for the most effective arbitrator in its midst, then throws its weight behind this individual to give him a broad base of support for guaranteeing peace and order. In this sense, then, there is a payoff to the control role: instead of coming from powerful friends, the return favor comes from those who at first glance appear powerless. Indeed, males in this role may benefit tremendously from grass-roots support if their position comes under fire from the "angry young men" of their species.

Another advantage for the control male is that by supporting the weaker of two combatants he may be leveling the hierarchy underneath him, thus creating a bigger gap between himself and potential rivals. His interventions frustrate attempts of other high-ranking individuals to enforce their positions. Not that such a tactic can explain all control activities observed—control males often stop aggressors who cannot possibly pose a threat to their position, as when they intervene in a quarrel between juveniles—but it is another benefit to consider.

The dissociation between a control male's social preferences and the way he manages intragroup conflict is unique, showing the first signs of equity and justice. A fair leader is hard to come by, hence it is in the community's interest to keep him in power as long as possible. Tensions among mothers, for example, flare whenever a friendly rough-and-tumble among juveniles turns into hair pulling, kicking, and screaming. Because each mother is inclined to protect her own offspring, her approach to the scene is enough to raise the hairs—literally—on the other mother. A higher authority who takes care of these problems with impartiality and minimum force must be a relief for all.

Even though we cannot go so far as to call chimpanzees egalitarian, the species has certainly moved away from despotism toward a social arrangement with room for sharing, tolerance, and alliances from below. Although high-ranking individuals have disproportionate privileges and influence, dominance also depends to some degree on acceptance from below.

An example of accepted dominance is the position of the current alpha male in our chimpanzee group at the Yerkes Field Station. After removal of the previous alpha male, we introduced two adult males. The females, who had lived together for many years, ejected both of them (that is, the males had to be treated for serious injuries). Several months later, two new males were introduced. One got the same reception, but the other male, Jimoh, was permitted to stay. Within minutes of his introduction, two older females contacted and briefly groomed Jimoh, after which one of them fiercely defended him against an attack by the alpha female.

Years later, during a background check on all the chimpanzees in our study, it was discovered that Jimoh had been housed with those same two females at another institution before coming to the Yerkes center. Apparently this contact more than fourteen years earlier had made all the difference.

Although nearly thirty years old, Jimoh is an unusually small male—considerably smaller than several of the adult females he has come to dominate through sheer energy and persistence. Every day he would make charging displays, asserting himself, sometimes supported by his female friends, but increasingly on his own. One by one the females began to bow and pant-grunt to him, including eventually the alpha female. Jimoh also took up the control role: I have known few males so alert at stopping the most minor squabbles before they get out of hand.

Only on rare occasions (such as his attack on Socko, described earlier) do we see the former female alliance against him. These incidents, in which Jimoh is invariably defeated, confirm that he is dominant only by virtue of the females' acceptance, a power balance reminiscent of the first-among-equals arrangement of human egalitarian societies. However atypical this undersized male's relation with the females may be, it illustrates that dominance is not always a matter of one party's imposing conditions on others: rank relationships resemble a mutual contract. In the wild, too, the stability of a male's position may depend on acceptance of his leadership.[38]

In short, the dismantling of despotic hierarchies in the course of hominoid evolution brought an emphasis on leadership rather than dominance, and made the privileges of high status contingent upon services to the community (such as effective conflict management). Community concern comes into play here. Boehm believes that arbitration in disputes helped keep communities numerically strong by reducing divisiveness, hence allowed them to stand up more effectively against hostile neighbors.[39] This trait became so important during human evolution that it gave rise to a far more anticipatory approach to controlling conflict. Thus, in addition to breaking up ongoing disputes, or reconciling afterward—as seen in our closest relatives—people make an explicit effort to instill community values in each member, and to lay down general principles for the resolution of conflict. Probably this development required every sector of society, from the highest to the lowest, to have some say in community affairs. Rather than being some irrelevant curve in our evolutionary path, the egalitarian ethos may have been a prerequisite for the origin of morality.

# 4

# QUID PRO QUO

The fine adjustment of social relations, always a matter of importance among primates, becomes doubly important in a social system that involves food exchange. Food sharing . . . probably played an important part in the development of reciprocal social obligations that characterize all human societies known about.

*Glynn Isaac*[1]

Who other than a crazed scientist would drag eight tons of dead livestock through the snow up a mountain just to see scavengers feast on the meat? Bernd Heinrich did just that in the Maine wilderness, conducting a series of experiments on the discovery of carrion by ravens and their communication about it. Ravens are about the smartest birds in the world, careful to check out any carcass before landing near it. After all, it could be a wounded or sleeping animal, or guarded by other interested parties. Thus, even the most conspicuous food bonanzas may go untouched for weeks, leaving the freezing zoologist with lots of time to fine-tune his theories.

In his enjoyable *Ravens in Winter* Heinrich notes that there are always a few ravens brave enough, despite their extreme caution, eventually to face the risks. Others will watch from the sidelines and join in only when the coast is clear. While the advantage of that attitude goes without saying, one wonders about the motivation of the birds testing the ground. Had they waited a bit longer, perhaps another raven would have done the job for them. Heinrich points out, however, that not all ravens hesitate to be the first: some seem to positively *court* danger. For example, ravens have been seen diving at a resting wolf, or sneaking up from behind to peck at its tail, only to jump away at the last moment to escape its snapping jaws.

I recognize this behavior all too well as I used to have jackdaws, small members of the same corvid family. On strolls with me through a park, a male named Johan made a habit of pestering dogs by flying just above their heads, so as to make them go after him. The poor wingless creatures would run and jump up each time Johan came close, until they were exhausted. I can only guess at the dogs' feelings, but I am familiar enough with human faces to know that the owners—especially of the bigger dogs—were not amused to see the bird return to my shoulder afterward.

Heinrich speculates that the occasional boldness of corvids serves to enhance status and impress potential mates by demonstrating that they have the courage, experience, and quickness of reaction to deal with life's dangers. Male birds may alternate between acts of bravery and courtship of female onlookers. They sometimes even treat risk-taking as a privilege rather than as anathema: tested with stuffed owls, male crows have been seen *competing* over who is going to attack the predator. In our own society, bravery may be rewarded with medals; in corvid society, according to Heinrich, it helps females tell the "men" from the "boys."

Ravens who locate a carcass, check it out, and communicate their discovery to the valley and beyond with loud yells are doing their fellow corvids a tremendous favor at a price to themselves. Without any positive impact on reproduction, bravery would long ago have been weeded out by natural selection. Wolves have been known to kill annoying ravens.

The rise of sociobiology is closely tied to successful attempts to account for the evolution of *altruistic behavior,* defined as actions that are at once costly to the performer and beneficial to the recipient. Cost-benefit analyses are the staple of evolutionary arguments. The premise is always that there must be something in it for the performer, if not immediately then at least in the long run, and if not for him then at least for his relatives. Heinrich follows this assumption when speculating that acts of courage may make male ravens attractive to the opposite sex. Showing off desirable qualities, they are rewarded by increased mating opportunities.

Because of the constantly changing composition of the feeding crowds, and of the raven population in general, it is almost impossible for these birds to achieve much more than such instant payoffs. Their encounters follow the laws of the singles-bar, not those of the marketplace. Other species are more amenable to a system in which favors are traded back and forth. Primate groups have a limited membership and tend to hold together over long periods of time. Durable relationships allow close monitoring of the exchange of favors. These animals do not need to operate on the basis of quick impressions of one another; they review entire histories of interaction.

## The Less-than-Golden Rule

The idea of exchange is central to the theory of *reciprocal altruism,* developed by Robert Trivers in the early 1970s. It is quite different from the theory of *kin selection,* proposed a few years earlier by William Hamilton. The two theories are by no means in conflict, however; they complement each another nicely. Hamilton's theory explains why animals often assist close relatives. Even if such altruism harms the actor's chances for reproduction, it does not necessarily prevent the genes involved from reaching the next generation. Kindred are by definition genetically similar, sometimes even identical, to the actor and will thus put the help received to good use by spreading the same genes. From a genetic perspective, helping kin is helping oneself.

Initially, kin selection completely overshadowed reciprocal altruism in discussions about the origin of altruism and mutual aid. The focus at the time was on social insects (which often live in colonies of close relatives), and there was a dearth of examples to support Trivers' theory. In recent years reciprocal altruism has begun to receive the attention it deserves, particularly in research on primates and other mammals. This is partly owing to the current fascination with cognitive abilities; reciprocal altruism is a complex mechanism based on the remembrance of favors given and received. Even more important from a moral perspective is that reciprocal altruism allows cooperative networks to expand beyond kinship ties.

Not that support of kin is morally irrelevant—family obligations weigh heavily in any moral scheme—yet the tendency is quite robust in and of itself. Sometimes it even leads to distinctly unfair situations, as when a power figure hands out government jobs to his relatives. In human society, a bias for kin is both assumed and a matter of concern.

Our strongest moral approval is reserved for the more fragile tendencies that underlie collective welfare, such as sharing and cooperation outside the family or clan. The most effective way to instill these tendencies is through some sort of linkage between taking and giving. The usual argument is that we are better off helping each other, that the benefits of such a system far outweigh the costs of contributing to it. This anticipation of gain is central to the human moral contract—not in each and every exchange, of course, but overall. This is why no one can withdraw from the contract without dire consequences, such as ostracism, imprisonment, or execution. All able-bodied men and women are in it together. What would be the point of contributing to a community in which others idly stand by?

Reciprocity can exist without morality; there can be no morality without reciprocity. If we accept this thesis, it is clear why the very first step in the direction of the Golden Rule was made by creatures who began following the reciprocity rule "Do as the other did, and expect the other to do as you did."[2]

Even though phrased here as straightforward tit-for-tat—whereas reciprocal altruism is quite a bit more flexible and variable—the first hints of moral obligation and indebtedness are already recognizable.


## Mobile Meals

A link between morality and reciprocity is nowhere as evident as in the distribution of resources, such as the sharing of food. To invite others for dinner—whether around a table or at a campsite fire—and to have the invitation returned on a later date is a universally understood human ritual of hospitality and friendship. It is difficult even to imagine a culture in which people believe that joint meals are to be avoided and that feasts are a bizarre habit. Inasmuch as such a concept would fly in the face of the most elementary solidarity, a culture embracing an eat-alone principle would strike us as a collection of individuals unworthy of the label "community," let alone "moral community."[3]

Rather more typical of our species is Japanese drinking etiquette, according to which one insults one's company by pouring oneself a drink. Friends around a table are supposed to be each other's hosts and guests at the same time: they constantly keep an eye on the glasses around them to fill them with beer or sake whenever necessary. No one goes thirsty. This custom epitomizes what human community is all about: reciprocity and sharing (see page 137).

# HELP FROM A FRIEND

For food-sharing primates, the arrival of food is a joyous event that leads to begging and a relatively equal distribution. Chimpanzees and capuchins are exceptions in this respect: very few other primates show high tolerance for sharing outside the mother-offspring unit. A more widespread form of mutual aid is coalition formation: most primates will support others in fights.

Chimpanzee politics are based on coalition formation. Here two adult males are united during a confrontation. Nikkie (behind) became alpha male with the assistance of Yeroen, an older male. Nikkie mounts Yeroen, while both scream at their common rival. *(Arnhem Zoo)*

When food arrives, chimpanzees engage in a celebration. They embrace each other, hooting loudly—here an adult male—drawing the entire colony into the festive atmosphere. Blackberry shoots, a favorite foliage, are eaten with withdrawn lips because of the spines (facing page). *(Yerkes Field Station)*

Gwinnie (left) extending an open hand to Mai, who is chewing a tasty morsel. Since Gwinnie does not share much herself, others have little to gain from sharing with her. Gwinnie's begging often meets with resistance. (*Yerkes Field Station*)

A cluster of four sharing chimpanzees and an infant (partially hidden beneath their food). The female in the top right corner is the possessor (as well as the infant's mother). The female in the lower left corner is tentatively reaching out for the first time; whether or not she can feed will depend on the possessor's reaction. *(Yerkes Field Station)*

Not all food is distributed by means of passive tolerance. Here an adult female feeds an unrelated juvenile a piece of sugarcane. *(Yerkes Field Station)*

Food sharing is a highly selective process: only half of the interactions result in an actual transfer. *(Yerkes Field Station)*

Chimpanzees look through a window to see what their lucky group mates may have discovered indoors during one of our food tests. During these tests, possessors (inside) sometimes hand food through the window to the members of the colony waiting outside. *(Yerkes Field Station)*

An adult male chimpanzee in the African rain forest eating a red colobus monkey. Capture of such agile prey requires close cooperation and task division among chimpanzee hunters. *(Courtesy of Christophe Boesch; Taï National Park, Ivory Coast)*

Hunting-related communication and food sharing are less developed in baboons than in chimpanzees. After a female savanna baboon encountered a gazelle fawn, she sat down next to it, looking repeatedly at her troop in the distance. The troop included adult males who no doubt would have killed the fawn had they known about it. The female left without doing it any harm. *(Gilgil, Kenya)*

One of the many traits capuchins have in common with chimpanzees is that they share food. A juvenile displays the typical hand-cupping of a begging capuchin. He presses his face close to the food of an adult male, proffering an open hand. *(Yerkes Primate Center)*

Despite their tolerant temperament, stump-tails do not allow subordinates to take food directly from their hands or mouth. While the alpha male feeds, everyone has come to watch, but no one is getting anything. The species also lacks begging gestures. *(Wisconsin Primate Center)*

Rhesus monkeys have a talent for aggressive cooperation. They form alliances mostly to advance their position within the group, but may also do so against other species—here a dog. First an adult male threatens the dog on his own. When there is no apparent effect, he recruits a friend and together they rout the dog. *(Wisconsin farm group)*

Three rhesus females of the third-ranking matriline oppose a single member of the number two matriline (viewed from back). Although barely an adult, this individual confidently holds her ground, returning the threats. Were she to get into trouble, her entire matriline would quickly descend on her opponents. *(Wisconsin Primate Center)*

Baboon friendships often translate into support between a male and a female. A resident male baboon (middle) defends a female against a stranger (left). The stranger, who recently immigrated into the troop, first chased the female, who ran straight to her protector, hiding behind his back while screaming at her attacker. *(Gilgil, Kenya)*

Three adult male yellow baboons engage in a tense confrontation. The male on the left screams in response to the threatening stares, with raised eyebrows, of the other two. The male in the foreground used to be the ally of the threatened male but has recently begun to shift his allegiance to the male in the background. The screaming male is thus faced with a rather unpleasant change in political reality. *(Courtesy of Ronald Noë; Amboseli National Park, Kenya)*

The etiquette of sharing is universal. Here its logic is discussed in an American television classic, *The Honeymooners*. Ralph Kramden, Ed Norton, and their wives have decided to share an apartment. The men have problems with food distribution:

**Ralph:** When she put two potatoes on the table, one big one and one small one, you immediately took the big one without asking what I wanted.

**Norton:** What would you have done?

**Ralph:** I would have taken the small one, of course.

**Norton:** You would? (in disbelief)

**Ralph:** Yes, I would!

**Norton:** So, what are you complaining about? You GOT the little one!

Sharing can be so prevalent, especially in the egalitarian cultures we have considered, that the thought of keeping anything for oneself does not even arise. Katharine Milton, an American anthropologist and primatologist, tells us about this trait in Indians of the Brazilian forest:

> Unlike our economic system, in which each person typically tries to secure and control as large a share of the available resources as possible, the hunter-gatherer economic system rests on a set of highly formalized expectations regarding cooperation and sharing. This does not mean hunter-gatherers do not compete with one another for prestige, sexual partners, and the like. But individuals do not amass surplus. For instance, no hunter fortunate enough to kill a large game animal assumes that all this food is his or belongs only to his immediate family.[4]

Because hunting success is subject to chance, the man who brings home the bacon one day may be glad to get a piece of someone else's a couple of days later. Sharing makes for a more reliable food supply. Moreover, like the ravens who impress each other with their bravery, the hunter who consistently contributes more meat than his fellows may gain prestige and sexual privileges. In a Paraguayan hunter-gatherer culture studied by Hillard Kaplan and Kim Hill, for instance, successful hunters were reported to have more than their share of extramarital affairs. The anthropologists speculate that women may have sex with these men to encourage them to stay in the band.[5]

Egalitarian people being who they are, one also expects counter-measures to prevent top hunters from rising above the rest. One way is to minimize the value of whatever they have killed, even the fattest buffalo. Knowing this penchant of their comrades, the wise hunter does not boast. According to Richard Lee, the !Kung San hunter comes home without a word, sits down at the fire, and waits for someone to come along and ask what he has seen that day. He casually replies something like: "Ah, I'm no good for hunting. I saw nothing at all (pause) . . . just a little tiny one."

The anthropologist's informant adds that such words make him smile to himself as they mean that the speaker has killed something big. Yet even those who then go out with the hunter to carve up the meat will restrain their joy. Upon arrival they will cry out, "You mean to say that you have dragged us all the way out here in order to make us cart home your pile of bones!" or "To think that I gave up a nice day in the shade for this!" Then, with much hilarity, they butcher the animal, carry the chunks of meat back to camp, and the entire band eats to its heart's content.

Another informant explains why it is necessary to ridicule the hunter:

> When a young man kills much meat he comes to think of himself as chief or big man, and he thinks of the rest of us as his servants or inferiors. We can't accept this. We refuse one who boasts, for someday his pride will make him kill somebody. So we always speak of his meat as worthless. This way we cool his heart and make him gentle.[6]

In this way hunter-gatherers maintain a delicate balance between honoring contributions to the food supply—if not with their mouths, then at least with their stomachs—and subverting personal pretensions. Their entire system of reciprocal exchange would collapse if major inequalities in status were allowed to emerge.

It is evident that meat has a unique significance. Even if we no longer assume that the subsistence of hunter-gatherers owes more to hunting than to gathering, it cannot be denied that hunting products do arouse great excitement. In proportion to its nutritional value, the importance attached to meat is actually quite excessive—and universally so. Carving the Thanksgiving turkey in front of the family remains part of a North American culture that otherwise seems to be moving away from collective meals. In most parts of the world, meat (or fish) is the traditional centerpiece at the dinner table, and it is the

Animal protein takes center stage at collective meals all over the world. The division of meat is so much part of the festivity that people insist on carving it at the dinner table, as shown here for the traditional Thanksgiving turkey of North American culture. (Photo courtesy of the Norman Rockwell Museum at Stockbridge; printed by permission of the Norman Rockwell Family Trust, copyright © 1943 the Norman Rockwell Family Trust)

kind of food most often subject to special privileges and religious taboos.

Apart from cultural explanations, which stress our kinship to the animals we consume,[7] it is not hard to find a very mundane reason for the status of meat. Meat differs from vegetables and fruits in that it *moved* before it was put into the cooking pot. Meat runs, swims, or flies away if approached with unfriendly intentions. And meat that comes in large quantities tends to defend itself with teeth, tusks, hooves, and horns; it is often too much for a single hunter to handle.

Could the dangerous, unpredictable, and often cooperative nature of hunting, as opposed to gathering, explain the significance attached to meat? If so, the issue would turn from nutritional to social.

Consider an enigma that has intrigued me for a very long time: chimpanzees are quite good about sharing prey, but hopeless when it comes to favored plant foods. In the wild, the capture of a monkey is a celebrated event, signaled with a characteristic call that attracts other chimpanzees. With a deafening outburst of screams, clusters of begging and sharing individuals gather and hand meat from one to another. Why do these apes not behave the same way when they find a pile of bananas? Excitement about this food leads to such violence that provisioning at Gombe's banana camp needed to be cut back and regulated so as to reduce competition. Documenting events at the camp, William McGrew did not notice much tolerance; sharing was mostly restricted to mothers and their youngest offspring.

Here we have two favorite foods: one consists of a number of bite-size snacks, the other comes as a single large piece. The first is fought over, the second shared. One possibility is that possessors of bananas are more often attacked because a quantity of fruits is easily divided (the owner may drop half and run off with the rest), whereas an animal carcass does not fall apart when one is in a hurry to escape. Could it be, then, that aggression toward meat possessors is rare because it is not worthwhile? This explanation only takes care of the violence, however: it fails to tell us why a highly prized food that is hard to divide is shared *at all*.

It may be more fruitful to take the perspective of the hunter. When chasing arboreal monkeys, chimpanzees often work in pairs, trios, or larger teams. It is obviously no simple task to capture agile targets in three-dimensional space. Since certain species, such as colobus monkeys, defend themselves fiercely to the point of injuring the hunters, there are additional reasons for chimpanzees not to try hunting them on their own. At Gombe lone males have been seen to remain quietly near a colobus troop, only to hunt immediately when joined by another male. In Taï National Park, Ivory Coast, the hunting technique of chimpanzees has been documented by a Swiss couple, Christophe and Hedwige Boesch. Their data indicate that capture success improves with the number of participating hunters, and that the speed of movement increases sharply when the magic number of three hunters is reached.

Now, why should chimpanzee B join chimpanzee A on a strenuous hunt if A's success would not translate into any reward for B? Under such conditions B might still join A, but not in order to do anything that gives A an undue advantage; B's primary goal would be to exploit A's effect on the prey and to catch something before A does. At best, the result would be synchronous action.

According to the Boesches, chimpanzees are much better coordinated than this: they arrive at a task division in which individual hunters perform different but complementary actions. Some of them drive the prey, others encircle them or block their escape to a distant tree. If meat is the incentive for working together, Taï chimpanzees should also share readily. Such indeed proved to be the case, particularly with regard to adult males. Rather than taking meat into the trees, where beggars can be avoided, Taï chimpanzees typically form feeding clusters on the ground, where there is room for everyone.

Meat sharing is not an entirely peaceful process. The captor usually manages to retain a significant portion, yet prey does tend to change hands immediately upon the hunt's completion. There is great commotion when a monkey has been caught; others may steal the prize during the flurry of excitement that follows. All the same, participation in a successful hunt usually leads to a payoff, whether directly from the captor's hands or from someone else's. When the entire group has settled down, the begging, whimpering, and waiting for scraps begins. Soon everyone is chewing meat and crunching bones.

Chimpanzees seem to recognize a hunter's contribution to this process. The Boesches found that participation in a hunt affects how much meat a male can expect at the end. Males attracted to the scene *after* the prey is captured, whatever their rank or age, tend to receive little or nothing. Females are not held to the same standard: they receive meat regardless of their role in the hunt. According to the primatologists, the linkage for male hunters between participation and payoff guarantees a high degree of collaboration in the Taï community.

At an international conference on chimpanzee behavior organized by the Chicago Academy of Sciences in 1991, two Japanese primatologists, Hiroyuki Takasaki and Toshisada Nishida, showed a videotape in which a male chimpanzee seemed to reward a female directly for assisting him in a hunt. Here is my summary of the sequence.

After an adult male had captured one monkey, a female discovered a second, which she cornered underneath some rocks. Instead of trying to catch it herself, she called the male while staring at the monkey. The male understood her signals, came over, and grabbed the second monkey. He killed it right away by flinging it forcefully against the ground. Despite the presence of other beggars, the male let this particular female have one of his two monkey carcasses.

Contrast this with an encounter I once witnessed between a female baboon and a Thompson gazelle fawn hidden in the high grass of a Kenyan plain. Even though baboons are known to eat fawns, the female merely stared at it. My guide, Ronald Noë, who has studied these baboons, suggested that the fawn was too large for her to kill; an adult male would not have hesitated. The female was more than 30 meters away from her troop. She looked around at the others several times, but did not vocalize or in any other way draw attention to the situation.

The fawn was lucky. Had food-related tolerance been as well developed in baboons as in chimpanzees, the female could have called in a male in the same way her chimpanzee counterpart did in the videotaped incident. Baboons do not share nearly as well as chimpanzees, however; the female would not have gotten any.

The orchestrated hunt of chimpanzees is unique among nonhuman primates. There are indications that their close collaboration, and the sharing that follows, also has profound implications for other aspects of social life. The Boesches note that generosity marks males of high status, and Nishida and his coworkers report on the specific case of an alpha male named Ntologi. This male appeared to use meat distribution to strengthen his power base in the Mahale Mountains community. Apart from being an effective hunter himself, Ntologi often claimed carcasses from other males: in about one-third of all meat-sharing sessions, he controlled the largest portion. To distribute food appeared to be his main intention; he occasionally secured carcasses from which he scarcely ate himself. He would merely hold the spoils and let others pull off meat until everything was gone.

There was a peculiar system to Ntologi's food distribution. When plundering a carcass from prime adult males, he always permitted these males to keep a substantial cut for themselves. Young adult males did not receive this courtesy, nor were they allowed to take scraps afterward. With Ntologi in control, males less than twenty years of age could do little other than watch from a distance while the rest feasted. Around the age of twenty, males are climbing the social ladder and begin to pose a serious challenge to high-ranking males. Similarly, Ntologi never permitted beta males, the most likely usurpers of the alpha rank, to join the meat-sharing cluster.

Kalunde became the beta male in 1986 and since then has become Ntologi's major rival. Although he is usually observed not far from Ntologi, Kalunde typically disappears from the scene during meat-eating episodes when Ntologi controls access to the carcass. Kalunde has never been seen to beg for meat from Ntologi. The former alpha male did not share meat with Ntologi when he was the beta male.[8]

Ntologi chiefly shared with females, as well as with those males who were unlikely to threaten his position; that is, influential aging males and prime adult males in stable midranking positions. While these males lacked the social status and/or physical capacity to rise to the top, they could be effective allies. Some were seen to join Ntologi's intimidation displays against rivals. Possibly the alpha male was "bribing" certain parties to support his position, or at least not turn against him. Ntologi's tenure at the top of the Mahale community lasted an exceptionally long time—more than a decade. Perhaps the way he distributed meat was part of the secret.

During one of the power struggles at the Arnhem Zoo, the challenging male, Luit, developed a sudden interest in live oak and beech trees on the island. Their foliage, much liked by the chimpanzees, was almost impossible to reach as every tree trunk was surrounded by electric wire. Luit would break a long branch from a dead tree, then drag it to a live tree to use it as a ladder to avoid being shocked—an act of great skill and bravery. Once high in the live tree, he would break off many more branches than needed for himself, only to drop them to the colony waiting below. Soon everyone, including rival males, would be munching on fresh leaves from the sky.

Because Luit accomplished this feat many times during his successful bid for alpha status, I speculated in *Chimpanzee Politics* that "it may have been accidental that Luit played Santa Claus on that first and later occasions, strewing food around for the group, but to me it immediately looked as if he had hit on a very clever way of drawing attention to himself."[9]

Possibly, then, generosity serves political ends: food distribution may enhance an individual's popularity and status. If so, the ancient top-to-bottom arrangement remains visible in the more recently acquired economy of exchange. Yet instead of dominants standing out because of what they take, they now affirm their position by what they give. Note that this is precisely the sort of status seeking that human egalitarian societies try to prevent.[10]

Early human evolution, before the advent of agriculture, must have been marked by a gradual loosening of the hierarchy. Food sharing was a milestone in this development: it both marked the reduced significance of social dominance and provided a launching pad for further leveling. It is therefore relevant for us to understand its origin. In a straightforward rank order, in which dominants take food from subordinates, the food flow is unidirectional. In a sharing system, food flows in all directions, including downward. The result is the relatively equitable distribution of resources that our sense of justice and fairness requires.

Reality may not always match the ideal, but the ideal would never even have arisen without this heritage of give-and-take.

## At the Circle's Center

In the animal kingdom as a whole, sharing is most prevalent in species that feed on high-energy foods of which the collection, processing, or capture depends on special skills or rare opportunities. Among non-primates, sharing is most notable in social carnivores, such as wolves, brown hyenas, mongooses, and vampire bats. In the primate order, we find it in two forms. In small, stable family units, such as those of gibbons and marmosets, food is freely shared with offspring and mates. Because the tendency benefits kin and reproductive partners, it is easily explained as a product of kin selection. Such intrafamilial tolerance may have laid the groundwork for the second kind, which could not have evolved without some degree of reciprocity: the group-wide sharing of chimpanzees, humans, and capuchin monkeys.

Certain food characteristics are conducive to this transition from kin-based to extrafamilial sharing. Whereas a few plant foods, such as giant fruits that are hard to open, show some of these characteristics, only large prey shows them all. Shared food typically has the following traits:

1. Highly valued, concentrated, but prone to decay.
2. Too much for a single individual to consume.

3. Unpredictably available.
4. Procured through skills and strengths that make certain classes of individuals dependent on others for access.
5. Most effectively procured through collaboration.

A hunting connection for the evolution of sharing seems obvious enough in chimpanzees and humans.[11] What about capuchins? Until recently, the sharing habits of this Neotropical monkey were relatively unknown to science. Remarkable tolerance had been reported by field workers such as Charles Janson, but mainly between mother and offspring or adult males and juveniles. My own observations of captive capuchins, however, showed tolerance to be far more pervasive. The capuchin is one of very few primates in which unrelated adults, including those of the same sex, peacefully remove food from each other's hands.

Capuchin monkeys exploit a great variety of plant and animal foods in their natural habitat. They do so through force, destructive manipulation, and perhaps tool use. I once followed a group by ear through dense forest: they were noisily breaking open palm fronds. Because of the strength involved, this foraging technique may itself provide a basis for sharing. Adult males (who are very muscular compared to females) may be able to reach foods that females and youngsters cannot obtain on their own.

Most animals eaten by these omnivores are insects, spiders, reptiles, tree frogs, and so on. Not all prey are too tiny to share, however. Susan Perry and Lisa Rose, anthropology graduate students, recently discovered that wild capuchins in Costa Rica raid coati nests and distribute the meat of the pups. Apart from raids on unguarded nests, the monkeys also managed to steal pups defended by adult coatis. Even for agile monkeys this is a risky business, as coatis have formidable jaws. Coatis are relatives of raccoons, roughly twice the size of capuchins.

While the degree of cooperation—if any—during these raids remains to be ascertained, subsequent sharing has been carefully documented. Because the capuchins ate the pups alive, without killing them first, beggars were attracted by the screams of the prey. Each carcass had between one and seven owners before it was consumed. Most of the sharing took the form of owners allowing others to collect scraps or tear off pieces. On occasion, however, they would set meat down in front of a beggar. The capuchin monkey seems no exception, therefore, to a connection between predation and food division.

If carnivory was indeed the catalyst for the evolution of sharing, it is hard to escape the conclusion that human morality is steeped in animal blood. When we give money to begging strangers, ship food to starving people, or vote for measures that benefit the poor, we follow impulses shaped since the time our ancestors began to cluster around meat possessors. At the center of the original circle we find a prize hard to get but desired by many, a situation that remains essentially unchanged. In the course of human evolution and history, this small, sympathetic circle grew steadily to encompass all of humanity—if not in practice then at least in principle. Some philosophers, such as Peter Singer in *The Expanding Circle,* even feel that all creatures under the sun deserve to be included, and that animals should therefore never be used for research, entertainment, or human consumption. Given the circle's proposed origin, it is profoundly ironic that its expansion should culminate in a plea for vegetarianism.

I am not saying that such arguments cannot or should not be made. Moral reasoning follows a logic of its own, independent of how the human inclinations that it works with (or against) came into existence. The moral philosopher simply takes for granted what the biologist seeks to explain.

## A Concept of Giving

Ever since the meat sharing of chimpanzees was dismissed as "tolerated scrounging" by Glynn Isaac, a paleontologist interested in the role of hunting and sharing in human evolution, anthropologists have felt absolved from the need to take its implications seriously. According to Isaac, only active food distribution deserves the label "sharing."

It is indeed highly unusual to see one chimpanzee spontaneously offer food to another. Yet, instead of stressing what these apes do not do, we may find it more profitable to focus attention on what they do do in comparison with most other species. Many primates do not seem to have even a *concept* of giving. When I for the first time hold out an apple to a rhesus monkey, he will most likely snatch it out of my hand with menacing stares and grunts, the only way he knows to obtain food from someone else. Because relaxed give-and-take is not part of his natural repertoire, it takes time for a rhesus monkey to learn not to bite the hand that feeds him.[12]

Not only do chimpanzees (and other apes) react more amicably to food offerings, they understand exchange. For example, if something that we wish to retrieve (such as a screwdriver) has been left behind in the ape enclosure, one of its inhabitants will quickly grasp what we mean when we hold up a tidbit while pointing or nodding at the item. She will fetch the tool and trade it for the food. I know of only one monkey species with which such deals can be struck without prior training, and it can be no accident that it is yet another food sharer: the capuchin.

Even though food donation is normally rare, situations can be created in which it becomes common. As long as sixty years ago, Henry Nissen and Meredith Crawford successfully did so. They conducted experiments with pairs of chimpanzees in adjacent cages separated by bars; only one of the two was given food. After the other begged with hand held out, some possessors shared with them, which obviously required active participation. Similarly, we recently conducted tests at the Yerkes Field Station in which chimpanzees were trained to enter a building individually and open a box. On some occasions the box was stuffed with fruits. The rest of the colony could watch the discovery through an open window too small to climb through. Soon it became known among us as the "take-out window" because of the occasional handouts to outsiders by the fortunate ape inside.

Although active sharing constitutes only a fraction of all food transfers in the wild, the phenomenon has been reported by many students of chimpanzee behavior. Most accounts concern meat sharing, but Jane Goodall once saw an adult female bring fruit to her aging mother.

> Madame Bee looked old and sick. It was very hot that summer, and food was relatively scarce. . . . When soft calls indicated that the two young females [her daughters] had arrived at the food site, Madame Bee moved a little faster; but when she got there, it seemed that she was too tired or weak to climb. She looked up at her daughters, then lay on the ground and watched as they moved about, searching for ripe fruits. After about ten minutes Little Bee climbed down. She carried one of the fruits by its stem in her mouth and had a second in one hand. As she reached the ground, Madame Bee gave a few soft grunts. Little Bee ap-

proached, also grunting, and placed the fruit from her hand on the ground beside her mother. She then sat nearby as the two females ate together.[13]

As for capuchins, the first evidence for active sharing is buried in a technical report by M. R. D'Amato and Norman Eisenstein. During experiments on food deprivation one subject, Lucy, failed to lose weight. The authors blamed this surprising result on Lucy's friends. "The most likely interpretation . . . is that Lucy received additional food supplies from unauthorized sources. We have observed more than once the passing of food from an animal on full rations to one in an adjacent cage on deprivation."[14]

Our ongoing research confirms this observation. Inspired by the Nissen and Crawford study, we place capuchin monkeys in adjacent compartments of a test chamber with a mesh partition between them. Rather than deprive them, we give them treats of attractive food.[15] One of the two receives a bowl of apple pieces for twenty minutes, after which the other receives cucumber pieces for the same amount of time. Many a colleague has been amazed by our video footage of capuchins handing, pushing, or throwing food through the mesh to their neighbor. This kind of exchange is simply unthinkable in most other primates.

Nevertheless, in these same tests the vast majority of transfers remain passive. The possessor generally transports handfuls of food

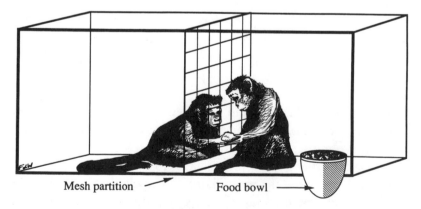

Mesh partition ➝        Food bowl ➝

A male capuchin (right) hands a piece of apple to a female. The mesh between the two monkeys prevents the female from getting any food without the male's cooperation. In the same test, the female will receive a bowl with cucumber pieces to see if her willingness to share is affected by what she received. This drawing (by the author) is based on an actual video still.

Science's first videotaped instance of what we interpret as spontaneous deception occurred unexpectedly during a food test on chimpanzees. It contains all the crucial elements desired in a case of deception: a clear motive, a benefit, and the absence of trial-and-error learning. The individual committing the apparent act of miscommunication had never before found herself in this exact situation.

The following description is based on an analysis of two videotapes—one recorded indoors, the other outdoors—as well as direct observation by four experienced chimp watchers. Time is in seconds from the onset of the test.

Date: May 21, 1993

Location: Yerkes Primate Center Field Station

## Time    Simultaneous Indoor and Outdoor Observations

000     Inside a building, Marilyn and her juvenile daughter discover a box filled with two dozen apples. Outside, the rest of the group is aware of the food because of an open window.

040     While Marilyn and her daughter gorge themselves, Georgia, an adult female, begins to collect handfuls of mud (it has rained) in the outdoor enclosure. Sticking her arm through the window, Georgia hurls the stuff with excellent aim at the two inside. Marilyn (although quite dominant over Georgia) goes to the window with complaining whimpers.

460     The indoor area is becoming dirty, slippery, and wet. Dirt throwing is not unusual in this colony for individuals who want attention, but what Georgia is doing amounts to serious pestering. Because she does not let up, Marilyn is forced to leave the box. She climbs to the ceiling, out of Georgia's range. Marilyn's daughter does not seem to mind and continues to feed, dodging the incoming mud balls.

620     During a brief spell of quiet, Marilyn's daughter hands a piece of apple through the window to Georgia's daughter outside.

635     Marilyn comes down from the ceiling and moves to the window while uttering soft calls. These particular calls normally signify mild alarm, as for a distant snake. Marilyn does not look at anything in particular, though, and the experimenter inside sees absolutely nothing disturbing.

645     Marilyn now utters louder alarm calls through the window. Georgia immediately responds by rushing to the fence of the enclosure to stare into the forest behind the building. She then rushes away from the fence; her startled response makes other apes do the same. The apes outside gather on a climbing frame (a normal response to danger).

Even though we inspect through binoculars the spot on which Georgia focused her attention, we detect nothing unusual. Furthermore, if anything is there, Marilyn can't have seen it as it is outside her visual range (blocked by the building's side wall).

710 Still staring in the same direction, the chimpanzees outside now utter a chorus of loud "woaow" barks. Marilyn joins them by calling from inside, looking out through the window.

725 Marilyn's daughter seems disturbed by the alarm—she does not approach the box any more and stays alert—as do the others outside. Marilyn is *the only one* who pays no further heed. Immediately after her last bark, she turns away from the window and moves to a far corner of the indoor area. There she picks up an apple and starts eating.

Georgia has lost interest in annoying Marilyn, who can finally enjoy her food bonanza.

---

to the partition, spreads it out on the floor, and starts eating. The partner needs only to reach through the mesh to collect pieces, or take them directly from the possessor's hands or mouth. Typically, capuchins cup an open hand under the possessor's chin in order to catch any dropping bits. Note that there is absolutely no need for possessors to bring food to this side of their compartment; they could just as easily keep everything for themselves in a far corner. Indeed, this is what occurs in intolerant pairs. Sharing is a *selective* process; we are able to predict on the basis of social relationships in the group which combinations of individuals will share, and which will not.

If active donation is rare in species other than our own, it is not because they are incapable of it. Rather, there seems little need for it. Whether transmissions of food are brought about by possessors or recipients is of secondary importance; the main point is that transmission takes place. Letting others gently remove food that is clearly in your possession is a tremendous change compared to animals without such tolerance. Chimpanzees and capuchins may not share exactly like people, but the outcome is identical: one individual obtains food from another on an apparently voluntary basis.[16]

## Testing for Reciprocity

The psychology of sharing is little understood. For example, our capuchins may carry food to the mesh partition simply because they prefer to eat next to their companion. That is, the sharing could be a combination of tolerance and affection. Alternatively, their behavior could reflect a concept of exchange and the expectation of return favors. Which of these two possibilities is the reality makes quite a difference. It is this sort of question that our experiment seeks to answer, issues difficult or impossible to resolve in the field. Now that we know *how* and *when* primates share food under natural conditions, it is time to manipulate this tendency in a controlled environment to establish *why* they do so.

The need for such research is particularly felt in relation to chimpanzees. Despite all the observations of meat sharing in the wild, virtually nothing is known about the degree of reciprocity, partly because participation in predatory episodes changes from one occasion to the next, as does the quantity of meat. Possibly the apes themselves keep track of who did what for whom, but the constantly changing composition of feeding clusters makes the establishment of reciprocity a statistical nightmare for the scientist. How much more convenient to conduct repeated standardized trials with the same individuals. This is precisely what I set out to do at the Yerkes Field Station.

What kind of food to select? I knew that a single pile of favored fruits, if provided on a regular basis, would be the surest way of destroying the colony through violence. We learned this lesson from the bananas at Gombe as well as from early attempts at establishing captive chimpanzee colonies. To allow the chimpanzees to catch and kill an animal might provide a natural context for a study of sharing, but was ruled out for ethical reasons. Instead, I gave the colony large bundles of branches tied together with honeysuckle vine.

Wild chimpanzees do not need to share the foliage that is all around them. In captivity, however, branches with fresh leaves are ideal to investigate sharing; they arouse quite a bit of excitement yet no excessive competition. When the chimpanzees see a caretaker arrive in the distance with two enormous bundles of blackberry, sweetgum, beech, and tulip tree branches, they burst out hooting. General pandemonium ensues, including a flurry of embracing and kissing. Friendly body contact increases one-hundred-fold, and status signals seventy-five-fold. Subordinates approach dominants, particularly the alpha male, to greet them with bows and pant-grunts. Paradoxically, the apes are confirming the hierarchy just before canceling it, to all intents and purposes.

I call this response a *celebration*. It marks the transition to a mode of interaction dominated by tolerance and reciprocity. Celebration serves to eliminate social tensions and thus pave the way for a relaxed feeding session.[17] Nothing even remotely similar occurs in species that do not share. If macaques notice the arrival of attractive food, they immediately move into a competitive mode: high-ranking monkeys come forward, supplanting those of low rank. Chimpanzees do the exact opposite, throwing themselves into each other's arms with obvious delight. Within minutes each and every member of the colony has obtained some food. They do show competition, occasionally even fight, but it is their peacefulness and civility that is most striking: only 3 percent of interactions between adults involve any sign of aggression.

Field-workers noted long ago that social dominance loses some of its luster during sharing sessions. It does not become totally insignificant—as illustrated by Ntologi—but it is not unusual to see the most feared and respected individual stretch out a hand to one of his underlings to beg for a few scraps. Why does he not claim the food by force? In our tests, subordinates avoid dominants if both approach unclaimed food, but once the food is firmly in a subordinate's hands, his or her ownership is generally respected. This pattern holds among adults only; juveniles are treated (and treat each other) with less inhibition.[18]

The generosity of high-ranking individuals is so striking that subordinates often flock around them rather than solicit food from low-status possessors, who tend to hold onto it more tightly. This observation contradicts a popular hypothesis, according to which possessors (human or nonhuman) part with their load out of *fear*. Nicholas Blurton Jones, a British anthropologist, proposed that sharing is a way of keeping the peace with potentially hostile beggars. If true, would we not expect low-status possessors to share the most, as they are the most easily intimidated?

Walnut, the previous alpha male of the Yerkes colony, was the most generous sharer in my studies. Huge and muscular, without rivals of his own sex, Walnut totally dominated all females and juveniles. To me it is unimaginable that there was one drop of fear in this male when he let females pull the juiciest branches out of his bundle. The sharing-under-pressure hypothesis also cannot explain why chimpanzees and capuchins still bring food to others when the risk of attack has been eliminated, as in the experiments previously described. Finally, the hypothesis fails to account for the predominant direction of aggression in my food trials with chimpanzees; possessors threatened beggars five times more often than that beggars threatened possessors.

It remains possible that sharing under pressure comes into play with highly valued foods, or with a large number of competing males. Yet the distribution of food is so well developed under more relaxed conditions that I see this as a secondary development only. In non-sharing species, a single dominant may feed undisturbed even if surrounded by a hundred hungry subordinates. That such perfect peace is not given to a chimpanzee or human owner of prized food is because of different *expectations* in the have-nots, who beg doggedly and throw tantrums if ignored. What needs to be explained is the origin of these expectations, rather than the pressuring tactics that spring from them. Only the theory of reciprocal altruism provides a satisfactory answer.

To test this theory, I recorded nearly five thousand interactions over "browse food" in the Yerkes chimpanzees. Half of these resulted in a transfer of food from one individual to another—a proportion nearly identical to that determined by Geza Teleki for meat sharing in the Gombe chimpanzees. That only one of two attempts is successful shows how discriminating the apes are. The most common ways of getting rid of beggars are to turn away when they approach, to pull branches out of their reach, to tap their hand when they reach out, or just to walk off with the food. Only rarely do possessors bark or scream at beggars, or whack them over the head with an entire food bundle to make clear how little they care for their presence. Low-ranking possessors are just as capable of rebuffing high-ranking beggars as the other way around. Obviously, sharing is no free-for-all.

Food transfers in the colony were analyzed in all possible directions among adults. As predicted by the reciprocity hypothesis, the number of transfers in each direction was related to the number in the opposite direction; that is, if A shared a lot with B, B generally shared a lot with A, and if A shared little with C, C also shared little with A.[19] The reciprocity hypothesis was further supported by the finding that grooming affected subsequent sharing: A's chances for getting food from B improved if A had groomed B earlier that day.

Even though my tests were conducted on a colony with an unusual sex ratio (several adult females and a single male), and with a food source that wild chimpanzees do not need to share, the data definitively support the *principle* of reciprocal exchange. And the principle is really all that matters. Individuals with the mental capacity to keep track of given and received favors can apply this capacity to almost any situation. Collaborative hunting and the sharing of meat, or grooming and the sharing of foliage, are only two possibilities. Female chimpanzees, for example, may follow reciprocity rules when protecting or baby-sitting each other's offspring, and sex is an obvious bargaining chip between males and females. This alternative is particularly used by bonobos: females of this species are known to receive food from males immediately following, or even in the midst of, intercourse.[20]

Once a quid pro quo mindset has taken hold, the "currency" of exchange becomes secondary. Reciprocity begins to permeate all aspects of social life.

## From Revenge to Justice

Tangible exchanges, such as those involving food, are often more convincing than intangible ones. Nevertheless, it is quite possible that before food sharing appeared on the evolutionary scene the trading of *social* services was already in full swing in our primate ancestors, and reciprocity had become the new way of doing business. A prime candidate for having set this process in motion is support in fights, also known as alliance formation.

As with the sharing of food, the importance of alliances is best illustrated by contrasting species that form them with species that do not. *Felis silvestris catus,* the domestic cat, belongs to the latter category. At home we have two neutered tomcats, Diego and Freddie. Diego used to roam and defend a large territory around the house. He did so effectively and diligently until he got older; then he began to withdraw (in the typical slow-motion fashion of cats) from younger and stronger rivals. Freddie, on the other hand, habitually overestimates his fighting abilities. He regularly loses against feral tomcats and does not seem to learn anything at all from these experiences.

One day Freddie, with all hair on end, stood opposite a rival who had emerged from the woods. When Diego joined him to stare at the same intruder, this looked to us like a promising approach. But when Diego took an additional step forward, Freddie immediately turned around and hissed at him, as if he was now dealing with two rivals at once. The tension of the moment had made him hostile to a cat with whom he normally was friendly. During the confusion, the enemy took off.

Because of the millions of years of alliance formation in my evolutionary heritage, I can wrap an arm around a friend's shoulder while hurling nasty insults at someone else. My friend will have no trouble appreciating that these insults have nothing to do with him. Such distinctions come naturally. Teaming up against a rival requires moving from general motivational states to differentiated states, depending on the precise role of the other. Freddie was unable to separate friend from foe, but many primates are masters at juggling attitudes. They (and a few other animals, such as dolphins) are perfectly at ease with the role differentiation of political animals. It is not that unusual for a chimpanzee to beg for A's support (with outstretched hand), while threatening B (with screams and barks), only to court C (with erect penis and foot stamping) immediately afterward.

The reciprocity of alliances is still very much under debate. Many alliances are kin based—witness the confrontations between matrilines in macaques and baboons. The evolution of such a support system does not require reciprocity; kin selection offers an excellent explanation. For nonrelatives to support one another, however, we assume that they must gain something by doing so.

Sometimes the act of support has an immediate payoff and so may not be truly altruistic. Take the way two male savanna baboons together displace a rival from a sexually receptive female. Altruism implies absorption of a cost for the sake of someone else, yet each male in these situations seems to be out for himself. Their goal is to claim the female at the expense of all other males present, including their allies. Once the previous owner has been defeated, both allies race to the female. The first to arrive will become her next consort. Sometimes the previous owner continues to do battle with one ally while the other sneaks out to the female. Clearly, "opportunism" better characterizes such behavior than "altruism." In independent studies in Kenya, both Frederick Bercovitch and Ronald Noë concluded that willingness to assist other males is not what drives these alliances. Rather, there are immediate advantages to be gained.

Not that there are no mutual benefits. There are males who operate consistently as a team; they would obviously not be doing so if, on balance, both of them would not gain. Whereas supportive relationships among male baboons may start out on an entirely opportunistic basis, some of them may gradually develop into well-established partnerships regulated by expectations of reciprocity.

Baboon males also support females and their offspring. By developing friendships with particular members of the opposite sex, males may win acceptance in a troop (male baboons migrate, whereas females stay all their lives in the same troop) while at the same time increasing the willingness of their protegees to mate. So the male offers protection—which he is eminently capable of doing, as he is almost twice a female's size—and the female offers opportunities for sex and, ultimately, reproduction. According to Barbara Smuts, these mutually profitable relationships may last for years, and are established through rather humanlike flirtations.

> First, the male and female looked at one another but avoided being caught looking. This phase was always accompanied by feigned indifference to the other, indicated by concentrated interest in grooming one's own fur or by staring intently at some imaginary object in the distance (both ploys are commonly used by baboons in a wide variety of socially discomfiting situations). Eventually, the coy glances were replaced by a more direct approach, usually initiated by the male. Grooming then followed. If the friendship "took," the couple would then sit together during daily rest periods, and eventually they would coordinate subsistence activities as well.[21]

Mixed-currency exchanges, such as a friendship to which each sex makes its own unique contribution, do not make it any easier for the investigator to establish reciprocity. Monkey groups may be veritable marketplaces in which sex, support, grooming, food tolerance, warnings of danger, and all sorts of other services are being traded. To us scientists falls the task of figuring out the worth of each service and of following relationships over a long enough period to understand the deals that are being struck. To be protected by a male might mean a lot to a female baboon—it could spell the difference between life and death for her offspring—yet is it worth enough for her to ignore the attentions of other males? Can any amount of grooming compensate the groomee for injuries suffered in an attempt to defend the groomer? We know far too little to answer such questions.[22]

For the moment, it may be simpler to isolate a single currency and determine how it is being traded against itself. We have already done so for food sharing. Applying the same procedure to thousands of alliances recorded over the years in both chimpanzees and two kinds of macaques, we were able to demonstrate that alliances too are reciprocal. That is, the tendency of A to support B in fights varies with the tendency of B to support A. While considerably stronger in chimpanzees than macaques, this relationship characterizes all three studied species.

Such reciprocity can come about in two quite different ways. The simpler is that monkeys and apes preferentially aid kin and friends, that is, partners with whom they spend much time. Does Sonja support Mira because they are always near each other, and does this also explain Mira's support for Sonja? Since association time is symmetrical (identical for both Sonja and Mira), it may be all we need to explain the mutuality of their support. There are statistical ways to remove the effects of a variable, however; reciprocity was found to persist after symmetry was taken into account. Therefore the first explanation cannot be enough, and a second mechanism must be assumed. Some of the events considered in this analysis occurred weeks or months apart. Perhaps primates keep track of favors given and received, and make assistance to others conditional on the way they have been treated in the past. This more calculative view is generally accepted for people; it may hold for other species as well.[23]

We further found that chimpanzees achieve more complete reciprocity than macaques. Not only do chimpanzees assist one another mutually, they add a *system of revenge* to deal with those who oppose them. When an individual takes sides in an ongoing dispute, his action does more than benefit one party; he cannot avoid hurting another. Each *pro* choice entails a *contra* choice. If Yeroen joins a fight between Luit and Nikkie, he simultaneously makes a *pro* choice (for Nikkie) and a *contra* choice (against Luit). This phenomenon is all too familiar in human politics. As soon as a public figure takes up a particular cause or endorses a particular candidate, he is perceived—rightly—as having chosen against other causes or candidates. It is impossible to make everybody happy.

Chimpanzees are unique in that not only the *pro* but also the *contra* interventions are reciprocally distributed; that is, if A often helps others against B, B tends to do the same against A. This tendency may sound natural enough—because people do the same—but it does not apply to macaques. To square accounts with dominant adversaries requires opposing the hierarchy, which is difficult or impossible for macaques. With the vast majority of their alliances directed down the hierarchy, there is no room for a revenge system. Chimpanzees are much less reluctant to stand up against those who normally dominate them; retaliaton is an integral part of their system of reciprocity.[24]

Thus, it is not unusual for a dominant chimpanzee to corner a group mate sometime after a confrontation in which the latter, along with a number of others, stood up against him. With his allies out of sight, this individual is in for a hard time if the dominant decides to get even. As a result, low-ranking chimpanzees need to think twice before poking their noses into disputes among higher-ups. On the other hand, once a subordinate has developed an antagonistic relationship with a specific dominant, it is only a matter of time until this dominant will become involved in a conflict that can be exploited. The subordinate—perhaps together with others in a similar mood—will side with the dominant's rival and make clear that having too many enemies involves a price.

Such retribution may be rare in macaques; it is not wholly absent. An exceptional yet dramatic instance was observed by one of my students, Brenda Miller, in a colony of Japanese macaques on an island at the Milwaukee County Zoo. The group's lowest-ranking female, Shade, was frequently harassed by a particular male. One day she finally summoned the courage to counter his aggression, turning around in the midst of a chase to face her tormentor.

What happened next explains why such behavior is rare. Within seconds Shade was subdued by an angry mob: a whole group of monkeys drove her straight into the moat. It was March, when the Wisconsin weather is still icy cold. According to Miller, attackers normally do not keep victims in the water for more than a few minutes, but Shade was forced to stay for more than twenty minutes. When she finally crawled onto the shore, she was seized and bitten by five aggressors simultaneously. Subsequent veterinary inspection showed her injuries to be superficial, but it was decided to keep Shade indoors overnight because of serious hypothermia.

Early next morning, Miller was at the zoo for the release, worried about renewed violence against Shade. Rather the opposite happened. As soon as Shade appeared, the other macaques on the island began to run away, and a high level of tension was evident. Shade, still weak and limping, walked straight to the male who had led the assault on her. During the next seventeen minutes she attacked him thirteen times, completely ignoring attempts by others (including the alpha male) to stop her. Each time she was distracted, her two offspring would take up the chase after the culprit. Eventually aggression subsided. The male approached Shade three times to make contact, but she obviously was not in a forgiving mood; she moved away from him an equal number of times. The male hit her, made a bouncing display with his tail in the air, and left Shade alone. Only then did the group return to normal activities.

Joint action by low-ranking against high-ranking macaques is extremely uncommon. Perhaps to compensate for this deficit, macaques are specialists in *indirect* revenge. Filippo Aureli and his colleagues discovered that victims of attack often vent their feelings on a relative of the opponent. Their targets are typically younger than the initial aggressor, hence easier to intimidate, and the vindictive action may occur after considerable delay. It is as if I respond to a reprimand received from my boss by looking for his daughter to pull her hair. I do not need to go against the peck order, yet I still inflict punishment on my offender. Unfortunately for me, my boss will have no trouble handling the situation! Macaques, in contrast, cannot be fired; all that can happen is an alliance in defense of the younger target, resulting in revenge upon revenge. Matrilineal politics are cyclic and complex.

I am the first to admit that we still have a long way to go before we can consider reciprocal altruism proven and understood, yet there is every indication that it is better established in our closest relatives than previously thought. Inclusion of negative acts considerably broadens the scope of the balance sheets they seem to keep on social affairs: not only are beneficial actions rewarded, but there seems to be a tendency to teach a lesson to those who act negatively.

It is to Trivers' credit as a theoretician that—before we knew much about alliances and mutual aid—he recognized that a system of favors and return favors would not last if the tendencies that undermine it went unchecked. There is a strong temptation to take advantage of the system without making a corresponding investment. Defined as "cheating"—that is, giving less than one takes—this attitude threatens the entire system, including the interests of honest contributors. The only way they can protect themselves is by making cheating costly. They do so through punitive action, also known as *moralistic aggression*. It is an apt label, as the reaction concerns how others "ought" to behave.

A human emotion specifically mentioned in this context by Trivers is *indignation*. We are indignant, for example, when refused a favor by a colleague whom we have helped numerous times in the past. Indignation is aroused by the perception of injustice; as such, it is part of the emotional underpinning of human morality. The outraged reaction that it may trigger serves to clarify that altruism is not unlimited: it is bound by rules of mutual obligation.

A first, tentative suggestion that chimpanzees may know this special emotion came from our experiments on food sharing. We found that some individuals, when approaching a possessor, were more often threatened away than others, and that this depended on how they themselves acted as possessors. The contrast between two females, Gwinnie and Mai, illustrates this point. If Gwinnie obtained one of the large bundles of browse, she would take it to the top of a climbing frame, where it could easily be monopolized. Except for her offspring, few others managed to get anything. Mai, in contrast, shared readily and was typically surrounded by a cluster of beggars. Guess who met with more resistance if she herself was in need and tried to get food? Gwinnie, Georgia, and other stingy personalities encountered far more threats and protestations than generous sharers such as Mai and Walnut.

This relationship between an individual's generosity as possessor and the resistance encountered as beggar is to be expected if moralistic aggression regulates food exchanges. It is as if the other apes are telling Gwinnie, "You never share with us, why should we share with you!"

A taste of revenge is the other side of the coin of reciprocity. To act negatively toward stingy individuals (along with direct and indirect retaliation) suggests a sense of justice and fairness. The eye-for-an-eye mentality of primates may serve "educational" purposes by attaching a cost to undesirable behavior. Although the human juridical process abhors raw displays of emotion and prefers arguments based on the greater good of society, there is no denying the role of such urges. In *Wild Justice* Susan Jacoby points out that human justice is built on the transformation of a primitive sense of vengeance. When relatives of a murder victim or survivors of war atrocities seek justice, they are driven by a need for redress even though they may present their cause in more abstract terms. Jacoby believes that one measure of a civilization's complexity is the distance it creates between the aggrieved individual and the administration of his or her urge for vindication.

> The struggle to contain revenge has been conducted at the highest level of moral and civic awareness attained at each stage in the development of civilization. The self-conscious nature of the effort is expectable in view of the persistent state of tension between uncontrolled vengeance as destroyer and controlled vengeance as an unavoidable component of justice.[25]

Thus, retributive justice ultimately rests on a desire to get even, a desire that needs to be reined in and subjected to powerful rationalization so as to keep society from being torn apart by eternal feuding. Like fire, revenge can be incredibly destructive if left untamed. According to the American anthropologist Napoleon Chagnon, it is hard even to imagine the terror that might invade our lives in the absence of laws prohibiting people from seeking lethal retribution when close kin have died at the hands of someone else. In a study of blood feuding among the Yanomamö Indians of the Amazonas, Chagnon estimated that approximately 30 percent of adult male deaths were due to violence.

A young Yanomamö man visiting the capital immediately saw the advantages of a more even-handed juridical apparatus:

> He excitedly told me that he had visited the governor and urged him to make law and police available to his people so that they would not have to engage any longer in their wars of revenge and have to live in constant fear. Many of his close kinsmen had died violently and had, in turn, exacted lethal revenge; he worried about being a potential target of retaliations and made it known to all that he would have nothing to do with raiding.[26]

Although human reciprocity and justice are undoubtedly far more developed than anything seen in other animals, there is more common ground than most students of law and ethics are aware of. Thus, reading *A Theory of Justice,* an influential book by the contemporary philosopher John Rawls, I cannot escape the feeling that rather than describing a human innovation, it elaborates on ancient themes, many of which are recognizable in our nearest relatives. Of course, everything is more explicit in human society because of our ability to formulate rules of conduct, discuss them among ourselves, and write about them in exquisite detail. Still, it is safe to assume that the actions of our ancestors were guided by gratitude, obligation, retribution, and indignation long before they developed enough language capacity for moral discourse.

A century ago Thomas Henry Huxley claimed that a purely competitive view of life cannot accommodate moral behavior.

> [The pursuit of virtue] repudiates the gladiatorial theory of existence. It demands that each man who enters into the enjoyment of the advantages of a polity shall be mindful of his debt to those who have laboriously constructed it; and shall take heed that no

act of his weakens the fabric in which he has been permitted to live.[27]

Instead of concluding that morality is a cultural construct that flies in the face of nature, Huxley and his followers would have done better to broaden their perspective on what the evolutionary process can accomplish. Petr Kropotkin had an inkling; Trivers formulated it with admirable precision. Given what we know now, the above statement about the advantages of mutual aid seems to hold reasonably well for monkeys, apes, and some other animals.

And could not the admonition at the end apply to Gwinnie?

# 5

# GETTING ALONG

Some stories cannot be literally true,
and among these are both our current
guiding myths—not only the Genesis
story, but the Social Contract myth as
well. The point is not just that there
never was a moment of contract.
Much more deeply, there was never
the need to which that contract would
have been an answer.

*Mary Midgley*[1]

In the 1960s and early 1970s, the funding floodgates for research on
aggression were thrown open by a single popular and hugely contro-
versial book. Konrad Lorenz's *On Aggression* defined a new area of
inquiry. Even his adversaries admitted as much, and took advantage
of the research opportunities. Entire libraries started to be written on
the topic, and soon a steady stream of articles compared definitions
and explanations of the phenomenon. Though still a graduate student
at the time, I was allowed to join a group of Dutch psychiatrists,
criminologists, psychologists, and ethologists who regularly came together to discuss the roots of aggression and violence.

In this stimulating intellectual climate, I embarked on a study of
aggressive behavior in long-tailed macaques—fairly small, brown-
green monkeys native to Indonesia, Malaysia, and the Philippines.
Working with a tape recorder and primitive black-and-white video
equipment—equipment so heavy that setting it up was a back-break-
ing enterprise—I would patiently wait for spontaneous fights in a
captive group. What struck me most while sitting and waiting was
how rarely these monkeys fought, even though they had a reputation
for belligerence: I calculated that they devoted less than 5 percent of

their time to this activity. Most of the time they played, groomed, slept in large huddles, or were otherwise peacefully occupied. Then in a flash they would be chasing one another, aggressors barking and victims screaming in shrill voices, with the ever-present danger of serious damage from the males' sharp canines. I became as fast as a play-by-play sports announcer in speaking what happened into a microphone, recording in great detail the maneuvers of a number of simultaneous actors. The next moment the combatants would settle down, and I would be out of work again.

The common view of aggression as the expression of an internal drive, or a sign of frustration, or a response to some irritating external stimulus rapidly lost appeal for me during this period. Not that these notions were wrong—they were heavily debated, and there was something to be said for each of them—but they stressed the individual, not the social context. To me, the individuals became more and more of an abstraction; it was their relationships that caught my attention. In the same way that, when gazing at the night sky, we see the Great Bear or Orion instead of a mass of stars, I saw a dominance order, kinship bonds, alliances, and rivalries among my monkeys. Aggression was our label for the sparks that flew when interests collided: it could only be regarded as an interindividual, not an individual, phenomenon. It also was not a phenomenon that could be investigated in isolation, as it was so clearly embedded in other aspects of social life. How did the 5 percent and the 95 percent mesh? I did not solve the puzzle at the time, but sometimes felt I was studying the yang without the yin.

The questions emerging from this project, however vague in my mind, prepared me for the answer when it appeared a couple of years later during my chimpanzee studies at the Arnhem Zoo. If this sounds like the Holy Apparition Theory of Scientific Discovery, it is often how insights are achieved. Lorenz himself notes how "one day, after a long period of unconscious data accumulation, the *Gestalt* that has been sought is there, often coming completely unexpectedly and like a revelation, but full of the power to convince."[2]

The *Gestalt* that gave me the key to my problem was an embrace and kiss between two chimpanzees shortly after a serious altercation. The event caused hooting tumult in the colony; the other apes evidently attached great significance to what had happened. Since the embrace occurred between the chief opponents of the preceding fight, it struck me as a *reconciliation*. This insight was no doubt facilitated by the fact that chimpanzees are so humanlike in everything they do; we know now that reconciliations are not limited to these apes.

Since that day twenty years ago, I have watched literally thousands of reconciliations, highly emotional to rather casual, ones that appeared to resolve tensions to those that did not. It still gives me special pleasure to see the rapprochement phase (which may be hesitant and tentative), the physical reunion, and the calming talk or grooming that ensues. While this pleasure derives from my human capacity for empathy, I also have the reassuring knowledge that aggression has been put into context. Instead of the evanescent fireworks of group life, aggression turns out to be an integral part of social relationships: it arises within them, it upsets their dynamics, and its harmful effects can be "undone" through soothing contact.

Every reconciled conflict is a choice against entropy. As with expressions of sympathy, conflict resolution by peaceful means would never have come into existence were it not for strong attachments based on mutual dependency and cooperation. Resolution reflects a level of social connectedness lacking in many other species, such as the territorial birds and fish studied by early ethologists. Their choice of subjects explains why aggression was initially depicted as a *spacing* mechanism, a way of maintaining individual distance and defending territories. Observations of monkeys and apes challenge this notion: aggression followed by reconciliation is the exact opposite. Instead of dispersal, we see mutual attraction after fights. This pattern may seem counterintuitive, but not if one knows how strongly these animals rely on each other; they just cannot afford alienation.

To view aggressive behavior as an expression of interindividual conflict, both determined by and functional within social relationships, removes us ever further from the Lorenzian "instinctivistic" view; it pays equal attention to social and biological factors. Of course, a broad definition of the biological covers the social (social predispositions are as much part of a species' biology as its physiology and anatomy), yet the term is not commonly used this way in the eternal debate about aggression. A 1986 document known as the "Seville Statement on Violence," for example, tries to free humanity from what it calls "biological pessimism" by an outright rejection of genetic explanations. Oddly enough, no one would ever bother to write a similar manifesto to dispute the genetic basis for attachment, cooperation, or sex. Most people accept these behavioral universals as core elements of human nature, so why not aggression?

The reason is that aggression is the one trait that our species does not like to see when it looks in the mirror. It is the ugly pimple on our face, and biologists are blamed for suggesting that it might be hard to get rid of.

The Seville Statement targets outdated views; it still lives in a time in which we were being depicted as Killer Apes.[3] Contemporary ethologists include environmental factors along with genetics in their analyses of aggressive behavior, and have accumulated detailed data on the social context and resolution of interindividual conflict. While writing *Peacemaking among Primates,* I was astonished to discover that we know more about how our animal relatives cope with aggression than about how we ourselves do. Most research on human aggression still isolates the phenomenon from other aspects of social life, and treats it as an antisocial rather than a social activity.[4]

In this penultimate chapter, I provide an update of the growing body of knowledge about primate conflict resolution. I challenge social scientists to move from a paradigm defined in opposition to a thirty-year-old book to one that looks at human aggression from *both* a biological and a social perspective. This viewpoint can be achieved without in any way reducing aggression to an uncontrollable drive or instinct.

## The Social Cage

Occidental culture enjoys a long-standing love affair with personal autonomy. We are individualists at heart, and what better way to stress this fact than by claiming that our primogenitor was self-sufficient? Jean-Jacques Rousseau engraved forever in our souls the image of the noble savage napping alone under the tree from which he had just collected his meal, satisfied in body and mind. What could he possibly need others for? His independence was not even compromised by love making: members of the two sexes simply forgot about each other once their passions had been stilled.

The total absence of social connectedness in this fantasy world did not bother Rousseau, who was a timid, retiring man most at ease during solitary botanical outings. For him, being *seul* was synonymous with being *libre.*

Though presented as a mere theoretical construct, not a historical truth, Rousseau's powerful image of autonomous savages lingers. It has become an article of faith among economists, who describe society as an aggregation of Robinson Crusoes, that is, a number of independent households engaged in free exchange. The same notion permeates theories of justice as a set of fairness principles agreed upon by free and equal human beings who have decided to compromise their autonomy so as to build a community. The concept of "rights" results: a morality that asks each person to respect the claims of each other person. John Rawls goes so far as to present the "initial situation" of human society as one involving rational but mutually disinterested parties.

Disinterested? As if our ancestors did not descend from animals that had lived for millions of years in hierarchically structured communities with strong mutual attachments. Any system of justice arising among them would have concerned individuals who were unfree, unequal, and probably more emotional than rational. There can be no doubt that they must have felt deep interest in one another as parents, offspring, siblings, mates, allies, friends, and guardians of the common cause. A morality exclusively concerned with individual rights tends to ignore the ties, needs, and interdependencies that have marked our existence from the very beginning. It is a cold morality that puts space between people, assigning each person to his or her own little corner of the universe.

How this caricature of a society arose in the minds of eminent thinkers is a mystery. Are we so painfully aware of the ancient patterns that we crave an antidote? Fairness and mutual respect do not come easily—we look at them as accomplishments, goals we fight for—and therefore, rather than admitting that we started out close but unequal, we like to give our quest for justice weight by constructing a story about how we were originally distant but equal. Like a nouveau riche claiming old money, we twist history to legitimize our vision of society.

The myth has served its purpose. With the French Revolution more than two centuries behind us, we now should be able to afford thought experiments that genuinely reconstruct the past. Although Rousseau himself briefly considered biology as a source of inspiration, he dropped the idea, lamenting the lack of knowledge in his day. Present chances to achieve a credible, scientifically grounded reconstruction are much better. We do not need to replace the noble savage with a killer ape, but we do need to abandon the romantic notion of an ancestor free as a bird.

While a wild male chimpanzee may roam a huge stretch of forest, there is a border beyond which he cannot venture, given the hostility between communities. He absolutely needs to get along with his male group mates: united they can stand against (and commit) brutal acts of territorial aggression. At the same time, he vies with these very same males for dominance. He must constantly keep track of his allies and rivals, as he may owe his rank to the first and run risks in presence of the second.

A chimpanzee female generally stays in a smaller home range within the males' territory; she is always surrounded by males who dominate her and offspring who appeal to her for assistance. I do not mean to imply a purely stressful existence, because wild chimpanzees also enjoy companionship, leisure time, and all sorts of gratifying activities—but I do believe that they are social captives.

It is like life in a small village where everyone knows everyone else: there is stability, closeness, and security in these relationships, but also intense control. This characteristic applies even more to monkeys than to chimpanzees. Chimpanzees live in so-called fission-fusion societies; that is, they move through the forest in small parties of a few individuals at a time, the composition of which changes regularly. All associations, except between mother and dependent offspring, are of a temporary nature.[5] Most monkey species form cohesive groups with all members present at all times; their social cage is even more confining.

Assuming that the face-to-face group with its attendant lack of liberty is the original condition of humankind, chimpanzees in captivity, such as the ones I work with, represent a unique experiment. Given the fluidity of their social network in the natural habitat, forcing them together in a permanent group seriously challenges their *adaptive potential,* defined as the range of conditions to which animals can adjust without compromising their health, ability to reproduce, or major portions of their species-typical repertoire of behavior. This range usually stretches well beyond the various habitats occupied in nature. The experience of the last two decades at enlightened zoos and research institutions, beginning with Arnhem Zoo's seminatural enclosure, demonstrates that chimpanzees are readily capable of living healthy lives, both physically and socially, in large captive colonies even if this situation implies forfeiting fission-fusion opportunities.

Under these conditions, social behavior resembles that of wild chimpanzees in many respects except, of course, that group life is considerably intensified. Adult females in particular show a social closeness unknown in their wild counterparts, who tend to be rather solitary. In captive settings, female chimpanzees protect each other against male violence, actively influence male power struggles through concerted action, groom one another regularly, and share food—behaviors rare or absent among females in the best-known wild populations.[6] Adult male relations seem less affected by living conditions; both in the wild and in captivity, males show a characteristic mixture of bonding and rivalry. In short, the chimpanzee's adaptive potential encompasses life in permanent associations similar to those of monkeys.

To say that these chimpanzees do not behave "naturally" misses the point. Few humans do. We spend long periods alone in small boxes on wheels, eat cooked foods, are in touch with relatives via wire, deal with strangers on a daily basis, and so on. Given this wholly artificial world, we may be pushing our adaptive potential to the limit; for this reason, the adaptability of other primates deserves close attention. People in modern societies and captive chimpanzees both successfully adjust to novel circumstances through psychological and social plasticity, which in and of itself is a natural ability.

The chimpanzees' capacity to live in stable groups is highly relevant in relation to human evolution. Without a similar capacity our ancestors could never have made the monumental step toward life in permanent settlements. As noted by Roger Masters, an American political scientist, the study of captive chimpanzee colonies may

> provide particularly valuable evidence of what happens to hominoids when they cannot easily leave their home community, and thus, like humans after the invention of agriculture, tend to substitute shifting social alignments for the group fission characteristic of hunter-gatherers and wild chimps.[7]

This observation brings us back to the issue of freedom. Regardless of circumstances, chimpanzees, monkeys, and humans cannot readily exit the group to which they belong. The double meaning of "belonging to" says it all: they are part of and possessed by the group. Migration between groups does occur in nature but tends to be limited to a particular life stage of one or the other sex. Despite opportunities for temporary distancing—opportunities that are considerably greater in the wild than in captivity, and greater in a populous "urban jungle" than in a village—in the long run, most group members are stuck with one another. My phrasing here is negative only to contrast the actual situation with the myth that we started out as a bunch of loners free to go wherever we wanted. Being social animals, we have no trouble recognizing the positive side. The definition of social animals is precisely that they seek and *enjoy* company; the social cage is their palace!

If group life is based on a social contract, it is drawn up and signed not by individual parties, but by Mother Nature. And she signs only if fitness increases through association with others, that is, if sociable individuals leave more progeny than do solitary individuals. We are seeing how social tendencies came into existence—via a genetic calculus rather than a rational choice. Even in our species, which prides itself on free will, we may find an occasional hermit who has opted for reclusion; yet we never encounter someone who has consciously decided to become social. One cannot decide to become what one already is.

It is not true that for us, or any other social species, life in groups has only pros and no cons; conflict resolution is necessary precisely because group life is not all upbeat. Its greatest disadvantage is that one is continuously surrounded by individuals searching for the same food and attracted to the same mates. Groups are breeding grounds for strife and competition, which ironically also pose the strongest threat to their existence. In an anonymous aggregation, animals may get away with back stabbing—in the way that schooling piranha occasionally take a quick bite out of each other—but an individualized society is doomed without checks and balances on aggression. In such a society, disruptive behavior has more consequences for the perpetrator as others tend to remember *who* is responsible. Cooperative relationships depend on trust that the other parties will act in a particular way under particular circumstances; troublemakers have difficulty gaining such trust.

I am assuming here that animals do not dampen competition for the sake of the group: the good of the group is a factor only insofar as it overlaps with that of the individual. Yet this overlap is considerable if group membership is a matter of life or death. Even apes have natural enemies, such as lions or leopards, and all monkeys suffer predation by birds of prey, snakes, and cats. The main benefit of group living, therefore, may be antipredator defense. Carel van Schaik and Maria van Noordwijk, two Dutch field biologists, traveled to different sites in Southeast Asia to see if group size in long-tailed macaques varied with predation pressure. One site, in Sumatra, had clouded leopards, golden cats, and tigers, whereas the other site, an island in the Indian Ocean, was cat free. Their study confirmed that in the absence of predation monkeys tend to live in smaller groups. In a theoretical paper van Schaik summed up: "The picture that emerges is quite simple: the lower threshold to group size is set by predation, the upper limit is posed by feeding competition among group members."[8]

Sue Boinsky, who followed squirrel monkeys in Costa Rica, noticed how females, upon giving birth (which they do with remarkable synchrony), shift from foraging on their own to traveling in close-knit groups. New mothers often sit side by side staring into the sky, continuously swiveling their heads. Boinsky ascribed their increased gregariousness to vigilance against birds of prey, and the fact that two pairs of eyes cover a wider angle than one.

> The amount of time that raptors were either directly above or near the troop rose from 2 percent to 10 percent when the babies were popping out like popcorn. Eight times I saw collared forest falcons try to grab a baby right off its mother's back; each time the falcons were mobbed and driven off. Some of the mothers that lost their babies had scratches and bleeding backs like those of monkeys I have seen attacked by falcons.[9]

The predator as the ultimate reason for group life is an idea with general applicability. Even elephants are thought to travel in herds because of the vulnerability of their calves to hyenas and lions. If this situation exists on land, imagine three-dimensional space, where surprises can come from any direction. In *Dolphin Days* Kenneth Norris discusses the features of dolphin "schools" that help them evade dangers lurking in the water. I use the quotation marks because an aggregation of dolphins is something quite different from a school of fish. Dolphins may look alike yet they recognize one another by special whistle sounds, and they lead complicated lives, including nursing of the young and lasting cooperative relationships, in a world in which they cannot lag behind for a minute. Even when dispersing in relaxed moments, they stay within what Norris calls their *magic envelope* of sights and sounds, a concept not unlike that of the social cage. When sharks or killer whales approach, the envelope tightens, sometimes in a flash, so as to confuse the predators with a coordinated response faster than their eyes can follow. It is virtually impossible to effectively pick out a potential victim among identically shaped, identically moving objects with little room in between.

Dolphins are a unique combination of a highly individualized society on the inside and faceless ranks on the outside. Norris describes their schooling reaction to Big Bear, a fisherman on a large vessel:

The dolphins leapt ahead of us, pouring from the water in ragged ranks. Suddenly Big Bear, steering with one hand, reached inside the cabin door for a rifle and began pumping shells in the water behind the dolphins to see, he said, if he could 'drive them.' The impact of those shells in the water near the dolphins must have been concussive, for they leapt out of the water as one, so tight to one another that you could not see between them.[10]

Apart from the survival value of belonging to a group with its multiple eyes and ears, its defense mechanisms, and (in case of social carnivores, such as wild dogs) its ability to overpower prey too fast or strong for a single predator—all of which concern external factors—there is the possibility of within-group collaboration to attain within-group goals. Many primates excel at this: their main tool for internal competition is the alliance of two parties against a third. Inasmuch as each individual tries to establish the best alliances, partners become commodities and social bonds become veritable investments, as Hans Kummer was the first to note.

Imagine that monkey A has managed over the years to cultivate a mutually supportive relationship with B, which allows the two of them jointly to keep lower echelons in line in the harsh manner typical of female macaques and baboons. A and B confirm and foster this partnership through mutual grooming and coordinated actions. Should A accept it when a third female, C, grooms B? If C is B's kin or of high rank, there is little A can do about it; blood is thicker than water, and the hierarchy is usually respected. But if C is neither, A will try to threaten C away from B, or simply push her aside. Such competition is commonplace and well documented in monkey groups indicating that social investments are carefully safeguarded.

Or take the triangle of Nikkie, the young alpha male of the Arnhem chimpanzee colony, his older ally, Yeroen, and their chief rival for the top spot, Luit. The extreme predictability with which Nikkie used to keep the other two males apart made me label it a "divide-and-rule" strategy. As soon as he saw Yeroen and Luit together, he would go over to break up the combination: not a single exception to this pattern was observed during Nikkie's years of leadership. Another indication of how much Nikkie valued his partnership with Yeroen—without whose support he could never have subdued Luit—was his eagerness to reconcile with him. Nikkie and Yeroen sometimes had tensions about mating rights. Initially Yeroen, the kingmaker, mated freely with the females; but over time the king himself became increasingly confident and bossy, hence less tolerant of his partner's sexual affairs.

Nikkie's disruptions of Yeroen's mating attempts invariably led to high drama, with Yeroen screaming and rallying female support and Nikkie nervously keeping an eye on Luit, who would grow in size and boldness as soon as the alliance was split. The only way for Nikkie to stay in control was quickly to mend the political base of his position, which he did by stretching out a hand to Yeroen. The ensuing embrace of the ruling males signaled the end of Luit's brief period of latitude. With Yeroen's backing, Nikkie would then make one of his spectacular jumps over Luit, who ducked for this display of dominance, shielding his head with both arms.

That Nikkie could not afford to estrange Yeroen became evident when the alliance finally collapsed after three years of cooperative rule. Overnight Luit took over.

## The Relational Model

Constraints on competition, like that between Nikkie and Yeroen, are hard to accommodate within the received scientific view of aggression as an individual expression, a stimulus-response pattern, or a personality trait. Let us call it the *individual model*. It inspired classical studies such as the one in which rats attack each other after having been shocked by the experimenter, or in which human subjects are instructed to punish strangers or to report their feelings after having watched a violent movie.

Without denying its merits, I feel the individual model fails to give primacy to the most common context of aggression: relationships among familiar individuals. These relationships could, of course, be construed as complex stimulus-response chains, yet I favor a more direct focus on social context. The *relational model* views aggressive behavior as resulting from conflicts of interest between individuals who share a history (and a future). It assumes an equilibrium between tendencies that pull individuals apart and those that bring them together. It focuses on individuals drawn together by attachment and a sense of belonging to the same group. Whenever open conflict shakes this emotional foundation, it causes discomfort not unlike that associated with physical separation. Because conflicts may occur despite a conflux of interest between the same parties, aggression usually is not a one-time event but part of a series of encounters, from positive to negative, through which the relationship cycles.

In an attempt to explain why, in his words, "we should be so constructed that we find comfort in companionship and seek it, and that we experience greater or lesser degrees of anxiety when alone," John Bowlby, the British psychiatrist who founded attachment theory, suggested that avoidance of being alone ultimately derives from avoidance of danger.[11] As we have seen, the same can be said of conflict avoidance. Each clash with a valued companion brings in a waft of chilly air from outside the social cage.

To pursue this parallel between physical separation and emotional distancing due to conflict, consider the logical opposite of separation anxiety, which we may call *reunion euphoria*. After a separation, elephants greet each other with much spinning around, urinating, ear-flapping, entwining of trunks, clicking of tusks, and a chorus of rumbles and piercing trumpets. Cynthia Moss has no doubt that they experience joy: "It may not be similar to human joy or even comparable, but it is elephantine joy and it plays a very important part in their whole social system."[12]

The greeting ceremonies of chimpanzees, both in the wild and in captivity, are well known; they involve charging about with erect hair, loud hooting, kissing, and embracing. There is always a hostile undercurrent, which explains the gestures of submission and appeasement with which subordinates approach dominants. I once watched a reintroduction of two captive adult males who had lived together previously but had not seen each other for nearly five years. We were concerned about the potential for a fight (common between unfamiliar males), but they embraced and kissed in great excitement, slapping each other's backs as old friends, and groomed with tooth-clacking for a long while afterward. Tensions did emerge the next day, but the initial response was undeniably one of elation.

I have experienced human-ape reunions firsthand. Each time I return to the Arnhem Zoo, even if I appear among hundreds of visitors, the oldest female, Mama, will move her arthritic bones to meet me at the moat's edge with pant-grunts. Whereas Mama and I go back a long way, I have been similarly greeted by apes who I thought might have forgotten me.

Kevin, an adolescent male bonobo, had been transferred from the San Diego Zoo, where I had known him, to the Cincinnati Zoo, which I visited six years later. Let me add that, at least in observational studies, I make a point of interacting little with my subjects,

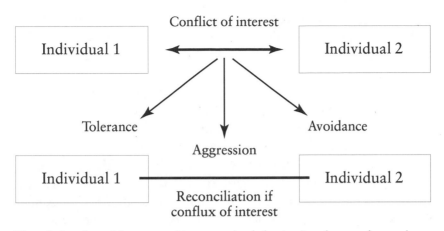

The relational model assumes that aggressive behavior is only one of several ways in which conflicts of interest can be resolved. Alternative solutions are the sharing of resources, priority claims based on previous encounters, or withdrawal from confrontation. If aggression does flare, the value of the relationship determines whether repair attempts will be made afterward; reconciliation is most likely if there is mutual interest in the maintenance of a valuable relationship. Parties negotiate the terms of their relationship by going through cycles of conflict and reconciliation.

and I certainly avoid feeding them or being directly involved in management. I want to reduce the attention they pay me; indeed, I feel honored if primates who jump up at the sight of a caretaker, veterinarian, or unfamiliar visitor accept my presence with hardly a glance, as if I have become part of the furniture. I do always say hello when I arrive, and with Kevin I recall a few close and friendly encounters in his night quarters.

Initially, Kevin just stared when I approached in the company of people familiar to him. As soon as I squatted down and said a few words, however, he pirouetted, clapped his hands, and invited me to play by locking eyes with me, then running away and looking over his shoulder. Distinctly happy to see me, he presented his back and started laughing with guttural sounds even before I dug my fingers into the base of his neck and under his arms (where all hominoids have their tickle spots). His immediate trust was so obvious that I was introduced later that day to my audience as "a good friend of Kevin," and most questions after my presentation were about our relationship. It also made me rethink my assumptions. I myself never forget a primate face that I have seen on a daily basis, and I certainly recognized Kevin instantly. Why had I expected it to be any different for him?[13]

But the most spectacular primate reunion I ever witnessed was among stump-tailed macaques at the Wisconsin Primate Center. After the approximately twenty monkeys returned from a long "vacation" in Puerto Rico (they had lived for a couple of years in an outdoor corral there), they needed to go through quarantine before they could go back to their enclosure at the Vilas Park Zoo in Madison. For months, each individual (except mothers with young infants) was kept in a separate cage in the same room: they could see and hear each other but had no contact. When they were finally put together, an incredible din resulted. In a species-typical "hold-bottom" gesture, the monkeys held each other's hips or embraced, all the while squealing at the top of their lungs. Running from one to the other, their goal seemed to be to go through this procedure with every possible partner, youngsters included. The excitement lasted for about half an hour, after which they settled down to groom each other with softer, more contented-sounding calls.

Given this celebration of togetherness, it is not surprising that stump-tails also reconcile fights more readily than almost any other species. A definite link exists between greeting and peacemaking: the first unifies parties who have been physically apart; the second, parties whose relationship has been strained. Both processes reflect the value attached to the relationship, and both confirm that, whatever has happened, the basic emotional connection is still intact.

## Peacemaking

Golden monkeys do it with mutual hand-holding, chimpanzees with a kiss on the mouth, bonobos with sex, and tonkeana macaques with clasping and lipsmacking. Each species follows its own peacemaking protocol. Many have evolved gestures, facial expressions, and calls specifically for this purpose, whereas other species lack such behavior: their reconciliations look the same as any other contact.

How do we know, then, that these creatures are reconciling? Because the criterion is not a particular behavior but a particular sequence of events. I define reconciliation as a reunion between former opponents not long after their fight. A few acccidental reunions are not enough: reconciliation is believed to occur only if there is a systematic increase in friendly interactions following aggressive ones. This pattern is verified by comparing behavior after conflict with behavior at other, more relaxed moments. Quite a few studies have been made and have concluded that former opponents are *selectively attracted,* that is, they tend to come together more often than usual, and more often with each other than with individuals who had nothing to do with the fight. The phenomenon seems widespread in the primate order: we now have systematic evidence for chimpanzees, bonobos, mountain gorillas, golden monkeys, capuchin monkeys, red-fronted lemurs, patas monkeys, vervet monkeys, baboons, and a variety of macaques (rhesus, tonkeana, stump-tailed, long-tailed, pig-tailed, bonnet, Barbary, and Japanese macaques).[14]

Reconciliations range from the rather uneasy and nervous encounters of patas and rhesus monkeys to the seemingly pleasurable eroticism of bonobos. Some species reconcile only a fraction of conflicts, whereas other species reconcile a majority. Although this variability is as yet unexplained, it is logical to assume that the more conciliatory a species, the more important group cohesiveness must be in the wild. We assume that making peace is an evolved adaptation to the natural environment. Not that it is a relatively immutable trait: reconciliation is such a complex skill that it is probably strongly modified by social experience.

Primates begin developing this skill early on. As with everything related to attachment, it starts with the mother-infant bond, and it gets its strongest impetus from the inescapable weaning trauma. The mother pushes the infant away from her nipple, yet allows it to return right away when it screams in protest. The interval between rejection and acceptance lengthens with the infant's age, and conflicts turn into major scenes. Eventually, the infant learns to time its demands so as to reduce the likelihood of maternal rejection. Older infants have become quite smart at assessing maternal accessibility, as noticed by Jeanne Altmann in baboons in Kenya:

> Sometimes I was following a mother and could not locate her infant at all. The mother began a grooming interaction or resting and immediately the infant would dart toward her from an activity over 20 meters away, make contact, and begin suckling.[15]

Maintaining a tie with the mother despite occasional discord lays the groundwork for all later conflict resolution. Reconciliations with peers, probably next in importance, appear early in life as well. An early observation in our developmental study involved two four-month-old rhesus females, Oatly and Napkin. The two were play-wrestling when they were joined by Napkin's maternal aunt. This adult "helped" Napkin by holding her playmate down. Napkin took advantage by suddenly jumping on Oatly and biting her. After a brief struggle they broke up. The incident was not too serious, but it was remarkable for its aftermath. Oatly walked straight up to Napkin, sitting with the same aunt, and groomed her from behind. Napkin turned around and they embraced belly to belly. To complete this picture of harmony, the aunt then put her arms around the reconciling infants.

Unfortunately, observations of young monkeys tell us little about the learned nature of behavior. We can see a behavior become more complex with age, but in order to know how exactly it is acquired we need to manipulate experience. This goal became a major obsession with me after a debate with a child psychologist who, in defense of the virtual absence of data on human reconciliation, had argued that it was easier to collect such information on monkeys because they act in a stereotypical manner based on "instinct," whereas humans show perplexing variability. Apart from the fact that this could hardly be considered a valid excuse (the task of science is precisely to make sense of variability), differences between human and animal behavior are never that absolute. I decided that the field of primate conflict resolution could use a learning experiment.

My test paradigm combined two ingredients present at the Wisconsin Primate Center, where the project was conducted. One was the availability of two related primate species with contrasting temperaments. The other was the long-standing tradition of rearing experiments by Harry Harlow, the founder of the center. One of his students, Melinda Novak, had used so-called monkey therapists to rehabilitate rhesus monkeys who had been removed from their mothers and raised in isolation. These poor monkeys showed all sorts of stereotypies and tics as a result of their unnatural upbringing and were terrified of body contact. Novak's experiments, conducted in the early 1970s, demonstrated that they could be helped by bringing them in contact with normal members of their species. The isolated individuals learned from these therapists that contact can be comforting and desirable rather than frightening. Their stereotypies gradually disappeared.

Because my aim was not to see if I could cure abnormal monkeys but rather to see if I could change normal ones, I will speak of "tutors" instead of "therapists." We gave stump-tailed macaques an opportunity to act as tutors for rhesus monkeys. Stump-tails are easygoing, tolerant characters, whereas rhesus have a strictly enforced hierarchy. Most important, reconciliation occurs three times more often after fights among stump-tails than among rhesus monkeys, and stump-tails possess a much richer repertoire of reassurance gestures, including the hold-bottom contact that we first noticed during their grand reunion.

Our question was whether we could get any of the stump-tails' gentleness to rub off on the rhesus. We established mixed-species groups of two-year-old rhesus monkeys and two-and-a-half-year-old stump-tails (on the assumption that older, dominant tutors would be more effective than younger ones). These groups were kept together day and night for five consecutive months—a long time in the life of a macaque. Macaques reach adulthood at the age of four or five, so our cohousing experiment might be compared to placing a human child for two years in a chimpanzee colony (which, I wager, would have a profound, perhaps not altogether desirable, effect on the child).

When we first put the two species together, surprisingly, the rhesus were scared. Not only are stump-tails a slightly larger species, they are very tough beneath their gentle temperament; the rhesus must have sensed this fact. So, with the rhesus clinging in a fearful huddle to the ceiling of the room, the stump-tails calmly inspected their new environment. After a couple of minutes some rhesus, still in the same uncomfortable position, dared to threaten the stump-tails with harsh grunts. If it was a test, they were in for a surprise. Whereas a dominant rhesus would have answered the challenge and a subordinate would have fled, the stump-tails simply ignored it. They did not even look up. For the rhesus, this was perhaps their first experience with dominant companions who did not feel a need to forcibly underline their position.

In the course of the experiment the rhesus learned this lesson a thousand times over. Whereas mild aggression was common, physical violence and injuries were virtually absent; friendly contact and play soon became the dominant activities. At first the groups were strikingly segregated, reflecting the preference of almost any animal for its own species.[16] When Denise Johanowicz, the student who deserves much of the credit for the study's completion, arrived in the morning she would find a huddle of rhesus in one corner and a huddle of stump-tails in the other, suggesting that they had slept apart. Play between the species was unusual, but grooming did cross the divide. The stump-tails, as their name suggests, have hardly any tails themselves but were obsessed by those of the rhesus. We had the distinct impression that they sometimes groomed the rhesus just so that they could manipulate and inspect these strange appendages. Although the species segregation never totally disappeared, it diminished with time; toward the end of the experiment, the two species got along very nicely indeed, sleeping together in a single huddle.

Our most significant finding was that, after having lived with stump-tails, the rhesus reconciled more easily. Initially, they made up after fights as seldom as is typical of their species; but gradually they approached the high rate of their tutors, until they reconciled exactly as often as the stump-tails. Even after the stump-tails had been removed and the rhesus were left to interact among themselves, they maintained this newly acquired pacifism. Like chemists altering the properties of a solution, we had infused a group of monkeys of one species with the "social culture" of another.[17]

Imitation did not explain our results. The rhesus did not adopt any of the behavior patterns typical of stump-tails, such as hold-bottom gestures and teeth-chattering. Instead, they acted in every way like rhesus monkeys except for a distinctly friendlier disposition. The rhesus more often uttered a soft, pleasant-sounding vocalization, known as "girning," that signals good intentions during affiliation or play. Possibly the stump-tails' mellow, lenient temperament, combined with their unquestionable dominance, had created a social atmosphere that allowed the rhesus to loosen up and become more conciliatory than would be possible in a group ruled by the typical despots of their own kind. This explanation fits the relational model: different group dynamics had produced a fundamental change in the way conflict was being handled.

The outcome of this study contains an optimistic lesson. If rhesus monkeys are able to learn peacemaking skills, why not human children? Extrapolating to educational efforts in the human species, our findings suggest that the nature of relationships is the key. Reward or punishment of specific behavior by parents and teachers, such as the interruption of aggressive acts or the encouragement of peacemaking, may be too narrow an approach. Even if Western, particularly American, education will always emphasize self-actualization over group values, conflict resolution cannot be taught without attention to the social environment within which it functions. Perhaps we should look at techniques employed in other cultures. For example, Joseph Tobin and his coworkers compared preschools in different countries and observed that fights are almost never broken up by Japanese schoolteachers. These teachers follow the philosophy that children need to learn by themselves how to handle aggression and how to get along.

Evidently their education focuses on the general quality of relationships rather than on desirable or undesirable behavior.[18]

The most important factor by far is the *worth* of relationships. We are learning that primates, including humans, suppress aggression or make peace not for peace's sake but in order to preserve something valuable. This tendency was demonstrated by Marina Cords and Sylvie Thurnheer in an experiment with long-tailed macaques at Hans Kummer's laboratory in Zurich. In earlier tests Cords had provoked quarrels between two monkeys by giving a tidbit to one and not to the other. After the incident the monkeys tended to come together in a friendly manner. In order to create both reconciled and unreconciled pairs, the investigator sometimes prevented a reunion by distracting the monkeys. After this diversion the monkeys were presented with two drinking nipples, side by side, from which they could obtain a sweet drink. As expected, the reconciled monkeys drank together more readily than the unreconciled ones.

Cords and Thurnheer then took the bold step of increasing the worth of the relationship—a manipulation never tried before in primate studies. They trained certain monkeys to feed cooperatively. These monkeys were presented with a series of small holes, each just large enough for one individual at a time, through which they could reach popcorn, a favorite snack. In order to get the popcorn, they needed to take their positions at the same time, at holes closer together than their usual feeding distance and without exchanging any threats. The holes would remain shut if they deviated from these table manners. Once all the monkeys knew how to behave, they went through the same procedure as before, but instead of receiving drinks, they ended up at the popcorn dispenser. Since it was now impossible to get a reward without coordination with the other, the monkeys were smart enough to resolve the problem between them first: their reconciliation rate jumped more than threefold. Here we have the first firm evidence for *strategic reconciliation,* that is, reconciliation mindful of the partner's value.

Rather than a blind process, primate reconciliation is a learned social skill, sensitive to the social configuration of which individuals are part and wielded as an instrument to preserve precious ties. If this conclusion sounds rather calculating, we should not forget its emotional underpinnings. It is unlikely that primates rationally weigh how life would be with or without the other; they probably react to general anxieties about the relationship. If emotional closeness between individuals varies with their degree of mutual support, the rate of grooming between them, their kinship relation, and so on, then these feelings provide an excellent guide for "rational" decisions. A breakup or separation creating strong anxiety will almost always concern a relationship worth restoring. Several studies have confirmed that the tendency to reconcile increases with bond strength, as measured by the amount of time monkeys spend together.

The anxiety involved in the process has been studied by Filippo Aureli. Making use of the fact that monkeys scratch themselves at times of stress or insecurity—the way a student scratches her head at a difficult question—Aureli took careful measures of self-scratching after spontaneous altercations among long-tailed macaques. First, he established that the rate of scratching increases sharply after an individual has been attacked by another. Insecure about the relationship with the aggressor, recent victims are torn between approach and withdrawal. Their caution is well founded; often more attacks come their way, and not only from the initial aggressor.

Second, Aureli demonstrated that reconciliations, even brief ones, immediately reduce the scratching rate. If we accept that scratching reflects stress—which is supported by a variety of studies—friendly reunions between opponents alleviate stress. One reason is increased physical safety: conflicts followed by reconciliation are less often revived than those that go unreconciled. Further, reconciliation normalizes the relationship and restores tolerance and cooperation, as shown in Cords's experiments.

These results may sound blatantly obvious. What else would one expect? Yet all this needed to be proved before postconflict contact in nonhuman primates could justifiably be called reconciliation. Well, it happened of course the other way around, as so often in science—the label came first and much of the evidence later. Without studies such as those cited, use of the term "reconciliation" might have remained vulnerable to charges of anthropomorphism. Now that many predictions from the relational model have been tested and borne out by data, we can turn our attention to the model's full implications.


## Rope Walking

Human aggression runs the entire spectrum from the little family quarrels, with which we are comfortable most of the time, to socially harmful forms, such as child abuse, rape, and murder. When the focus is on the most extreme expressions, it is too easy to generalize our concern and condemnation to all forms. The result is the unworkable mix of moral judgments, policy suggestions, and scientific insights that has plagued research in this field from the beginning.

To present all aggression as undesirable, even evil, is like calling all wild plants weeds: it is the perspective of the gardener, not the botanist or ecologist. Neither of the latter thinks in terms of the utility or beauty of plants, but studies their morphology, size, habitat, taxonomic status, and so on. From this perspective, the plant thrown out by the gardener is just as interesting and exciting, perhaps even more so, than the plant that is allowed to stay and flourish. It is this nonjudgmental, open-minded attitude that I advocate with regard to the question of how aggression functions in social relationships, and in society at large.

Even the verb "to function" is considered problematic because of its positive connotations. The "Seville Statement on Violence," for example, takes the interest of biologists in function to mean that they are out to "justify" aggression and violence, which of course they are not. Biologists rather make the point that a behavior that is universal in the human species, and widespread in the animal kingdom, simply cannot be as detrimental as social science would have us believe. There must be advantages associated with it—perhaps not for the recipients, but definitely for the performers. Biologists are not asking anyone to admire or encourage the behavior, only to step back enough to see that it is part and parcel of the social dynamics around us. So much so, in fact, that we may seriously question the tenet that aggressive behavior is by its very nature antisocial.

When demand exceeds supply—a common condition in nature as well as in human society—a collision of individual interests is inevitable. Some of the resulting conflicts will be resolved contentiously, perhaps with threat or use of violence. Therefore, we can dismiss absolute peace as utopian. Only two realistic alternatives exist in our imperfect world of limited resources: (1) unmitigated competition, or (2) a social order partly shaped and upheld by aggression.

Monkeys, apes, humans, and a host of other animals have clearly opted for the second possibility. Fighting fire with fire, we have made the use of force part of the solution to the problem of the use of force. One kind of aggression restrains other kinds, including the raw contest springing from unevenly distributed resources. Threats and intimidations signal interest in food and mates, back up or stake out priority rights (which in the long run help reduce conflict), or prevent physical harm to the young and weak by putting a halt to bullying by others. Through these regulatory functions an order is created that in complexity far exceeds that of animals, such as grazing herds of bovids, characterized by low levels of competition owing to evenly distributed resources.

Thus, some of humanity's most cherished social institutions are firmly rooted in and upheld by aggression. Systems of justice, for example, can be regarded as the successful transformation of a deep-seated urge for revenge—euphemized as retribution—which keeps this urge within acceptable boundaries. Law enforcement, which is little else than governmental violence—euphemized as force—is often, but by no means always, sanctioned by the majority of the population. There is also abundant historic evidence of violence as a means to bring about much-needed societal change, the threat of which makes elites realize that they can ignore the plight of the poor and the disadvantaged only at their own peril.

Notwithstanding the claim of the British ethologist Robert Hinde that the cumulative unhappiness produced by individual acts of aggression rivals the threat of the nuclear bomb, the above examples make it hard to deny the existence of constructive forms of aggression at the societal level. The same applies at the interpersonal level. Whether aggression has healthy or unhealthy consequences for social relationships depends on how and when it is used, how far it is allowed to escalate, and what is at stake. It also depends on the power balance: if aggression always comes from one side, and only serves the interests of one party, it obviously is not much of a constructive mechanism for the other party. It is a matter of dosage and context. In the same way that one can drink beer without being an alcoholic, one can express anger without being abusive.

We can all distinguish a mean-spirited attack from charges that express love and concern, such as the shouting and screaming of a parent at a child who has almost fallen off the roof. Anger is so much part of our daily relationships that it is rarely pure: it mixes with all sorts of other feelings. One of the most notable fictional sagas of "prosocial" aggression, at least from the perspective of the recipient, is cartoonist George Herriman's creation *Krazy Kat*. This feline is so much in love with Ignatz, a mouse, that every brick thrown by the mouse is perceived as a sign of affection. Thus, instead of stars we see little hearts around the cat's head when it is hit by Ignatz's bricks. And if no brick has been forthcoming for a while, Krazy Kat gets bored and says such things as "He'll not fail me—that dollin."

Recent data on human marital relationships have begun to chal-

Even if Krazy Kat and Ignatz have a somewhat dysfunctional relationship, brick throwing is not necessarily antisocial. (Cartoon by George Herriman; reprinted with special permission of King Features Syndicate)

lenge the conventional wisdom that the best way of handling conflict is invariably by "talking things out." Marriage counselors used to steer couples away from bickering and explosive fights, convinced that such conflicts poison the relationship. We prefer couples to fight with words rather than fists or heavy objects, yet one can hardly expect them to negotiate the most important relationship of their lives without occasional anger and frustration. Extensive research on marriage and divorce by the American psychologist John Gottman suggests that much more important than *whether* people fight is *how* they do it.

Gottman distinguishes three kinds of marriages: the *avoidants* (who dodge and minimize conflict), the *validators* (who carefully listen to each other's arguments), and the *volatile* (who argue and fight on a grand scale). Even though the last kind of marriage may seem to court disaster, the investigator observes that

it turns out that these couples' volcanic arguments are just a small part of an otherwise warm and loving marriage. The passion and relish with which they fight seems to fuel their positive interactions even more. Not only do they express more anger but they laugh and are more affectionate than the average validating couple. These couples certainly do not find making up hard to do—they are masters at it. As intense as their battles may be, their good times are that much better.[19]

I sometimes imagine people as having ropes between them. The thicker the rope, the harder they can pull each other around without breaking the tie. If it is less of a problem to express hard feelings to a spouse than to a colleague, it is because the thickest ropes best endure conflict. Thus, conflict engagement may follow a simple law: the more easily reconciliation can be achieved, the less reluctant we are to fire a salvo.

Lest this leave the impression that conflict and reconciliation are desirable under any circumstances, I should add that the rope metaphor comes with other images, including that of getting entangled. Sometimes a tie that is not worth preserving is kept alive by giving in too readily to the demands of the other—or by accepting apologies for unacceptable behavior. If aggression reaches damaging levels or individual interests are not served equitably, reconciliation becomes a maladaptive process. Relationships can unravel either because a tie is too weak to sustain serious negotiation or because one of the parties systematically shortchanges his or her own interests.

The relational model is agnostic about whether aggression, or reconciliation, is good or bad. Its main purpose is to study how conflicts of interest are worked out, under which conditions this process results in overt hostilities, and how these are dealt with. Aggressive behavior is viewed as one of a multitude of tools available to shape a relationship. Use of the tool may be compatible with harmonious, mutually beneficial relationships, may create tensions and depressions, or may result in the "traumatic bonding" sometimes seen between victims and victimizers. The exact interplay of factors makes us decide whether to resort to aggression or not, whether to emphasize our own interests or not, and whether to preserve a tie or not. I would argue that understanding the normal, acceptable forms of aggression needs to be part of any endeavor to understand the more severe forms that worry us.

## Baboon Testimony

The view of social relationships as arenas in which interests are traded back and forth, partly via stormy encounters, recently received a boost from macaque research. It has been known since the pioneering fieldwork of Japanese primatologists in the 1950s that the strongest ties in macaque society are those of female kin. Grandmothers, mothers, daughters, and sisters often groom each other, tolerate each other around food and water, and band together against other matrilines. Now studies on both free-ranging and captive monkeys have demonstrated that the highest level of fighting occurs *within* the matrilines. Thus, rather than automatically marking poor relationships, aggressive clashes are common between individuals who by any other standard have strong and positive relationships.[20]

This finding should not be pushed too far. Related monkeys do not spend all their time squabbling—peaceful association is the rule. The point is that fights occur in the best of families, and that strong relationships are not necessarily characterized by the absence of conflict. As in the "volatile" marriages, what matters more than the frequency of conflict is how the conflict is weathered. If aggressive behavior serves to negotiate the terms of relationships, a high rate among individuals who are close and mutually dependent makes perfect sense. There is plenty of opportunity in long-term relationships to go through repeated conflicts so as to achieve a fine-tuning of expectations about each other. Once the terms have been accepted, the intensity of conflicts will diminish.

Every day I can see endearing compromise in the chimpanzees at the Yerkes Field Station. Some of the juveniles suck on their mother's lower lip or ear, or nap while sucking on the skin right next to her nipple rather than holding the nipple itself in their mouth—which they are no longer allowed to do. Such substitute nursing is the result of an extended period of discrepant desires between their mother and themselves, in which access to milk has become increasingly restricted despite vociferous protest. Toward the end of the process, youngsters often bury their face close to their mother's breast, in her armpit for example, only to sneak up to the real thing when they get a chance. Occasionally she gives in, but at other times a major falling-out results. Most four-year-old juveniles have learned not even to try the underhanded maneuver anymore; they may stick a finger or toe in their mouth, but they prefer to create an *illusion* of being nursed. We observers have to watch carefully, because from a distance one would swear it is for real.

Mother and offspring bring different weapons to the weaning battlefield. The mother has superior strength; the offspring, a well-developed larynx and subtle blackmailing tactics. After all, the mother has no desire to lose the time and energy she has put into gestation, nursing, and protection. The youngster cajoles her with signs of distress, such as pouts and whimpers, and—if all else fails—a temper tantrum, at the peak of which he may almost choke in his screams or vomit at her feet. This is the ultimate threat: a literal waste of maternal investment.[21] In addition, the commotion may attract unwanted attention to the mother, whereby an adult male, for instance, may hit her for causing all the noise. Thus, apart from undermining his mother's determination by raising concern about his well-being, the offspring exerts social pressure.

Wherever there is a clash of wills, negotiation takes place. Each party develops expectations about the other's behavior, which in time converge on a tacit agreement about what is acceptable. The agreement is not a rational decision, but an adjustment to how the other reacts to one's own behavior. Since the end product is that the wants and needs of the other are taken into account, we are looking at the prototype of a social contract.

The feelings guiding this adjustment are central to human morality, ranging from sympathy and a desire to please to anger and insistence on what one has come to expect. William Charlesworth, a child psychologist and ethologist, sees a child's protest against diminishing maternal care as the first expression of moral outrage.

> One of the infant's earliest perceptions of its world is in terms of how advantageous or disadvantageous it is to its well-being. What is advantageous is perceived as just; what is disadvantageous as unjust. Anger is . . . a clear-cut instance of the earliest sense of a disadvantageous or unjust world.[22]

Charlesworth is not saying here that the child is interested in justice for anyone except itself; that would require more advanced moral understanding than the child has. The negotiations I am describing are driven by self-interest, and just outcomes are by no means guaranteed.

Mother and offspring have so many interests in common that, with increased juvenile independence and the mother's readiness for the next pregnancy, the weaning conflict usually works itself out to their mutual advantage. Exceptions do occur, however. Jane Goodall watched Flo, who used to be an excellent mother, lose the battle as she became too old. Lacking the energy to put up with her last son's aggressive tantrums, Flo carried him on her back until she could no longer bear his weight: by that time he was eight. We also know how in our own species, if one party brings superior muscle power to the domestic arena and is willing to use it, equitable outcomes may as well be forgotten.

How conflicts of interest are settled depends substantially on the kind of relationship two individuals have, which in turn depends on their species. It is easy to see how the mother-offspring relation shares fundamental characteristics across all mammals, but other relations vary tremendously. Some species enforce dominance rigidly, thereby delineating the amount of negotiation space. As a result, members of different species often end up with strikingly different expectations about how they will and should be treated. Each species has its own sense of social regularity.

How much expectations matter became evident when I began working with capuchin monkeys. In a major departure from my previous hands-off approach, in the capuchin project I wanted to investigate social behavior experimentally. Rather than putting the monkeys in single cages to facilitate testing—as is still often done—I dreamed of keeping the entire colony together in a large pen with outdoor space, and the testing area in the same facility, so that subjects could stay vocally in touch with their group during the brief tests I planned. This arrangement seems to me the best way of maintaining captive primates. Moreover, it is the only way to work with monkeys who have long-term social relationships that they care about, which is essential for my research.

The entire plan hinged on our ability to separate individuals from the group without causing too much stress. To this end, they needed to learn to enter a carrier. We interacted freely with them so that they became used to us, and soon some of the capuchins were so tame that they would jump on my shoulder, or check my pockets without permission. A few of the older individuals, however, remained so shy that they would not even accept a peanut from my hand. I naively assumed that my "friends" in the colony would be the first to learn what I wanted, and that the timid individuals would take longer. Was I wrong! The shy ones quickly grasped that when I clapped my hands and chased them, their problems were over as soon as they jumped into the carrying cage. I then immediately released them into another pen with lots of good food; after a few trials they were more than happy to follow the procedure.

The tamest monkeys were the ones who gave me the most trouble. It was not just that they refused to go into the carrier—they were obviously less fearful of me—but they started a major brawl with this man whom they had come to trust and who had the temerity to violate all their expectations. They screamed and barked, lunged at me, slapped at my face, but also made friendly sounds in between their bouts of rage, as if pleading with me to call off the whole business. We had, after all, established a bond, and they very reasonably assumed that this gave them some leverage. Not wanting to hurt them, but also not prepared to let them get away with their behavior, I simply showed more patience and determination than they were willing to invest. In a few cases it took an hour before the monkey finally entered the carrying cage, leaving both of us exhausted. The same individuals would enter in ten minutes on the next day, then in five, until they would try to go into the transport cage even before I had opened it.

I still work with these monkeys today, and they must now be among the easiest in the world to handle. The Yerkes Primate Center made the setup possible, and the capuchins, smart and small, turned out to be an ideal choice. The strenuous disagreement the capuchins and I had to go through before reaching this point was entirely in line with the temperament of the species. Capuchin society is closer to the chimpanzee's tolerant arrangement than to the rhesus monkey's despotism.

This experience also made me appreciate the claim of Vicki Hearne, an American horse trainer, that trainers and their charges enter what she calls a morally loaded pact; that is, they develop expectations about each other through a process of mutual agreement, not plain coercion. With animals as physically intimidating as horses, it is perhaps easier to see why. Discussing her approach to a "crazy" horse named Drummer Girl, Hearne explains:

> If, for example, I were to approach her believing some febrile nonsense of the sort I quoted earlier, about training as coercion, then my beliefs would be manifest in my body as I approached her, and she, reading this, would plain old kill me, that's all, if she could find a way, thus underlining a remark of William Steinkraus's—that the horse is the ultimate authority on the correctness of our theories and methods. It is wrong to talk about coercion not only because that doesn't happen to be what's going on in places like the Spanish Riding School, where horses are trained to the highest pitch, but also because it cannot go on with horses performing at high levels: horses have souls, and there is an inexorable logic consequent on that which makes coercing them into high performance impossible. I don't mean that you

can't coerce horses—only that if you do you will end up, if you are lucky, with a dull, unenthusiastic mount or, if you are unlucky, with a Drummer Girl emerging murderously from the trailer.[23]

Although coercion and the threat of force are very much part of primate (including human) relationships, the ropes tying individuals together would fray quickly indeed if these tendencies were not held in check. A mother chimpanzee could stop her offspring's suckling attempts at once, and a dominant chimpanzee could keep all food for himself—but this is not how things are done if there is an interest in maintaining good relationships. So, rather than coercion, much of the time we see a process closer to *persuasion*.

Perhaps the best-known form of negotiation among primates is the way adult male baboons greet other males in their troop.[24] As described by Barbara Smuts and John Watanabe, who studied greetings in the field in Kenya, one male will typically walk up to another with a rapid, swinging gait. He looks the other straight in the eye with some friendly expression, such as lipsmacking, which makes it absolutely clear that he only wants to initiate a greeting. To communicate intention is essential, given the fierce rivalry of males over females and the formidable canines with which males can cause a deep gash in a split second.

The encounter itself follows a certain protocol that varies with the kind of relationship the two males have. Often, the other welcomes the approach with a similar friendly expression, and one male presents his rear end while the other touches or grasps his hips. They may then proceed to mounting, or, if they really get intimate, one male may fondle the other's scrotum or pull at his penis. Known as "diddling," it is a sign of tremendous trust. The contact lasts only a few seconds, after which the two males separate again. Male baboons do not seem comfortable enough in each other's presence to associate or groom; their predominant modes of interaction are fighting and greeting.

The same behavior was studied by Fernando Colmenares in a large colony at the Madrid Zoo. He found the encounters to be extremely tense, occasionally erupting into fights. The reason is that they often serve to test and confirm who is on top, hence the jockeying for position to decide which male is going to be the mounter (generally the dominant) and which the mountee. Greetings thus seem a way of assessing intention: a male who used to elicit presentation in another learns from his partner's refusal that their previous roles are no longer working, and that a serious challenge may be in the air. Since tensions remain under control in the vast majority of greetings, the advantage of this sort of information exchange is that matters can often be worked out without physical confrontation.

Smuts and Watanabe found the youngest, most pugnacious adult males to be the most preoccupied with dominance. They are extremely edgy during greetings. Senior males who usually have known each other a long time, are less nervous, and instead of competing have learned to cooperate. With one another, that is: their old-boy network effectively keeps younger and stronger males from claiming every attractive female. Concomitantly, the older males' greetings are conducted at a leisurely pace, as they have changed from negotiations about dominance to confirmations of partnership. A few combinations of older males have even reached the point at which dominance hardly matters anymore; they have moved from asymmetrical to symmetrical greetings.

Take Alexander and Boz, two devoted allies. On one occasion Boz heard Alexander scream from 50 meters away, hurried over to the spot, and jumped without hesitation on the back of his buddy's attacker. Alexander would have done the same for Boz. This alliance served them so well that every day, first thing in the morning, the two males would go through a series of intimate greetings so carefully balanced that one would think they were keeping count. Boz would present to Alexander to let him touch his genitals, while both gazed into the other's face and lipsmacked. Two minutes later Alexander would present to Boz for the reverse procedure. If they were agreeing on something, the symmetry of their encounters made it evident that it was on mutual support and shared profits for the fresh day, not on who could push around whom.

The formalization of roles and the remarkable involvement of vulnerable body parts made Smuts and Watanabe draw a parallel with biblical oaths in which one man places a hand under another's loins. Considering that the words "testify," "testimony," and "testicle" share a common Latin root, it does not seem too far-fetched for these primatologists to speculate that

> the genital touching that sometimes occurs in greetings perhaps serves to enhance the truth value of whatever these males are 'saying' to each other within the formally circumscribed context

of greeting. Lacking articulate speech, and unable to swear oaths, perhaps male baboons make a gestural equivalent by literally placing their future reproductive success in the trust of another male. Such risky gestures may help to enhance whatever verity is presumed in the greeting because they impose a potential cost on the presenting male.[25]

## Draining the Behavioral Sink

Some of the most destructive aggression in modern society takes place between strangers or individuals who share few or no interests: it is the bloodshed of gang warfare, drive-by shootings, rioting, muggings, and random violence. This sort of aggression hardly fits the relational model, for it concerns people without ties; attackers and victims may not even view themselves as part of the same community. Much of this violence takes place in cities, and unfortunately (or perhaps fortunately) these massive collections of strangers have no parallel in the social life of monkeys and apes. Not that this fact has prevented the highest levels of those in the U.S. science and government from embroiling themselves in primatological discourse about the issue.

The matter burst into the open when Frederick Goodwin, the head of a large federal organization (the Alcohol, Drug Abuse, and Mental Health Administration), proposed at a committee meeting of the National Institutes of Mental Health on February 11, 1992, that monkey behavior may hold clues for an understanding of inner-city crime:

> If you look, for example, at male monkeys, especially in the wild, roughly half of them survive to adulthood. The other half die by violence. That is the natural way of it for males, to knock each other off. . . . Now, one could say that if some of the loss of social structure in this society, and particularly within the high-impact inner-city areas, has removed some of the civilizing evolutionary things that we have built up and that maybe it isn't just a careless use of the word when people call certain areas of inner cities jungles. (excerpted verbatim from a transcript of the meeting)[26]

These remarks caused such an outcry that Goodwin ended up resigning his position. Part of the problem was that a comparison between inner-city youth and male monkeys struck some politicians as racial stereotyping, even though Goodwin himself never mentioned race. Actually, the affair went much deeper, reflecting profound disagreement about the role of biology in human behavior.

On the one side stand scientists who believe that human aggression cannot be purely cultural. Genes, brains, and hormones must be involved, otherwise why would, for example, the vast majority of violent crimes all over the world be committed by young adult males? The other side is deeply suspicious of the policy implications they fear may emerge from a biomedical approach, such as the screening of children for possible genetic or neurological markers of a violent predisposition, and the decision on how to treat such children. It is the familiar problem of whether we want to gain knowledge that might lend itself to abuse. According to this school of thought, all we really want and need to learn about aggression is its socioeconomic and environmental dimensions.

In a peculiar twist, the chief spokesperson for this group, Peter Breggin, has argued that if comparisons with animals are going to be made at all, they should be with chimpanzees, not monkeys. In a letter to the *New York Times* (March 15, 1992), the psychiatrist explains: "The chimps are relatively nonviolent, family-oriented and settle conflicts within the community through loving activities, such as playing, hugging, kissing and mutual grooming. We would do well to mimic them."

I could almost have said that myself, and I agree wholeheartedly that we could learn a thing or two from these apes. Yet I also believe that the point can be made just as effectively without downplaying the lethal "warfare" observed between chimpanzees in the wild, and their occasional infanticide and cannibalism. Chimpanzees are no angels of peace. It is precisely because they *can* throw overboard all inhibitions that their usual restraint is so impressive.

With scientists publicly hitting each other over the head with primate examples, a golden era of research in this field seemed to be dawning until two politicians, Senator Edward Kennedy and Congressman John Dingell, issued the verdict that "primate research is a preposterous basis for discussing the crime and violence that plague our country today."[27]

Looming behind this entire controversy is the dreadful image of the *behavioral sink*. Intentional or not, Goodwin's remarks about the loss of civilization and structure in the inner-city "jungle" echoed the popular view of disorder and depravity under crowded conditions. We owe this perspective to John Calhoun's experiments on domesticated rats, published in 1962 under the title "Population Density and Social Pathology." Calhoun opened his paper with Thomas Malthus' observation that population growth is automatically slowed by increased vice and misery. The scientist added that while we know overpopulation causes misery such as disease and food shortages, we know virtually nothing about its impact on vice.

This reflection inspired the nightmarish experiment of an expanding rat population in a crammed room killing, sexually assaulting, and eventually devouring each other. Much of this scenario took place among the occupants of a central feeding area. Despite the presence of food hoppers elsewhere in the room, the rats were irresistibly attracted by the social turmoil of this particular area; as a result, great numbers of them jostled and trampled each other for a position at the hoppers. It was this magnetism of the crowd and the attendant chaos and deviancy that made Calhoun speak of a "behavioral sink."

In no time, popularizers were comparing politically motivated street riots to rat packs, inner cities to behavioral sinks, and metropolitan areas to zoos. Warning that society was heading for either anarchy or dictatorship, Robert Ardrey, an American science writer, remarked on the voluntary nature of crowding: "Just as Calhoun's rats freely chose to eat in the middle pens, we freely enter the city."[28] In jumping from rodents to people, however, these writers missed something terribly important: the connection between population density and aggression is far from straightforward in our species.

I am particularly skeptical myself, having moved from the country with the highest population density in the industrialized world to a country with lots of empty space and by far the highest murder rate: the United States has fourteen times fewer people per square kilometer than the Netherlands, yet ten times more homicides per capita. It is not simply a matter of whether people live in large or small agglomerations. Cities are the most crowded places, but why should Washington have an annual homicide rate of 34.6 per 100,000 inhabitants and New York 14.4, compared to Berlin's 1.4, Rome's 1.2, and Tokyo's 0.5? Population density cannot be the answer.[29]

What is most amazing is that our species is able to survive in cities at all, and how relatively *rare* violence is—as eloquently expressed in 1976 by the American ethologist Nicholas Thompson:

My students were New York citizens who rode the subways and daily saw the spectacle of hundreds of people of every age, sex, race, religion, mode of dress, smoking habit, eating habit, and degree of wakefulness compressed peaceably into an intimacy rarely shared between husband and wife in our society, much less by strangers. Yet despite this spectacle, my students were eager to interpret the handful of aggressive incidents which occur daily in the subways as evidence that man's simian nature ill suits him to live in an urban environment. To an ethologist, what is surprising about people in subways is not their hostility; on the contrary, it is the degree of coordination and habituation which permits thousands of people to move daily through an environment so physically hostile as to stampede the herds of any sane animal.[30]

Like Thompson's students, however, the general public preferred to listen to authors who exaggerated the problems of the city, to make the point that humanity lacks the capacity to handle the situation, and blamed this on our brutish past.[31] Initially, primatologists went along with this pessimistic position, claiming that captivity gives rise to bullying monkey bosses who terrify the group, that dominance hierarchies are mere artifacts of stress, and that the rate of aggression skyrockets when monkeys lack space. Combined with the then-prevailing view of total peacefulness in nature, scientists saw striking similarities between primates and rodents.

Things changed when field-workers began to report sporadic but deadly violence in a wide range of species—from langurs to gorillas—as well as strict and clear-cut hierarchies that remained stable for decades. They also measured remarkable hardship in low-ranking monkeys. For example, Wolfgang Dittus saw food competition result in what he termed "socially imposed mortality": no less than 90 percent of the males and 85 percent of the females born in a wild population of toque macaques in Sri Lanka died before reaching adulthood, mostly from malnutrition. Compared to the food abundance and absence of predators in captivity, one would think that stress would be higher, instead of lower, in natural habitats with such dim survival prospects.

At the same time that the Rousseauian image of primates in their natural state was crumbling, questions were being raised about the supposed connection between population density and aggression. It was felt that density needed to be clearly distinguished from other factors. For example, in 1971 Bruce Alexander and E. Roth reported serious fighting, even killing, when a group of Japanese macaques at the Oregon Regional Primate Research Center were released into a corral seventy-three times *larger* than their original enclosure. After then living for years in this corral, crowding the group into a small pen produced a similar rise in aggression. The investigators concluded that "removal from a familiar habitat is adequate to provoke mobbing and this effect is independent of the characteristics of the new habitat."[32]

As a consequence of these and other puzzling findings, new research tried to circumvent novelty effects of environments and companions through a focus on well-established groups in familiar habitats. The results were inconclusive, with some investigators reporting more aggression under crowded conditions, and others equal or even less aggression.[33]

Whereas it is logical to expect social friction under conditions of high density, we know that primates have ways of managing this problem. To see if their control techniques might be the reason why they respond differently than rats, one of my students, Kees Nieuwenhuijsen, carefully compared long-term behavioral records on the Arnhem chimpanzee colony collected over hundreds of hours of observation both indoors and outdoors. The indoor hall in which the colony spends the cold winters is only 5 percent of the size of the outdoor island, so we were dealing with an exceptionally high crowding factor. The apes were thoroughly familiar with both environments, which eliminated novelty effects.

In the winter the chimpanzees seemed irritable, at times tense, but not overly aggressive. For example, two females who normally would stay out of each other's way because they do not get along, had trouble doing so in the hall. A problem might ensue if the infant of the one naively crawled into the lap of the other. Rather than open conflict, however, this situation usually was resolved by the second female, even if she was dominant, moving out of the youngster's range. Alternatively, the mother might go over to her for a grooming session that would have been unthinkable on the island.

Males ready to challenge the existing order would "lie low" during the winters, frequently paying their respects to the alpha male by greeting him with bowing and pant-grunting. Opportunities to maneuver without being cornered, and to engage in one-on-one battles without all the others on the sidelines, would only open up after release onto the island. Within weeks trouble might start; almost all major power struggles in the Arnhem colony's history have occurred outdoors.

While the frequency of aggressive incidents went up less than two-fold in the winter hall compared to the island, their intensity barely changed, and we did not notice more injuries. The effect was very modest, given the crowding factor. Other kinds of behavior, such as submissive greetings and grooming, increased even more than aggression. Inasmuch as grooming and greeting serve appeasing and calming functions, they may have smoothed strained relationships. Most important, we found that some measures were affected during the first couple of weeks only. Their subsequent return to summer levels implied that the traditional test paradigm, in which animals or human volunteers are crowded for a brief period, measures initial reactions only, not any long-term effects of the situation.[34]

Because nothing remotely resembling the extreme violence and hypersexuality of the behavioral sink occurred with crowded chimpanzees, I developed an alternative theory. It is not a complete alternative, as it incorporates Calhoun's idea that crowding puts individuals and their social system under stress. The big difference is that the new hypothesis assumes that primates do not take this tension lying down: they utilize countermeasures to keep their society from collapsing. According to the theory, we expect the strongest crowding effects in "naive" populations facing this challenge for the very first time, and weaker effects in populations that have had time to adjust.

Preliminary support came from studies by Michael McGuire and coworkers on vervet monkeys, and from my own inspection of published reports on rhesus monkeys. Both comparisons concerned existing populations under free-ranging as well as captive conditions, and both indicated fairly uniform levels of aggression. Furthermore, crowding in a highly social nonprimate, the dwarf mongoose, was studied by Anne Rasa. She found a rise in aggression but also in affiliative behavior, resulting in stabilization of the social system. Possibly, then, coping mechanisms are not unique to primates.

The next logical step was to cast the net as widely as possible, and have a single investigator with a standardized method evaluate populations under various conditions. I selected groups of rhesus monkeys in small indoor pens and large outdoor enclosures at the Wisconsin Primate Center, in spacious outdoor corrals at the Yerkes Field Station, and monkeys set free on a large island off the coast of South Carolina. The four conditions differed dramatically in the number of monkeys per square meter: the island offered 646 times more surface area per individual than the small pens. And this is not even a fair comparison, as the island is covered with oak and palm trees: taking three-dimensional space into account, the crowding factor exceeded 6,000!

Peter Judge, an American primatologist, joined my team in 1989, as a traveling observer. Over the years he collected thousands of "focal follows" (observations on one monkey at a time) at the various sites, entering each one into a computer. Here is what we found.

*Minor aggression increase:* The average rate of aggressive acts per adult per hour ranged between 1.6 and 2.6 across conditions. Although the top rate was not reached under the most crowded condition, the general trend was for more aggression under higher densities. In view of the great variation in space, however, the effect on aggression was astonishingly small.

*Increased aggression intensity:* Under all conditions, most aggressive encounters consisted of mere threats and chases. Under crowded conditions, however, severe aggression, such as biting, increased more than the low-intensity forms and monkeys suffered more injuries as a result.

*Sex difference:* Only females showed the two trends above; male aggression and wounding were unaffected by spatial conditions. Perhaps the competition and the posturing that males must engage in to be successful is always high or at an upper limit. Females generally perform less aggression than males and often can avoid direct competition under low-density conditions. Unlike males, they have room for increase: their aggression level rises as they become more crowded.

*Increase in grooming and appeasement:* The hourly rate of grooming per adult ranged from 2.6 to 4.2 across conditions, increasing steadily in both sexes with population density. Submission and appeasement gestures also went up under crowded conditions.

These data suggest that if a monkey population lives long enough in a particular environment, aggression rates will stabilize at a species-typical level that varies little with density. The social system, with its matrilineal hierarchy and kinship network, remains essentially the same under all conditions, and apparently gives rise to similar amounts of social friction. In addition, monkeys groom each other more and show more appeasement gestures when densities are higher, which may dampen tensions. The one detrimental correlate of density—and a far from trivial one—is the rate of damaging fights. Yet, rather than being the product of density per se, fights may have more to do with reduced escape opportunities. If so, instead of concluding that crowding makes monkeys aggressive, it would be more appropriate to say that once aggression does erupt, the consequences are more serious when space is limited.

In further support of the idea that primates actively cope with environmentally induced stress, reconciliation is more common under crowded conditions. There is a serious catch here, however: should we not correct for the number of fights? And should we not also correct for the general level of affiliation in the group? There simply is more opportunity to run into a former opponent accidentally in a cramped space. After we had applied these corrections, three specifically designed studies failed to confirm an increase in conciliatory tendencies under crowded conditions. Angeline van Roosmalen and I compared the reconciliation rate of the Arnhem chimpanzees indoors and outdoors, Josep Call did the same for rhesus monkeys in a corral and in a more crowded enclosure, and Filippo Aureli journeyed to Indonesia to see if long-tailed macaques in the rain forest reconciled as often as those in captivity. All three studies failed to demonstrate environmental effects on peacemaking tendencies.

One way to look at this finding is from the perspective of the social cage and the ties that bind individuals together. If the sense of belonging to a group, and the value of particular relationships, are similar across conditions, there is no reason to resolve fights more often in a corral or enclosure than in the wild or on an island. The alternative to peacemaking, namely avoidance between aggressor and victim, may not be a realistic option under any condition. Judge speculated that low-ranking rhesus monkeys on the island cannot leave their group for too long as they are probably better off being the last to feed among their group mates than competing on their own with strangers (the island is occupied by many different groups). Similarly, Aureli speculated that the risk of encountering large cats or birds of prey in the forest prevents monkeys from leaving the protection of the group even if they have serious problems with some of their group mates.[35]

The picture emerging from this research is that of a close-knit social system that produces $x$ conflicts and requires $y$ reconciliations for its maintenance regardless of whether it is held together by a moat, a fence, dangerous predators, or hostile groups. The tighter the perimeter, the more work needs to be put into keeping tensions down, partly because it is harder to escape physical damage if they do erupt.

It is well to realize, though, that coping with stress is by no means

# WAR AND PEACE

Even in the closest group, conflicts are inevitable. One way to regulate and resolve them is through a clear-cut hierarchy. Nevertheless aggression may erupt, causing damage to valuable partnerships. To restore the peace, most primates engage in friendly reunions following fights.

Many animals have special signals to communicate who is dominant and who is subordinate. Two male chimpanzees demonstrate rank by creating an illusory size difference; the dominant walks upright with raised hair, the subordinate bows and pant-grunts. In reality, they are about the same size. *(Arnhem Zoo)*

As chimpanzees grow up, particularly the males, their youthful teasing gradually turns into serious challenges of the status quo. Here an adolescent swaggers in front of an adult female. In order to impress her, though, he still has to grow a little. She lashes out, hitting him in the stomach. *(Yerkes Field Station)*

An adolescent male chimpanzee (right) teases his adult sister to the point that she cannot stand it any longer and bursts out screaming and gesticulating. *(Yerkes Field Station)*

Luit, Nikkie, and Yeroen (left to right) during a strategic reconciliation. The alpha male, Nikkie, has been fighting with his ally, Yeroen, providing their rival, Luit, with an opening to show off his strength. Without Yeroen's help, Nikkie is unable to restore order. Here he reaches out to Yeroen to mend their alliance before putting Luit in his place. *(From* Chimpanzee Politics; *Arnhem Zoo)*

Chimpanzees may not kiss exactly as we do, but the principle is the same. A kiss on the mouth (here by a female to a male) is this ape's conciliatory gesture par excellence. *(Yerkes Field Station)*

Browse food at the center of this scene has created conflict between the two female chimpanzees on the extreme left and right. As soon as one of them screamed, the alpha male, Jimoh, arrived with both arms spread as if beseeching them to stop quarreling. Despite his small size, Jimoh is an effective arbitrator of disputes. *(Yerkes Field Station)*

Even though bonobos and chimpanzees are closely related, they make peace in a strikingly different way. Bonobos do so via sexual and erotic contact, with partners of both the opposite sex and their own. One adult male offers a brief genital massage to another after a fight between them. Two adult females bare their teeth and squeal during genito-genital rubbing, and two juveniles engage in tongue-kissing (next page). *(San Diego Zoo)*

Savanna baboons during a greeting ritual in which one male tries to mount the other. *(Gilgil, Kenya)*

Two Chinese golden monkey females holding hands after a fight. One female opens her mouth widely, a conciliatory expression of this species. *(Courtesy of RenMei Ren; Peking University, Beijing)*

Capuchin monkeys make it clear when expectations have been violated. A juvenile male (right), trying to get a close look at an infant, is pushed away by the mother. The juvenile screams in protest; his tantrum is sustained for more than a minute. Immediately afterward, the juvenile spreads his legs and shows his erect penis. The mother responds to this typical appeasement posture by inspecting his genitals. *(Yerkes Primate Center)*

Kinship bonds provide a common context of conflict. A rhesus mother grabs the head of her pubertal daughter, who came too close to her new offspring (barely visible on the mother's belly). Her daughter grins submissively in response. *(Wisconsin Primate Center)*

One juvenile long-tailed macaque confronts another with an unmistakable threat face: open mouth, staring eyes, raised eyebrows, and spread ears. *(Photograph by Han van Beek; Courtesy of University of Utrecht)*

The hold-bottom gesture is characteristic of reunions and reconciliations among stump-tailed macaques. *(Yerkes Field Station)*

A free-ranging rhesus family on Morgan Island in South Carolina. The differences between captive and free-ranging monkeys are sometimes exaggerated. It is easier for monkeys to avoid attack where there is more space, but the sources of conflict never disappear. Social behavior and group organization have been found to be essentially the same under both conditions.

The elegant and elusive muriqui, or woolly spider monkey, may be one of the most peaceful primates on earth. *(Fazenda Montes Claros, eastern Brazil)*

the same as getting rid of it; constant behavioral (and probably also physiological) countermeasures are necessary under crowded conditions. All of these techniques are part of the impressive adaptive potential of the primate order. I often feel that the traditional approach of measuring how often primates fight or groom can only reveal the tip of the iceberg. If these measures show little variation, it may be because they do not adequately probe the modus vivendi each population arrives at after having lived for generations in a particular environment. The notion of negotiation and integration, of animals adjusting their intentions and expectations to those of others, is probably essential to an understanding of how social arrangements specific to the circumstances are agreed upon.

The outcome may parallel cultural variation. Human populations with long crowding histories, such as the Japanese, the Javanese, and the Dutch, each in their own way emphasize tolerance, conformity, and consensus, whereas populations spread out over lands with empty horizons may be more individualistic, stressing privacy and freedom instead. Inasmuch as the balance between individual and community values affects moral decisions, morality is an integral part of the human response to the environment, and an important counterweight to the social decay predicted for crowded conditions. Adjusting the definition of right and wrong is one of the most powerful tools at the disposal of *Homo sapiens,* a species of born adaptation artists. Morality is not the same during war and peace, or during times of plenty and scarcity, or under high or low population densities. If certain conditions persist for a long time, the entire moral outlook of a culture will be affected.

Even if the capacity to cope with social stress reaches its absolute peak in our species, it evidently has a long evolutionary history. Where it ultimately comes from can perhaps be answered by fieldwork on other primates. It is in the natural habitat that their behavior evolved, and no artificial environment, however well conceived, can replace the plants on which the species foraged for millions of years, the predators it tried to escape, the climate it had to deal with, and other environmental factors. If captive studies evaluate the adaptive potential of a species, fieldwork illuminates the adaptive significance of its behavior. *Adaptive significance* is defined as the advantages associated with a behavior that may have promoted the transmission of that behavior from one generation to the next until it became widespread in the species. Ideally, its study requires pristine ecosystems that have retained all their original qualities. These are hard to find nowadays because of worldwide pollution and habitat destruction, although it is generally assumed that current primate habitats are close enough to the hypothetical originals to at least shed *some* light on evolutionary adaptation.[36]

One such site is a remnant forest of 800 hectares in eastern Brazil, atop a mountain covered with coffee plantations. For the past ten years Karen Strier has raced up and down the ridges and valleys, cutting her way through an entangled understory, in order to keep up with muriquis effortlessly swinging through the canopy. These monkeys, weighing up to 15 kilograms, are the New World equivalent of the mountain gorilla: they are the largest indigenous primates on their continent—and one of the most endangered, with perhaps fewer than five hundred left in the wild. They are also true gentle giants.

One might object that we have heard false claims of peacefulness before, but in twelve hundred hours of observation, Strier counted a total of only nine aggressive chases among muriquis. Although she, like any primatologist, expected males near a sexually attractive female to compete with one another, she found that male muriquis simply wait their turn without any scuffles among them. Females have full control, writes Strier in *Faces in the Forest:* "I have often seen a female avoid a [genital] inspection by one male only to present herself with suggestive grins and twitters to another."[37] Similar sexual patterns and tolerance among males have been observed at another Brazilian site.

Males spend much time together, often embracing in clusters of two or more individuals while uttering a sound called the chuckle. The virtual absence of aggression is explained by Strier as a combination of separate foraging, egalitarian relations between the sexes, and the huge testicles of male muriquis. The last factor suggests that the arena of sexual competition may have shifted from direct contest over who gets to mate to the production of enough sperm to win the fertilization race against the sperm of other males. After copulation the female's vagina is blocked by a plug of fresh ejaculate, which is unceremoniously removed by the next male, to be dropped to the ground or eaten before he himself mates with her. Why things evolved in this direction is ambiguous, but it is this sort of field research that may reveal under which conditions evolution discards aggression as a conflict-settling strategy.

It is evident that the problem with which we started—that of aggression and violence in human society—cannot be solved by giving men bigger testicles. We have to work within our biological endowment, which is quite different from that of muriquis and rodents in that it includes both a rather combative temperament and powerful checks and balances.[38] Debates such as the one surrounding the Goodwin affair—about whether it is biology or environment that holds the key to society's woes—start from the erroneous assumption that the dividing line between the two is as clear-cut as that between the natural and social sciences.

If we accept that the biology of a species includes its typical behavior and adaptability, human biology has everything to do with environment: not only has it been shaped by past environments, it also determines how we respond to current environments. Insofar as we share these responses with other primates, study of their group life under a variety of conditions may help us see where the remarkable human plasticity comes from, and what it takes to stay out of the behavioral sink.

## Community Concern

Socko, an adolescent chimpanzee at the Yerkes Field Station, teases Atlanta at his own peril. Atlanta may be fat and slow, but she makes up for it with an excellent memory. One moment, Socko throws dirt at her; more than an hour later, while Socko is absorbed in one of his exuberant games, we see Atlanta sneak up on him to grab an arm quickly and deliver a bite. Socko bursts out screaming, touching and squeezing the hurt body part. He runs to his "aunt" Peony and lets her take a look at it, all the while yelling indignantly. Peony gently takes the young male's arm and grooms him until he quiets down.

Still afraid of Atlanta, Socko walks in a wide arc around her to Rhett, her son. He tickles and wrestles with the juvenile, until both are rolling around over the ground uttering hoarse laughs. If it were not for the numerous quick glances he throws at Atlanta, one would think that Socko has forgotten the whole incident and is really enjoying himself. Instead, he is demonstrating good intentions and getting close to his opponent through contact with someone connected to her. Indeed, after a few minutes he moves from son to mother and sits down just out of reach of Atlanta, staring at something in the distance. Atlanta nods her head and shifts her position slightly in the way of a chimpanzee getting ready for a grooming session. Socko immediately responds by coming closer and picking through her hair. Soon Atlanta herself is grooming her tormentor.

Involvement of extra parties in the reconciliation process (Rhett in this instance) was first investigated by Peter Judge at the same field station but in a different species, the pigtail macaque. Like all macaques, pigtails form a matrilineal society in which female kin associate with and support one another. Apart from direct reconciliations between former combatants, Judge found that relatives of the victim tend to seek contact with the aggressor. A mother may approach the attacker of her daughter for what appears to be a reconciliation "on her offspring's behalf." If such so-called *triadic reconciliation* protects the victim's matriline against further hostilities, all of its members benefit, including the one who went to see the aggressor.[39]

Such may indeed be the case: tensions between individuals tend to generalize to their respective families. Cheney and Seyfarth noted in wild vervet monkeys that if the members of one matriline confront those of another, there is a reasonable chance that later in the day *other* members of the same matrilines will carry on the fight. These individuals must have watched the original incident and have developed hostile feelings toward the relatives of the monkeys who confronted their own kin. Triadic reconciliation, shown by vervets as well, is simply the other side of the same coin. Instead of getting even with a matriline that opposed their kin, they now try to mend relationships.

Reconciliation by proxy requires that monkeys know not just their own kin, but also to which kin group everyone else belongs. There are indeed growing indications that primates recognize the relationships around them. Crucial evidence has been produced by Verena Dasser, a Swiss primatologist. Showing macaques photographed portraits of adult females and juveniles of their group, she gave them the task of classifying the pictures on the basis of whether or not the depicted individuals were related to each other. Her subjects handled the task well, demonstrating that, like Socko, they recognized the mother-child connection.[40]

Knowledge of relationships in which they are not directly involved explains why fights among primates do not always remain restricted to the parties who started them, and why peacemaking may ripple well beyond a conflict's epicenter. Some species, such as the stumptailed macaque, even utter special squeals during reconciliation that alert and attract the entire group to what is going on. Yet there is probably no nonhuman primate that keeps a closer eye on reconciliations, and has a better grasp of their significance, than the chimpanzee. I have even seen members of this species react *negatively* when one among them offered an olive branch to another.

It is not unusual for females in a captive chimpanzee colony to band together to protect themselves against an abusive male. Given that such female coalitions can deliver quite a beating, the male is in an understandable hurry to get out of their way. He watches the other sex from a safe distance if he has been lucky enough to escape. Because none of the females matches him in strength and speed, their solidarity is crucial. During these standoffs, I have seen females turn all their pent-up fury against the first among them to approach the adversary to present her behind, or kiss him. Apparently, the other females were not finished with him yet and saw this one female's peace initiative as treason.

Much more commonly, though, responses to reconciliation are positive, even celebratory. After a major confrontation, juvenile chimpanzees may hang around unreconciled adult males, looking from the one to the other, only to jump with loud hooting on the males' backs as soon as they hug each other. And, as described before, adult females sometimes serve a catalytic function by bringing rival males together, an intervention that requires quite a degree of social awareness. Such mediation demonstrates the value chimpanzees attach to harmonious coexistence, as also reflected in the pandemonium and embracing by an entire colony following a dramatic reconciliation in its midst.

Triadic reconciliation, third-party mediation, and mass excitement about evaporated tensions suggest that monkeys and apes care about the state of relationships in their group or community. And not just their own private relationships, but also those around them. I have labeled this *community concern*. It is not that I believe monkeys and apes worry about the community as an abstract entity; they seem rather to strive for the kind of community that is in their own best interest. Insofar as the interests of different individuals overlap, community concern is a collective matter.

If a female chimpanzee, for example, confiscates the heavy rock in the hand of a male who is about to challenge a rival, or acts as go-between after an actual confrontation between the two, the whole group benefits even if she did so only for her own sake. It is not hard to see what she stands to gain by improved male relations. A group of savagely brutal and continuously edgy males poses a grave threat to every female and the offspring she is trying to raise. Moreover, in the wild, such males would have trouble presenting a united front to the outside, thus inviting raids and territorial takeovers by neighboring males.

If individual interests were to overlap completely, everything would be straightforward; there would be total agreement on the value of social harmony. But individuals have clashing interests as well. A young male's climbing of the rank order may stir up a lot of trouble, throwing the group into chaos for weeks or months on end. Or a matriarch may seek confrontation after confrontation with members of a higher-ranking matriline weakened by the death of its own matriarch. There is high tension between private goals relating to status and access to resources and common goals relating to the group's success in its particular ecological setting. When individual members jockey for the best social position, or for the largest share of food, the wider network of relations and the group as a whole may suffer.

This situation is dangerous, given the reliance of social primates on each other for defense against outside threats and for finding food and water. They can ill afford to be at war with the companions on whom they depend. Community concern takes as its starting point each organism's vested interest in a social environment optimal for survival and reproduction. The drawbacks of competition can be summarized as follows.[41]

*Harm to specific partnerships:* Social primates face the dilemma that they sometimes cannot win a fight without losing a friend. Profitable partnerships need to be nursed and protected, a process that requires the suppression of aggressive outbursts. In a few species these inhibitions are so powerful that resources are peacefully shared instead of generating competition. Occasionally even the best relationships explode, as described for the ruling alliance in Arnhem between Nikkie and Yeroen. Reconciliation serves to contain the damage.

*Bodily harm to others:* Companions who are limping, bleeding, and suffering from infections are of little use against predators or neighboring groups. Hyperaggressive individuals who cause frequent injuries compromise the quality of the social environment on which their very survival depends.

*Harm to group unity:* Given the value of the group, preservation of social cohesion serves each and every member. Exceptions do occur when individuals immigrate into a group and disrupt it by efforts to attain an advantageous position, or when resident members start a protracted dominance struggle. The payoffs of such activities are evidently high enough to outweigh social disruption. In the long run, however, members who regularly and seriously disrupt group life damage—along with the interests of everyone else—the interests of themselves and their relatives in the group.

Community concern can be defined, then, as *the stake each individual has in promoting those characteristics of the community or group that increase the benefits derived from living in it by that individual and its kin.* This definition does not hinge on conscious motives and intentions; it merely postulates benefits associated with particular behavior. It says that social animals have been selected to inhibit actions that may destroy group harmony and to strive for an optimal balance between peaceful coexistence and the pursuit of private interests. Whether animals realize how their behavior impacts the group as a whole is not critical for the evolution of community concern any more than that it is critical that animals know how sex relates to reproduction in order to pursue optimal reproductive strategies.

This said, motives and intentions are fascinating to contemplate, particularly because human morality can be looked at as community concern made explicit to the fullest degree. The higher a species' level of social awareness, the more completely its members realize how events around them ricochet through the community until they land at their own doorstep. This understanding allows them to become actively involved in shaping community characteristics. It starts with interest in relationships close to them (as between their kin and an attacker), then extends to more distant relationships that impact their lives (strained relations between rival dominants), and culminates in collective support for actions that enhance group harmony (arbitration by a central individual, who performs the so-called control role).

Not satisfied with a society fashioned by uncoordinated individual efforts, one of humanity's chief accomplishments is to translate egocentric community concerns into collective values. The desire for a modus vivendi fair to everyone may be regarded as an evolutionary outgrowth of the need to get along and cooperate, adding an ever-greater insight into the actions that contribute to or interfere with this objective. Our ancestors began to understand how to preserve peace and order—hence how to keep their group united against external threats—without sacrificing legitimate individual interests. They came to judge behavior that systematically undermined the social fabric as "wrong," and behavior that made a community worthwhile to live in as "right." Increasingly, they began to keep an eye on each other to make sure that their society functioned in the way they wanted it to function.

Conscious community concern is at the heart of human morality.

# 6

# CONCLUSION

I question whether the spiritual life
does not get its surest and most ample
guarantees when it is learned that the
laws and conditions of righteousness
are implicated in the working processes of the universe; when it is found
that man in his conscious struggles, in
his doubts, temptations and defeats, in
his aspirations and successes, is moved
on and buoyed up by the forces which
have developed nature.

*John Dewey*[1]

Even if animals other than ourselves act in ways tantamount to moral
behavior, their behavior does not necessarily rest on deliberations of
the kind we engage in. It is hard to believe that animals weigh their
own interests against the rights of others, that they develop a vision
of the greater good of society, or that they feel lifelong guilt about
something they should not have done.

## What Does It Take to Be Moral?

Members of some species may reach tacit consensus about what kind
of behavior to tolerate or inhibit in their midst, but without language
the principles behind such decisions cannot be conceptualized, let
alone debated. To communicate intentions and feelings is one thing;
to clarify what is right, and why, and what is wrong, and why, is quite
something else. Animals are no moral philosophers.

But then, how many *people* are? We have a tendency to compare
animal behavior with the most dizzying accomplishments of our race,
and to be smugly satisfied when a thousand monkeys with a thousand
typewriters do not come close to William Shakespeare. Is this a reason

to classify ourselves as smart, and animals as stupid? Are we not much of the time considerably less rational than advertised? People seem far better at explaining their behavior after the fact than at considering the consequences beforehand. There is no denying that we are creatures of intellect; it is also evident that we are born with powerful inclinations and emotions that bias our thinking and behavior.

A chimpanzee stroking and patting a victim of attack or sharing her food with a hungry companion shows attitudes that are hard to distinguish from those of a person picking up a crying child, or doing volunteer work in a soup kitchen. To classify the chimpanzee's behavior as based on instinct and the person's behavior as proof of moral decency is misleading, and probably incorrect. First of all, it is uneconomic in that it assumes different processes for similar behavior in two closely related species. Second, it ignores the growing body of evidence for mental complexity in the chimpanzee, including the possibility of empathy. I hesitate to call the members of any species other than our own "moral beings," yet I also believe that many of the sentiments and cognitive abilities underlying human morality antedate the appearance of our species on this planet.

The question of whether animals have morality is a bit like the question of whether they have culture, politics, or language. If we take the full-blown human phenomenon as a yardstick, they most definitely do not. On the other hand, if we break the relevant human abilities into their component parts, some are recognizable in other animals (see page 211).

*Culture:* Field primatologists have noticed differences in tool use and communication among populations of the same species. Thus, in one chimpanzee community all adults may crack nuts with stones, whereas another community totally lacks this technology. Group-specific signals and habits have been documented in bonobos as well as chimpanzees. Increasingly, primatologists explain these differences as learned traditions handed down from one generation to the next.[2]

*Language:* For decades apes have been taught vocabularies of hand signals (such as American Sign Language) and computerized symbols. Koko, Kanzi, Washoe, and several other anthropoids have learned to effectively communicate their needs and desires through this medium.

It is hard to imagine human morality without the following tendencies and capacities found also in other species.

**Sympathy-Related Traits**
Attachment, succorance, and emotional contagion.
Learned adjustment to and special treatment of the disabled and injured.
Ability to trade places mentally with others: cognitive empathy.*

**Norm-Related Characteristics**
Prescriptive social rules.
Internalization of rules and anticipation of punishment.*

**Reciprocity**
A concept of giving, trading, and revenge.
Moralistic aggression against violators of reciprocity rules.

**Getting Along**
Peacemaking and avoidance of conflict.
Community concern and maintenance of good relationships.*
Accommodation of conflicting interests through negotiation.

* It is particularly in these areas—empathy, internalization of rules and sense of justice, and community concern—that humans seem to have gone considerably further than most other animals.

*Politics:* Tendencies basic to human political systems have been observed in other primates, such as alliances that challenge the status quo, and tit-for-tat deals between a leader and his supporters. As a result, status struggles are as much popularity contests as physical battles.

In each of these domains, nonhuman primates show impressive intelligence yet do not integrate information quite the way we do. The utterances of language-trained apes, for example, show little if any evidence of grammar. The transmission of knowledge from one generation to the next is rarely, if ever, achieved through active teaching. And it is still ambiguous how much planning and foresight, if any, go into the social careers of monkeys and apes.

Despite these limitations, I see no reason to avoid labels such as "primate culture," "ape language," or "chimpanzee politics" as long as it is understood that this terminology points out fundamental similarities without in any way claiming *identity* between ape and human behavior. Such terms serve to stimulate debate about how much or little animals share with us. To focus attention on those aspects in which we differ—a favorite tactic of the detractors of the evolutionary perspective—overlooks the critical importance of what we have in common. Inasmuch as shared characteristics most likely derive from the common ancestor, they probably laid the groundwork for much that followed, including whatever we claim as uniquely ours. To disparage this common ground is a bit like arriving at the top of a tower only to declare that the rest of the building is irrelevant, that the precious concept of "tower" ought to be reserved for the summit.

While making for good academic fights, semantics are mostly a waste of time. Are animals moral? Let us simply conclude that they occupy a number of floors of the tower of morality. Rejection of even this modest proposal can only result in an impoverished view of the structure as a whole.

## Floating Pyramids

It is hard to take care of others without taking care of oneself first. Not that people need a mansion and a fat bank account before they can be altruistic, but certainly we do not expect much assistance from someone in poor health without the most basic means of subsistence. Paradoxically, therefore, altruism starts with an obligation to oneself.

The form of altruism closest to egoism is care of the immediate family. In species after species, we see signs of kin selection: altruism is disproportionally directed at relatives. Humans are no exception. A father returning home with a loaf of bread will ignore the plight of whomever he meets on his path; his first obligation is to feed his family. This pattern of course says nothing about the inherent value of his own children compared to the others living in the neighborhood. If his family were well fed and everybody else were starving, it would be a different matter—but if his family is as hungry as the rest, the man has no choice.

The circle of altruism and moral obligation widens to extended family, clan, and group, up to and including tribe and nation. Benevolence decreases with increasing distance between people. Going against the grain of this natural gradient meets with sharp disapproval. Spies are despised precisely because they help an out-group at the expense of the in-group. Similarly, we are shocked that people under the East German communist regime informed on parents and spouses, putting nation before family. And if the father in the above example had come home empty-handed because of sympathy for strangers, his family would have shown very little understanding.

Altruism is bound by what one can afford. The circle of morality reaches out farther and farther only if the health and survival of the innermost circles are secure. For this reason, rather than an expanding circle I prefer the image of a floating pyramid. The force lifting the pyramid out of the water—its buoyancy—is provided by the available resources. Its size above the surface reflects the extent of moral inclusion. The higher the pyramid rises, the wider the network of aid and obligation. People on the brink of starvation can afford only a tiny tip of the moral pyramid: it will be every man for himself. It is only under the most extreme conditions, however, perhaps like those described for the Ik by Colin Turnbull, that such "lifeboat ethics" apply.

As soon as the immediate threat to survival is removed, members of our species take care of kin and build exchange networks with fellow human beings both inside and outside their group. Compared

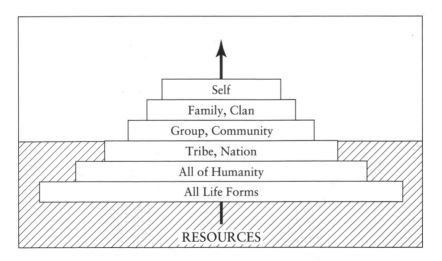

The expanding circle of human morality is actually a floating pyramid. Altruism is spread thinner the farther away we get from our immediate family or clan. Its reach depends on resources and affordability; the pyramid's buoyancy determines how much of it will emerge from the water. The moral inclusion of outer circles is thus constrained by obligations to the inner ones.

to other primates, we are a remarkably giving species. Moral inclusion does not imply, though, that every person is valued exactly the same. In principle they may be equal, but in practice human kindness and cooperativeness are spread thinner the farther we get from kin and community.

The ideal of universal brotherhood is unrealistic in that it fails to distinguish between these innermost and outermost circles of obligation. The American human ecologist Garrett Hardin disdainfully refers to indiscriminate kindness as "promiscuous altruism." If altruism evolved because of a need to cooperate against hostile forces, solidarity with what is close against what is distant is an integral part. As observed by the French anarchist Pierre-Joseph Proudhon more than a century ago: "If everyone is my brother, I have no brothers."[3]

Depending on what a society can afford, then, the moral pyramid may swell to giant size, in principle embracing all of humanity, but always retaining its fundamental shape. Life forms other than our own may be included. Recent studies of animal behavior, mine included, provide ample reason to reconsider the way animals are used for science, entertainment, food, education, and other purposes. We need to re-evaluate traditional attitudes developed over a long history without realistic alternatives, and without awareness of the sensibilities and cognitive abilities of animals. This process is well under way at zoos and research institutions, and in society at large.

Because I feel close to the animals with whom I work, I welcome this development. I certainly do not subscribe to the position that we have a God-given right to do with other animals whatever pleases us. If apes, elephants, dolphins, dogs, and the rest indeed possess the intelligence and incipient morality we have talked about, how could we ever subscribe to Descartes' view of them as machines unable to suffer and therefore unworthy of compassion?

At the same time, I must express discomfort with attempts to phrase these issues in terms of *rights*. Emphasis on autonomy rather than on connection has given rise to a discourse that is cold, dogmatic, and leaning toward an absolutism that fails to do justice to the gray areas of which human morality is composed. The ultimate result is a call for the abolition of *all* use of *all* animals under *all* circumstances, from hunting to meat consumption, from keeping them in zoos to having them work on the farm. In the process, we sometimes ignore our first obligation, which is to fellow human beings.

A particularly radical proposal is that of Paola Cavalieri and Peter Singer. Together with a number of prominent scientists, in a volume entitled *The Great Ape Project,* they advocate a "community of equals" consisting of apes and humans. They see no good reason why animals as close and similar to us as the great apes should fall into a different moral category. Why not elevate them to the same legal status as their bipedal relatives?

The logical flaw in this proposal is its blatant anthropocentrism. How can one make similarity to a particular species the touchstone of moral inclusion without ranking that species above the rest? If rights increase in proportion to the number of humanlike characteristics possessed by a species, it is hard to escape the conclusion that humans themselves deserve the most rights of all.

A second problem is that rights are normally accompanied by responsibilities, which cannot possibly apply to apes. The authors reply that since mentally retarded people are exempt from this linkage, why not apes?

To my mind, Cavalieri and Singer's plea reflects profound condescension. Have we really reached the point at which respect for apes is most effectively advocated by depicting them as retarded people in furry suits? And while we are at it, why should we not then classify a baboon as a mentally challenged ape? It seems endless: once apes are granted equal status on such questionable grounds, there is no way to keep out cockroaches. My own feeling is that we must take the inherent beauty and dignity of animals as our starting point.

No matter how well intentioned the concerns of animal rights advocates, they are often presented in a manner infuriating to anyone concerned about *both* people and animals. Human morality as we know it would unravel very rapidly indeed if it failed to place human life at its core. Again, there is no judgment here about the objective value of our lives compared to the lives of other creatures. Personally, I do not feel superior to a butterfly, let alone to a cat or a whale. But who can deny our species the right to construct its moral universe from a human perspective?

It will be up to society to decide whether it will continue to support certain kinds of research on certain kinds of animals. It is already common practice in biomedical research that if a particular experiment on monkeys is considered no more effective than on rats, the monkey study will never be conducted. Similarly, if an experiment on chimpanzees is judged no more effective than one on monkeys, the first study will simply not take place.

Unfortunately for the animals, they are not the only ones hanging in the balance. Human lives are also at stake. Anyone who enters a hospital or picks up a prescription at the pharmacy makes use of animal testing. Few people consider it trivial to fight diseases such as AIDS, that affect millions. If a vaccine could be developed without using animals, of course that would be preferable. But there are no signs that this stage will be reached anytime soon. Choices must be made, and these get more difficult the more complex the life forms serving as guinea pigs.

How much do we care and what can we afford? There are excellent reasons to insist on respect and concern for animals that serve the human cause. Apes do warrant special consideration. We should either phase out experiments on certain species altogether, or if humanity cannot forgo the benefits derived from them, we must at least enrich and enhance their lives in captivity and reduce their suffering. Phrasing the issue, as I do here, in terms of our *responsibility* to other life forms leaves the moral pyramid intact, and may lead to less radical conclusions than phrasing it in terms of rights. All the same, it is no easier to resolve the dilemmas facing us.[4]

## A Hole in the Head

On September 13 of 1848 Phineas Gage, while leveling terrain for a railroad track in New England, suffered a hideous accident that would make him a neurological *cause célèbre*. Owing to a momentary distraction, Gage triggered a blast while leaning over a hole filled with explosive powder. The pointed tamping iron that he held in his hands was hurled like a rocket straight through his left eye, brain, and skull. Incredibly, Gage was only briefly stunned. He instantly regained consciousness and was able to walk and talk immediately afterward. The meter-long iron lay in the sand, meters away.

The twenty-five-year-old foreman recovered completely, retained all elementary mental functions, and remained able-bodied for the rest of his life. His speech was normal, he absorbed new information as before, and he showed no lapses of memory. However, his personality changed. From a pleasant and reliable fellow, popular among his peers, he turned into someone who could not hold a job because he had lost all respect for social conventions. He would lie and curse uncontrollably. Perhaps the greatest change was that his sense of responsibility vanished: he could not be trusted to honor commitments. According to his physician, the equilibrium between intellectual faculties and lower impulses had been disturbed by the accident.

## THE FAR SIDE By GARY LARSON

Larson 12-2

"Fair is fair, Larry . . . We're out of food, we drew straws — you lost."

Lifeboat ethics with dog (1981 The Far Side cartoon by Gary Larson is reprinted by permission of Chronicle Features, San Francisco, California. All rights reserved.)

The neurologist Hanna Damasio and her coworkers recently reported on an inspection of Gage's skull and the tamping iron—both preserved in a museum at Harvard University. They made computer models of the brain damage. Apparently the transformation from an upright citizen into a man with serious character flaws had been brought about by lesions in the ventromedial frontal region of his brain. This pattern fits that of a dozen other brain-damaged patients known to science who have intact logical and memory functions but compromised abilities to manage personal and social affairs. It is as if the moral compass of these people has been demagnetized, causing it to spin out of control.

What this incident teaches us is that conscience is not some disembodied concept that can be understood only on the basis of culture and religion. Morality is as firmly grounded in neurobiology as anything else we do or are. Once thought of as purely spiritual matters, honesty, guilt, and the weighing of ethical dilemmas are traceable to specific areas of the brain. It should not surprise us, therefore, to find animal parallels. The human brain is a product of evolution. Despite its larger volume and greater complexity, it is fundamentally similar to the central nervous system of other mammals.

We seem to be reaching a point at which science can wrest morality from the hands of philosophers. That this is already happening—albeit largely at a theoretical level—is evident from recent books by, among others, Richard Alexander, Robert Frank, James Q. Wilson, and Robert Wright. The occasional disagreements within this budding field are far outweighed by the shared belief that evolution needs to be part of any satisfactory explanation of morality.

Gardener and garden are one and the same. The fact that the human moral sense goes so far back in evolutionary history that other species show signs of it plants morality firmly near the center of our much-maligned nature. It is neither a recent innovation nor a thin layer that covers a beastly and selfish makeup.

It takes up space in our heads, it reaches out to fellow human beings, and it is as much a part of what we are as the tendencies that it holds in check.

# NOTES

## Prologue

1. Huxley, 1989 (1894), p. 83.
2. Williams, 1988, p. 438.
3. Dewey, 1993 (1898), p. 98.

## 1. Darwinian Dilemmas

1. Dawkins, 1976, p. 3.
2. Gould, 1980, p. 261.
3. Dettwyler, 1991, p. 382.
4. Kurland, 1977, p. 81.
5. Midgley, 1991, p. 8.
6. Wilson, 1975, p. 562.
7. According to Kenneth Lux, opposition to welfare assistance (the so-called Poor Laws) was most evident in the second edition of Malthus' *Essay on the Principle of Population* and was expunged from subsequent editions: "A man who is born into a world . . . if he cannot get subsistence from his parents on whom he has a just demand and if the society does not want his labour, has no claim of right to the smallest portion of food, and, in fact, has no business to be where he is. At nature's mighty feast there is no vacant cover for him. She tells him to be gone,

and will quickly execute her own orders, if he does not work upon the compassion of some of her guests. If these guests get up and make room for him, other intruders immediately appear demanding the same favour" (quoted in Lux, 1990, pp. 34–35).

8. Rockefeller quoted in Lux, 1990, p. 148.
9. History is not as simple as presented here. Charles Darwin, Alfred Russell Wallace, Thomas Henry Huxley, and Herbert Spencer each took a different position with regard to the (im)possibility of an evolved morality. Well-documented accounts of this early debate may be found in Richards (1987) and Cronin (1991). See also Nitecki and Nitecki (1993).
10. Yerkes and Yerkes, 1935, p. 1024.
11. Gene-centric sociobiologists often speak of "a gene for behavior $x$," regardless of what is known about the heritability of behavior $x$ (usually, little or nothing). In reality, each gene acts in conjunction with hundreds of others. So every behavior is likely to depend on a wide range of genetic factors. Even if we grant gene-centric sociobiologists that their one-gene–one-behavior scheme is not to be taken literally—that it is a mere shorthand for discussion—it is advisable to balance it with another generalization, one that is at least as close to the truth: "Every character of an organism is affected by all genes and every gene affects all characters" (Mayr, 1963, p. 164).
12. Apparently Dawkins is not convinced that we are born selfish, in the vernacular sense. In response to Midgley (1979) he admits that selfish-gene rhetoric may well be out of touch with actual human motives: "To the extent that I know about human psychology (a rather small extent), I doubt if our emotional nature is, as a matter of fact, fundamentally selfish" (Dawkins, 1981, p. 558).

This is a message to bear in mind, for it certainly is not evident in the author's writings. A general problem with pop sociobiology is that complex issues are compressed to such a degree that even if the author is fully aware of what is left out, the reader has no way of knowing. The simplifications are then perpetuated ad nauseam by less-informed writers until they haunt the field in general and must be countered as if they represented serious ideas (Kitcher, 1985).

In *The Ethical Primate,* Midgley (1994, p. 17) has reiterated her views on the pitfalls and illusions of reductionist science, giving scathing attention to sociobiology's forays into the psychological domain: "Darwinism is often seen—and indeed is often presented—not as a wide-ranging set of useful suggestions about our mysterious history, but as a slick, reductive ideology, requiring us, in fact, to dismiss as illusions matters which our experience shows to be real and serious."

13. Hamilton, 1971, p. 83; Dawkins, 1976, p. 215.
14. Williams, 1989, p. 210.

15. Williams, 1989, p. 210. One may wonder if Williams really meant to condemn Mother Nature as a wicked old witch. Perhaps, instead of *immoral,* he intended to say that nature is *amoral,* which is of course exactly what Huxley meant by "morally indifferent." However, Williams makes it quite clear that he sees a contrast between the biological and the physical order: "I would concede that moral indifference might aptly characterize the physical universe. For the biological world a stronger term is needed" (p. 180). When he distinguishes being struck by lightning (physical process) from being struck by a rattlesnake (animal action), Williams calls the behavior of the snake and other animals "grossly immoral." In normal usage this judgment would imply disapproval, yet he does not believe that an animal can be held accountable for its actions. But since there can be no morality without individual responsibility, Williams selected the wrong term: he does mean that nature is amoral, and his whole tirade unravels.

16. NSF Task Force, Newsletter of the Animal Behavior Society, vol. 36 (4).

17. Frank, 1988, p. 21.

18. The only similar report that I am aware of concerns captive dolphins. Two females showed interest in the labor of a third, remaining close to her until the fetus was expelled. The older of the two attending females and the mother then swam under the baby dolphin, one on each side. Had the infant not been able to reach the surface by itself, the two females most likely would have lifted it between their dorsal fins (McBride and Hebb, 1948).

19. Gould, 1988, title.

20. Kropotkin, 1972 (1902), pp. 18, 59.

21. To say, as Lorenz (1966) did, that animals rarely kill members of their own species because then the species would die out, assumes that animals care about the well-being of their group or species. Such naive group selectionism was dismissed by Williams (1966), who argued that variants pursuing this goal would rapidly lose out to variants placing private interests first. Natural selection favors individuals who procreate more successfully than others; the interests of groups or species are relevant only insofar as they overlap with those of individuals.

    Extreme sacrifices, however, such as human warriors endangering or giving their lives in combat, pose a serious challenge to this line of thought. Do these warriors not place the good of their group above private interests? To explain their behavior, it has been speculated that status and privilege accrue to surviving heroes, or to the families of those who actually lost their lives. If this is indeed the case, heroic acts on behalf of the community may increase the warrior's reproduction or the survival of his offspring, an argument attributed to R. A. Fisher by Alexander (1987, p. 170). Note, however, how this explanation injects moral mechanisms, such as approbation and gratitude, into a discussion about the origin of morality, creating a rather circular argument. Furthermore, it is hard to believe that, in practice, the families of fallen soldiers are better off than the families of soldiers who return alive from battle.

22. Pronouncements of the demise of group selection theory have been premature. Selection at the level of groups probably operates along with selection at the level of individuals and genes. Such "nested" selection models by no means introduce noncompetitive principles; rather, they transpose conflict up one level, from individual against individual to group against group (Wilson, 1983; Wilson and Sober, 1994).

23. Darwin, 1981 (1871), vol. 1, p. 166.

24. De Mandeville, 1966 (1714), pp. 18–24.

25. Smith, 1982 (1776), bk. 3, p. 423.

26. Smith, 1937 (1759), p. 9.

27. Ethologists distinguish sharply between proximate and ultimate causes. *Proximate causes* concern learning, experience, and the direct circumstances and motivations underlying behavior. *Ultimate causes* promoted a behavior in the course of evolution. If a behavior assists survival and reproduction, for example because it repels predators or attracts mates, this is the ultimate reason for its existence. Since evolution takes place on a timescale that escapes perception, only proximate causes exist in the minds of animals and most humans. Students of evolutionary biology are unique in that they care about ultimate causes.

   Unfortunately, proximate and ultimate levels are frequently confused, particularly when the function of a behavior seems so obvious that it is hard to imagine that the actors are oblivious to it. Popular nature documentaries contribute to the mixup by describing animal behavior in ultimate terms. They will explain that two male walruses fight over the right to impregnate a female, whereas these males neither know nor care about what happens in the female's womb after they have mated.

28. De Waal and van Roosmalen, 1979, p. 62.

29. Once, after I had explained these theories to a political scientist with antisociobiological sentiments, he commented with some *Schadenfreude,* "Oh, but then you are getting into exactly the same mess we are in." He meant that instead of having the neat, crisp, reductionist picture of human behavior advertised by the early sociobiologists, we are introducing so many layers and refinements that the complexity may begin to overwhelm us as does the hodgepodge of theories confronting the social sciences. The big difference, of course, is that biologists have a single core theory within which everything must somehow make sense, whereas the social sciences lack such an integrative framework.

30. The first use of the word "ethology" in its current meaning was a reaction against the laboratory-based biological science of the influential Baron Cuvier. Cuvier's most important adversary in the debates at the

Académie des Sciences was Etienne Geoffroy-Saint-Hillaire, the father of Isidore, who proposed the ethology label. The term referred to the study of animals as living beings in nature, as opposed to the Cuvierian cadavers that smelled of formaldehyde. At approximately the same time, however, the renowned German evolutionist Ernst Haeckel coined *Ökologie* (which became the English "ecology") for the relation between the organism and its environment. This term immediately overshadowed "ethology" and generated confusion about the exact meaning of the latter. Jaynes (1988) believes that the closeness in meaning, combined with the association of early French ethology with Lamarckism, prevented ethology from developing into a significant movement in the nineteenth century.

31. Age-specific symbol-learning sensitivity may extend to nonhuman primates. When Sue Savage-Rumbaugh tried to teach symbols to a fully adult bonobo, she met with little success. The ape, despite being cooperative and bright, learned only seven symbols; her two-and-a-half-year-old son, on the other hand, learned from just sitting in on the training sessions. Without instruction or reward, he picked up the use of many symbols and comprehended hundreds of spoken English words (Savage-Rumbaugh et al., 1986).

32. Special learning abilities or sensitivities involved in the acquisition of moral consciousness have also been discussed by Lewin (1977), Simon (1990), and Wilson (1993, pp. 148–152).

33. Well-known ethologists, such as Wolfgang Wickler, Irenäus Eibl-Eibesfeldt, and Konrad Lorenz, have extensively speculated in popular books about the biological roots of human ethics. It must have been increased awareness of the naturalistic fallacy that compelled Wickler (1981) to add a subtitle to the second edition of his best-seller, *Die Biologie der Zehn Gebote* (The biology of the Ten Commandments), which literally reads *Warum die Natur für uns kein Vorbild ist* (Why nature does not serve us as example). This literature was critically reviewed by the late German anthropologist and primatologist Christian Vogel (1985, 1988).

34. The fatal incident in the Arnhem colony was interpreted as political murder. It resulted from a collapse of the ruling coalition because of the leader's failure to grant sexual privileges to his ally. In the resulting power vacuum, another male suddenly rose to the top. He paid for this ten weeks later when the two frustrated former allies banded together at night to injure him so badly that his life could not be saved (de Waal, 1986a; 1989a, pp. 59–69).

Since this was the very first report of such severe fighting within an established group, it may be tempting to dismiss it as a product of captivity. Recently, however, a similar event was described by Goodall (1992) for wild chimpanzees. The reigning alpha male fell from power after a gang attack that resulted in serious damage to his scrotum (the ensuing infection might have killed him had it not been for veterinary intervention). This intracommunity aggression was by far the most savage observed during thirty years at Gombe; such belligerence is more typical between communities (Goodall, 1986).

35. Lorenz, 1966 (1963), p. 167.
36. Hume, 1978 (1739), p. 469.
37. A wide range of views exists on biological constraints on morality. My personal opinion is that the evolutionary process provided us with the ability and the prerequisites for morality, as well as with a set of basic needs and desires that morality needs to take into account. The moral decisions themselves, however, are left to be negotiated among the members of society, hence are by no means specified by nature. Ruse (1986), in contrast, believes that "ought" feelings, such as a felt duty to assist others, have been put in place directly by natural selection: "We are talking of more than a mere feeling that we want to help others. It will be an *innately based sense of obligation* towards others" (p. 222; italics added). These differences of opinion need to be worked out within the framework of evolutionary ethics, the basic tenet of which is that the moral sense is not antithetical to but an integrated part of human nature (Ruse, 1988; Wilson, 1993).

## 2. Sympathy

1. Darwin,, 1981 (1871), vol. 1, pp. 71–72.
2. Wispé, 1991, p. 80.
3. On the basis of this incident, Porter (1977, p. 10) comments that he would not automatically discount the numerous reports of people who claim to have been saved by porpoises or some of the smaller whales. Accounts of Cetacea helping humans generally describe one of the following: (a) a drowning person is lifted to the surface; (b) a boat or ship is guided to safety (around submerged rocks, out of a storm); or (c) a swimmer is protected against sharks by a dolphin cordon. Reviews of both interspecific and intraspecific succorant behavior of Cetacea may be found in Caldwell and Caldwell (1966), Connor and Norris (1982), and Pilleri (1984).
4. Porter, 1977, pp. 10, 13.
5. Eibl-Eibesfeldt, 1990, p. 156.
6. Did Yeroen intentionally manipulate the other male's perception, or had he simply learned that limping reduces the risk of attack? The first possibility would have required him to imagine how he himself looked from the other's perspective; the second would have required little else than a rewarding experience during a period when he had been limping of necessity.

Even if it is increasingly believed that great apes possess a capacity for intentional deception, it is impossible to prove this capability in each instance. Moreover, the false distress described for a female gorilla (Hediger, 1955, pp. 150–151) and for Yeroen (de Waal, 1982, pp. 47–48) is paralleled by similar occurrences in species supposedly lower on the cognitive scale. Dog owners tell me of faked limps by pets trying to get attention, and Caine and Reite (1983, p. 25) describe a female macaque with signs of malingering: "Whenever she was placed in her social group she limped badly, although, upon examination, no evidence of injury or disease was found. Furthermore, the limping disappeared when the animal was housed alone."

This female's behavior may have had more to do with how veterinarians treat limping monkeys than with the reaction of conspecifics. Perhaps preferring to be alone, she may have learned from a real physical trauma in the past how to get people to remove her from the group. If so, Yeroen's deception differed from this monkey's, as well as from that of the gorilla and the dogs mentioned previously, in at least one aspect: it was intended to appeal to members of his own species.

7. Lieberman, 1991, p. 169.
8. Play inhibitions obviously are not limited to primates. As the owner of any large dog can testify, they are even more dramatic in animals such as carnivores that are equipped to do horrible damage in a fraction of a second. The acquisition of such inhibitions was observed in two female black bear cubs, Kit and Kate, raised by Ellis Bacon for a wildlife project in the Smoky Mountains. Bear cubs, although very appealing, can be quite aggressive in play and enter wrestling matches with an energy and force that totally overwhelm a human partner. Human skin being paper-thin compared to that of a bear, the legs and arms of the cubs' caretakers were covered with scratches, bites, and bruises. A dramatic, welcome change in play style occurred, however, when the cubs were approximately eight months old: "They acted as if they discovered he [Bacon] was different from a bear: there was a rapid decline of inadvertent scratching and biting, and they distinguished clothing (which was still fair game) from flesh. From then on, with the exception of occasional dominance testing, Ellis considered himself physically safe in their presence. In contrast, the cubs were still very rough with each other in play or fights" (Burghardt, 1992, p. 375).

Moss (1988, p. 163) describes how the world's most formidable play partner, a bull elephant, learned to downsize in order to have fun: "Earlier in the year I had seen a large adult bull, Mark, lie down in an upright position in order to spar with another bull who was considerably smaller than he was. They had sparred playfully and briefly with both standing, but the young bull, M140, turned away, and although Mark followed, M140 would not spar with him again. Then Mark sank down on his knees with his rear legs out behind him, and as soon as M140

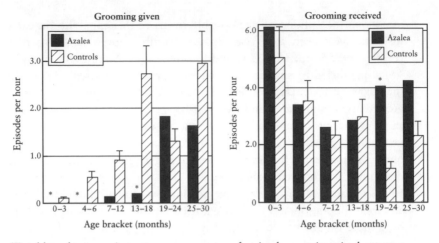

Total hourly grooming rates per age group for Azalea, a trisomic rhesus monkey, and the mean (plus standard error of mean, SEM) for twenty-three normal female peers of the same age (controls). Asterisks denote periods in which Azalea ranked at the extreme top or bottom of the distribution.

saw him he came straight over and started sparring. M140 was now the taller of the two."

9. After having devised this example, I heard from Sue Savage-Rumbaugh a striking story about an orangutan named Marie who had lost both arms early in life. Marie made precisely the kind of connection between her own body and that of another individual required for cognitive empathy. Savage-Rumbaugh, one of whose fingers is missing its tip, was grooming and talking to Marie, when the latter suddenly noticed the stumpy finger. She inspected it closely, holding Savage-Rumbaugh's hand with one of her feet. Marie then brought Sue's finger into contact with the stump of one of her own arms. She looked questioningly into her companion's eyes as if wondering if she saw the same connection.

10. As can be seen from the accompanying figure, Azalea's grooming activity was far below that of her peers until the age of 18 months. She received an average amount of grooming until this age, after which she began to receive substantially more than her peers. It is not clear whether these two developments were related. Data from de Waal et al. (1995).

11. Fedigan and Fedigan, 1977, p. 215.

12. In the sort of experiment that, in the words of Silk (1992a), makes one wonder about taxonomic bounds for compassion, Berkson experimentally blinded a number of young rhesus monkeys in a free-ranging population. These young monkeys, groping for roots as they went, had great difficulty in finding their way through the mangrove. Their mothers stopped often and waited for them, and the group as a whole was extra vigilant and alarmed if the blind infants were approached by human

observers. "The blind babies were never left completely alone. . . . It is remarkable that there was always another animal in the group near them. In addition, two individuals who were unrelated to the mothers often stayed with the blind infants during this time" (Berkson, 1973, p. 585).

13. Scanlon, 1986, p. 107.

14. It is surprising how little we know about precisely which situations trigger succorance and which generate intolerance. Pavelka (1993, p. 92) describing free-ranging Japanese macaques, comments that incapacitated group members may meet with hostility. This was the reaction to staggering and stumbling individuals who were recovering from anesthesia after routine veterinary checkups. Even though the mothers would protect their drowsy infants, they sometimes bit and shook their offspring as if punishing them for inappropriate behavior. Over the years the monkeys became used to the sight of half-sedated group mates, and aggressivity toward them diminished.

15. Moss, 1988, p. 73.

16. Goodall, 1990, p. 196.

17. Flint was perhaps too old to be adopted by others. Younger orphans are frequently taken care of by female relatives, sometimes by unrelated females, and enjoy remarkable tolerance from adult males (Goodall, 1986, pp. 102–103; Nishida, 1979, p. 106). For a review of adoption in nonhuman primates see Thierry and Anderson (1986).

In the Arnhem chimpanzee colony, Fons lost his mother when he was four. Soon afterward he was seen associating with adult males, particularly his presumed father, Luit, who became his mighty protector. Fons resembled Luit even at an early age (de Waal, 1982, p. 75), but he looks, acts, and sounds uncannily like the older male now that he is fully grown. Unfortunately, Luit died before the colony could be subjected to a paternity analysis.

18. Smuts, 1985, p. 23.

19. No agreed-upon explanation for human weeping exists. Outside the primate order, copious tear production is associated with marine habitats (probably because of the increased need for salt excretion). Thus, fresh-water crocodiles do not shed tears, whereas sea crocodiles do. Tears can also be observed in sea otters and seals. Because of this link with marine ecology, proponents of the "aquatic ape" theory view human tears as evidence that there must have been an aquatic phase during human evolution (Morgan, 1982).

Accounts of tears in primates other than humans are extremely rare, and need to be considered with reservation. Most likely, people *expect* tears, hence project or imagine them. The only report by an experienced primatologist is in Fossey (1983). Despite my profound skepticism— could the "tears" have been due to excessive perspiration?—I present it here because Fossey was certainly aware of the extraordinary nature of her observation.

The account concerns Coco, a young mountain gorilla whose entire family had been wiped out by poachers. Following weeks of mistreatment and life in a tiny box, the young gorilla was claimed by Fossey and brought to her camp. There Coco for the first time saw her natural environment again. "Coco sat on my lap calmly for a few minutes before walking to a long bench below the window that overlooked nearby slopes of Visoke. With great difficulty she climbed onto the bench and gazed out at the mountain. Suddenly she began to sob and shed actual tears, something I have never seen a gorilla do before or since. When it finally grew dark she curled up in a nest of vegetation I had made for her and softly whimpered herself to sleep" (p. 110).

20. Yerkes and Yerkes, 1929, p. 297.
21. Temerlin, 1975, p. 165.
22. Boesch, 1992, p. 149.
23. The German naturalist Bernhard Grzimek was once attacked by an adult male chimpanzee, an event he was lucky to survive. When his rage had died down, the ape seemed very concerned about the outcome. He approached the professor and tried, with his fingers, to close and press together the edges of the worst wounds. Lorenz (1967, p. 215), who described this incident, adds that "it is highly characteristic of that dauntless scientist that he permitted the ape to do so."
24. The accompanying figure shows data from de Waal and Aureli (forthcoming) concerning 1,321 spontaneous aggressive incidents in an outdoor colony of twenty chimpanzees at the Yerkes Field Station. The graph demonstrates that immediately after fights (in the first two minutes) bystanders often make contact with participants in the conflict, particularly with the recipients of serious aggression.
25. Skinner (1990) saw both cognitive psychology and creationism as heavily influenced by religion. This element is obvious enough with regard to creationism, sometimes mislabeled creation science ("mislabeled" because creationists work with a single hypothesis, determined a priori to be true, whereas science tries to choose among alternative hypotheses). The effect of religion on cognitive psychology may be less evident—hidden as it is by centuries of sophisticated philosophizing, it is revealed in the persistent mind/body and human/animal dualisms. These dualisms lack a factual basis, and psychology would be much better off without them (Gibson, 1994).
26. Most readers would long ago have laid aside this book if I had limited myself to purely descriptive, technical language. There is a fine but important line between the use of anthropomorphism for communicatory purposes or as a heuristic device, and gratuitous anthropomorphism that projects human emotions and intentions onto animals without

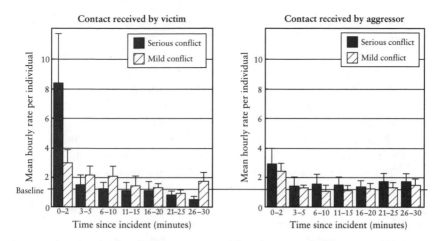

Mean (plus standard error of mean, SEM) hourly rates of affiliative contact (kissing, hugging, grooming, gentle touching) received from bystanders by individuals recently involved in fights. Contacts between former opponents (reconciliations) are excluded from the analysis. The thirty-minute window following each incident has been divided into blocks of two, three, and five minutes. Data are presented separately for incidents involving vocalizations and/or physical contact (serious conflicts) and mere silent threats and lunges (mild conflicts). The baseline shows the mean hourly contact rate received per individual.

justification, explication, or critical investigation. Strong opinions about the use and abuse of anthropomorphism can be found in Kennedy (1992), Marshall Thomas (1993), Masson and McCarthy (1995), and in Mitchell, Thompson, and Miles (forthcoming).

27. Burghardt, 1985, p. 917.

28. Diogenes Laertius, quoted in Menzel, 1986, p. 167.

29. Promises and problems of the cognitive approach to animal behavior have been extensively debated among ethologists. See Griffin (1976, 1984), Kummer (1982), Kummer, Dasser, and Hoyningen-Huene (1990), de Waal (1982, 1991a), and Cheney and Seyfarth (1990).

30. Carpenter, 1975, pp. 452–453.

31. This passage was translated from the Dutch by Kortlandt (1991, p. 11). Anton Portielje was a remarkable observer: he was also the first to notice enough difference between a chimpanzee and a bonobo to suggest, in 1916, that they might be different species. The distinction became official only in 1929 (de Waal, 1989, pp. 177–178).

32. Oddly enough, gorillas were long assumed incapable of passing Gallup's mirror-recognition test (reviewed by Povinelli, 1987). Since Westergaard, Hyatt, and Hopkins (1994) found that bonobos recognize themselves, the gorilla would have been the only anthropoid ape without self-recognition. Apart from not making much evolutionary sense (if the common

ancestor of apes and humans had self-awareness, why should it have been lost in one species?), this conclusion is open to doubt.

A videotape featuring a language-trained gorilla, Koko, shows the ape deliberately using a mirror to stare into her mouth, tilt her head to get a better look, pick at her teeth aided by the mirror, and so on. A recent report confirms that Koko is able to make a connection between herself and the gorilla in the mirror (Patterson and Cohn, 1994). Perhaps Koko's special education brought forward this talent (Povinelli, 1994), yet it makes one wonder if other gorillas can lag far behind.

The familiar problem with negative evidence applies here. Even if we accept that passing the mirror-test demonstrates self-awareness, failing the test certainly does not prove its absence. For debate about these issues, the reader is referred to Parker, Mitchell, and Boccia (1994), volume 11(3) of *New Ideas in Psychology*, pp. 295–377 (1993), Heyes (1993), and Cenami Spada et al. (forthcoming). An experiment promising to turn the presumed gap between monkeys and apes into a gray zone was presented recently by Howell, Kinsey, and Novak (1994).

33. Hatfield, Cacioppo, and Rapson (1993, p. 96) define emotional contagion as "the tendency to automatically mimic and synchronize expressions, vocalizations, postures, and movements with those of another person and, consequently, to converge emotionally."

34. This correlation was reported by Johnson (1982) and Bischof-Köhler (1988). According to the latter study, the link between mirror self-recognition and the emergence of cognitive empathy holds up even after correction for age.

35. The main alternative to a cognitive explanation of the absence of consolation in macaques is the so-called social constraints hypothesis. It posits that macaques run serious risks in associating with an individual who has just been attacked. With their more tolerant and flexible relationships, chimpanzees may not be operating under the same constraints. We plan to conduct experiments to eliminate the risk of approaching a victim of aggression. If macaques still fail to contact distressed group members under these circumstances, the social constraints hypothesis would be weakened (de Waal and Aureli, forthcoming).

36. Certain birds weave leaves into their feathers, and hermit crabs tote around entire houses, replacing them as they grow with larger residences. These self-enhancements are identical in all members of the species and probably have nothing to do with self-awareness. The only nonprimates in which self-decoration might accompany awareness of its effect on others are dolphins and killer whales. Marine mammal trainers speak of their subjects' *jewelry*, meaning the bits of seaweed they string around their pectoral fins or flukes, or the dead fish they carry on their

snouts (Pryor, 1975). Wild dolphins, too, tend to drag "stuff" around (Christine Johnson, personal communication).

If this is indeed self-decoration and not mere object play, it is intriguing in view of the highly developed succorant tendencies in the same mammals. Could the Cetacea, which after all have unusually large brains, be another group with increased awareness of the self? See some fascinating speculations by the neuroanatomist Harry Jerison (1986), and the first studies of dolphin self-recognition by Marten and Psarakos (1994) and Marino, Reiss, and Gallup (1994).

37. Even if apes are the most conspicuous behavioral copiers, they may not be the only ones. An intriguing monkey example comes from Breuggeman (1973, p. 196), who saw a juvenile rhesus monkey follow her mother while the mother carried a newborn. The daughter picked up a piece of coconut shell, carrying it ventrally in the same way that her mother held her new brother. When the mother lay down on her side, with one hand resting on the infant's back, the daugher did the same a few feet away, adopting the exact same posture while holding the shell.

38. Garner, 1896, p. 91.

39. Renewed experimentation on observational learning in monkeys and apes was pioneered by an Italian ethologist, Elisabetta Visalberghi, and an American developmental psychologist, Michael Tomasello. Thus far their findings have failed to support claims of full-blown imitation in nonhuman primates.

Field-workers, such as Boesch (1991a, 1993) and McGrew (1992, pp. 82–87), are not convinced that absence of imitation in the laboratory implies absence in the natural habitat. Although not saying in so many words that captive chimpanzees are backward, they imply it when pointing out that one cannot expect individuals under impoverished conditions to be competent to perform complex tasks. This hypothesis is contradicted by the masterly tool use for which captive orangutans are known, whereas their wild counterparts rarely demonstrate anything close to this ability (Lethmate, 1977; McGrew, 1992). Furthermore, it has been argued that free time under captive conditions actually *promotes* innovation and social sophistication (Kummer and Goodall, 1985).

Clearly, the real issue is not whether captive or wild primates are smarter, but whether the relevant variables have been controlled. The laboratory wins hands down on this count: observational learning covers a wide range of processes that cannot easily be disentangled in the field. For further discussion see Galef (1988), Visalberghi and Fragaszy (1990), Whiten and Ham (1992), Tomasello, Kruger, and Ratner (1993), and Byrne (1995).

40. Menzel, 1974, pp. 134–135.

41. The ability to attribute knowledge, feelings, and intentions to others is now often phrased as the possession of a "theory of mind" about others. This expression derives from an experiment by Premack and Woodruff (1978) in which apes were challenged to infer the intentions of other individuals by watching their efforts on video. The apes seemed to have an idea of the mental states of others. Theory-of-mind research covers both child and nonhuman primate behavior (reviewed in Buttersworth et al., 1991; Whiten, 1991; Byrne, 1995).

According to Cheney and Seyfarth (1991, p. 253), even the most compelling examples of attribution in monkeys and apes "can usually be explained in terms of learned behavioral contingencies, without recourse to higher-order intentionality. What little evidence there is suggests that apes, in particular, may have a theory of mind, but not one that allows them to differentiate clearly or easily among different theories or different minds." This passage was written, however, before Povinelli's experiments strengthened the case for attribution and perspective-taking in the chimpanzee (Povinelli et al., 1990, 1992).

A serious problem with studies of the ape's theory of mind is the interpretation of negative results. The experimental subjects are sometimes presented with rather unusual situations, such as blindfolded persons or persons instructed to stare into the distance. Like us, apes are very sensitive to body language: an unresponsive human experimenter is likely to confuse and disturb them. In addition, the rules of eye contact are different in apes than in humans: rather than gazing directly at others—which they do under exceptional circumstances only, such as during a reconciliation—apes are masters at monitoring companions by means of peripheral vision and quick glances that are barely noticeable. Negative test results may therefore say more about the apes' expectations about normal social interaction and the species barrier in this regard than about their grasp of the connection between looking and seeing.

The fairest comparison of apes tested by humans would be human children tested by apes; who knows how poorly children would do under such circumstances.

42. Example 1: de Waal, 1986b, p. 233; Example 2: de Waal, 1992d, p. 86; Example 3: de Waal, 1986b, p. 238; Example 4: de Waal, 1982, p. 49.
43. Menzel, 1988, p. 258.
44. Salk (1973) discovered the left-side cradling preference of human mothers, and Manning, Heaton, and Chamberlain (1994) report the same bias in gorillas and chimpanzees but not orangutans. See Hopkins and Morris (1993) for a review.
45. Mercer, 1972, p. 123.
46. Goodall, 1971, p. 221.
47. One notably different reaction to polio victims involved two adult males

suspected to be siblings or nephews: Mr. McGregor (with paralyzed legs) and Humphrey (unafflicted). Humphrey stood by McGregor until the end, defending him against even the most dominant aggressors. After McGregor's death, Humphrey kept returning for nearly six months to the place where his possible relative had spent the last days of his life in great pain and misery (Goodall, 1971, pp. 222–224).

48. Nevertheless, members of one species are sometimes vicariously aroused by those of another species. Recently the entire chimpanzee colony at the Yerkes field station was intently following how animal care staff caught an escaped rhesus monkey in the forest around their enclosure. Attempts to lure the monkey back into his cage had failed. The situation became hairy when he climbed a tree. I heard one of the watching chimpanzees, a juvenile named Bjorn, suddenly utter whimpers while seeking reassurance from an ape next to him, reaching out to her. When I looked up, I saw that Bjorn's distressed reaction coincided with the monkey's clinging desperately to a lower branch of the tree; he had just been shot with a tranquilizer dart. People were waiting beneath the tree with a net. Although it was not a situation Bjorn himself had ever been in, he appeared to empathize with the monkey: he uttered another whimper when the escapee dropped into the net.

49. Turnbull, 1972, pp. 112, 230.

50. It is hard to imagine being delighted by the misery of others unless one has a bone to pick with them. Turnbull's (1972) observations have not gone unchallenged; one fascinating speculation has been that the anthropologist felt so isolated and frustrated living with the Ik that *he himself* began to derive joy from their misfortune (Heine, 1985).

51. Weiss et al., 1971, p. 1263.

52. In a careful review of the psychological literature, Batson (1990) compares the attitude of science toward human altruism to that of the Victorians toward sex: it is denied and explained away. All too often, caring for others is interpreted as caring about oneself.

Experiments have failed to confirm this interpretation. Because there is no evidence for selfish motives behind *all* helping behavior, Batson concludes that people do possess a genuine caring capacity. Wispé (1991) supports this view, arguing that feelings of sympathy evaporate the moment self-interest enters as a conscious motive. This is not to deny an internal reward, but the reward seems specifically tied to the other's well-being. Alleviating another person's pain or burden gives a special satisfaction that is simply unavailable to those who base their help on hope for return favors, a desire for praise, or a wish to go to heaven. Such calculations may *mix* with sympathy, but they cannot replace it because "rewards are what sympathy is *not* about . . . Even if one always derived pleasure from helping others, it would not follow that one helps others in order to feel pleasure" (Wispé, 1991, p. 81).

Note that the issue of unselfishness is treated here from the perspective of motivation and conscious intent. Nothing is said about the possibility that acts of sympathy and cognitive altruism may, in the long run and perhaps quite circuitously, serve the actor's self-interest. Indeed, without such benefits the entire complex of empathy and helping behavior could never have evolved. The main point is that these benefits need not factor into the actor's conscious decision-making.

53. Wilson, 1993, p. 50.


## 3. Rank and Order

1. Hall, 1964, p. 56.
2. Example 1: author's translation of Trumler, 1974, pp. 52–53; Example 2: Lopez, 1978, p. 33; Example 3: Barbara Smuts, personal communication; Example 4: von Stephanitz, 1950, p. 814.
3. Modified from de Waal, 1991b, p. 336.
4. See de Waal (1982, p. 207). Nishida (1994, pp. 390–391) reports similar outraged reactions to violations of the social code. For example, he once saw a wild chimpanzee attack another from behind after a stealthy approach. This tactic is highly unusual: chimpanzees normally signal aggressive intentions in advance. Loudly screaming, the victim chased the attacker, who, although dominant, kept his distance. Speculating that the dominant did not fight back because he felt guilty about the sneak attack, Nishida concludes that "unusually fierce, prolonged retaliation on the part of a subordinate party and the corresponding reluctance to escalate the fight on the part of the dominant party may be one of the factors discriminating moralistic aggression from a conventional counterattack by a subdominant." This characterization of moralistic aggression may also apply to the extraordinary retaliation by Shade, a Japanese macaque, recounted in Chapter 4.
5. Hobbes, 1991 (1651), p. 70.
6. For decades the received view has been that animals engage in approach-retreat encounters, fights, and competitions that may *reveal* who dominates whom, but that the rank order itself is a mere construct of the human observer: animals neither classify themselves in terms of who dominates whom nor do they deliberately strive for better positions (Bernstein, 1981; Altmann, 1981; Mason, 1993).

   Less prominent in the textbooks, yet present at least since Maslow (1936), is the alternative that social dominance does exist in the minds of animals. For example, research on chimpanzees has produced evidence supporting what appear to be calculated, Machiavellian strategies to attain high status (de Waal, 1982). Theory formation tends to follow a pendulum pattern, and future students of animal behavior will no doubt revisit the issue of status striving. It is unclear at this point, for instance, how much the "striving" position really differs from the following formulation of the "nonstriving" position: "The critical issue is not social status per se, but the extent to which the relationship is oppressive and the type of satisfactions it affords. When the oppressive constraints in a relationship consistently exceed the satisfactions for one of the participants, the potential for conflict is high. . . . Primates generally act so as to maximize their personal freedom and mobility under demanding circumstances" (Mason, 1993, p. 25).

7. Whereas the outcome of conflict varies with the presence or absence of allies, or the resource at stake, expressions of submission are virtually immune to such effects. The bared-teeth face of some macaque species or the chimpanzee's bobbing and pant-grunting are completely predictable: it is hard even to imagine a situation in which a dominant would give these signals to a subordinate (Noë, de Waal, and van Hooff, 1980; de Waal and Luttrell, 1985). The simplest explanation for the independence of context is a cognitive one, namely that primates know in which relationship they are dominant or subordinate and that they communicate these evaluations to one another. In this view, submissive gestures and facial expressions reveal how the animals *themselves* perceive dominance relationships.

8. My text speaks of male, not female, rivals because it is written with an eye on chimpanzees, a species in which males are by far the more hierarchical sex. Most male animals compete about mates; females compete over food for themselves and their offspring. Whereas male chimpanzees are no exception to this rule, female chimpanzees at the best-known field sites avoid competition by living dispersed throughout the forest, each female occupying her own core area (Wrangham, 1979). This tendency may explain the lesser development of the female hierarchy in these apes. Most monkeys, on the other hand, form permanent mixed-sex groups in which food competition is common: females of these species are as dominance oriented as males.

   Accounts of status competition in both male and female monkeys may be found in Bernstein (1969), Chance, Emory, and Payne (1977), de Waal (1977; 1989a, pp. 133–140), Leonard (1979), Walters (1980), and Small (1990).

9. Koestler, quoted in Barlow, 1991, p. 91.

10. The effect of submission on social relationships was investigated during three months of instability between two male chimpanzees, Yeroen and Luit, at the Arnhem Zoo (de Waal, 1986c). Over two hundred hours of observations were collected in order to document changes around the time of first submission. During the weeks prior to this moment, friendly contacts became increasingly rare, whereas aggressive confrontations and intimidation displays between the two males reached their peak. As usual during power struggles, the exchange of status signals ceased

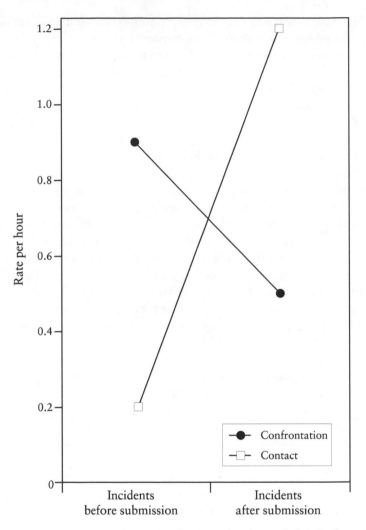

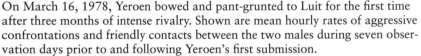

On March 16, 1978, Yeroen bowed and pant-grunted to Luit for the first time after three months of intense rivalry. Shown are mean hourly rates of aggressive confrontations and friendly contacts between the two males during seven observation days prior to and following Yeroen's first submission.

completely. The low level of contact occurred because the future dominant, Luit, walked away each time Yeroen approached.

Luit's attitude changed dramatically the day Yeroen uttered his first submissive pant-grunts: Luit suddenly became receptive to Yeroen's overtures. Aggression diminished and contact between the rivals increased over the next few days. Significantly, the longest grooming session of the entire period took place only a few hours after Yeroen's acknowledgment of Luit's status. This case study confirmed that peaceful coexistence among male chimpanzees depends on a formal clarification of their dominance relationship.

11. Dog owners who believe in the efficacy of punishment after the fact may be right for the wrong reasons. Instead of having taught their pet to associate a bad habit with punishment, they may have taught them merely to avoid certain sights, smells, or locations associated with the transgression. For example, a dog learns to avoid a bedroom in which he was admonished for chewing a pair of shoes, hence stops the chewing inasmuch as he does not encounter the same shoes again (Vollmer, 1977).

12. The overly submissive macaques illustrate the advantage of attributional capacities found in humans, and perhaps in apes (Chapter 2). A chimpanzee confronted with similar behavior in a subordinate would probably suspect that something had been going on, in the same way that we guess from the absence of a happy greeting by a dog that a rule must have been broken. Because of this more complete understanding of what may lie behind an expression of emotion, chimpanzees and people need to be more careful: better lie-detecting abilities require more sophisticated lies. I have never seen subordinate male chimpanzees react in the same way as these macaques. Even when caught in the middle of a prohibited act, they tend first to try concealment of the evidence (such as dropping their hands over their penis) before responding with fear and submission.

13. Coe and Rosenblum, 1984, p. 51.

14. Davis, 1989, p. 88.

15. Scott, 1971, p. 81.

16. Darwin, 1965 (1872), p. 309.

17. Starting with Trivers' (1971) theory of reciprocal altruism, we now seem to have the first elements of a plausible scenario for the evolution of conscience. My discussion closely follows recent theorizing by Alexander (1987), Frank (1988), and Simon (1990) about susceptibility to social influence (Simon's *docility*) and emotional commitment (Frank). A central concept is reputation, or status, as defined by Alexander (1987, p. 95): "Systems of indirect reciprocity, and therefore moral systems, are social systems structured around the importance of status. The concept of status simply implies that an individual's privileges, or its access to resources, are controlled in part by how others collectively think of him as a result of past interactions."

18. A sharp distinction between the reason for the evolution of a behavior and its underlying motivation is assumed in discussions of evolutionary ethics by Frank (1988), Simon (1990), and myself (Chapter 1).

Alexander (1987, 1993), in contrast, defends the position that, consciously or not, selfish motives guide all human behavior, including behavior that the actors themselves believe to be unselfish. Similarly,

Badcock (1986) tries to reconcile our species' true nature—which he sees as literally selfish—with altruistic motives. To the rescue comes Freudian repression theory: the ego defends itself by presenting a distorted picture of internal processes. It hides selfish motives from our conscious self, presenting them in the most favorable light. In the view of Alexander and Badcock, then, the human mind expends a good deal of energy in concealing selfish agendas: we are sophisticated hypocrites.

In a review of Wright (1994), who adopts the same position, Steven Pinker (1994, p. 35), a cognitive neuroscientist, makes the by-now-familiar point (Chapter 1 notes 12 and 27) that this view confuses proximate and ultimate causation: "When a person's public stance is selfless but his private motives serve his interests, we can call it hypocrisy. However, when a person's public stance and private motives are both selfless but those motives came about because they once served the interests of his ancestors' genes, we have not uncovered hypocrisy; we have invoked a scientific explanation couched at a different level of analysis. . . . The evolutionary *causes* of our motives can't be judged as if they *are* our motives."

19. Lever, 1976, pp. 482, 483.
20. Gilligan, 1982, p. 104.
21. Gilligan has been accused of giving in to popular expectations about gender roles without careful research to back her position (Colby and Damon, 1983; Walker, 1984; Mednick, 1989; Smetana, Killen, and Turiel, 1991). Some believe that her ideas stand in the way of progress, a criticism leveled most harshly by Broughton (1983, p. 614): "Gilligan does not seem very concerned with societal transformation given her desire to imbed women even more deeply in the domestic and personal aspects of welfare in civil society."
22. Walker, 1984, p. 687.
23. Hoffman, 1978, p. 718.
24. Applying ethological methods of data collection in the field, Edwards (1993) found consistent sex differences across a dozen cultures in countries from Kenya to India, and from the Philippines to the United States. During middle childhood, boys spend more time away from the home than girls, and girls have more contact with and responsibility for infants. The latter difference probably reflects both girls' greater attraction to infants and socialization practices (mothers preferentially assigning child care to daughters).
25. Strier, 1992, p. 85.
26. The Finnish study is special in that it did not focus on open conflict only—which universally is most common in boys (Maccoby and Jacklin, 1974)—but included *indirect* conflict by asking children what they do when angry. A rather cruel picture of girls emerged: they said they could

stay mad forever, whereas boys measured their anger in minutes (Lagerspetz, Björkqvist, and Peltonen, 1988).

A work of fiction detailing female-style conflict is Margaret Atwood's *Cat's Eye*. The author contrasts the torments to which girls subject one another with the more straightforward competition among boys. At one point, the principal female character complains: "I considered telling my [elder] brother, asking him for help. But tell what exactly? I have no black eyes, no bloody noses to report: Cordelia does nothing physical. If it was boys, chasing or teasing, he would know what to do, but I don't suffer from boys in this way. Against girls and their indirectness, their whisperings, he would be helpless" (Atwood, 1989, p. 166).

Unfortunately, sex differences in the domain of interpersonal conflict have been only poorly investigated. We are in the curious situation of knowing more about spontaneous aggression and reconciliation in nonhuman primates than in our own species (de Waal, 1989a).

27. Tannen, 1990, p. 150.
28. In well-established chimpanzee societies, males reconcile more readily after fights than females, and the male power structure is well defined and fiercely contested compared to the rather informal female hierarchy (Goodall, 1971, 1986; Bygott, 1979; de Waal, 1982, 1986c). As explained by Nishida (1989, p. 86), females decide dominance issues on the basis of seniority: "Unlike males, whose reproductive success depends on social status, female reproductive success may depend primarily upon acquiring a core area near the center of the unit-group's territory. Therefore, females who have acquired their own core areas have no pressing reason to strive for higher rank. Thus, a female's rank will be more or less fixed sometime after her immigration. Thereafter, her promotion in rank will be caused mainly by the death of senior high-ranking females and by the addition of younger low-ranking females to the hierarchy."

The rarity of overt conflict between female chimpanzees, and their relatively vague hierarchy, should not be interpreted as a lack of interest in competitive goals. Under particular circumstances, such as when wild females migrate into another community or when captive females are introduced to strangers, females do compete fiercely. In Arnhem, females did not give up their top positions willingly when adult males were introduced into the colony (de Waal, 1982); and when a new colony was established at the Detroit Zoo, females engaged in dominance strategies remarkably similar to those of males (Baker and Smuts, 1994).

Given the plasticity of the behavior of chimpanzees and other primates, researchers have moved away from deterministic explanations of sex differences. Discussions of these differences increasingly pay attention to potential, context dependency, social values, and payoff curves

(Goldfoot and Neff, 1985; Smuts, 1987; de Waal, 1993b; Baker and Smuts, 1994).

29. The effect of social context on the nurturing abilities of rhesus monkeys was investigated by Judith Gibber and Robert Goy (Gibber, 1981, pp. 63–66). In one series of tests, individually-caged monkeys received an unfamiliar infant. Rhesus males normally pay little attention to young infants, but under these conditions they proved remarkably friendly. This response was not seen in the second test series, however, which involved pair-housed subjects. Males who individually had picked up and held infants failed to do so in the presence of a female companion: the female did most of the infant handling. Males apparently defer to the other sex when it comes to infant care.

30. Andries Vierlingh, translated by Schama, 1987, p. 43.

31. See Schama (1987, pp. 25–50) for a remarkable outsider account of Dutch history. That the tendencies noted are still part of the culture was demonstrated in 1995, when river levels in the Netherlands rose to the point that thousands of families had to be moved to higher land. In a show of solidarity, Queen Beatrix appeared in rubber boots at the threatened dikes.

32. These socioecological theories were developed by, among others, Wrangham (1980), Vehrencamp (1983), and van Schaik (1989). Another important variable, emphasized by van Schaik, is within-group competition. The energy invested in rank-related affairs obviously depends on the advantage of high rank. This advantage varies with the kind of food a species lives on: there is little point in trying to monopolize scattered low-energy foods, such as foliage; but it does pay to be dominant in the case of clumped high-energy foods such as fruits. A steep dominance hierarchy is therefore more likely under the latter condition. For a discussion of contrasting dominance styles in monkeys and apes see de Waal (1989b) and de Waal and Luttrell (1989).

The idea that despotic dominance requires a closed exit door most likely applies to humans as well. For example, domestic abuse may persist especially when a victim's (perceived) options to quit the relationship are minimal. Conversely, a totalitarian regime may lose its grip once the national border has become porous. This happened when changes in neighboring countries created an opening for an exodus from East Germany. Erich Honecker's power evaporated as soon as people began voting with their feet.

33. For anthropological and evolutionary perspectives on despotism and egalitarianism see Woodburn (1982), Betzig (1986), Knauft (1991), Boehm (1993), and Erdal and Whiten (1994, in press). Boehm was the first to fully develop the idea that egalitarianism is not simply the absence of social stratification but the product of vigilance against excessive individual ambition.

If hierarchical tendencies are counteracted in egalitarian societies, it is precisely because they have not disappeared. Thus, rather than fitting a naive, idealized picture of human nature, egalitarianism occurs in full recognition of the ubiquitous tendency of men to accumulate power and privilege. There is only one way to neutralize this tendency: alliances from below. Ridicule and social control are important in holding ambition in check, but cannot work without sanctions. And sanctions against the top ultimately require joint action by lower levels.

Alliances from below are also recognizable in the balance-of-power arrangements of chimpanzees (de Waal, 1982, 1984). Most likely, therefore, the common ancestor of humans and apes already had a dominance orientation *and* leveling tendencies. Knauft (1991) is no doubt correct, however, that humans took the leveling tendency a giant step further by means of cultural norms and institutions.

Inasmuch as democracy can be interpreted as a hierarchical arrangement achieved by egalitarian means, the evolution and history of leveling mechanisms is relevant in relation not only to small-scale human societies but also to state organization.

34. Erdal and Whiten, in press.
35. De Waal, 1982, p. 124.
36. Usually, the control role in primate groups is restricted to a single dominant male. Although female macaques without relatives have been known to perform control activities (Varley and Symmes, 1966; Reinhardt, Dodsworth, and Scanlan, 1986), and a female chimpanzee may stop a fight if she is the highest-ranking individual present (de Waal, 1982; Boehm, 1992), the strong commitment of female primates to close relatives—and perhaps by extension to close friends—hampers impartial arbitration.

    In the early years, the Arnhem chimpanzee colony was dominated by Mama, a female without offspring. Unfortunately, we have little information on her rule. We do know from veterinary records that after males took over, the number of serious injuries in the colony dropped sharply. One possible explanation is that males were more effective than Mama at controlling fights (de Waal, 1982).

    In a cohousing experiment at the Wisconsin Primate Center with juvenile rhesus and stump-tail monkeys (Chapter 5), one mixed-species group was dominated by a male stump-tail, the other by a female stump-tail. Only the male performed control interventions, a task overriding the typical own-species bias. He intervened far more often than any other monkey, usually protecting losers even if it meant favoring rhesus monkeys over stump-tails (as he did in 67 percent of forty-six interventions). All other stump-tails favored their own species. The dominant female in the other group intervened only seven times, five of which were in support of other stump-tails.

For discussion of the control role see de Waal (1977, 1984), Ehardt and Bernstein (1992), and Boehm (1992, 1994).

37. Boehm, 1992, p. 147.

38. When Goblin, after having lost his top position in the Gombe community, tried to stage a comeback, he was defeated by a ferocious mass attack. The unusually hostile reception may have had something to do with the fact that Goblin had been a very tempestuous alpha male who frequently disrupted the group with his charging displays. "Possibly, his return would have roused a less dramatic response had he himself been a more peaceful and calm individual" (Goodall, 1992, p. 139).

39. The role of external threats, particularly from enemy groups of the same species, in the evolution of moral systems is a recurrent theme treated also in Chapters 1 and 5, and emphasized by both Darwin (1871) and Alexander (1987).

## 4. Quid pro Quo

1. Isaac, 1978, p. 107.

2. This rule cannot explain how altruistic exchanges started. A mere response tendency ("Do as the other did") does not suffice. According to computer simulations of tit-for-tat strategies, an initial cooperative attitude is necessary (Axelrod and Hamilton, 1981).

3. Indeed, this attitude is so unhumanlike that it may develop only under the most extreme circumstances. See Chapter 2 for Turnbull's (1972) claim that the Ik abandoned morality in the face of severe food shortages.

4. Milton, 1992, p. 39.

5. These ideas have been summarized by another anthropologist, Kristen Hawkes, who argues (1990) that men have an interest in providing food bonanzas that can feed many hungry mouths. Hunting success and generosity increase a male's attractiveness as a mate and help foster political ties. The meat distribution strategies of male chimpanzees discussed later on in this chapter seem entirely compatible with Hawkes's "showing off" hypothesis. See also note 20 to this chapter.

6. Lee, 1969, p. 62.

7. According to the French sociologist Claude Fischler, meat blurs the line between ourselves and what we eat. We both challenge and confirm our self-identity when consuming another being made of blood, bones, brains, secretions, and excretions. In this view, human flesh is the superlative meat; and Fischler (1990) indeed argues in L'Homnivore (a wordplay making a maneater out of an omnivore) that our obsession with animal foods ultimately derives from ancient practices of cannibalism and human sacrifice. A link with this past is also preserved in the Roman

Catholic ritual of ingesting bread and wine as representations of Christ's flesh and blood.

8. Nishida et al., 1992, p. 169.

9. De Waal, 1982, p. 110.

10. According to Sahlins (1965), human reciprocity takes two forms: (a) "vice versa" movements of goods and services within dyadic relationships, and (b) centralized exchanges via a recognized authority who pools and redistributes resources. The latter function may be performed by a chief or, in modern society, the government.

Centralized reciprocity is recognizable in both the food distribution strategies of top-ranking chimpanzees and their control role—their tendency to defend the weak against the strong (Chapter 3). In both cases a dominant individual dampens competition to the advantage of low-ranking members, in return receiving support and respect.

Studies on aid giving and sharing in human children, too, fit this pattern. Apart from reciprocity at the dyadic level, they demonstrate increasing protectiveness and generosity with increasing status (Ginsburg and Miller, 1981; Birch and Billman, 1986; Grammer, 1992).

11. Detailed information about chimpanzee predation and meat sharing can be found in Teleki (1973b), Goodall (1986), Boesch and Boesch (1989), Boesch (1994ab), and Stanford et al. (1994a).

Whether bonobos fit the predation hypothesis of the evolution of sharing is still ambiguous. Despite reports of meat sharing (Badrian and Malenky, 1984; Ihobe, 1992; Hohmann and Fruth, 1993), predation seems relatively insignificant. For example, bonobos have not been observed to hunt monkeys; on the contrary, their relations with monkeys seem rather friendly (Ihobe, 1990; Sabater Pi et al., 1993).

Plant food sharing, in contrast, is common. At a provisioning site for bonobos in Zaire, sugarcane was widely shared (Kuroda, 1984), and bonobos have also been seen to divide large *Treculia* and *Anonidium* fruits, some weighing 30 kilograms apiece (Hohmann and Fruth, forthcoming). Perhaps consumption of these fruits helped promote sharing tendencies. It should be added, though, that my own captive studies suggest that the bonobo's food-related tolerance is no match for that of the chimpanzee (de Waal, 1992b; and note 16 to this chapter).

12. Sharing between mother and offspring occurs in most or all primates, including rhesus monkeys, as does cofeeding on a clumped yet abundant food source. When I speak of "nonsharing" species, I mean primates with a predominantly competitive mode of interaction around food, in which subordinates never remove food directly from the hands or mouth of unrelated dominants. Generally, these species also lack communication signals specific to the sharing context, such as gestures and vocalizations to solicit food.

13. Goodall, 1986, p. 357.

14. D'Amato and Eisenstein, 1972, p. 8.
15. The main effect of food deprivation is to increase interest in food. But the same effect can be achieved by presenting favorite foods. I feel that there is so much to be discovered in this way that food deprivation is wholly unnecessary. The capuchins and chimpanzees in our tests receive foods that they particularly like but do not normally get, at least not in such abundance.
16. Feistner and McGrew (1989), who review primate patterns of food distribution, define sharing as the "transfer of a defensible food-item from one food-motivated individual to another, excluding theft" (p. 22).

    Below is a classification of four methods of interindividual food transfer during interactions relative to plant food in chimpanzees at the Yerkes Primate Center (de Waal, 1989d), bonobos at the San Diego Zoo (de Waal, 1992b), and capuchins at the Wisconsin Primate Center (de Waal, Luttrell, and Canfield, 1993). All methods of transfer occurred in all species, but chimpanzees showed more tolerant transfers (cofeeding and relaxed taking) and bonobos more intolerant transfers (forced claims and theft).

    *Forced claim or theft:* One individual supplants another at a food source, grabs food by force, or snatches a piece and runs. The first two patterns are typical of high-ranking individuals; the last, of subordinates and juveniles.

    *Relaxed taking:* One individual, in full view of the possessor, removes food from his or her hands in a relaxed or playful manner without threat signals or use of force.

    *Cofeeding:* An individual joins the possessor to feed peacefully on the same source, which both may hold. This category includes active food donations: 0.2 percent of all transfers in chimpanzees, 2.7 percent in bonobos, and 1.8 percent in capuchins.

    *Nearby collection:* An individual waits for dropped pieces and scraps, which are collected from within arm's reach of the possessor.

|                       | Chimpanzees | Bonobos | Capuchins |
|-----------------------|-------------|---------|-----------|
| Number of transfers   | 2,377       | 598     | 931       |
| Forced claim or theft | 9.5%        | 44.5%   | 26.2%     |
| Relaxed taking        | 37.1%       | 15.7%   | 26.5%     |
| Cofeeding             | 35.9%       | 17.6%   | 9.2%      |
| Nearby collection     | 17.6%       | 22.2%   | 38.0%     |

17. The effect of celebration was investigated through a variation in the method with which bundles of foliage were provided to the chimpanzees:

*Keeper delivery:* A caretaker brought bundles from a distance, giving the colony one to two minutes for celebration before the bundles were thrown into the enclosure.

*Self-delivery:* Well before the trial, I concealed the bundles behind me on the observation platform. At an unexpected moment, I threw them into the enclosure, giving the colony no chance to prepare for the event.

Aggression at the moment that the food arrived was rare under either condition; most of it occurred when individuals tried to join existing feeding clusters, or begged from possessors. On average, self-delivery trials involved 1.5 times more aggressive incidents than keeper-delivery trials. This finding is consistent with the idea that celebration increases social tolerance. The ambiance seemed less explosive during sessions preceded by this flurry of body contact and rituals confirming the hierarchy (de Waal, 1992b).

18. Respect for possession was first investigated in relation to sexual partners in hamadryas baboons. Males of this species do not interfere with each other's bonds with females: even large, totally dominant males are inhibited from taking over the female of another male after having seen the two together for a couple of minutes (Kummer, Götz, and Angst, 1974). Recently, Kummer and his coworkers conducted further experiments on possession and property rules, which showed similar inhibitions in relation to objects (Sigg and Falett, 1985; Kummer and Cords, 1991; Kummer, 1991).

19. The accompanying graph (p. 246) illustrates that shared amounts are correlated and well balanced within pairs of dominant and subordinate chimpanzees. Since a few rank relationships were ambiguous, only thirty of the thirty-six pairings among the nine adults are included. Reciprocity, tested on the entire 9 x 9 matrix, resulted in a correlation of $r = 0.55$ ($P = 0.001$). See de Waal (1989d) for details.

20. Sex-for-food transactions have been documented by Kuroda (1984) for wild bonobos, and by de Waal (1987, 1989a) for captive bonobos. Such exchanges are less prominent but not absent in chimpanzees (Yerkes, 1941; Teleki, 1973b). Thus, the best predictor of hunting by male chimpanzees in Gombe National Park is the presence of estrous females in their traveling party. One motivation for hunting, then, may be to increase mating success through sharing with females (Stanford et al., 1994b).

21. Smuts, 1985, p. 223.

22. In our own economy, the value of various services is expressed in a common currency: money. The evolutionary equivalent of money, reproductive fitness, is hard to measure. A discussion of this issue by Seyfarth and Cheney, with reference to their own field data, is contained in a collection of papers on the current state of knowledge of reciprocal

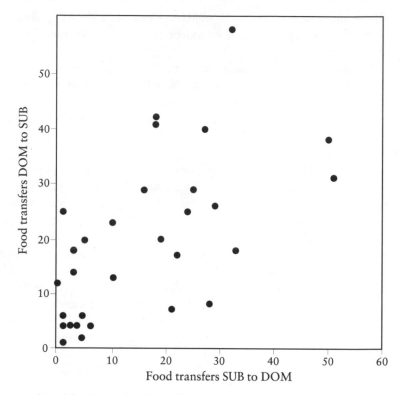

Scatter plot of food transfers from dominant to subordinate chimpanzees (DOM to SUB) against transfers in the opposite direction (SUB to DOM). Each dot represents one adult-adult partner combination.

altruism. See *Ethology and Sociobiology* 9 (1988, pp. 67–257). Reciprocity is also a central theme in Harcourt and de Waal's volume on alliance formation (1992).

23. For details see de Waal and Luttrell (1988). The same statistical elimination procedure was applied to food sharing, with identical outcome: a significant level of reciprocity remained after controlling for symmetrical relationship characteristics, such as kinship and association time (de Waal, 1989d).

24. Silk (1992b) challenges the claim that only chimpanzees have a system of direct revenge. The author reports reciprocal *contra* interventions among male bonnet monkeys. Because interventions against the established order were as uncommon in these monkeys as in other macaques, it remains to be seen how comparable their behavior is to that of chimpanzees, who retaliate regardless of the hierarchy (de Waal and Luttrell, 1988). For further data on revenge in monkeys and apes see de Waal (1982, 1989d), Aureli (1992), and Cheney and Seyfarth (1986, 1989).

Discussions from an evolutionary perspective have been provided by Trivers (1971) and by Clutton-Brock and Parker (1995).

25. Jacoby, 1983, p. 13.
26. Chagnon, 1988, p. 990.
27. Huxley, 1989 (1894), p. 140.

## 5. Getting Along

1. Midgley, 1994, p. 119.
2. Lorenz, 1981, p. 45.
3. Ardrey (1967) called our species the Killer Ape, based on Dart's (1959) depiction of *Australopithecus* as a carnivore who loved to devour writhing flesh and slake its thirst with warm blood (a truly imaginative conclusion, given the limits of fossil data). Dart saw the lust to kill as humanity's "mark of Cain," a feature that sets us apart from our anthropoid relatives. This line of thinking led others to seek the origin of war in hunting, and to present aggressiveness as a prerequisite to progress (Cartmill, 1993).

   One of several problems with the Killer Ape myth is that it equates carnivorousness with violence against one's own kind. We need to distinguish aggression definitively from predation, as Lorenz (1966, p. ix) wisely did when he defined aggression as "the fighting instinct in beast and man which is directed against members of the same species." Thus, it is assumed that a leopard killing an antelope is motivated by hunger, whereas a leopard driving another leopard out of his territory is motivated by aggression. For one thing, members of the same species communicate extensively during confrontations. They have ritualizations and inhibitions to prevent bloodshed, whereas predators usually assail their prey without warning signals and without pulling any punches. The difference in form and purpose of the two kinds of attack is obvious if we compare a cat stalking a mouse with one bristling and hissing at a rival.

   In light of Lorenz's emphasis on this crucial distinction, the most preposterous cover under which his *On Aggression* ever appeared (undoubtedly selected for marketing purposes) was one featuring a dramatic painting of a lion sinking teeth and claws into a frightened horse.
4. Notable exceptions are developmental studies by Sackin and Thelen (1984), Hartup et al. (1988), and Killen and Turiel (1991). Consistent with the theoretical framework presented in this chapter, Killen and Turiel note that fights among children are not always destructive; they often have a social orientation. "Children's conflicts are not solely struggles about selfish desires or aggressive impulses. Children are responsive to others and engage in negotiations to resolve their conflicts" (p. 254).
5. Initially, this flexibility baffled field-workers. Did chimpanzees know

stable groups at all? After years of documenting the composition of chimpanzee parties in the Mahale Mountains, Nishida (1968) was the first to crack the puzzle. He discovered that the ever-changing parties belong to an umbrella group, the members of which mix freely among themselves yet never with members of another such group. Nishida called this higher level of organization a "unit-group," yet the literature came to favor Jane Goodall's term "community" (mere "group" would hardly do, given the fission-fusion character of chimpanzee society).

6. The qualifier "best-known wild populations" is necessary, given the remarkable behavioral diversity—sometimes called cultural variation—of wild chimpanzees. Even populations in similar habitats in the same part of Africa differ in communication gestures and tool technology (Nishida, 1987; McGrew, 1992; Wrangham et al., 1994).

   Female-female relations are probably the most variable element of chimpanzee social organization (de Waal, 1994; Baker and Smuts, 1994). These relations range from close in all captive colonies known to me, to rather loose in wild populations at the Gombe and Mahale Mountains national parks in Tanzania (Nishida, 1979; Goodall, 1986) as well as in the Kibale Forest in Uganda (Wrangham, Clark, and Isabirye-Basuta, 1992).

   This variability may not represent an absolute difference between captive and wild conditions, however. Female bonding appears to exist in a small chimpanzee population "trapped" by agricultural encroachment in a forest of approximately 6 square kilometers on top of a mountain in Bossou, Guinea. Despite the substantial amount of available space, Sugiyama (1984, 1988) often saw the majority of individuals in this forest travel together in a single party, and measured relatively high rates of female-female grooming. Similarly, female chimpanzees seem more sociable in Taï Forest, Ivory Coast, than at other sites: they frequently associate, develop friendships, share food, and support one another. Boesch (1991b) attributes this sociability to cooperative defense against leopards.

7. Masters, 1984, p. 209.

8. Van Schaik, 1983, p. 138.

9. Boinsky, 1991, p. 187.

10. Norris, 1991, p. 187.

11. Bowlby, 1981, p. 172.

12. Moss, 1988, p. 125.

13. Using portraits of familiar individuals of both species, Matsuzawa (1989, 1990) compared facial discrimination by chimpanzee and human subjects as measured by latency with finding the correct name (the chimpanzees had first learned to match faces with name-keys on a computer keyboard). He found that recognition of human faces is easier for humans than chimpanzees, and recognition of chimpanzee faces easier

for chimpanzees than humans. Similar experiments in which human subjects select among people of different races have documented an own-race bias, that is, we find it easier to differentiate members of one's own race than members of another race (Brigham and Malpass, 1985).

14. The technique of comparing postconflict and matched-control observations, introduced by de Waal and Yoshihara (1983), has been followed in most observational studies in both captivity and the field. Different control procedures have yielded essentially the same results. See de Waal (1993a) for an overview of the methods used in reconciliation research on nonhuman primates.

15. Altmann, 1980, p. 163.

16. The human own-species bias has been declared morally equivalent to sexism and racism by the Australian animal-rights philosopher Peter Singer (1976). The term he uses for this bias is "speciesism." Although Singer traces its origin to the ancient Greeks and the Bible, thus positing that speciesism is a Western peculiarity, own-species bias certainly antedates humanity itself. Virtually all animals, given a choice, will accord their own kind the better treatment, and cross-species exploitation is absolutely rampant in nature (for instance, some ant species keep aphids as livestock, or force other ant species into labor; Holldöbbler and Wilson, 1990).

17. As expected, stump-tails were characterized by high reconciliation rates (see figure, p. 250). Rhesus monkeys not exposed to stump-tails (rhesus controls) had low rates throughout the experiment. Rhesus living with stump-tails (rhesus subjects), in contrast, started out at the same level as the controls, but rose steadily during the cohousing phases (Co-1, 2, and 3), remaining high even after removal of the stump-tails in the postphase (from de Waal and Johanowicz, 1993).

18. This insight is not limited to Japanese teachers. An early American student of child behavior, Helen Dawe (1934, p. 154), noted that "the mother or teacher who continually interferes is depriving the child of excellent opportunities to learn social adjustment." When Peter Verbeek, a graduate student, observed children at an outdoor playground in Florida, he found that approximately one-third of the fights were broken up by teachers. The teachers would tell the children to "make peace," yet only 8 percent of the combatants continued to associate after a forced reconciliation compared to 35 percent after an independently resolved dispute.

19. Gottman, 1994, p. 41.

20. Kurland (1977) was the first to report high rates of aggression between kin in free-ranging Japanese macaques. This paradoxical observation was confirmed for rhesus and stump-tail monkeys in outdoor enclosures by Bernstein and coworkers (Bernstein and Ehardt, 1986; Bernstein, Judge, and Ruehlmann, 1993) and de Waal and Luttrell (1989). Further-

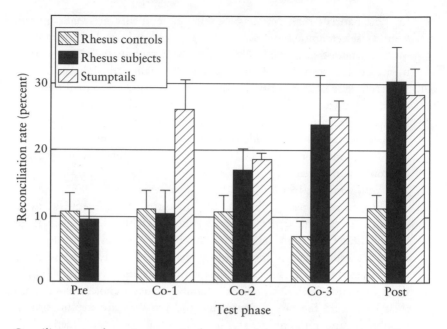

Conciliatory tendency increases in rhesus monkeys housed with stump-tails. Shown are individual means (plus standard error of means, SEM) of aggressive conflicts followed within three minutes by reconciliation. Before and after the experiment (pre- and post-phases), subjects were housed with members of their own species only (no pre-phase data are available on stump-tailed monkeys).

more, kinship ties are not the only bonds characterized by frequent aggression; the same applies to ties among nonkin (de Waal and Luttrell, 1986).

The number of fights among kin ceases to be exceptional if time spent together is taken into account. The high aggression rate is therefore partly a product of proximity. Yet the same is true of other kinds of interaction, so that a connection with proximity cannot be used to devalue high aggression rates among kin unless one is prepared to do the same for grooming and other affiliative behavior (Bernstein, Judge, and Ruehlmann, 1993).

There is no evidence that aggression among kin is relatively mild: injuries do occasionally result. How, then, does the matrilineal organization survive all this infighting? The key is that fights among kin and other close associates are relatively often reconciled (reviewed by Kappeler and van Schaik, 1992). A parallel report in human children finds friends preserving proximity despite high conflict rates (Hartup et al., 1988).

21. Obviously, juvenile chimpanzees do not vomit as a conscious threat; they simply get extremely frustrated and upset. My "investment" language is

inspired by Trivers' (1974) provocative analysis of parent-offspring conflict as a genetic tug-of-war.

In this battle of wills mothers have weapons, too. Jane Goodall offered a striking example at a symposium entitled "The Great Apes Revisited" (Mexico, 1994). In Gombe National Park, chimpanzee Fifi had shown regular five-year interbirth intervals, almost like clockwork. Her last birth, however, occurred when her previous child, Faustino, was only three and a half years old. The abrupt drop in maternal attention caused Faustino to have incredible tantrums. More than a year too young for weaning, he must have found life definitely "unjust." Fifi did not completely wean him, though; she continued to allow him to sleep in her nest, even to nurse along with his new sibling.

One of Fifi's original answers to Faustino's tantrums was to climb high in a tree and throw him literally to the ground, at the last instant holding onto an ankle. The young male would hang upside down for fifteen seconds or more, screaming wildly, before his mother retrieved him. Fifi was seen to employ this scare tactic twice in a row, after which Faustino stopped having tantrums that day.

22. Charlesworth, 1991, p. 355.
23. Hearne, 1986, pp. 43–44.
24. This discussion is based on the work of Smuts and Watanabe (1990) and of Colmenares (1991). The study of baboon greetings has a much longer history, however, going back to Kummer's (1968) observations of so-called notification in hamadryas baboons. It seems a particularly promising area for research into nonverbal negotiation. Colmenares (1991, p. 59) summarizes the ingredients of negotiation as follows: (a) conflict of interest, (b) attempts to reach nonaggressive solutions, (c) assessing and influencing the other's intentions, and (d) accommodating one's initial goals to those of the other. For further thoughts on animal negotiation see Hinde (1985), Dunbar (1988, pp. 238–248), Noë (1992), and Chadwick-Jones (1992).
25. Smuts and Watanabe, 1990, p. 169.
26. Goodwin, quoted in Haglund, 1992, p. 140.
27. Quoted in *Washington Post*, February 28, 1992.
28. Ardrey, 1970, p. 62.
29. The reported homicide rates for the Netherlands and the United States come from the *World Health Statistics Annual* of 1987 and 1988. Homicide statistics per city were reported in the *New York Times* of August 5, 1990.
30. Thompson, 1976, p. 226.
31. The general public loves to hear about the biological roots of vice and depravity. Ever since de Mandeville (1714), authors have been more than willing to cater to this desire (Montagu, 1968). We first met this genre of literature in Chapter 1, in relation to the evolutionary process, but the

aggression literature has, if possible, produced even more bad news about our species.

The standard trick is to present mean and selfish acts as proof of our true character, and to either overlook human kindness and sympathy, or demonstrate a hidden agenda behind it. Thus, in the same paradoxical way that the sexlessness of a dream can be taken as evidence for sexual repression, the manifest civility of most people can be explained as a facade hiding a brutish nature (Thompson, 1976).

32. Alexander and Roth, 1971, p. 82.

33. Perhaps the closest primate parallel to Calhoun's (1962) expanding rat population was a group of Japanese macaques in a corral of 0.8 hectare that grew from 107 to 192 individuals over a five-year period. Despite this increase of 79 percent in population density, the mean individual rate of aggressive acts per hour did not significantly vary over the years (Eaton, Modahl, and Johnson, 1980). For reviews of crowding research on nonhuman primates see Erwin (1979) and de Waal (1989c).

34. The table below summarizes the effect of a twentyfold area reduction on the Arnhem chimpanzee colony, based on data from Nieuwenhuijsen and de Waal (1982). Weighted individual rates of behavior during two summer periods (outdoors) are compared with those of three winter periods (indoors), resulting in factorial increases. Note that all measures except play were higher during the winters.

| Measure | Outdoors | Indoors |
|---|---|---|
| Aggression | 1 | 1.7 |
| Proportion of severe aggression | 1 | 1.1 |
| Submissive greetings | 1 | 2.4 |
| Social grooming | 1 | 2.0 |
| Social Play | 1.4 | 1 |

35. Given that macaques live in permanent groups in the wild, whereas chimpanzees form fission-fusion societies, it is entirely possible that the observed similarity in conciliatory tendency between captive and wild macaques does not generalize to captive and wild chimpanzees: distancing between adversaries *is* a realistic option for wild chimpanzees.

Even though chimpanzees on the Arnhem island have a great deal of space, they cannot get out of each other's way for more than a couple of hours. The observed similarity in conciliatory tendency during indoor and outdoor periods may be due, therefore, to the chimpanzees' having learned that it is better to reconcile right away than to run into an ill-willed opponent later on.

Some of the most spectacular reconciliations in Arnhem took place in the late afternoon, when the chimpanzees were being called into the building for their evening meal. If rival males had avoided each other following a confrontation, they might find themselves in the awkward and dangerous situation of having to spend the night unreconciled together in the same room. Under these circumstances, males were often seen circling each other outside, near the entrance door, testing preparedness to make up. These tense scenes usually ended with an outburst of screaming and embracing between the two—a highly emotional moment followed by grooming. Sometimes they groomed each other so long that the keeper proceeded to feed the rest of the colony while we waited until the two males had calmed down sufficiently to come in together. These reconciliations, clearly forced on the males by the anticipation of proximity, are oriented to the future. Accordingly, I have called them "truces" (de Waal, 1982, pp. 113–114).

36. For chimpanzees there is no such thing as "the" natural habitat. Environments in which these apes survive today range from relatively open, wooded savannas to dense rain forests. Moreover, most known chimpanzee populations have been affected by human activity, such as hunting or food provisioning. On the basis of her reading of the literature, Power (1991) has argued that provisioning at some field sites (such as Gombe's banana camp) turned the chimpanzees more violent and less egalitarian, and thus changed the "tone" of relationships both within and between communities. Power's analysis—which blends a serious reexamination of available data with nostalgia for the 1960s image of apes as noble savages—raises questions that will no doubt be settled by ongoing research on unprovisioned wild chimpanzees.

The issue of provisioning is also relevant to this chapter's comparison of macaques under different conditions, because all populations (except the one studied in the field by Aureli, 1992) were provisioned. It is not well understood how the behavior of provisioned free-ranging monkeys compares to that of wild monkeys subsisting on dispersed natural foods. Asquith (1989) has reviewed the pros and cons of provisioning in the field.

37. Strier, 1992, p. 70.

38. In light of the current advances in genetic technology, a statement such as "We have to work within our biological endowment" is rapidly becoming outdated.

39. If monkeys sometimes reconcile "for" their matriline, the same mechanism might operate between groups. Intergroup relations were documented in a free-ranging population of rhesus monkeys at Morgan Island, South Carolina. The vast majority of intergroup encounters were hostile, but on eleven separate occasions adult females belonging to *different* groups were seen to assemble for grooming. Remarkably, these contacts involved alpha females of the respective groups, particularly of groups between which much fighting occurred. In a parallel with international diplomacy, several of these high-level contacts took place

shortly after an intergroup fight, and may thus have served to reestablish peaceful relations (Judge and de Waal, 1994).

40. See de Waal (1989a, pp. 107–110) and Cheney and Seyfarth (1990, pp. 72–86) for further discussion of nonegocentric social knowledge.

41. Bodily harm to self is no doubt the first and foremost constraint on competition. According to Maynard Smith and Price (1973), the advantages of winning a fight are weighed against the cost of injury in case the adversary fights back. Van Rhijn and Vodegel (1980) refined this model by including the role of individual recognition.

These early evolutionary models, however, considered physical damage only. Elsewhere I have discussed constraints on competition from the perspective of *social* damage. The social environment may be regarded as a set of resources (for example, cooperative relationships) the effective exploitation of which requires that energy be put into their preservation (de Waal, 1989b). Thus, Sigg and Falett (1985) speculated that the main function of tolerance in relation to food is that it permits high-ranking and low-ranking baboons to forage side by side, which in turn helps all of them to close ranks and defend themselves in times of danger.


## 6. Conclusion

1. Dewey, 1993 (1898), pp. 109–110.

2. The father of Japanese primatology, Kinji Imanishi, defined culture as "socially transmitted adjustable behavior" (Nishida, 1987, p. 462). Early data and concepts in the study of animal culture may be found in Kummer (1971), Menzel (1973), and Bonner (1980). Cultural transmission is usually contrasted with the acquisition of behavior through individual learning and/or genetic transmission: cultural transmission implies *learning from* others, and in its most effective form (perhaps limited to our species) *teaching by* others. Two recent books reviewing primate cultural phenomena are McGrew (1992) and Wrangham et al. (1994).

3. Proudhon, quoted in Hardin, 1982, p. 184.

4. For a balanced account of the controversy over the use of monkeys and apes in biomedical research, see Blum (1994). This science journalist's book ends with a description of the Yerkes Field Station as the sort of model facility that animal advocates should be able to accept. As a behavioral scientist working at this facility and a few others devoted to research, education, and conservation, I often feel caught in the middle of the controversy. I fully recognize the need to treat animals with respect and compassion, and I am a strong proponent of social housing for nonhuman primates (see, for instance, de Waal, 1992c). At the same time, I greatly appreciate the benefits derived from biomedical research, benefits that even the staunchest critics of such research are not prepared to decline.

The strategy of both sides in this acrimonious debate has been to depict the other as inhumane or immoral. Ironically, a debate such as this one is precisely what defines us as moral beings. As with all true dilemmas, the majority of people feel torn between two undesirables: inflicting pain upon animals and forgoing the medical advances produced thereby.

# BIBLIOGRAPHY

Adang, O. M. J. 1984. Teasing in young chimpanzees. *Behaviour* 88:98–122.
——— 1986. Teasing, harassment, provocation: The development of quasi-aggressive behaviour in chimpanzees. Ph.D. diss., University of Utrecht.
Alexander, B., and E. Roth. 1971. The effects of acute crowding on aggressive behavior of Japanese monkeys. *Behaviour* 39:73–89.
Alexander, R. D. 1987. *The Biology of Moral Systems.* New York: Aldine.
——— 1993. Biological considerations in the analysis of morality. In M. H. Nitecki and D. V. Nitecki, eds., *Evolutionary Ethics,* pp. 163–196. Albany: State University of New York Press.
Altmann, J. 1980. *Baboon Mothers and Infants.* Cambridge, Mass.: Harvard University Press.
Altmann, S. A. 1981. Dominance relationships: The Cheshire cat's grin? *Behavioral and Brain Sciences* 4:430–431.
Ardrey, R. A. 1967. *The Territorial Imperative.* London: Collins.
——— 1970. The violent way. *Life,* Sept. 11, pp. 56–68.
Arnhart, L. 1993. How animals move from "is" to "ought": Darwin, Aristotle, and the ethics of desire. Paper presented at the annual meeting of the American Political Science Association, Washington, D.C.
Asquith, P. 1984. The inevitability and utility of anthropomorphism in description of primate behaviour. In R. Harré and V. Reynolds, eds., *The Meaning of Primate Signals,* pp. 138–176. Cambridge: Cambridge University Press.

——— 1989. Provisioning and the study of free-ranging primates: History, effects, and prospects. *Yearbook of Physical Anthropology* 32:129–158.

Atwood, M. E. 1989. *Cat's Eye*. New York: Doubleday.

Aureli, F. 1992. Post-conflict behaviour among wild long-tailed macaques *(Macaca fascicularis)*. *Behavioral Ecology and Sociobiology* 31:329–337.

Aureli, F., and C. P. van Schaik. 1991a. Post-conflict behaviour in long-tailed macaques *(Macaca fascicularis)*: I. The social events. *Ethology* 89:89–100.

——— 1991b. Post-conflict behaviour in long-tailed macaques *(Macaca fascicularis)*: II. Coping with the uncertainty. *Ethology* 89:101–114.

Aureli, F., et al. 1992. Kin-oriented redirection among Japanese macaques: An expression of a revenge system? *Animal Behaviour* 44:283–291.

——— 1993. Reconciliation, consolation, and redirection in Japanese macaques *(Macaca fuscata)*. *Behaviour* 124:1–21.

——— 1994. Post-conflict social interactions among barbary macaques *(Macaca sylvana)*. *International Journal of Primatology* 15:471–485.

Axelrod, R., and W. D. Hamilton. 1981. The evolution of cooperation. *Science* 211:1390–96.

Badcock, C. R. 1986. *The Problem of Altruism: Freudian-Darwinian Solutions*. Oxford: Blackwell.

Badrian, N., and R. Malenky. 1984. Feeding ecology of *Pan paniscus* in the Lomako Forest, Zaire. In R. L. Susman, ed., *The Pygmy Chimpanzee: Evolutionary Biology and Behavior,* pp. 275–299. New York: Plenum.

Baker, K., and B. B. Smuts. 1994. Social relationships of female chimpanzees: Diversity between captive social groups. In R. W. Wrangham et al., eds., *Chimpanzee Cultures,* pp. 227–242. Cambridge, Mass.: Harvard University Press.

Barlow, C. 1991. *From Gaia to Selfish Genes*. Cambridge, Mass.: MIT Press.

Batson, C. D. 1990. How social an animal: The human capacity for caring. *American Psychologist* 45:336–346.

Bauers, K. A. 1993. A functional analysis of staccato grunt vocalizations in the stumptailed macaque *(Macaca arctoides)*. *Ethology* 94:147–161.

Bercovitch, F. B. 1988. Coalitions, cooperation, and reproductive tactics among adult male baboons. *Animal Behaviour* 36:1198–1209.

Berkson, G. 1973. Social responses to abnormal infant monkeys. *American Journal of Physical Anthropology* 38:583–586.

Bernstein, I. S. 1969. Spontaneous reorganization of a pigtail monkey group. *Proceedings of the 2nd International Congress of Primatology, 1968,* vol. 1, pp. 48–51. Basel: Karger.

——— 1981. Dominance: The baby and the bathwater. *Behavioral and Brain Sciences* 4:419–458.

Bernstein, I. S., and C. Ehardt. 1986. The influence of kinship and socialization on aggressive behavior in rhesus monkeys *(Macaca mulatta)*. *Animal Behaviour* 34:739–747.

Bernstein, I. S., P. G. Judge, and T. E. Ruehlmann. 1993. Kinship, association, and social relationships in rhesus monkeys. *American Journal of Primatology* 31:41–54.

Betzig, L. L. 1986. *Despotism and Differential Reproduction: A Darwinian View of History.* New York: Aldine.

Birch, L. L., and J. Billman. 1986. Preschool children's food sharing with friends and acquaintances. *Child Development* 57:387–395.

Bischof-Köhler, D. 1988. Über den Zusammenhang von Empathie und der Fähigkeit sich im Spiegel zu erkennen. *Schweizerische Zeitschrift für Psychologie* 47:147–159.

Blum, D. 1994. *The Monkey Wars.* New York: Oxford University Press.

Blurton Jones, N. G. 1987. Tolerated theft, suggestions about the ecology and evolution of sharing, hoarding and scrounging. *Social Science Information* 26(1):31–54.

Boehm, C. 1992. Segmentary warfare and the management of conflict: Comparison of East African chimpanzees and patrilineal-partrilocal humans. In A. H. Harcourt and F. B. M. de Waal, eds., *Coalitions and Alliances in Humans and Other Animals,* pp. 137–173. Oxford: Oxford University Press.

—— 1993. Egalitarian behavior and reverse dominance hierarchy. *Current Anthropology* 34:227–254.

Boesch, C. 1991a. Teaching among wild chimpanzees. *Animal Behaviour* 41:530–532.

—— 1991b. The effects of leopard predation on grouping patterns in forest chimpanzees. *Behaviour* 117:220–242.

—— 1992. New elements of a theory of mind in wild chimpanzees. *Behavioral and Brain Sciences* 15:149–150.

—— 1993. Towards a new image of culture in wild chimpanzees? *Behavioral and Brain Sciences* 16 :514–515.

—— 1994a. Chimpanzee—red colobus monkeys: A predator-prey system. *Animal Behaviour* 47:1135–48.

—— 1994b. Cooperative hunting in wild chimpanzees. *Animal Behaviour* 48:653–667.

Boesch, C., and H. Boesch. 1989. Hunting behavior of wild chimpanzees in the Taï National Park. *American Journal of Physical Anthropology* 78:547–573.

Boinski, S. 1988. Use of a club by a wild white-faced capuchin *(Cebus capucinus)* to attack a venomous snake *(Bothrops asper)*. *American Journal of Primatology* 14:177–179.

—— 1992. Monkeys with inflated sex appeal. *Natural History* 101 (7):42–48.

Bonner, J. T. 1980. *The Evolution of Culture in Animals*. Princeton: Princeton University Press.

Bowlby, J. 1983 (1973). *Attachment and Loss*, vol. 2, *Separation Anxiety and Anger*. Harmondsworth: Penguin.

van Bree, P. 1963. On a specimen of *Pan paniscus*, Schwarz 1929, which lived in the Amsterdam Zoo from 1911 till 1916. *Zoologische Garten* 27:292–295.

Breggin, P. R. 1992. We could all learn a thing or two from the chimpanzees. *New York Times*, Mar. 15.

Breuggeman, J. A. 1973. Parental care in a group of free-ranging rhesus monkeys *(Macaca mulatta)*. *Folia primatologica* 20:178–210.

Brigham J. C., and R. S. Malpass. 1985. The role of experience and contact in the recognition of faces of own- and other-race persons. *Journal of Social Issues* 41:139–155.

Brothers, L. 1989. A biological perspective on empathy. *American Journal of Psychiatry* 146:10–19.

Broughton, J. M. 1983. Woman's rationality and men's virtues: A critique of gender dualism in Gilligan's theory of moral development. *Social Research* 50:597–642.

Burghardt, G. M. 1985. Animal awareness: Current perceptions and historical perspective. *American Psychologist* 40:905–919.

——— 1991. Cognitive ethology and critical anthropomorphism: A snake with two heads and hog-nosed snakes that play dead. In C. A. Risteau, ed., *Cognitive Ethology*, pp. 55–90. Hillsdale, N.J.: Erlbaum.

——— 1992. Human-bear bonding in research on black bear behavior. In H. Davis and D. Balfour, eds., *The Inevitable Bond: Examining Scientist-Animal Interactions*, pp. 365–382. Cambridge: Cambridge University Press.

Buttersworth, G. E., et al. 1991. *Perspectives on the Child's Theory of Mind*. Oxford: Oxford University Press.

Bygott, J. D. 1979. Agonistic behavior, dominance, and social structure in wild chimpanzees of the Gombe National Park. In D. A. Hamburg and E. R. McCown, eds., *The Great Apes*, pp. 405–428. Menlo Park, Calif.: Benjamin Cummings.

Byrne, R. W. 1995. *The Thinking Ape*. Oxford: Oxford University Press.

Byrne, R. W., and A. Whiten. 1988. *Machiavellian Intelligence: Social Expertise and the Evolution of Intellect in Monkeys, Apes, and Humans*. Oxford: Oxford University Press.

——— 1990. Tactical deception in primates: The 1990 database. *Primate Report* 27:1–101.

Caine, N., and M. Reite. 1983. Infant abuse in captive pig-tailed macaques: Relevance to human child abuse. In M. Reite and N. Caine, eds., *Child Abuse: The Nonhuman Primate Data*, pp. 19–27. New York: Liss.

Caldwell, M. C., and D. K. Caldwell. 1966. Epimeletic (care-giving) behavior in Cetacea. In K. S. Norris, ed., *Whales, Dolphins, and Porpoises,* pp. 755–789. Berkeley: University of California Press.

Calhoun, J. B. 1962. Population density and social pathology. *Scientific American* 206:139–148.

Campbell, D. T. 1975. On the conflicts between biological and social evolution and between psychology and moral tradition. *American Psychologist* 117:1103–26.

Canetti, E. 1963 (1960). *Crowds and Power.* New York: Viking Press.

Caporael, L. R., et al. 1989. Selfishness examined: Cooperation in the absence of egoistic incentives. *Behavioral and Brain Sciences* 12:683–739.

Carey, S. 1985. *Conceptual Change in Childhood.* Cambridge, Mass.: MIT Press.

Carpenter, E. 1975. The tribal terror of self-awareness. In P. Hockings, ed., *Principles of Visual Anthropology,* pp. 451–461. The Hague: Mouton.

Cartmill, M. 1993. *A View to a Death in the Morning: Hunting and Nature through History.* Cambridge, Mass.: Harvard University Press.

Cavalieri, P., and P. Singer. 1993. *The Great Ape Project: Equality beyond Humanity.* London: Fourth Estate.

Cenami Spada E., et al. Forthcoming. The self as reference point: Can animals do without it? In P. Rochat, ed., *The Self in Infancy: Theory and Research.* Amsterdam: Elsevier.

Chadwick-Jones, J. K. 1992. Baboon social communication: The social contingency model and social exchange. In F. D. Burton, ed., *Social Processes and Mental Abilities in Non-Human Primates,* pp. 91–108. Lewiston, N.Y.: Mellen.

Chagnon, N. A. 1988. Life histories, blood revenge, and warfare in a tribal population. *Science* 239:985–992.

Chance, M., G. Emory, and R. Payne. 1977. Status referents in long-tailed macaques *(Macaca fascicularis):* Precursors and effects of a female rebellion. *Primates* 18:611–632.

Charlesworth, W. R. 1991. The development of the sense of justice. *American Behavioral Scientist* 34:350–370.

Cheney, D. L., and R. M. Seyfarth. 1986. The recognition of social alliances by vervet monkeys. *Animal Behaviour* 34:1722–31.

——— 1989. Reconciliation and redirected aggression in vervet monkeys, *Cercopithecus aethiops. Behaviour* 110:258–275.

——— 1990. *How Monkeys See the World: Inside the Mind of Another Species.* Chicago: University of Chicago Press.

——— 1991. Reading minds or reading behaviour? Tests of a theory of mind in monkeys. In A. Whiten, ed., *Natural Theories of Mind; Evolution, Development and Simulation of Everyday Mindreading,* pp. 175–194. Oxford: Blackwell.

Ci, J. 1991. Conscience, sympathy and the foundation of morality. *American Philosophical Quarterly* 28:49–59.

Clutton-Brock, T. H., and G. A. Parker. 1995. Punishment in animal societies. *Nature* 373:209–216.

Coe, C. L., and L. A. Rosenblum. 1984. Male dominance in the bonnet macaque: A malleable relationship. In P. R. Barchas and S. P. Mendoza, eds., *Social Cohesion: Essays toward a Sociophysiological Perspective*, pp. 31–63. Westport, Conn.: Greenwood.

Colby, A., and W. Damon. 1983. Listening to a different voice: A review of Gilligan's *In a Different Voice*. *Merrill-Palmer Quarterly* 29:473–481.

Colmenares, F. 1991. Greeting behaviour between male baboons: Oestrus females, rivalry, and negotiation. *Animal Behaviour* 41:49–60.

Connor, R. C., and K. S. Norris. 1982. Are dolphins reciprocal altruists? *American Naturalist* 119:358–372.

Cords, M. 1988. Resolution of aggressive conflicts by immature male long-tailed macaques. *Animal Behaviour* 36:1124–35.

Cords, M., and S. Thurnheer. 1993. Reconciling with valuable partners by long-tailed macaques. *Ethology* 93:315–325.

Coser, L. A. 1966. Some social functions of violence. *Annals* 364:8–18.

Cronin, H. 1991. *The Ant and the Peacock*. Cambridge: Cambridge University Press.

Crook, J. H. 1989. Introduction: Socioecological paradigms, evolution and history: Perspectives for the 1990s. In V. Standen and R. A. Foley, eds., *Comparative Socioecology: The Behavioural Ecology of Humans and Other Mammals*, pp. 1–36. London: Blackwell.

Damasio, H., et al. 1994. The return of Phineas Gage: Clues about the brain from the skull of a famous patient. *Science* 264:1102–05.

D'Amato, M. R., and N. Eisenstein. 1972. Laboratory breeding and rearing of *Cebus apella*. *Laboratory Primate Newsletter* 11(3):4–9.

Darley, J. M., and C. D. Batson. 1973. From Jerusalem to Jericho: A study of situational and dispositional variables in helping behavior. *Journal of Personality and Social Psychology* 27:100–108.

Dart, R. A. 1959. *Adventures with the Missing Link*. New York: Harper.

Darwin, C. 1965 (1872). *The Expression of the Emotions in Man and Animals*. Chicago: University of Chicago Press.

——— 1981 (1871). *The Descent of Man, and Selection in Relation to Sex*. Princeton: Princeton University Press.

Dasser, V. 1988. A social concept in Java-monkeys. *Animal Behaviour* 36:225–230.

Davis, H. 1989. Theoretical note on the moral development of rats *(Rattus norvegicus)*. *Journal of Comparative Psychology* 103:88–90.

Dawe, H. C. 1934. An analysis of two hundred quarrels of preschool children. *Child Development* 5:139–157.

Dawkins, R. 1976. *The Selfish Gene*. Oxford: Oxford University Press.

——— 1981. In defense of selfish genes. *Philosophy* 56:556–573.

Demaria, C., and B. Thierry. 1990. Formal biting in stump-tailed macaques *(Macaca arctoides)*. *American Journal of Primatology* 20:133–140.

Deputte, B. L. 1988. Perception de la mort et de la séparation chez les primates. *Nouvelle Revue d'Ethnopsychiatrie* 10:113–150.

Dettwyler, K. A. 1991. Can paleopathology provide evidence for "compassion"? *American Journal of Physical Anthropology* 84:375–384.

Dewey, J. 1993 (1898). Evolution and ethics. Reprinted in M. H. Nitecki and D. V. Nitecki, eds., *Evolutionary Ethics*, pp. 95–110. Albany: State University of New York Press.

Dickey, L. 1986. Historicizing the "Adam Smith Problem": Conceptual, historiographical, and textual issues. *Journal of Modern History* 58:579–609.

Dittus, W. P. J. 1979. The evolution of behaviors regulating density and age-specific sex ratios in a primate population. *Behaviour* 69:265–302.

Dittus, W. P. J., and S. M. Ratnayeke. 1989. Individual and social behavioral responses to injury in wild toque macaques *(Macaca sinica)*. *International Journal of Primatology* 10:215–234.

Dugatkin, L. A. 1992. Sexual selection and imitation: Females copy the mate choice of others. *American Naturalist* 139:1384–89.

Dunbar, R. I. M. 1988. *Primate Social Systems*. London: Croom Helm.

Dutton, D., and S. L. Painter. 1981. Traumatic bonding: The development of emotional attachments in battered women and other relationships of intermittent abuse. *Victimology* 6:139–155.

Eaton, G., K. B. Modahl, and D. F. Johnson. 1980. Aggressive behavior in a confined troop of Japanese macaques: Effects of density, season, and gender. *Aggressive Behavior* 7:145–164.

Edwards, C. P. 1993. Behavioral sex differences in children of diverse cultures: The case of nurturance to infants. In M. E. Pereira and L. A. Fairbanks, eds., *Juvenile Primates: Life History, Development, and Behavior*, pp. 327–338. New York: Oxford University Press.

Ehardt, C. L., and I. S. Bernstein. 1992. Conflict intervention behaviour by adult male macaques: Structural and functional aspects. In A. H. Harcourt and F. B. M. de Waal, eds., *Coalitions and Alliances in Humans and Other Animals*, pp. 83–111. Oxford: Oxford University Press.

Eibl-Eibesfeldt, I. 1990. Dominance, submission, and love: Sexual pathologies from the perspective of ethology. In J. R. Feierman, ed., *Pedophilia: Biosocial Dimensions*, pp. 150–175. New York: Springer.

Erdal, D., and A. Whiten. 1994. On human egalitarianism: An evolutionary product of Machiavellian status escalation? *Current Anthropology*, 35:175–183.

——— In press. Egalitarianism and Machiavellian intelligence in human evolution. *Cambridge Archeological Journal*.

Erwin, J. 1979. Aggression in captive macaques: Interaction of social and spatial factors. In J. Erwin, T. L. Maple, and G. Mitchell, eds., *Captivity and Behavior,* pp. 139–171. New York: Van Nostrand.

Fedigan, L. M., and L. Fedigan. 1977. The social development of a handicapped infant in a free-living troop of Japanese monkeys. In S. Chevalier-Skolnikoff and F. E. Poirier, eds., *Primate Bio-Social Development: Biological, Social, and Ecological Determinants,* pp. 205–222. New York: Garland.

Feistner, A. T. C., and W. C. McGrew. 1989. Food-sharing in primates: A critical review. In P. K. Seth and S. Seth, eds., *Perspectives in Primate Biology,* vol. 3, pp. 21–36. New Delhi: Today and Tomorrow's Printers and Publishers.

Fiorito, G., and P. Scotto. 1992. Observational learning in *Octopus vulgaris*. *Science* 256:545–547.

Fischler, C. 1990. *L'Homnivore: Le goût, la cuisine et le corps.* Paris: Odile Jacob.

Fisher, A. 1991. A new synthesis comes of age. *Mosaic* 22:3–17.

Fossey, D. 1983. *Gorillas in the Mist.* Boston: Houghton Mifflin.

Frank, R. H. 1988. *Passions within Reason: The Strategic Role of the Emotions.* New York: Norton.

Freedman, D. G. 1958. Constitutional and environmental interactions in rearing of four breeds of dogs. *Science* 127:585–586.

Freud, S. 1961 (1930). *Civilization and its Discontents.* New York: Norton.

Galef, B. G. 1988. Imitation in animals: History, definitions, and interpretation of data from the psychological laboratory. In T. Zentall and B. G. Galef, eds., *Psychological and Biological Perspectives,* pp. 1–28. Hillsdale N.J.: Erlbaum.

Gallup, G. 1982. Self-awareness and the emergence of mind in primates. *American Journal of Primatology* 2:237–248.

Garner, R. L. 1896. *Gorillas and Chimpanzees.* London: Osgood.

Gibber, J. R. 1981. Infant-directed behaviors in male and female rhesus monkeys. Ph.D. diss., University of Wisconsin–Madison.

Gibson, E. J. 1994. Has psychology a future? *Psychological Science* 5:69–76.

Gibson, J. J. 1979. *The Ecological Approach to Visual Perception.* Boston: Houghton Mifflin.

Gilligan, C. 1982. *In a Different Voice: Psychological Theory and the Women's Movement.* Cambridge, Mass.: Harvard University Press.

Ginsberg, H., and S. Miller. 1981. Altruism in children: A naturalistic study of reciprocation and an examination of the relationship between social dominance and aid-giving behavior. *Ethology and Sociobiology* 2:75–83.

Goldfoot, D. A., and D. A. Neff. 1985. On measuring sex differences in social contexts. In N. Adler, D. Pfaff, and R. W. Goy, eds., *Handbook of Behavioral Neurobiology,* vol. 7, pp. 767–783. New York: Plenum.

Goodall, J. 1971. *In the Shadow of Man.* Boston: Houghton Mifflin.

———— 1986. *The Chimpanzees of Gombe: Patterns of Behavior.* Cambridge, Mass.: Belknap Press, Harvard University Press.

———— 1990. *Through a Window.* Boston: Houghton Mifflin.

———— 1992. Unusual violence in the overthrow of an alpha male chimpanzee at Gombe. In T. Nishida, et. al., eds., *topics in Primatology,* vol. 1, *Human Origins,* pp. 131–142. Tokyo: University of Tokyo Press.

Gottman, J. 1994. *Why Marriages Succeed or Fail.* New York: Simon and Schuster.

Gould, S. J. 1980. So cleverly kind an animal. In *Ever since Darwin,* pp. 260–267. Harmondsworth: Penguin.

———— 1988. Kropotkin was no crackpot. *Natural History* 97(7):12–21.

Grammer, K. 1992. Intervention in conflicts among children: Contexts and consequences. In: A. H. Harcourt and F. B. M. de Waal, eds., *Coalitions and Alliances in Humans and other Animals,* pp. 258—283. Oxford: Oxford University Press.

Guisso, R. W. L., and C. Pagani. 1989. *The First Emperor of China.* New York: Birch Lane.

Hadwin, J., and J. Perner. 1991. Pleased and surprised: Children's cognitive theory of emotion. *British Journal of Developmental Psychology* 9:215–234.

Haglund, K. 1992. Violence research is due for attention. *Journal of NIH Research* 4:38–42.

Hall, K. R. L. 1964. Aggression in monkey and ape societies. In J. Carthy and F. Ebling, eds., *The Natural History of Aggression,* pp. 51–64. London: Academic Press.

Hamilton, W. D. 1971. Selection of selfish and altruistic behavior. In J. F. Eisenberg and W. S. Dillon, eds., *Man and Beast: Comparative Social Behavior,* pp. 59–91. Washington, D.C.: Smithsonian Institution Press.

Harcourt, A. H., and F. B. M. de Waal. 1992. *Coalitions and Alliances in Humans and Other Animals.* Oxford: Oxford University Press.

Hardin, G. 1982. Discriminating altruisms. *Zygon* 17:163–186.

Hartup, W., et al. 1988. Conflict and the friendship relations of young children. *Child Development* 59:1590–1600.

Hatfield, E., J. T. Cacioppo, and R. L. Rapson. 1993. Emotional contagion. *Current Directions in Psychological Science* 2:96–99.

Hawkes, K. 1990. Showing off: Tests of an hypothesis about men's foraging goals. *Ethology and Sociobiology* 12:29–54.

Hearne, V. 1986. Reflections: Questions about language. I—Horses. *New Yorker* 62 (Aug.):33–57.

Hediger, H. 1955. *Studies in the Psychology and Behaviour of Animals in Zoos and Circuses.* London: Butterworth.

Heine, B. 1985. The mountain people: Some notes on the Ik of north-eastern Uganda. *Africa* 55:3–16.

Heinrich, B. 1989. *Ravens in Winter.* New York: Summit.

Heyes, C. M. 1993. Anecdotes, training, trapping and triangulating: Do animals attribute mental states? *Animal Behaviour* 46:177–188.

Hinde, R. A. 1970. Aggression. In J. Pringle, ed., *Biology and the Human Sciences,* pp. 1–23. Oxford: Clarendon.

———— 1985. Expression and negotiation. In G. Zivin, ed., *The Development of Expressive Behavior: Biology-Environment Interactions,* pp. 103–116. Orlando, Fla.: Academic Press.

Hobbes, T. 1991 (1651). *Leviathan.* Cambridge: Cambridge University Press.

Hoffman, M. L. 1978. Sex differences in empathy and related behaviors. *Psychological Bulletin* 84:712–722.

———— 1981. Perspectives on the difference between understanding people and understanding things: The role of affect. In J. H. Flavell and L. Ross, eds., *Social Cognitive Development,* pp. 67–81. Cambridge: Cambridge University Press.

Hohmann, G., and B. Fruth. 1993. Field observations on meat sharing among bonobos *(Pan paniscus). Folia primatologica* 60:225–229.

———— Forthcoming. Food sharing and status in provisioned bonobos *(Pan paniscus):* Preliminary results. In P. Wiessner and W. Schiefenhövel, eds., *Food and the Status Quest.* Oxford: Berghahn.

Holldöbbler, B., and E. O. Wilson. 1990. *The Ants.* Cambridge, Mass.: Harvard University Press.

Hopkins, W. D., and R. D. Morris. 1993. Handedness in great apes: A review of findings. *International Journal of Primatology* 14:1–25.

Howell, M., J. Kinsey, and M. A. Novak. 1994. Mark-directed behavior in a rhesus monkey after controlled reinforced exposure to mirrors. *American Journal of Primatology* 33:216.

Hume, D. 1978 (1739). *A Treatise of Human Nature.* Oxford: Oxford University Press.

Huxley, T. H. 1888. Struggle for existence and its bearing upon man. *Nineteenth Century,* Feb., 1888.

———— 1989 (1894). *Evolution and Ethics.* Princeton: Princeton University Press.

Ihobe, H. 1990. Interspecific interactions between wild pygmy chimpanzees *(Pan paniscus)* and red colobus *(Colobus badius). Primates* 3:109–112.

———— 1992. Observations on the meat-eating behavior of wild bonobos *(Pan paniscus)* at Wamba, Republic of Zaire. *Primates* 33:247–250.

Isaac, G. 1978. The food-sharing behavior of protohuman hominids. *Scientific American* 238(4):90–108.

Itani, J. 1988. The origin of human equality. In M. R. A. Chance, ed., *Social Fabrics of the Mind,* pp. 137–156. Hove: Erlbaum.

Izawa, K. 1978. Frog-eating behavior of wild black-capped capuchin *(Cebus apella). Primates* 19:633–642.

Jacoby, S. 1983. *Wild Justice: The Evolution of Revenge.* New York: Harper and Row.

Janson, C. H. 1988. Food competition in brown capuchin monkeys *(Cebus apella):* Quantitative effects of group size and tree productivity. *Behaviour* 105:53–76.

Jaynes, J. 1969. The historical origins of "ethology" and "comparative psychology." *Animal Behaviour* 17:601–606.

Jerison, H. J. 1986. The perceptual worlds of dolphins. In R. J. Schusterman, J. A. Thomas, and F. G. Wood, eds., *Dolphin Cognition and Behavior: A Comparative Approach,* pp. 141–166. London: Erlbaum.

Johnson, D. B. 1982. Altruistic behavior and the development of self in infants. *Merrill-Palmer Quarterly* 28:379–388.

Johnston, K. D. 1988. Adolescents' solutions to dilemmas in fables: Two moral orientations—two problem-solving strategies. In C. Gilligan, J. V. Ward, and M. Taylor, eds., *Mapping the Moral Domain: A Contribution of Women's Thinking to Psychological Theory and Education,* pp. 49–71. Cambridge, Mass.: Harvard University Press.

Joubert, D. 1991. Elephant wake. *National Geographic* 179:39–42.

Judge, P. G. 1991. Dyadic and triadic reconciliation in pigtail macaques *(Macaca nemestrina). American Journal of Primatology* 23:225–237.

Judge, P. G., and F. B. M. de Waal. 1994. Intergroup grooming relations between alpha females in a population of free-ranging rhesus macaques. *Folia primatologica* 63:63–70.

Kant, I. 1947 (1785). Groundwork of the metaphysic of morals. In H. J. Paton, trans., *The Moral Law.* London: Hutchinson.

Kaplan, H., and K. Hill. 1985. Hunting ability and reproductive success among Ache foragers: Preliminary results. *Current Anthropology* 26:131–133.

Kappeler, P. M., and C. P. van Schaik. 1992. Methodological and evolutionary aspects of reconciliation among primates. *Ethology* 92:51–69.

Kaufman I. C., and L. A. Rosenblum. 1967. Depression in infant monkeys separated from their mothers. *Science* 155:1030–31.

Kennedy, J. S. 1992. *The New Anthropomorphism.* Cambridge: Cambridge University Press.

Killen, M., and E. Turiel. 1991. Conflict resolution in preschool social interactions. *Early Education and Development* 2:240–255.

Kitcher, P. 1985. *Vaulting Ambition: Sociobiology and the Quest for Human Nature.* Cambridge, Mass.: MIT Press.

Knauft, B. M. 1991. Violence and sociality in human evolution. *Current Anthropology* 32:391–428.

Kohlberg, L. 1984. *Essays on Moral Development,* vol. 2, *The Psychology of Moral Development.* San Fransisco: Harper and Row.

Köhler, W. 1925. *The Mentality of Apes.* New York: Vintage.

Kortlandt, A. 1991. Primates in the looking glass: A historical note. *Animal Behaviour Society Newsletter* 37:11.

Kropotkin, P. 1972 (1902). *Mutual Aid: A Factor of Evolution.* New York: New York University Press.

Kummer, H. 1968. *Social Organization in Hamadryas Baboons.* Chicago: University of Chicago Press.

——— 1971. *Primate Societies.* Chicago: University of Chicago Press.

——— 1978. On the value of social relationships to nonhuman primates: A heuristic scheme. *Social Science Information* 17:687–705.

——— 1982. Social knowledge in free-ranging primates. In D. Griffin, ed., *Animal Mind—Human Mind,* pp. 113–130. Berlin: Springer.

——— 1991. Evolutionary transformations of possessive behavior. In F. W. Rudmin, ed., *To Have Possessions: A Handbook on Ownership and Property.* Special issue of *Journal of Social Behavior and Personality* 6(6):75–83.

Kummer, H., and M. Cords. 1991. Cues of ownership in long-tailed macaques, *Macaca fascicularis. Animal Behaviour* 42:529–549.

Kummer, H., and J. Goodall. 1985. Conditions of innovative behaviour in primates. In L. Weiskrantz, ed., *Animal Intelligence,* pp. 203–214. Oxford: Clarendon.

Kummer, H., V. Dasser, and P. Hoyningen-Huene. 1990. Exploring primate social cognition: Some critical remarks. *Behaviour* 112:84–98.

Kummer, H., W. Götz, and W. Angst. 1974. Triadic differentiation: A process protecting pair-bonds in baboons. *Behavior* 49:62–87.

Kurland, J. A. 1977. *Contributions to Primatology,* vol. 12, *Kin Selection in the Japanese Monkey.* Basel: Karger.

Kuroda, S. 1984. Interactions over food among pygmy chimpanzees. In R. Susman, ed., *The Pygmy Chimpanzee,* pp. 301–324. New York: Plenum.

Kyes, R. C. 1992. Protection of a disabled group member in hamadryas baboons. *Laboratory Primate Newsletter* 31:9–10.

Lagerspetz, K. M., K. Björkqvist, and T. Peltonen. 1988. Is indirect aggression typical of females? Gender differences in aggressiveness in 11- to 12-year-old children. *Aggressive Behavior* 14:403–414.

Lee, R. B. 1969. Eating Christmas in the Kalahari. *Natural History* 78(12):14–22, 60–63.

Lee, V. 1913. *The Beautiful: An Introduction to Psychological Aesthetics.* Cambridge: Cambridge University Press.

Lethmate, J. 1977. *Fortschritte der Verhaltensforschung,* vol. 19, *Problemlöseverhalten von Orang-Utans (Pongo pygmaeus).* Berlin: Paul Parey.

Lethmate, J., and G. Dücker. 1973. Untersuchungen zum Selbsterkennen im Spiegel bei Orang-Utans und einigen anderen Affenarten. *Zeitschrift für Tierpsychogologie* 33:248–269.

Lever, J. 1976. Sex differences in the games children play. *Social Problems* 23:478–487.

Lewin, R. 1984 (1977). Biological limits to morality. In G. Ferry, ed., *The Understanding of Animals*, pp. 226–234. Oxford: Blackwell.

Lieberman, P. 1991. *Uniquely Human: The Evolution of Speech, Thought, and Selfless Behavior.* Cambridge, Mass.: Harvard University Press.

Lippa, R. A. 1990. *Introduction to Social Psychology.* Belmont, Calif.: Wadsworth.

Lopez, B. H. 1978. *Of Wolves and Men.* New York: Scribner's.

Lorenz, K. Z. 1960. *So kam der Mensch auf den Hund.* Vienna: Borotha-Schoeler.

—— 1966 (1963). *On Aggression.* London: Methuen.

—— 1981. *The Foundations of Ethology.* New York: Touchstone.

Lux, K. 1990. *Adam Smith's Mistake.* Boston: Shambhala.

Maccoby, E., and C. Jacklin. 1974. *The Psychology of Sex Differences.* Stanford: Stanford University Press.

de Mandeville, B. 1966 (1714). *The Fable of the Bees: or, Private Vices, Public Benefits,* vol. 1. London: Oxford University Press.

Manning, J. T., R. Heaton, and A. T. Chamberlain. 1994. Left-side cradling: Similarities and differences between apes and humans. *Journal of Human Evolution* 26:77–83.

Marino, L., D. Reiss, and G. G. Gallup. 1994. Mirror self-recognition in bottlenose dolphins: Implications for comparative investigations of highly dissimilar species. In S. T. Parker, R. W. Mitchell, and M. L. Boccia, eds., *Self-Awareness in Animals and Humans: Developmental Perspectives*, pp. 380–391. Cambridge: Cambridge University Press.

Marshall Thomas, E. 1993. *The Hidden Life of Dogs.* Boston: Houghton Mifflin.

Marten, K., and S. Psarakos. 1994. Evidence of self-awareness in the bottlenose dolphin *(Tursiops truncatus).* In S. T. Parker, R. W. Mitchell, and M. L. Boccia, eds., *Self-Awareness in Animals and Humans: Developmental Perspectives*, pp. 361–379. Cambridge: Cambridge University Press.

Maslow, A. H. 1936. The role of dominance in the social and sexual behavior of infra-human primates. I. Observations at Vilas Park Zoo. *Journal of Genetical Psychology* 48:261–277.

—— 1940. Dominance-quality and social behavior in infra-human primates. *Journal of Social Psychology* 11:313–324.

Mason, W. A. 1993. The nature of social conflict: The psycho-ethological perspective. In W. A. Mason and S. P. Mendoza, eds., *Primate Social Conflict*, pp. 13–47. Albany: State University of New York Press.

Masson, J. M., and S. McCarthy. 1995. *When Elephants Weep: The Emotional Lives of Animals.* New York: Delacorte.

Masters, R. 1984. Review of *Chimpanzee Politics*. *Politics and the Life Sciences* 2:208–209.

Matsuzawa, T. 1989. Spontaneous pattern construction in a chimpanzee. In P. Heltne and L. Marquardt, eds., *Understanding Chimpanzees*, pp. 252–265. Cambridge, Mass.: Harvard University Press.

––––––– 1990. Form perception and visual acuity in a chimpanzee. *Folia primatologica* 55:24–32.

Maynard Smith, J., and G. R. Price. 1973. The logic of animal conflict. *Nature* 246:15–18.

Mayr, E. 1963. *Populations, Species, and Evolution*. Cambridge, Mass.: Belknap Press, Harvard University Press.

McBride, A. F., and D. O. Hebb. 1948. Behavior of the captive bottle-nose dolphin, *Tursiops truncatus*. *Journal of Comparative Physiological Psychology* 41:111–123.

McGrew, W. C. 1975. Patterns of plant food sharing by wild chimpanzees. In *Contemporary Biology 5th International Congress of Primatology, Nagoya 1974*, pp. 304–309. Basel: Karger.

––––––– 1992. *Chimpanzee Material Culture*. Cambridge: Cambridge University Press.

McGuire, M., M. Raleigh, and C. Johnson. 1983. Social dominance in adult male vervet monkeys: General considerations. *Social Science Information* 22:89–123.

Mednick, M. T. 1989. On the politics of psychological constructs: Stop the bandwagon, I want to get off. *American Psychologist* 44:1118–23.

Menzel, E. W. 1973. *Precultural Primate Behavior*. Basel: Karger.

––––––– 1974. A group of young chimpanzees in a one-acre field. In A. M. Schrier and F. Stollnitz, eds., *Behavior of Non-human Primates*, vol. 5, pp. 83–153. New York: Academic Press.

––––––– 1986. How can you tell if an animal is intelligent? In R. J. Schusterman, J. A. Thomas, and F. G. Wood, eds., *Dolphin Cognition and Behavior: A Comparative Approach*, pp.167–181. London: Erlbaum.

––––––– 1988. Mindless behaviorism, bodiless cognitivism, or primatology? *Behavioral and Brain Sciences* 11:258–259.

Mercer, P. 1972. *Sympathy and Ethics: A Study of the Relationship between Sympathy and Morality with Special Reference to Hume's Treatise*. Oxford: Clarendon.

Midgley, M. 1979. Gene-juggling. *Philosophy* 54:439–458.

––––––– 1991. *Can't We Make Moral Judgements?* New York: St. Martin's.

––––––– 1994. *The Ethical Primate: Humans, Freedom and Morality*. London: Routledge.

Miller, B. L. 1990. Aggression and other social behaviors in a captive group of Japanese Monkeys, *Macaca fuscata fuscata*. Master's thesis, University of Wisconsin–Milwaukee.

Milton, K. 1985. Mating patterns of woolly spider monkeys, *Brachyteles arachnoides:* Implications for female choice. *Behavioral Ecology and Sociobiology* 17:53–59.

—— 1992. Civilization and its discontents. *Natural History* 101(3):37–42.

Mitchell, R. W. 1993. Mental models of mirror-self-recognition: Two theories. *New Ideas in Psychology* 11:295–325.

Mitchell, R. W., N. Thompson, and L. Miles. Forthcoming. *Anthropomorphism, Anecdotes, and Animals.* Albany: State University of New York Press.

Montagu, M. F. A. 1968. The new litany of "innate depravity" or original sin revisited. In M. F. A. Montagu, ed., *Man and Aggression.* London: Oxford University Press.

Morgan, E. 1982. *The Aquatic Ape.* New York: Stein and Day.

Moss, C. 1988. *Elephant Memories: Thirteen Years in the Life of an Elephant Family.* New York: Fawcett Columbine.

Nieuwenhuijsen, C., and F. B. M. de Waal. 1982. Effects of spatial crowding on social behavior in a chimpanzee colony. *Zoo Biology* 1:5–28.

Nishida, T. 1968. The social group of wild chimpanzees in the Mahale Mountains. *Primates* 9:167–224.

—— 1979. The social structure of chimpanzees in the Mahale Mountains. In D. A. Hamburg and E. R. McCown, eds., *The Great Apes,* pp. 73–121. Menlo Park, Calif.: Benjamin Cummings.

—— 1983. Alpha status and agonistic alliance in wild chimpanzees. *Primates* 24:318–336.

—— 1987. Local traditions and cultural transmission. In B. B. Smuts et al., eds., *Primate Societies,* pp. 462–474. Chicago: University of Chicago Press.

—— 1989. Social interactions between resident and immigrant female chimpanzees. In P. Heltne and L. Marquardt, eds., *Understanding Chimpanzees,* pp. 68–89. Cambridge, Mass.: Harvard University Press.

—— 1994. Review of recent findings on Mahale chimpanzees. In R. W. Wrangham et al. eds., Chimpanzee Cultures, pp. 373–396. Cambridge, Mass.: Harvard University Press.

Nishida, T., et al. 1992. Meat-sharing as a coalition strategy by an alpha male chimpanzee? In T. Nishida et al., eds., *Topics in Primatology,* vol. 1, *Human Origins,* pp. 159–174. Tokyo: University of Tokyo Press.

Nissen, H. W., and M. P. Crawford. 1936. A preliminary study of food-sharing behavior in young chimpanzees. *Journal of Comparative Psychology* 22:383–419.

Nitecki, M. H., and D. V. Nitecki. 1993. *Evolutionary Ethics.* Albany: State University of New York Press.

Noë, R. 1992. Alliance formation among male baboons: Shopping for profitable partners. In A. H. Harcourt and F. B. M. de Waal, eds., *Coa-*

*litions and Alliances in Humans and Other Animals,* pp. 285–321. Oxford: Oxford University Press.

Noë, R., F. B. M. de Waal, and J. A. R. A. M. van Hooff. 1980. Types of dominance in a chimpanzee colony. *Folia primatologica* 34:90–110.

Norris, K. S. 1991. *Dolphin Days.* New York: Avon.

Novak, M. A., and H. F. Harlow. 1975. Social recovery of monkeys isolated for the first year of life. I. Rehabilitation and therapy. *Developmental Psychology* 11:453–465.

Nucci, L. P., and E. Turiel. 1978. Social interactions and the development of social concepts in preschool children. *Child Development* 49:400–407.

Parker, S. T., R. W. Mitchell, and M. L. Boccia. 1994. *Self-Awareness in Animals and Humans: Developmental Perspectives.* Cambridge: Cambridge University Press.

Patterson, F. G. P., and R. H. Cohn. 1994. Self-recognition and self-awareness in lowland gorillas. In S. T. Parker, R. W. Mitchell, and M. L. Boccia, eds., *Self-Awareness in Animals and Humans: Developmental Perspectives,* pp. 273–290. Cambridge: Cambridge University Press.

Pavelka, M. S. McDonald- 1993. *Monkeys of the Mesquite: The Social Life of the South Texas Snow Monkey.* Dubuque, Iowa: Kendall/Hunt.

Perry, S., and L. Rose. 1994. Begging and transfer of coati meat by white-faced capuchin monkeys, *Cebus capucinus. Primates* 35:409–415.

Piaget, J. 1962 (1928). *The Moral Judgment of the Child.* New York: Crowell-Collier and Macmillan.

Pilleri, G. 1984. Epimeletic behaviour in Cetacea: Intelligent or instinctive? In G. Pilleri, ed., *Investigations on Cetacea,* pp. 30–48. Vammala, Finland: Vammalan Kirjapaino Oy.

Pinker, S. 1994. Is there a gene for compassion? *New York Times Book Review,* Sept. 25.

Porter, J. W. 1977. Pseudorca stranding. *Oceans* 4:8–14.

Povinelli, D. J. 1987. Monkeys, apes, mirrors and minds: The evolution of self-awareness in primates. *Human Evolution* 2:493–507.

———— 1994. How to create self-recognizing gorillas (but don't try it on macaques). In S. T. Parker, R. W. Mitchell, and M. L. Boccia, eds., *Self-Awareness in Animals and Humans: Developmental Perspectives,* pp. 291–300. Cambridge: Cambridge University Press.

Povinelli, D. J., S. T. Boysen, and K. E. Nelson. 1990. Inferences about guessing and knowing by chimpanzees *(Pan troglodytes). Journal of Comparative Psychology* 104:203–210.

Povinelli, D. J., K. E. Nelson, and S. T. Boysen. 1992. Comprehension of social role reversal by chimpanzees:Evidence of empathy? *Animal Behaviour* 43:633–640.

Povinelli, D. J., A. B. Rulf, and M. A. Novak. 1992. Role reversal by rhesus monkeys, but no evidence of empathy. *Animal Behaviour* 44:269–281.

Power, M. 1991. *The Egalitarians: Human and Chimpanzee.* Cambridge: Cambridge University Press.

Premack, D., and G. Woodruff. 1978. Does the chimpanzee have a theory of mind? *Behavioral and Brain Sciences* 1:515–526.

Pryor, K. 1975. *Lads before the Wind.* New York: Harper and Row.

Rasa, O. A. E. 1976. Invalid care in the dwarf mongoose *(Helogale undulata rufula). Zeitschrift für Tierpsychologie* 42:337–342.

——— 1979. The effects of crowding on the social relationships and behaviour of the dwarf mongoose *(Helogale undulata rufula). Zeitschrift für Tierpsychologie* 49:317–329.

Rawls, J. 1972. *A Theory of Justice.* Oxford: Oxford University Press.

Regal, P. J. 1990. *The Anatomy of Judgment.* Minneapolis: University of Minnesota Press.

Reinhardt, V., R. Dodsworth, and J. Scanlan. 1986. Altruistic interference shown by the alpha-female of a captive group of rhesus monkeys. *Folia primatologica* 46:44–50.

Ren, R., et al. 1991. The reconciliation behavior of golden monkeys *(Rhinopithecus roxellanae roxellanae)* in small breeding groups. *Primates* 32:321–327.

van Rhijn, J., and R. Vodegel. 1980. Being honest about one's intentions: An evolutionarily stable strategy for animal conflicts. *Journal of Theoretical Biology* 85:623–641.

Richards, R. J. 1987. *Darwin and the Emergence of Evolutionary Theories of Mind and Behavior.* Chicago: University of Chicago Press.

Rousseau, J. 1965 (1755). *Discours sur l'origine et les fondements de l'inégalité parmi les hommes.* Paris: Gallimard.

Ruse, M. 1986. *Taking Darwin Seriously: A Naturalistic Approach to Philosophy.* Oxford: Blackwell.

——— 1988. Response to Williams: Selfishness is not enough. *Zygon* 23:413–416.

Sabater Pi, J., et al. 1993. Behavior of bonobos *(Pan paniscus)* following their capture of monkeys in Zaire. *International Journal of Primatology* 14:797–804.

Sackin, S., and E. Thelen. 1984. An ethological study of peaceful associative outcomes to conflict in preschool children. *Child Development* 55:1098–1102.

Saffire, W. 1990. The bonding market. *New York Times Magazine,* June 24.

Sahlins, M. D. 1965. On the sociology of primitive exchange. In M. Banton, ed., *The Relevance of Models for Social Anthropology,* pp. 139–236. London: Tavistock.

Salk, L. 1973. The role of the heartbeat in the relations between mother and infant. *Scientific American* 228:24–29.

Salzinger, K. 1990. B. F. Skinner 1904–1990. *American Psychological Association Observer* 3:1–4.

Savage-Rumbaugh, E. S., et al. 1986. Spontaneous symbol acquisition and communicative use by two pygmy chimpanzees. *Journal of Experimental Psychology* 115:211–235.

Scanlon, C. E. 1986. Social development in a congenitally blind infant rhesus macaque. In R. G. Rawlins and M. J. Kessler, eds., *The Cayo Santiago Macaques,* pp. 94–109. Albany: State University of New York Press.

van Schaik, C. P. 1983. Why are diurnal primates living in groups? *Behaviour* 87:120–144.

——— 1989. The ecology of social relationships amongst female primates. In V. Standen and R. A. Foley, eds., *Comparative Socioecology: The Behavioral Ecology of Humans and Other Mammals,* pp. 195–218. Oxford: Blackwell.

van Schaik, C. P., and M. A. van Noordwijk. 1985. Evolutionary effect of the absence of felids on the social organization of the macaques on the island of Simeulue (*Macaca fascicularis fusca,* Miller 1903). *Folia primatologica* 44:138–147.

Schama, S. 1987. *The Embarrassment of Riches: An Interpretation of Dutch Culture in the Golden Age.* New York: Knopf.

Scott, J. F. 1971. *Internalization of Norms: A Sociological Theory of Moral Commitment.* Englewood Cliffs, N.J.: Prentice-Hall.

Scott, J. P. 1958. *Animal Behavior.* Chicago: University of Chicago Press.

Seton, E. T. 1907. *The Natural History of the Ten Commandments.* New York: Scribners.

Seville Statement on Violence. 1986. Middletown, Conn.: Wesleyan University.

Seyfarth, R. M. 1981. Do monkeys rank each other? *Behavioral and Brain Sciences* 4:447–448.

——— 1983. Grooming and social competition in primates. In R. Hinde, ed., *Primate Social Relationships: An Integrated Approach,* pp. 182–190. Sunderland, Mass.: Sinauer.

Seyfarth, R. M., and D. L. Cheney. 1988. Empirical tests of reciprocity theory: Problems in assessment. *Ethology and Sociobiology* 9:181–188.

Sherif, M. 1966. *In Common Predicament: Social Psychology of Intergroup Conflict and Cooperation.* Boston: Houghton Mifflin.

Sigg, H., and J. Falett. 1985. Experiments on respect of possession in hamadryas baboons *(Papio hamadryas). Animal Behaviour* 33:978–984.

Silk, J. B. 1992a. The origins of caregiving behavior. *American Journal of Physical Anthropology* 87:227–229.

——— 1992b. The patterning of intervention among male bonnet macaques: Reciprocity, revenge, and loyalty. *Current Anthropology* 33:318–325.

Simon, H. A. 1990. A mechanism for social selection and successful altruism. *Science* 250:1665–68.

Singer, P. 1976. *Animal Liberation.* London: Jonathan Cape.

——— 1981. *The Expanding Circle: Ethics and Sociobiology.* New York: Farrar, Straus and Giroux.

Skinner, B. F. 1990. Can psychology be a science of mind? *American Psychologist* 45:1206–10.

Small, M. F. 1990. Social climber: Independent rise in rank by a female Barbary macaque *(Macaca sylvanus)*. *Folia primatologica* 55:85–91.

Smetana, J. G., M. Killen, and E. Turiel. 1991. Children's reasoning about interpersonal and moral conflicts. *Child Development* 62:629–644.

Smith, A. 1937 (1759). *A Theory of Moral Sentiments*. New York: Modern Library.

———— 1982 (1776). *An Inquiry into the Nature and Causes of the Wealth of Nations*. Indianapolis: Liberty Classics.

Smuts, B. B. 1985. *Sex and Friendship in Baboons*. New York: Aldine.

———— 1987. Gender, aggression, and influence. In B. B. Smuts et al., eds., *Primate Societies,* pp. 400–412. Chicago: University of Chicago Press.

Smuts, B. B., and J. M. Watanabe. 1990. Social relationships and ritualized greetings in adult male baboons *(Papio cynocephalus anubis)*. *International Journal of Primatology* 11:147–172.

Sober, E. 1984. *The Nature of Selection: Evolutionary Theory in Philosophical Focus*. Cambridge, Mass.: MIT Press.

———— 1988. What is evolutionary altruism? *Canadian Journal of Philosophy* 14:75–99.

Stanford, C. B., et al. 1994a. Patterns of predation by chimpanzees on red colobus monkeys in Gombe National Park, 1982–1991. *American Journal of Physical Anthropology* 94:213–228.

———— 1994b. Hunting decisions in wild chimpanzees. *Behaviour* 131:1–18.

von Stephanitz, M. 1950 (1918). *The German Shepherd Dog*. 8th rev. ed. Augsburg: Verein für Deutsche Schäferhunde.

Strier, K. B. 1992a. Causes and consequences of nonaggression in the woolly spider monkey, or muriqui *(Brachyteles arachnoides)*. In J. Silverberg and J. P. Gray, eds., *Aggression and Peacefulness in Humans and Other Primates,* pp. 100–116. New York: Oxford University Press.

———— 1992b. *Faces in the Forest: The Endangered Muriqui Monkeys of Brazil*. New York: Oxford University Press.

Strum, S. C. 1987. *Almost Human: A Journey into the World of Baboons*. New York: Random House.

Sugiyama, Y. 1984. Population dynamics in wild chimpanzees at Bossou, Guinea, between 1976 and 1983. *Primates* 25:391–400.

———— 1988. Grooming interactions among adult chimpanzees at Bossou, Guinea, with special reference to social structure. *International Journal of Primatology* 9:393–408.

Tannen, D. 1990. *You Just Don't Understand: Women and Men in Conversation*. New York: Ballantine.

Taylor, C. E., and M. T. McGuire. 1988. Reciprocal altruism: Fifteen years later. *Ethology and Sociobiology* 9:67–72.

Teleki, G. 1973a. Group response to the accidental death of a chimpanzee in Gombe National Park, Tanzania. *Folia primatologica* 20:81–94.

—— 1973b. *The Predatory Behavior of Wild Chimpanzees.* Lewisburg, Penn.: Bucknell University Press.

Temerlin, M. K. 1975. *Lucy: Growing up Human.* Palo Alto, Calif.: Science and Behavior Books.

Thierry, B., and J. R. Anderson. 1986. Adoption in anthropoid primates. *International Journal of Primatology* 7:191–216.

Thompson, N. S. 1976. My descent from the monkey. In P. Bateson and P. Klopfer, eds., *Perspectives in Ethology,* pp. 221–230. New York: Plenum.

Tinklepaugh, O. L. 1928. An experimental study of representative factors in monkeys. *Journal of Comparative Psychology* 8:197–236.

Tobin, J. J., D. Y. H. Wu, and D. H. Davidson. 1989. *Preschool in Three Cultures.* New Haven: Yale University Press.

Todes, D. 1989. *Darwin without Malthus: The Struggle for Existence in Russian Evolutionary Thought.* New York: Oxford University Press.

Tokida, E., et al. 1994. Tool-using in Japanese macaques: Use of stones to obtain fruit from a pipe. *Animal Behaviour* 47:1023–30.

Tomasello, M., A. Kruger, and H. Ratner. 1993. Cultural learning. *Behavioral and Brain Sciences* 16:495–552.

Trivers, R. L. 1971. The evolution of reciprocal altruism. *Quarterly Review of Biology* 46:35–57.

—— 1974. Parent-offspring conflict. *American Zoologist* 14:249–264.

Trumler, E. 1974. *Hunde Ernst Genommen: Zum Wesen und Verständnis ihres Verhaltens.* Munich: Piper.

Turnbull, C. M. 1972. *The Mountain People.* New York: Touchstone.

Varley, M., and D. Symmes. 1966. The hierarchy of dominance in a group of macaques. *Behaviour* 27:54–75.

Vehrencamp, S. A. 1983. A model for the evolution of despotic versus egalitarian societies. *Animal Behaviour* 31:667–682.

Visalberghi, E., and D. M. Fragaszy. 1990. Do monkeys ape? In S. Parker and K. Gibson, eds., *"Language" and Intelligence in Monkeys and Apes: Comparative Developmental Perspectives,* pp. 247–273. Cambridge: Cambridge University Press.

Vogel, C. 1985. Evolution und Moral. In H. Maier-Leibnitz, ed., *Zeugen des Wissens,* pp. 467–507. Mainz: Hase und Koehler.

—— 1988. Gibt es eine natürliche Moral? *Civis* 1:65–78.

Vollmer, P. J. 1977. Do mischievous dogs reveal their "guilt"? *Veterinary Medicine Small Animal Clinician* 72:1002–5.

de Waal, F. B. M. 1977. The organization of agonistic relations within two captive groups of Java-monkeys *(Macaca fascicularis). Zeitschrift für Tierpsychologie* 44:225–282.

—— 1982. *Chimpanzee Politics: Power and Sex among Apes.* London: Jonathan Cape.

—— 1984. Sex-differences in the formation of coalitions among chimpanzees. *Ethology and Sociobiology* 5:239–255.

—— 1986a. The brutal elimination of a rival among captive male chimpanzees. *Ethology and Sociobiology* 7:237–251.

—— 1986b. Deception in the natural communication of chimpanzees. In R. W. Mitchell and N. S. Thompson, eds., *Deception: Human and Nonhuman Deceit,* pp.221–244. Albany: State University of New York Press.

—— 1986c. Integration of dominance and social bonding in primates. *Quarterly Review of Biology* 61:459–479.

—— 1987. Tension regulation and nonreproductive functions of sex among captive bonobos *(Pan paniscus). National Geographic Research* 3:318–335.

—— 1989a. *Peacemaking among Primates.* Cambridge, Mass.: Harvard University Press.

—— 1989b. Dominance "style" and primate social organization. In V. Standen and R. A. Foley, eds., *Comparative Socioecology: The Behavioural Ecology of Humans and Other Mammals,* pp. 243–264. Oxford: Blackwell.

—— 1989c. The myth of a simple relation between space and aggression in captive primates. *Zoo Biology Supplement* 1:141–148.

—— 1989d. Food sharing and reciprocal obligations among chimpanzees. *Journal of Human Evolution* 18:433–459.

—— 1990. Do rhesus mothers suggest friends to their offspring? *Primates* 31:597–600.

—— 1991a. Complementary methods and convergent evidence in the study of primate social cognition. *Behaviour* 118:297–320.

—— 1991b. The chimpanzee's sense of social regularity and its relation to the human sense of justice. *American Behavioral Scientist* 34:335–349.

—— 1992a. Aggression as a well-integrated part of primate social relationships: Critical comments on the Seville Statement on Violence. In J. Silverberg and J. P. Gray, eds., *Aggression and Peacefulness in Humans and Other Primates,* pp. 37–56. New York: Oxford University Press.

—— 1992b. Appeasement, celebration, and food sharing in the two *Pan* species. In T. Nishida et al., eds., *Topics in Primatology,* vol. 1, *Human Origins,* pp. 37–50. Tokyo: University of Tokyo Press.

—— 1992c. A social life for chimpanzees in captivity. In J. Erwin and J. C. Landon, eds., *Chimpanzee Conservation and Public Health: Environments for the Future,* pp. 83–87. Rockville, Md.: Diagnon/Bioqual.

—— 1992d. Intentional deception in primates. *Evolutionary Anthropology* 1:86–92.

—— 1993a. Reconciliation among primates: A review of empirical evidence and unresolved issues. In W. A. Mason and S. P. Mendoza, eds., *Primate Social Conflict,* pp. 111–144. Albany: State University of New York Press.

———— 1993b. Sex differences in chimpanzee (and human) behavior: A matter of social values? In M. Hechter, L. Nadel, and R. Michod, eds., *The Origin of Values,* pp. 285–303. New York: Aldine de Gruyter.

———— 1993c. Co-development of dominance relations and affiliative bonds in rhesus monkeys. In M. E. Pereira and L. A. Fairbanks, eds., *Juvenile Primates: Life History, Development, and Behavior,* pp. 259–270. New York: Oxford University Press.

———— 1994. The chimpanzee's adaptive potential: A comparison of social life under captive and wild conditions. In R. W. Wrangham et al., eds., *Chimpanzee Cultures,* pp. 243–260. Cambridge, Mass.: Harvard University Press.

de Waal, F. B. M., and F. Aureli. Forthcoming. Reconciliation, consolation, and a possible cognitive difference between macaque and chimpanzee. In A. E. Russon, K. A. Bard, and S. T. Parker, eds., *Reaching into Thought: The Minds of the Great Apes.* Cambridge: Cambridge University Press.

de Waal, F. B. M., and D. L. Johanowicz. 1993. Modification of reconciliation behavior through social experience: An experiment with two macaque species. *Child Development* 64:897–908.

de Waal, F. B. M., and L. M. Luttrell. 1985. The formal hierarchy of rhesus monkeys: An investigation of the bared-teeth display. *American Journal of Primatology* 9:73–85.

———— 1986. The similarity principle underlying social bonding among female rhesus monkeys. *Folia primatologica* 46:215–234.

———— 1988. Mechanisms of social reciprocity in three primate species: Symmetrical relationship characteristics or cognition? *Ethology and Sociobiology* 9:101–118.

———— 1989. Toward a comparative socioecology of the genus *Macaca*: Intergroup comparisons of rhesus and stumptail monkeys. *American Journal of Primatology* 10:83–109.

de Waal, F. B. M., and R. Ren. 1988. Comparison of the reconciliation behavior of stumptail and rhesus macaques. *Ethology* 78:129–142.

de Waal, F. B. M., and A. van Roosmalen. 1979. Reconciliation and consolation among chimpanzees. *Behavioral Ecology and Sociobiology* 5:55–66.

de Waal, F. B. M., and D. Yoshihara. 1983. Reconciliation and re-directed affection in rhesus monkeys. *Behaviour* 85:224–241.

de Waal, F. B. M., L. M. Luttrell, and M. E. Canfield. 1993. Preliminary data on voluntary food sharing in brown capuchin monkeys. *American Journal of Primatology* 29:73–78.

de Waal, F. B. M., et al. In press. Behavioral retardation in a macaque with autosomal trisomy and aging mother. *American Journal on Mental Retardation.*

Walker, L. J. 1984. Sex differences in the development of moral reasoning: A critical review. *Child Development* 55:677–691.

Walker Leonard, J. 1979. A strategy approach to the study of primate dominance behaviour. *Behavioural Processes* 4:155–172.

Walters, J. 1980. Interventions and the development of dominance relationships in female baboons. *Folia primatologica* 34:61–89.

Weiss, R. F., et al. 1971. Altruism is rewarding. *Science* 171:1262–63.

Wendt, H. 1971. *From Ape to Adam.* London: Thames and Hudson.

Westergaard, G. C., C. W. Hyatt, and W. D. Hopkins. 1994. The responses of bonobos *(Pan paniscus)* to mirror-image stimulation: Evidence of self-recognition. *Journal of Human Evolution* 9:273–279.

Whiten, A. 1991. *Natural Theories of Mind: Evolution, Development and Simulation of Everyday Mindreading.* Oxford: Blackwell.

Whiten, A., and R. W. Byrne. 1988. Tactical deception in primates. *Behavioral and Brain Sciences* 11:233–273.

Whiten, A., and R. Ham. 1992. On the nature and evolution of imitation in the animal kingdom: Reappraisal of a century of research. In P. J. B. Slater et al. eds., *Advances in the Study of Behavior,* vol. 21, pp. 239–283. New York: Academic Press.

Wickler, W. 1981 (1971). *Die Biologie der Zehn Gebote: Warum die Natur für uns kein Vorbild ist.* Munich: Piper.

Wilkinson, G. S. 1984. Reciprocal food sharing in the vampire bat. *Nature* 308:181–184.

Williams, G. C. 1966. *Adaptation and Natural Selection.* Princeton: Princeton University Press.

——— 1988. Reply to comments on "Huxley's evolution and ethics in sociobiological perspective." *Zygon* 23:437–438.

——— 1989. A sociobiological expansion of "Evolution and Ethics." In *Evolution and Ethics,* pp. 179–214. Princeton: Princeton University Press.

Wilson, D. S. 1983. The group selection controversy: History and current status. *Annual Review of Ecology and Systematics* 14:159–187.

Wilson, D. S., and E. Sober. 1994. Reintroducing group selection to the human behavioral sciences. *Behavioral and Brain Sciences* 17:585–654.

Wilson, E. O. 1975. *Sociobiology: The New Synthesis.* Cambridge, Mass.: Belknap Press, Harvard University Press.

Wilson, J. Q. 1993. *The Moral Sense.* New York: Free Press.

Wispé, L. 1991. *The Psychology of Sympathy.* New York: Plenum.

Woodburn, J. 1982. Egalitarian societies. *Man* 17:431–451.

Wrangham, R. W. 1979. On the evolution of ape social systems. *Social Science Information* 18:335–368.

—— 1980. An ecological model of female-bonded primate groups. *Behaviour* 75:262–300.

Wrangham, R. W., A. P. Clark, and G. Isabirye-Basuta. 1992. Female social relationships and social organization of Kibale Forest chimpanzees. In T. Nishida et al., eds., *Topics in Primatology,* vol. 1, *Human Origins,* pp. 81–98. Tokyo: University of Tokyo Press.

Wrangham, R. W., et al. 1994. *Chimpanzee Cultures.* Cambridge, Mass.: Harvard University Press.

Wright, R. 1994. *The Moral Animal: The New Science of Evolutionary Psychology.* New York: Pantheon.

Yerkes, R. M. 1925. *Almost Human.* New York: Century.

—— 1941. Conjugal contrasts among chimpanzees. *Journal of Abnormal Social Psychology* 36:175–199.

Yerkes, R. M., and A. W. Yerkes. 1929. *The Great Apes: A Study of Anthropoid Life.* New Haven: Yale University Press.

—— 1935. Social behavior in infrahuman primates. In *A Handbook of Social Psychology,* pp. 973–1033. Worcester, Mass.: Clark University Press.

Zahn-Waxler, C., B. Hollenbeck, and M. Radke-Yarrow. 1984. The origins of empathy and altruism. In M. W. Fox and L. D. Mickley, eds., *Advances in Animal Welfare Science,* pp. 21–39. Washington, D.C.: Humane Society of the United States.

Zahn-Waxler, C., et al. 1992. Development of concern for others. *Developmental Psychology* 28:126–136.

# ACKNOWLEDGMENTS

This book reflects more than two decades of primate research—and a lifelong love of animals. As a child, I caught and kept sticklebacks, raised jackdaws, and bred mice, always fascinated with the details of their behavior. It was only later that I discovered that some of these creatures also happened to be the favorites of two renowned ethologists, Konrad Lorenz and Niko Tinbergen. No wonder I identified with these men and their groundbreaking work.

I was educated in the Dutch ethological tradition by eminent scientists such as Gerard Baerends, Jaap Kruijt, Piet Wiepkema, and particularly Jan van Hooff, under whose supervision I conducted my first primate studies. My six years with the chimpanzees at the Arnhem Zoo are still a highlight. Core ideas of the present book were developed during this period, if not in full-fledged form then at least in utero. I am grateful to everyone involved, from the zoo director, Anton van Hooff, to the many students of the University of Utrecht.

Most material for this book was collected in the 1980s at the Wisconsin Regional Primate Research Center in Madison. I did make a few expeditions to San Diego and Atlanta to study bonobos and chimpanzees, but Wisconsin was the home base where I had rhesus, stump-tailed, and capuchin monkeys. Two people were absolutely crucial: Robert Goy, the director who invited me to the center, and

Lesleigh Luttrell, who assisted me with great dedication in my many projects. Peter Judge and RenMei Ren joined my team as scientists, and students of the University of Wisconsin contributed to the research: Kim Bauers, Eloise Canfield, Charles Chaffin, Karen Friedlen, Lisa Jeannotte, Denise Johanowicz, Brenda Miller, Katherine Offutt, Amy Parish, and Kurt Sladky. I very much enjoyed my interactions with fellow ethologists and primatologists in Madison, especially Charles Snowdon and Karen Strier.

In 1991 I moved to Atlanta, Georgia, to join the scientific staff of the Yerkes Regional Primate Research Center as well as the faculty of the Department of Psychology at Emory University. The principal reason was my desire to continue working with chimpanzees, an understudied species in relation to the interest it deserves. The Yerkes Primate Center and its director, Frederick King, have been most generous in helping me set up a research operation that today includes a team of approximately fifteen enthusiastic people. Of these, let me mention in particular technicians Lisa Parr and Michael Seres and postdoctoral associate Filippo Aureli; they have made invaluable contributions to the research reported in this book.

Atlanta and nearby Athens, Georgia, probably have the world's largest concentration of both nonhuman primates and primatologists; the intellectual environment has proved most stimulating. Colleagues in the psychology department have taught me to think critically about a number of issues with which, as a zoologist, I had little familiarity.

Over the years my research has been generously supported by two regional primate research centers, as well as by funding from the National Science Foundation, the National Institutes of Mental Health, the National Institutes of Health, the Harry Frank Guggenheim Foundation, and Emory University.

The genesis of this book was a 1989 meeting in Monterey, California, of the Gruter Institute for Law and Behavioral Research. For many years Margaret Gruter, a legal scholar with a keen interest in evolutionary theory, has brought together international experts to explore the interface between law and biology. This particular meeting, entitled "Biology, Law, and the Sense of Justice," first made me realize how the phenomena that I was studying in nonhuman primates could shed light on the origin of justice and morality in our own species. By assembling scholars of widely disparate disciplines, Margaret has rendered all of us a tremendous service. The influence of her institute will reverberate throughout academic life for a long while.

Because morality is such a broad topic, I invited comments on drafts of the manuscript from many scholars—from economists to philosophers, and from cognitive psychologists to fellow ethologists and biologists. I learned much from their reflections and sometimes was given references to significant literature that I had not been aware of. Much of this was done with the convenience of the Internet. Naturally, not every reviewer agreed with me, and not every disagreement could be resolved. I remain fully responsible for the opinions expressed in this book.

Commentators on portions of the manuscript and contributors of observations or citations include Otto Adang, Richard Alexander, Filippo Aureli, Kim Bard, Christopher Boehm, Sue Boinsky, Gordon Burghardt, Josep Call, Richard Connor, Marina Cords, Hank Davis, Lee Dugatkin, Robert Frank, David Goldfoot, Harold Gouzoules, Christine Johnson, Peter Judge, Melanie Killen, Bruce Knauft, Stella Launy, Elizabeth Lloyd, Rudolf Makkreel, Anne McGuire, Ulric Neisser, Toshisada Nishida, Ronald Noë, Mary McDonald Pavelka, Michael Pereira, Susan Perry, Daniel Povinelli, John Robinson, Philippe Rochat, Sue Savage-Rumbaugh, Laele Sayigh, Carel van Schaik, Jeanne Scheurer, Rachel Smolker, Elliott Sober, Volker Sommer, Emanuela Cenami Spada, Karen Strier, Hiroyuki Takasaki, Ichirou Tanaka, Michael Tomasello, Robert Trivers, Peter Verbeek, Elisabetta Visalberghi, Kim Wallen, Andrew Whiten, and David Sloan Wilson.

In addition, I was fortunate to receive comments from four exceptionally incisive readers who went over the manuscript intensively, each from his or her own perspective. These were Barbara Smuts, well versed in the theoretical controversies that run through this book as well as an expert on baboon behavior; Lesleigh Luttrell, who as my assistant of twelve years knows every monkey subject by name and background, and in addition has excellent editorial judgment; Michael Fisher, my editor and champion at Harvard University Press; and my wife, Catherine Marin, who read every draft as it came off my printer. The detailed feedback from these four persons helped enormously in shaping the book's content and form. I also thank Vivian Wheeler for the thoroughness with which she edited the final text.

The majority of the photographs are mine, taken on black-and-white Kodak film with a Minolta camera and lenses ranging from 50 to 500 millimeters. Robert Dodsworth and Frank Kiernan, photographers at the Wisconsin and Yerkes primate centers, respectively, did much of the darkroom work. For additional illustrations I thank

Donna Bierschwale, Christophe Boesch, Gordon Burghardt, Susan Meier, Emil Menzel, Cynthia Moss, Ronald Noë, and RenMei Ren.

Catherine created the environment that made it possible for me to complete this challenging yet enjoyable task, providing support, warmth, and humor at home despite a demanding academic career. I could have no greater pleasure, therefore, than to dedicate this book to her.

# INDEX

For ease of identification, main entries that are names of individual primates are italicized.

Egoism. *See* Self-interest
Eibl-Eibesfeldt, Irenäus, 43, 223n33
*Einfühlung*, 79, 85
Eisenstein, Norman, 148
Elephants, 53–54, 63, 171, 225n8
Embarrassment. *See* Shame
Emotional contagion, 69–70, 80, 81, 121, 211; defined, 230n33
Empathy: among chimpanzees, 19–20, 56–57, 58, 85, 210, 233n48; sympathy and, 41; absence of, 47–48; as term, 79; sex difference in, 121. *See also* Play, inhibitions in; Succorant behavior; Sympathy
Erdal, David, 128
Ethics: ethology and, 34–39; intentions of animals and, 73; evolutionary, 224n37
Ethology: sociobiology and, 13; ethics and, 34–39; as term, 35, 222n30. *See also* Zoo biology
Evolutionary parsimony, 64–65
Exchange, concept of. *See* Reciprocal altruism: Reciprocity; Social contract; Trading, concept of
Expectations about others: social rules and, 95–96; observability of, 96; food-sharing and, 153; species differences and, 189; negotiation and, 189–193; theory-of-mind research and, 232n41

*Fable of the Bees* (de Mandeville), 27, 28
Facial discrimination, 248n13
Fairness, 85–86, 160. *See also* Justice
Falett, J., 254n41
*Faustino*, 251n21
*Fawn*, 45–46, 60
*Faza-71*, 9
Fear: of punishment, 106–109; sharing and, 152–153
Fedigan, Laurence, 50
Fedigan, Linda, 50
Feistner, A. T. C., 244n16
*Fifi*, 251n21
Fighting. *See* Aggression; Conflict; Reconciliation
Fiorito, Graziano, 71
Fischler, Claude, 242n7
Fisher, R. A., 221n21
Fission-fusion societies, 168–169, 247n5

Fissioning, 8, 26
Fitness. *See* Natural selection
*Flint*, 54
*Flo*, 54, 188
Floating pyramid model, 212–216
*Fons*, 227n17
Food-sharing: origin of kissing in, 43; rules and, 93, 95; reciprocal altruism and, 136–144; chimpanzees and, 140–142, 147–148, 149–150; traits of shared foods, 144–145; extrafamilial, 144–146; concept of giving and, 146–150; methods of transfer, 244n16. *See also* Generosity; Reciprocity
Formal dominance: changes in, 100, 235n10; distinguished from everyday contests, 100; acceptance from below and, 131–132; food-sharing and, 142–144, 152–154; "divide-and-rule" strategy and, 172–173; received view of, 234n6. *See also* Hierarchy, social; Power; Rules
Fossey, Dian, 227n19
Frank, Robert, 18, 116, 218
Freedman, David, 108
Freud, Sigmund, 17, 238n18
Friendship: among nonhuman primates, 19, 24, 26–27, 101, 156; human-ape, 174–175, 189–190

Gage, Phineas, 216–217
Gallup, Gordon, 68, 70
Gardener-and-garden metaphor, 2, 218
Garner, Robert, 72
Gender relations: mediation and, 31–33, 205–206; group sanctions and, 91–92, 205–206; dominance and, 99, 131–132; sneaky matings and, 109–111; food-sharing and, 141–142; captivity and, 169; among muriquis, 201; inhibition in, 245n18. *See also* Mating; Sex differences
Gene-centric sociobiology, 13–20, 220n11
Generosity, 142–144, 152–153, 160, 242n5
Geoffroy-Saint-Hillaire, Etienne, 223n30
Geoffroy-Saint-Hillaire, Isidore, 35
*Georgia*, 13–14, 160
Gibber, Judith, 240n29
Gibson, J. J., 68

Ik (tribe), 85–86, 213, 242n3
IM (two-headed snake), 37
Imanishi, Kinji, 254n2
Imitation, 19–20, 71–73, 180, 231nn37,39. *See also* Learning
Impartial spectator, 33–34, 109
Imprinting, 35, 36
Indignation, 159–160. *See also* Moralistic aggression
Indirect reciprocity, 33, 237n17
Indirect revenge, 159
Individual and society, tensions between, 171–172, 206–208. *See also* Self-sacrifice
Individual model of aggression, 164, 173
Infants. *See* Mother-infant bond
Injuries, responses to, 56–60
Innate releasers, 80–81
Intentions: human moral judgment and, 15, 73; gap between consequences and, 28–29; of animals, 46–47, 73, 96–97, 113, 232n41; communication of, 191–193, 203
Interests, conflux of, 27
Intergroup conflict, 29–31
Internalization of rules, 105–111
Invisible hand metaphor, 28
Isaac, Glynn, 133, 146

Jacoby, Susan, 160
*Jakie,* 83
Janson, Charles, 145
Japanese culture: drinking etiquette in, 136; conflict resolution in, 180–181
Japanese macaques: treatment of the handicapped, 6–7, 8, 9, 50–51, 227n14; matrilines and, 8, 9, 187; friendship among, 26; aggression in, 158–159, 196–197
Jigokudani Park, 6, 8, 26, 48
*Jimoh,* 91–92, 131–132
*Johan* (jackdaw), 134
Johanowicz, Denise, 179
Johnston, Kay, 119–120
Joubert, Beverly, 53
Joubert, Dereck, 53
Judge, Peter, 199, 200, 204
Justice: human social regulation and, 125; control role and, 131; revenge and, 160–162, 184; individual autonomy and, 167

*Kalind,* 82
*Kalunde,* 143
Kant, Immanuel, 10, 87
*Kanzi,* 210
Kaplan, Hillard, 137
Kaufman, Charles, 54
Kennedy, Edward, 194
*Kevin,* 174–175
Keyes, Randall, 52
Killen, M., 247n4
Killer Ape myth, 38, 167, 247n3
*Kindchenschema,* 81
Kin selection, 12, 15, 135, 144, 155, 212. *See also* Group selection; Reciprocal altruism
Kinship: in macaque society, 8; nepotism and, 18; conflict mediation and, 36; reciprocal altruism and, 135; triadic reconciliation and, 203. *See also* Matrilines
Kissing, origin of, 43
Knauft, B. M., 241n33
Knowledge of relationships, 100–101, 203, 235n7
Koestler, Arthur, 102
Kohlberg, Lawrence, 92–93, 105
Köhler, Wolfgang, 68, 85
*Koko,* 210, 230n32
Kortlandt, A., 229n31
*Krazy Kat* (cartoon), 184, 185
Krebs, Dennis, 25
*Krom,* 72, 83
Kropotkin, Petr, 21–23, 27, 29, 162
Kummer, Hans, 172, 181, 245n18, 251n24
Kurland, Jeffrey, 9, 249n20

Language: human acquisition of, 36; role in morality, 45, 79; anthropomorphism and, 63–64; research on ape use of, 111, 210
Langurs. *See* Golden monkeys
Larson, Gary, 217
Law-and-order mentality, 93
Leadership, and dominance, 128–132
Learned adjustment, 48–53, 56–57, 211
Learning: age specificity and, 36, 223n31; black box approach to, 62; of rules, 94–95; of conflict-resolution skills, 178–180, 249n17; active teaching and, 211; observational, 231n39;

Morality *(continued)*
group life as context for, 166–168; ingredients of, 211; neurobiology of,
216–218
Moss, Cynthia, 53–54, 174, 225n8
Mother-infant bond: maternal protection and, 89–91; double-holding and,
101–102; socialization and, 112–114,
122–125; weaning conflict and, 177,
187–189, 251n21; development of
reconciliation skills and, 177–178;
food-sharing and, 243n12
*Mountain People, The* (Turnbull), 85–
86
Mouth feeding, 43
*Mozu,* 6–7, 8, 26, 48
Muriquis, 201

*Napkin,* 177–178
National Science Foundation, 17
Naturalistic fallacy, 38–39, 223n33
Natural selection, 5, 9, 11–12, 16–17,
18, 39
Nature: amorality of, 2, 16, 221n15;
communal principle and, 22–23
Negative evidence, 230n32, 232n41
Negotiation: group life and, 34, 39,
201; conflict as, 187, 188; expecta-
tions and, 189–193; as ingredient of
morality, 211; nonverbal, research
on, 251n24. *See also* Conflict; Media-
tion; Social contract
Nepotism, 18
Neurobiology, 216–218
Nieuwenhuijsen, Kees, 197
*Nikkie,* 97, 130, 157, 172–173
Nishida, Toshisada, 141, 142, 234n4,
239n28, 248n5
Nissen, Henry, 147, 148
Noë, Ronald, 142, 155
van Noordwijk, Maria, 170–171
Norris, Kenneth, 171–172
Novak, Melinda, 178
*Ntologi,* 142–143
Nucci, Larry, 105
Nurturant behavior, 123, 124, 240n29

*Oatly,* 177–178
Octopus, 71
*Of Wolves and Men* (Lopez), 94
*Oortje,* 55–56
*Orange,* 112–113

Orangutans, 67, 71, 226n9
Oregon Regional Primate Research Cen-
ter, 196–197
Orphans, 124, 227n17. See also *Flint;
Fons*

Parsimony, principle of, 64–65, 66
Pavelka, M. S. McDonald-, 227n14
Peacefulness, among muriquis, 202
Peacemaking. *See* Conflict resolution;
Mediation; Reconciliation
*Peacemaking among Primates* (de
Waal), 31, 82, 166
*Peony,* 203
*Pepe,* 84
Pereira, Michael, 59
Perner, Josef, 74
Perry, Susan, 145
Perspective taking, 69–70, 73–78
Persuasion, 191
Philosophy, and morality, 10, 146,
218
Piaget, Jean, 118
Pigtail macaques, 204
Pinker, Steven, 238n18
Plato, 65
Play: inhibitions in, 47–48, 225n8; de-
ception using, 76; sex differences
among humans and, 118–119; cross-
species, 179
Polio victims, reactions to, 83–84,
232n47
Politics, primate, 77, 142–144, 211. *See
also* Alliance formation; Formal
dominance
Population density, 194–196. *See also*
Crowding
Porter, James, 42, 224n3
Portielje, Anton, 67, 229n31
Povinelli, Daniel, 74–75, 232n41
Power: in human societies, 97–98, 97–
105, 125; will to, 99–100; aggression
against infants and, 113; leveling
mechanisms and, 128, 131, 241n33;
struggles for, among chimpanzees,
223n34, 235n10. *See also* Formal
dominance; Hierarchy, social
Power, M., 253n36
Predation: and group life, 170–171; dis-
tinguished from aggression, 247n3.
*See also* Hunting; Meat, status of
Premack, D., 232n41

Price, G. R., 254n41
Primate order, evolutionary tree for, 4
Promiscuous altruism, 214
Prosimians. *See* Ring-tailed lemurs
Proudhon, Pierre-Joseph, 214
Provisioning, 253n36
*Puist,* 76, 97
Punishment: assertive reconciliation and, 104; after the fact, 107–108, 237n11; rule acquisition in juveniles and, 112; revenge and, 157–159, 160

Quid pro quo. *See* Reciprocity

Rank. *See* Formal dominance
Rasa, Anne, 80, 198
Rats, 105–106, 107, 195
Ravens, 133–134
Rawls, John, 161, 167
Reciprocal altruism, 12, 24–27; characteristics of, 24; distinguished from cooperation, 24; link between morality and, 136–144; expectations and, 153–154; revenge and, 157–159, 160; evolution of conscience and, 237n17. *See also* Kin selection; Trivers, Robert
Reciprocity: similarity principle and, 26; among hunter-gatherers, 137–138; experimental evidence for, 150–154; alliances and, 154–159; as ingredient of morality, 211; indirect, 237n17; centralized, 243n10; forms of, in human societies, 243n10. *See also* Reciprocal altruism; Revenge
Reconciliation: as label, 18–19; mediation and, 32–33; assertive, 103–104; sex differences in patterns of, 123–124, 239n28; nature of aggression and, 164–166; defined, 176; protocols for, 176; learning of, 177–182; strategic, 181; maladaptive, 186; crowded conditions and, 200, 252n35; teasing and, 203; triadic, 204; research methods and, 249n14
Reductionism, 17, 102, 220n12
Reite, M., 225n6
Relational model of aggression, 173–176, 186, 193
Relationship, value of, and conflict resolution, 181, 200. *See also* Relational model
Religion, 17, 30, 117

Ren, RenMei, 31–32
Repression theory, 238n18
Reproductive success. *See* Mating
Reputation, 115–116, 237n17
Retribution. *See* Revenge
Reunion euphoria, 174–176
Reunions, 174–176. *See also* Greetings
Revenge: direct, 157–158, 246n24; indirect, 159; justice and, 160–162, 184; as ingredient of morality, 211
Rhesus monkeys: friendship among, 26–27, 101; empathy among, 45–46, 47, 61, 69; treatment of the handicapped and, 49–50, 51–52; food-sharing and, 93, 95; social hierarchies and, 99, 101–102, 104, 109–111; double-holding among, 101–102; reconciliation and, 104, 177–180, 200, 249n17; punishment among, 112–113; rule learning among, 112–113; dominance style among, 126–127; levels of aggression among, 198–200; imitation and, 231n37; nurturant behavior among, 240n29; conflict mediation and, 241n36; intergroup relations among, 253n39. *See also* Macaques
*Rhett,* 203
van Rhijn, J., 254n41
Right and wrong, 2, 39, 105, 123, 201
Rights: sex differences in human morality and, 119–122; individualism and, 166–167; of animals, 214–216. *See also* Cross-species empathy
Ring-tailed lemurs, 59–60
*Rita,* 47
*Rix,* 56
Robinson, John, 81–82
*Rock,* 73–74
Rockefeller, John D., 11
Role-taking, 69–70, 73–78
van Roosmalen, Angeline, 200
*Ropey,* 26, 61, 101–102
Rose, Lisa, 145
Rosenblum, Leonard, 54, 110
Roth, E., 196–197
Rousseau, Jean-Jacques, 166–167, 196
Rule-based morality, 119
Rules: group sanctions and, 89, 91–92; descriptive *vs.* prescriptive, 90–92, 211; acquisition of, 94–95, 111–114; intentionality of, 96–97; internaliza-

Stump-tailed monkeys: treatment of the handicapped by, 52; treatment of infants among, 90–91; reconciliation and, 104, 178–180, 204, 249n17; teasing and, 114; dominance among, 127; mediation among, 129, 241n36

Submissive behavior, 99, 100, 235n10, 238. *See also* Formal dominance; Hierarchy, social

Succorant behavior: defined, 41; of whales, 42–43; in social development, 44–47; in nonhuman primates, 45–46, 80; absence of, 47–48, 61, 227n14; as ingredient of morality, 211. *See also* Empathy

Sugiyama, Y., 248n6

Symbol learning, 223n31. *See also* Language

Sympathy: Adam Smith on, 28; *vs.* empathy, 41; in young children, 44–45; elements of, shared with nonhuman animals, 78–83; as indestructible instinct, 87; James Q. Wilson on, 88; sex differences in human morality and, 119–122; self-interest and, 233n52. *See also* Succorant behavior

Sympathy-based morality, 119

Taï National Park, Ivory Coast, 58, 140–141

Takasaki, Hiroyuki, 141

Tanaka, Ichirou, 8

Tannen, Deborah, 120, 123

Tears in primates, 227n19

Teasing, 114, 203

Teeth-baring, 76

Teleki, Geza, 56, 153

Temerlin, Maurice, 57, 58

Temper tantrum, 61, 93, 188, 251n21

Theft, tolerated, 146, 244n16. *See also* Sharing

Theory-of-mind research, 232n41

Thompson, Nicholas, 195–196

Thurnheer, Sylvie, 181

Tinklepaugh, O. L., 96

Tobin, Joseph, 180

Todes, Daniel, 22

Tomasello, Michael, 231n39

Tool use, 72–73, 145, 210, 231n39

Trading, concept of, 147, 211. *See also*

Alliance formation; Reciprocal altruism; Reciprocity; Social contract

Triadic reconciliation, 204

Trisomy, autosomal, 49–50

Trivers, Robert, 24, 27, 135, 159, 162, 237n17; interview with, 25

Truces, 253n35

Trumler, Eberhard, 94

Turiel, Elliot, 105, 247n4

Turnbull, Colin, 85–86, 87, 213, 233n50, 242n3

Vampire bats, 20–21, 144

Verbeek, Peter, 249n18

*Vernon*, 82

Vervet monkeys, 198

Visalberghi, Elisabetta, 231n39

Vodegel, R., 254n41

Vogel, Christian, 223n33

Vollmer, Peter, 107, 237n11

Walker, Lawrence, 120

Wallace, Alfred Russell, 220n9

*Walnut*, 152, 160

*Wania-6672*, 50–51, 81

Warfare, 29–30. *See also* Aggression; Conflict, intergroup

Warriors, and self-sacrifice, 221n21

*Washoe*, 210

Watanabe, John, 191, 192–193, 251n24

Weaning conflict, 177, 187–189, 251n21

Weiss, Robert, 87

Westergaard, G. C., 229n32

Whales, 40–43, 230n36

Whiten, Andrew, 78, 128

Wickler, Wolfgang, 223n33

Wild chimpanzees: responses to death among, 54, 56; learning among, 72–73, 231n39; control role and, 129–130, 231n39, 234n4; sharing and, 151; group life and, 167–168; moralistic aggression among, 234n4; cultural variation and, 248n6. *See also* Chimpanzees

Wilkinson, Gerald, 21

Williams, George, 2, 16, 221n15

Wilson, Edward O., 10, 12

Wilson, James Q., 88, 218